DIAMONDS ARE FOREVER

THE COMPLETE TRILOGY

CHARMAINE PAULS

Published by Charmaine Pauls

Montpellier, 34090, France

www.charmainepauls.com

Published in France

Photography by Wander Aguiar Photography LLC

Cover design by Simply Defined Art

ISBN: 978-2-491833-05-3 (eBook)

ISBN: 979-8-689583-89-1 (Print)

Created with Vellum

DIAMONDS IN THE DUST

BOOK 1, DIAMONDS ARE FOREVER TRILOGY

A DIAMOND MAGNATE NOVEL

PROLOGUE

The screaming in the kitchen turns louder. Mommy and Daddy's voices travel through the thin wall and sting my ears. It doesn't hurt like when I had an ear infection, but it hurts in my chest, and I'm really scared.

I crouch in the corner on the bed I share with my brother, Damian, and hold Vanessa, my doll, close. I wish Damian was here, but it's Sunday, and he's delivering newspapers.

A thump shakes the bunker beds of my older brothers, Leon and Ian, against the opposite wall. Cups and plates rattle on the other side.

"Always the fucking same." Daddy's voice is too loud.

The neighbors will hear. I cringe, because they'll look at me weird tomorrow when I play on the stairs.

"You're all the fucking same."

My heart flaps like the wings of that poor bird I saw in the awful cage in Auntie May's kitchen with the poo scattered around it on the floor. I concentrate on the moldy patches on the wall and the crack that runs down the middle, holding my breath as I wait for the next thud to shake the floor. The dark stain in the corner looks like the head of a wolf with a long snout and a floppy ear. The one in the middle looks like a flower growing from the crack.

I knew it was coming, but when something crashes against the other side of the wall, I gasp quietly, careful not to make noise.

"It's all right," I whisper to Vanessa, clutching her tighter. I wish my name was something pretty like Vanessa. I hate my name. Zoe is a stupid name.

"How many times must I tell you, woman?" Daddy bellows. "You don't—"

Mommy's voice is shrill. "You don't tell me what to do!"

I lay Vanessa on the bed, trembling as I try to block out the angry voices. "Shh." She stares at me with big, happy eyes, but I know she's just as scared as I am. I know how to smile to look brave.

Maybe they'll stop.

Sometimes, they do.

I push Vanessa's arm through the hole I've cut from one of granny's napkins with Mommy's nail scissors and tie the ends in a knot. It doesn't matter that she only has one arm. It's a pretty dress all the same.

Something crashes. The noise is sharp and dull, like when grandpa chops wood.

"I'll fucking kill us all!" Daddy shouts.

Mommy's footsteps fall hard on the floor. "Don't touch me! I'll stab you! I'm not kidding, you fucking prick!"

It hurts to breathe. My eyes burn and tears start to drip. They plop on my hands, warm and wet. I'm dizzy and hot, like when I had the flu. Scrambling off the bed, I grab Vanessa and my book and dash down the short hallway to the broom closet at the end.

Please don't let them see me.

I close my eyes as I pass the kitchen door, but nobody calls my name or grabs the collar of my dress. The closet door squeaks as I open it and slip inside the darkness that smells of shoe polish and dust. I close it tightly, so tightly you can't even see the light through the crack, and feel under the cushions on the scratchy blanket of my nest for the flashlight. Huddling in the corner of my hiding place, I flick on the light and rock with Vanessa and my book in my arms.

The book is big and heavy. It's my only other possession, and I take it everywhere I go. The pages are dirty from all the times I've licked my fingers to separate them. Damian says they have dog ears, although I'm not sure where he sees the dogs. When I ask him, he just laughs at me. The spine is cracked and slack with stitches sticking out like my dresses when Mommy takes out the seams so I can wear them another year. When I open the book, it falls open at the same place it always does, on the first page of my favorite story about the princess and the frog.

The tinkling of breaking glass pierces my safe place. Pinching my eyes shut, I block out the terrible sound that's scarier than monsters.

More stuff falls over somewhere.

I force myself to open my eyes and look at the picture. I know each outline and every color of the princess in her puffy, pink dress, the golden ball lying next to the pond, the green leaves of the water lilies, and the frog sitting on them.

Pushing my finger on the page, I drag it along the letters as I whisper, "Once upon a time…"

I can't read yet, but I know the story by heart.

"…there was a beautiful princess who lived in a castle."

The book is like magic. The world in the story becomes real, and the sounds coming from down the hallway fade as I turn into the princess in the pink dress, standing next to the pond on the softest, greenest grass in my silk slippers with my golden ball. I'm a beautiful girl with yellow hair just like in the picture, not the boring color of dark-brown coffee like my own hair, and—

I jerk when the door opens.

"Hey, Zee," Damian says, calling me by his special name for me when his face appears in the crack. "Can I come in?"

He doesn't wait for me to say yes. He crawls in, bending double to fit under the shelf because he's ten and not only twice my age, but also twice my size.

When he's closed the door and settled opposite me, he asks, "What are you reading?"

The space is so small even with our knees pulled up our legs press together.

Sniffing, I shrug. He knows the stories by heart, too, because he's the one reading them to me. It's not like I have another book.

He nudges me. "Want me to read it to you?"

I shrug again but turn the book around for him to see the letters.

He ruffles my hair. "Next year, when you go to school, you'll learn to read, then you don't have to wait for me, and you can read other books, better books."

I hold Vanessa tighter. "I like it when you read to me. I like *these* stories."

Ian and Leon are older. When they're not in school, they're in the street with their friends, getting up to no good as Mommy always says. I don't see them much, and when I do, they mostly tease me. Damian is only in grade five and not allowed to go out in the street alone after school. He has to stay and look after me, so Mommy won't be cross when she comes home from work.

"You won't want to read these silly stories anymore when you're in school," he says.

Fresh tears prick behind my eyes. "They're not silly."

"This isn't like life at all," he says, sounding all grownup.

I jut out my chin. "It is, too."

"Is not."

"Is, too! One day, I'll find a prince, and marry him, and be a princess, and live in a castle, and we'll live happily ever after. You'll see."

His sigh is deep and heavy, sounding just like Daddy when he comes back from a day of what he calls *deep diggin'*. I always imagine *deep mine diggin'* to be making a big hole in the middle of a lawn for a sparkling blue swimming pool.

"Life isn't a fairytale, Zee. There's no knight on a white horse who's going to rescue you. You have to do it yourself."

Pressing my hands over my ears, I block him out. I block out the nasty words, because they're not true. I know they're not.

He pulls away my hands. "I'm not telling you this to be mean. I'm telling you this, so you won't be disappointed one day."

"Stop it," Mommy yells.

A glass shatters somewhere.

"You want me to stop, huh?" Daddy yells back. "Why not destroy everything?"

"You know what?" Mommy is sobbing. "Go ahead. Break everything. That's all you're good for, you son of a lousy bitch."

A curse. A loud bang. Then, the awful, awful silence.

Sometimes, the silence is worse. Daddy won't come home until tomorrow. Mommy will cry all night and not come out of her room. Damian will butter toast, and we'll eat it under the tent he'll make of our blanket on our bed, but there's nowhere to hide from the guilt.

Father Mornay says guilt is good because it tells us when we've done something wrong. I don't like feeling guilty. Mommy will scream at us and say it's our fault, all because there are so many mouths to feed. I'll feel really bad and not know how to be better or less of a mouth to feed.

Daddy will come home stumbling up the stairs and crashing into furniture, and he'll ignore Mommy and be angry with us. He'll give me a hiding for not cleaning the kitchen, even if the dishes are done. He'll take his belt to Damian for not taking out the trash, even if the trashcan is empty. I'll cry quietly in our room, and Damian will get broody and glary-eyed, but Daddy won't touch Ian or Leon. They're too big, almost as tall as Daddy, and stronger.

"Once upon a time..." Damian starts, his voice cracking a little as if it's on the brink of breaking, becoming deeper like Ian's, "...there was a princess..."

One day, Damian will be strong and tall, too.

I don't care what Damian says. One day, I'll find my prince. He'll buy me beautiful dresses and lots of pretty glasses, and he'll never break them. He'll take me very, very far away from here, and I'll never come back. Just wait and see.

CHAPTER 1

Johannesburg, South Africa

Zoe

My gaze is trained on the pavement to keep from stepping in the dog poo that litters the four blocks from the sweatshop to my apartment, but I'm not present in the glorious summer afternoon. My thoughts are where they usually dwell, dreaming up fantastic plans of escaping the hellhole I'm living in. Dreaming makes my existence more bearable. Dreaming *is* my escape.

Near the flea market, the air is thick and heavy with the smell of carbon from the coal train tracks. Everything underneath the train bridge is gray, covered in layers of soot and smog. I glance at the sky. Up there, the air is blue and clear, pure and unobtainable.

With a sigh, I fall in line at the fresh produce stall, using the waiting time to stretch my sore muscles. My back aches from being bent over a sewing machine all day. In my head, I count how far the coins I have left in my purse will go. The end of the month is always the worst, but on the upside, payday is around the corner. When it's my turn, I take a banana and two tomatoes.

I drag myself the last two blocks home, weary to the bone. I'm eager to feed my empty stomach and soak in a warm bath. Then I'll collapse into bed with my new stack of library books.

At my building, I curse under my breath. The door that gives access to the street is ajar. The lock is broken again, and it will take ages before it's fixed. The landlord doesn't maintain the building. That's why the façade is black with years' worth of grime and the inside walls moldy from permanent damp.

With my gaze trained on the floor so I don't step on one of the cats always begging for food, I push the door open with a shoulder while balancing my tote in one hand and my shopping bag in the other. The gloomy entrance is quiet, strangely absent from meows and furry bodies rubbing against my legs.

My eyes are still adjusting from the bright daylight to the somber interior. The light switch has been broken for years. I frown, scouting the stairs in the sliver of light that falls in from outside before the door swings shut with a creak and basks the space in semi-darkness. The weak glow from the single bulb on the upstairs landing is the only light preventing the inhabitants from not tripping on the stairs.

I'm about to call for the cats when something crashes into me from behind. My mouth opens on a scream, but no sound escapes as a large hand clamps over my mouth and an arm knocks the wind from my stomach as it wraps around my waist and lifts me off my feet.

The bags in my hands drop to the floor. Fear slams into my chest. In a distant corner of my mind, I notice the tomatoes that roll to the foot of the stairs, and a logical, detached part of me worries about the spoiled food even as I start fighting for my life. I twist and buck. With my arms constrained at my sides, I can only kick. I try to bite, but I can't force my lips apart. The hold over my mouth is too tight. It feels as if my jaw is about to snap. A button on my blouse pops from my efforts. It drops on the floor with a clink and bounces three, four, five times before it finally surrenders quietly in some corner. A smell of spices and citrus invades my nostrils—a man's cologne. My senses are heightened. In the life that passes in front of my eyes, everything seems louder and clearer.

"Shh," a male voice says against my ear, only making my terror spike.

I want to twist my head to the side to evaluate the threat, but I can't turn my neck. Two men manifest from the shadows. One has long, blond hair and the other is bald with a beard. They move quickly. The blond one snatches up my bags while the bearded one goes up the stairs. He looks left and right before giving a nod.

At the signal, my captor follows with me. I have to breathe through my nose as he climbs the single flight of stairs to my floor. Like this, the smell of the urine on the stairs and the mold on the walls is stronger. It makes me gag. Or maybe it's how our bodies are pressed together, and what he has in store for me.

The blond has taken my keys from my bag and has the door to my apartment open by the time we hit the landing. I glance at my neighbor's door, praying to God Bruce isn't playing his X-Box with his headphones on, but the sounds of his favorite game hits me before the stranger carries me inside.

Lowering me to the floor, he keeps his hand over my mouth. "My men are going to leave." His voice is deep and his accent strong. The way he rolls the R makes the dangerous words sound sensual. "I don't want to hurt you, Zoe, but if you scream, I'll have to. Understand?"

Dear God. He knows my name. I pinch my eyes shut, my chest heaving with every breath. How does he know my name?

He speaks softly, pressing the words to my ear. "I asked you a question."

I give a tight nod. What choice do I have?

He removes his hand slowly. "That's better."

The minute he releases me, I spin around and back up to the couch. "I don't have money. I have nothing valuable."

He smiles. "Do I look like I need to steal money?"

I take him in. His face is square with sharp lines, his nose slightly askew as if it has been broken many times. Thick, black hair is styled with fashionable sideburns. The tone of his skin is warm, but his eyes are cold, their color the gray of an overcast sky. He's not a handsome man, and the broken skin of his knuckles tells its own story.

Swallowing, I drop my gaze to his body. He's taller and broader than anyone I've seen. His chest and legs fill out every inch of his suit. It's a gray pinstripe—pure wool, judging by the thread—but it's the perfect cut that differentiates him. He screams money and power. No, he wouldn't have broken in for money. The alternative makes me break out in a cold sweat.

He advances on me, his gaze slipping to my chest. "However, you do have something of value I need."

I look down. My blouse is flaring where the button tore off, exposing my bra. Clutching the ends together, I ask through trembling lips, "What?"

When he nods at the two men, I look over at them. The blond one has a model-pretty face. He's lean and tall. The one with the beard is stockier with eyes so black the pupils bleed into the irises. Both are dressed in dark suits and carry guns.

The bearded man goes through my tote, unpacking the overall I use for work on the table with my purse and hairbrush. The bag with my banana lies next to it. He picked up my tomatoes, the split skins visible through the transparent plastic. When he finds my phone, he hands it to the man who grabbed me. The man pockets it. Then, like my captor promised, his men leave. The key sounds in the lock. I'm locked in with the stranger.

Fear heats me from the inside, making me feel nauseous. Even my hunger disappears. "What do you want from me?"

The man doesn't answer. As soon as his accomplices are gone, he turns his attention from me to inspecting my living space. His gaze moves from the ratty couch with the broken springs to the framed photos on the wall and finally to the daisy in the vase on the table. His evaluation is invasive. I know what he sees, but I refuse to be ashamed of my poverty, especially in front of a man with an expensive suit who snatched me off the street.

He walks to the daisy and touches the stem. "Nice touch."

"What?"

"The flower." Meticulously, he strokes every petal. "Where did you get it?"

What the heck does that matter? "From the pavement."

He gives me a doubtful smile. "You didn't take it from someone's garden."

Despite my fear, my anger blooms. "No, I didn't *steal* it. It grows wild."

He doesn't react to the silent accusation. He only continues to watch me intently. After a moment, he asks, "A boyfriend didn't give it to you?"

"No." Where is he going with his line of questioning? Why doesn't he tell me what he wants?

"No boyfriend, then."

"No." I watch him as he moves to the wall to study the photos, my heart pounding like a pendulum against my ribs.

"Your family?"

"Yes."

He points at the tallest boy on the yellowed Polaroid picture. "Who's this?"

"Why do you care?"

He looks back at me with a quiet warning in his eyes. He doesn't need his foreign-sounding words to instill fear.

"That's Ian," I say reluctantly, "my oldest brother."

"The others?"

"Next to him is Leon, then Damian, and me."

Leaning closer, he studies the girl with the pigtails and too short dress. "You were cute. How old were you?"

I grip my blouse tighter. "Ten."

He motions at Mom and Dad. "These are your parents?"

"Late parents."

"My condolences."

He picks up the book about Venice from the couch and turns the cover. I don't want him to touch it. I don't want this man who stole into my privacy to also invade my dreams. My dreams are mine. They're private, but I'm helpless from stopping him as his gaze skims over the table of contents and the library stamp before he drops it back onto the couch and opens the book on the coffee table. It's on loan from the library, too, about the same topic, just like the book next to the bath and the one on my nightstand. When he's done inspecting that one, he goes to the bookshelf and tilts his head to read the titles. Shelf by shelf, he goes through them.

Losing interest in the books, he makes his way to the kitchen. He stops in the doorframe and assesses the shelf with two chipped glasses and a dented pot, the only inherited items that haven't yet broken or rusted. His attention moves to the geranium on the windowsill. The sturdy, green plant is my pride and hope. I found it in the trash and managed to save it. Whoever discarded it must've thought it was dead, but there was still a tiny bit of green in the stalk. It was dry, neglected, and I felt sorry for it. The fact that it fought and survived to bloom and thrive is a reminder to myself to never to give up.

He looks at the darker square on the lanoline floor where the fridge used to stand. I long since sold it when I couldn't pay the rent, just like the rest of the furniture and everything else that were worth a few bucks. Without groceries, I don't need a fridge. A few minutes ago, where tomorrow's dinner was going to come from was my biggest problem. I never imagined my life could get worse.

Suddenly tired, I hug myself. "Look, just tell me why you're here and then leave me alone."

He doesn't acknowledge me. He's staring at the food cupboard. Instead of a door, it's covered with a curtain, which I left open, exposing the almost empty jar of peanut butter and crust of bread.

"I suppose an introduction is in order," he says when he finally turns back to me. "Since I already know your name, it seems only fair."

"I don't want to know your name," I blurt out. The less I know, the better my chances of survival.

He extends a hand. "Maxime Belshaw."

My shaking gets worse. This doesn't look good for me. When I don't move, he strides over, grips my fingers, and presses his lips to my knuckles. The gesture seems taunting instead of chivalrous, and I yank my hand away from his touch.

"Now that we know each other, *Zo,* we're going to have a conversation."

"Don't call me that." Only people who care about me call me Zo.

He raises a brow. "Isn't that what your friends call you?"

The fact that he knows is disturbing. "Exactly. They're *friends*."

Rather than upset, he appears amused. "Zoe, then. Your older brothers, they left town a long time ago. Am I right?"

"If this is about Ian or Leon, I haven't heard from them since they left."

"No." Reaching out slowly, he drags a thumb along my jaw. "This isn't about them."

The gentleness of the touch catches me off guard. I have to bend backward to escape the odd caress because my calves are pressed against the couch.

"This is about Damian," he says.

When he drops his hand, I straighten, trying to hold his gaze without letting him see the fear in my eyes.

"This is how our talk is going to work," he says. "I'm going to ask you a few questions, and you're going to answer them."

"Never."

I'm not ratting on Damian. Of all the people in our dysfunctional family, he's the only one who cares. Damian is only five years older than me, but he single-handedly raised me. He looked out for me when no one else did. He's suffered enough. He didn't deserve any of the terrible things that have happened to him.

Maxime looks me over. "You're tougher than I expected. The poor ones usually break easily."

My anger makes me forget to be frightened. "Fuck you."

"Did I hit a nerve?"

"Go to hell," I hiss.

"Fine. We'll play it your way." He takes his phone from his pocket and swipes over the screen.

My heart pumps so furiously I feel every beat in my temples. He rests the phone against the book on the coffee table with the screen turned toward me. A video call connects. The video and audio functions on his side are deactivated. Whoever he's connecting to can't see or hear us.

A second later, an image fills the screen. I freeze. A chill runs down my spine. Maxime's cronies are next door with Bruce, and my neighbor is tied up in a chair.

"Bruce!" I jump for the phone, but Maxime easily grabs me, holding me by my arms. I struggle in his hold, but I'm no match for his strength. "What are you doing to him?"

"Quiet," Maxime says.

I try to kick him, but he easily restrains me.

"Why are you doing this?" I cry out, fighting to free myself while his fingers dig harder into my flesh.

The bald bastard pulls back his arm and plants his fist in Bruce's face. The chair topples over, Bruce landing on his back.

"No!" I strain forward, trying to reach the phone, but Maxime holds me tightly.

The guard picks up the chair. Bruce spits blood, his eyes filled with venom as he glares at his assailant. The bastard hits him again, this time with a blow on the jaw that sends his face flying sideways.

"Stop it," I scream. "Leave him alone."

Bruce grunts as fists fall on his stomach and ribs. A vicious blow splits his eyebrow open. I can't watch any more. My legs buckle. Sobbing, I fall to my knees. Maxime's grip moves to my hair. His fingers fasten in the bun I always wear to work. Pulling my head back, he forces me to meet his eyes.

"Are you ready to have a conversation now?"

"Please, stop," I say through my tears. "I'll tell you what you want to know."

He picks up the phone, flicks a finger over the screen, and says, "Give it a break."

After pocketing the phone, he takes my elbows to help me to my feet. Gently almost, he wipes the tears from my cheeks. "It doesn't have to be like this. It can be as easy or difficult as you make it." He pushes me down onto the couch.

Teeth chattering, I scoot into the corner, getting as far away from him as I can.

"Stay there," he says.

He goes to the kitchen. The pipes creak as he opens the tap. A moment later, he returns with a glass of water, which he pushes into my hand.

"Drink," he says.

I take a sip on autopilot, even if I'm not thirsty.

He sits down so close to me our bodies touch. "Let's have that little chat. Are you and Damian close?"

I nod, unable to stop the tears running down my cheeks.

"Shh." He threads his fingers through my hair, massaging my scalp. A pin comes loose and drops into my lap. "Do you visit him in jail?"

I shake my head.

"Use your voice, Zoe."

The word comes out on a croak. "No."

"Good. You're doing well." He twists a lock of hair that came free from my bun around his finger. "Why not?"

"He doesn't want me to visit."

"Why's that?"

"He doesn't want me around the people doing time with him. He says they're dangerous, and they won't hesitate to use me against him."

It's tough surviving on the inside. Damian doesn't tell me what happens, but one of my friends dated a warden. The stories she told me gave me nightmares.

"Wise guy." He takes the glass from me and leaves it on the coffee table. "A prison full of hard, unscrupulous men is definitely not a place for a beautiful, young woman."

"Damian is innocent." I look into Maxime's cool gaze. "He didn't deserve that sentence. Whatever you think he did, he didn't do it."

"How can you be so sure?"

"He told me. I believe him. I *know* Damian. He didn't steal that diamond. Someone planted it on him."

"What kind of contact do you have? Do you call?"

"He says the phones are bugged. I write."

He lifts a brow. "Letters aren't monitored?"

"Damian knows the wardens in charge of reading the letters. They're safe. Besides, I don't share personal information."

"What do you write about, then?"

"My job." I shrug. "Everyday life."

"You mean your lack of a life."

My cheeks heat with more helpless anger. "You're an asshole."

"If you're so close, why doesn't he take care of his little sister?"

I glare at him. "How is he supposed to do that from a jail cell? Besides, I'm capable of taking care of myself."

He casts a glance around the room. "I've noticed."

"Times are hard for everyone." Dragging my gaze over his expensive suit, I add, "Well, not everyone. The thugs seem to thrive."

"Don't be so defensive, and it'll be wise to watch your tone with me. Do I need to remind you of the consequences of bad behavior?"

Tears choke me up when I think about Bruce. My answer is bitter. "No."

"Has Damian mentioned his plans for after his release?"

"He still has six of the ten-year-sentence to go." My heart hurts when I say it. "What plans can he make?"

"He never told you anything about acquiring a mine?"

"Are you joking? A mine must cost millions."

"Billions." Almost absent-mindedly, he rubs the stray strand of my hair between his fingers. "Did Damian tell you about money making schemes he's running in jail?"

"No." Unease starts digging into my gut. "Why? What is he involved in?"

He drops my hair. "Nothing. Just checking. Have you met any of his fellow inmates?"

"I told you, he doesn't want me to."

"Does the name Zane da Costa ring a bell?"

"He's Damian's cellmate, but that's all I know."

Getting up, he extends a hand. "I think you're telling the truth, but I'd like to see his letters."

I let him pull me to my feet. "There are no letters. Damian never writes back."

"Why not?"

"The wardens who read the outgoing letters aren't the same ones in charge of incoming mail. Damian doesn't trust them. He doesn't like them to know about my existence."

"What about photos? You must have some more of your brother."

I don't want to give him more information he can use against Damian. I don't want him to witness our poverty growing up. "Those are private."

"Zoe." He cups my cheek. "You need to understand that the only choices you have from now on are the ones I give you. I advise you to make those choices carefully. Don't waste them, because you'll have little enough. More importantly, don't test me. I'm not a patient man."

Gripping his wrist, I move his hand away. "Don't touch me."

His lips curve into a lazy smile. "I have a feeling you're going to swallow those words."

"Never," I say through clenched teeth.

"We'll see." He points at the hallway. "Get a move on."

I hurry away from him as fast as I can, but he follows close on my heel down the short hallway and into the room I once shared with my three brothers. Opening the dresser drawer, I take out the box of old photos and hand them to him. Doing so guts me, because those rare moments of our lives captured on film aren't meant for his hateful, emotionless eyes.

"Thank you," he says, accepting the box.

"I've given you what you want. Let Bruce go."

"What's Bruce to you?" He says the name with disdain.

"A kind neighbor." My look is accusing. "He's only ever been watching out for me."

"There's nothing romantic between you?"

I cross my arms. "No, not that it's any of your business."

"Do I need to remind you of your place?"

I avert my eyes, resenting him for taking my power. "You got what you wanted. Please, go."

"I'm not here for the photos."

Sick with fear, I look back at him. "What more do you want? You said you'd let us go."

"I never said that."

I take several steps back until my body hits the wall. "Did you lie? Are you going to kill us?"

"No."

"What then?" My whole body is shaking. Even the hem of my skirt is trembling.

"First things first. We're going out for dinner." His gaze drops to my gaping blouse again. "Make yourself presentable."

I stare at him. "Dinner?"

"You know," his tone is dry, "the meal you have between seven and nine."

"I have to go see Bruce," I exclaim. "He's hurt."

He opens the top drawer of my dresser and starts going through it. "He'll survive."

Dashing forward, I grab his arm. "Hey! What are you doing?"

He stops and looks at where I'm touching him.

I loosen my fingers and remove my hand. "That's mine, and it's private."

He sweeps aside my underwear and socks and checks underneath my sweater. He does the same with every drawer, and then pulls away the curtain to check inside the closet.

Without another word, he walks from the room and goes through the broom closet in the hallway before searching the closet in my late parents' room.

Satisfied that there's nothing of interest, he pulls out his phone. "We're leaving in five. This is one of those precious choices I'm allowing you, Zoe. You can either fix your clothes, or we go as you are."

"If I go with you, will you let Bruce go?"

"You're not in a position to bargain. You *are* coming with me, but don't worry about your neighbor. My business isn't with him."

Lifting the phone to his ear, he asks for a table for two while making his way back to the lounge. My chest is tight and my breathing shallow. Who *is* this arrogant man? What does he want? Is Damian in trouble? Is Bruce all right?

My tears are useless, but they flow anyway. Slipping into the bathroom, I lock the door. The window is too small to climb through. There's no backdoor. I'm trapped in my apartment with a dangerous man, a foreigner with cruel eyes and unknown intentions, but Bruce is even worse off.

I stare at my face in the mirror. I'm a mess. My mascara is smeared under my eyes. The neat bun of this morning is partly undone, my hair wild. I open the tap and rinse my face, washing away the mascara. The pins drop to the floor as I undo my hair with shaky fingers. I don't bother to pick them up. My brush is on the table in the lounge, and I'm not going there because *he* is there. Using my fingers, I comb through my hair to tame the tangles. Both my spare blouses are in the wash. I get a safety pin from the box with my needles and thread and pin the edges of the blouse together as best as I can. It takes longer than what it should because of how much I'm shaking. By the time I'm done, a knock falls on the door.

"Open the door, Zoe."

For a fleeting moment, I consider not complying, but I can imagine how that will go. It won't take much to kick down the door, and Bruce will suffer again because of my resistance. With my heart in my throat, I turn the key, but I don't push down the handle. My brain refuses to obey the command. It takes me a moment to search for the courage, but before I find it, Maxime opens the door.

"Let's go." He takes my arm and leads me to the lounge.

The blond man must've been standing just outside, because Maxime only has to knock once before the door is unlocked. When Maxime drags me through it, I know my life as I knew it has ended.

CHAPTER 2

Zoe

A black Mercedes with tinted windows is parked in the alley around the corner. It's new—judging by its shiny and flawless exterior—and a target for hijackers.

I glare at the blond guard as he opens the backdoor for Maxime who shoves me inside. Immune to my hostility, the blond gets behind the wheel while the bearded guy takes the passenger seat in the front. Unlucky for me, I share the backseat with the devil.

There's ample space, but he takes up all of it, making me shift into the corner against the door. His energy envelops me like a shadow eating up light until only the darkness of his intentions is left. The cologne that overwhelmed my senses since the moment he took me is more prominent in the confines of the car. He smells of cloves and citrus, a faint mix of winter that matches the cold color of his eyes and the frost that never melts in their depths.

The driver starts the engine while the bald one watches the road like a soldier looking out for danger in enemy territory. When the car pulls away, I twist around to look at my building. There's no movement behind Bruce's window.

Sagging back in my seat, I ask, "What do you want from me?"

Maxime doesn't answer. He's taken out his phone and is typing something.

The luxury car is so out of place in this suburb pedestrians slow down to stare. However, crime is nothing new. Women are kidnapped all the time. I won't be the first person to disappear from Brixton.

Has the driver locked the doors? Locals do it habitually, but my kidnappers are foreigners. There's a chance they might not have activated the central locking system.

It's rush hour. We're moving slowly. I have to take my chance while Maxime's attention is on his phone. By now Bruce would've alarmed someone. Hopefully, he's on his way to a hospital. Maxime can't hurt him anymore. Taking a shaky breath, I prepare myself for hitting the tarmac.

Now!

I yank the door handle.

It's locked.

Fuck.

"No," I moan, fresh tears welling up in my eyes.

Panic overwhelms me anew. My mind knows it's futile, but my body acts on survival instinct, demanding I try harder. Pulling with all my might, I shake the handle in a fit of hysteria.

A strong, warm hand folds over mine. I look down to where my kidnapper's fingers are curled around my fist, stilling me with minimal effort. His grip is firm without being too tight. I have no doubt he can easily crush my bones.

His voice is calm, a controlling force in the madness raging in my chest. "Look at me, Zoe."

I only comply because I don't know what he'll do if he loses his cool.

He regards me with those flat, frank eyes. "It'll be easier for both of us if you calm down."

The driver looks at me in the rearview mirror. He's clutching the wheel hard. His friend has one hand on the gun in his holster. I take it all in, jumping to the obvious conclusions.

"Over here." The clicking of Maxime's fingers draws my gaze. He's pointing at his face. "Eyes on me. That's better."

To my utter shame, my lip starts to wobble. "Are you going to kill me?"

"No." Maxime squeezes my hand and places it in my lap. "Why would I feed you if I was going to kill you? I already told you, I don't want to hurt you."

But he will if I don't do what he wants. If he doesn't want to tell me what he wants, it must be bad. This isn't a random kidnapping. Maxime targeted me for a reason. It has something to do with Damian. Maxime knows who I am. He knows where I live. He knows I live alone. He waited for me, knowing at what time I'd be arriving home from work.

Oh, my God. "Have you been stalking me?"

His smile is as flat as his eyes, like soda that's lost its bubbles. "The old lady in your building was only too happy to tell me everything I wanted to know."

"Mrs. Smit?" I gasp.

"It's amazing what a cup of tea and a slice of cake can buy."

"That's disgusting. You used that poor old lady."

"At least I'm not a stalker."

"Great." I stare through the window. "That makes me feel so much better."

"Sarcasm doesn't become you."

I turn my head back to him. "Really? You're lecturing me on my attitude?"

Focused on his phone again, he says, "I'll lecture you whenever I deem it necessary."

"Bruce would've called the police by now. They'll be looking for your men." I glance at the two guards again, but their eyes are trained on the road.

"Not for the theft of a cellphone. Your police have enough murders to keep them busy."

"You stole his cellphone?" I cry out.

He lifts a shoulder. "Motive for the forced entry and assault."

"You bastard."

The lines around his eyes tighten. "This is the last time I'm going to warn you about your language."

"Bruce is innocent. He's not rich like you. He can't afford another phone. How can you be so cruel?"

He chuckles. "You haven't seen cruelty yet, little flower."

"This is Brixton, in case you haven't noticed."

"I've noticed," he replies in a dry tone.

Meaning, the man who is carrying me off is worse than the neighborhood I've been trying to escape my whole life. I can't help but laugh in a hysterical fit at the irony.

"Something funny?" he asks.

"My life."

"You'll feel better when you've eaten."

I snort.

He takes a packet of tissues from the side of the door and drops it in my lap. "Any allergies or food dislikes I need to know about?"

I'm not going to wipe my eyes on his tissues. I use the back of my hand instead. "Couldn't find that out, huh? Why, your power does have limits."

Gripping my jaw, he doesn't squeeze hard enough to hurt, but with enough force to let me feel the underlying threat. "If you went for your regular health checks, I would've known."

I jerk free. "Yeah, well, doctor visits cost money."

"We'll correct that shortly."

"Correct what?" My pulse jumps again. "Why?"

"Just focus on what's important now. I asked you a question."

"I'm not answering your questions any longer. By now Bruce is safe. You can't manipulate me by hurting him anymore." I lift my chin. "When you let me out of this car, I'll run. I'll scream. You can't just take me."

Cruel calculation flashes in his eyes as he leans closer, pressing me against the door. "Do you know what an easy target a man in jail is?"

He brushes his knuckles over my cheek. "You see, Zoe, a man behind bars is nothing but a sitting duck. One word from me and your brother is dead."

Tears blur my vision. I slap away his hand. "I don't believe you."

He gets out of my face, giving me space to breathe. "Zane works for me. That, my pretty flower, you better believe."

The punch hits me straight in the gut, because what I do know is that Damian loves his cellmate like a brother. I feel sick. I want to spit in Maxime's face.

"I'll only ask you one more time," he says. "Do you have allergies or is there any food you hate?"

I clench my hands in my lap. "I'm not a fussy eater, and I don't have allergies."

"Medication?"

I frown. "What?"

His harsh features are emphasized by the shadows playing over his face as we pass under the bridge. "Are you on any medication?"

I fumble with my sleeves, a nervous habit. "Why are you asking?"

"Alcohol is prohibited with some medications."

"No, nothing."

Glancing at my restless fingers, he folds his hand over mine. "In that case, I hope you'll let me order for you."

Normally, I'd take offense to anyone making my decisions, especially deciding what I should eat, but this situation is so far removed from normal it feels unreal. What feels too real is where he's touching me. I'm like a kid with a vicious dog, tensing up, waiting for the moment it's going to bite, but then he pulls his hand away. My chest expands with a breath.

After dropping the threat on Damian's life like a hand grenade in my lap, Maxime continues to work on his phone quietly.

I have to warn Damian.

I look at the passing landscape while scheming, noting the landmarks as we drive north. Since we were kids, Damian and I had a secret code language. Our code words for trouble at home were apple pie.

I'll get word to Damian. I'll warn him Zane isn't his friend.

My turbulent thoughts are cut short when we stop at Seven Seas in Sandton. Only the wealthy and famous eat here. My monthly salary won't even cover a starter. I've seen pictures, but the private mansion converted into a restaurant is much more imposing in real life. The modern double story building is encased almost entirely in glass and situated on a vast, green lawn.

The blond guy opens my door. Ignoring his proffered hand, I get out. Maxime comes around to take my arm and steer me to the entrance. I can't help but stare at the lights in the double story foyer when we enter. A modern chandelier reaches all the way from the top level to the ground floor in a cascade of golden bulbs.

A hostess bustles over. "Max." She kisses his cheeks before taking his jacket. "Welcome back."

I suppress the urge to push the toe of my shoe into the carpet to hide the scruff where the color has worn off.

Her gaze flickers over me. "No bag for the lady?"

From her red Balenciaga number, it's obvious my antique lace blouse and mermaid skirt don't fit here, but I made them, and I love them.

Maxime lays a hand on my shoulder. "No bag."

His palm burns through the thin silk lining of the blouse. When the hostess turns away, I shake his touch off.

After putting Maxime's jacket in the cloakroom, she leads us down a red carpet to a veranda overlooking a fishpond that stretches the whole length of the lawn. A fountain with a sea snake spouting water from a forked tongue stands in the middle. Lilies drift on the water. It reminds me of an illustration of The Frog Prince in a book I owned, only this is no fairytale. I've stepped right into a nightmare.

Not having a choice, I sit down in the chair Maxime pulls out for me. A waiter drapes a linen napkin over my lap and hands me a menu. It's all very pretty and fancy, but I hate the place. We've entered a different world where unfamiliar rules and manners apply, a world where someone takes your jacket and judges you for the price tag on your clothes. Several other diners in eveningwear cast curious glances my way. With his European style, Maxime fits right in. I must stand out like the underprivileged kid in the candy store.

When Maxime opens his menu, I do the same, not because I'm eager to participate in this charade, but to block out his hateful face behind the big leather folder. There are no prices on mine. Going through the list of entrées and main courses, I understand why Maxime suggested ordering for me. It wasn't so much a gesture of control than saving me the embarrassment of admitting I understand nothing. The dishes all have foreign names. I'm guessing they're French. There's nothing I recognize.

The waiter returns with appetizers. "Sea urchin on Melba toast with truffle oil."

I stare at the disc of bread with a dollop of red cream, a sprig of chive, and three dots of oil on the side.

"Do you like urchin?" Maxime asks.

"I don't know." Isn't it's obvious I can't afford food like this? "I've never had it."

"Some people love it. Others hate it. Go ahead. Try it."

I haven't eaten since breakfast, but I don't have an appetite. Even if I were starving, which technically I am, I would've declined on principle. I'm not selling my soul to the devil for a meal.

I push the plate away. "No, thanks."

His eyes crinkle in the corners, but the set of his mouth is hard. "I'll feed you if you prefer." He pronounces the words carefully in his accent, making sure I understand. "On my lap."

He'll do it. I have no doubt. He's callously uncaring about how people are looking at us, or rather at me. Defeated, I give him a cutting look as I take the morsel between two fingers and place it in my mouth. It's salty and smoky with a strong but not off-putting iodine aftertaste.

"Do you like it?" he asks.

I cross my arms. "No."

"I'll order you something more ordinary, then."

The insult is payback for my ungrateful and bad-mannered reply, but I couldn't care less. Yes, I'm poor. Yes, I'm not used to much, certainly not urchin, and caviar, and whatever else they serve here, but at least I'm not a criminal who breaks into people's homes and kidnaps them.

Picking up the knife and fork on the far outside of his plate, Maxime scoops up the bite and brings it to his lips. I want to crawl under the table for demonstrating just how uneducated I am by eating with my hands. It's not that I care what he or the people around us think. I just hate giving them the pleasure of being right about me.

The waiter returns with a bottle of wine and pours us each a glass, after which he takes our order. Maxime has no problem pronouncing the names of the dishes.

When the waiter is gone, I decide to go for a blunt approach. I already know my kidnapper's name. Knowing less or more about him won't make a difference in my fate.

"Are you French?" I ask.

His lips quirk in one corner. "What gave me away?"

"Your accent."

"It was a rhetorical question, Zoe. It's called humor."

Some of the fear makes place for anger. "Don't patronize me."

"I wasn't patronizing you." His smile grows into a full, mocking curve. "I was just pointing out the obvious."

I hate him. He did this on purpose, making me feel stupid for asking. Not wanting to talk to him anymore, I turn my head away.

"Why so angry, my little Zoe? Is it because I didn't fall for your transparent way of fishing for information about me?"

I look back at him. "I'm not your little Zoe, and actually, I brought it up because your accent is rather unpleasant on the ear."

He raises a brow. "Is that so?"

I'm not going to tell him he makes talking sound like sex. I bet that's what he's used to hearing.

"Strange," he drawls. "You're the first woman to complain."

"Oh, I'm sorry." I bat my eyelashes. "Did I hurt your fragile ego?"

"No teacher ever managed to rid me of this accent, no matter how many private tutors I had."

There's honesty in that statement, like an olive branch he's offering. I'm too desperate to know why he took me not to take it. "You speak English well enough."

He takes a sip of wine. "A business requirement."

"What kind of business are you in?" I can't stop myself from adding, "Human trafficking?"

He only smiles broader. "When necessary."

The waiter arrives with our starters. It looks like some kind of seafood soup. In different circumstances, the spicy aroma would've made my mouth water, but my stomach churns when the waiter puts a bowl down in front of me.

"Bisque," Maxime says. "I hope you'll like it."

I stare at the lobster tail drifting in the center of the bowl.

"The secret is in the sherry," he says, bringing his spoon to his mouth.

I drag my gaze from the bowl to his face. "So, France is home."

"Eat your food, Zoe. If you need to know something, I'll tell you."

My anger escalates. "Ah, so we're on a need-to-know basis."

"Exactly."

"What about after dinner? What happens then?"

He stills. "You really need to live more in the present, to enjoy the moment."

"Because something bad is going to happen later?" I ask a little louder.

His gaze hardens. "Keep your voice down and eat your food."

If I eat one bite, I'm going to vomit. "I'm not hungry."

"I'm not feeding you again until tomorrow morning."

The last two words get stuck in my head. *Tomorrow morning.* They add to my barely controlled panic. "Why do you need me until the morning? Why are you doing this?" He reaches over the table for my hand, but I pull away. "Tell me. Tell me now."

"Calm down. I don't want to embarrass you in front of all these people by teaching you your place."

"On your lap?" I say in a catty tone.

"*Over* my lap, and then you'll eat *on* my lap with a smarting ass."

Tears that refuse to dry up burn behind my eyes. "I hate you."

"I know. You'll hate me even more if Damian gets a beating tonight." He motions with his spoon at my untouched soup. "Now eat."

"I can't. I'll be sick."

He wipes his mouth on his napkin. "You have two choices. You can either eat the delicious food and enjoy the conversation or be treated like a child and go to bed hungry and sulking. You can see why the first option is hands down the winner. You'll nourish your body and make the best of a moment you don't have any control over. It's up to you. Just know I won't hesitate to execute my threat. I don't make idle ones."

I'm crying with helpless anger by the time his speech is done. I don't even care any longer that everyone is staring. I just want to go home.

"What will it be, Zoe?"

Picking up my spoon, I grip it so hard the metal pushes painfully into my palm.

"Good decision." His voice is calm but his gaze attentive, waiting for the moment I crack.

I dunk the spoon with a shaking hand in my bowl. The tremors running over my body are no longer only from fear, but also from anger and injustice. I force the liquid down my throat, tasting nothing.

Maxime continues to watch me until I've cleared my bowl. Every swallow is a battle I fight. I drink more wine than I'm used to, downing the first glass and throwing back another straight after.

The waiter doesn't look at me as he clears our bowls and serves the main dish—lobster for Maxime and *ordinary* pasta for me. I somehow manage to eat everything and keep it down, although in the morning I'll probably not even remember what I ate.

Through it all, Maxime makes conversation and even lighthearted jokes. When our dessert and herbal tea arrive, he pours a cup and hands it to me.

"What do you do at the sweatshop?" he asks.

"I'm a seamstress."

His gaze drops to my blouse. "Did you make that?"

"Yes."

"I didn't notice a sewing machine in your apartment."

"I use the machines at work."

"Doesn't the manager have a problem with that?"

"The supervisor lets us use them after hours."

He brings the cup to his lips. "Is that what you always wanted to do?"

"It's a steppingstone."

"To designing."

I nod. He saw the books on my bookshelf.

"Honey?" He pushes the pot toward me.

"No." I take sugar, but I don't say so.

"You're talented."

I shrug.

The conversation continues in this manner until he asks for the bill. He pays with a stack of cash that would've covered my rent for a couple of months. He asks if I need to use the bathroom and waits outside the door until I'm done.

The guards are smoking in the garden. They put out their cigarettes when we approach. The blond one hurries to get my door, but Maxime waves him away.

"I've got this, Gautier."

Once inside, Maxime turns to me. "Would you like to go for a drink somewhere, maybe show me another part of your city?"

I rub my temples where a headache is building. "I've played your game. I've eaten my food. I just want to go home."

"As you wish," he says, "but you're not going home."

My body goes rigid. "Where am I going?"

He nods at Gautier, who pulls off as Maxime says, "To my hotel."

CHAPTER 3

Maxime

Glass skyscrapers and modern office blocks dominate the view as we drive to my hotel in Melrose Arch. It's nothing like the crumbling buildings and weed-infested pavements of Zoe Hart's suburb. I've seen worse neighborhoods. In my line of work, there's always worse. Yet for some reason, the empty buildings with planks crossed over their broken windows in Brixton made me tense. We're armed with enough weapons to defend ourselves should anyone be stupid enough to attack us, but it's not my safety I fear. The uneasiness eating at me is for the woman I just found and can't afford to lose. Her apartment doesn't even have an alarm, for God's sake.

In a place like that, it's only a matter of time before she turns into a statistic. The fact that I'll be the one to turn her into that statistic doesn't faze me, which says a lot about the kind of man I am.

I regard my petite charge. She's quiet now, her worry bigger than her anger. It's not that I don't want to put her at ease. It's just that I can't tell her the truth. Her hands are clutched together in her lap.

Every now and then, she untangles those long, slender fingers to rub at a temple. That should teach her for downing two glasses of the most expensive wine in the restaurant without even tasting it. Not that I blame her.

She's right to be nervous. She should be wary of me. I'm angry with her, even if it's not her fault. I'm angry that she put me in this position, a position that makes me give a damn. How could I not look at her as a person after going through her apartment and witnessing the dreams so obviously strewn around? She wears them like the emotions in her expressive eyes—on her sleeve. Hope shines in those wide blue irises, and hope makes a person human.

The problem is I've never dealt with an innocent. Everyone in my business has dirt on his hands, but Zoe is only a pawn. If I hand her over to my younger brother, as planned, she'll be broken and nothing but a shell of herself, those beautiful dreams and naïve hope crushed and forgotten by the time we send her back to her brother. If we ever do.

I had to drive the last woman unfortunate enough to have ended up in Alexis's bed to hospital. Her injuries weren't pretty. Even without the payoff from my father, she wouldn't have pressed charges. The consequences are too terrifying. Our family is feared. It's not fair, but that's life for you.

Zoe tenses more when we pull up at the hotel. Part of her fault is that she's pretty and exactly Alexis's type. He'll like her dark hair and pale skin. He'll want her. That makes her my problem, one I don't need and shouldn't want. Yet I do. Maybe that's the real problem. I've wanted her since I pressed her body against mine and slammed my hand over her mouth.

I liked the head rush I got from holding her in my power. I liked how clean her apartment was amidst the filth of the buildings surrounding hers. I liked the simple wildflower and the cherished green plant on her windowsill. Just like her. She's a pretty little daisy that pushes through a crack on a dirty pavement, resilient and beautiful, surviving against the odds.

She's poor as fuck, but she's proud. I like that, too. Judging by the books she reads and the clothes she fancies, she's a romantic. That, I like the most. It fascinates me. I want to know how she can believe in something so abstract and idyllic that doesn't exist. Even if it did, she certainly wouldn't have found it in Brixton.

I want to know how the fuck she can still believe in something beautiful, in anything at all, when everything around her is dilapidated, rotten, and hopeless. I want to know how someone with her fragile body and meager means survives. I want to know how her soul can crack concrete and flourish with no one's care to shine like a daisy amidst the grime. Maybe, just maybe, if I know her secret, I'll know how to be happy. Maybe if I can catch her spirit, I can steal her dreams and make her hope mine.

Zoe glances at me when we pull up at the hotel. She's been wringing her hands since we left the restaurant. Instead of quieting her fiddling, I let her have the outlet even if it distracts me from my thoughts of what the fuck to do with her. I get out and go around to get her door. I don't give her a chance to reject my offer to help her from the car like she did with Gautier. With him, I allowed it, preferred it even. I didn't like him touching her. My grip on her waist is firm as I swipe my access card to open the door and lead her inside. There's no receptionist or lobby staff, part of the reason why I chose to stay here. It's more like an aparthotel with the services of a hotel.

Gautier and Benoit scout the area before they follow, as much from habit as a necessity in a high crime area. We ride the elevator together. I tell them in French to have dinner before catching a few hours of sleep. It's only after eight. The kitchen staff deliver meals to the rooms until ten. We have a long day ahead of us tomorrow.

On the top floor, we split. They go to the room they share at the end while I take Zoe to the penthouse suite.

She pulls back when I unlock the door with my card, but it doesn't take much to push her over the threshold. She doesn't weigh more than a cat. A small kitten, really. When I lock the door, she puts distance between us, backtracking to the middle of the floor.

The suite is three times the size of Zoe's apartment. She looks lost, hugging her slight frame in the middle of the lounge in her frilly blouse and hip-hugging skirt, and even more petite than usual against the floor-to-ceiling window framing Melrose Arch. With those black curls and pearly skin, she's more than easy on the eye. Long lashes frame her blue eyes, and her mouth is pouty like a budding rose. The blush on her cheeks is as pink as the petals of that rose, the darker hue closer to the stem if I were to pull the flower apart.

At my evaluation, she folds into herself like a flower that curls up at night. I'm staring too openly, the lust I don't care to show in public probably visible on my face. I remove my jacket and hang it over the clotheshorse. Then I put my Glock and access card in the safe, making sure my body blocks the code so the little flower I plucked from her life isn't baited with temptation.

When I turn back to her, her eyes are swimming with trepidation. The way the tears make them glitter are gorgeous. They seem bigger and even more expressive. It's a pretty sight, but I don't want to torture her. She did nothing to deserve what's coming to her.

Folding back my shirt sleeves, I advance slowly so I won't frighten her. She tilts her head back to meet my gaze when I stop in front of her.

Her voice is as silky as her flower-petal skin. "Why am I here?"

I know what she's really asking. "Don't worry. I'm as little a rapist as I'm a stalker." Only a killer.

Swaying a little, she frowns and rubs at her temples. "Then why did you bring me to your hotel?"

She's exhausted, has been since she came home with sagging shoulders, dragging feet, and two tomatoes for dinner. "To sleep."

"I have a bed. I have a home."

Not any longer. I walk to the wet bar and pour a glass of water, which I carry back to her. "You had too much wine too quickly. Drink."

She takes the glass and gulps everything down. I refill it and take the pill from the box waiting next to the decanter. It's a good thing I had the foresight. Being kidnapped can be draining on all counts, both the spirit and the body.

"What is it?" she asks when I hand the pill to her with the water.

"Something for your headache."

She regards me with mistrust, as she should. It's not a lie. It will take away her pain. It's just not the full truth. It's not the first time I don't give her the truth, and it won't be the last.

"How did you know I have a headache?"

"It's obvious from the way you rub your temples."

She studies my face with wide, weary eyes. I see the exact moment she decides to believe me. Putting the pill in her mouth, she swallows it down with the water.

I take back the glass. "I have some business to take care of. Why don't you have a nice, warm bath?"

She glances at the bedroom door.

"This way." I take her arm and lead her to the opposite door that gives access to the bathroom. "I'll be a while. Take your time."

She looks around the room, seeming as lost as when I brought her into the suite.

"Do you need help with operating the facilities?"

Her look is scathing. "I can open a tap."

Ah, her fire hasn't burned out. It pleases me. I smile. "Call if you need me."

She scoffs before pushing past me and slamming the door in my face. The lock turns on the other side. As if she has any power. Grinning, I shake my head and drag a hand over my face. The stretch of my lips is a foreign feeling, something I haven't experienced in long time. Maybe never.

Leaving the little flower to her bath, I steel myself for the call I have to make. Certain she can't escape, I go onto the balcony for privacy and check the hour. It's the same time in France.

It takes a while for my father to take the call. From the cutlery sounding in the background, he's having dinner.

"Did I catch you at a bad time?" I ask in French.

It's my brother who replies. He's jovial, a few glasses of wine already in his stomach. "How are things working out in South Africa?"

I roll my shoulders, but my voice comes out tight, anyway. "Fine. I didn't know Maman invited you for dinner."

"We're at the club."

My spine goes stiff. The club is where the deals are made. Alexis is greedy to undermine my power. "Let me speak to our father."

"Do you have her?" He sounds excited.

Something dark stirs in my chest. I can't discuss her with him. Even that little will soil her.

"Max?" Alexis's voice rises in volume. "We have a bad connection. I can't hear you."

"Put Father on, Alexis. It's late."

He laughs. "Getting old?"

I let the jab slide, but get one of my own in. "Pronto, *little brother*."

The diminutive works. A moment later, my father's cigar-rough voice comes on the line. "Did you meet with Dalton?"

Good evening to you, too, Dad. "You're at the club."

"The business doesn't go on hold when you're not here."

I force nonchalance into my tone. "What's Alexis doing there?"

The way my father changes from brusque to overly friendly tells me everything I want to know. "It's just dinner, Max."

"I thought you said it's business."

"For me. Your brother is networking. Enough of family. Tell me about Harold Dalton. Did you see him?"

"Last night." I hated every minute of the dinner I shared with that shark.

"And?"

"He's not going to last."

There's a moment of silence. "Is he as bad as our dealers say?"

"Worse. His mine reeks of mismanagement, and his board is corrupt."

"Did you have a look at the books?"

"Only the ones he wanted me to see. He did a good job of trying to hide it, but they're definitely cooked." I have a nose for figures. It only takes me a moment to know when one and one don't add up to two.

"I see." Another short silence. "In that case, we won't interfere with Damian Hart's scheme."

"I'll advise against it. From looking at all the facts, Hart is the best man to revive that mine. Plus, his motivation is personal." *Personal* always guarantees the best results.

"Then we let Dalton go under when the time comes."

"In two years' time, we won't be making any more money out of him. He's running the mine into the ground."

Literally.

Harold Dalton is the owner of one of the most lucrative diamond mines in South Africa. He sells to us directly, cutting out the brokers and wholesalers, which earns us a big fat saving of thirty percent. When you're talking billions, thirty percent is a considerable chunk, enough to bribe and, if needed, kill for.

Word has it that the mine is running empty and will soon go bankrupt. We keep a close ear on the ground. In our business, it's imperative. We have informants everywhere, even in Dalton's mining workforce, and we're not the only ones who play that game.

It turns out Damian Hart has informants, too. He knows about the mine's pending failure. According to his cellmate and our informant, Zane da Costa, the mine has unyielded potential that Dalton is too thick in the head to exploit. Da Costa sold us information about Hart's plans to take over the mine when he gets out of jail. According to Hart, Dalton stole his discovery, and he has every intention of taking it back.

From what I've learned about his strategy and how he's planning on going about it, my money is on Hart. For the time being, Dalton is giving us the first buying option for a kickback. Hart wants to bring back the wholesalers and cut out the shady dealers like ourselves, which poses a problem for our business. If Hart takes away thirty percent of our business, everything will fold—the casinos, shipping companies, our whole empire. Our mission is ensuring Hart honors the deal, and for that to happen, we need a sword we can hold over Hart's head.

My father sighs. "I hate change. Too damn unpredictable."

At least that's one thing we agree on. "Better the devil you know."

"I take it you found Hart's sister."

Dipping a finger into the knot of my tie, I loosen it. "Why else would I call?"

"Are they as close as da Costa said?"

"I don't doubt it." If I had a sister like Zoe, I'd protect her with my life.

"Good. Bring her in."

I hesitate. "It'll take some time." With enough time, I could let her become used to me and even brainwash her into believing it was her idea to leave.

Impatience infuses his tone. "Tomorrow."

"Why the rush?"

"Business is like a game of chess, son. You've got to have your pieces in place before your opponent has as much as thought about moving his. I'm not taking any chances. It'll be checkmate before Hart even enters the game."

"We have six years before Hart has served his sentence. He's only starting to gain power in jail."

A glass clinks. It's time for my father's after-dinner cognac. "I heard from da Costa. Hart may be released from prison early for good behavior."

"How early?"

"In two years."

Someone on the outside is paying Hart for services rendered on the inside. He doesn't have access to that money yet, but in two years' time he'll be considerably wealthier. With wealth comes power, which is the second reason we're not taking him out. Number one is he has the ability to revive a mine that sustains our business, and number two is he's wasted no time in making powerful allies in jail. Some of the families who run Hart's country and pull the politician's strings have members on the inside. They're not the kind of enemies we want or can afford to make.

"How sure are you of this informant?" I've always had a bad feeling about the rat.

"Nothing is ever sure, but this one is power hungry."

They're the easiest to buy, the ones without honor or loyalty.

My father exhales. I imagine him sucking on his cigar. "Let me know at what time you'll arrive."

Staring at the city lights, I consider this new dilemma I didn't expect. I consider what I'm going to do, telling myself it hasn't crossed my mind even once. "Expect me back after the weekend, not before."

"Why the delay?" my father asks.

"I have loose ends to tie up."

Laughter sounds in the background.

"I've got to go," my father says. "The girls have arrived."

I clench my fists. My words are measured. "Say hello to Maman for me."

My father doesn't like the rebuke. The line goes dead. I stare at the phone in my hand. Fuck. If I had more time—

"Maxime?"

I turn around.

Zoe stands in the open sliding door, barefoot and drowning in a hotel robe. Her dull eyes show the medication is kicking in. "What was that about?"

I pocket the phone. "Nothing that concerns you."

"It sounded like a fight."

"Go inside." My body is tense, my cock taking notice of how little there is between my hand and her skin. "You'll catch a cold."

"I don't feel well."

It's not a lie or an attempt at manipulation. The pill will do that. In a minute, she'll be a little nauseous, too.

I close the distance and take her arm. "You're tired. You'll feel better after you've rested."

"I need my clothes." Her tongue slurs a bit. "I have nothing to wear to bed."

In the room, I stop to take one of my T-shirts from the dresser. "Put that on. You can take the bed."

She watches me with drooping, albeit wary eyes. "What about you?"

"I'll take the couch."

"Okay," she says with obvious relief. She takes the T-shirt and stumbles on her way to the bed.

I catch her around the waist before she hits the floor. "I'm sorry, little flower." She smells like the hotel shampoo. When I first pressed her against me, her skin and hair smelled like roses. I make a mental note to get the same brand of shampoo I saw in her apartment before we go.

Helping her into a sitting position on the bed, I stay close in case she pukes.

She puts a hand over her stomach. "I feel sick."

"You'll be fine."

Her long lashes lift, her eyes scanning my face with an ingrained desire to trust. "I think I ate something. The urchin maybe."

"There was nothing wrong with the food. Relax. It'll get better in a minute."

"May I please have some water?"

"Wait it out." I don't want her to puke up what's left of the pill in her stomach.

"Maxime?" There's panic in her sleep-heavy voice.

"Shh." I brace her nape with one hand and cup her cheek with the other, brushing my thumb over the soft skin under her eye as I watch them lose more focus until her eyelids finally close and unconsciousness takes her.

Gently, I lower her to the bed and take a step back. Her hair is spread out around her face, the curls framing her beautiful bone structure. My T-shirt is still in her hand, her dainty fingers folded around it softly. The robe gapes slightly where her legs are bent over the edge. I grow hard looking at her like this. I imagine stripping the robe and spreading her legs to watch her. I imagine dragging my hands over the contours of her body and getting to know her curves while she's out cold. The dark, invasive thought makes me even harder. I could tell her I had to dress her in the T-shirt, so she'd sleep more comfortably. She'd never know if I stroked her or stroked myself while looking at her.

But not like this.

My thoughts are sick. They make me sick.

Disgusted, I grab my testicles and squeeze until my eyes water. The pain is good. It grounds me. I deserved that.

I arrange her like a princess on the bed and cover her with the duvet. Then I sink down into the armchair with my head in my hands, watching, thinking. When I've decided, I get up. I'd like to watch her all night, but there's plenty to do.

It takes a lot of work to make a person disappear.

CHAPTER 4

Zoe

I wake up groggy. My throat is dry, and my eyes burn. I'm lying in a big bed, covered by a soft blanket, instead of on the lumpy mattress of my single bed. Memories from yesterday return, of a man with big hands and a winter's day eyes. I shoot upright.

Blinking, I look around the room, but it's not the hotel room from last night. Wait. What happened before I passed out? The last I recall was feeling sick. Maxime took me to the bedroom and gave me a T-shirt. After that, my mind is a blank.

I glance down at the hotel robe I'm wearing. No T-shirt. I don't remember putting it on or going to bed. My panic escalates as I survey the room with the Renaissance furniture and golden brocade curtains I don't remember.

Where am I?

Jumping from the bed, I rush to the window and yank the curtains open. The view makes me stumble a step back, gasping as I take in the dome roofs and towers over the canal.

My heart beats furiously as I turn back to the room for clues. My bare feet are quiet on the thick carpet as I run to the adjoining room and peer inside. It's a bathroom. I'm desperate, so I lock the door and use the facilities before washing my hands and splashing cold water on my face to clear my head.

The bathroom is even bigger than the one of last night. The shower has twin nozzles. A spa bath window overlooks more sandstone buildings and cobblestone streets. I run to the window and check for a handle, but there isn't one. It doesn't open. Light streams into the room, the sun still high. It's sometime in the morning, maybe around ten.

I go back into the room and open the closet. It's empty. I check the nightstand for stationary or a complimentary pen, any clue, but there's nothing. I have a terrible suspicion, one so unreal it's absurd to even think it. I hurry to the other door and push the handle down. It opens onto a lounge as luxuriously decorated as the bedroom. Maxime sits in an armchair, a cup of espresso on the coffee table. He stands when I enter. Dressed in a dark suit and silver tie, he's as impeccably groomed as yesterday.

"Where am I?" I cry out, going to the lounge window. The view over the square is strangely familiar, yet I know this isn't home. This isn't South Africa.

"Calm down, Zoe. Come have breakfast, and I'll explain."

I spin around. "I don't want breakfast."

He walks to a table and lifts the silver lid from one of the dishes. A waft of pancakes fills the air. He points at the chair. "Please."

The word is a command. Not hungry in the least, I pad over cautiously and lower myself into the seat. He adjusts my chair and serves two pancakes on the plate in front of me before reaching for a bowl of cream.

I can't stand it. I have to know. "Did you touch me?"

His hand stills on the serving spoon. It's minute, but I notice. He drops a dollop on each pancake. "No."

I don't know if I believe him, but he definitely didn't rape me. I would've felt the difference in my body, wouldn't I? "What's going on? Please tell me where we are."

Offering me a bowl of strawberries, he waits with an outstretched arm. It's clear he's not going to budge until I serve myself. I take a strawberry without paying attention to what I'm doing. I'm too focused on his face, looking for answers.

He pours tea that smells like roses into a porcelain cup and puts it next to my plate before taking the seat opposite me. "We're in Venice."

The strawberry drops from my fingers. It rolls over the carpet under the table. I can feel the blood drain from my face as he gives me the verbal confirmation of what I suspected.

"Why?" I whisper.

"I thought you wanted to come here."

He saw the books in my apartment. I clench my jaw. He stole me. That's terrifying, but somehow this, the fact that he invaded my dreams, feels so much worse.

"Eat," he says. "You need your strength."

I grab the knife. The shaft shakes in my hand. Am I capable of stabbing him? Can I drive the blunt end into his black, devious heart? "How did I get here?"

"I have a plane."

"You abducted me." I can't make sense of the facts staring me in the eyes. "I don't even have a passport."

"You didn't. You do now."

"How...You can't just get a passport overnight."

He doesn't answer.

Oh, my God. He came prepared. He came to South Africa with a passport. My kidnapping was well thought out. Premeditated. "Just tell me what you want."

He crosses his legs as he considers me with his emotionless eyes. Does he even feel anything? Is he a psychopath? His face is rough and unsightly to look at, but it's the flatness of those sharp, gray eyes that scares me the most.

"Eat," he says again, "and then we'll talk."

I eat, not because I want to, but so he'll tell me what's going on. The pancakes are fluffy, but I don't taste anything.

"Have a strawberry," he says. "They're out of season. I had them flown in especially."

I stare at the bowl of fat, red strawberries. Each one is perfect, almost too pretty to be real. Taking one, I bite into the flesh. Juice runs over my chin. I catch it with my palm. He reaches over the table, offering me a linen napkin. I snatch it from his hand, scrunching it up in my fist before dumping it next to my plate in an impulsive act of defiance.

The warm drink is the only thing I really want. I reach for the tea. "I ate. Now talk."

Rubbing a thumb over his lips, he seems to weigh his words. After an awkward silence, he says, "We need to borrow you for a while."

The warm tea scalds my throat as I almost choke on the sip I took. "Borrow me? We?"

"My family."

I replace the cup on the saucer lest I drop the hot liquid in my lap. "What for?"

"You don't need to concern yourself over the details. What you need to know is Damian's life is in your hands."

Shock runs through me. He—they—intend to keep me. If I don't comply, Damian will pay. "I have a job, a home, friends—"

"You resigned," he says. "I already gave up your lease and took care of your outstanding bills."

"You can't do that," I exclaim. "My plant… the cats… nobody else will feed them."

"Your neighbor kindly took your plant, and I'm paying for the food he'll feed the cats. He also promised to return your library books."

I jump to my feet. "You went back to see Bruce?"

"He sent a text to your phone to tell you what happened. He wisely thought he should warn you about the thieves targeting your building. I explained you were with me and wanted me to check on him."

"You told him I was going away with you. Is that the lie you told him?"

"He was happy for you. Oh, and you'll also be glad to know I replaced his phone. He was very grateful for the gesture."

I swallow down my tears. I can't believe this is happening. "You drugged me."

"It was easier that way, less stressful for you."

I curl my hands into balls at my sides. "You don't know what's easier for me."

"Sit down and finish breakfast. We have work to do before I can show you the city."

"You want to go fucking sightseeing?"

"Mind your tongue, Zoe. We're really going to have to do something about your language."

"Is that why you brought me here?" Every muscle in my body is trembling in rage. "As payoff for *borrowing* me?"

"No," he says softly. "Not for that."

"How long exactly is this borrowing supposed to last?"

"Three, four years. It's hard to say. It all depends."

Four years? I place a hand over my stomach, feeling sick again. "On what?"

"I can't say."

His calm indifference infuriates me. I want to slap him. Kill him. My gaze darts to the teapot. If I throw it into his face—

"Don't even think about it," he says. "Gautier and Benoit are right outside. I really don't want to punish you, but I will. I'm not going to threaten you with Damian again. The next time you disobey me, I'll put those threats into action." He gets up and walks over, stopping close to me. "This," he waves an arm around the room, "is not going to happen every day, maybe never again, so I suggest you make the most of it. Enjoy the food. Enjoy the trip. I went to a lot of effort and spent a lot of money to make this happen for you. Whether you hate it or set aside your pride to enjoy it won't change your fate. You may as well make the wise choice and make the most of it."

With his speech done, he watches me with a raised brow, waiting for me to make my decision. I want to fling myself at him in a fit of fury and punch him in his ugly face, but I can't surrender to my anger. That's not an option he gave me, not unless I want to suffer the consequences of getting my brother hurt. The wiser option is to tamp down my bitter anger and mad rage, and to obey like a dog.

It takes all the strength I possess to sit back down and fold my hands around the teacup. It hurts. It hurts my self-esteem and my pride, but I swallow it with my tears, not only for Damian, but also for myself.

"Good decision," he says, squeezing my shoulder.

My body stiffens under his touch. Thankfully, he pulls his hand away.

While I force pancakes and strawberries down my throat, washing it down with rose petal tea, he makes phones calls in French. He stays on the far side of the lounge, as if giving me space would help to keep down my food.

When my plate is empty, he calls me over with a flick of his fingers.

I stand and walk over like the obedient dog he's making of me.

Approval softens his features. He likes my obedience, or maybe it's just easier for him not having to fight and threaten me constantly. "Would you like to have a shower? I'm having clothes sent over for you in a while."

"I have clothes." Which I love.

"They won't serve you here."

I give him a hateful look.

His smile is patient. "The weather here is much less forgiving than in your country."

"I'll have a shower," I bite out.

"Another good choice." Another mocking smile. "You'll find everything you need in the bathroom."

I go to the bathroom and lock the door for good measure. As he promised, the cabinet is stocked with cosmetics and toiletries. I even find my normal brand of shampoo as well as the conditioner I could never afford.

Opting for the shower instead of the bath, I quickly wash and dry off. I apply some body lotion to alleviate the dryness of my skin. I don't know if it's a side effect of the drugs or the flight. I've never travelled. I do know from reading that Venice is a fourteen-hour-long flight from Johannesburg. The surrealism of it all still shakes me to my core. When I'm done, I pull on a clean robe with a hotel logo.

Maxime is waiting in the lounge when I step out. There's a rail with dresses, jackets, and coats. Several pairs of boots are displayed on the floor. A box with underwear stands on the coffee table.

"I think this is your size," he says.

Despite my resolution to take as little from Maxime as possible, I can't help but go over to admire the clothes. My fingers itch to touch the fabric. I lift a tag and nearly faint at the price. It's Valentino. I've never shopped in a department store, let alone a boutique. My clothes are either self-made or bought at the flea market. Owning a piece from a world-renowned designer has only featured in my dreams, which is why I drop the tag. I'm not giving Maxime more of my dreams.

"What's wrong?" he asks. "Don't you like the clothes?"

I turn to face him. "No."

He shrugs. "Then I'll choose what you wear."

I watch with mounting anger as he takes a navy wool dress with white sailor collar and matching coat from the rail.

"I think this will look good on you." He pushes the items into my hands. "Go put that on."

I jut out my chin. "No."

"You prefer to go out naked?" Something sparks in his eyes, something dark and demented, as if the idea appeals to him. "Maybe I should let you walk around without clothes. I could put a collar and chain on you instead. Would you like that? Would the way people look at you make you wet?"

"You're sick," I spit out.

He puts his nose inches from mine. "Right now you still have a choice. Remember what I said about not wasting the little you have."

Dumping the blue set on the couch, I back away. "Fine. You win. You can have your way in this, but you'll never have a piece of my soul."

He smiles. "I never asked for your soul."

Seething, I spin away from him and flip through the clothes with more force than necessary. My hand stills on a beautiful pink coat with a scrunched collar. The matching dress is a fitted cut with puffy sleeves.

"Good choice," he says.

Grabbing the box with the underwear, I escape to the room. The dress fits perfectly. I finish off the outfit with nude winter tights and boots.

A knock falls on the door just as I finish drying my hair. I pull a brush through it and reluctantly open the door.

Maxime's gaze trails over me. There's nothing in his eyes to tell me what he thinks, not that I care.

"Time for work." He takes my hand and pulls me into the lounge.

I jerk free but follow him to the writing desk pushed against a window. A writing block with the hotel logo and pen lie on the desk. He pulls out the chair in silent command. Once I'm seated, he puts the pen in my hand.

"You're going to write a letter," he says.

I already know before I ask, "To who?"

"To Damian. You're going to tell him you met someone, a foreigner visiting your country, and that he swept you off your feet. Love at first sight. You went out for dinner. It was beautiful, like a fairytale. You were devastated when he had to go back to his country. He couldn't bear leaving you behind, so he asked you to come with him. You didn't think twice. He got you a passport, and you left the country. You're in Europe with him now, and you're very, very happy."

He presses his palms on the desk, putting our faces close together. His eyes are cold, as always, but it's a different kind of cold, a cold that frightens me, because flames can burn a cold shade of winter.

"So happy, that you're never going back."

It's that spark flickering under the deepest layers of gray ash that makes me lean back. It's the story he told, the one he stole from my books that parts my lips on a soundless gasp. It punches a hole straight through my heart, because this will be the most terrible lie I've ever told, and I've never lied to my brother, not even once.

My nostrils stir in the stare-off between us, faint tremors running over my body and accumulating in my fingers where he pushed the pen.

I was holding out for that story, for that love. That man. He has no right to steal that place, to take my fantasy and twist it into a hopeless lie. I can't write it. If I do, I'll lose a piece of myself, and I swore I wouldn't.

The pen drops from my fingers. It rolls to the edge of the desk where he catches it.

I shake my head. "I can't."

He puts the pen back in my hand, folding my fingers around it. "You will."

"I'll come up with something." My voice is hoarse. "Something Damian will believe."

"He'll believe this." He pushes a strand of hair behind my ear. "Nothing else."

How does this stranger know so much about me from going through my belongings? There's more to this than cooking up a believable story. Maxime wants to make my fantasy his own. He wants to feature in it. That's what those cold flames signify —excitement.

"I've never lied to my brother," I say in a feeble attempt to appeal to his compassion, even if I'm starting to believe he has none.

"I wouldn't corrupt you if I had a choice." His gaze moves to my lips, then to the neckline of the dress. "In this, there is no choice."

He says it with so much conviction, regret almost, that I'm silent for a moment. The statement is false. Of course, he has a choice, but he believes he doesn't. I want to beg him not to make me do it, but he tightens his fingers over mine where I'm clutching the pen and brings my hand to his mouth. I'm shocked to an immobile state as he kisses every knuckle, five times of reverence. It's only when the warmth of his lips fades that I get the function of my body back, enough to pull away my hand, enough to put pen to paper, and start the destruction of a part of my dream.

This is important to me. Was important to me. My hand shakes as I spin the tale, so much that he stills me, tears off the page, and makes me start over.

He kisses my head tenderly, whispering in a soothing tone, "It's all right, little flower. You're doing well."

The untruth burns into my heart as I write it. It's more than lying to my brother. It's admitting that my dream is over, destroyed. That I held out for nothing. That it's never going to happen. No knight is going to charge in on a white horse and save me, just like Damian had said.

So, I do. I write it. I say Maxime's words. At the end, I sign off with, *I love you, always.* It's the only piece of truth in the letter, the part that will tell Damian the rest is false. I never say I love him. I don't have to. He knows. Damian and I don't use that kind of language with each other. Maybe it's because our parents couldn't tell us they loved us, and we've always felt awkward admitting the words.

I turn my face to look up at Maxime. He's shaking his head, giving me a disapproving tsk of his tongue. "That's one of the things I find so endearing about you. It's your will to survive." He strokes a hand over my head. "Just like a little wildflower."

Feigning innocence, I ask, "What do you mean?"

He straightens, takes his phone out of his pocket, swipes over the screen, and turns it to me.

I suck in a breath. On the screen is a copy of a letter, the last one I wrote to Damian. He flicks his finger again. Another letter. Again and again. All my letters.

"Where did you get these?" I cry out.

He tilts his head, giving me time to figure it out for myself.

"Zane da Costa." I say the name like a curse.

"You'll sign it Zoe with two x's and two o's like you always do." He tears off the page, crumples it in his fist, and indicates the blank sheet.

With no choice, I start again, writing Maxime's words but signing as myself.

"That's better," he says, folding the page exactly in the middle and sliding it into one of the matching envelopes with the hotel logo, proof that I've truly left the country, and proof that I'm in a luxurious hotel on my dream vacation.

Oh, my God. That's why Maxime did it. That's why the sly bastard brought me here. It's for appearances sake. If Damian had any doubts after reading my letter, this would convince him I met a wealthy stranger who treats me like a princess. It will smooth over any concerns Damian may have, because princesses are loved and adored.

I twist in the chair to face the man who made me a hostage. Hostages aren't loved and adored. They're used and manipulated. "You're a bastard."

"Shh." He plants a kiss on my head, looking smug as he slips the envelope into the inside pocket of his jacket. "You've been a good girl. Get your coat. It's time for your reward."

I stand on wooden legs. When I don't move for several seconds, Maxime fetches the pink coat and throws it over my shoulders. He hands me a fur-trimmed wool hat and matching scarf. I feel frozen, my fingers too stiff to obey the signals from my brain as he helps me into the coat and buttons it up. He fits the scarf and hat, and finally the gloves, dressing me like a child.

He seems like a happy tourist looking forward to exploring a new city when he pulls on his own coat, scarf, and gloves.

"Have you been here before?" I blurt out, because the guard I should be keeping on my tongue seemed to have shut down with my mental and physical functions.

"Many times," he says.

My tone is biting. "Then this should be very boring for you."

"But it makes me the perfect tour guide." He offers his arm.

I let him hook his arm through mine. I've already fought too many battles with him that I can't win. I need to save my energy for the ones that matter.

Outside the room, Gautier and Benoit stand guard, just like Maxime had said. They nod at Maxime in greeting but ignore me. We go down a hallway with beautiful paintings and mirrors and descend a staircase with a carved wooden rail. The lobby is extravagantly furbished with tones of burgundy and gold. We cross a marble foyer, and then we're in a cobblestone street.

A blast of cold air hits me, making my eyes water. Of course. It's winter here. I didn't think about it, not even when Maxime dressed me up in warm clothes. Abstractly, the knowledge registered, but my brain was on shutdown. The sudden chill makes me shiver.

Maxime pulls me closer. "Warm enough?"

I stiffen. I'm not, but I nod. I walk next to him, deflated, while Gautier and Benoit follow. I absently take in the sights Maxime points out, not to spite him or myself, but because I simply can't gather any enthusiasm, let alone excitement. My mind takes in the beautiful city, but my heart doesn't process the sensory experiences as joy.

We visit Saint Mark's Basilica, Dodge's Palace, and the Rialto Bridge. At each one, we pose for photos Benoit takes with Maxime's phone. I smile when Maxime tells me to, the gesture stiff and unnatural, but when he shows me the photos we look like every other couple in a pose—happy and carefree. It's the trickery of the scenery, of the wind that blows wisps of hair across my face, hiding my expression and making us look breathlessly windblown instead of cruel and trapped. I suppose the photos are more evidence in case my friends back home ask questions. Maybe Maxime will even include one in the letter to Damian.

In the afternoon, we stop for pizza. Maxime says the restaurant is famous throughout the world and that I'll spot some of the Italian *families* dining there. I don't care about spotting infamous mafia members. I eat the pizza and drink the wine, noticing in the back of my mind that the bill is the price of buying a pizza franchise back home. Maxime does all the talking, keeping a steady conversation, but the words float into one ear and out of the other. I'm in a strange kind of limbo. It feels as if I'm not present but staring down at myself from somewhere else, somewhere safer.

"Coffee?" Maxime asks, pulling my attention to him after the waiter has cleared our dessert plates. "Or maybe tea?"

"No, thank you."

"Did you like the tiramisu?"

I look at him. I don't answer, because I really don't know.

His mouth tightens. "Zoe."

"Yes."

He smiles. "Good." Getting up, he holds out a hand. "Come."

Outside, he stops at the flower market to buy a huge bouquet of pink roses. They really are pretty and smell divine. I expect him to take more photos with the flowers as another one of his props, but he seems to be done with the photos. Benoit carries the flowers while Maxime helps me into a gondola. The oarsman speaks to Maxime in Italian. I'm not sure what they say, but Maxime is fluent in the language.

The oarsman steers us down the canal, under bridges and archways, singing passionate songs of love while I sit next to Maxime with a blanket draped over our legs. He's holding my hand as if we are lovers and not as if he has a gun tucked in his waistband under his jacket and his two guards aren't following in their own gondola a short distance behind.

Around the bend, the oarsman stops for us to admire the sunset. It's chilly, and I'm grateful when we finally get off and start making our way back to the hotel. My legs are tired, and I want to crawl into bed and curl into a ball, hiding from *him*, from myself, and most of all from the next four years.

We stop on the square. It's not until Maxime frames my face between his broad palms that I notice Gautier and Benoit have fallen slightly behind, giving us space.

"Zoe." Just from the way my name is a sigh on his lips I know what's to follow is going to be heavy. "Did you have fun today?"

I return from whatever spell I'd been in, my consciousness being thrown back into the moment. Like when he grabbed me in the lobby of my apartment block, my senses become heightened and my awareness sharp. Instinctively, I sense this is important, that the moment has detrimental effects on my wellbeing.

I nod, because I don't want to displease him.

"Good." He smiles, rubbing his thumbs over my cheeks. "Now use your words."

"Yes." Belatedly, I add, "Thank you."

"I want you to listen very carefully to me," he continues. "Remember what I said about choices?"

I nod again, my anxiety mounting.

"I'm going to give you one, maybe the most important one you'll ever make, and I want you to think carefully. I want you to make it wisely. Understand?" He shakes me a little when I don't answer. "Do you understand?"

I don't, but the word he expects slips from my lips. "Yes."

Letting me go, he takes a step back. For a moment, he hesitates, but then he takes my hand and leads me toward an alley. He's walking so fast I have to run to keep up, and by the time we enter a dark, narrow, passageway, he's almost dragging me behind him.

"Maxime." I pull on his hand, trying to get him to slow down, but he won't look at me.

We follow another passageway, this one even narrower, that cuts toward the canal. Under a bridge, we take a staircase that descends to a level below the buildings. The staircase is cold and moldy, the stone walls wet. It leads to a room that seems to be under the water level, maybe an old part of a house before the foundations of the city sank below the sea.

"What is this?" I ask, blinking for my eyes to adjust.

The only light comes from a ventilation hole with an iron grid high up on the wall, just below the ceiling.

Maxime turns to look at me, his eyes flat and emotionless in the dusky interior. He pulls me closer, flush against his body, and folds my arms behind my back. Something clips around my wrists.

"Maxime," I cry out on a whisper.

He slams my back against the wall and takes something from his pocket. I watch in horror as he peels away the backing of a piece of duct tape.

"Maxime! What are you—?"

He seals my lips with the tape, pressing so hard my head knocks against one of the stone bricks. Stars explode behind my eyelids. I shake my head, trying to clear my vision, and when I open my eyes again, I'm just in time to see him fling an iron gate shut, and then a heavy wooden door.

CHAPTER 5

Zoe

Semi-darkness folds around me with the turn of the key. Running to the door, I slam a shoulder against it. The only noises I can get out are panicked mm's. All I get in return is Maxime's retreating footsteps. His heels clack on the stairs, then farther overhead, and finally nothing.

Silence.

I sag against the wall, shaking from head to toe. I can't believe he did this. I can't believe he left me here. Alone. But why is that so hard to believe? He's cruel, not kind.

The shadows are creeping up on me fast. Soon, it will be completely dark. I look around while I can still make out shapes in the dusk. A bench is pushed up against the wall. Other than that, there's nothing.

A sense of abandonment washes over me. I feel lost and alone, but that's nothing compared to the betrayal that burns in my stomach.

Panic.

I have to get out of here. The only hole in this godforsaken place is the ventilation gap, and that's not big enough for a cat to squeeze through, not that I'll ever reach that high, not even standing on the bench.

I go still, taking in the quiet.

Think, Zoe. Think.

It's not completely quiet. The silence I registered after the absence of human voices—Maxime's and my own—is in fact, now that I listen, permeated with the lap of water and the distant hum of a motorboat.

Maybe if I make enough noise someone will hear me. I grab the idea like a life buoy, kicking the walls with the heels and toes of my boots until my feet hurt. When that doesn't work, I kick over the bench and drive it repeatedly into the wall with my feet, but I'm under the water level, and the stone walls must be thick. No one will hear me through the massive door.

The hopelessness of the situation drives me to my knees. I hit the wet, cold, hard floor with my hands handcuffed behind my back, staring up at the hole that goes black as the night sets in.

Despite my coat, hat, scarf, and gloves, I'm cold. I force myself back onto my feet, struggling to do so with my hands tied, but I eventually manage by using the wall as a support. I trace the diameter of the room, turning in circles to create heat and stay warm, but the space is too small for the exercise to work effectively. I jump up and down for as long as I can, but eventually I tire too much.

I turn the bench back over with a foot and sit down. The only way I'm getting out of here is if someone lets me. Maybe nobody will. Maybe that's why Maxime left me here.

To die.

I start crying shamefully as the notion takes form like a living, breathing monster in my chest. A squeaky noise stills me. Something scurries over my hands. Screaming behind the duct tape, I jump up. More squeaking sounds.

Rats.

My teeth start to chatter. I huddle in a corner just like I used to when I was a child. Only, my fairytales can't save me any longer. This is a nightmare, and it's real.

Is Maxime coming back?

He has my letter and the photos. He has my phone. He can send the photos to Damian and my friends, showing them what a great time I'm having. Everyone who knows me even a little knows I've always wanted to come to Venice. Everyone knows I've stupidly been waiting for love to find me, for the right man to save me. Eloping with a stranger is such a *me* thing to do. No one is going to come looking for me. I'll vanish off the face of the earth. My bones will rot in this burial chamber under the canals of Venice, the city of my dreams.

I can't help but laugh hysterically through my tears. What a stupid idiot I've been. So naïve.

Sniffing, I wipe my cheek on my shoulder. Feeling sorry for myself isn't going to help. It's not the fear of dying that hits me hardest in the gut. It's the regret. It's not paying closer attention when Maxime said it wouldn't always be like this. His meaning was obvious, yet my mind rejected it, choosing not to see it. It's not heeding Maxime's words when he told me to make the best of the day, most probably the last day of my life.

CHAPTER 6

Maxime

Back at the hotel, I dismiss my guards and have a long, warm shower. Then I order room service, put on a classical music collection, and arrange the roses in the vase while I wait for my food to be delivered.

It arrives promptly, a steak the way I like—rare—with garlic and parsley potatoes on the side and a bottle of their best red. The cutlery is silver and the glass crystal. The candle on the table is scented. It smells of lavender. Tomorrow, I'll ask them to get some rose-scented ones.

I eat everything, enjoying the warmth of my suite and the view over the square. When I'm done, I pour four fingers of cognac from the wet bar and walk to the window to stare at the canal. It's pretty at night with lanterns hanging over the bridges. So romantic. Such an illusion. Under the beautiful streets where tourists eat, laugh, and shop, lies my buried treasure. Somewhere down there under the dirty water is a little flower, a yellow daisy that will wilt and die without sunlight or water.

I stopped smoking years ago, but I wrap my coat around my body and take the packet I nicked from Gautier out onto the balcony. Lighting one up, I drag the smoke into my lungs. If she's suffering, so will I. It's the least I can give her. Stripping naked, I bare my body to the cold. As always, the freezing pain settling in my toes and fingers grounds me.

I don't finish the cigarette.

I put it out on my chest.

CHAPTER 7

Zoe

When I doze off, the rats soon discover I'm a harmless target and nip at the exposed flesh of my wrists and even at my legs through my tights. I swat and kick at them, but they're becoming fearless, even taking their chances when I'm awake. The broken skin burns at first, but after a while the cold numbs everything, so much so I don't feel the bite of pain as their sharp teeth gnaw at my flesh. The best way of warding them off is moving, but they follow and try to climb up my legs when they can't bite through my boots.

By the time the sun comes up, I'm exhausted and cold to my core. It's as if the damp has infiltrated my bones. I can't stand on my feet anymore. I think the rats may kill me before I starve. I'm not sure which is the most merciful. My stockings are torn and the expensive clothes ruined, dirty from the damp and black mold on the walls. It stinks worse than my apartment building down here.

Leaning against the wall, I kick at a rat that climbs onto the toe of my boot. The slosh of the water is quieter. It's low tide. There's something else, too, like the fall of a hammer. It comes closer. No, it's the fall of footsteps. My heart starts thundering in my chest when they descend down the steps. I brace myself, praying for rescue, but the door swings open on Maxime's face.

He's wearing a pale suit with a pink tie, and his face is clean-shaven. When he opens the gate and enters my prison, a whiff of winter reaches my nostrils. It's clean and fresh, a stark contrast to my dirt and exhaustion, like a magnifying glass on his cruelty. He's cold and monstrous.

He's not my savior.

I back away, but he grips my hair with one hand, and carefully pulls off the tape with the other. It hurts. The skin on my lips stretches and cracks. I drag my tongue over them and taste blood.

Something inside me snaps. My vision turns blurry.

He turns me around to undo the cuffs. The moment my hands are free, I jump at him. I claw and hit, screaming like a mad person. I must be mad, because what I should be doing is escaping. I kick. I punch him in the gut. He only stands there and takes it, my blows doing no damage. After the next fist I jam into his stomach, I shove him and run.

I'm not even on the first step before he grabs hold of my ankle. I go down, stopping my fall with my hands. The heels of my palms burn as the skin comes off, but I kick with all my might. I dig my fingers into the stone, my nails breaking as he drags me back into my cell.

"No!"

He flips me onto my back and covers my mouth with his hand. My lips are pulled back, my jaw wide. I bite down until the pressure of his hand becomes so severe, I think my skull may crack.

"Are you done?" he asks through thin lips.

I shake my head, but we both know I am. The fight goes out of me, my energy spent.

"If you scream," he says, "I'll leave. I can do this for days until you're ready to listen."

When I go still, he removes his hand. "That's better."

I lie on my back on the damp stones, the wetness seeping through my coat and dress, through my very skin and into my heart. He's crouching next to me, studying me with one arm braced on his knee. His frame is big and powerful. The shadow he casts over me swallows me whole. Somehow, it seems darker and colder than the winter night I spent in my cell.

"I want you to listen to me, Zoe."

My gaze homes in on his face, on the non-symmetrical lines of his features and the bump on the bridge of his nose.

"When I take you home," he continues in his musical accent, "you have a choice."

My hope lifts a fraction. "To South Africa?"

"To France."

The words are a punch. I don't know how many more punches I can take. I force the question from numb lips. "What choice?"

"It can be like yesterday, like the day we spent, or it can be like this." He motions around the space. "What you decide is entirely up to you, but you should know that each choice comes with a price."

I hold my breath, waiting for him to carry on.

"If I take you to my family in France, this is what awaits you. You'll be locked up, a prisoner. The men will take turns with you, starting with my brother, and he's not a kind man. He'll keep you alive, but you'll wish you were dead. The only way I can protect you is to lay claim to you." His gaze pierces mine. "Do you understand what I'm saying?"

My body is shaking uncontrollably, my mind refusing to give meaning to the words.

"Do you understand, Zoe?" he asks in his musical accent.

I shake my head.

"You're going to have to become my mistress." The flames in his eyes burn glacially. "You're going to have to let me fuck you, convincingly and often."

CHAPTER 8

Maxime

Zoe's pretty, blue eyes flare, as always giving away her heart. She finds the idea of me fucking her disgusting. I didn't expect otherwise. Nonetheless, it stabs into my chest.

I bet she'll find Alexis handsome. All the women do, until they discover his fetishes.

She licks her cracked lips. "Are you asking me to sell my body in exchange for your protection?"

"I don't need to buy sex, little flower." Despite my physique, I have enough eager bed partners.

"You mean your mistress as for real?"

I nod, a sadistic part of me enjoying her discomfort for making her distaste so obvious. "For real."

I can almost see her brain kicking back into action. "Why can't we pretend? Why do I have to sleep with you?"

"Because my family will know." More accurately, my father and brother.

"How?"

"Believe me, there are signs that will be obvious." I fuck hard. My family knows me. My lovers don't walk straight in the morning, not that they're complaining. There will be medical checkups, birth control, and our doctor is a family friend. He'll report back to my father. Changing to a different practitioner will be suspicious, a dead giveaway. No, there's only one way of playing this.

For real.

She swallows. "Why would you help me?"

Yes, why indeed? "Because I'd hate to see your life wasted."

She blinks, her lashes wet with unshed tears. "Isn't it already wasted?"

"Choice, Zoe. It all depends on how you choose to look at it."

Sniffing, she turns her face to the light that falls in a wedge from the hole in the wall. Between the two options, I know, and she knows what her choice is going to be. I let her have the moment, let her bask in denial for a little while longer.

When she finally looks back at me, her tears are spilling over. It both pains and pleases me how little she wants me and that she's already admitting her defeat, because when she opens her pretty, little mouth, she's going to give me her consent.

She nods, a small movement that barely tilts her head.

I wipe a strand of hair from her dirty face. "Say it." The quicker she consents, the quicker I can carry her out of here, clean her, and give her sunlight and water so she'll flourish again.

"Yes," she says in a faint voice.

"Yes, what?"

"I'll be your mistress."

"That's a good choice, Zoe." I drag my palm over her cheek. "You made it wisely."

I don't waste time. I scoop her up from the cold floor, cradling her against my chest. The demonstration was a hard one, but it was necessary. It hurt me as much as it hurt her. The fresh cigarette burns on my stomach and chest are proof of that.

She weighs nothing in my arms as I mount the stairs. I hold her tighter, sheltering her against the cold as much as I can. She's mine now. I'll take care of her every need.

Gautier waits at the street level with a blanket. He drapes it over her, careful not to touch her, and I tuck it around her body. She's shivering like a petal caught in a storm. We don't go down the alley but take the steps to the jetty where the motorboat is tied. Benoit is aboard. At our approach, he unties the boat. I lower Zoe to her feet and help her inside. When we're all in, I sit, drawing her into my lap and making sure she's covered with the blanket.

Benoit starts the engine and turns the boat into the canal. The wind nips at my face and ears. In the fight, Zoe lost her hat. She draws deeper under the blanket, huddling close to me. It feeds a hungry part of me. I open my jacket and pull it around her under the blanket so the heat from my body can warm her better.

After a short ride, we moor the boat in front of our hotel. It's early. Few people are about. I lift Zoe out and carry her inside while my men scout the area ahead of us. We don't run into anyone in the lobby or on the stairs, and a few minutes later we're back in the suite.

Carrying her straight to the bathroom, I lower her onto the bench next to the bath before crouching in front of her. When I reach for the blanket, she clutches it tighter to her chest.

"What are you doing?" she asks.

"You need a shower." When the pleat on her brow doesn't smooth out, I explain my intention. "I'm not going to hurt you. I need to take care of you."

"Then get out."

I stand. The rejection stings, but I welcome the hurt. Feeling something after nothing, after thinking I'd never feel again, is a miracle and joyful in itself.

She agreed. I want to remind her, but I have to be patient. In fact, it's better I don't see her naked before tonight. The drawn-out expectation will only heighten the pleasure.

Still, I'm not comfortable leaving her in this state. She's tired and weak. She can slip in the shower and crack open her head.

"Please?" she says.

The word pulls at my heart, another foreign sensation, because I do want to please her.

"Call if you need me." I turn and leave but stop in the door. "Maybe it's better if you have a bath."

"I'll be fine," she says, her eyes sparking with annoyance.

I smile in return. "I'm right outside."

Her rosebud mouth turns down. "Isn't that good to know?"

I let it slide. I'm so happy to have her consent.

Closing the door to give her privacy, I settle down at the bureau in the bedroom so I can hear her in case she changes her mind about needing my help. I summon Benoit and give him the letter to mail with an instruction to bring back a tetanus shot. We have contacts everywhere. I can get anything I want, no matter where I am.

The water in the shower comes on. By the time it turns off, I've ordered brunch and made arrangements for tonight. When Zoe steps out dressed in a bathrobe, I point at the loveseat.

She trots over, but falters before she reaches the seat. "Are you going to do it now?"

My grin is diabolic. I know what she means, but I want her to say it. "Do what?"

"You know." She waves at the bed.

"You mean fuck you?"

Her cheeks turn a deep pink, pretty like a fuchsia rose.

I watch her with my hands folded behind my back, enjoying her shyness. "We don't need a bed to fuck. We can do it on other furniture, in many different places, and in a variety of positions." But for our first time, it will be in the bed.

She swallows. "I'm not ready."

What does she need to be ready? Definitely not clothes. I enjoy playing this game of cat and mouse with her, but I want her relaxed, not stressed. I want her to enjoy it. It's in both our interest that I put her mind at ease.

"Don't worry." I walk closer. "You have time."

Her shoulders sag. Does she know how openly she shows her relief? "Until when?"

"Tonight."

Nighttime is when lovers do it, at least the first time. Or so I presume. I've never been the romantic type. I've never been anyone's lover. I've fucked enough times to have refined the technique of giving a woman pleasure to an art, but I've never been with the same woman more than a couple of times. I'm actually looking forward to exploring long-term sex with Zoe, which is why the first time is important. The first time of everything determines how the rest of it will go.

Taking her hand, I pull her down onto the seat. Then I crouch in front of her and brush the robe away to expose her legs. She sits quietly, albeit tensely, as I inspect the bite marks on her legs. I push back the sleeves and turn her wrists this way and that to do the same. Finally, I straighten to drag my fingers through her hair and over her scalp, feeling for bumps. There's a small one at the back of her head.

"Do you have pain?" I ask.

She shakes her head.

"Are you hungry?"

"Thirsty," she says.

"I'll feed you soon."

I leave her on the loveseat to take the medicine kit from my bag. I never travel without one. It's a must in our business. Meticulously, I disinfect every mark and scratch on her skin, including the heels of her palms.

The brunch arrives just as I've finished. I don't make her sit at the table but order her to bed and fluff out the pillows behind her back. I serve a savory muffin, bacon, and scrambled eggs onto a plate and let her eat in bed while I pour rose petal tea into a cup to cool.

Benoit returns with the tetanus vaccine as I carry her empty plate away. I first give her an anti-inflammatory pill to drink with her tea, and then I take a hypodermic syringe from the kit.

Her eyes widen when I insert the needle into the vial. "What are you doing?"

"It's a tetanus shot," I explain, "for the bites."

She says nothing as I push the sleeve of the robe up and lock my fingers around her arm. She flinches when I insert the needle into her skin and empty the syringe, but she's a brave girl. She doesn't complain.

With my charge taken care of, I'm a lot happier, certainly less miserable than last night. The only thing left is for her to get some rest.

Stroking her soft hair that's still damp after her shower, I say, "Close your eyes. Sleep. You must be tired."

She doesn't argue. Her long lashes flutter over her eyes, and her face muscles go slack as she eases down onto the mattress. With an unusually docile acceptance, she allows me to pet her hair.

Someday, she'll long for me to touch her like this. There will come a day she won't have to simply tolerate my touch.

When I'm done with her, she's going to need it like a drug.

CHAPTER 9

Zoe

It's dusk when I wake up. The room is basked in a soft, rose-gold glow. I feel a lot better than this morning. My belly is full, my aches are gone, I'm warm, and I'm fully rested. Then a ball of trepidation tightens my stomach, spoiling my good physical state.

In an hour, it will be dark. Sinful things happen in the dark. Prey is hunted and monsters thrive, but vows must be honored, no matter if dreams are destroyed.

I swing my legs over the bed and look around. Thankfully, I'm alone in the room. Not knowing how much I'll be granted in the future, I make the most of the privacy by going to the bathroom to use the facilities, but when I open the door, I'm met with shimmering candlelight and the sensual smell of roses. The tub is filled with steaming water, rose petals drifting on top. Candles burn on the vanity, floor, and edge of the bath. Petals are scattered around them. The scene is so pretty I forget to be angry and even to be anxious for a moment, but then I remember who's set it all up, and my shoulders snap tight with tension again.

I glance back at the room, expecting *him* to be standing there, gauging my reaction, but I'm still alone. The fragrance and the warm water are too enticing to waste. I lock the door and let the robe slip from my shoulders. Tying my hair in a bun on top of my head, I climb into the tub and lower myself into the water.

It's heaven. The warmth seeps into my skin, melting the tightness in my muscles. A flute with bubbly, golden liquid stands within my hand's reach on the windowsill. It's a beautiful glass with intricate engraving. I bring it to my lips and take a sip. The champagne is dry and yeasty. I've had a couple of glasses in my lifetime, at year-end work parties on both occasions, and instantly loved the taste. It's a luxury I could never afford on my grocery budget.

It takes a bit of playing with the settings before I figure out how to make the bubbles work. A stream of water massages my lower back and another my feet. I lay back—there's even a bath pillow for my head—and admire the view of the canal and the bridge below. Lights are twinkling on the bridge, and the streetlamps illuminating the cobblestone street look antique, like something straight from a fairytale. Except, this isn't a fairytale, and I shouldn't forget it.

As reality wiggles back into my consciousness, wiping away the beauty of the moment, I down the champagne in one go. I no longer want to sip it for enjoyment. I only want to use it to dull my senses.

I do have a little buzz when I get out a long while later and dry myself. My thoughts run ahead to what will follow, but they're interrupted by what I find when I walk back into the room. The bed has been freshly made with clean linen. A pink dress is arranged at the foot end. It's the most beautiful creation I've seen. Unable to help myself, I step closer.

It's a long, off-shoulder evening dress. The cut is simple. What makes it extraordinary is the diamante tulle. It's shimmery, delicate, and so faintly pink the color is a mere blush. I love it. It's completely me. The thought makes me go rigid. Of course, Maxime knows. He probably went through my books and sketches when he went back to see Bruce and wipe away the evidence of my existence.

Pink silk underwear and thigh-high stockings with a lace trimming are set out next to the dress. A velvet box catches my eyes. My curiosity piqued, I reach for the box and flip back the lid. A pair of solitaire diamonds sits on a black velvet cushion, their light brighter than sunrays or a rainbow. They're enormous, at least a couple carats. I've never owned a diamond, but I know a lot about them from the clippings I collected of my dream ring, the one the man who loved me was going to offer me.

I close the lid and throw the box back onto the bed.

What am I doing?

How can I admire objects my kidnapper bought? Soon to be my lover. A chill breaks out over my body. When I think of the alternative, of what Maxime showed and told me, I drop the towel and pull on the clothes.

Everything fits perfectly, even the heels that are the same color as the dress. I'm about to go to the bathroom to brush my hair when I notice the silver brush and cosmetics on the bedroom dresser. I go over and trace the embossed rose on the back of the brush. It's beautiful, a piece of art. After removing the elastic keeping up my bun, I pull the brush through my hair, almost closing my eyes at how the soft bristles massage my scalp.

I sit down and look at my reflection in the mirror. I'm pale. I don't want to look pretty for Maxime. I don't want to give him me. Tonight, when I give him my virginity, I want to be someone else, someone I don't care about so I can still face the real me in the mirror tomorrow.

I inspect the makeup. It's an expensive French brand. Other than mascara and lip gloss, I usually don't wear makeup and not because I don't like it. I can't afford it. Now I go for a dramatic look, using smoky eye shadow and black eyeliner that I round off with a pale lipstick. Definitely not me. The sparkling earrings add the finishing touch.

A clutch bag covered with the same cloth as the dress and an intricately sewn rose fastened to the clip stands next to a bottle of perfume. I dab a drop on my wrist to smell it and notice the marks from last night's ordeal. My breathing turns shallow, but I inhale deeply and blow the breath out slowly. I can do this. I can put up this act.

Standing, I regard my image in the mirror. I don't recognize the woman staring back at me. Good.

A knock sounds on the door. When I answer it, Maxime stands on the threshold with a bouquet of flowers. He's dressed in a tux and bowtie, and his hair is damp.

"You showered," I say stupidly, wondering if he's renting another suite.

"I showered in Gautier and Benoit's room. I wanted to give you privacy." His gaze trails over me and fixes on my face. "You look beautiful, Zoe." He holds the flowers out to me. "These are for you."

I take them uncertainly. I don't understand this man who'll lock me up in a dungeon and buy me flowers before stealing what's left of my dream. He doesn't need to woo me. It's not as if we're dating.

"Don't you like them?" he asks.

I look at the cellophane-wrapped bouquet. It's a colorful collection of sweet peas, poppies, daisies, and cornflowers. The arrangement is informal and uninhibited, just like the wildflowers. It's lovely.

"Thank you."

"You'll want to put them in water before we go."

I scoot around him, pulling in my stomach to avoid touching him when he doesn't move out of the way. He watches me as I find a vase on the table and carry it back to the bathroom to fill it with water.

While I take care of the flowers, he blows out the candles, presumably so the suite doesn't burn down while we're out to wherever he's taking me.

"Your bag," he says when I turn to go.

For lipstick, tissues, and powder, and whatever else a woman on a fuck date may need. He really thought about everything. I drop the tube of lipstick and compressed powder inside for the sake of placating him and hold my head high as I walk to the door.

He stands aside for me to exit ahead of him. In the lounge, he drapes a long white coat around my shoulders and hands me a faux-fur scarf.

"Where are we going?" I ask when he offers me his arm.

He smiles down at me. "You'll see."

If this is supposed to be a surprise, it's not the good kind.

I'm happy that a car and not a boat waits, because the air is wet and cold. He takes my hand and helps me inside. As before, he sits next to me in the back while Gautier and Benoit sit up front.

I stare at the buildings as we pass, trying not to fidget. After a long drive, we stop in front of a building I recognize from my travel books —the Teatro La Fenice. I've read about it extensively. Is this why he brought me here? Because he saw various books about the landmark building in my apartment? I've always wanted to see an opera, just not with Maxime.

The façade is the only part of the opera house that survived the two fires that almost destroyed the building in 1836 and 1996. It's stunning. It bears the theater's insignia in the center, a phoenix rising from the flames. Two statues in niches represent the muses of tragedy and dance. Above them are the masks of Comedy and Tragedy.

The opulence inside is overwhelming. The photos I've seen don't do it justice. I can't help but stare at the golden pillars and detailed ceiling paintings. Maxime steers me to the Royal Box, the best seats in the house. We're barely seated before the first curtain call sounds.

I gasp when the curtains rise to reveal the set of a scene in Egypt. The life-size sphinx and pyramid look so real I'm transported to a different place and time. When the opera starts, I forget about Maxime for a moment. It's Nabucco, goosebumps-worthy and incredibly sad. I loathe to admit I love every minute. When I dare to turn my head in Maxime's direction, I catch him watching me with undisguised fascination, as if my reaction is the real attraction. It makes me feel like a monkey in a zoo.

During intermission, he gets me a glass of freshly squeezed lemon juice with mint. I eye the glass of wine he sips. I could do with more alcohol courage. Too soon, the beautiful performance comes to an end.

Gautier and Benoit stand guard at the entrance to our box when we exit. Maxime says something to Gautier in French, who nods and leaves. Benoit stays behind, following in our footsteps.

"Do you always have protection?" I ask.

Maxime places his hand on the small of my back to steer me down the stairs. "Yes."

"Why? Because your family is involved in criminal activities?"

He glances around and says in a lowered voice, "Because we're powerful."

"That makes you a target?"

"Always." He brushes his thumb over a vertebra. "You have to fight to get to the top, and then you have to fight twice as hard to stay there. There's always someone eager to take your place."

His touch makes me shiver. "Does being at the top matter so much?"

"Yes." His voice is filled with conviction. "In this world, only the strongest survive."

I want to say it's a cynical outlook, but we've arrived at the cloakroom. He gets my coat and makes sure I'm covered before leading me to the car. His attention is unsettling. He's behaving like the perfect gentleman, but I know who he truly is.

I expect us to go back to the hotel, but Gautier pulls up in front of a small but cozy-looking restaurant. Surely, we're overdressed. When I mention it to Maxime, he only laughs.

Once inside, I understand why Maxime wasn't fazed. We're the only customers. A man in his late fifties pushes through a swing door to greet us. I get a glimpse of the kitchen through the open door. Meat is sizzling on a grill and something is bubbling in a pot. An aroma of oregano and garlic fills the air.

"Max." The man slaps him on the back and says something in Italian.

Maxime replies, after which the man addresses me in English. "Welcome to my humble restaurant. I will do my best to satisfy your appetite. I'm Matteo, but you can call me Teo."

I smile stiffly, my nerves getting the better of me. "Thank you."

Teo leads us to a small veranda where a table with a crisp white tablecloth is set with crystal and silverware. The terrace is encased in glass, keeping the cold out while allowing a view over the canal. A creeper grows over the trellis, and glass balls with tea candles dangle at different heights from the ceiling. It's breathtaking. With the moon hanging low over the water between the buildings, it's picture perfect.

Teo seats us, then bustles off and returns with olive bread and tapenade.

"I thought you'd be more at ease with an informal setting tonight," Maxime says when Teo is gone.

I glance at the empty tables. "You booked out the whole place?"

"It's more intimate, no?"

Intimate isn't where I want to go. When I toy with the stem of my glass, Maxime asks, "Thirsty?"

I nod.

He serves sparkling water for me and wine for himself.

"Is there a reason I'm not allowed to drink wine?" I ask.

"A good one."

"That is?"

His eyes darken. "I want you lucid tonight."

My stomach flips. He wants me to remember our first time.

Teo saves me from a response by arriving with a selection of small dishes.

"I thought we'd just nibble," Maxime says, "as you may be too nervous for a heavy meal."

His seductive accent chills me to the bone. His insight sets me further on edge. I don't want him to know what I think or feel. Especially, not what I feel.

He leans closer, his gaze sharp and predatory. "I can make it very good for you, Zoe. All you have to do is relax. I'll take care of everything."

My cheeks heat, as Teo is still busy shifting the dishes around to fit everything on the table.

When Teo is gone again, Maxime drops the lustful tone and talks about the opera while he serves me. Like the night he took me to

Seven Seas, he proves how skillful he is at the art of making conversation, keeping it light while the stone in my stomach is heavy and I don't have words.

If not for the circumstances, the evening might've been pleasant, but I can't wait for it to be over. I'm half relieved and half terrified when Maxime finally stands and offers me a hand.

His gray stare is as intense as his words are charged. "Shall we go?"

Clearing my throat, I push back my chair. I consider not taking his hand, but after a moment's hesitation I accept. This is one of those battles not worth fighting.

The closer we get to the hotel, the tighter my stomach grows. I think I may be sick. I hate him, even if he's saving me from a worse fate. If he hadn't taken me to start with, I wouldn't have been in this awful position.

I glance at his face from under my lashes as we drive. The man I'm about to accept as my lover is harsh, unfeeling, unattractive, and a kidnapper. I don't understand why he went to so much trouble for me tonight. I do, however, believe he does nothing without purpose, and that makes me question his motives. He doesn't need to give me consideration, attention, or lavish treatment.

He turns his head a fraction, catching me staring. "Don't like what you see?"

Unable to admit the truth, I avert my eyes.

His easy acceptance of the unspoken insult tells me that one, he gets that a lot, and two, it doesn't faze him.

By the time we're back at the hotel, I'm a wreck. I climb the stairs ahead of the men, my back stiff and chin high. Maxime bids the guards good night on the landing and opens the door for me.

Once inside, my bravado falters. I stop in the lounge. What now? How is this supposed to happen? Do I go to the room and get naked? Wait for him in the bed? At the thought, a shiver crawls over my skin.

In no hurry, Maxime removes his jacket and drapes it over the clotheshorse. He undoes his tie and pours himself a whiskey from the wet bar. Sipping it, he studies me quietly. Unlike me, he doesn't seem uncertain. It looks as if he knows exactly what he's going to do next.

I have an urge to wring my hands together. Instead, I force them behind my back. I'm not giving him the satisfaction of knowing he'll be my first. I lock that knowledge away, hanging onto it selfishly for as long as I can. He doesn't deserve it. Hopefully, he won't even notice.

"Zoe."

I jump at the sound of his voice, giving away my anxiety. The timbre is deep and velvety, the way he says my name in his foreign accent like a caress. I barely suppress the rebellious instinct to defy him.

"Do you need to use the bathroom?" he asks.

Not trusting my voice, I shake my head.

He says in a low voice, "Then go to the room, *cherie*."

CHAPTER 10

Zoe

The words are like a sentence, the lash of a whip on my back. A sense of pending loss hangs over me, but I squash it and lock down my emotions as I do what he says and go to the room. I throw the clutch onto the loveseat where he treated my wounds this morning and stop next to the bed. When he enters the room, courage hangs around me like a shroud.

I square my shoulders, my false bravado back in place. "How do you want me?"

He tilts his head and studies me curiously. "How do you mean?"

I curl my fingers until my nails cut into my palms. "Naked or clothed?"

A slow smile curves his lips. "I don't fuck a woman with her clothes on."

"Naked, then," I say with a bite in my tone. "On the bed? Bent over the dresser?"

"Zoe." He shakes his head, amusement making the flat gray of his eyes seems livelier, like quicksilver. "Slow down."

"Just do it already." I only want this to be over.

He walks to me slowly, working his bowtie free. "Fucking isn't only about me driving my dick into your pussy."

My cheeks heat at his crass language. When he hands me his tumbler, I take it in a reflex reaction. He unbuttons his collar before taking back the glass and leaving it on the dresser. His actions are fluid, self-assured. He stares deep into my eyes, penetrating every corner of the parts I try to hide from him as he cups my face between his broad palms.

His skin is warm and calloused on my cheeks. I gasp as he tilts my head back and lowers his with slow purpose. I know he's going to kiss me, but nothing prepares me for the moment his lips touch mine.

I expected to be repulsed, as I expected him to strip me naked and use me. I didn't expect him to kiss me and certainly not like this. It's tentative, exploring. His lips are warm and soft, and the gentle pressure on mine wakes the nerve endings under my skin. When he releases my lips, I stare up at his face with a mixture of surprise and confusion.

"What are you doing?" I manage on a whisper.

He scans my face, studying my eyes before his gaze drops to my lips. Instead of answering, he presses our mouths together again. This time there's a crackle of a spark where his lips brush over mine. I gasp, a soft intake of breath. His eyes darken at the sound. The lust burns brightly in his, but before apprehension can take root, he deepens the kiss.

The only parts of our bodies touching are his hands on my cheeks and our lips, but it's already a sensory overload. His clean smell infiltrates my nose—citrus and spices. The warmth of his hands seeps into my skin. I'm unprepared, and the new sensations catch me off-guard. Maybe I wouldn't have been so susceptible if this wasn't my first kiss. I can only blame myself for holding out for a futile fantasy. I can only blame my inexperience for being so utterly defenseless against his skillful lips.

Goosebumps break out over my arms when he sucks my bottom lip into his mouth. He nips the flesh softly with his teeth and then lets go to plant a butterfly kiss on the same spot. Heat surges through my veins, my body reacting violently to the light stimulation. When he traces the seam of my lips with his tongue, my lips open of their own accord. He steals inside, intensifying the kiss further. He tastes of whiskey and man. The gentle way he molds his lips over mine weakens my knees. My body starts to hum, electricity tingling under my overly sensitive skin. All the while, he holds me carefully, framing my face like I'm a fragile doll.

My breathing spikes. My breasts tighten. An ache starts to pulse between my legs. A moan escapes my lips, bursting like a bubble in our kiss. Need rises in my body as the kiss becomes more demanding. I answer it without thinking, tangling my tongue with his. The minute I return the caress with equal measure, he walks me backward until my body collides with the window. The curtains haven't been drawn. The pane is cold on my back, emphasizing how overheated my skin is.

He leans in, pressing his body against mine. There's something about being held like this by a man. I can't put my finger on it, only that it makes me want to submit to his possession, to be dominated by his strength and protected by his power. I fall effortlessly into the trap. My lifelong tendency to escape via dreaming is a well-practiced skill. It easily aids my mind away from reality to the fantasy that's played off so many times in my dreams that I'm longing for it with constant desire.

He's hard and solid, a wall of muscle. His erection presses against my stomach, feeding me my own measure of power. Male power has always featured in my fantasies about sex, but I never knew I'd have some of my own. It's liberating, soothing my resentment of our unequal standing. The small part of my mind that still functions processes and stores the new knowledge. The only place I'll ever have power is in his bed.

His hands leave my face to slide down my neck and over my shoulders. They roam over my arms and come to rest on my hips. Through it all, he doesn't break the kiss. Our life forces are mingled, the air we inhale the same. My breathing becomes more labored as Maxime lays a palm over my stomach. I know he can feel the rapid movement of my in- and exhales, my need for more. It's as if he does just that, measures my reaction, before moving his hand to the underside of my breast. I gasp, my body going still in anticipation. Cautiously, he drags his hand higher until his thumb brushes my nipple. When the tip hardens under his touch, a growl escapes his chest.

Our kiss turns frantic, my fantasy urgent and his victory a foregone conclusion. I can't describe what his hands on me feel like. I've never experienced such crazed need. I don't even know what to expect, only that it's natural when he bunches the dress in a fist and pulls it up to my hip so his free hand can slip underneath and cup the heat between my legs.

My moan is mindless, shameful. My underwear is wet. The sound he makes when he discovers this is closer to animal than man. Abandoning the private place no man has ever touched, he grips the zipper on the side of the dress. It makes a scratchy sound as he pulls it down. He's gentle as he slips the sleeve off my shoulder. The fabric pools around my waist. He holds my gaze as he pushes it over my hips, letting the dress fall around my feet. The gray of his eyes is smoky, the usual coldness burning hot. I'm mesmerized by their transformation, staring at the way the color darkens to molten mercury as he takes a step back and drags his gaze over me.

The distance leaves me cold. It breaks the feverish spell. It shocks me back to the moment, dousing my desire with shame. I flatten by back against the glass, trying to put distance between us, but Maxime scoops me up in his arms and carries me to the bed. He lowers me carefully to the mattress, leaving my legs dangling over the edge. When he crouches down, I push up on my elbows with anxious expectation, but he only reaches for my foot. He takes off first the one, then the other shoe, kissing the bridge of each foot. Then he straightens again and grips the elastic of my thigh-high stocking. I watch as he rolls it down and discards it before doing the same with the other. It's when he reaches for the panties that I stiffen.

"Shh." He leans over me, kisses my lips, and pushes me back with a palm on my chest until my arms give out and my back hits the mattress. "Just relax."

I don't. I pinch my eyes shut as he pulls the underwear over my hips and feet. I feel him move over me and jerk when he places a kiss at the top of my sex.

"Look at me, Zoe."

Reluctantly, I open my eyes.

"That's better," he says. "I want to see your expression when I make you come."

When he reaches for the bra, I automatically put a hand over his to still him.

He doesn't force it. Instead, he says, "Take off your bra for me. I want to see all of you."

I'm already naked from the waist down, but I hesitate. Somehow, I'm reluctant to remove this last barrier. He waits patiently. He's not going anywhere until I comply. Refusing is only pulling this out longer.

My hands shake slightly as I unclip the front clasp.

"Take it off completely," he says.

I push the straps from my shoulders, pulling one arm free at a time.

He does a slow evaluation of my body. "You're beautiful, my little flower. Gorgeous, just like I knew you'd be."

He pushes to his feet and unbuckles his belt. He lets it hangs loose as he removes his shoes and socks, and then the pants. He watches me intently as he pushes his briefs over his hips, so much so that I can't look at him and have to turn my head to the side.

"Eyes on me, Zoe."

The stern command is in stark contrast to the gentleness of earlier. Slowly, I face him again as he opens two buttons of his shirt from the bottom up. The shirttails don't hide his hardness. His cock is thick and long, jutting out proudly. He's huge. The sight is more erotic than I expected, making my lower body heat. I've never seen a man so close to naked or a stiff cock peeking out from the folds of his shirt front.

I try to scoot back when he steps between my legs, but he grabs my thighs and spreads them wide before going down on his knees.

"What are you doing?" I cry out.

His lips quirk in one corner. "What does it look like?"

He lowers his head, watching me watching him as he presses a kiss right in the center of my legs. My whole body jerks.

He gives me a knowing smile. "No one has ever gone down on you?"

I want to say yes, to tell a lie, but the sweep of his tongue over my folds steals my words. It's hot. It's delicious. Grabbing my knees, he keeps my legs open and licks from the bottom to the top of my slit. My thighs quake. The swipe of his tongue over my clit makes my back arch.

"So responsive," he says, sounding pleased.

When he sucks lightly on the bundle of nerves, my body bows. The pleasure is exquisite. Heat unfurls and coils in my lower body, spinning a web of need. It climbs, transporting me to a place I desperately need to go, but then he slows down. I fist my hands in the sheets in frustration. Devouring me, he keeps his gaze on my face, gauging my reaction. He uses his thumbs to spread me, then nips and licks until the tightly coiled tension is about to snap, but just before it does, he slows down again.

I moan in frustration. "Maxime."

His tone is lazy, teasing almost. "What is it, *ma belle?*"

"Please." Make it stop.

"Do you want to come?"

No, not like this but being kept on the edge of something unknown is torture.

"You have to say it," he says.

Even in this, he forces my consent. Yet just like with our warped arrangement, he doesn't give me a choice. Not really. Not when he's tormenting me with his erotic administrations.

The word escapes on a defeated breath from my lips. "Yes."

He immediately complies, focusing all his wicked attention on my clit. He drags his tongue in circles and bites down gently before flicking the tip of his tongue over the flesh that feels engorged and needy.

At last, the tension snaps. Fireworks set off in my core. My muscles contract, my legs hugging his face as he continues his assault and pushes me higher, still. It's better and worse than I imagined. Better because the pleasure is unique, a powerful sensation unlike any other. Worse, because the surrender tastes like defeat. The relief is physical. The agony is mental.

The thoughts lash at me as I lie naked and spread with my ecstasy on display, little shocks tightening my sex while Maxime studies me, studies his work. I wish I could disappear within myself like yesterday when he forced me to write the letter, but the pleasure grounds me. I'm fully present in the moment.

As Maxime shifts me to the middle of the bed and stretches out over me, I tell myself I'm someone else, the woman with the dark makeup. When he aligns his cock with my entrance, I don't want to feel the heat that liquefies my center. I want to be cold and frigid, but I'm aroused and on fire.

He threads his fingers through my hair, holding my head gently as he stares into my eyes. The moment imprints in my memory. What we're about to do, neither of us can ever erase. It's nothing, just sex, and yet it's everything. It's my whole life's worth of dreaming combined. Destroyed. When the head of his cock nudges my folds apart and my wetness coats him, I see the pleasure in his eyes. I hope he can see the hate in mine. I hate him, but not nearly as much as I hate myself for what he makes me feel.

When he pushes forward, parting me, I grab his upper arms despite my intention not to touch him. It burns. It feels like he'll split me in two.

"Shh." He kisses my forehead. "You'll adapt in a minute."

I don't, but he's patient. He moves slowly. When he slides another inch inside, I start to panic. He's too big. It hurts too much.

"It'll soon be better," he says.

His promise is a lie, because the more he stretches me the more it hurts. He seems to have difficulty entering me deeper. My breath catches. I clench my teeth, trying not to show him my agony.

Bringing his hands to my face, he brushes his thumbs over my cheeks. "You're tight, my little flower." His voice is strained. "Has it been a while?"

I can't speak for the fear of giving myself away. I don't deny or admit it. I only focus on breathing through the intrusion that burns like fire and makes me regret not choosing a cell full of rats over this.

He pulls out a fraction and pushes back gently. My inner muscles clench in an effort to expel the cause of my pain. He curses under his breath, sweat beading on his forehead.

"You're going to make me come before I'm fully inside you," he says with a tight jaw.

It sounds like a reprimand, but I don't know what he wants from me. I moan when he moves again, and it's not a sound of pleasure.

"Relax, *ma cherie*," he says. "Take a deep breath for me."

I do, and it helps a little.

"That's good." He kisses my cheek. "Like that."

Just as the tension in my muscles ease marginally, he surges forward, driving past the barrier that prevents his entry. My inner muscles protest. It feels as if he's tearing me apart. The stretch is unbearable, the pain white-hot. I forget to breathe. My lips part on a soundless gasp.

Maxime stills. His entire body tenses on top of mine. His gaze goes wide. Shock settles in the winter-gray pools and bleeds into male pride.

"Ah, Zoe." He clicks his tongue and shakes his head, but possessive satisfaction burns in his eyes. "You should've told me."

Unbidden tears gather in my eyes. I try to blink them away, but they spill over when I lower my lashes.

He kisses the corner of my eye, his lips tracing the path of my tears. "I would've prepared you better."

Him having this knowledge only makes it worse.

"Don't cry." His big hands cup my jaw, holding my head carefully. "I'll take care of you."

He moved as he spoke, his shallow thrusts making the burn flare. I dig my nails into the fabric of his shirt, clutching his arms as he punishes me with every roll of his hips, but then his lips are on mine. The kiss is sweet and tender. It somehow settles me as his hands find their way to my breasts, his fingers brushing softly over my nipples. They harden, and the pleasure his touch elicits echoes in my clit.

The burn doesn't abate, but I turn slicker. He presses deeper, his entry slightly easier. The more he kisses me, the more my body softens around him until he's fully sheathed and our groins press together.

"Zoe," he says into my mouth, his voice drenched in arousal.

I can only cling to him as he lets me get used to the feeling for a moment before increasing his pace. He releases my mouth and pulls away to look at my face. Pushing up on one arm, he slips a hand between our bodies. When his fingers find my clit, the pleasure of earlier returns, the need I'm now familiar with rising above the hurt and somehow diminishing the pain.

"That's my girl," he says.

I don't want to touch him, but as the pleasure climbs, and I'm spiraling out of control I need to hold onto something. My arms go around him of their own accord, finding an anchor in his strong body.

He starts moving faster, and my body follows instinctively. He groans when I wrap my legs around him in an automatic move to hold on. The pain is still there, but I don't register it any longer. I only feel the tension of the building release I need like food or water. I'm almost at the crescendo when he pulls out of me violently. I cry out in discomfort.

Reaching over me for the nightstand drawer, he takes out a condom, and tears the packet open with his teeth. I can't believe I didn't think about protection in my haze of lust. When he sits back on his heels to fit the condom, I look at his cock. He's covered in my blood and arousal. The sheets are a mess. My cheeks heat in shame of how badly I want him to finish this, how badly I need this from a man I hate.

After rolling on the condom, he pushes back inside me. A perverse part of me mourns the loss of his naked skin and resents the new barrier. Then all thoughts fly from my head as he pushes deep and slides almost all the way out before burying deep again. The movement strokes over nerve endings, adding new pleasure to the familiar. He massages my clit in slow circles as he takes me with an increasingly demanding pace. Only when my body starts to tighten and the pleasure reaches a new height does he lose his control.

He moves harder, chasing his own release faster. I moan, the sounds coming from my mouth belonging to a wanton woman. When my orgasm explodes, he throws back his head on a low groan, driving himself as deep into me as he can. His body hardens, his muscles growing taught under my palms. I can feel the knots and grooves of the maleness that defines his back under his shirt. He drops his head next to mine, breathing hard.

Turning his face a fraction, he plants a soft kiss on my temple. "You'll be my destruction."

I sag back, letting the mattress absorb my weight.

He's already my destruction.

I'm no longer the woman I used to be.

I can never go back to how things were.

CHAPTER 11

Zoe

When Maxime rolls off me, I push up onto my arms. My thighs are covered in blood, much more than I expected there'd be. The sheets are soiled. Traces of my lost virginity mark the white fabric of Maxime's shirt. He scans my face as he removes the condom. I need to escape that piercing stare. The invasion of my body was enough. I don't want him digging through my feelings.

He gets up and walks to the bathroom. The moment the door closes, I'm on my feet. I have to escape this bed. I want to run, but the lounge is as far as I can go. The ache between my legs is persistent, an unpleasant reminder of my new reality.

I go straight to the wet bar and pour myself a whiskey. I'm not a big drinker, and I've never had whiskey, but I down the shot in one go. It steals my breath, burning all the way to my stomach. Spotting the packet of cigarettes next to the decanter, I snatch it up with the lighter and look around the room for something to wear. I'm not going back to the bedroom. Not yet. My gaze falls on the clotheshorse with Maxime's tux jacket. I don't give it a second thought. I pull the jacket on and push the sliding door wide open, not caring that the cold blasts inside or that my body feels frozen the minute I step barefoot onto the terrace.

I light a cigarette and inhale deeply. My gaze is trained on the beautiful view, the reflection of the streetlights in the water, but I don't really see it. My thoughts are trained inward. They're turbulent. How do I reconcile the woman I became in that bed with the one I used to be? How could I find pleasure at the hands of a man I loathe? Because he was gentle? A good lover? Considerate? Because he did everything right?

My fingers curl into a ball at that admission. It would've been easier and less confusing if he was cruel. I don't know how to place the man, and I need to know. He's my enemy. An unpredictable enemy is the most dangerous kind. I don't understand him, and that scares me. I don't understand his actions or motivations.

A shadow stretches over the floor. Maxime steps up next to me, dressed in tracksuit pants and a T-shirt. I don't turn my head to acknowledge him. I keep my gaze trained on the water and the lights, an image as pretty as it is traitorous, because I know what ugliness lies underneath the foundations of this city.

He takes the cigarette from my fingers. I only notice now how much I'm shaking and how my teeth are chattering from the cold. I sense him looking at me. I'm aware of him, no longer lost in my head, but I don't look at him or acknowledge his existence.

He takes a drag before putting the cigarette out in the ashtray. "Do you smoke?"

"No." I experimented a little after school but decided I didn't like it. "Do you?"

"No."

My question was meant to be sarcastic, but his answer surprises me, and even more so his placating tone. Leaning my elbows on the rail, I finally turn to face him. The jacket falls open, but I don't care. I don't care that I'm cold. I welcome the frozen numbness of my body. I don't care that he sees. He's seen it all. There's nothing left to give.

The wind blows his fringe over his forehead. He must be cold, but he just stands there quietly, watching me. It infuriates me. I want him to talk, to tell me why I'm here, to explain this twisted game he's playing.

"Why did you do it?" I ask.

He dips his head, his stance casual but his eyes sharp and aware. "Do what?"

"The dress, the flowers, the opera…the extravagant dinner. Why?"

His gaze is level. "For the same reason I brought you here."

"You've already done the convincing role-play for Damian's sake yesterday. You didn't have to repeat it today."

"I could've done that anywhere."

I still. I've had it figured out. Didn't I? If not to convince my brother I was here out of my own free will, a loved and pampered woman, then why? I will him to speak, to say it, but he's keeping that little distance between us, waiting patiently for me to connect the dots.

"I don't get it," I finally say.

His monotone voice is flat, a robot conveying facts. Or maybe reserved, as if he's not sure how I'm going to take this. "To give you your fantasy."

The words bowl me over. For a moment, I still don't understand, but then, slowly, the meaning sinks in. Oh, my God. My chest constricts. It hurts to breathe. He didn't bring me here to show my friends and Damian how lucky and happy I am. Maybe that too, but that was just a convenient bonus.

My lips part in shock. "You brought me here to fuck me." Because he knows my most intimate ideals. He knows about Venice, my fixation with this particular opera house, and my version of the perfect dress. He stole my life and my dream, mixed them together in some fucked-up fantasy, and served them to me in a twisted version of reality. He knows my desires and used them against me. "You son of a bitch. You used my dream to create this whole romantic little scenario."

His regard remains cautious. "Would you have preferred the crueler version?"

"I prefer the truth."

He closes the two steps between us. Grabbing the lapels of the jacket, he brings the edges together to cover my body. "Is that why you didn't tell me, Zoe? Because you prefer the truth?"

I look away.

His tone is gentle, one you'd use trying to coax the truth out of someone. "Why were you still a virgin?"

"I was waiting for the right man," I say like it doesn't matter.

He nods, a silent acknowledgment of understanding. There's no remorse in his voice when he says, "No man can be more wrong than me."

I'm shaking violently when he picks me up, sheltering me against his chest. He carries me inside and easily closes the door balancing me in one arm. He goes to the bathroom and lowers me onto the rug next to the bath. I wrap my arms around myself, shivering as I watch him open the tap to let the water run warm. The petals and candles are gone. The bath has been cleaned. Housekeeping came in while we were having dinner.

The bath is only a quarter full when he slips his palms under the jacket and brushes it off my shoulders, carelessly disregarding the expensive garment crumpled on the floor. He picks me up and puts me on my feet in the bath. Taking a jar of bath salts from the edge, he empties the whole jar in the bath and scoops water into the jar that he empties over my shoulder.

The warmth dispels the cold. My skin contracts with goosebumps. He refills the jar and drains it over my other shoulder. He does the same with my front and back, and then he crouches down to soap a sponge. He starts at my waist, dragging the sponge from my hip to my thigh before squeezing out the sponge and letting the soapy water run down my calf. Meticulously, he washes me, stroke by gentle stroke removing the blood and the cold.

The bathroom is warm, but I'm still shivering. When the bath is half-full, he turns off the water and guides me to lie down. Twisting my hair in a knot, he trails it over the edge of the bath. The water stings between my legs, but heat envelopes me, melting the last of the bitter frost under my skin and calming my shivers. All the while, he continues to bathe me, washing away the remnants of our coupling in a strangely humble way as if I'm the princess and he the servant.

When my skin starts to wrinkle, he pulls the plug and takes my hand to help me out of the bath. Draping a fluffy towel around me, he dries my body. When not a patch of wetness is left on my skin, he leads me back to the room and makes me sit on the loveseat while he strips the sheets off the bed, leaving the duvet. Folding it back, he looks at me in silent command.

I'm spent. My fight is cold. I get up without arguing, dropping the towel at the side of the bed before getting in. Turning on my side, I face the wall. He gets in beside me, flicks off the lamp, and spoons me from behind with an arm he throws over my stomach to anchor me to him.

Our breathing is quiet. We're both awake, but neither of us speaks. Light from the streetlamps falls through the window into the room. It plays over the walls, creating a shadowed reflection of the free world outside.

After a long while, he says into the darkness, "If I had the time, I would've made you fall in love with me first."

At the words, I stop breathing.

They're meant to be a consolation, but they're stunningly cruel.

CHAPTER 12

Maxime

The day is gray, the Mistral blowing at full force when we land in Marseille. It was a bumpy flight and a rough landing, but my pilot is skilled. A car is waiting when we exit the plane, Alexis leaning against it. I'm not fooled into seeing it as a one-man welcoming committee. My brother isn't here for me. He looks beyond me at the woman who stiffly descends the steps. His curiosity is palpable and his excitement sickening.

In an impulsive, possessive act, I find Zoe's hand and close my fingers around hers. Alexis's gaze homes in on the gesture. His face folds into a frown as he takes in her fashionable wool coat and patent leather boots.

He straightens as we approach. Not sparing Zoe another glance, he addresses me in French. "What's going on, Max?"

My smile is fake. "You tell me." My cousin, Jerome, informed me that Alexis negotiated a deal with the Italians.

He watches me with the attention of a hawk. "Why is our hostage wearing Gucci?"

My voice betrays my tension. "She's no longer our hostage."

He lifts a brow. "You were supposed to hand her over to me."

"The plan has changed."

"To what? The whore is now our guest?"

I narrow my eyes. My tone is quiet but the violence underneath anything but. "Mind your mouth. She's my mistress."

He laughs softly, shaking his head. "You're something else, Max. Father won't be pleased."

I open the car door for Zoe. "Does it look like I give a damn?"

"No, you don't. That's part of the problem, isn't it?"

It's not the first time he accuses me of putting my selfish needs before the business. He's a hypocrite. Alexis has never done anything unless it benefits him.

"Why?" he asks. "Does she have a golden cunt?"

I'm not going to let that remark slide, but I'm not taking him on in front of Benoit and Gautier who are following with our luggage. Alexis will own up to his filthy tongue later.

I keep my smile intact. "Jealous?"

He turns his attention back to Zoe, looking her over as if she's livestock. "Nah. She's not much for the eye. Too thick around the hips for my liking."

That's because he hasn't been in her space, hasn't seen her hopeless faith and quiet resilience. He'd crush a pretty little flower under his two-thousand-dollar moccasins and never even notice it.

"Shut up and drive." I add mockingly, "Isn't that why you're here?"

He grins, not taking the bait, and shifts to behind the wheel.

Benoit and Gautier load our suitcases into the trunk before making their way to the hangar where we keep a couple of cars. They'll follow.

We don't talk on the way home. I keep holding onto Zoe's hand, feeling her tense as we turn through the gates of my property forty-five minutes later. The house stands on an acre of land on the outskirts of Cassis. It's built on the edge of the cliff, overlooking the sea.

Alexis parks in the front but doesn't get out. "Welcome home, brother. I'm not going to hang around for the victory drinks."

Ignoring his mocking tone, I get out and open Zoe's door. A guard rushes over from his post by the entrance to take our bags from the trunk. Zoe looks up at the two-story mansion with its double chimneys, shutters, and ivy-covered walls. I try to look at it through her eyes, try to see what she sees. It's a typical southern French design, the house dating from four centuries back. I went to great pains to restore it, as well as with the design of the formal garden and its maze. It must be unfamiliar and strange, not what she's used to.

The front door opens just as Alexis pulls off. My mother exits, wearing her cooking apron over a Chanel dress. As always, she's impeccably groomed, her white-gray hair styled into a bob and her makeup cleverly invisible. Despite her age, her face is youthful, a lucky trait she's inherited from her long line of purebred aristocracy.

"Max." Her features light up with a smile that freezes when she notices the woman at my side. Her mouth draws down. It's minute, quickly replaced with a friendly expression, but I noticed. I know her too well.

She pulls herself to her full petite height, her spine going stiff. "I cooked. I reckoned you'd be hungry. God only knows what you had to eat in that godforsaken country. I didn't expect you to come home with a guest." She looks at Zoe. "There won't be enough food."

"Never mind, Maman." I kiss her cheeks. "We'll make do." I switch over to English. "This is Zoe. Zoe, this is my mother, Cecile."

My mother doesn't kiss Zoe's cheeks, but offers her hand, a gesture that demeans Zoe for a lower class but that someone not familiar with our culture won't grasp.

Zoe glances at me. I give a small nod, a warning, at which she shakes my mother's hand. My mother isn't up to speed with the grittier details of our business, even if she knows how we conduct it is shady. My father prefers to keep her in the dark, to protect her as he claims, not only from the blood on our hands, but also from his mistresses. If my mother knows, she's never given on, but her reaction to Zoe tells me she may be less ignorant about my father's infidelity than what I've thought, or, for her sake, hoped.

"Well," my mother says in English, her accent worse than mine, "you better come in."

She steps aside for us to enter. The guard follows with the suitcases.

"Where must I put this, sir?" he asks in French.

"In my bedroom."

My mother purses her lips. Her gaze flicks over Zoe's pleated coat and killer heel boots with distaste.

As I help Zoe from her coat, my mother, reverting back to French, asks, "How long is she staying?"

I put the coat on the stand by the door before removing my own. "A while."

Her silence communicates her displeasure.

"You didn't have to come out all the way here to cook for me," I say.

She pinches my cheek. "I'm your mother. That's my job."

"In English, please."

She irons out her apron and switches back to English. "Go freshen up. Lunch will be ready when you're done."

I show Zoe to the guest bathroom downstairs and wait outside.

When she exits, I take her arm, squeezing harder than necessary. "Not a word to my mother or anyone for that matter. Say anything out of line, and Damian pays the price. Understand?"

She stares at up me, her big, blue eyes shimmering with apprehension and a twist of hostility. "Yes."

"Good." I kiss the top of her head just because I can and lead her to the dining room.

Her arm brushes against mine as we walk. I'm overly aware of her, my usual business-focused mind distracted. I don't know many twenty-one-year-old virgins. I never could've guessed. The knowledge surges in me with heated satisfaction. Her innocence suits me even better. I've never liked to share my toys as a child. That hasn't changed once I turned into an adult. If anything, the trait became more imbedded in my making. I guess Alexis is right. I am a selfish bastard.

My mother waits at the table, her apron removed and the rings she takes off for cooking back on her fingers. The five-carat emerald surrounded by diamonds is a family ring, passed on for generations from mother to daughter. We don't have a sister. Alexis and I are the only children. As the first-born, the ring will be passed on to my wife, and I know exactly what my mother is thinking as she twists the ring on her finger while studying Zoe with a tight expression.

I seat Zoe on my right and take the head of the table. My mother already sits on the left, a place normally reserved for the lady of the house. A veal roast with Parisian potatoes and green beans are set out. There's enough to feed ten people.

"It smells delicious," I say, taking the carving knife.

"Your favorite." My mother gives me a tender look, a look that speaks of family intimacy and customs, one that excludes outsiders such as Zoe. Our clan has always been a clique.

After I've carved the meat, my mother serves while I pour the wine. She fills me in on the watering of the plants she's managed in my absence, which ones have flowered, and the groceries she's ordered to be delivered. We talk about my cousins, Sylvie and Noelle, who will be home soon from the university they attend in Paris.

"I got you some tangerines," my mother says after we've finished the main course, pushing the bowl toward me. "They're the ones from Corsica you like so much."

"You shouldn't have gone to so much trouble." I take one, peel it, and place it on Zoe's plate. "I have a cook, you know."

My mother sniffs. "She doesn't know you like I do. Neither does she cook like me." She pushes to her feet. "I've been in the kitchen on my feet all morning. I need a break."

I stand. "Who's driving you?"

"One of your father's men."

I kiss her cheeks. "Thank you for lunch."

She pats my arm. "Take care of yourself." To Zoe, she says, "Goodbye, then."

Zoe mumbles a barely audible greeting.

"Have some tea," I say to Zoe. In other words, stay.

I see my mother out.

While pulling her coat and scarf on at the entrance, she asks, "How did you meet this..." she waves a hand, "...whatever her name is?"

"Zoe. By chance."

My mother fits her gloves. "She's a foreigner, Max."

"I'm well aware, Maman."

"Is she Catholic?"

"You know I'm not religious."

She sighs and pats my cheek. "I have to be home before the charity meeting this afternoon. Do think about making a donation. Those poor kids can do with the aid."

"I'll write a check."

"Good."

I signal the guard waiting on a bench next to my father's Mercedes and walk my mother to the car.

My mother hesitates when I open the door. "Max, you know how this is going to look."

I feel one of those long talks coming. "I'm thirty, not ten."

Sighing again, she gets inside and waves as the driver pulls off. I lift a hand in greeting, waiting until they clear the gates before going back inside.

I find Zoe in the dining room where I left her, a teacup in her hand. She looks up when I enter, her expression uncertain.

"Come," I say. "I'll show you the bedroom."

The way she tenses gives me the same jabbing sensation in my chest as when she showed me so openly how repulsive the idea of me fucking her is. My face may put her off, but she had pleasure last night. She may hate the idea, but she liked what I did to her. In time, she'll get used to looking at me.

We go upstairs to the master suite. I open the door and usher her inside. The room is spacious with a sitting area and dressing room that connects to the bathroom. The French doors open onto a balcony. The view is magnificent. She goes to the window to look out at the sea. I'm proud. My home is more than an investment. It's the only place I can let my guard down and relax.

"What do you think?" I really want to know. Why it's important to me that she likes my home I don't know.

She turns on me, ire shining in her pretty, blue eyes. "What do you want me to say? That it's lovely? That my prison is beautiful? Shall I swoon over how big and fancy your property is, over how much it's worth?"

I give her a warning look. "A simple thank you will do."

"Oh, my mistake. I guess this is the part where I thank you for saving me from being locked up and raped."

I let it go. She's tired. She's been through a lot in the last three days, especially last night. "If you need anything, my housekeeper, Francine, will see to your needs. My home is yours, and I won't go out of my way to make you miserable."

I step closer. "However, don't make the mistake of thinking I'm a forgiving man. You will act your part, or Damian pays. If you run, your brother is dead. Live by my rules, and we'll get on fine. It doesn't have to be unpleasant for you. If you try, I'm sure you'll like living here."

Her look is cutting. What the hell am I doing? I took on a mountain of problems for myself by claiming Zoe. I could've just handed a faceless, nameless, meaningless woman over to my brother, just another pawn in a strategy to protect our business. No, I had to make it personal. I had to see her for who she is. I allowed her to fascinate me. I allowed her secrets to tempt me. Whatever the case, no matter how ungrateful she is or how much she hates me, I can't go back on my decision. After last night, it's much too late for that now.

I cup her cheek, giving her affection, because that's what she needs. "I'll be back tonight. Feel free to look around the house, but don't go outside. In case you're tempted, I have guards stationed on the grounds and at the gate. If you get hungry, Francine will fix you a snack."

I kiss the top of her head and walk away before I'm tempted to strip her naked and do more. Leaving her alone so soon isn't ideal, but facing my father is a bigger priority.

After giving my guards instructions not to let her off the property, I leave a note for Francine, who is out on her lunch break. My guest isn't allowed to use the telephones. I unplug all the landlines and lock them in my study. Then I take one of the cars in the garage, preferring to drive. I need to think, and I'd rather be alone.

On the way to Marseille, I consider how to present the decision to my father. He won't be happy, especially not now that our negotiations with the Italians have started. He'd want no complications, nothing to interfere with the fragile business development.

My father's office is near the harbor. I pull up front and throw the keys to the valet to park the car. Raphael Belshaw sits on his throne behind his desk when I enter. His thick, gray hair is brushed back, the waves neatly tamed. As always, he's dressed in a black suit and white shirt. My uncle, Emile, my father's younger brother, sits in the visitor's chair.

My father looks at me through narrowed eyes, the left one drooping. "You're late."

His displeasure isn't about the hour. I bet Alexis wasted no time in sharing the news.

"Bad weather. We had to circle for a while before we could land." I bend down to hug my uncle and slap his back in the habitual way of greeting. "How are Sylvie and Noelle?"

He scoffs. "Spending too much money in Paris."

"At least they're getting a good education."

My uncle raps his fingers on the desktop, the gold ring with our family crest knocking against the wood. "I don't know why they bother. They'll marry and have babies. What good is a career going to do them, then? If you ask me, they're only throwing money into the water."

I take the seat next to him. "Some women like to work, just like men."

He stands. "Times have changed, and I'm not sure it's for the better." He nods at my father. "I'll leave you to catch up with Max. Don't forget Hadrienne is organizing a lunch on Sunday to welcome the girls home from Paris. We expect you all to be there." He takes his hat from the coat stand. "You included, Max."

The minute the door closes behind him, my father says, "You have some fucking explaining to do."

I give a wry smile. "Ah, Alexis stopped by."

"Alexis said you took Damian's sister as a mistress. Tell me it's a joke."

"I'd never play a joke like that."

My father leans forward, his gaze harsh. "Then what are you playing at, son?"

"Damian Hart may be behind bars, but he's powerful and becoming more so by the day. He's snide, clever, merciless, and resourceful. He's wasted no time in making the right kind of connections on the inside. He's got people looking out for him on the outside, managing the money he earns by getting information and doing dirty jobs. He can't put his hands on that money now, but he will be able to when they let him out in two years." My father knows money and connections mean power, enough to start a war. "We don't want him for an enemy."

"Wasn't that the point of taking his sister? Tell me how that doesn't make him our enemy."

"The point was having something to hold over his head." To blackmail him into honoring our deal with Dalton when the ownership of the mine transfers to Hart. "This way will be even better."

My father grumbles. "Better how?"

"He'll honor the deal if his sister is happy. If he thinks she's here because she wants to be, he'll want to make sure she continues to be happy, and we won't have to fight a war." One we may very well lose.

He gives me a skeptical look. "How do you expect to pull that one off?"

It's simple, really. "By making her happy."

His belly shakes with a laugh. "We kidnapped her. How is that going to make her happy?"

"I have my ways. The idea will grow on her."

"The chances of you two meeting accidentally are too big a coincidence." My father interlaces his fingers on the tabletop. "Hart won't fall for it."

"I already thought about it." On the drive over, in fact. "I went to South Africa to meet Dalton about business. We talked about the mine, and I asked how the diamond deposit was discovered. We've had a couple of bottles of wine, so he told me about Damian Hart, the discoverer, who ended up in jail for stealing a diamond from Dalton's house during a dinner party. I was curious. Something about the story didn't add up. Why would Hart steal a diamond if he's discovered a whole riverbed full of them? So, I visited Hart's only remaining family, Zoe Hart, to hear her opinion of the story. We went out for dinner. There was an instant attraction, and I decided to save her from her miserable life and give her a better one."

He sneers. "You're a fucking Hallmark movie director now? You think you've got it all figured out, don't you?"

I cross my legs. "I do."

His nostrils flare. His fingers curl around the Montblanc pen on his desk, squeezing so hard that thick, blue veins pop out on his hand. I bet he'd love to stab me with that pen. I've often wondered if there'd come a day I'd shove him over that edge. I've always pushed his buttons by being the defiant son, the one who doesn't follow orders. I guess that's why he prefers Alexis. Alexis doesn't pose questions. As long as it's for the business, and therefore for himself, Alexis does what he's told. He's easier to handle, not unimpressionable like me, and a lot more like my father. Which makes me my mother's favorite. She doesn't hate my father, but she doesn't exactly love him, either. Alexis reminds her too much of Raphael Belshaw, the man she wedded as a business arrangement. I wouldn't say Maman loves Alexis less, but she's always treated me differently, favoring me.

The skin on my father's brow plows into grooves as his mind

works at full speed, but there's no way out of this. A lover is a lover, entitled to protection and a certain amount of respect. You can't mess with the unspoken rules of *les beaux voyous* without upturning the apple cart.

He slams a fist on the desk. "Why couldn't Alexis make her *happy*?"

He says *happy* like it's a curse, and my whole body snaps tight at the mere thought of that. I'm unable to filter all the anger from my voice. "We both know Alexis isn't capable of making anyone happy, let alone an unwilling woman. We both know, too, how it would've turned out for Zoe if Alexis took her. That would've definitely made Hart our enemy. He would've sent an army to save her. He wouldn't have stopped until he destroyed us."

"What about the Italians? We can't afford any complications now."

"We'll be discreet." I add a jibe. "Just like you are."

His droopy eye twitches. "What prevents her from running or telling her brother?"

"She doesn't know why we took her. I told her if she runs or tries anything Hart will pay." Of course, we have no intention of harming Hart. We need him to revive the mine or our business will sink, anyway.

"In other words, you're blackmailing *her* instead of us blackmailing Hart."

"Genius, no?"

He leans back, his words sounding bitter with unwilling acceptance. "I suppose it's easier to manipulate the girl."

"She's young. Hart is worldly and hardy."

He drums his fingers on the desk, considering my words. He's unwilling to admit it, but he doesn't have a choice. If we take a family vote on the decision, he'll lose. Half of the power of running the business has already transferred to me at my thirtieth birthday, like it had to my father, and his father, and every other Belshaw before him. The other half I'll get when I marry. My father is a loose cannon. He's made too many bad decisions. His love for overindulgence and unnecessary violence has stained our reputation and name. The family likes the stability I bring to the business. They'll vote for me.

After a while, he says, "Fine. You have two years to tame her before Hart gets out."

I stand. "That's doable."

"You better hope so. If this backfires—"

"It won't backfire."

He grimaces. "We'll see. Now get out of here. I have work to do."

"Where's Alexis?"

"Overseeing the docks."

I straighten my tie. "I'll see you on Sunday."

I GET my car and drive to the end of the docking area where the debt collectors hang around, playing cards. Alexis is having a conversation with one of the men.

Walking up to my brother with brisk strides, I say, "A word with you."

He saunters around the corner, his hands in his pockets. The minute he turns back to me, I slam my fist into his face. His head bounces back, hitting the wall. Blood pours from his nose.

Grabbing his nose between his hands, he gives me an incredulous look. "What the fuck, Max?"

"That," I point a finger at him, "is for mentioning Zoe's cunt."

"Are you fucking crazy?" He fumbles for the decorative handkerchief in his top jacket pocket and presses it against his nose. "You just said it yourself."

"Only me." I stab his chest with the finger I was waving in his face. "I'm the only one who mentions, breathes, fucks, and eats out Zoe's cunt. I'm the only one who thinks about her cunt. Get it?"

He raises his palms. "Calm the fuck down, man."

Now that I've put him back in his place, I am calm. The problem with being part of the family is that if you don't enforce the rules, every dick like my brother will try to break them. If I can't stand up for what's mine, no one will respect my property. It's an important lesson. No one will fuck with Zoe after this.

I turn and walk back down the road that stinks of diesel and fish.

"You're fucking nuts," Alexis calls after me.

I don't look back. Doing so would mean I care about the insult. Alexis's laughter follows me into the car. I start the engine and clench the wheel. I should be going to the office in the city. I should catch up with the Italian deal. Instead, I turn the car in the opposite direction.

I need a vent for my anger, and my vent is at home.

CHAPTER 13

Zoe

The moment I hear the front door shut, I go to the writing desk standing in the far corner of Maxime's room and go through it. I find what I'm looking for in the second drawer. Pulling out the writing pad and pen, I sit down in the chair and write a letter to Damian.

I tell him I've arrived safely in France after a short holiday in Italy. I tell him Venice was magical. I tell him I'm settling in nicely in my new home, baking apple pie. I tell him I can't wait for the day he gets out, that I'll bake apple pie to welcome him, and I hope he'll bring his cell mate for me to meet. I'm sure his friend will love apple pie. I make sure to mention the address and give a detailed description of the property. I paid attention to the road signs on the way and the address on the letterbox by the gate. I mention how wealthy and important my white knight is, so much so that his property is guarded. Then I sign off as always, my name with two x's and o's.

To anyone reading it, it's just a letter from a happy girl who got lucky by landing a rich guy, but Damian will understand the code. He'll get the message. He'll know Zane and Maxime are his enemies, and that I'm being held against my will.

Folding the letter neatly, I seal it in an envelope I find in the same drawer and write the address on it. Then I go through the room, looking for a phone. I doubt Maxime would've left one, which is why my priority was writing the letter, but I still try.

There are no landline plugs in the room, so I take the letter and exit onto the landing. The house is quiet. No sounds come from the kitchen. The hallway is dark and spooky. Faded tapestries and portraits of men and women dressed in clothes from centuries ago hang on the walls. The space smells of wood polish and cedar. I shudder but force myself to walk out onto the creaking wooden floor, opening doors as far as I go.

The one next to Max's room gives access to a bedroom the same size as his but decorated with feminine pinks and lilacs. The two rooms share the same bathroom and balcony. The other rooms on the floor are all bedrooms with en-suite bathrooms. A heavy wooden door at the end of the hallway gives access to a spiral staircase. Unable to squash my curiosity, I climb the stone steps to the top. The staircase exits into a circular tower room. A narrow bay window with a built-in bench overlooks the sea. I can't make out much of the view through the stained-glass window. The only furniture is a small desk. Other than that, the floor and walls are bare. It's cold and noisy with the wind cutting around the tower.

Shivering, I go back to the first-floor landing and descend the steps to the foyer. I pass the guest bathroom and dining room, a big and smaller lounge, and am about to reach for the door at the end when it opens in my face.

Gasping, I clutch the letter to my chest. A woman dressed in dark slacks and a button-down blouse stops dead when she sees me. Her green eyes widen. She sweeps her gaze over me, taking in my face, clothes, and boots. Slender and willowy, she's a head taller than me. Her blond hair is twisted into a bun, and her smooth skin is pale like porcelain, but unlike mine, hers is blemish free. She's wearing mascara and a glossy pink lipstick. Her perfume is faint but smells expensive.

"Oh," she says, "you must be Zoe." Her accent is less pronounced than Maxime's.

"You must be Francine."

"I just got back from my lunch break and found Max's note." She gives me another quick once-over. "Is there something you wanted?"

I hand her the letter. "I was hoping someone could mail this for me. I don't have a stamp."

She reaches for it hesitantly. "I'll leave it with Max's mail. He usually drops it in the mailbox on his way to work."

My spirits sink. He'll read it, no doubt. He won't understand the hidden messages, but he may not like the details I conveyed about his house, such as how well protected it is and where it's situated. I can only hope he won't burn it.

For a moment, I hold onto the envelope, reluctant to hand it over, but when Francine pulls a little, I have no choice. I have to let go if I don't want to give her a reason to be suspicious.

"If there's nothing else?" She folds her arms, the envelope clutched in one hand. She's posed like a ballerina, one knee bent with her foot turned out and her long fingers resting elegantly on the sleeve on her blouse. Her nails are painted with a French manicure.

"No, thanks."

"If you'll excuse me, I have to start dinner."

"Of course."

Going back inside the kitchen, she closes the door. She might've well put a sign on it that reads *stay out*.

Not knowing what else to do with myself, I go through the rest of the house. Every room is decorated with antique furniture. There's even a knight's armor and medieval weapons. The place is like a museum. I don't find a phone anywhere, and the empty wall plug in the entrance indicates the phone has been unplugged. I would've given anything to call Damian now, to tell him what my letter may not convey if Maxime decides not to send it.

One of the doors is locked, presumably a room Maxime doesn't want me to have access to, and next to it I find a library with a fireplace. The house is cold. My wool dress barely keeps me warm. I use the chopped wood stacked in the basket to build a fire and stoke it until the flames leap high. To my dismay, all the books are in French. I settle on one about the region with photographs and drag the armchair closer to the fire.

In no time, my cold muscles thaw. My face warms, and my fingers prick with pins and needles as the frozen stiffness melts away. A gust of wind enters as the front door opens across the foyer. Maxime stands on the step, looking windblown and angry.

The physical heat remains, but a blast of coldness settles over me when he closes the door. My stomach tightens with apprehension as he removes his coat, scarf, and gloves, and hangs everything neatly on the coat stand before making his way to the library. I'm in full sight of the open door, and he watches me darkly as he advances.

I shut the book when he enters. My mouth goes dry when he closes the door and turns the key. I'm uncertain of him. I can't place him. I don't know who he is right now, the man of the cold cell or the man of the luxurious hotel suite.

CHAPTER 14

Maxime

Working my tie loose, I walk to the chair where Zoe is draped so prettily and stop in front of her. I'm hard. I want her. I've never wanted with such abandon. Certainly not a woman. My dirty pleasures are money and power. Sex is a recreational activity, a form of release. I enjoy it, but I enjoy work more. Not today, it seems. Today I chose her over the office, and I do need release.

As I take the book from her hand and leave it on the coffee table, I blame Alexis. I blame my anger as I pull her to her feet and take her place on the chair. It's warm, her body heat lingering in the flowery upholstery.

I unbutton my jacket and cross my legs. I rest my hands on the armrests, a casual pose that belies how badly I want to lay them on her. I trail my gaze over her, taking in her luscious curves before pausing on the pussy at my eye level, the cunt I've assaulted my brother over.

"Sore?" I ask, lifting my eyes back to hers.

She stares down at me with her beautiful face, the pink flush on her cheeks from the fire deepening to a red. "Yes."

I can't take her again so soon, but there are other ways. "Undress."

Her blue eyes go wide. "What?"

"Take off your clothes."

She inhales audibly. "Why?"

I raise a brow.

Her curls tumble over her shoulders as she shakes her head. "I don't want to have sex."

"I won't fuck you with my cock, but I did say often and convincingly."

Her hands fist into the skirt of her dress. "It hurts."

"I'm not going to hurt you."

"I didn't enjoy it."

My little liar. "You came, didn't you?"

"That doesn't mean I liked it."

I cock a shoulder. "You don't have to come if you don't want."

"Then why do it?"

"That's what lovers do."

"Get naked in the study?"

My lips twitch. "Anywhere I want. You better get used to it, Zoe. These are the games grownups play."

Her dainty nostrils flare. "Fuck you. I'm inexperienced. That doesn't make me a child."

"We're going to punish that mouth of yours, but first things first. Are you going to undress, or do you find it more romantic if I undress you?"

She glares at me with her dress bunched in her tiny fists.

"It's my job to teach you how to please me, and apparently also yourself, but I'm not going to force you."

"But we are going to sleep together," she says, a glint of rebellion in her eyes.

"Naturally. Unless you've changed your mind?"

"No," she says, unclenching her fingers. "I haven't changed my mind."

"Then trust me."

"Trust you?" She laughs.

"Trust me with your body. I know what I'm doing."

"You certainly have the experience," she throws back at me. "Don't you?"

Bringing up my experience isn't going to help win her over. "You're the most important person in this room. Only your needs matter."

"I don't have needs."

Such a wordy little girl. "Are you going to trust me? You're only wasting your own time. Whether today, tomorrow, or next week, you will take off your clothes for me and ask me to make you come."

She narrows her eyes. "I won't ask to come."

My smile holds a challenge. "Prove it."

She glares at me some more but does reach for the zipper of her dress at her back. I don't offer to help. I sit and watch. That's my job. It's showing her how lovely she is.

She pulls the zipper down and pushes the dress from her shoulders and over her hips. Her underwear is chocolate-brown, the same color as the dress. It's lacy and pretty, but I prefer her naked. She removes the boots and stockings, and then the underwear.

Standing naked in front of me, she asks bitingly, "I'm supposed to need this?"

I take in her firm breasts and pink nipples, her narrow waist, and curved hips. The dark, unshaven triangle between her legs. She's voluptuous, small but rounded where it matters. "You're very beautiful, Zoe."

The pink of her cheeks flares again. "What now, Maxime?"

"Come sit on my lap and tell my what you did while I was away."

Her lips part. "What?"

"You heard me."

She pads over uncertainly. When she stops in front of me, I

uncross my legs and spread them. Turning sideways, she steps between them. I hook my hands under her arms to lift her onto my thigh, arranging her with her legs draped over the armrest and her back in the crook of my arm.

I brush her curls over her shoulder before trailing my fingers down her arm, keeping the touch light. "Did you explore the house?"

Goosebumps break out over her skin. "Yes."

I drag my fingers up to her shoulder and back down to her wrist. "Do you like it?" Up, down, and up again. "And no more sass like earlier."

She shivers a little. "What do you want me to say? You have a nice house. A little spooky, but impressive."

I smile at the spooky bit, tracing the arch of her neck. "It has a great view. Have you looked outside?"

She turns her face to me. "You told me I wasn't allowed to go outside."

I explore the elegant curve of her collarbone with my fingertips. "On the balcony."

"No, but I went up in the tower."

"Mm." I brush the back of my knuckles over a pink nipple. The tip hardens. The darker skin around contracts. "I don't go there much, but women seem drawn to it. It must be the princess in the tower thing."

She stiffens. "I was just curious. I didn't go up there with some repressed fantasy."

I place my palm on her waist, the touch meant to be calming. "That's not what I said."

"No, what you said is that you bring many women here."

"You're the only one here now, aren't you?"

She doesn't answer.

I bring my hand back to her breast, stroking the underside with a thumb. "Did you meet Fran?"

"Yes." She leans her full weight against me, settling in deeper. "She speaks English very well. She almost doesn't have an accent."

I move to the other breast, tracing the areola with a finger. The tip buds beautifully, growing hard even before I flick a finger over it. "She studied at a culinary school in London. Her food is very good. I'm sure you'll enjoy it."

She squirms when I move lower, tracing her navel. "How long has she worked for you?"

"A couple of years." I drag a line from her navel to the apex of her sex, rolling my middle finger over her clit.

She sucks in a breath and presses her knees together. "I gave her a letter. She said you'll mail it for me."

"To your brother?" I trace her pussy lips with my thumb.

"Yes," she says, hardly suppressing a moan before biting her lip. "I wanted to tell you before Francine mentions it."

Ah, she was hoping to get her letter mailed without my knowledge but realized Francine will never undermine me. "You can write to Damian as much as you like."

She gives me a surprised look. "You don't mind?"

"Not in the slightest."

At the declaration, her body sags. I use the opportunity to part her slightly, playing just inside her opening without penetrating her with my finger. Her back arches. She moans. I slip a hand between her thighs and push them open wide, then urge her to settle back in my hold. She's so goddamn pretty spread over my lap with her nipples tight and arousal glistening on her pussy. Her breathing is shallower, her stomach rising and falling faster. I'm harder than before, painfully so, but I ignore the torturing feel of her ass on my cock, focusing only on her as I promised.

My play is soft and teasing, enough to stimulate but not enough to make her come. I won't take her pleasure unless we're fucking, unless I'm taking mine, or unless she asks me. I carry on with my stroking, extending the caresses to the inside of her thighs. She's trembling with full-blown shivers now.

Lowering my mouth to her ear, I press a kiss to the shell. "Do you want to come?"

"No," she says quickly, unwilling to surrender and admit defeat.

"It's no big deal." I tease her earlobe with my teeth. "We all need release. All you have to do is say yes."

She sighs, tilting her head to give me better access. I love how responsive she is to my touch, how I can coax her into the pleasure I want her to have. I love the smell of roses in her silky hair and the velvety petal smoothness of her skin. I love how wet and slick she is for me and how her ass lifts a little every time I rub a finger over her swollen clit. She's spread and on display, her lower body resting snuggly in my lap. Her eyes are closed and her head thrown back. She's a sight to behold. Since she's not saying no, I gather her wetness, careful not to overstretch her sensitive skin, and slip the tip of my finger into her heat. The hot tightness is torture. I can't help but imagine sinking my cock into her just like last night.

She gasps, her arms going rigid at her sides. It doesn't take long for her hips to follow my shallow thrusts. When her inner muscles go softer around my finger, I push in all the way to the knuckle.

Her thighs clench on my finger. "Maxime."

I lay her out like a sacrifice and bring my mouth down to kiss her nipple. I lick it lightly at first, then close my lips around the hard, little tip and lathe it with my tongue. She tastes delicious. I can't stop myself from French kissing her breast, covering her skin with sloppy kisses until her curve is wet. Her nipple hardens when I finally let go and cooler air washes over it.

Whimpering, she lifts her arms and rests them on her forehead.

"Do you want to come, Zoe?"

She keeps her eyes hidden from me, her expression sheltered under her arms. I feel her desire, how badly she wants to give in, but I won't take if she doesn't give it to me freely.

"Will it be bad if I say yes?" she asks in a small voice.

"No, Zoe. It won't be bad. Quite the contrary."

Her cry is defeated, a tremulous sigh. "Yes."

I increase the pace of my finger, pressing my thumb on her clit. She's so close, it only takes a few seconds before her body pulls as tight as a bow, her legs forming a V as the arrow hits right where I intended—in her soft little heart.

Women like Zoe feel the physical explosion of an orgasm on every level, most of all with their emotions.

She comes undone with a climax that locks her inner muscles around my finger and a tear that rolls over her cheek. It's victory and defeat, all rolled into one.

I withdraw slowly, taking care not to hurt her. Then I take her arms and arrange them around my neck where she most needs them to be, even if she doesn't know it herself. I hold her and give her something to hold onto as she comes back down to reality, to seeing herself naked in my arms like a shameful Eve saw herself for the first time before paradise turned into the garden of sin.

Grabbing the throw from the chair back, I cover her body, not only because the logs in the fire is burning out, but also because she'll feel vulnerable when the haze of passion dims. Reality is like winter, cold and unforgiving.

Her tears wet my neck, but she doesn't pull away. She burrows closer. I revel at the victory. There's nothing that can feel better, not my own release, not even the success of saving our business. The tenseness of my muscles is gone. The anger I felt when I entered this room has dissipated, vanished in the throes of her orgasm.

"There now." I kiss the top of her head. "It'll get better."

It's the vow I made to myself long before I made the promise to my father.

As we sit quietly in front of the last embers of the fire, Zoe dozes off. We didn't sleep much last night. The journey was tiring. I'm reluctant to wake her—I much prefer to stay like this with her in my arms—but it's dark outside. She has to eat.

I brush a strand of hair from her face and kiss her forehead. "Are you up for a shower?"

She yawns. "What time is it?"

I check my watch. "Almost six."

She stretches like a lazy cat. "I suppose."

My arms tighten around her involuntarily. She's cute, this little flower of mine. Balancing her in my arms, I stand to adjust my erection. I haven't forgotten about punishing her mouth. I've just moved it back to prioritize her needs. I unlock the door and carry her to my room. The hallway is lit, courtesy of Francine.

In the room, I switch on the light and turn up the heat before ordering Zoe to the bathroom.

She obeys wordlessly. The water in the shower comes on. I walk closer and put my ear to the door, listening to the sounds of cascading water, imagining her under the spray and wishing I could be there with her. Not yet. She's not ready for that.

A knock sounds on the door. I go over and open it. Fran stands on the step.

Her eyes dart toward the bathroom. "You've been away for less than a week."

"Meaning?"

"Meaning *that*," she points at the bathroom door, "was fast."

I swallow down my irritation. Fran is a loyal employee. "My private life isn't your concern."

"No?" She tilts her head. "It used to be."

"It's over, Fran. We've been through this."

Her eyes cloud over. "A couple of rolls between the sheets are enough to make you grow tired of a woman?"

Sadly, yes.

She motions with her head toward the bathroom. "How long do you think she'll last?"

"None of your business."

"She asked me to mail a letter."

"She told me."

"Why are the phones locked away, Max? Why isn't she allowed to leave the house?"

I clench my jaw. "As I said—"

"Not my business."

"Exactly."

She takes a step forward, putting our bodies flush. "I'm loyal to you." She snakes her arms around my neck. "You know that."

I grip her arms to pull them away. "But?"

"But I can't deal with having another woman flaunted—"

The bathroom door opens. We both turn our heads that way.

Zoe freezes on the threshold in a billow of steam. Clutching a towel to her chest, she looks between Fran and me. I don't like what I see in her expressive eyes. I don't like that wounded look or the sag of betrayal that sets in her shoulders.

I untangle Fran's arms and put her a step away from me.

Giving Zoe a cold look, Fran says, "Dinner is ready. I'll leave it in the warmer drawer before I go."

My voice is measured. "You do that."

With a last glance at me, Fran leaves.

"More than just your cook, I see." Zoe's chin is lifted but her eyes brim with emotions that spoil our earlier moment.

"It was a long time ago."

"Then you don't deny it. You fucked her."

I'm not going to lie. Not about that. "Yes."

"Thanks for that." She walks past me to the suitcase that lies unpacked on the bed. "I needed the reminder."

I catch her wrist. "You're not going to do this."

"Do what?"

"Look for excuses to shut me out."

"They're not excuses. They're facts, and why would I shut you out if you've never been inside to start with?"

I drop my voice an octave. "Careful, little flower. You don't know me. If you did, you wouldn't push me."

She yanks her arm free. "I know you better than you think."

It's a laughable generalization, a terrible misjudgment. Putting my hand on her shoulder, I push her down to her knees.

She fights it, straining back, and then fights the towel that threatens to fall open.

Unzipping my fly, I stare down at her shocked face. "I said we were going to punish that mouth. You owe me twice already." I pull out my cock, heavy and hard, thick with need. My balls ache with unspilled release.

She knows where I'm going with this when I stroke myself three times and aim for her lips. She clamps them shut. I grab her jaw and squeeze the pressure points next to her ears. It opens her mouth wide, wide enough to slide my cock through those plump lips. She gags and tries to pull back, but I grab the back of her head.

"You're going to take me," I hiss, "and swallow everything."

She grabs my thighs when I push her face forward, making her swallow my cock. Not caring so much about the towel now, it falls to the carpet, leaving her naked on her knees. Stunning. Struggling for air. I let her. She needs to learn this little lesson. Her very breaths belong to me. I can be kind or what she makes me out to be, either a cultured gentleman or the monster of her nightmares.

I count carefully, controlled. I'm in charge even as her saliva coats my dick and her tongue is warm on the underside, making me want to explode. I twist her locks around a fist and pull out when I get to ten. She gulps in air. Her big, blue eyes are watering, spit running down her chin. I'm being easy on her. She should be able to hold her breath to thirty without effort. I give her time for one more drag of air before I drive back. Then I move. I pump with two short thrusts and a long one, my cock hitting the back of her throat at every third count. I fuck her face on the beat of a waltz. It's a dance designed to limit her gag reflex and prevent her from vomiting.

My balls draw tight. Her lips are stretched thin around me, the noises she makes only spurring me on. I can last for a long time. Practice makes perfect. I can drag this out until she faints. I give her two more breathing reposes before I let myself go, aiming my cock deep and shooting my load down her throat. Her delicate white neck convulses as she tries to swallow with the intrusion in her throat. I spend every last drop, not sparing her before I pull out.

She sags in my hold, her chest heaving as her small body sucks in air. I don't let her go down. I keep her up by her hair. Using the long, silky tresses, I wipe my dick clean. Then I go down on my haunches, putting us on eye level.

Tilting back her head, I make her face me. "The choice, little flower, is always yours." I kiss her ravaged lips. "One punishment down. One to go."

Only then do I release her.

I go to the bathroom and shut the door. I need a shower. I strip and turn the water on the hottest setting I can handle. I let the burn scald me until fire rains over my skin.

I'm a depraved man.

I'll defile my little flower's body many times yet to come.

CHAPTER 15

Zoe

Hunched over, I catch my breath on the floor. My shoulders rise and fall rapidly with the air I try to suck in quietly, but I can't stop the loud panting completely. It's the sound of my humiliation. The warm tears blurring the pattern on the carpet is the sight and the carpet burns on my knees the feel. The taste is a lingering afterthought in my mouth. This is the portrait of degradation.

As oxygen feeds my lungs, the harshness of my breathing evens out. It turns from a perverse fight for air and dignity to searing anger that flares my nostrils and curls my shoulders outward like the edges of a piece of paper furling in a flame. Sitting back on my heels, I wipe the saliva from my chin. I still feel Maxime in the stretch of my lips and in the little tears in the corners. I still taste him on my tongue. The message was clear. My behavior has consequences. Play nice and be treated in kind.

My pride won't let me.

I want to hurt Maxime like he's hurting me. I want to insult him and crush him in every way I can, even as I give him my body. He just showed me he won't let me. He won't let me use him as a punching bag to gain the satisfaction of extracting some kind of revenge. He wants everything. He's not happy only with my body. He wants me to give it with a pretty please and a kind thank you. That's why he wants me to like the house and the food. He wants me to adapt, accept my fate, and give my body freely in return for his protection.

He'll make it as good for me as I make it for him.

Rationally, I know all of this, but my pride is a monster and my anger a dragon that live in my chest. They breathe fire into my soul until I'm blind to anything but the flames burning in my gut.

Fixing my gaze on the bathroom door, I push to my feet. I keep the target in sight as I move forward with balled hands and shoulders rolled inward. I grip the handle and fling the door open, stepping into the steam.

Maxime's body is a blurry image, an apparition in the fog through the glass. His back is turned to me, his head tipped back and big hands with bruised knuckles brushing over his skull. He's huge. His body dominates the space, but I don't miss a beat. I yank the shower door open.

He spins around, his gray eyes widening as he takes me in. Before the shocked expression on his face has vanished, I draw back my arm and slap him hard enough across the face to make his head fly sideways. Turning his face back to me, he touches his fingers to the imprint of mine on his cheek.

The fight leaves me with the outlet of violence. Just like that, the fire burns out. I've never been a physical fighter. I never wanted to be, not after my father, and shame and disappointment replace the anger, becoming the new monsters in my chest.

He doesn't give me a second to process what I'm becoming. Fast like the lash of a whip, he strikes out, grabbing my neck and arm and jerking me inside the shower. The breath leaves my lungs with an oomph as my back hits the tiles. Fear finds the front seat in my chest now as he stares at me with a clenched jaw and retribution burning in his eyes.

I expect him to hit me back. An ugly part of me wants him to so I can hate him more. Men like my father, those I understand, but Maxime is a complex mix of confusing signals. If my words made Maxime all but suffocate me with his cock, the mark I left on his skin should do much worse. I can't look away from his eyes. I watch their molten gray transform to a darker storm. With grinding teeth, he stares at me, his fingers tightening around my neck and pinning me against the wall. Just when I think he's going to snap my neck, he brings his head down and crushes our mouths together.

The kiss is brutal. His teeth cut my lip. I taste the blood as our tongues tangle. His breathing is harsh, his growl a primitive sound. He mashes our lips together, sucking the very life out of me as if this is a new kind of war. I fight back. I kiss him like my life depends on it. I don't know where my desperation comes from, only that this mutual roughness feels purging.

He takes, but I take, too. I bite down on his lower lip until our blood mingles. I use the aggression as an outlet for my pain like he won't allow me to use my sharp words or self-preserving pride. I stop being a passive participant, trying to hold onto something precious with both hands, something I don't want to share, and take something from him for myself.

It's a tipping point. To take, your hand has to be open, not clutched tightly around your heart. When I take from Maxime, I open myself. I'm vulnerable to the unknown, susceptible to the sensations of a violent kiss, surprised to find I like it. It's like a fight for life, a fight to death. Only one of us will be left standing when this is all over. The desperation transforms into arousal. Heat blooms between my legs. It's not gentle and slow building like in the study. It's instant and demanding. I moan, a keening sound of need that triggers Maxime's tipping point in turn.

He grows gentle. The warning hold on my neck loosens to a possessive caress. He drags his tongue over the cut on my lip and molds his mouth around mine with tender precision. It's a skilled kiss, a seductive kiss. I lean into it, pushing our bodies together. Placing one hand next to my face on the wall, he drags his hand from my neck to my breast, squeezing softly. My back arches. He tilts his hips toward mine, pressing his hard-on against my stomach. Water washes over us, drawing an abstract picture with blurry lines, but right and wrong vanishes with the need that pulses in my body as if it has a life of its own.

Like my aggression stoked his, his slower pace awakens new needs in me, a need to touch and to be held. Lifting my hands from the tiles where they're plastered next to my hips, I place them on Maxime's chest. The muscles are hard and unrelenting under my palms as I expected, but it's the bumpy texture of his skin that stills me.

I lean back, blinking the water from my eyes. Maxime freezes. His eyelids lift with wary apprehension. My gaze skims down. The skin of his chest is red and angry, patchy all the way to his stomach and covering half of his abdomen, an aggressive pattern of pain painted on a man. I've never seen anything like it. My heart squeezes in involuntary empathy. What happened to him? What caused such scars?

When I splay my fingers to inspect the damage, he catches my wrist.

The pressure of his grip is too hard. "Don't." The single word is harsh, but there's a plea in his eyes, and it's mixed with agony to reflect a portrait of stunning suffering in those ash-colored pools.

"What happened?" I whisper.

"Fire."

He moves my hand away, down, and places it over his erection. I close my fingers involuntary. He hisses. The sound gives me power. I stroke. He growls.

I know what he's doing. He's using distraction to prevent me from asking the questions turning in my mind, and it's working. His cock twitches under my palm, hardening more. I look at my fist, my fingers barely meeting, and back at his gaze.

He's watching me with sharp attention. I watch him in turn as I slide my fist up and down. I see what I do to him. I see the angry hunger in his eyes.

He cups my hip, angling his erection toward my opening. "Actions have consequences, little flower." He grabs my wrist and moves my hand away. "You came in here knowing full well what could happen."

I came in here to avenge myself for how he used me. Instead, I find myself pressed up against a wall, wet and needy. He grabs the base of his cock in one hand and presses the head against my clit while holding my hip with the other like I'm fragile and about to break. He rubs in a circle, sending flushes of heat through my body. Slickness covers my sex. He drags his cock over my opening, bringing my arousal back to my clit. I open my legs to give him better access. I'm panting, needing this now that I know what it feels like and how good the release is.

He rubs a thumb over my hip, a soft backward and forward brush. "I wasn't going to do this so soon."

When he grips my thigh and drapes it around his ass, I place my palms on his shoulders. I'm not going to let him make me forget why I came in here. There are lines he can't cross. "I won't let you bully me."

"Then stop bullying me."

His words take me by surprise. Is that how he sees my actions, my sharp tongue and spiteful attitude? I gasp, but not because of his words. He's parted me and slipped inside an inch. It burns, but not as much as last night.

"This isn't punishment," he says. "I don't want to hurt you. You can tell me to stop."

I don't. A spark ignites when he slides over sensitive nerve endings. Leaning my head against the tiles, I bite my lip, feeling the fire steal over my body, incinerating me from the inside out.

I adapt faster than yesterday. The stretch still hurts, but my body is suppler, welcoming the intrusion instead of trying to push it out. He's excruciatingly gentle, moving inch by inch until he is fully sheathed. He cups a hand between my legs, massaging my dark entrance with a middle finger. The stimulation makes me clench my knees together, trapping him inside me. My inner muscles squeeze. He curses and lets go, giving me room to relax and take him deeper.

I cling to his shoulders when he starts to move. His pace is slow and careful. He locks his hands around my middle, circling my waist. Bringing down his head, he catches my bottom lip between his teeth, sucking it gently into his mouth. He kisses me softly, reverently, as he drags his hands over my ribs to the sides of my breasts. He pushes the curves together between his palms until my nipples brushes over his chest. I feel the quick intake of his breath in our kiss. I hear it as he lets my breasts touch him where he wouldn't allow my hands.

His soft kiss and gentle touch stoke the fire inside me higher. Its fuel is as effective as the aggressive kiss that started this. Tilting my hips forward, I urge him to move faster and send me over the edge.

He's good at this dance. He knows the rhythm and the steps. He knows how to lead me. The way our bodies rub together stimulates my clit. I feel it coming, a band that stretches to breaking point.

"I'm going to—" The orgasm hits. It's white-hot and a symphony of pleasure exploding in every cell of my body. I dig my nails into his arms. A cry escapes my lips as he rips himself from me.

I want to mourn the premature ending of the fireworks under my skin, but when ribbons of cum erupt from his cock and fall over my thighs, I understand. I've almost forgotten a fundamental precaution. The consequences of him coming inside me make me go cold. Dammit. How could he disarm me this much? I haven't even asked if he's clean.

I'm scolding myself for my irresponsible behavior when he presses his forehead against mine. He's breathing heavily. We both are.

"Maxime."

He cups my cheek, this thumb hooking under my jaw. "What is it, Zoe?"

"We almost forgot."

He leans away to look at me. "I'm careful, but you're right. I'll take care of it first thing tomorrow."

"You're my first, but…" I bite my lip. I don't want to insult him again, not until I've decided how to move forward, if I'm willing to fight to the death of my soul or if I'm going to take the white flag he's offering.

His lips pull up in one corner. "Do you seriously think I'd risk giving you diseases?"

I study him. "I don't know." Despite what I said earlier, I don't really know him, and I'm having a tough time figuring him out. He's too confusing, a dangerous cocktail of mixed signals.

His mouth tightens. "I'm clean."

"Okay." It's a meek word, a feeble attempt at guarding our fragile peace.

"The water is getting cold."

He reaches for the sponge, soaps it, and starts to wash me. By the time he's done, the scalding hot water of earlier is lukewarm. He turns off the water and wraps me in a thick towel before taking one for himself. After drying me, he pulls on a T-shirt and a pair of tracksuit pants.

I'm lethargic and sore, and I have a strange glowing feeling in my body. I'm also hungry, and my stomach rumbles to announce it.

"Go to bed," he says, watching my reflection in the mirror as I'm brushing out my hair. "I'll bring up a tray."

I turn in surprise. "I can go down to eat."

"You're tired."

He doesn't wait for my response. He walks from the bathroom, leaving the door open. I go back to the room and rummage through the suitcase Maxime had packed, but there are no pajamas. He didn't get me any. I settle for a pair of silk panties, the ones that cover my bottom the most, and one of his T-shirts. Then I slip between the cold sheets, resting my back against the headboard.

I really am tired, and by the time he returns my eyes are drawing close.

He sits down next to me with a chuckle. "My little hellcat is exhausted."

I don't say anything. I'm not sure how I feel about what I did, about hitting him then kissing him like an animal and fucking as if we were having make-up sex. I don't want to turn into my father, my mother either.

He brushes a strand of hair behind my ear. "What's wrong?"

"Nothing." Except that I almost apologized to my kidnapper for slapping him. Am I losing my mind?

"Fran made *magret de canard*." He forks a bite-sized piece of meat and holds it to my lips.

I stiffen a little at the mention of his lover, or ex-lover as he's claimed, but I open my lips. I'm too hungry to refuse, hungrier than I've ever been. I'm surprised that I have an appetite at all. Maybe it's the sea air, or the colder winter, or the sex.

The duck is delicious. He alternates the meat with grilled potatoes, feeding me until the plate is empty.

"What about you?" I ask when he hands me a glass of red wine.

"I still have work to do. I'll eat later."

"Oh." I take a sip of wine, contemplating the man who fed me, taking care of my needs before his. Does he have a split personality? How can he be so caring in one moment and cruel in the next? Because he doesn't harbor feelings for me. I'm an object, his hostage.

He gathers the tray and stands. "It'll do you good to have an early night."

As if that will make everything all right.

"Goodnight, Zoe."

With that, he walks from the room. I stare at the closed door. I'm unsettled. Uncertain. It's only my first day in his house. How will I get through four years? I take another sip of the wine. It's good, rounded and smoky. It makes me feel warm and relaxed. What I need is some fresh air to clear my head. I need to decide how to handle this. I can't do this see-saw thing with Maxime. It's too exhausting. I'm either consenting to my fate or defying him to the point of my soul's destruction. What I can't do is become a person I hate. We'd vowed this to each other, Damian and I, that we'd never repeat our parents' mistakes.

I pull on a pair of socks and Maxime's thick robe that hangs behind the bathroom door. Taking my wine, I open the balcony doors and step outside. It's freezing. The wind nips at my skin, making me shiver. It's dark over the ocean save for the wedge of moonlight that illuminates the cove. A half-moon of sand shines in the light. There's a small beach at the bottom of the cliffs.

A movement on the boulder catches my eye. Someone is walking along the edge of the cliff. It's impossible not to recognize Maxime's powerful frame and purposeful stride. He's dressed in the same clothes from earlier, no coat. I suck in a breath. He'll catch his death out there.

I rest my arms on the rail, leaning over farther for a better view. He stretches his arms over his head. What the hell is he doing? He's taking off his T-shirt. Stunned, I watch as he strips naked. I'm caught so much off guard, I don't come to my senses until he steps right up to the edge and jumps.

CHAPTER 16

Maxime

The water is like icicles driving into my skin. The shock is thermal. It makes me feel alive. I go down deep, a place I've gone many times before, and not just literally. I don't swim. I don't fight. I let the cobalt hole swallow me, and I count. When I get to sixty, I start to kick. Another sixty, and I break the surface. Six times as much as I made Zoe take. If she suffered, I have to suffer too.

Gasping for air, I fight the cramps that set in due to the cold. My lungs burn. The punishment blazes through my chest like a fire while the cold encases my skin. I embrace it. Fuck, it feels great. Power surges through me. Strength bursts in my veins. I turn away from the shore and swim deeper into the ocean with strong breaststrokes. The cold vanishes until only the invincible sensation remains. In the stretch of moonlight that falls over the water, I float on my back to look at the stars. The sky is clear. It's a cold kind of clear, that dry, iciness that settles over the night and frosts the landscape like icing sugar sifted over a cake.

This is part of what I love so much about this place—the silence. I drift about aimlessly, enjoying the quiet and weightlessness for as long as I can. Chaos awaits on the shore. With a life like mine, there's always chaos. I should turn back soon. I may not feel the pain, but hypothermia will set in after a few more minutes. I drag my fingers over the scar tissue on my chest. The skin is dead. There's no feeling. There hasn't been since the multiple skin grafts.

That's the problem with men like me. We're unfeeling. It goes deeper than my scarred skin. It goes all the way down to the hardened, black, rotten organ I call my heart. In my occupation, we *do* things, *see* things. It desensitizes us. It makes us monsters to others and dead to ourselves. Until Zoe touched me.

When I held her against me in the lobby of her building, I felt something. It was different to the usual physical arousal that comes with sex. She stirred *things* inside me, things I thought were dead. She stirred my curiosity about life, about staying pure and beautiful amidst the sins that make grown men unfeeling. When she put her hands on my chest in the shower tonight, I swear my dead skin crawled. There was something there underneath the flesh and blood. I felt her touch in my heart. Longing. Compassion. Admiration. A need to protect. A need to please.

It's new. It's confusing. Fuck me if I know what to do with it.

What shall I do with her, my little flower? I look at the house that stands on the cliffs, a beacon of status and wealth with the lights shining from its windows. My gaze finds the room where she's sleeping, and then I still. A figure stands on the balcony, small and vulnerable against the evil myths and unfortunate truths that lurk in the night. A gust of wind rips her hair across her face. She shouldn't be out there. She'll catch pneumonia.

Turning back to the shore, I swim fast. I can find the passage between the sharp rocks blindfolded. In no time, I walk out on the sand, and when I look up, she's no longer there. I take the path, climbing up the steep steps to the cliff top where I left my clothes. I pull them on over my wet body and make my way back to the house.

I push the front door open, and Zoe stands there, hugging herself.

She's dressed in my robe, one of my T-shirts, and a pair of socks. A different kind of power surges through me. It has nothing to do with being invincible and everything about vulnerability. It's possessive. I'm overwhelmed with male pride, with owning what stands in front of me. My clothes mark her as mine. The way I took her body is an irrevocable claim. I'm jealous of her. I'm jealous of the men who'll have her when we're over, and suddenly the thought is unthinkable.

She's looking at me with parted lips, questions in her eyes. I lock away my revelations, the strangeness of these new feelings, and shut the door behind me.

Sleeking back my wet, windblown hair, I ask, "What are you doing up?"

"My God, Maxime." She steps toward me, her eyes big. "You'll freeze to death." She scans my face. "Your lips are blue."

Her concern warms my chest. Pathetically, I want more of her worry. "I thought you would've been glad if I dropped dead."

She grabs my arm and drags me deeper into the house. "Don't joke about that."

A smile plucks at my lips. It's not a forced gesture, but one of those spontaneous ones that feels so unfamiliar it must look unnatural. "About what? Death?" I'm not afraid of it. Not for myself. Yet for her I'm terrified.

She slaps my arm. "Shh. If you say it, you'll make it happen."

That makes me smile. It's not just a quirk of my lips. It's the full nine yards. "If I talk about my death, I'll die?"

Her blue eyes grow even rounder. "We attract what we think."

I'm intrigued. It's this part of her that fascinates me. "Do you believe in that hocus pocus hippy stuff?"

She gives me a chiding look. "It's not hippy stuff. It's quantum physics. It's the law of energy. What you give is what you get." Lifting a cocky brow, she continues, "You are what you think. Never heard about that?"

I cross my arms. "Is this a misguided lesson in morals?"

She scrunches up her nose. "No, it's science. For every action there's an equal reaction." She cocks her hip, her posture a challenge.

"You said so yourself, didn't you? Not in so many words, but if you think about it, we really believe in the same thing." She shrugs. "Actions have consequences."

She's cute, this tiny woman. I want to throw her over my shoulder and carry her away to somewhere nicer, someplace happier, but this is who we are, and we've already set the chain of actions in motion. It does give me insight into her mind and her thought process though, and I'm hungry to understand her.

I study her sassy little stance and saucy mouth. "It sounds as if you were thinking in my absence."

She clutches her hands behind her back. "I was."

I remain quiet, waiting for her to carry on, because I want to know how she operates. I want to know how she survives. Will she roll over and play dead, biding her time until it's up? Will she go into denial and pretend this isn't happening by living out some bullshit fantasy in her mind? Will she surrender? Or will she fight me until the end? What makes her tick? What will her strategy be in our war?

She blushes a little. "I'm not going to give you any more trouble."

I'm guessing the color in her cheeks is due to shame and not shyness. It's the knock she takes in willingly being the lesser, submitting to a fate she'd otherwise never have chosen. But her shoulders are square, and her head is high. This isn't surrender. She's either playing dead or fighting the only way she can, by choosing her battles wisely.

Uncrossing my arms, I move closer. "Is that what you were doing outside on the balcony? Making important decisions?"

She takes a step back. "You saw me?"

"You should've dressed warmer. The wind is cold."

"You're one to talk. I saw you jumping off that cliff in nothing but your birthday suit."

"Is your concern for the cold, the jump, or the fact that I was naked?"

"None." She backtracks when I advance another step. "I'm not concerned about you."

"No? Then why do you behave like you are?"

"The only thing I'm concerned about is what happens to me if you die."

Ah. That sours my mood a little, not that I could've expected differently. "Right. You should be since I have your passport, not to mention that you'll be given to Alexis."

The pink disappears from her cheeks.

"You don't have to worry your pretty little mind over things like that. I'm not planning on dying soon, and I'm glad we can put the fights aside." I cup her cheek. I'm going to figure her out, this clever little daisy. "I meant what I said. You can be happy here."

She nods. "Okay."

"What made you change your mind?" Jokingly, I add, "Seeing me jump off a cliff?" Had I known it would be this easy, I'd have done it sooner.

She looks away. "The way I behaved reminded me too much of my father."

Gripping her chin, I turn her face back to me. "The way you behaved how?"

She averts her eyes. "When I slapped you."

I don't like where this is going. "What did your father do, Zoe?"

"He was violent."

My back goes rigid. "With you?"

"Mostly with my mother and Damian, but he broke things, and it scared me."

I try to picture Zoe as a child, a little girl, scared and defenseless, and I don't like it. I don't fucking like it one bit. I admire her for fighting her genes, for wanting to be better. I sure as hell didn't manage.

"I see." I drop my hand. "Do I remind you of your father?"

She lifts her gaze back to mine. "No." Just as my spine relaxes, a sliver of fear creeps into her tone. "You're in a different league. My father wasn't a tenth of what you are."

She fears me more. I both hate and love it. I can't decide which feeling I want to embrace. Just when I thought I almost had her figured out she confuses me again. Confused isn't something I've ever been. I don't like it.

Staring at her big, frightened eyes, I move even closer, my body shadowing hers. I want her. I want her fear and pleasure. I want her happiness and submission. I want to take her right here on the stairs. I barely manage to grit out, "Go to bed."

She doesn't let me tell her twice. She runs up the stairs like a mouse fleeing from a cat. I stand at the bottom, staring after her while mulling over her words and dissecting my feelings. Making sense of thoughts and sensations is a logical process. I don't trust my heart. I only trust my mind.

I suppose what she said about being worse than her father is true. I've broken a lot more than material things. There's more blood on my soul than on the hands of a soldier. I suppose I do scare children, and puppies, and pretty little innocent flowers, but I'm neither coward nor fool. Her father was a coward for terrorizing his own daughter and a fool for not seeing the pure, perfect girl right under his eyes.

An insight hits me. Zoe grew up with violence. However wrong that is, she should be used to it, at least to an extent. What I am should scare her, but it shouldn't surprise her. She shouldn't be as innocent as she is. She avoided reality. The only means she had of escaping a traumatic childhood was hiding in herself by going someplace else in her head. That's why Zoe is a dreamer. That's why she's a romantic. Her reality was a shithole, but she desperately held out for cupids and happily-ever-after. That's why she's a princess, down to the way she dresses.

Warfare is an art. It requires a certain finesse. There's little finesse in slaying your enemy by cutting off his head. It's much more challenging to turn him into an ally. It's much more rewarding to have your enemy worship at your feet. This new insight tells me exactly what my strategy with Zoe should be. I'm not going to be her father. I won't allow her to live in her head where she can hide from me. In the art of warfare, it's crucial to know your enemy's vulnerability. Now that I know hers, I'll fill that gap. I'll give her what she most wants.

Before her time here is up, she'll be eating out of my hand. When the time comes to set her free, she'll beg me to stay. Yes, I like this outcome much better than keeping her chained with threats. My chest heats just thinking about it. My cock hardens at the challenge.

My own daisy, in a vase on my table. I didn't steal it from someone's garden. It was growing wild on the pavement, right there for the taking.

CHAPTER 17

Zoe

Persistent shaking pulls me from my sleep. I fight it, but I can't ignore the deep voice or the French accent. I wake with a gasp when I remember where I am.

"Easy, Zoe." Maxime brushes a hand over my shoulder. "You have to wake up. We have an appointment in Marseille."

Rubbing my eyes, I turn to face him. He sits on the edge of the bed, dressed in a dark suit. His hair is still damp from his shower. The smell of winter hangs like a faint cloud around him, but it's pierced with the summery fragrance of roses. A cup of steaming tea stands on the nightstand.

"I brought you an infusion," he says. "Fran can make you coffee if you prefer. Breakfast is waiting downstairs."

"Thank you," I say uncertainly, my manners still intact while I'm half asleep.

"You're welcome." He takes my hand and kisses the back, then puts something in my palm.

I lift my hand and stare at the cellphone.

"My number is programmed." He gets to his feet. "Come down when you're ready. We're leaving in thirty minutes."

I only get to my senses when he's gone. Maxime had opened the curtains. The sky outside is still dark, dawn barely breaking through a thick layer of clouds. I look at the telephone screen again. The time says it's eight o'clock.

Wait. I have a phone.

Shooting upright, I type in the number for the correctional service where Damian is held and press dial. A message comes on in English, announcing I don't have access to the service. I check the settings. Of course. I can only dial Maxime's number. I didn't expect anything different, but my shoulders sag in disappointment.

Dejected, I reach for the tea on the nightstand. Folding my hands around the cup, I inhale the fragrant herbal tea. It smells of roses and raspberries, the same tea Maxime served me in Venice. I take a sip. It's a delicious blend. The brew warms and somewhat fortifies me.

Memories of last night's discussion turn in my head as I shower and change into a pair of slacks and a cashmere sweater with frilly sleeves that have been neatly arranged in the dressing room. Maxime must've unpacked the suitcase either last night or this morning. I thankfully fell asleep before he came to bed. I wasn't going to unpack. Putting the clothes he'd bought for me in his closet doesn't only feel wrong, but also way too final. After putting on a pair of ankle boots, I go downstairs where a breakfast of croissants and orange juice is set out in the dining room. Maxime is seated at the table, reading something on his phone. Judging by the pastry flakes in his plate, he's already eaten.

When I enter, he gets up and pulls out a chair for me.

"Sleep well?" he asks.

"Yes." Surprisingly. "Why are we going to Marseille?"

"You have a doctor's appointment."

Of course. Relief flows through me. The last thing I want is an unplanned pregnancy.

He checks his watch. "I have a few instructions to give to Fran before we leave. Any meal preferences for this week's menu?"

I shake my head. I don't care what I eat. I hate that I have to eat Maxime's food at all.

"Maybe later," he says with a stiff smile.

I eat quickly, and when he returns, I'm ready.

Like yesterday, Maxime drives us while two men follow in their own car. I stare at the scenery outside, at the cliffs, the beach, and the city that comes into view forty minutes later. From afar, the buildings aren't impressive. The only piece of architecture that stands out is the church on the top of the hill. As we enter the center of town, the buildings change from white concrete blocks to beautiful old ones with French windows, blue shutters, and ornate balcony rails. He parks in front of a building with a sculptured entrance, each top corner supported on a marble angel's shoulders.

"Wow," I say as I look up at the carved wooden door.

Putting a hand on my back, he buzzes us in and leads me up a stone staircase to the third floor. A middle-aged man with mousy hair and glasses opens the door when Maxime rings.

"Max." He pats Max on the back before extending a hand toward me. "Mademoiselle Hart. I'm Dr. Olivier."

I accept the handshake automatically. From the fact that he speaks English, Maxime must've briefed him about me before we arrived. What did he tell the doctor? That I'm his willing lover? Or does the doctor know the truth?

"Come through," the doctor says, showing us into an examination room.

The far end next to the fireplace serves as a sitting area. Maxime takes my hand and leads me to the sofa. He pulls me down next to him, not letting go of my hand but arranging it on his thigh instead. It's an intimate act, a loving one almost, and the doctor's gaze slips to our intertwined fingers as he takes the chair. It's acting, all part of the role Maxime plays. That means the doctor doesn't know the circumstances of why I'm here.

"So." The doctor adjusts his glasses and gives me a curious look. "You're here for birth control."

My cheeks heat at the implication. My fingers involuntarily clench on Maxime's thigh. He rubs a thumb over my knuckles in a soothing gesture as he replies, "We want what's least invasive for Zoe."

"The injection is very efficient with minimal hormonal side effects. It also eliminates the possibility of forgetting to take the pill, which makes it more effective."

"The shot, then," Maxime says.

"I've prepared everything." Dr. Oliver clears his throat. "Do you have any questions, Zoe?"

I glance at Maxime.

"Go on," he says with a smile. It's a practiced smile, one he puts up for show.

"How long before it's safe?" I ask.

"Seven days," the doctor replies, "so use additional protection for the next week or two." He stands. "You can sit over there in the examination chair."

While the doctor prepares the shot, Maxime takes me to the chair and rubs a finger over my pulse.

"This won't hurt," Dr. Oliver says, approaching with a hypodermic needle.

I've never liked needles or blood. I get queasy at the sight of both, so I turn my head away while he works. It doesn't hurt much, just a small prick, but I jump nevertheless when he inserts the needle.

Maxime brushes a strand of hair from my forehead. "Does it hurt?"

"No," I say. "I'm just not good with sharp things being stabbed into my skin."

Maxime's smile is genuine this time—amused—and the usual frost in his eyes a few degrees warmer. "Do you have a low pain threshold?"

I narrow my eyes. "Are you making fun of me?"

"Never," he says, but his smile doesn't fade.

A short while later, the doctor has also taken a blood sample. Maxime thanks Dr. Olivier and writes out a check. They shake hands, and we're on our way.

In the car, Maxime takes my hand as he steers the automatic into the traffic. "You look pale."

"It's the blood. It makes me feel like fainting."

He squeezes my fingers. "You need a hearty lunch. Have you tried *bouillabaisse?*"

"No."

"It's a local specialty. I'll take you to a place. I just have to take care of some business first."

We drive through the old town to the hilly part until we're on the outskirts of town. A property twice the size of Maxime's comes into view. The mansion is built in the same style with wooden shutters and a balcony that runs around the first floor.

"This is my parents' place," he says. "You'll wait here."

I sit up straighter. "With your mother?"

He glances at me. "Is that a problem?"

"She doesn't like me." It was clear in every part of her body language.

He presses a button on an intercom at the gate. "My mother is old-fashioned. She doesn't believe in sex before marriage."

"Then she won't want me here," I say as he pulls up to the house and parks in a circular driveway.

He pats my hand that still rests on his thigh. "She'll get used to the idea."

I doubt that very much, but he's already coming around to get my door. Taking my hand, he pulls me toward the main entrance. The wind is freezing. It penetrates my very bones. A woman in a maid's uniform opens the door. She's young and pretty with chestnut hair.

Maxime greets her in French and exchanges a few words while she takes our coats before leading me through the lobby to a sitting room that overlooks the garden.

"We're lucky," he says. "Maman is having a friend over for tea."

I pull back. "I hate to impose."

He stops to look down at me. "You're with me, Zoe. That makes you a guest. Guests don't impose."

I'm not sure what to say to that, but before I can find my words, we enter the lounge where Cecile Belshaw sits with another woman. The remnants of a tea party are spread out on the coffee table. In the middle of the teacups and saucers stands a pink mousse cake with a couple of slices missing.

"Max?" Cecile's tone is friendly, but her eyes tighten as she puts down her teacup.

She says something in French. The other woman, who's around the same age as Cecile, looks between Maxime and me. I don't know what they're saying or if it's about me, but her spine stiffens as she takes me in. Her smile is so fake it looks painted on her face. Cecile addresses her son in a pleasant voice that's no less fake.

Maxime switches to English. "This is my aunt, Hadrienne. She's my mother's sister-in-law." He bends down and kisses her cheeks. "How are you, Hadrienne? This is Zoe."

She nods and says with a heavy accent, "How do you do?"

"Pleased to meet you." What else can I say?

"I'll be back before lunch." Maxime kisses my forehead and then turns to his mother. "Take good care of her."

I watch his back as he strides away. The door shuts behind him with a click. Silence prevails. I turn back at the two women who are looking at me as if I'm garbage that blew in from the street.

Cecile sighs. "You better sit, Zoe."

The only free space is the seat next to Hadrienne, unless I'm to take one of the chairs standing on the other side of the room. She scoots up when I sit, putting as much distance between us as the couch allows.

"Tea?" Cecile asks in an icy tone.

A drink to warm me up will be welcome, but that's not why I accept. I agree because I need something to do with my hands. If not, I'll fidget. "I'll get it."

She gives me a startled look. "I'll remind you this is my house."

"Oh, I didn't mean to be rude. I only wanted to save you the trouble."

"I can pour my tea in my home, thank you very much." She exchanges a look with Hadrienne. "Foreign customs."

Hadrienne raises a brow.

I let Cecile pour my tea, and thank her as I take the cup, but decline a slice of cake.

An uncomfortable silence falls over the room again.

"Where were we?" Cecile asks after a few beats. "Oh, yes. We were talking about gooseberry tart for dessert on Sunday. It's so complicated to think and speak in English."

Fine. I understand her irritation. I'm an uninvited guest, disrupting their tea party, but does she have to be so rude? I'm not Maxime's girlfriend. I owe them nothing. I don't have to take this.

"You don't have to speak English on my behalf." I wave a hand. "Just carry on in French. Your chatter will most probably bore me, anyway."

Cecile's cheeks light up, two red apples on a pale background. "I beg your pardon?"

Leaving the cup on the table, I stand. "I'll have a walk in the garden, if you don't mind. It's stopped raining, and I can do with some exercise."

Hadrienne laughs. "Oh, do sit down, girl." To Cecile she says, "You have to admit, she's got some backbone."

Cecile clenches her jaw. "Maybe you should have some cake, Zoe. I think eating is a better occupation for your mouth than speaking."

My lips part. I'm about to tell her to go to hell, but Hadrienne grabs my wrist and pulls me back down. "Enough of that. It's a long time to lunch. I'm sure we can find something neutral to talk about."

"What is your problem?" I ask Cecile.

"Me?" She makes big eyes. "You're imagining problems where there are none."

Right.

"There now." Hadrienne smoothes out her skirt. "Why not tell us how you met."

"In South Africa," Cecile says. "A speedy romance. Then again, money makes everything go faster, doesn't it?"

"You think I'm after Maxime's money?" I ask.

Raising a pinky, Cecile lifts the cup to her lips. "I never said you're after his money."

"You implied it." I move to the edge of my seat. "That's the same thing."

Cecile rolls her eyes. "Oh, it's not. Don't overreact."

I don't care what Maxime's reaction will be. I can't just sit here any longer. Pushing to my feet, I say, "Excuse me. If I stay, I'm afraid I'll say something disrespectful."

"You know what's disrespectful?" Cecile puts down her cup. "Coming here and attacking me in my own house."

"Attacking you?" I ball my hands. "Do you really expect me to keep quiet and accept your insults?"

"Yes," she says evenly. "I expect you to shut up. That's the least you can do."

What's wrong with these people? Turning on my heel, I walk to the French doors and push them open. Escaping outside, I walk down a path that leads to a gazebo at the end of the garden. At the edge, I stop to breathe in the salty air and let the small freedom fill my lungs.

I hate them. I hate them all. I wish I could run. I wish I could climb down the steps to the street at the back and sneak onto a train and go wherever it takes me. I don't care that I don't have a passport or money. I can work. I can always make a plan. What I can't do is let Damian get hurt.

My fingers curling into fists, I take in the view of this strange and unwelcome place.

Four years. Give or take a few, to quote Maxime's words.

I feel like screaming. I feel like hurling the bird feeder that hangs from the branch of a pine tree into the street, but that won't help me one bit. I can't let Cecile get to me. I don't care what she thinks. Why should I care about how she treats me?

I settle on the bench in the gazebo, staring out at the sea. Why did Maxime even help me? He didn't have to. He could've just left me to my fate. I don't understand his motives. I'm not even sure it's about sex. He said he's had many lovers. Francine seemed quite willing.

"Well, look who's here," a male voice says behind me.

I jump.

Alexis comes around the bench with my coat in his hand. "I didn't mean to scare you." Holding out the coat, he says, "You forgot this."

Thinking of the devil. When I reach for the coat, he holds it open like a gentleman, instead. Warily, I get up so he can help me slip into it. His hands rest on my shoulders for a second before he sets me free. I step away and turn back to face him. He's handsome in the blond hair and fair skin kind of way. The color of his eyes leans more toward blue than his brother's. Recalling what Maxime had said about him, a shiver runs over my body.

Watching me with his head tipped down, he asks, "How are things with my brother?"

I fold one side of the coat over the other. "Why don't you ask him yourself?"

He smiles. "Touché. Is he treating you all right?"

"What do you care?"

"I don't know what my brother told you, but I'm not your enemy, Zoe."

"No?" I look him over. "Then what are you? My *friend*?"

"There's no need to say it like that."

My fingers tighten on the fabric I clutch to my chest. "How would you like me to say it? My kidnappers? My jail keepers?"

He holds up a hand. "Maybe friends isn't the right term, but no one wants it to be bad here for you. We're not monsters, you know."

His expression and words are so sincere I have a hard time processing them.

"That's why I asked how Max is treating you," he continues.

"You're concerned?" I ask mockingly. "You expect me to believe that?"

He taps his temple. "Max isn't always right up here. Ever since the accident..."

My heart starts beating faster. "What accident?"

"The fire. Didn't he tell you?"

I shift my weight, eyeing the distance to the gazebo steps. I feel like a bird trapped by a cat. "He mentioned it."

"Arson. Someone set fire to one of our warehouses. Max was trapped inside." He rubs his forehead. "No one should've been able to survive those flames. The pain must've been excruciating. After Max walked out of there, he never was quite the same."

I shudder at the mental picture. "Are you saying he's insane?"

"What I'm saying," Alexis says, "is that you have to be careful."

"Talking about me?" a deep, familiar voice asks.

I spin around to see Maxime approaching with a dark look on his face.

"We were just getting acquainted," Alexis says with a cold smile.

Maxime steps up next to me. "You don't speak to her when I'm not around."

"That'll be a tad difficult," Alexis says, "seeing that she's part of your household now and our paths are sure to cross more often than not. You can't always be everywhere, can you?"

Maxime grabs my arm. "It's time to go."

Alexis salutes. "I'm looking forward to seeing you on Sunday, Zoe."

"She's not going," Maxime bites out.

Alexis pulls his face into a shocked expression. "You're leaving her all by herself in that stuffy old house while we're having a party? How rude of you, brother. Don't worry, Zoe. I'm happy to keep you company. My social skills are not as unpolished as my brother's."

Maxime puts his face in Alexis's. "You don't want to test me."

"Having authority issues, Max?"

Maxime's hold on my arm turns painful. His other hand clenches at his side. "I dare you, little brother." His smile is thin and cruel. "I'd love a reason to give you the treatment you deserve."

Maxime pulls me roughly down the steps and onto the path, walking with such long strides I'm battling to keep up. Cecile and Hadrienne get up when we enter the lounge.

"Max." Worry is etched on Cecile's face. "What happened?"

"Nothing." He kisses his mother's cheeks. "See you on Sunday."

He all but drags me to the car and shoves me inside. When he comes around and takes the wheel, I try to make myself small against the door. My heart is still thumping in my chest. I can't stop thinking about what Alexis said. There's not much love lost between the brothers. There's no question that they're both manipulating me, but which one is telling the truth?

CHAPTER 18

Maxime

Alexis loves fucking with me, but I won't let him fuck with Zoe. She doesn't know this family and their layers of nuances. She has no way of protecting herself against the mind games we play. It'll take her years to figure us all out.

I glance at her as I change the gears. "No more talking to Alexis."

She gives me an incredulous look. "What am I supposed to do when he talks to me? Ignore him? Pretend I don't hear?"

"Just say I don't want you to talk to him." Possessiveness is something every man in this family understands.

She shrugs. "Fine."

"What did he say to you?"

"That you're insane."

I laugh. "He's probably right."

She gapes at me. "You're not upset?"

"I don't get upset about things that don't matter."

She looks back at the road. "Wait. Why are we heading home? I thought you wanted to eat in town."

"I changed my mind."

"Just like that."

"Yeah. Just like that."

"I see."

"No, Zoe. You don't."

"What's that supposed to mean?"

I pull over at the outlook point and park. "Get out."

Her eyes grow large. "What?"

"Get out of the car."

"You're leaving me here?"

"Did I say I was leaving you here?"

She looks around the unbuilt area, and then up the deserted road. No doubt escape is at the forefront of her mind. It probably will be for a while still to come. She'll dream about it like recovered addicts dream about drugs and ex-smokers dream about cigarettes. A turning point will come when her dreams will evolve around staying and building a nest for herself.

Giving me an uncertain glance, she grips the handle and opens the door. She steps into the somber day, her hair blowing in every direction.

I shut down the engine and get out. "Walk to the edge."

She turns her face toward the cliff. When she looks back at me, her face is pale with fear. "Are you going to make me jump?"

"No." I move around the car, closer to her. "Go."

She gives me a pleading look. "I don't want to."

"Go, Zoe." She needs to learn to trust me, even when she's frightened.

She walks to the edge, carefully peering down. A frown mars her features. "What is that?"

"What does it look like?"

"A picnic?"

I take her hand. "Come. There's a path this way."

She pulls free. Her voice is angry. "You scared me. You could've just told me why we stopped here."

"Then it wouldn't have been a surprise."

"I thought…"

"I was going to kill you?"

"Yes," she whispers.

"I've told you before. I'm not going to kill you."

"How do I know you won't change your mind?"

"You don't."

Her chest rises with a deep breath. "Is this one of your lessons?"

"Yes."

Her beautiful eyes are filled with apprehension. "What am I supposed to learn from this?"

"To do something when I tell you to."

She scoffs. "Blind obedience?"

"As long as you do as you're told, I'll watch out for you." I take back her hand. "Now come."

We climb down the path to the small beach below. It's private, part of our territory. I was going to take her for the best bouillabaisse in town until I called to make a reservation and found out my uncle and father were lunching there. The picnic is improvised, a stab at fulfilling her romantic needs, but right now there's nothing romantic about the way I feel. Volatile is more like it.

When we reach the beach, Zoe pulls her hand free and walks to the edge of the water. She stares out over the ocean, a small, lonely, sad figure, and something stirs in my chest. I pop the cork of the champagne and pour her a glass.

"Come here," I say.

She turns away from the water and sits down on the blanket. I hand her the champagne, and then prepare a plate of cheese, charcuterie, and baguette.

"Hungry?" I ask as I put the plate between us.

"A little."

"Eat up."

I let her eat and drink, filling her glass twice while only having one myself. I'm driving, but that's not why I'm pumping her full of champagne. I'm getting her drunk. I need her uninhibited.

"That's enough for me," she says when I offer her another piece of Brie.

Setting the food aside, I push her down.

"What are you doing, Maxime?"

I straddle her legs. "Having my dessert."

"Here?" she cries out.

"Wherever I want."

"What if someone—"

Her words cut off when I push up her coat and unfasten her pants. I pull them down her hips with her underwear and flip her around.

There's a tremor in her voice. "Maxime."

I wrap my arm around her waist and pull her to her knees. She looks at me from over her shoulder, her pretty face tense, but it's only until I bury my fingers in the tight flesh of her globes and drag my tongue over her pussy. The frown on her brow evens out as she pinches her eyes shut. I repeat the action, this time spearing my tongue through her folds. Her lips part. The tension in her pretty features turns to desire. She's not complaining about the location any longer. All thoughts of our unsuitable spot have vanished from her mind, courtesy of a small dose of lust and three glasses of expensive French champagne.

She moans when I sink my tongue deeper. I don't waste time. I suck her clit and work a finger inside her wet heat, getting harder as I remember exactly how tightly her inexperienced pussy grips my cock. She comes with a cry, her back arching and her fingers burying in the blanket.

My pants are unzipped and my cock free before her orgasm is over. I take a condom from my pocket and make quick work of sheathing my cock. She's wet. She's ready. Gripping her hips, I push in carefully. Her moans are loud. She's tight and warm, gripping me like a fist. I can go harder on her because of the alcohol. Her body is supple and relaxed. She pushes back, taking me deeper, and I slam all the way home. Her cry makes me even harder. It makes me take her with punishing strokes. Twisting her long hair around a fist, I use it like a rein, pulling her head up and to the side until she faces me. I want to see the ecstasy on her face as I fuck her into oblivion.

I'm rough, but she arches her back and makes sexy, needy little sounds. I fuck her until her arms give out and she goes down on her elbows, until pleasure erupts at the base of my groin and fills up the condom instead of her body. One day, I'll empty myself inside her. I'll mark her. When I do, no man will ever touch her again. She'll belong to me forever, not only for four years.

I ease her down gently and cover her body with mine, making sure to keep my weight on my elbows.

Pressing a kiss behind her ear, I say, "No more talking to Alexis."

She turns her head to the side, her cheek flat on the blanket and her breathing heavy. "Is that what this is about? That's what you're trying to teach me? That you'll fuck me like it's a punishment in broad daylight where anyone can see if I speak to your brother?"

I pull out, causing her to whimper. The beach is secluded. You can't see it unless you look over the cliff, and the boats don't sail past this cove. There are too many rocks in the shallow water. I wasn't planning on doing this, either, when I set up the picnic. Fucking her here became a part of my intentions after I caught her with Alexis. Yes, I want her to accept me inside her body anywhere and anytime, and yes, I don't want her to talk to Alexis, but that's not what this is about.

She's mine. All mine.

That's the lesson.

CHAPTER 19

Zoe

It must be the effect of the champagne, but it's after nine when I wake up the next morning. The cup of rose tea on the nightstand is cold. Maxime's side of the bed is empty. He must've gone to work.

After showering and changing, I use the same stationary to write another letter to Damian. Emails aren't allowed, although he has limited access to a computer for the studies he took up in jail.

I seal the letter in an envelope and go downstairs. A breakfast of croissants and oranges are laid out on the dining room table. I eat quickly, then carry my plate to the kitchen. Francine is standing at an island counter, chopping onions. She's dressed in black pants and a silk blouse with a white apron tied around her waist. She lifts her eyes when I enter but doesn't say anything.

I put the plate in the dishwasher and lean against the counter. "I have another letter. If you tell me where to leave it—"

"In the silver tray in the entrance."

"Look, I…" I get why she doesn't want me here, but I can't tell her I don't have a choice. I remember Maxime's threat all too well, and he's a man of his word. That's another lesson he's taught me.

"I'm busy," she says. "I'm here to cook, not to chitchat when you're bored."

"Does Maxime read the letters?"

She gives me an irritated look. "I'm not psychic. You'll have to ask him."

Fine. This is how she's going to play it. I straighten and walk to the door.

Her words stop me in the frame. "You won't last, Zoe."

My name is like an insult on her lips. I look back at her from over my shoulder. "It seems you didn't."

Her cheeks flush red. "I'm here, am I not?" She smiles. "We'll see where you are when he grows tired of you."

A rather frightening thought. I hope not on the bottom of the ocean.

For the rest of the day, I install myself in front of the fire in the library. I page through the coffee table books with photos of the region, but I can't focus. I switch on the television and figure out how to set the language to English. I've never owned a television, and I lose myself in a spy series, but by late afternoon I'm hungry and bored. I've skipped lunch.

Pushing the throw aside, I go in search of something to eat in the kitchen and find a salad and a glass of water set on the table in the dining room. I eat listlessly before washing my plate and glass in the kitchen. Francine has already left. A casserole stands on the stove.

I walk to the window and peer out. It's rainy today. Drops lash at the windows. The ocean is obscured in a haze of fog. The grounds that stretch to the edge of the cliff are green with hedges and bushes trimmed into shapes. A maze stands in the middle.

I go from window to window, looking at the garden from different angles. I arrange the books in the library in alphabetical order. I switch the television on and off. Finally, I sit down in my favorite chair in front of the fireplace and stare at the flames. Normally, I would've daydreamed to pass the time, but dreaming isn't my go-to escape any longer. That dream, the one about Venice and love, has been vandalized. It hurts too much to poke at it or to try and construct something new from the debris that's left.

It's dark when the front door opens. The fire has long since burnt out. A light flicks on in the entrance. Heavy footsteps approach. I turn my head toward the sound. Maxime stops in the frame.

"What are you doing in the dark?" he asks.

"I haven't noticed."

He flicks on the light. He's wearing a black suit and purple shirt. "That you can't see your hand in front of your face?"

"I was looking at the fire."

He glances at the ashes, and then at the photo book on the coffee table. "What did you do with yourself today?"

"I arranged the books alphabetically." A belated thought strikes me. "I hope you don't mind?"

He looks at the shelves. "You didn't strike me as the OCD type."

I shrug.

His steps are purposeful as he walks over and stops in front of the chair. "Come here."

I made a promise. I said I wouldn't give him trouble. Slowly, I rise.

Approval sparks in his gray eyes. "Take off my tie."

Reaching up, I untie the knot and pull the tie from his collar.

His face is harsh, his features always frightening, but there's something friendly, playful almost, in his expression when he says, "Go pour me a drink."

My first reaction is resistance. It's like telling a dog to fetch a newspaper. I'm not his damn servant. Yet yesterday's lesson with the picnic gives me pause. Fine. I'll trust him on this. I'll play along.

I go to the wet bar and pour a few fingers of whiskey the way I saw him do it, then carry the glass back to him. Our fingers brush when he takes it.

"Thank you," he says, holding my gaze as he takes a sip.

The way he looks at me heats my belly. It's a stare that communicates want, need, shared secrets, and praise. It's the praise that makes the warmth spread to my chest. I've always been a pleaser.

His lips curve as he hands me the glass. It's more than offering to share his drink. It's sharing a private moment and a part of himself with me. He's opening up, letting me in. He's making himself vulnerable. That's what this lesson is. He didn't order me to fetch his drink to humiliate me. He's showing me how to be kind to him, and how my kindness will be rewarded in return.

I turn the glass and put my lips on the spot where his has been. His eyes widen a fraction, surprise thawing their usual coldness. The alcohol burns down my throat when I swallow. Taking the glass back from me, he leaves it on the table and reaches for the zipper of my dress. Without the fire it's cold, but I let him push the dress over my shoulders and hips. My breasts tighten in the lace cups of my bra. The matching panties grow wet. Now that I've had a taste of the forbidden, my body craves it.

He drags his gaze over me, lingering on the underwear and long boots. "I think I'll leave those on."

The approval of earlier turns into a different kind of approval, something more carnal than appraisal. He likes what he sees, and he doesn't mind making himself vulnerable by showing me. No. He's exposing himself on purpose, rewarding my trust by giving me power. The exchange feeds the part inside me that needs approval and above all kindness. I'm starving for this kindness. I *need* this kindness.

As he shrugs out of his jacket and starts unbuttoning his shirt, a revelation hits me. This is nothing but science, the law of energy. The more he tortures me, the more I need kindness to restore the imbalance in my soul. What he proved yesterday when he forbade me to speak to his brother is that the only person permitted to give me kindness is Maxime himself. The man who torments me is the only man who can make it better.

The cure for my pain is the cause of the pain.

It's confusing. It feels like a mind-fuck. It's messing with my head as he unbuckles his belt and pulls down his zipper. I need distance from this, to figure out what he's doing to me, but his cock is hard and huge. I know it'll hurt a bit, and I need that, too. Maybe it's to punish myself for giving in to the emotional needs I allow him to fulfill. Maybe I'm flogging myself with physical pain for my weakness.

He removes his shoes and socks and straightens to stand naked in front of me. He shows me his scars and ugliness, a gift for my kindness. He's exposed—vulnerable—but so am I, and I can't tell the difference between manipulation and lessons any longer. Not that it matters, because when he touches me, my mind recedes to a place where thoughts don't matter. All that matters is the burning desire for him to hurt and please me, to bring me relief from the torment he orchestrates with such clever design in both my body and soul.

He steps up against me, letting his cock brush my stomach. "Don't think so hard, my little flower."

No, he wouldn't want me to think, because thinking leads to the truth. "What do you want me to do?"

His voice is husky, a foreign accent targeted on seduction. "Just feel."

I don't argue when he lifts me and carries me to the desk. As much as I made a deal, I need this. *He* made me need this.

Posing me on the edge, he spreads my legs and steps between them. He reaches over, lifts the lid of an antique silver box, takes out a condom, and hands it to me. As I tear the packet open with my teeth like I saw him do, he rubs a thumb over my clit. My body tightens where he touches me, pleasure already starting to build. My hands shake when I roll the condom over his thick length.

Grabbing a fistful of my hair, he kisses me softly. "How do you want it?"

I don't have to think about it. The tender kiss is sweet, but it makes me inexplicably sad. It's the pull on my hair that makes me wet. "Hard."

He brushes his knuckles over the lace that covers my nipple. "You surprise me, Zoe." He drags his lips over my neck, planting another sweet kiss on my shoulder. "Rough it'll be."

His hands lock around my waist, yanking me flush against him. Impatiently, he moves aside the elastic of my panties and aligns his cock with my entrance. He doesn't move slowly this time. He drives in deep, taking me with a single, hard thrust. I'm wet, but it hurts. It burns. I gasp, embracing the pain, wanting the punishment. He doesn't disappoint. He fucks me like I wanted, so roughly my eyes water and my insides feel raw. He must know I can't handle this pace for long, because he rolls my clit between his fingers until that pain also turns to pleasure, and I come with a wail as relief floods my body. He slams into me while the aftershocks ebb out, and then he climaxes with a grunt.

We're both spent, perspiration beading on our skins. I'm tender when he pulls out, and he's gentle when he picks me up and carries me to the shower. He's careful when he washes me, especially with the part that aches between my legs. He dresses in a tracksuit and I in one of his T-shirts and his robe, and then we have dinner in the formal dining room like two normal people, like the sex in the study never happened.

~

THE FOLLOWING DAY, Maxime comes home with a tablet on which almost a hundred books are uploaded in English. They range from romance and thrillers to books about clothing design and traveling. I delete the ones about Venice.

Reading brings a measure of relief, but I'm developing cabin fever. I'm lonely, too, being cooped up in the big old house with no one but Francine who goes out of her way to avoid me. The only person I see and speak to is Maxime. I'm losing my concept of time. I don't know what day it is, let alone what hour. I look at my face in the library's antique mirror with a network of cracked spider webs under the glass. I have the odd sensation I'm not real, that life is an illusion slipping through my fingers. The thought scares me. The last thing I can afford is to lose my sanity.

I'm quiet when Maxime comes home, reflecting on this new state of mind. We fuck where he finds me in the library, have a shower, and eat dinner. Now that my body has grown accustomed to being used, he fucks me more often. When we go to bed, he takes me more gently.

Draping me over his chest afterward, he drags a hand through my hair. "What did you do today?"

"Read."

"What did you read?"

"Dunno. Can't remember."

He sweeps my hair over my shoulder, caressing the curve of my neck. "You were reading *Gone with the Wind*. You said it's a long one. Did you finish it?"

"Oh." I rub my cheek over his chest, craving the warmth and contact. "Yes."

"Did you like it?"

I frown. "Mm." The truth is, I can't remember. The words registered but the meaning didn't. I'm filling my brain with empty phrases, with letters and lines that don't form pictures. I'll pay better attention tomorrow. Right after I've written Damian's letter. I write to him every week, saying how happy I am but planting clues about the truth via our code language.

"Zoe?"

"Mm?"

His hand stills on my shoulder. "Did you hear what I said?"

"Sorry, what was that?"

He grips my chin and turns my face toward him. "I said you need exercise."

"Oh. Right." The thought of it alone makes me tired.

"I'll have an indoor bike and walker installed."

"Don't waste your money. I'm not the walker-biker type."

He frowns. "You're pale."

"I have a pale skin."

"Paler than usual. Do you feel sick?"

"I'm fine."

He lets my face go to sweep a hand over my back. "I've tired you out. Go to sleep."

I close my eyes and do exactly that, because I've learned something new.

Avoidance doesn't only come with daydreaming.

The best way to avoid reality is the dreamless state of sleep.

CHAPTER 20

Maxime

She's bored, my little flower. Isolating her in a house far removed from a city and the bustle of life isn't ideal, but the Italian negotiations Alexis so graciously started in my absence is complicated. I'm needed at work now more than ever. I don't trust my brother, and my father is like a fucking child that needs overseeing all the time. Between keeping Alexis in check and making sure my father doesn't sate his greed by doing something stupid like over-charging our Italian connection, I've got my hands full.

I've neglected Zoe. I've neglected her needs. She's shown me she'll be good. She's given me trust. I have to reciprocate by giving her leash a little farther reach. I don't like the idea of my men looking at her, but I've agreed to let her outside. She needs the air and the exercise. She's too pale, too listless. I'm not an idiot. I know what the signs of depression are. I know she's lonely. She needs human contact. I wasn't planning on taking her back to my parents' house, but the lunch on Sunday may be just what she needs.

It's lunchtime when I push the doors of the club open. The usual mob is already there—uncle Emile, my father, and a few of his men, the muscles and specialists. Me, I'm the brain. Benoit and Gautier flank me.

"You're late," my father says, clipping a cigar.

"Traffic." I adjust my jacket and sit. A topless waitress puts an espresso next to me. I push it away. "Where's the contract?"

My father shifts it over the table to me. I flip the pages, scanning over the print to make sure nothing new has been slipped in. I wouldn't put that past my father. I'm at the second-last page when Paolo Zanetti arrives with an entourage of guards. The Italian is short and stocky with shrewd eyes. Thank God the man's daughters take after their mother.

I stand. "Mr. Zanetti."

He shakes my father's hand, then mine.

Taking the pen, I turn to the last page of the contract, but Zanetti grabs my arm before I can sign. He nods at one of his men who puts a ledger on top of the contract.

I eye the gleeful man, addressing him in Italian. "What's this?"

"The new contract."

My father pushes to his feet. "We've negotiated terms."

"The terms have changed," Zanetti says. "I want ten percent extra on everything you move through my territory plus free rights to the Riviera."

"What?" My father pushes his palms on the table.

"We'll take it," I say.

That's a better deal than what I was hoping for. I've been bidding low, knowing Zanetti would come with a counteroffer. I've done my homework. There's nothing Zanetti loves better than winning, not even money, and I've just made him feel like we're the biggest fucking losers on the planet. I've got him by the balls, and he doesn't even know it.

My father clenches his fingers on the edge of the table. He can't challenge me in front of everyone. We have to appear united. Raphael

Belshaw's sincere anger only makes Zanetti smugger, playing right into my hand.

Opening the ledger, I read through the contract, and then sign on the dotted line.

"Wonderful," Zanetti says, snatching up his copy. "I can't wait to take the tour."

"After lunch." I indicate the seat next to me. "I'll show you around. How long are you staying in town?"

"We're leaving tomorrow."

Good. We have a family lunch tomorrow. Inviting Zanetti would've been obligatory.

It's not the kind of trouble I need right now.

CHAPTER 21

Zoe

The house where Maxime parks is not as big as his parents' place, but it's just as imposing. A table with champagne is set out in the foyer. Maxime hangs my coat in the closet next to an array of expensive labels before handing me a glass. I drink it all. I'm nervous about being here, especially after how the last visit with his family went.

He places a palm on my back and lowers his head to whisper in my ear, "We're going to get separated. Men in the lounge, women in the kitchen. Yell if you need me."

I stare up at his face. There's a spark of humor in his gray eyes, an easiness that's unusual for him.

"You look happy with yourself."

"I signed off on a deal. It was a trying negotiation."

"In gemstones?"

He smiles. "No."

"What then?"

He takes my empty glass and puts it back on the table. "Come."

Putting an arm around my waist, he leads me through the foyer to the lounge, which is packed with people. I recognize Cecile and Hadrienne, but none of the others.

His arm tightens around me as we stop in front of a thickset man with a drooping eye. "Zoe, this is my father, Raphael."

Raphael holds out a hand. His expression is neutral, but I get the feeling he doesn't like me.

"My father doesn't speak much English," Maxime says.

"Isn't Belshaw an English surname?" I ask.

"Very French, in fact. One of the oldest."

"Max!" Two women storm up to us, throwing their arms simultaneously around Maxime.

Sandwiched in the middle, he chuckles. "And these are my cousins, Noelle and Sylvie."

The young women turn to me. They both have dark hair and green eyes. They look so much alike, they could've been twins. The only difference between them is that Sylvie is a little taller. They're both wearing Dior, matching vintage dresses with a cinched waist. Noelle's gaze moves over my off-shoulder jersey and jeans. I'm underdressed. This isn't the laid-back Sunday barbecues I'm used to being invited to back home.

Sylvie takes Maxime's arm. "I have to talk to you about something."

She drags him away, leaving me stranded with Noelle. The silence is uncomfortable.

"I'm going to help in the kitchen," Noelle says after a strained moment, slipping past me.

I look over to the terrace where Maxime and Sylvie are talking outside. It looks serious.

Hadrienne approaches me with a stiff back and places her hand on the shoulder of the man who's chatting to Raphael to catch his attention. "This is my husband, Emile."

Emile turns sideways to look at me. He nods but doesn't shake my hand.

"Well," Cecile says, joining our circle. "Look who's here." Pushing past me, she says, "I smell something burning in the kitchen."

"Oh, dear," Hadrienne exclaims, following on her heels.

Emile turns back to his conversation with Raphael. I stand awkwardly, feeling out of place. After another few moments, I don't have a choice but to offer my help in the kitchen.

I go back through the foyer and follow the smell of rosemary and garlic to the kitchen where the women are gathered, talking in French.

I stop in the door. "Can I help with anything?"

They fall quiet. Cecile and Hadrienne exchange a look. Noelle glares at me.

"I suppose you could prepare the coffee tray," Hadrienne says, waving a hand at a coffee maker on the shelf.

The atmosphere is toxic. What have I done? They don't know Maxime is keeping me against my will. As far as they know, we met in South Africa, and now we're together. Why would they hold that against me?

Unable to take the tension any longer, I ask, "Why are you acting like this?"

Cecile tilts her head. "What makes you think we're acting in any way? You're not that important. In fact, you're nothing, neither family nor friend."

My lips part in shock at her blatant hostility. Before I can say anything, the three women carry on with their conversation in French, acting as if I don't exist. I'm tempted to run away, but I won't give them the satisfaction. Instead, I go through the cupboards like I own them until I find the ground coffee and filters. A nasty part of me notices Hadrienne's displeasure with ugly satisfaction. It only spurs me on. I open and close the cupboards loud enough to disturb their talking. Since I don't see any mugs, I take the small espresso cups and place them on a tray with teaspoons and the pot of sugar. I arrange everything just so. There. Only then do I walk from the room.

My chest is tight with tension when I reenter the lounge. The men are nowhere to be seen. Walking out onto the terrace, I lean against the wall and stare into the distance to where the water glitters with sparklers of sun. It's a clear day, sunny and cold. I shiver without my coat.

Sylvie steps out with two glasses of red wine. She holds one out to me. "It's pretty, isn't it?"

I take the drink hesitantly.

"It must be tough," she says.

"What?"

She takes a sip of her wine. "Being the new girl."

"I suppose adaption is always tough," I say vaguely.

"They're cliquish, my family." She smiles. "It's not easy to get in."

"I've noticed."

"You can call me if you'd like to talk or grab a coffee in town."

I look at her in surprise. "Thanks."

"I'm only here until the end of the month before the new semester starts, but feel free to call me in Paris."

"What are you studying?"

"Law. My father isn't happy about it." She laughs. "He thinks I'm wasting my time."

"Why?"

She sits down on the bench. "Because he'll marry me off to some wealthy guy who probably won't allow me to work."

"How can a husband make decisions for his wife?"

She crosses her legs. "This is *le milieu,* baby. It's just how it works." Her gaze trails over me. "I'm not sure what I envy you more for, your ignorance or your freedom."

I look away. How ironic. As for ignorance, there's nothing to envy. She unknowingly takes the prize. She has no idea how wrong she is about my freedom.

"Hey." She gets up and nudges my shoulder. "The men are smoking cigars in the study. They'll be in there for a while. I can bum a cigarette from one of the guards. Want one?"

I think about the night Maxime had taken my virginity. "No, thank you."

"Suit yourself." She pushes off the wall. "Will you cover for me?"

"What should I say?"

"That I'm in the bathroom touching up my makeup or something."

"Sure."

She winks. "I love your outfit, by the way."

"Thanks, I guess."

Backtracking to the steps, she rambles off a number. "That's my telephone number. Remember it. You're going to need a friend to go shopping." She salutes before cutting across the lawn to where a man stands guard.

I'm not ready to go back inside, but I'm cold. I leave the wine on the coffee table. Rubbing my arms, I go over to the mantelpiece and inspect the photos. Most of them are of a younger Sylvie and Noelle.

"Lunch is ready," Noelle calls from somewhere in the house.

Maxime comes to find me, smelling of cigars and winter. He drags his nose through my hair. "What have you been doing with yourself?"

"I spoke to Sylvie." I scan his face for his reaction.

"Good."

"You're not upset?"

He cups my neck and brushes his thumb over my nape. "Why would I be?"

"I didn't think you'd want me to speak to your family."

"Sylvie is a good girl." He kisses my lips. "What I said about Alexis stands."

"Where is he, by the way?"

His face darkens. "Miss him?"

"That's not what I said. I was just wondering."

"No need to waste your wonderings on my brother, little flower."

Taking my hand, he leads me to the dining room. A table is set with the finest porcelain and crystal I've seen. I'm out of my depth, even more so when Hadrienne announces I'll sit between Sylvie and Noelle, separated from Maxime.

I hold onto his hand when he moves to take his seat.

He looks at me. "What is it?"

"What are we eating?" I whisper.

He frowns. "Why?"

I look from under my lashes at the array of knives and forks next to each plate. "I'm not educated in all those eating utensils."

A laugh bursts from his chest. It's loud and uninhibited, and it makes everyone look at us, but he doesn't seem to care.

Lowering his head to my ear, he says in a low voice, "Just follow my lead."

Embarrassed about the room's attention on us, I pull away to take my seat, but he holds me back.

"For the record, Zoe, you're a little uncultured, but you're not uneducated."

Raphael clears his throat. My cheeks are hot when I take my seat. Cecile sits as straight as a statue, her eyes on her plate.

I don't know how I get through the three hour-long, five course ordeal. The only people who speak to me are Maxime and Sylvie. The rest pretend I don't exist. Still, they speak English, which leaves the two older men mostly quiet. The afternoon is a disaster. It was a mistake to bring me.

When the table is cleared, we move to the lounge for coffee. Noelle carries in the tray I've prepared.

"Oh, dear," Cecile says, eyeing the tray.

Noelle giggles.

I look between them. "Is something wrong?"

Sylvie snatches up the sugar pot. "Nothing." She disappears down the hallway and returns with a silver pot filled with sugar cubes.

"That's such an Anglo Saxon thing," Cecile says.

Hadrienne lights a cigarette. "Don't get me started on the clothes."

Maxime stands. "Emile, Hadrienne, thank you for lunch."

"You're leaving?" Hadrienne asks. "Already?"

Maxime takes my hand and helps me to my feet. "We have a long way home."

It takes almost thirty minutes to say goodbye, and by the time we get in the car I'm emotionally exhausted. I don't want to repeat one of these lunches any time soon.

"Did you enjoy yourself?" Maxime asks as he turns the car onto the coastal road.

"It was nice meeting Sylvie."

"I've been busy with work, but now that the deal's done, we'll go out more." He takes my hand. "I promise."

I give him a sideway glance. "You don't have to make an effort. It's not like we're dating."

"I said I'd look out for you if you behave, and you've been behaving very well."

I scoff. "I'm glad you approve."

"Don't spoil it now."

"I've been thinking."

He smiles. "What has been going through my little flower's mind?"

"I want to learn to speak French."

He raises a brow. "I didn't expect that."

"Will you teach me?"

He lifts my hand to his lips and kisses my knuckles. "I can do better. I'll get you a tutor."

"Really?"

"Of course."

"Why would you do that for me?"

"Because I can. Why do you want to speak French?"

I shrug. "Because I can." So that no one can talk about me behind my back ever again.

His eyes darken but the humor remains in his voice. "You and that sassy mouth of yours. I can think of ways to tame it, and I'm not going to hold out until we're home."

Clenching the wheel with one hand, he pulls down his zipper with the other and frees his cock. Seeing him so hard for me just from a game of words makes me horny and wet. When he cups the back of my neck, I go down on him willingly, swallowing him like he taught me. I swirl my tongue around the head and suck until my cheeks hollow. He curses, saying filthy words in French. I don't need a tutor to understand those. I take the power he gives. I own the groan that erupts from his chest. I own his release.

CHAPTER 22

Maxime

I watch Zoe through the open door of the dressing room while buttoning up my shirt. She sits in front of the dresser, applying her makeup. Her hair is twisted on her head in pretty curls. She's wearing a red dress with black heels, and the diamonds I gave her in Venice as a gift to commemorate our first time shines in her ears. She's a vision. It's hard tearing my gaze away to fit my cufflinks.

I check my watch. We have an hour before the dinner. It's a charity event to raise money for cancer research. I hate these galas, but I'm hoping it'll do Zoe good. She objected, said she didn't want to go, but she needs to be around people.

Now that the Italian deal has been negotiated, I can focus on her again. I feel both lighter and heavier. We need the alliance with the Italians. It gives us access to their infrastructure, a broadened scope to move our diamonds safely, while the tax they're paying to ship from our port doesn't hurt, either. We've been at war for too long, wiping out each other's men and resources. Hence, the deal is a good thing. Complicated, but good. It's going to require some finesse in the foreseeable future. In the short term, it means I can spend more time with my flower.

Yesterday's lunch didn't go as well as I've hoped. The men owe Zoe the respect she deserves as my lover. It's an unbendable rule. However, I didn't foresee how the women would react. I can't really blame them. Of course, they'd frown upon her sharing my bed. Mistresses are a common occurrence among the menfolk in our circles, but you don't bring them to a family lunch. A charity event, yes. A weekend in the Bahamas, definitely. While mistresses wear diamonds and sip champagne on yachts, the wives are home raising their cheating husband's kids. I'd hoped Maman would've been more open-minded, if not for Zoe then for my sake, but I'd misjudged my mother's tolerance and Catholic values. For as staunch as her values are, her tolerance is low.

I still don't know why Alexis didn't show. If I haven't fucked Zoe from the minute we got home to sunrise, I would've called him. He's probably scheming behind my back like he tried to weasel his way into the Italian deal. Taking my phone from my pocket, I send a text to Gautier, telling him to tail my brother and find out what he's so busy with that's more important than a family lunch. For all the times the married men in my family have entertained their lovers on exotic islands and faraway dream escapes, they don't back out when there's a family lunch at home. Another one of our unspoken rules.

"I'm ready," Zoe says.

I lift my head to look at her. The breath is knocked from my lungs. The dress clings to her body, accentuating her curves. The gown was my choice. I know she hates it, but she has no idea what a knockout she is with her slender neck and the milky skin of her shoulders exposed. There's a flush on her cheeks again since she started taking long walks outside. Her skin and eyes glow, the freckles on her nose like a dusting of golden stars. She's the epitome of innocence and purity. Only, I know she likes sex both sweet and rough. I know how to read her, how to give her what she needs, and I burn with satisfaction knowing I'm the one who corrupted her. Her moans and dirty little acts are all mine.

"I don't know about this," she says, smoothing her palms over her hips. "I really don't like these formal parties."

I take her wrap from the chair and drape it around her shoulders. "So you've said."

"I should stay. I'd rather watch a movie here where it's warm."

"Not an option." Hooking my arm through hers, I lead her downstairs. "I want to show you off." Every man in Marseille and to the ends of the world needs to understand she's mine. No one will ever stake a claim on her again, no man in the mob, and no man outside of the families. No one will be foolish enough.

Her spine stiffens. "I'm not a showpiece."

"You are whatever I want you to be."

She pulls to a stop. "I don't want to be auctioned."

"It's for charity."

"What happens after the bidding?"

"You dance with the highest bidder."

"Just a dance?"

Unfortunately, no. Mostly not. The high society of Marseille enjoys a bit of swinging while raising money for a good cause.

She yanks on my sleeve. "Is the winner going to expect sex?"

"Most probably."

Her nostrils flare. "Is this why you dressed me up like a slut?"

"Careful, Zoe. One, you look beautiful, and two, you should really remember to trust me."

"To trust you to whore me out?"

A nerve pinches between my shoulder blades. We were doing so well with her obeying me blindly. I grip her arm. "You're not a whore, and I'm not tempted to make one of you."

Her words are spoken breathlessly. "You already have."

My anger starts to simmer. A curl slips loose from her updo as I shake her. "Take that back."

"I can't." Tears pool in her eyes, giving them that expressive edge I love so much. "I can't take back my virginity."

Bringing that up now makes me angrier, because I don't like how she puts it. I don't like how she sees it.

"We made a deal," I say through clenched teeth.

"Exactly." She stares up at me, fearless but wary. "For which I'm paying with my body. Tell me that doesn't make me your whore."

I shake her harder. More curls fall to her shoulders. "It's nothing like that."

"If that's what you believe, you're lying to yourself."

I march her backward with a palm on her chest and slam her body against the wall. "When have I ever treated you like a whore?"

"Whores get paid." Emotions swirl in her eyes, teardrops trapped behind a brilliant blue. "You're paying me with my brother's life."

Grabbing her neck, I fold my fingers around the slender column. "You'll be wise to shut up now, Zoe."

Her chest heaves with breaths. Her palms are pressed flat on the wall next to her hips. She's scared, but she doesn't back off. She keeps on fucking pushing me. "Can't face the truth? The diamonds, the clothes, the tutor, what are they if not payment?"

I squeeze harder. "Gifts. Fucking gifts, you unthankful little—"

She lifts her chin, defying the hold than can snap her neck. "Say it."

Goddamn. My grip slackens.

"Go ahead," she says. "Finish what you were going to say."

"Bitch," I grit out, my whole body shaking with anger. "You unthankful little bitch."

Fuck dammit. It's true. Every word she said is chiseled down to its naked, hurtful truth. I made her a whore, but a cherished one. Alexis would've done so much worse.

Her body sags against the wall, her tiny frame crumbling. "Is this what showing me off means?" She sweeps a hand over the dress. "I look pretty for your friends? You share me when the mood hits?"

Slamming a palm next to her face on the wall, I lean in. "You don't know me, remember? *If* I'm ever inclined to share, you'll do as I tell you, and you'll do it with a smile on your face. If I tell you to swallow my best friend's cock and take it in your pussy and up your ass, you'll do that, too."

I don't have a best friend, and I'd rather saw off my dick than share her, but she doesn't need to know that. She doesn't deserve the power of that kind of knowledge. What she does need to know by now is to fucking trust me. I guess we have a few more lessons to go.

Her blue eyes are awash with anger. "You're an asshole."

No arguing that fact. It's the hurt in those pretty baby blues that hits me squarely in the chest.

"We're going to be late." I grip her wrist and drag her behind me, my earlier good mood down the drain.

She doesn't say a word as we get into the car and drive to Marseille. She stares from her window at the dark landscape. I clench the wheel so hard the ring with our family crest, the same one my father wears, presses a groove into my finger. It's the ring the head of the family wears, the man who makes the decisions. The weight of it leaves a mark on my soul. Of all the sins I've committed, Zoe is the biggest one, the stone that drags me under and drowns me. She consented, but I didn't give her a choice. The only choice I gave her was how to look at the situation, how to see herself. I wanted to give her pretty, and she had to go choose the ugly truth.

Fuck.

I slam the wheel. Zoe jumps. She huddles closer to the door, her shoulders turned away from me. I want to remind her of that choice, but it'll be a lie dressed up in glitter, in diamonds and red, and it looks like Zoe is done pretending. She's done living in a dream.

As paparazzi are flocking the main entrance to the casino, we use a back entrance. I promised my father I'd be discreet. The casino belongs to a distant uncle. The annual charity event is held in the big hall. I greet a few people, mostly business associates, and introduce Zoe as my date. She's tense on my arm. I'm still angry, too angry to set her at ease. Where I was looking forward to bringing her here only an hour ago, I now wish this night was already over.

"Max." A sickeningly handsome man with dark hair, brown eyes, and an olive skin tone pats me on the shoulder. "Good to see you," he says in French.

Fuck. Paolo Zanetti's son. We've only met once. It was a couple of years ago when we had our first talks about making a French-Italian connection. He's one of Zanetti's specialists, a genius at money laundering. At twenty-seven, he's young for the high position he holds in their organization, but I respect his brains. I hate his pretty face though, and when he smiles at Zoe, I downright detest it.

What the fuck is he doing here? There can only be one reason.

"I didn't know you accompanied your father," I say, barely holding the ice from my tone.

"I'm getting to know our new partners." His brown eyes tighten the minutest fraction when he turns them to Zoe. "Aren't you going to introduce me to your lovely companion?"

I switch to English. "This is Zoe. Zoe, this is Leonardo, a business associate."

Taking Zoe's hand, he asks, "Zoe who?"

"Zoe Hart," she says, not knowing the man looking at her with such kindness is a snake about to strike.

"Leonardo Zanetti." He brings Zoe's hand to his lips, intelligently not making contact with her skin. "It's an honor, Zoe. However did this brute catch such a beauty?"

"We met in South Africa during a business trip," I say quickly. Directing my gaze to where he's clutching Zoe's fingers in his paw, I make sure he sees the warning in my eyes.

"If you don't mind me asking," he finally drops Zoe's hand to motion between her and me, "is this casual or serious, because if it's not serious I'd love to meet up in town before I head back to Italy. I've always wanted to go to South Africa, and I could use some travel advice." He turns to me, all false respect. "Of course, if it's serious, I'm not going risk your jealousy, Max."

Zoe glances at me. There's no way she can answer that question. If she says it's not serious, she's accepting his offer. If she says it's serious, she's admitting to something neither she nor I can confess. Something I definitely shouldn't admit to Leonardo Zanetti.

He's pushing me into a corner. Clever motherfucker. I wish I could plant my fist between his troubadour eyes. The only thing preventing me is my strong control, something that has started unraveling earlier tonight. If I'm honest about it, it's been unraveling ever since I've abducted Zoe. I shouldn't let my emotions get the better of me. It'll kill our business. There's too much at stake. I'm about to say Zoe isn't available—indefinitely—when she speaks.

"We're kind of, uh, committed."

Leonardo gives me a smug smile. "I suppose you have to enjoy it while you can."

A tall woman with an athletic build makes her way over with two glasses of champagne. She's dressed in a black number with a slit that starts on her hip.

I tilt my head in the direction of the woman who's heading straight for Leonardo. "Like you are?"

"Oh." He straightens his bowtie. "I'm not committed to anyone. She's just my date for tonight."

"Well, hello," the woman says, shoving a glass in Leonardo's hand. Her eyes roam over Zoe. "You're a pretty little thing."

I put an arm around Zoe's waist and pull her against my side. "We'll go find our table and let you mingle."

"We're at the same table." Leonardo raises his glass. "Let me show you."

Of course, we are. With the newly forged deal, Leonardo is as good as family, part of my clan. Clenching my jaw, I follow them to our table.

We greet the other people, my cousin, Jerome, as well as an elderly court official and his young fiancée, but I hardly pay them attention. I'm too busy listening in on the conversation between Zoe and Leonardo. They talk about safaris and wine farms, and then about Tuscany. I only relax when Jerome demands Leonardo's attention and Zoe starts talking to Leonardo's date.

My hand wanders to Zoe's thigh under the table. I need the physical reassurance of her presence as much as I need her to understand who's in charge. She stiffens at the gesture, her hand tightening on her water glass. The court official, a man called Big Ben for his unusual height and weight, is staring openly at her. It takes everything I have and some to not crush his skull with the bottle of champagne.

There are speeches about research developments between the courses of salmon terrine, sea bass, and strawberry mousse. I donated handsomely. Ploughing money back into the community keeps doors open for us. It helps make the influential corporate players and government officials turn their heads the other way where our illegal business is concerned.

Zoe pushes the food around on her plate. During the meal, she downs two glasses of champagne, and when the MC announces the start of the auction, she's like a rice paper kite in a storm, looking as if her wings are about to be ripped off.

The sponsors—lovers or spouses—who volunteered the women participating in the auction proudly present their protégés when the MC calls their names. When it's Zoe's turn, I stand and offer her my hand.

She stares up at me with defiant eyes. There's a moment's hesitation, a moment of mistrust when her hate for me is written so clearly on her face it spears my unfeeling heart. I narrow my eyes in warning. If she defies me in front of all these people, I'll make her pay in so many ways she'll wish she'd never brought that lesson upon herself. My pulse beats in my temples as another second passes and the MC clears his throat. Just when I think Zoe is going to decline, she slips her small hand into mine.

I pull her to her feet, my face decorated with the smile I've adopted for the gentry, but the gesture goes no further than my mouth. Behind my tightly stretched lips, my teeth are clenched. Zoe's hesitation only lasted a moment, but a moment is long enough, especially for the sharp eyes of the predators surrounding us. I thought I'd made better progress with my flower, but it seems I've underestimated her. She may need a stronger hand.

Lifting her arm, I turn her in a circle. The hall breaks out in applause. Men nod enthusiastically while women stare daggers. In the midst of salivating wolves and hateful envy stands an innocent little lamb, my virgin sacrifice.

"Fifty," someone calls from the back before the MC has even opened the bidding.

It's what I wanted, for everyone to see who owns her, but the over-eager interest makes my hackles rise. Laughter erupts. Someone pats the impatient bidder on the back. Red-hot jealousy burns in my gut.

"Since the bidding seems to be open," the MC says with a chuckle, "who'd like—"

"One hundred," someone calls.

I turn around. The actor is a national celebrity.

Zoe looks at me quickly. One hundred thousand is the highest bid of the evening yet.

"One hundred and fifty," a fat parliament member says.

Zoe's eyes are burning on my face. I'm not looking at her, but I can feel her stare, her plea.

"Going once," the MC calls.

She lays a hand on my arm, her fingers digging into my skin.

Don't worry, my little flower. Be quiet and learn your lesson in trust.

"Going twice." The MC lifts his hammer.

"Two hundred," I say.

Zoe's chest deflates. Her relief is so great her body sags against mine.

A strong voice with an accent reverberates through the space. "Five hundred."

The room goes quiet. All heads turn toward the owner of the voice. I isolate him in my vision like a torpedo homes in on a target. Our eyes meet across the table.

Leonardo.

There's a challenge in his, a deviant intention. I want to squash him like a bug. My body tenses, every muscle preparing to rip him apart when Jerome's hand falls on my shoulder.

"Don't let him get to you," Jerome whispers.

No. I'm not going to let him get to me. Neither is he getting Zoe. Over my dead body.

"She's not worth it," Jerome continues. "Not the Italian deal."

Wrong fucking words. I shake him off. "One million."

Gasps sound around the room. Zoe stares at me with big eyes, her lush lips parted.

"Wow, uh…" The MC gives a high-pitched laugh. "That sets a new record. I have one million euros for Miss Zoe Hart. Do I have one million and one?"

Leonardo shakes his head at the MC, but his smile is aimed at me. Instead of looking slain, he appears victorious.

"One million going to Mr. Belshaw."

Jerome looks at me as if I've lost my marbles. If only he knew. I would've paid two million. I would've given everything I own to keep another man's hands off the woman I've claimed. Mission accomplished. The message was dealt. Zoe belongs to me. She doesn't know it, but I've just painted a big hands-off sign all over her delectable body. She'll be mine for all eternity.

The lights dim and music comes on. A disco ball throws shards of light over the floor. The MC declares the dance floor open. People stare at us as sponsors lead their protégés to the men who won their bids.

"I believe this dance is mine," I say, pulling Zoe with me to the floor.

She blinks. "Why did you do this?"

"You preferred Leonardo?" My tone is mocking, but there's nothing mocking about the notion driving like a splinter under my skin, that a woman like her would want a man like him. I bet he's the kind of handsome that featured in her dreams, those pretty dreams she exchanged for the cold, hard truth. Me.

Before she can answer, Leonardo walks into my personal space. "Thank you." He leans closer. "You showed me what I wanted to know." Bumping my shoulder, he walks off into the milling crowd.

My skull pricks when I draw Zoe close.

"What's that about?" Zoe asks, her eyes as round as earlier when I had her pushed up against the wall.

"Nothing."

I put my arm around her waist and lead her to the center of the floor where several couples are already dancing. It's a slow dance. I'm a good dancer, courtesy of my mother who insisted on sending me to dance classes when I dropped out of piano lessons. A refined education has always been important to Maman.

Zoe misses the first step. She trips, bracing herself with her palms on my chest. I catch her around the waist to straighten her and lower my head to whisper in her ear, "Relax. Just follow."

Uncertainly, she places her palm in mine and lays a hand on my shoulder. I lead us into the two-step, enjoying the closeness of her body and the familiar smell of roses in her hair. A few tendrils still fall around her face from our earlier fight. She's always pretty, but she's stunning when she's disheveled.

She pulls back to look at me. "Why did you do that?"

"You know why."

"You could've just told me you were going to bid on me. You made me stress all night. Why be so cruel?"

"You know why, Zoe."

"To teach me to trust you?"

Cupping her head, I press her cheek to my chest. "Always."

Our bodies sway to the rhythm, the curves of her small one fitting to the hollows of mine. She fills the emptiness and brings light to my darkness, but when she doesn't trust me, she creates that gaping emptiness that brings out the monster in me.

I'm hard for her. Too hard. I'm not myself, not one hundred percent in control. It's a combination of factors. It's my jealousy. It's our fight. What Leonardo said is pulsing in my brain. Zoe's hesitation needs to be punished. I can't let her relapse go unanswered. Actions have consequences. She said so herself. What respect will she have for me if I'm not a man of my word? Most of all, it's how she sees herself, as nothing but my whore.

When the dance is over, I take her arm and lead her across the hall. The other couples are dispersing, some moving in the same direction as us—to the bedrooms upstairs.

Before we reach the door, Jerome stops me. "You've made a mistake, cousin," he says in French.

I raise a brow. "Have I?"

Zoe looks between us with a frown marring her beautiful features.

"You've just showed everyone the woman means something to you."

Something may be a bit of an understatement. "Good night, Jerome. I'll catch up with you tomorrow."

He shakes his head as we walk off, clearly not impressed with me.

"Where are we going?" Zoe asks when I usher her into the elevator.

We could've just gone home, but I don't want her to have negative connotations to the place I want her to consider as her safe haven.

She follows me out on the top floor, blindly this time. Too little, too late. Blind obedience won't serve her now.

At the presidential suite, I swipe the access card and step aside to let her in. She looks around much like she had that first night in South Africa. The view over the city is stunning.

Turning to me, she asks with a shaky voice, "Why are we here?"

I turn the lock. "Strip."

"You're going to fuck me?"

"I paid a million euros for your pussy. I'm going to make sure I get my money's worth."

Hurt contorts her features. "Why are you doing this, Maxime?"

Advancing on her, I grab a fistful of her hair and pull her head back. "To show you what it's like to be treated like a whore."

"Please." She grips my forearms, her neck straining from my hold on her hair. "Don't do this."

"I'm done talking."

She stumbles as I let her go. Before she falls on her ass, I catch her arm and fling her around. She cries out as I walk her to the window and plaster her body against it. She fights me, but I easily grab her wrists in one hand behind her back and pin her to the pane with my hips while I use my free hand to pull the zipper of her dress down. I shove it over her hips to pool around her feet. With the low back of the dress, she couldn't wear a bra. Her bare breasts press flat against the glass. I rip away the flimsy thong and let it fall on top of the dress. Then I work a knee between her legs, spreading them apart.

"Maxime, please."

I don't listen to the tremor in her voice. I unzip my pants, not bothering to push it over my hips. My cock is ready. Her body isn't, but that's the point of this lesson. That's how whores are treated, without consideration for their pain or pleasure. Taking the base of my cock in my hand, I press the head against her tight opening and thrust inside. She cries out, her face scrunching up and her eyes pinching closed.

She's warm and almost unbearably tight. A hiss leaves her lips as I pull back, bend my knees, and slam my hips up again, claiming my million-euro pussy, showing her the difference between being my lover and my whore. She thought she'd seen that side of me? Not even close.

I fuck her hard, knowing she's dry. My lust mounts, feeding the dark cravings I usually keep in check for her. My breathing is heavy when I unfasten my buckle and pull my belt through the loops. Excitement courses through my veins when I fold the leather double in one hand and pin her wrists hard against her lower back.

"Maxime." Her voice is panicked. "What are you doing?"

"Quiet."

I pull out of her body and take a step away. The head of my cock is slick with pre-cum. I've already gone too far. With any other woman, I would've put a condom on before I started. Zoe is my exception. She's the only woman I've ever fucked bareback. Taking a rubber from my pocket, I sheathe my cock and drop the packet on the carpet, not caring where it falls.

She knows what's going to happen. Still, she deserves a fair warning. I drag the belt over her ass, following the line of the enticing curve. She's toned and round, an ass made for spanking and fucking.

Taking aim, I swing my arm back. The leather makes a hissing sound as it cuts through the air. It falls with a sharp crack on her skin. She sucks air in loudly, her globes clenching and her body flattening against the glass to escape the pain. I don't spare her. I pull back and lash her again, carefully controlling my strength. Red welts mar her porcelain skin. I don't like to see them there. I don't like spoiling what's perfect, but she left me no choice. I have to prove that I'm trustworthy, that I make good on my promises. I can be as cruel as I can be kind. She must learn this lesson about choice.

She's fighting me, twisting and bucking, but it doesn't take much to keep her pinned to the window.

"Keep still," I say against her ear, "and this will be over quicker."

"Please." Her breath catches on a hitch. "Please, stop."

"I'm afraid not yet, *ma belle*."

With the next lash, I hit her like I mean it. It makes me harder. It's the depraved part of me that enjoys inflicting pain when I torture my enemies. It's the twisted excitement I feel at killing.

Tears roll over her cheeks, but she's brave. She doesn't give in. She remains on her feet. I dip my fingers between her legs. She's still dry. It doesn't stop me from entering her with three fingers. Stretching her with my hand is the only mercy I give her before I shove my cock back into her tight little cunt, greedily taking everything I've paid for. If she's my whore, this is how it is. This is about me. I don't owe her anything other than the price we agreed on. I honored my end of the bargain. She'll honor hers.

My lust is burning white-hot. The violence brings that out in me. I fuck her so hard the breath leaves her lungs in a feminine whimper with every thrust. It's a grueling pace, and it's not enough. Yet she's growing slicker.

Brushing away the tendrils of hair that stick to the sweaty skin of her neck, I nip the soft flesh where her shoulder starts. "Such a naughty little slut. You're getting wet. You like it when I'm rough."

Her nails dig into my skin of my hands where I'm restraining her. "Don't do this."

I gather her arousal and spread it to her asshole. "You're a dirty little whore, and I'm going to fuck every hole I paid for."

She gasps. "Maxime, please."

I slap her ass hard. "Don't you dare say my name. Whores call me Mr. Belshaw."

Pulling her globes apart, I admire the rosebud pucker of her ass, the forbidden entrance I have every right to take. Using her arousal as a lubricant is more than what I would've given any other whore. Still, she's a virgin, so I spit in my palm and coat her well before sinking a finger through the tight ring of muscle. Her inner muscles grip me like fist. When I start pumping, she whimpers. It's when I add a second finger that she fights. She only wiggles and twists until I remove my fingers and press my cock on her dark entrance. Then she stills. I use the moment to press forward, applying pressure until her muscles relent and her ass swallows the head of my cock.

It's a beautiful sight. Her globes are glowing red and her asshole stretching to take my cock. Her pussy is dripping wet. Arousal glistens on her clit. The bud is dark pink and engorged. I could easily slam all the way up, hurt her and get off on her screams. But this is her first time, and I don't want her to keep bad connotations.

Instead, I pull out of her ass, spin her around, and push her down to her knees. I bury one hand in her hair while I use the other to get rid of the rubber. Then I spear through her lips and down her throat. I don't deep-throat her like the first time. I just use her mouth to come. I do it fast, relief surging through me as I shoot my load on her tongue and mess up her face with my cum, but I don't find calm. The anger and darkness linger.

She's served her purpose. I let her go. She's sucking in deep breaths, trembling on her knees. Her mascara and lipstick are smeared; her cheeks and lips streaked with my cum.

"Stay," I say.

I go to the bathroom, wash up, and adjust my clothes. When I come back, she's still on her knees on the carpet with her back against the exposed window.

I stop in front of her. "That's a good slut. Do you want to come?"

She looks broken, her eyelashes wet with tears.

I crouch down in front of her. "You do, don't you? That's what dirty whores want. Go ahead. Touch yourself."

Her lips part as she stares at me with a mixture of shock and hurt.

I chuckle. "You didn't think I was going to touch you like that, did you?"

Her chin trembles but her voice is strong. "You're a bastard."

I shrug. "It's your choice. Get up."

Using the window as a support, she pushes herself up.

"What did this lesson teach you, Zoe?"

She hugs her breasts and crosses her legs, hiding as much of her nakedness as she can. "That nothing we've shared is real," she bites out with tears shining in her eyes. "The kindness isn't real. It means nothing, which means this means nothing, too." Spitting the words at me, she continues, "You mean nothing to me, and you never will."

It's my turn to stare at her. I don't like it. I don't like it one bit that she thinks what I've given her isn't real. It's true, though. Isn't that what I said to my father, that I was going to manipulate her into wanting to stay by giving her what she wants?

I've underestimated her, but not as much as I've underestimated how her answer would affect me. This isn't how this lesson was supposed to go at all.

Gnashing my teeth, I say, "Make your choice, Zoe. My lover or my whore?"

She's trembling, her frail body shaking, but from the way she drops her arms and stands up straighter as she bravely exposes herself, I know what her answer is going to be. She's going to choose the spiteful route.

My phone rings just as she opens her mouth to speak. I take it out of my pocket and check the screen. It's Gautier.

I answer with, "Not now."

"It's your brother, sir," he says. "You better come now."

CHAPTER 23

Zoe

"Put on your dress," Maxime says in a curt tone.

The string of expletives he utters makes me rethink disobeying him in this. Something happened. He doesn't wait to see if I'm complying. He hurries to the door and yanks it open. Standing there waiting, he drags a hand over his head. I've never seen Maxime behaving so worried. Angry, yes. Cold and cruel, yes, but never with such obvious concern.

I shimmy into the dress as quickly as I can. Anyone can walk past the open door, but I also instinctively know whatever the phone call was about is bigger than this, than me. The fabric is light, but even the soft brush against my backside hurts. The ache between my legs and in my dark entrance is an extension of my punishment as I walk over to where my captor waits.

He looks at me as if seeing me for the first time. "You're a mess. Grab a towel from the bathroom."

I do as he says. My reflection in the mirror shocks me to a standstill. My makeup is smudged, and my hair is wild. Streaks of cum are mixed with dark rivulets of mascara on my cheeks. Shame burns in the pit of my stomach. Tears burn behind my eyes. Who am I becoming?

Maxime's loud voice booms through the space, making me jump. "Now, Zoe."

Grabbing a facecloth, I wet it with cold water and rub it over my face until my skin turns red. Not everything comes off, so I bring it with me to wipe away the evidence of what I can't face. Maxime's expression is tight. He's taken off his jacket. At the door, he holds the jacket out for me. I pull it on, hating the smell of winter that clings to the fabric.

Taking my hand, he pulls me behind him to the elevator. I almost trip in my heels trying to keep up. We ride down straight to the basement parking, not going back for our coats or my clutch in the cloakroom.

He unlocks the car and shoves me inside. "Buckle up."

Sitting hurts my butt. I shift to the most comfortable position I can find. Before I've fastened my seatbelt, Maxime is already pulling out of the parking with screeching tires. His hands are clenched on the wheel and his shoulders tense. When we hit the road, I understand why he told me to buckle up. He's driving like a daredevil, breaking the speed limit. I have to grab onto the door handle to prevent my body from being thrown to his side as we round a bend.

On a straight stretch of road, I rub the cloth over my face again, but I don't dare look in the sun visor mirror. I'm not sure I can cope with what I'll see.

Maxime doesn't say a word. All of his attention is fixed on the road. Fortunately, he's a skilled driver. We skip several red lights. I'm waiting with my stomach pulled tight for a police siren to sound or for us to crash into another car, but nothing happens. I'm one big ball of nerves when he finally parks in front of an apartment block near the harbor.

"Come," he says, throwing open his door.

I get out and scurry after him to the entrance. Gautier stands there, a dark look on his face. They exchange a few words. Gautier nods, then takes off.

Maxime punches in a code and lets me in.

"Where are we?" I ask, looking around the modern lobby.

His voice is tight. "My brother's place."

I want to ask what we're doing here, but a voice in the back of my head tells me this isn't the moment for questions. An unsettling sensation steals over me. Alexis seemed nice enough when I met him, but I'm sure it was all acting, just like Maxime is always acting with me, playing nice or decent and kind when it's nothing but a show, a sick game to manipulate me.

Maxime and I climb into the elevator. He punches in another code and watches the floors light up with a broody expression. Alexis's apartment is on the top floor. The elevator gives direct access to Alexis's lounge. We step into a spacious room with futon sofas and a low table. A lamp casts a soft light over the wooden floor. An electric fire burns in a black metal pit in the center. It's all very cozy, but goosebumps break out over my skin. The hair on my neck pricks. Something isn't right.

Alexis stands in front of the window that overlooks the harbor with his back turned to us and a drink in his hand.

"Alexis." Maxime's deep voice thunders through the space.

Alexis turns around, unsteady on his feet. Is he drunk?

Maxime advances on him with big steps. "What the fuck have you done?"

A whimpering noise comes from somewhere down the hallway. The sound makes me stop breathing. There's something horrifying about it, something that's not right. It's the sound a wounded animal would make. It's hopeless and scared, lost in pain.

Maxime grabs Alexis by the collar of his shirt. "*Qu'est-ce que tu as fait?*"

Alexis stumbles, spilling his drink over Maxime's sleeve. He says something in French that makes Maxime draw back an arm and punch him in the face. Alexis goes down on his ass, the glass flying through the air and breaking in shards on the floor.

The violence is unsettling enough, bringing back unpleasant memories of my drunken father I don't care to play over in my mind. My reaction is involuntary, a flashback to my youth that makes me retreat to the corner and try to make myself invisible, but it's not Maxime's pounding fists that hold my attention. It's the sickening grunts dispersed with pitiful moaning coming from elsewhere. Maxime is straddling his brother, dealing punch after punch to his jaw. My whole body drawn tight, I turn away from the fight and pause in the doorway. A low howl makes my stomach turn. Cold sweat breaks out over my body.

Light spills from a room at the end of the hallway. My mind screams for me to hurry, but my feet refuse to obey. It's as if I'm stuck in slow motion, in a very bad dream. When I finally reach the open door from where the light and sounds come, I battle to take in the scene. My brain refuses to process it. Nausea boils in my stomach, and bile pushes up in my throat.

A naked woman is tied to a cross in the middle of the floor, hands and feet spread. A man is pounding into her. He doesn't see me, because his back is turned to the door. A horrible pattern of criss-crossing lines covers what I can see of her breasts and thighs, blood dripping from the cuts. Her left arm is bent unnaturally at the elbow. Her face is bruised and her eyes swollen shut. Cuts mar her legs and feet.

My God. I swallow and swallow again. I've never seen anything as gruesome. The shock that froze me fizzles into a fit of blinding rage. My gaze settles on a whip that lies on a bed covered with a plastic sheet. I move like a demon, grabbing the instrument of torture from the bed and swinging it with all my might at the naked man's back.

He freezes with a curse at the fall of the strap, his eyes wild and confused as he turns his head my way. He shouts something violent in French as he rips free from the woman and charges for me. The lash I dealt hadn't drawn blood. To do so is harder than I thought. Lifting my arm, I put more effort into it as I swing the whip his direction, bringing it down over his face and chest.

He utters a cry, followed by a curse. Before I have time to hit him again, he's on me, wrestling the whip from my hand.

"Let her go," a frighteningly cold, hard voice says from the door.

The man stills. A sliver of fear slips into his voice. "Monsieur Belshaw?"

When he obliges, I rush to the woman. Maxime's words are murderous. The man starts pleading.

"It's okay," I whisper when I reach the woman. "I'm going to untie you."

She can't see me through her swollen eyes, but at the sound of my voice she starts sobbing.

"You're going to be all right," I say, working on the rope that ties her right wrist.

It's knotted too tightly. My fingers are shaking too much. I look around the room for something I can use when Maxime pushes me out of the way. He's clutching a big carving knife.

"Fuck," he mumbles under his breath as he takes in the woman.

"What are you doing with the knife?" I ask, placing myself between him and the woman.

"Cutting her loose. Move out of the way."

I step aside, casting a glance at the door, but the naked man is gone.

Maxime cuts through the rope tied around her wrist.

"I think her arm is broken." I'm having a hard time keeping my voice even. "I'm calling an ambulance."

"No."

His harsh tone makes me pause. "She needs to go to a hospital."

"She will. Put an arm under her shoulder. She's going to need support when I cut her loose."

I wiggle my arm between the cross and her back, holding her up as best as I can while Maxime frees her arms and legs. My heart is pounding between my ribs, my breathing erratic, but I push everything else to the back and focus on helping this poor woman.

Who does something like this? Alexis is ten times worse of a monster than the man who claimed me.

"Go find me a blanket," Maxime says, lifting the limp woman into his arms. "Second door on the left."

I rush down the hallway and push open the door Maxime has indicated. It's dark. I fumble for a light switch. When I find the button, I flick it on. It's a bedroom. The sheets are tangled on the bed. It smells of whiskey and sex. A blanket lies discarded on the floor. Snatching it up, I run back to the room at the end. Maxime exits just as I arrive. I cover the woman's body as best as I can.

"Let's go," Maxime says tersely.

I follow him down the hallway. Through the doorway of the lounge, I see Alexis and the other man. The stranger is dressed, and Alexis is holding a bag of frozen peas against his eye. I get the door and the elevator while Maxime carries the woman and says soothing things to her in French even if she seems unconscious.

Downstairs in the street, Gautier, who's returned, jumps to attention. He gets the passenger door while Maxime lowers the woman onto the seat and secures her safety belt. He says something to Gautier, then races around the car, gets in, and starts the engine. I watch dumbfounded, my words all dried up, as he takes off like a racing devil, the taillights of his car two red eyes in a dark evil of the night.

"I'm taking you home," Gautier says.

I turn to face him. At first his words don't make sense. Nothing makes sense. I'm shivering in Maxime's jacket, but not from cold.

"Come, Miss Hart. Please."

I look at his outstretched arm. A realization dawns on me. I don't know how I figure it out because the dots from my mind to my thoughts won't connect. He's not allowed to touch me.

"Please," he says again.

Numb, I follow him to a car parked on the side of the road and get in when he holds the door for me. I can't breathe. I can't calm the frantic beat of my heart. For the first time since Maxime took me from my home and brought me here, I'm grateful to my kidnapper. I'm grateful he didn't hand me over to his brother.

What I've seen tonight changes everything. It changes the answer I was going to give Maxime back at the hotel.

CHAPTER 24

Maxime

On the way to the hospital, I call Dr. Olivier.

"Another one?" he asks curtly when I've explained the situation.

"I know." I glance at the unconscious woman. "This is ending tonight."

He sighs. "I'll meet you there in ten."

I park underground and take the elevator to the ground floor. It's late. It's quiet. Dr. Olivier meets me at the side entrance. Together, we install the woman in a private room. The good doctor will treat her and give her something for the pain. He'll also handle the tricky logistics of the paperwork.

I take a picture of her injuries with my phone. Pocketing it, I say, "Text me an update on her progress."

The doctor looks up from examining her. "Where are you going?"

"To deal with my brother."

He nods. It's not his place to ask questions. "Do you know her identity? I'll need a name for the forms."

I'll need it to pay a hefty compensation, not that money can atone for Alexis's actions. Plus, her family will have to be informed of her *random assault*. She'll say someone got rough on her while she was working the streets. That's what they all say, but the prostitutes talk among themselves. Hopefully, they'll stay far away from my brother in the future.

"I'll get her name to you," I say. "Send me the bill." Of course, it'll include a big fat bonus for the doctor.

Without wasting more time, I get my car and drive to my parents' house. On the way, I call my father and tell him I'll be there shortly. It's almost three in the morning, but he doesn't share a bedroom with Maman, so I don't risk waking her up.

My father replies with, "I'll wait downstairs."

He knows I won't call at this hour unless there's a problem, usually one that involves a traitor or an unauthorized killing.

I kill the headlights before I pull through the gates. Maman's window faces the front lawn. Father stands in the dark by the door, flanked by two guards.

"Come in." He walks ahead of me to his study and only flicks the lights on when the door is closed. He's dressed in his silk robe and a pair of slippers. He pours two glasses of whiskey before taking the chair behind his desk. "What happened?"

I take out my phone and show him the picture I took of the woman in the hospital.

He lifts his gaze to me. "Alexis?"

My voice is clipped. "Yes."

Sighing, he rubs a hand over his face. "Is she going to make it?"

"I'm waiting for the doctor to text me, but I think so. She's not much worse than the previous one, and that one survived." I move closer. "However, the next one may not be so lucky."

"Fuck." My father slams a palm on the desk.

He understands the implications of murder. Taking out your

enemies is one thing. Taking out the very prostitutes you're pimping is quite another.

"We have to deal with Alexis," I say.

My father looks at me, his bad eye drooping more than usual. He doesn't want to punish his favorite son, but he knows he's let it go too far. If Alexis doesn't end up in jail soon, he'll end up with a bullet in the back of his head. These women have families. They're locals. Their fear of our power is only going to last so long before someone vengeful gets trigger happy. Besides, this is not the example we want to set.

"Fine," he says, pushing his chair away from the desk and getting to his feet. "Deal with him."

He can fucking count on that.

I leave his study with long steps. In the car, I dial Gautier. "Is Zoe home?"

"Yes, sir."

"Meet me at Alexis's and bring Benoit. Keep it discreet."

Back at Alexis's place, I find him a lot more sober than I left him. He's frightened, as he should be. He knows he fucked up one time too many. The fucker who was with him is still there. Good. At least the man was intelligent enough to do as I've instructed, to stay put. He knows better than to let me hunt him, because then he would've been a free kill.

Alexis is pacing the floor, a bag of peas pressed to his swollen eye. "What the fuck took you so long? Where have you been?"

"Home."

He stops. The color drains from his face. "Home?"

Crossing my arms, I enjoy his palpable fear. "To see father."

He swallows. "Max, listen, I—"

I turn to his buddy, one of the men I've seen frequently at the port. "What's your name?"

The man is so rigid it looks like his spine may snap. "Francois Leclerc, sir."

Alexis may be my father's son, but I'm the fucking underboss, and they both know I come with my father's blessing. Right now that makes me the boss.

"Who's the woman?"

Alexis points at a handbag that lies on the table. I go over and pick it up. It's imitation leather, a cheap quality. The plastic is cracked. Unzipping it, I take out a wallet. There's an ID card inside. I pocket it and take the bag, then tilt my head toward the door. "Let's go."

Alexis drops the bag of peas. "Where?"

I smile. "For a ride."

Francois turns as white as baguette pastry.

"Bring your toy," I say to him.

He frowns, looking at me with a retarded expression.

"Your whip," I say. "Go fetch it."

He starts to tremble. "It's not mine." He points at Alexis. "It's his."

"Did I fucking ask you whose it is?"

"No, sir."

"Then move your ass."

Looking at me from over his shoulder as if he expects me to shoot him in the back, he scurries down the hallway and returns with the whip.

"After you." Stepping aside, I wait for them to pass in front of me.

They don't argue. Arguing will only make what's waiting for them worse. Alexis grins as he passes, but it's all acting. The coward is shaking in his pants.

Benoit and Gautier have arrived. They're waiting downstairs. Benoit drives Francois while Gautier and I take Alexis with us. We don't speak. It's only when we near the warehouse at the docks where we torture our rivals that Alexis start to shift in the backseat.

"You're going to shoot me?" he asks snidely. "Your own brother?"

I don't bother to grace him with a reply.

After we've parked, Gautier escorts the two men to the warehouse. I take my Glock from the cubbyhole and slip it into my waistband before taking the whip. Benoit unlocks the warehouse door and flicks the light on.

"Wait by the car," I tell Gautier. I hand the woman's ID card and handbag to Benoit. "Get this to Dr. Olivier."

They nod and leave.

Alexis and Francois stand in a pool of light that falls from a single naked bulb when I enter the warehouse.

"Strip," I say. It's the same order I've given Zoe only a few hours ago and for the very same reason—to punish and teach a lesson.

The men don't move.

I take out the gun. "I can motivate you with a bullet in your foot." I step closer. "Maybe one in the hand, too."

At that, Francois starts unbuttoning his shirt. My reputation is solid. I'm a man of my word. No idle threats. I've worked hard on establishing that honor. That's why I let no one off the hook, not even my flower.

Alexis follows suit, hatred burning in his swollen eyes. His nose is askew. I've broken it. Good. I love the bruises blooming on his jaw.

I circle them like a shark, gun clutched in my hand, until they stand naked. Their cocks are flaccid.

Tapping the barrel of the gun against Francois's temple, I say. "Get him hard."

He turns his head quickly to look at me, slobber flying from his mouth. "What?"

I point at Alexis's soft dick. "Get it up."

Alexis growls. "What the fuck?"

"Shut up." I press the gun barrel on Alexis's hand, right above his trigger finger. "Do you need motivation?"

He's seen me torture our enemies before. He knows what I'm capable of. Gritting his teeth, he shakes his head.

Francois faces my brother reluctantly. Sweat beads on his forehead as he grips my brother's cock in his fist. Pinching his eyes shut, he turns his head away and starts pumping. The sick pervert that my brother is, he gets hard.

I kick a bench toward Francois. "Bend over."

He stumbles a step back. "What?"

"You heard me."

Walking with slow steps to the bench, he bends over, leaning his shaking arms on the wood. He looks at me from over his shoulder, his chin wobbling.

I give Alexis a shove. "Fuck him."

Alexis rounds on me, his eyes huge. "What?"

"Shove your dick in his ass and fuck him like you mean it, or you both get a bullet in the hand. I can guarantee you'll never use a gun again."

Alexis curses, but he goes forward. Inwardly, I smile. My brother isn't only a coward, he's also the worst kind, the kind who'd turn on a friend to save his own skin. He'd rather fuck his buddy in the ass than be the one who's fucked, which is why I'm letting him have a go first. I can't wait to see his face when it's his turn. They're going to fuck each other until their dicks are limp and then again. I'm going to whip them to shreds while they do it.

Picking up the whip, I tighten my fingers around the handle. I've been looking forward to this for a long time, and I have all night.

CHAPTER 25

Zoe

It's dawn, and Maxime is still not home. I've been pacing up and down, unable to think about anything but that woman, unable to get the images out of my head. I'm still dressed in the red ballroom gown and Maxime's jacket, my ass smarting from his belt, yet I feel extremely lucky, lucky that I'm not that girl. Knowing how easily that could've been me makes me sick. It leaves me with unanswered questions about who this family is and why they took me. If only I had access to the internet, I could've done my own research. I wish I could've called Maxime, but my phone is in the clutch bag we left at the hotel.

When I can't stand on my feet any longer, I go to the foyer and sit on the bottom of the stairs. I don't know how much time passes, if it's minutes or hours, but when the front door finally opens, I jump up and rush forward. Maxime stands on the step, my coat and clutch in one hand. For a second, we just look at each other. His hair is messy and his jaw dark with stubble. His coat hangs open. Splatters of blood decorate his white shirt. He's lost the bowtie, the top two buttons of his shirt undone.

"How is she?" I ask breathlessly.

"Fine." He strides past me into the house, leaving the door open.

A gust of cold wind follows him inside. I shut the door and just stand there, feeling useless, left in the dark.

"Maxime."

He stops, but he doesn't turn to look at me.

"What did the doctor say?" I ask.

"She'll be discharged by tomorrow. Stop worrying your pretty little head over her."

Stop worrying? I go after him, catching up just as he reaches the stairs. Moving around him, I climb two stairs to put us on eye level. "Do you hear yourself? Are you insane?"

The corner of his mouth pulls up. "We've established that already. Move aside, Zoe. I need a shower."

"Do you even give a damn?" I cry out.

"Yes." His jaw bunches. "Which is why Alexis and his friend have been punished."

"Is that where you've been all night?"

He looks me over. "You should've changed and gone to bed."

"There's no way I could've just put my head down and gone to sleep without knowing if she's all right."

"I told you." He lifts a brow. "Anything else you need to know?"

I consider my question and the impact it will have on an already fragile situation, but I can't go another day without the truth. "Why did you take me? What do you want from Damian?"

He watches me steadily, his gray eyes flat, but there's something underneath the coldness, something he's hiding.

"Tell me, Maxime. I deserve the truth." It's the least he can give me for stealing my life.

He mounts one step, two, putting our bodies flush. "Have you learned nothing, tonight?"

"That I'm supposed to trust you blindly?" I bite out, craning my neck to look up at him.

He grips the tangled mess of hair at the back of my head, but it's not an angry move. It's tender. "There are things I can't tell you. I can't always explain my actions. If you don't give me reason to do otherwise, I will always act in your best interest." His steely gaze pierces mine. "That's why you have to trust me. Always. No matter what."

I blink up at him, letting the information sink in, pondering a different question that has been haunting me all night. "Why didn't you give me to Alexis?"

He releases me. "We've been through this."

He's not giving me anything, nothing to piece the puzzle together, only the bit about trusting him without question. My life is spiraling out of control, and I feel lost. I don't have the facts to gather my ammunition and shield myself from the mind games he's playing. I'm at a disadvantage in our war, and I'm afraid I'm losing my grip.

Reading my expression correctly, he asks, "What are you so scared of, Zoe?"

I give him the truth. "I don't even know who I am anymore."

He trails his gaze over me, taking me in from my bare feet to my clean-scrubbed face. His words are soft-spoken, a complete contrast to earlier tonight. "When I look at you, I don't see a whore."

Tears spring to my eyes. No matter how he looks at me, I can never wipe those stains on my soul away. I am what he made me, and suddenly the truth I've been avoiding all night hits me squarely in the chest. I want to believe him. Badly. I want to believe that I'm somehow something more, but it's just my psyche's way of trying to protect itself.

Cupping my cheek, he draws a thumb over my jaw. "How you look at yourself is entirely up to you." Then he moves me aside and climbs past me up the stairs.

I'm drowning in helplessness, torn between wanting to grab the lie he offers between both hands and clinging to the last shreds of truth in my soul. I'm weak, so damn weak, because I don't want to end up like that woman—fuck, I don't even know her name, like she's no one—and I hate myself for it.

"Maxime."

He stops again.

"Please let me go outside," I say. "I need some air."

He hesitates.

"I'm not going anywhere." My hand trembles on the balustrade. "You've made that clear."

Keeping his back turned to me, he nods once before continuing his ascend.

When the bedroom door slams upstairs, I go through the kitchen to the backdoor. A guard stands aside when I exit. He seems surprised, but he doesn't stop me. I walk barefoot over the gravel to the maze, but I don't want to lose myself in more puzzles. Instead, I take the path to the cliffs and follow it to the spot from where Maxime had jumped. The pebbles and sticks are sharp under my feet. I welcome the pain. Even after last night, I still need the punishment. I'm freezing. The wind is cold and relentless, blowing the edges of Maxime's jacket open and exposing my naked shoulders. I embrace the bite, hoping it will freeze everything inside me, but the burning in my gut continues, eating me up like a ravenous monster. My pain shines like precious stones in the dusty bed of a river. My feelings are discarded like diamonds in the dust. Wasted.

I STARE out over the sea. It's breathtakingly beautiful. The sun is kissing the horizon. It gives the cold blue of the ocean a golden glow. Even in the stark gray of dusk, the water in the cove below is turquoise. A white beach hugs it, just like the one where we had the picnic. Sharp rocks are scattered treacherously throughout the bay, I'm guessing making it difficult for boats to anchor here. It's like a small slice of paradise in hell.

Slowly, I edge forward, until my toes hang over the cliff. My body screams at me to go back to safer ground as fear claws its way through my chest. It's a fear I'm no longer unfamiliar with, the fear for my life. Self-preservation kicks in, making me tremble and sweat, making me feel sick when I peer down. I'm a coward. I could've fought Maxime harder. I surrendered too easily. I hate myself. I hate feeling helpless and weak. I take another pace until only my heels are resting on the rocks, my stomach climbing up in my throat as my body sways in the strong wind.

"Zoe."

I turn my head at the sound of my name. It's instinctive. It's a trained reaction, like a dog minding a whistle. Maxime stands on the path, a distance away from me. He's wearing nothing but a pair of tracksuit pants. His chest and feet are bare, his scars exposed to the elements.

He raises an arm. "Give me your hand, little flower."

I look back down at the sea, scary but oh so pretty. I'm tired of being weak. I want to jump like him. I want to jump and know I can survive. Carefully, I lift my right foot, posing it over the abyss.

"Zoe! Look at me."

The last I hear is Maxime's howl as I face my demons and step over the edge.

~ THE END ~

DIAMONDS IN THE ROUGH

BOOK 2, DIAMONDS ARE FOREVER TRILOGY

A DIAMOND MAGNATE NOVEL

CHAPTER 1

Maxime

Jesus.

I dive for the edge, going after Zoe over the cliff. The thought of losing her hurts my chest. It hurts a thousand times more than the cold water. When I hit the surface, I don't go down far. I turn and swim up like a madman. The sea is flat. I should easily spot her, but there are rocks all around. Shouting her name, I scout the water like a lunatic as a vise of fear closes around my heart.

Then I see her. Thank fuck. The relief is so great I'm not even angry. I swim with powerful strokes and reach her in five seconds. She's gasping and splashing, treading water. Grabbing her around the waist, I turn her onto her back and swim us to the shore. There's no way she could've made it out on her own, not knowing where the underwater rocks give way to form a channel.

I'm out of breath when we reach the beach, but not from exertion. It's the fear. I've never felt anything like it, never cared enough. Dragging her out onto the sand, I put the revelation to the back of my mind to dissect later. I peel my jacket Zoe is still wearing off her body and cover her slender frame with my body, letting some of my heat warm her skin. Her teeth are chattering, and her limbs are shaking.

Fuck, fuck, fuck.

I lift her into my arms and start the steep ascend. The guards are waiting at the top, staring down with concerned faces, offering hands and assistance.

I brush them away. "We're fine."

Holding her close to my chest, I hurry to the bathroom where I run a shower. When the water is warm, I push her under the spray and undress her. Since I destroyed her underwear, she's wearing nothing but the red evening dress. Her lips are blue. So are her fingernails. I rub each of her hands between mine to warm them, and then her arms to aid the blood flow and increase her body temperature.

Somewhere between soaping her body and rinsing her hair, her teeth stop chattering. I brace her against the wall and drop to my knees in front of her. Droplets of water cling to her eyelashes as she stares at me, keeping her balance with her hands pressed on my shoulders. Her dark hair, normally wavy or curly, hangs straight and silky over her shoulders. Her breasts are big for her small body, her nipples a dark shade of pink. She doesn't shave or trim the triangle between her legs, but even there her hair is soft and perfect, a pretty womanly shape. There are many kinds of beautiful and plenty of norms to define it, but she's all of them, everything condensed into one.

Lifting her thigh, I hook it over my shoulder and worship her body with my hands. I circle her narrow waist and drag my palms over the curve of her hips, all the while watching her telltale eyes. They go hazy with need, the blue turning a shade darker, like the depths of the ocean. Her cheeks turn pink, and her nipples harden. I sweep a path down the outside of her legs and back up inside to her pussy. She's slick and swollen, her flesh needing what I've denied her earlier at the hotel.

I hold her eyes as I go down on her, eating her like she's my last meal. It doesn't take long for her to break. When she comes in my mouth, her long lashes brush her cheeks, and she catches her bottom lip between her teeth. I eat her out through the aftershocks of her orgasm, lapping up all her honey with lazy strokes of my tongue.

She's legless when I wrap her up in my robe and towel her dry. The exhaustion is a combination of my earlier punishing lesson, the sleepless night, the shock of what she's seen at Alexis's place, the afterglow of the orgasm, and coming down from the adrenaline of her goddamn jumping stunt. That's a lot for one small flower to take in all at once.

She doesn't protest when I carry her to my bed and pull the covers over us. I curl up with her back against my chest and her ass in my groin. I fold one arm under her head and the other around her waist. Like this, she's secure in the prison of my arms, finally warm and sated.

Kissing her neck, I inhale the sweet scent of her skin. "What the hell were you thinking, Zoe?"

"I wanted to know if I could do it," she says, her voice already thick with sleep.

"You could've fucking died."

"That would've been a bad thing?"

"Yes," I say vehemently. "You're never to do that again. Ever. Understand?"

"You did."

"I know what I'm doing."

"I did it, didn't I?"

I sigh. "You did, but there was no way you could've come out on the beach on your own. The rocks would've shredded you to pieces."

"Don't worry. I know why you're concerned." Her tone turns bitter. "It's this thing going on with Damian. Rest assured, I'm not going to kill myself."

Damn right, she isn't. Damn wrong, too. It's not just the *thing* with Damian. It's not about the diamonds or the business. It's about what I realized out there in those dangerous waters.

"Go to sleep," I say, tightening my arms around her.

She abides with a little sigh, her breathing soon evening out. Me, I lie awake, my heart thundering in my chest as I hold the woman who makes me feel, the only person in the world who makes me fear.

CHAPTER 2

Zoe

In the days that follow, Maxime behaves differently toward me. Sometimes, he worships me on his knees like he can never get enough of me, and at other times he pushes me away, deliberately keeping me at a distance. It's a never-ending push and pull. Through it all, he treats me well. As long as I'm sticking to my end of the bargain, he does. He's proving to me that he's good for his word, that he'll make my stay pleasant if I'm obedient, but he won't hesitate to punish me cruelly if I step out of line.

When I ask about the woman Alexis tortured, he only tells me she's fine. I ask about Alexis too, but Maxime says he's paid for what he's done and that's that. He refuses to divulge anything more. I know his family is wealthy. I've seen their properties and the lifestyles they live. Maxime told me they were powerful, but I didn't register exactly how much until now. Who gets away with what Alexis did? It's wrong. There's something disturbing about it, something significant, but there's already so much to deal with I block it out. Survival isn't only about the physical. It's also about the emotional and mental, and I'm processing as much as my mind can handle.

On a spring evening when Maxime seems to be in a good mood, I dare to bring up the subject that has been bothering me ever since the night he saved that woman from his brother. We're sitting on the couch in the library, me with a book in my hands and my feet in Maxime's lap. He's reading work related documents while massaging my feet.

"Maxime?"

He doesn't look up from the paper in his hand. "Mm?"

"Why wasn't Alexis convicted?"

He strokes a thumb along the curve of my sole. "Some punishments are better doled out by ourselves."

"You mean taking the law into your own hands."

Flicking over the page with one hand, he says, "Something like that."

I drop the book in my lap, no longer interested in the story. "Didn't the woman lay charges?"

"She didn't have to." Abandoning the massaging, he drags a palm over the bridge of my foot. "Alexis was punished, and she was compensated."

"She was okay with that?"

He lowers the papers. "Not with what happened, obviously, but she was satisfied that justice was done." His mouth tightens. "What's with all the questions? It's over. You should stop thinking about it."

"I just don't understand."

"What don't you understand?" he asks with impatience.

"How you could get away with something like that. Is it because your family is powerful? Because you have the right connections?"

He squeezes my foot. "Don't worry your pretty little head over that. As I said, you should forget that night happened."

"Just like that." I sit up straighter. "It's not something I'll ever be able to forget."

He sighs. "I regret taking you there. In hindsight, it was an error."

"Why did you?" When I try to pull my foot from his grasp, he holds tight.

"I've been asking myself the same thing." He stares at the empty fireplace. "I knew I'd need your help and that the woman was going to be more comfortable with the presence of another woman than more men descending on her, but I also wanted you to know who Alexis truly is."

"You took me there to see for myself."

He meets my eyes squarely. No remorse shines in his. "That was part of the reason, yes."

"Are you involved in worse crimes than kidnapping?"

His smile is cold. "What do you think?"

"What is it?" I pull my leg again, and this time he lets my foot go. "Drugs? Is that why you have all the guards around? I mean, the diamonds are legal if you buy them from Dalton's mine like you claimed, right?"

"You think too much."

"But—"

"No more."

The harsh tone shuts me up.

In a gentler voice, he continues, "No more speaking of this. Understand?"

Holding his gaze, I lift my chin. I hate how he keeps me in the dark. His look turns more predatory, lust bleeding into the gray pools that were flat and emotionless only a second ago as he grips my jaw in his big hand. Sexual awareness filters into the moment. The air becomes charged. With the innocent foot massage suddenly forgotten, I turn into prey. When he drags me closer, a tinge of fear mixes with anticipation. I do forget. I forget as long as he kisses me, and when he undresses me, we no longer speak.

THERE ARE many subjects Maxime doesn't like to discuss. We don't mention my jump, but I do feel better for it. Stronger. I did something scary and pushed my boundaries. It reinforced my spirit. It helps me keep my soul intact while I give my body to my captor on a daily basis. It helps me ignore that I come every time, that I crave his touch and sometimes his roughness. It helps me cope with who I've become.

No matter how I look at it, I can't see myself like Maxime wants me to. He claims he doesn't see me as a whore. That isn't real. It's make-believe, a fantasy he stole from my dream to enact in a castle on the edge of a cliff in France. He treats me like the princess I've always wanted to be, showering me with every possible material luxury, but it doesn't change the fact that I'm selling my body or being locked up in his tower.

However, he still allows me outside at free will, and I walk the grounds frequently, spending long hours looking out at the ocean. I walk in the gardens, the maze, and go down to the beach. It should be nice in summer. His guards never speak to me, not even when I greet them, but they do keep a close eye on me. If Maxime is home when I'm outside, I often see him standing on the terrace, watching me from afar, and from closer whenever I dare it near the cliffs again. I'm not going to jump a second time. Once was enough.

We go out often, eating in restaurants in town or visiting the sights. We walk around hand in hand like a couple in love while Maxime buys me treats at ice cream and strawberry stalls. He dresses and feeds me, and I say thank you with a smile. I don't like being the eye candy on his arm, but he insists the outings are good for me. Maybe they are. Maybe they keep me from going insane.

Francine comes in every weekday and every second weekend, but she avoids me. I keep out of the kitchen. I don't have any friends. I have no one to confide in. All I have are my letters to Damian, which I write faithfully every week.

A tutor arrives and I take up learning French. The course is intensive, four hours of classes a day plus two hours of homework. It's a good distraction for my mind. I've always enjoyed languages, and I'm a fast learner. It amuses Maxime to no end. He enjoys holding me on his lap in front of the fire in the evenings, making me repeat phrases and testing my vocabulary. He says my accent is adorable. It makes him smile. When I'm not working in the library with my tutor—an elderly man Maxime no doubt appointed only because of his age—I'm doing homework in the tower. I've pulled the desk to the window, using the window seat as a chair, and now that the weather is changing it's not so cold up there.

My life takes on a routine, a predictable one that makes it easier to cope, and when the jasmine starts to bloom and poppies bleed all over the wild grass near the cliffs, I can hold a basic conversation in French and understand most of what's spoken. My reading isn't bad, either.

On a sunny afternoon when the birds are loud in the garden Maxime comes home with a big box. His granite eyes are unusually bright with excitement. He installs the box on the table in the dining room and takes my hand to pull me closer.

"For you," he says, watching me with eager attention.

"Me?" There's nothing printed on the outside, no clue as to what's inside.

"Open it."

I pull at the masking tape, but I don't manage to break the seal.

"Fran," he calls toward the kitchen. "Bring a pair of scissors."

We're still speaking English when we're together, a habit from when we met that stuck.

Francine enters with a pair of scissors, eyeing the box with curiosity.

"What is it?" I ask, taking the scissors. I can't help my smile. Maxime's excitement is contagious. I've never seen him like this before.

"A gift," he says.

"A gift?" Francine looks at him. "That's a first."

He shrugs. "Are you going to open it today, still?"

I laugh. "Maybe you should open it."

"I'm tempted, but that's not how it works with gifts." Stepping closer, he cups my cheek, giving me a look so tender the foundations of the fortress around my heart shake a little.

Remembering Francine is watching us, I step back to escape the intimate touch. "What?"

Maxime smiles, soft and genuine. "I like it when you laugh. I should buy you gifts more often."

"You do," I say. "All the time." I'm not going to tell him I still feel like the extravagant clothes and jewelry are payments for my obedience and payoffs for my body. I don't think I can handle a repeat of what I went through on the night of the auction.

"Those things are utile," he says. "It's not the same."

It makes me all the more curious. Attacking the box with the scissors, I make both of us laugh. It's easy and carefree. It's been a long time since I've laughed like this.

Finally, I manage to pry the edges of the box open and peer inside. It's filled with shredded paper. I glance at him.

"Go on," he says, waving me on.

I brush the paper aside and catch a glimpse of white metal. I still, then scoop the paper aside faster, making it fall over the table and floor.

Oh, my God. I lift the owner's manual from the box. A Singer Quantum Stylist computerized portable sewing machine.

I gape at him. "Maxime."

"Do you like it?" There's uncertainty in his tone.

Emotions clog up my throat. I've had only one true gift in my life—a book of fairytales. The clothes Maxime buys are to make me look pretty for him and to be a showpiece worth looking at on his arm. The flowers he bought in Venice were a pre-consolation price for locking me up in a cell. This? This is different. This is not for him or the benefit of outside onlookers. This isn't a prelude to a lesson. This is for me. This is the first thing he's given me with no strings attached. It serves no other purpose than making me happy. I don't know what makes me sadder, that he's the first person other than my late mom to gift me anything or that he's the only one who's paid enough attention to me to know what I love. No matter that I hate it, he understands my dreams. No matter that I hate myself for it, his gesture moves me. Tears well in my eyes, unbidden and unwelcome but very sincere as I digest the enormity of his offering.

He frowns. "What's wrong?"

He looks so dejected I can't stop myself from wrapping my arms around him and leaning my cheek on his chest. His gift is a beautiful gesture, a pure one, and I'm not going to twist it into something ugly by throwing it back into his face. It will kill any shred of kindness left in his dark heart, proving to him kind acts are rewarded with cruelty. I refuse to be the teacher of such an inhumane lesson.

"Thank you," I whisper, hugging him tightly.

He folds his arms around me. "You're welcome."

Francine stands stiffly with a downturned mouth. With all the emotions coursing through me, I've all but forgotten about her. We've shut her out in our private moment. When she catches my eye, she turns on her heel and heads back to the kitchen.

Maxime kisses the top of my head. "I didn't want to give it to you before you've finished your French exams. I was afraid you wouldn't focus."

He's right. I can hardly focus on anything other than the designs already running through my head. "I haven't written my exams yet." It's only in two days.

"Knowing what a nerd you are, I'm sure you've already mastered everything."

"Almost."

"You'll have to go shopping for fabric and thread and whatever else a clothing designer needs."

Sniffing away my tears, I pull back to look at him. "You mean a seamstress."

"No." He wipes a thumb under my eye, catching a tear. "I think you should go to a design school."

I stare at him. "What?"

"It's a good school, one of the most prestigious in the country right here in Marseille. I've already looked into it. You can start after the summer break."

I'm battling to process the information. "Don't you have to pass very strict tests to be admitted?" They only take the best of the best, and I know how selective places are.

"Of course, but I have no doubt you'll pass. I've seen your drawings."

"You think they have merit?"

He smiles. "Without a doubt."

Excitement surges through me, but confusion, too. "Why would you do something like that for me?" I also know how much designing schools cost. I can't even begin to think how much he'd have to fork out to send me to a prestigious French one.

"It's good to have a purpose in life. I don't believe in wasting talents. Hard work is rewarding. All the more if said work is your passion."

He wants me to have purpose, to live my passion? To make me happy or to prevent me from jumping off cliffs? I'm not clear about his motivations. I've never understood them. There's still so much I don't know about the man who both holds me captive and protects me from people like his brother. I know nothing about his passion or purpose.

"Do *you* live your passion?" I ask.

"I was born to do what I'm doing."

"Dealing in diamonds?" I don't even know if he's a broker or the owner of a jewelry chain.

"That's just a part of the business." Taking my hand, he says, "We'll unpack your sewing machine later. Walk with me to the beach."

I'm eager to please him, not because he gave me a gift or is willing to let me study at his expense, but because he showed me he's capable of true kindness, that not everything in his heart is dark.

We take the path, using the steep steps to climb down. I'm wearing a summer dress and sandals, even if the days are not yet warm. Maxime is still wearing his business suit. On the sandy part, the cliffs shelter us from the wind. Nevertheless, he removes his jacket and hangs it over my shoulders before taking off his shoes and socks. We sit down close to the edge of the water. The sun sparkles on the turquoise surface. A seagull calls from close by.

The smell of salt is stronger here, and the sun is warm on my back. It's nice. Peaceful. Pleasant. But the weather and the view aren't alone in creating this feeling of contentedness. It's sitting beside him in silent harmony. It's being something other than an object, someone with a purpose in life that doesn't revolve around my brother and Maxime's mysterious reasons for keeping me.

"What are you thinking?" he asks in his sensual accent.

I turn my face toward him. His features are as sharp and unattractive as the day we met, but after all these months, I look at him differently. There's a term for that. It's called sex appeal.

"Zoe?"

I look away from the face I shouldn't find handsome in the slightest, digging my fingers into the soft sand. "I was thinking about Damian."

He covers my hand with his. "What about him?"

"I miss him."

"He's doing fine. You don't have to worry about him."

I turn my head back to him quickly. "You have news?"

"I'm keeping tabs on him."

I frown. "You didn't tell me."

"It goes without saying, doesn't it?"

I search the gray depth of his eyes, the secrets he keeps from me. He still hasn't answered the question I posed on the night I jumped into the sea. "Why are you keeping me, Maxime? Why are you threatening me with Damian's life?"

His gaze turns flat. My heart sinks. He's not going to let me in.

Letting go of my hand, he drags his fingers through his hair. "Stop asking questions I can't answer."

"Can't or won't?"

He rises. "It's time to head back. I have work to do."

Not yet. I don't want this to end so soon. If there's one lesson captivity has taught me, it's to make the most of the good moments. You never know when there will be another one, if ever.

Reaching up, I close my fingers around his to hold him back. His eyebrows snap together as he looks at me. I think back to our picnic, to how he pushed me down onto the blanket in the open, and how it aroused me.

"Oh, my little flower." His voice is deeper, his gaze sharper. "You're taking a risk showing your lust so openly."

Yes, it must be showing on my face. I yearn for him to stretch and fill me. Pulling on his hand, I drag him back down beside me. Every time he takes me, I open up my body, making myself vulnerable, but he makes himself vulnerable, too. That's why he keeps on pushing me as hard as he's pulling. He's scared. Just like me. The revelation filters intuitively into my mind as our gazes remain locked in a heated stare.

This time it's me who shoves him down with my hands on his shoulders. His pupils widen. He resists a little, as if he's uncertain about submitting to me, but then lets me push him flat onto the sand.

I unbuckle his belt and pull down his zipper. He's hard already, his cock bulging in his underwear. I don't look up to see if there are guards on the perimeter of the cliff. I'm too scared to break our fragile eye contact, too afraid he'll reject me. This is different. He's always done the taking and set the rules. With the exception of the night of the auction, he's always taken care of my pleasure, but sex happens on his terms. Even the times I've craved release, he's given it by using the signals of my body to predict and fulfill my needs. I've never asked for it, not like this, and it's so damn scary because deep inside, in a hidden part of me, I hunger for more.

I crave affection.

True affection.

My body is sated, but my heart is so empty. I have no one else to turn to but him. He's made sure of that. He's the only man who can give me anything as long as I'm locked up in his house and he owns my life.

"Maxime." His name is a broken whisper.

Until this moment, I never would've clutched this knife of hope in my hands, ready to shred my own heart with the betrayal of my emotions, but he showed me kindness. He put that knife in my hands when he gave me hope. The rest is science. I've been open and vulnerable for too long. I'm a receptive reservoir. I'm a romantic. It's just who I am. I'm desperate for a few crumbs of affection. He wants my body, but I want to mean more.

I want to be more than a whore and a pawn.

It's the biggest risk I've taken, freeing his cock. Straddling him, I press a kiss to the tip. He leans back on his arms, watching me with wary attention. I grip the base in one hand. He's so hard, so much man. He shudders when I lick the underside, and when I take him to the back of my throat he surrenders. Something inside me gives as he folds his arms under his head in the sand, his guard relaxing. I reward him by sucking him the way he likes, the way he taught me. He groans, lifting his hips a fraction, but he maintains his position of immobility, allowing me to choose.

I do. I choose to move my underwear aside and lower myself over his hard length. With every inch I take him deeper, I let the cold, hurtful blade of hope into my heart. I moan at how completely he fills me, at the bite of pain that comes with the stretch. My fingers clench in the fabric of his shirt, his jacket falling over us like a cloak when I lean forward and slide my body up and down. The pleasure is exquisite. Hard. Dark. I whimper as our groins press together. The angle is just right, adding friction to my clit, but I need to see his face. I need to look into his eyes when I fall, hoping to God there will be just one small spark of warmth for me.

Leaning back, I brace my hands on his thighs and ride him. I hold onto his gaze as release starts winding through my body. His jaw is tight, his gray eyes gleaming. He's ablaze just as I am, but his flames only go skin deep. Still, I cling to the sharpness in those pools that cut into my soul. If he could only give me a drop, just a little to survive.

I rock faster, my sounds and thoughts already splintering as my climax builds. My cry is desperate. "Maxime, please."

Satisfaction bleeds into his eyes, sharpening his edges, making him seem crueler as he recognizes his power over me. "Please, what?"

The words spill over my lips, a request that leaves me utterly powerless. "Please, love me."

He freezes. A shutter falls over his eyes. In a blink, he switches off.

No.

Tears burn at the back of my eyes. "Please," I whisper, "just a little."

A vein pulses in his temple. For a moment, we're stuck in a terrible limbo. It's a defining moment. It's the moment I fall for my captor, admitting I want—need—more from him than sex.

Just like that, the show is over. He moves from spectator to orchestrator. Grabbing my upper arms, he flips us around. I'm pinned in the sand by his heavy body and hard cock. The fever in his eyes is new. Cold. Buttons fly as he rips open the bodice of my dress. He flips the cups of my bra down, exposing my breasts. His fingers are punishing on my nipples, twisting and pinching. He pulls out and slams into me as if he's trying to break me in two.

The breath leaves my lungs with every thrust. Tears leak from the corners of my eyes. I hold onto his shoulders as he pivots his hips with a furious tempo, eradicating any earlier softness. It's animalistic and carnal. It's us. I was stupid to think it could ever be different. Stupid to want things I can never have. I should've known better, but now it's too late.

I climax with a raw cry, my body and heart falling apart as he rips his cock from me and comes over my breasts. His breathing is ragged and his expression wild. The birth control is long since effective, but he's still using a condom. And now, he didn't come inside me.

Shame surges through me. He humiliated me. On purpose. Another lesson. He'll never have feelings for me. I can blame it all on him, but I've also humiliated myself by opening up to him. The pain is brilliant. It slices me up with cruel, precise cuts. I can't stand for him to see me like this—something used and discarded. Gripping the shredded fabric of my dress, I cover my breasts.

"Zoe."

I lift my gaze to his. For the first time since I've known him, he's at a loss for words. Whatever is going through his mind, I don't want to hear it.

"Please," I say, "don't say anything."

Indecision plays over his features as he scans my face. Then he leans in and kisses me. The kiss is violent. I make a protesting sound, trying to turn my head away, but he catches my face in his hand. His fingers hurt my jaw. His teeth cut my tongue. I relent, going slack in his hold. At least like this, we don't have to talk.

He only lets me breathe when stars explode behind my eyes. I can't meet his gaze any longer. I'm looking at the sun from over his shoulder, letting the bright rays blind me.

"I'm sorry," he says, sitting up with his knees straddling my hips.

I laugh. "For what?"

"For spoiling your moment. I shouldn't have taken over."

I shrug, sinking a little deeper into the sand. "It wasn't my moment."

Tilting his head toward the sky, he scrubs a hand over his face. He opens his mouth, closes it again, and finally says, "If it's any consolation, I've never said sorry to anyone before."

"Okay." I close my eyes, seeing red spots from the sun.

I could be on an island, a castaway, trying to survive alone. It'll be an exciting game, a loveless dream in which to escape, but dreaming is no longer my escape. I think I've lost the ability altogether.

His sigh caresses my ears. I open my eyes when he buttons his jacket up over my torn dress and adjust his clothes. Getting to his feet, he offers me a hand.

I don't accept it. I stand on my own.

I did something despicable. I fell for my kidnapper in a yearning need for affection. I opened my heart, and I did it willingly. I exposed myself to his rejection and took it like a punch in the chest.

I may have lost this bet, but I'm still standing.

From now on, it's me on my own.

CHAPTER 3

Maxime

Zoe wants love. I'll give her anything in my power, except for letting her go, but love is the one thing I can't give. I'm not capable of loving. I care for her more than anyone. She makes me terrified that anything should happen to her, for fuck's sake. I've long since dissected my fear and categorized it. I fear because I care. I've accepted it. But love? That's a step I don't know how to take.

I stole her because I wanted her hope. I wanted her secrets. I thought if I could figure out how she could survive her dysfunctional family in her disadvantaged neighborhood and still shine like a light in the dark, maybe so could I. I took her for purely selfish reasons, because I saw her as my ticket to happiness. My little experiment, but then, she became my own little wildflower in a vase, and I no longer wanted to let her go.

Of course, keeping her here is detrimental to our plan to guarantee her brother supplies us with diamonds when he takes back his mine. To my family, she's our pawn. To me, that's just a bonus. I promised my father I'd make sure she'd want to stay. I've planned everything so carefully, how I was going to make her happy. I gave her every clue she scattered around in her apartment that pointed to a dream—the trip to Venice, more pretty clothes than she can ever need, and a place in an elitist fashion design school. Yet I've forgotten about this crucial little detail. Love. Love features so lowly in my spectrum of feelings, I sometimes forget it exists. What did I expect? Of course, Zoe wants love. She's a romantic. A dreamer. Above all, she deserves love. Maybe if she learns to love me she can love enough for the both of us.

My thoughts are dark as I head to my father's office in the morning. I'm berating myself for my slipup, for overlooking such an important factor in my shrewd plan to keep her. One thing is for sure. I'm not planning on sending her back to her brother. Ever.

She's mine.

Mulling over this new development, I walk into the office. My father is already behind his desk, even if it's earlier than his usual arrival time. Alexis stands by the coffee machine. He doesn't look at me as I enter, but the paper cup dents in his hand. We don't speak about what happened in the warehouse. I practically left him and his buddy for dead. It took him more than a couple of weeks to recover. I have no idea if his buddy survived. All I know is he's no longer around. He's either six feet under or he bailed. My father knows about the lashing, but not about the rest. I left the details up to Alexis to share, and it seems he's too proud to let anyone else know his fat friend came twice in his ass. He hasn't touched a prostitute since. Point taken. Lesson learned. I'd say the unfortunate event was successful. I grin as I pour my coffee, taking pleasure from how Alexis's jaw snaps tighter.

The toilet in the adjoining bathroom flushes. The door opens, and Leonardo steps out. I tense. What the fuck is the Italian doing here? Since my father is watching me closely, I don my poker face.

"Max." Leonardo walks over, his eyes scanning my face like a shark. "How are you? We don't see much of you in the club."

I raise a brow. "I didn't know you were frequenting the club."

"I've been over on a few weekends." He rolls his shoulders. "You know, to get a feel for the territory."

"So you've said." Sitting down, I leave my coffee on the desk and steep my fingers together.

"We have a situation." My father indicates the free chairs facing his desk.

Leonardo and Alexis each takes a seat.

"The *Brise de Mer* is sending more men to Marseille," my father continues. "Their number has doubled in one week."

I tap my fingers on the desk. "Under what guise?"

My father's voice is gravelly, a sign of his irritation. "An annual gathering."

Alexis moves to the edge of his seat. "Let me take out a few of those Corsican fuckers. That should send a message."

"No," I say. My brother has always been too bloodthirsty, just like my father. "That'll start a war."

"Maybe that's what they want," Leonardo says.

My reply is sharp. "Then they can start it. We'll fight, and we'll win, but we sure as hell won't take responsibility for a bloodbath." That'll put us in the bad books of our government supporters. As long as we play by the rules, no one will blame us for defending ourselves.

"What do you suggest?" Alexis asks. "That we sit on our asses and do fucking nothing while they invade our territory?"

I give him an easy smile that only infuriates him more. "That we give them the benefit of the doubt."

My father's chair protests with a squeak as he leans back. "It's too soon to make a move, but I want our men to keep tight tabs on these motherfuckers. There's no way they're taking back Marseille."

"We've kicked them out once," Leonardo says. "We'll kick them out again."

The *we* grates on my nerves. The young fuck is already taking credit for a history that has nothing to do with him, for blood that never soiled his hands. I, however, know why my father wants him here. We're using the legal money from our diamond business to sponsor the illegal activities, and we're constantly looking for new ways of laundering that money.

The second reason why my father wants him here is the real thorn in my side. It's not a done deal yet, but soon I'll have to take Leonardo under my wing and treat him like a protégé. One, I work alone, even if I still answer partially to my father, and two, Leonardo is clever. He's already seen what's important to me. He's ambitious. He's not going to be content with tagging along in my shadow forever. At some stage, he's going to want to climb the ladder, and he'll use any weakness he can exploit against me. Meaning Zoe, the beautiful woman I can't let go.

"Agreed." My father slams a hand on the desk to indicate the meeting is over.

When Alexis and Leonardo get to their feet, he motions for me to stay. Alexis shoots me a hateful glare on the way to the door. I catch the way he locks eyes with my father before he leaves. I often think Raphael is disappointed that I'm the first-born who inherited the power instead of his favorite son.

My father waits until the door closes before speaking. "You haven't been home for months."

"I've been busy."

His fixes me with his droopy-eye stare. "Your mother misses you."

"She could come over."

His hand curls into a fist on the table. "She won't as long as you're keeping that woman in your house."

"Her name is Zoe."

He clenches his jaw. "I know what her name is."

I lean forward. "Then use it."

His smile is slow to come, his patience forced. "Family comes first."

"Yes, a point you're proving well."

He narrows his eyes. "You better watch your tone with me, son."

My smile matches his. "No disrespect intended. Just stating the facts."

"You've taken this game far enough."

One by one, my muscles lock. "What's that supposed to mean?"

"She compromises everything—the Italian connection, our family. It will be in everyone's best interest to hand her over to Alexis as agreed. He's learned his lesson. He won't make such a mistake again."

The last part makes my body coil like a predator preparing for an attack. My voice is even, betraying nothing of the fury running under the surface. "I won't let her come between business or the family. It's working fine as it is." This discussion is over. To prove it, I get up. "Anything else?"

"No." My father's tone is cold. "Not for now." As I turn, he says, "Go visit your mother." I'm already across the floor when he calls after me, "You're breaking her heart."

I slam the door on my way out. It's true that I've been avoiding my parents' home after the way the women treated Zoe, but I'm not insensitive to their point of view. I know it's hard for Maman. I'm not behaving like the good, Catholic son she raised. In her eyes, I'm acting more like my father.

When I've done the round at the docks and poured over the books, I head out to the house of my childhood. It's been more or less a happy childhood, with Maman always fussing over me and Father being absent for most of my younger years. It's only when I entered high school that he started involving me in the business, trying to forge a bond that was never there to start from the beginning. In a way, he resented me for how Maman babied me, and Maman lavished me with attention because she had no one else.

I park out front and go through the house. The housekeeper—a new girl whose name I can never remember—tells me Maman is out back. I find her in a deckchair on the terrace with a book.

She puts the book aside when she sees me. "Max."

I bend down to kiss her cheeks. "How are you?"

She waves a hand. "As you can see."

I sit down in the chair. It's not her fault that she's lonely. She has always looked out for me. I shouldn't forget that. "I've been busy."

Her mouth puckers. "Too busy for your family?"

"You know why I didn't come."

"Because you can't bring *her*?"

I sigh. "She was a guest, Maman. I expected better from you."

"You thought it was all right to flaunt your lover around for all your family to see, to gloat over, gossip about, and point fingers at me?"

"Why would anyone point fingers at you?"

She sits up straighter. "For failing in my job to raise you well."

"This has nothing to do with raising me well."

Her voice takes on a pleading tone. "Max, what you're doing isn't right."

"Maman, stop it. We've been through this."

She falls back against the cushions. "I never thought I'd say this, but you're your father's son, after all."

I smile. "Emotional blackmail won't work with me. You can drop the act."

She takes my hand. "If you must, then do it, but get her out of your system and fast. This can't end well for either of you."

Squeezing her fingers, I stand. I owe my mother much, but Zoe isn't negotiable. "I'm sure you'll like her if you give her a chance."

Her expression is pained. "How can you even expect such a thing from me? My loyalty is with the family. *Our* family."

She's right, of course. What I've been asking is impossible. "I'm sorry for putting you in a difficult position. It was selfish of me."

Her face softens. "Get this girl out of your system and send her home."

My smile is grim. If only it was that simple.

"Come over for lunch on Sunday. I'll invite your cousins."

I hesitate. A few months ago, I never would've declined a family lunch. Now I can't make peace with leaving Zoe on her own. It wouldn't be fair to her, either. "We'll see."

My mother's face falls.

Kissing her forehead, I say goodbye and break every speed limit to get home to my mistress as my mother's words repeat in my head. I can no longer deny that I'm gambling with both of our futures—Zoe's and mine. But where there's a will there's a way, and if anyone has a will where she's concerned, it's me.

CHAPTER 4

Zoe

After Maxime's rejection that day on the beach, he becomes even more invested in me. He's making up for the affection he can't give with lavish attention. We visit the theatre and swim in the cove when spring turns to summer. Sometimes, he reads to me in the garden on a picnic blanket with his head resting in my lap. He rubs my body with suntan lotion, worried my pale skin will burn, and helps me with my French exercises. I still do them, even if I've passed my exam. I like keeping my mind busy.

My body is constantly sore from being used, the ache between my legs never preventing me from wanting him. He's all I have. Sometimes I think this can be enough, but sometimes, when I sit alone with a book in the tower, I long for someone to love me, someone to need me for more than my body. The more attention Maxime lavishes on me, the more my insecurity grows. Beauty is a feeble currency. It doesn't last forever. Bodies grow old. How long before he goes hunting for the next woman, someone younger and fresher, someone less used than me?

The day will come when he'll discard me—four years, give or take, from now—and by then there will be nothing left of my soul. He would've devoured it all. Everyday, I'm losing a little more of myself to him. The hole in my heart, the one I've cut myself with my stupid yearning for love, is tearing wider with each passing day. I can't stop it. I can't help the feelings filtering in, the treacherous loving Maxime only feeds with his twisted kindness and devotion.

The summers here are as unforgiving as the wet winters with its icy winds. It gets so hot most days I feel wilted, but the old house is fresh inside and sometimes there's a breeze from the sea that cools the air down. On those days, we have dinner prepared by a grumpy Francine on the terrace.

I work hard on my designs during summer and have a collection ready when the school submissions open in July. I'm nervous until August, much to Maxime's amusement, who says he finds my enthusiasm endearing. When the results finally come, Maxime calls me downstairs for dinner. The table in the garden under the old pine tree is set with a white tablecloth and a silver candelabra. It's a windless evening with no breeze to blow out the candles.

I eye the crystal flutes and the champagne in the ice bucket. "What's going on?"

"We have something to celebrate."

My chest expands. My cheeks heat in a rush of excitement. "We do?"

He pours two glasses and offers me one. "Congratulations."

I clutch the stem so hard I fear it may snap. "Really? I'm in?"

"I told you." He kisses my lips. "I never had a doubt."

"Oh, my God." I slam a hand over my mouth. "I can't believe it."

"To you," he says, raising his glass.

I watch him from under my lashes. "Thank you."

His voice turns husky. "Don't look at me like that."

"Like how?" I bite my lip.

The cold color of his eyes darkens to a stormy gray. "Like you want it rough."

He knows I do. I've never asked again, nor taken, not after the beach, but he's good at reading my body language. He's a master at predicting my needs.

Taking the glass from my hand, he places it with his on the table. Drops of condensation run in rivulets over the two glasses that stand side by side in the setting sun.

"Everyone out," he barks out in French.

The guards scatter, disappearing to wherever. For a rare moment we're alone in the garden and our exchange unobserved.

"Francine can—" I was going to say come out any minute, but Maxime has already fastened his hands around my waist and lifted me onto the table.

Impatiently, he pushes the candelabra away. His rugged features are heated and his concentration one-track minded as he sweeps his palms under my dress and up my inner thighs. I shiver when he reaches my sex. My underwear is already wet. Holding my eyes, he pushes the elastic aside and shoves three fingers inside. I like it when he's tender and gentle, but this is what I love. I love it when he doesn't prepare me, when the friction is unbearable and the stretch too much, when I can lose myself in the sensations and fall into the oblivion of ecstasy.

He rests his thumb on my clit and curls his fingers inside. He doesn't play with my clit. He just keeps his touch there. It drives me insane. I need more. He knows. Bracing my body with a palm on my lower back, he brings his lips to my nipple. When he sucks it through the fabric of my bra and dress, I arch against him, shamelessly surrendering to the pleasure he offers. I moan as he grazes the hard tip with his teeth. My nipples are sensitive. Just sucking on them is enough to bring me close to orgasm. He knows my body inside out. He knows what makes me beg and scream.

I know what he likes too. I cup his length while he twirls a tongue around my nipple, teasing me through too many layers of clothes.

When I squeeze, he leans into my palm. My favorite way of feeling him is outlining the shape of the broad head with a finger. The light caress drives him crazy. With a growl, he rips his fingers from my body and brushes my hand away to center his cock between my legs. His hard length rubs over my clit, pushing the wet fabric of my panties over the bundle of nerves, but it's not the silk I want to feel on my skin.

Digging my hands into the lapels of his jacket, I pull him to my mouth and take the kiss I want. He never denies me. He kisses me back with abandon and skill, making my body melt against his as all my nerve endings hum in need. I reach for his belt, fumbling with the buckle. He rips away my underwear. I'm starving, moaning as I pull down his zipper and sighing into his mouth when I finally fold my fingers around his cock. I stroke twice before catching the pre-cum on the tip and letting it lubricate my palm. It's the firm downward slide of my hand that makes him lose control. His groan is guttural as he grabs my wrist and forces my upper body down. My free hand is in his hair, pulling at the silky strands, holding his lips to mine, but he easily catches that one too, pinning both wrists in one hand above my head. He grips the base of his cock and guides it to my entrance. I brace myself, but never enough.

When he enters me fully with a single thrust, my body shifts up the table. He fastens a hand on my hip to hold me in place, pulls almost all the way out, and slams back. My back arches from the intense stimulation. It's more than I can take, but I lift my hips when he lowers his, meeting every thrust.

"Goddamn, Zoe."

His eyes are glittering darkly, hard granite cut from a rocky cliff. The candlelight plays over his face, the shadows making the hollows of his cheekbones deeper and the harsh lines of his nose and jaw starker. I long to trace the bump on the bridge of his nose, but when I test his hold he doesn't let go.

Kissing a path up my neck, he presses feverish words against my ear. "Do you know how beautiful you are?"

I still. The words trigger my suppressed insecurity, things I shouldn't and don't want to think about, but I can't stop myself from saying, "Not forever."

He slows his pace and lifts his head to look at me. "You'll always be beautiful."

"Not when I'm old."

"Then as much as now."

"Don't lie to me."

The lines around his eyes tighten. "I'm not lying to you."

"Just withholding the truth?"

"You need to know what you must. That's enough."

"Then tell me honestly, when will you tire of me?"

He stills completely. His expression becomes veiled. "You don't want me to answer that."

My passion turns to rage. The embers of everything adrift in my chest have caught fire, and the fear I've been pushing away for the last few months jumps into flames of fury. "When the next woman you can abduct comes along?"

His jaw bunches. "I'm not interested in other women."

"Only in whatever the hell you want from Damian?"

"No, my flower." Despite his clipped tone, his voice is soft. "I like to see the world through your eyes."

The answer is not what I expected. "Why?"

"You're everything I'm not."

I'm not sure what that means. It's strange to have this argument with my wrists pinned above my head and his cock buried deep in my body. I don't even know why or how the fight started, only that I can't finish this.

I pull on his hold. "Let me go."

His nostrils flare. "You're five seconds from coming and you want me to let you go?"

"That's what I said."

His smile is one I both fear and hate, a cruel one. "As you wish."

I'm empty when he pulls out of me, so incredibly cold that I fold my arms around my stomach. He flicks my skirt up over my hips and takes his cock in his hand. It only takes a few pumps before he comes, ejaculating thick streams of cum over my sex and my thighs.

When he's finished, he takes a napkin and cleans himself. Dumping the crumpled napkin on the table, he adjusts his clothes. "It seems you'll be happier with your own company tonight. As it's supposed to be a celebration, I won't spoil it for you."

The venomous words are hardly out before he turns and walks back into the house. I cover myself with shaky hands, pulling my dress down over my sticky thighs. My legs are wobbly when I push off the table. The setting is in disarray with the tablecloth full of folds and the crockery pulled askew. It's the remains of a wasted evening, the bitter result when feelings get in the way.

Francine exits with a tray. She places a platter on the table, but I'm too distraught to pay attention.

"Dinner for one?" she asks with a chuckle.

I stare at her face. Since when has this turned into a war between us? I suppose since the minute I set foot into this house.

"You're an unthankful bitch," she says, straightening the tablecloth.

"Excuse me?"

"This house, Maxime's protection, the gifts...Do you know how lucky you are?"

"I didn't ask for any of this."

"Most women will give anything for what you have, but don't worry." She winks. "You won't have to live here forever."

"What's that supposed to mean?"

Tilting her head, she gives me a smug smile. "Enjoy your meal."

I stare at her back until she disappears through the kitchen door. A part of me wants to go after Maxime. Another part wants to never see him again. That part is a lie. No matter how much I hate this inequality between us—the fact that I can't express myself freely and am only treated kindly when I behave—it's too late for me. I've formed a bond with Maxime. The fact that it's forced doesn't make the attachment weaker. If anything, it's stronger. He made me dependent on him in every sense—materially, physically, and emotionally. There's nowhere else to turn to. There's only this house now, this beautiful place I both love and hate, and him. Love and hate. That's an accurate description for what we share.

Taking the bottle of champagne, I kick my sandals off and make my way down to the beach. The sun is setting when I flop down in the sand, letting the water wash over my feet. It must be just after nine. By now it'll be pitch black, dark in South Africa. It took me a while to get used to the longer days. Some days are just too damn long. Tipping back the bottle, I swallow a mouthful. The champagne is deliciously dry. I finish half the bottle before my spirit is gratifyingly numbed.

It's so hot out here. Even at this hour, it's still over thirty degrees Celsius. Pushing to my feet, I fumble with the zipper of my dress. I stumble a little as I step out of the dress and unclasp my bra. Oh, dear. I think my torn underwear is still lying somewhere under the table. I better pick it up before the poor gardener finds it.

The water is clear and cool. I walk in until it reaches my waist, flinching as the salt burns the abused skin between my legs. I take another swig of the champagne and make a face. Yuk. It's lukewarm now.

After downing what's left in one go, I fling the bottle out on the sand and wade deeper into the water until I can drift on my back. The lights of the house on the cliff are blurry in my view. It forms a hazy picture as I try to fit the puzzle pieces of tonight together, of what Maxime said. No, wait. What Francine said. Oh, crap. Whatever. I think I'm a little drunk.

I'm such an idiot.

"Why's that, my little flower?" a husky voice asks.

Maxime? He's not supposed to be here. He should be upstairs in his big house, ruling over cliffs and kingdoms of diamonds with his iron fist.

"For falling for you," I reply.

Strong arms fold around me from behind, pulling me against a hard body. An impressive erection presses against my back. "I didn't give you a choice."

My words slur a bit. "What are you doing?"

"Making sure you don't drown."

"No," I say, wiggling when he slips his cock between my legs. "I mean what are you *doing*?"

Big hands cup my hips. Soft lips press on my shoulder and a warm breath washes over my neck. "Shh. I'm just going to make you come."

The broad head of his cock rubs over my clit before dragging through my folds. I want to ask why. I want to make sense of it all but then that hardness presses against my forbidden opening. I go still.

"Relax." He breathes against my ear.

Even in my drunken state, I can feel his dark excitement in the way his fingers tighten on my hips. I can hear it in the raw note of his voice. It stokes my fire. I've only had a taste of it once, and it hurt. I'm not sure I'm going to like it.

"You will," he says. "I'll make sure."

I said that out loud? Oh, God. I'm a lot drunker than I thought.

A burning sensation explodes in my dark entrance as he pushes through the tight ring of muscle. I cry out, trying to scoot away, but his fingers are on my clit, rubbing the way I like.

"Wrap your legs around me," he says.

The pleasure makes me blindly obedient, just the way he always wants me. I open my legs wider and hook my ankles around his thighs. My toes brush over sand. He's sitting on his heels with my back against his chest. We're shallow. He must've steered us closer to the shore.

I let my head fall on his shoulder. The act pushes out my breasts. I'm spread open. My body is a sacrifice, every hole accessible for his use. One hand finds my breast, gently rolling my nipple, while the other plays with my clit. I suck in a breath when he pushes his cock deeper. He holds still, letting me adjust. It still hurts, but I don't want him to stop. I want him to push me to my limits. I want to fly over the edge.

As he pushes two fingers inside my pussy, his cock slips deeper into my asshole. He curls his fingers inside and rolls his thumb over my clit until I'm soft and pliant enough to take all of him. This is nothing like the night at the hotel. This is twisted lust, not punishment. It's dark, and scary, and strangely exhilarating. He groans when

I push back, a lustful sound that spurs me on. I lift higher and slide down over his length, focusing on the magic work of his fingers and how everything seems so full, stretched so tightly.

The pain is like a hot branding iron, but pleasure surfaces through the fire, sending mixed signals to my brain. I can't distinguish any longer. I can only feel the pleasure coiling around my insides, squeezing until my breath is gone.

"Breathe," he says, locking his fingers around the column of my neck.

I drag in a ragged breath, and then come so hard my teeth chatter. He doesn't let me go. He continues to massage my oversensitive clit, milking every ounce I have left until his cock grows even thicker and he yanks me to his body so hard I'll have bruises on my neck and hip tomorrow. He punches his hips up, even if he's already sheathed to the hilt. He thrusts twice more, grunting as he empties himself in my ass. It must be the singular most powerful orgasm of my life.

"You did beautifully," he whispers, "like I knew you would."

It burns when he pulls out. My body sags in his arms. He catches me around the shoulders and under my legs, holding me to his chest. Out of nowhere, right in the middle of my drunken state, the reason why I was so upset earlier hits me. I've fallen for him, and since he's incapable of returning my feelings I have no reassurance he won't replace me with someone else. Wait. Shouldn't I want him to replace me? Am I not supposed to want to get away? Isn't being his captive the reason for my anguish and unhappiness?

I don't know how I get back to the bedroom. Somewhere between the burn and gentle kisses I black out. My dream is weightless and painless, a place where broken hearts and bodies don't exist. Idle words float in and out on a moonlight breeze, words that bring both terror and salvation as they promise to never let me go.

CHAPTER 5

Zoe

There are nine girls in Madame Page's class at the Marseille-Mediterranean College of Art. Smelling of cigarette smoke, she's an elderly woman with red hair and overlarge, square-rimmed glasses.

A delicate girl with jet black hair and slanted eyes sits next to me.

"Hi," I say, taking my sketchpad from my satchel. "I'm Zoe."

She gives me a sidelong glance, then moves an inch toward her side of the drafting table. Lifting her chin, she says, "I'm Christine."

The woman on the other side of me snickers. She has dark brown hair and eyes, and freckles like mine. "I suppose you want to know my name, too," she says. "I'm Thérèse."

Madame Page walks into the center of the room. She's wearing a straight white dress with square pockets and black piping. It's a Saint Laurent number.

"Quiet, please. For your first lesson, I want to get a sense of each of your unique styles." She claps her hands together. "Quick now. Open your manual on module one."

I take out my notepad and pens while the others open the module on their laptops or tablets. Maxime won't allow me a laptop or tablet. I didn't even have the concession when I was studying French.

Madame Page pushes a printout titled Module One over the table without looking at me.

"Thank you," I say, accepting the stack of papers stapled together.

Going through the introductory module, Madame Page explains we'll start with the basics such as design principles, drawing, building form, textile science, business practices, and history, and work our way up to pattern creation. Practical design will only start in the second year for those who make it. A panel of independent judges will judge a design contest at the end of the second year, including compulsory evening wear and a wedding dress, to determine which scholars will make it to the third and final year. The competition is severe. Only six of us will be accepted into next year's level. She talks about perseverance and discipline before pointing out a few class rules. No eating and drinking. No chitchatting. No copycatting.

"I'm looking for a fresh perspective, for a unique style," she says. "Each of you shows potential." She locks eyes with Thérèse. "Thérèse, you have an eye for lines but you're lacking detail. In this class, we're going to work on your strengths and weaknesses." Skimming over me, she moves to Christine. "Christine, I love your dare, but there's a fine line between eccentric and flamboyance. Juliette, your simplicity is refreshing. I love how you play with color and texture. I'm looking forward to seeing more of your work."

One by one, she goes around the table, ignoring me. I shake it off. It was probably just an innocent oversight.

For the next hour, we make rough sketches and notes. Madame Page gathers the sketches and goes through our notes. She gives detailed feedback on each one with praise and critique, but she only glances at mine without making any comments.

My chest pulls tight as she places my pad back on the table. I flip the page back to find nothing written in red, not like on Thérèse and Christine's sketches.

"I bid you a good day, ladies," she says. "I'll see you tomorrow."

Taking my time to gather my stationary, I wait until everyone has left before approaching her worktable. "Madame Page?"

She looks up with a pinched expression. "Yes?"

"Is there a problem with my work?"

She goes back to what she was writing. "No."

I'm tempted to just leave, but this is too important to me. "I'm sorry, but I don't understand. Why didn't you critique my work?"

Her pencil makes a scratching sound as she pulls it over the paper. "You don't need my input, Mademoiselle Hart. You'll pass with flying colors."

The words don't elicit the warmth of pride in my chest. Instead, they leave me cold, a terrible notion making me shrivel. "You don't think I merit to be here, do you?"

"If that's all, I have work to do." She waves me off, not bothering to grace me with another glance.

Clutching my satchel under my arm, I make my way into the warm sunlight while coldness creeps over every inch of my skin. Maxime waits across the road, leaning on his fancy sports car. His eyes are trained on me, following my progress with undivided attention. Giving me this much freedom is a big deal for him, but I can't appreciate it. Not right now.

A few of the women from my class are gathered on the lawn in front of the building. They're looking my way, whispering as they too follow my progress toward the blue Bugatti.

I block them out. I block everything out. When Maxime kisses my lips, I can't help but pull back. He stills. The coldness I feel in my bones settles over his eyes, turning the gray to winter instead of molten skies.

"How was the first day?" he asks, his observation sharpening on me as he gets my door.

I don't bother to answer. There's a tick to his jaw, but I can't even bring myself to be scared. I just feel numb like on the night that was supposed to be a celebration when I drank myself into a stupor and spent the next day being sick. That sickness descends on me now, turning my stomach.

He says nothing as he starts the engine. The powerful hum of the motor is the only sound in my ears as he heads toward town.

When he doesn't take our exit, I snap out of my haze. "Where are we going?"

"To celebrate."

My stomach clenches. I dig my nails into my palms.

"We're having dinner in town." He glances at me. "There's an opening of a new casino."

"You have to be there," I say in a flat tone.

He changes gears and accelerates too abruptly. "Yes, but it'll still be a celebration."

I register his fancy suit and tie. "I'm not dressed for a party."

"I have a dress for you in the trunk."

I can't face one of his fancy affairs. Not today. "Maxime, please. I just want to go home."

His eyebrows pull together. "What's wrong?"

I'm suddenly so tired I sag in my seat. "I don't want to be your eye candy tonight."

His knuckles turn white on the gearstick. "Is it so terrible to be seen with me? Is that what was going on back there? You're happy enough for my money to pay for your classes, but you don't want your friends to know who's paying?"

They're not my friends. He made sure they'd never be. Rubbing a hand over my forehead, I say quietly, "They already know."

He brings the car to a screeching halt in front of a white building with a water fountain. Grabbing my jaw in his hand, he squeezes painfully. "You're mine, Zoe, for the whole fucking world to see. Is that clear enough, or is it time for another lesson?"

Tears gather in my eyes. I shake my head. "Please, Maxime. I can't do this. Not tonight. Just take me home."

He lets go, the momentum shoving me against the door. "You will go inside and get changed. You will wait for me in the room until I come and fetch you." His expression hardens. "How tonight turns out is up to you."

He gets out, comes around, and opens my door. Gautier and Benoit must've followed behind us. They get out of a Mercedes. Gautier takes a dry-cleaning and overnight bag from the trunk of Maxime's car. Benoit scans the entrance of the casino and steps aside for me to enter. I'm halfway across the pavement when Maxime catches my wrist.

"You forgot something." Yanking me against him, he cups my nape and kisses me.

The kiss is hot and intense, but I'm not in it.

Maxime tears his lips from mine and pushes me aside. "Make sure you're ready in an hour."

I walk on wooden legs to the door, following Gautier and Benoit through the lobby to an elevator. Gautier pushes the button for the top floor. Always the penthouse. He leaves the bags on the bed and checks the suite before locking me in.

I stand awkwardly in the middle of the floor, the lights of Marseille stretching out below like a bed of diamonds. The ache in my heart bleeds and grows. The shame and betrayal are like stains on my soul. I can almost forgive Maxime for making me fall in love with him. Almost. At least that wasn't intentional. It happened all on my part because I opened my stupid heart when I opened my body, but this I can never forgive.

Rushing to the telephone, I lift the earpiece and dial zero.

"Good evening, Miss Hart," a male voice says. "How may I assist you?"

"I'd like to make a local call, please." If I can reach the embassy, I can ask for help. "Can you connect me?"

He clears his throat. "Sorry, ma'am. No calls. Mr. Belshaw's instructions."

Of course. It was worth a try. "Thank you, anyway," I say before hanging up.

My gaze falls on the bottle of champagne cooling in the ice bucket, the cork already popped. I pour a glass, but stop before bringing it to my lips. I said I wouldn't become my father. Drowning my problems isn't going to help. I leave the glass on the table and unzip the bag on the bed. It's a pink dress—simply beautiful. Silk rose petals are sewn onto the skirt with teardrop crystals. I brush my fingers over the stretch velvet fabric, admiring the craftsmanship. The dress looks as if it's made from rose petals that are scattered with drops of dew. It must've taken hours to hand-sew the detail. It only intensifies the ache in my chest that Maxime should know my taste so well.

The overnight bag contains my toiletries and makeup. I shower, take my hair up like Maxime likes it, and apply a light coat of makeup before putting on the dress. It has a high neck and low back, the fabric kissing my breasts and legs. I haven't touched the new sewing machine yet. I wanted to focus on my sketches first. Now I'm not sure I can.

After fitting the strappy heels, I go out onto the balcony and let the breeze cool my skin as I inhale the fragrance of the night. Salt drifts in from the sea. It's mixed with the smell of industrial oil and grilled sausage wafting from the hotdog vendor on the street corner four stories below. It's the smell of night and the city, of potential and freedom. In Johannesburg, it was smoke and coal, fabric dye near the flea market, and leather coming from the shoe factory. Each city holds its own prison, a life I yearn to escape. Yet here I am, a prisoner of my own making, bound to the heart of a merciless man.

The door opens and closes. There's a silent pause. I imagine him crossing the floor on the soft carpet. A moment later, his heels fall hard on the balcony tiles.

He comes to a stop next to me. Citrus and cloves reach my nostrils, wiping the city and night away and its feeble promise of freedom.

"I have something for you." Taking my hand, Maxime turns me to face him. His gaze slips over me, evaluating my efforts. "You look beautiful."

We haven't laughed since the sewing machine. I was going to laugh with him tonight. I imagined us like this, at home, maybe on the beach, sharing a moment from my day. He'd pull me into his lap and make me tell him everything while listening attentively like he always does.

"You never tell me about your day," I say.

He drags his knuckles over my cheek. "You didn't drink the champagne I ordered for you."

"I've learned my own lesson."

He smiles. "One glass isn't going to hurt."

No, but it'll take the edge off, and I don't want to dull my senses tonight. I want to punish myself with the truth for being so repeatedly, stupidly naïve.

I don't know where the words come from. They're out before I can stop them. "You used me that night."

His look is amused. "The night you got drunk? You let me."

True.

Leaning closer, he brushes his lips over my neck. "You liked it."

I did.

"It's on the table," he says. "Go open your gift."

I don't want another one, but I don't have the energy to fight this war, too. I let him pull me back inside. A velvet box lies on the table. I flip the lid back to reveal a diamond choker. The stones are brilliant and beautifully set. It looks invaluable. It looks like a really expensive collar.

"Turn around," he says, lifting it from the velvet cushion.

I face the mirror, watching my reflection as he puts the choker around my neck and secures the clasp at the back. The woman who stares back at me isn't me. She's the woman who sold her body in exchange for a life and a reprieve from lessons, a woman who's just accepted another magnificent token of ownership.

Cupping my hips, he meets my eyes in the glass. "You're so perfect it hurts to look at you."

Yes, it hurts. I turn away from the picture, condemning it to the place where I lock away all my painful memories.

He takes my hand and kisses my fingers. "Every eye will be on you tonight."

When he puts my hand on his arm, I don't protest. I follow him out in the hallway and into the elevator. We exit on the first floor. The ballroom is already buzzing with people. I'm relieved it's a seated dinner and not a cocktail, which means I don't have to follow like a puppy while Maxime mingles. I can sit down and drift away while the speeches drone on.

A hostess shows us to our table. The hall fills up even more. Maxime pours me a glass of water. It seems the couple who were seated with us didn't show up, because when the speeches finally start, we're alone at our table.

Maxime drapes an arm around the back of my chair. He drags his fingers over my shoulder and along the curve of my neck to my nape where his thumb traces the choker before brushing over a vertebra.

Leaning over, he whispers in my ear, "Talk to me, Zoe."

I look at him. He wants to talk here? Now?

"You're upset," he says in a low voice. "Tell me. I'll make it right."

"You can't make it right," I whisper back.

"Try me."

Tears burn behind my eyes again. "I never entered that school on my own merit, did I?"

He stiffens. "Who told you?"

"No one. It wasn't that hard to figure out."

Anger sweeps over his features. "If you're being treated unfairly just because—"

"No." I don't want trouble for Madame Page. It's bad enough he forced my way in with his powerful family connections. "How did you do it? Did you donate a ridiculous amount of money to the school?"

His lips tighten. "No one says no to me, not in this city."

"I see." I look away so he won't see the tears I can't contain.

Gripping my chin, he turns my face back to him. "Is it so bad that I want to make you happy?"

"Yes, Maxime. This is bad. This is really bad."

"Why?" he asks though clenched teeth.

"You made me believe I *earned* it."

"You did," he says with conviction.

"That's not for you to decide. You're not a fashion design expert. It was up to the board and Madame Page."

He looks confused. "I thought you'd be happy."

"I *was* happy until I found out it's a lie."

Gripping my hand hard under the table, he says, "I pulled a lot of strings to make this happen for you, so you're going to swallow your pride and be a good girl and go to school and do what you love. It's that simple."

"You'd think it is."

"If you're implying I don't care, you're damn right. I don't give a damn what *Madame* or your classmates think. You shouldn't either."

I guess that's the difference between us, and the crux of the problem. He doesn't give a damn. Unfortunately, I do.

"No more talking about this," he says, bringing my hand to his lips and kissing my knuckles.

I breathe in deeply to abate my tears and put a stopper on my emotions. I can't give the people around us the satisfaction of witnessing my distress. It's too personal. Too vulnerable.

I eat as much as I can stomach, feeling raw inside. Feeling cheated. What else is Maxime hiding from me? I'm peeling away these layers of truth one at a time, and I'm scared of what I'll find at the core. I'm so tired of floating in the dark and drowning in his secrets.

It's after midnight when the dinner is finally over and Maxime has greeted everyone he wanted to. Networking is important.

"I know you're tired," he says, placing a palm on my lower back. "We can sleep here if you like."

"If you don't mind, I prefer to go home."

Home. It's not the first time I've said it tonight, but we both pause when the word leaves my lips. Maxime is kind enough not to make a big deal out of it, even as more of the possessive satisfaction I've come to recognize washes over his face. He tells Gautier to fetch my overnight bag from upstairs and ask at reception for a valet to bring his car around.

The same questions as always repeat through my mind when he escorts me outside. Why is Maxime keeping me here? I know it has something to do with the diamonds from the questions he posed before kidnapping me, but why is he holding Damian's life over my head? I'm distracted, but simultaneously hyperaware of the warm night and how the heat seems to lift for a brief reprieve even as Maxime's broad palm burns hot on the exposed skin of my back. Benoit and Gautier move ahead of us, Gautier carrying my overnight bag. The valet rounds the corner with Maxime's Bugatti. The Mercedes in which the guards came is parked across the street.

A black car with tinted windows rolls slowly down the road. The back window lowers when they're almost next to us. It must be someone Maxime knows, maybe someone from the party who wants to call out a last goodbye. I look at Maxime to catch his attention. He's slowed down beside me, staring at the car with a strange expression.

"Get down," Maxime yells at the same time as a string of shots blast through the air.

He throws his body in front of mine, taking me down to the pavement as the glass door of the casino explodes behind us. I hit the concrete with a thud, his arms cushioning the fall but my head taking a knock that makes my teeth clatter. My elbows and hip burn. My bones are crushed against the hard surface by Maxime's weight.

Another round of shots go off. People scream. The couple who exited behind us scurry for the casino lobby. My cheek is pressed to the pavement. The concrete is rough and warm against my skin. It smells of dust and car exhaust. I register everything as the black car speeds off.

Someone shot at us.

"Maxime!" I push on his shoulders. Oh, my God! Is he hurt?

His eyes are the color of pale marble, cold and hard, when he lifts his weight and drags his hands over my body in clinical, examining strokes. He's calm. Collected. Only his voice is urgent. "Are you hurt? Have you been shot, Zoe?"

"I'm fine."

"Fuck." He gets up and helps me to my feet.

Benoit is waving a gun. Gautier is lying in the gutter.

What? No! I slam a hand over my mouth.

Maxime bends down and presses two fingers on the jugular vein in Gautier's neck. His face hardens. "Follow them," he says to Benoit.

Benoit runs for the Mercedes.

"Get in the car, Zoe," Maxime says.

I'm aware of him touching my arm, dragging me a little, but I can't focus on anything other than the blood oozing from Gautier's temple. I can't look away from his open eyes and the way the light is missing from their depths.

"Zoe." Maxime's fingers dig into my upper arms. My teeth clack together as he shakes me. "I need you to keep it together. Can you do that for me, *cherie?*"

He turns me toward the Bugatti. The valet stands on the pavement with a stunned expression. I somehow manage to fold my stiff body double and get into the passenger seat when Maxime opens the door for me. He gets in and secures my safety belt, then his own.

Not looking back, he pulls off with screeching tires. We're driving too fast. It makes me nervous, especially with the narrow road and the steep abyss dropping into the sea. I grip the door handle as he dials Raphael on voice command.

"We have a situation at the casino," Maxime says when his father replies. "Gautier is down."

Raphael's voice is tight. "Motherfucking damn."

"I'm dealing with it. I'll keep you posted."

Maxime switches over to another call, telling someone he needs cleanup. Another call demands backup, the next puts the guards at the house on alert, and the last instructs his lawyer to take care of the police. By the time we arrive home, Maxime seems to have everything, including himself, under control.

It's only me who's shaking, unable to process what's happened.

He comes around and helps me from the car. The front garden is swarming with guards. Two stand at the door. Another waits inside.

"Guard her with your life," Maxime says.

"Yes, sir."

Maxime makes his way with long strides to the room he always keeps locked.

I run after him. "Maxime, wait!"

He takes a key from his pocket, unlocks the door, and pushes it open. Reflexively, I remain on the threshold when he hurries inside. It's an instinctive reaction to knowing he doesn't want me in there. There's a big desk against the window and photos on the walls. It looks like a study. He opens a tall safe in a corner cabinet and removes a gun that he pushes into his waistband.

"Maxime, please. What are—?"

The automatic rifle he takes out next makes my words dry up.

Without giving me another look, he locks the door and walks from the house.

I stand in the foyer, staring at the front door he slammed behind him, hearing the echo bouncing off the emptiness.

The guard catches my eyes. "Maybe you should have a drink," he says in a strong voice. "And a hot shower."

I rest a palm against the wall. My body is shaking with cold chills. The lie whispers past my lips. "I'm fine."

I want to be, but I'm not. Gautier is dead. Someone tried to kill Maxime in the middle of the street, right there in the open. That's not normal. That's not a simple drawback of being part of a rich and powerful family. That's not taking the law into your own hands to punish your brother. That's the truth. That's the little worm that's been niggling its way into my brain, the one I've been trying so hard to ignore.

Making my way to the stairs, I grip the balustrade. My back is straight for the sake of the guard who's still watching. He can't see my shaky knees as I make my way to Maxime's bedroom. I stop in front of the mirror. The beautiful dress is torn. My arms are scraped and dirty. My hair is a mess. My face doesn't look much better.

I function on autopilot. I strip, shower, disinfect the scrapes, and put ointment on the bruise on my hip where I hit the concrete. I dress in a T-shirt and soft cotton shorts, and go down to the kitchen to make a pot of tea. I carry it to the bedroom and install myself there, waiting for Maxime to return, telling myself it's my future I'm worried about and not his life.

CHAPTER 6

Maxime

Benoit followed the motherfuckers to a house near the hill. I park a distance away and gather my men around me. The backup arrived a few minutes before me.

"Whoever pulled the trigger," I say, "is mine."

They nod.

"How many?" I ask Benoit.

"Three guys got out of the car and entered the house. The curtains are pulled, but the light came on downstairs. The only other movement is on the first floor, second window to the left."

I cock my gun. "Let's go."

We creep along the shadows, staying low behind the bushes. The front door opens on the street. I motion for Benoit to go around the back. He returns promptly, giving me the all clear.

Gun pointed in front of me, I stand back for one of the men to kick down the door. I'm inside before the three motherfuckers on the couch can blink. Four of my men rush up the stairs.

"Put your hands on the table," I say, circling the three idiots.

The one on the left is the last to comply. He holds my eyes with defiance, his lip curled up in a mocking smile. It's him I choose. I've always loved a challenge.

"Tie these two up," I say to Benoit, motioning at the other two.

"With pleasure, sir," he replies with cold hatred just as my guards drag a man, dressed in black combat gear with his arms tied behind his back, down the stairs.

"Anyone else?" I ask.

"No, sir," one of my men says. "We've searched upstairs."

The other guards return from the kitchen. "No one else downstairs, sir."

Benoit binds the arms of the men on the couch. Except for the cocky one. Him, I push into a chair.

"Secure his feet and hands," I say.

My men work fast. They tie him to the chair and use more rope to bind his wrists to the armrests and his ankles to the legs of the chair.

"Who pulled the trigger?" I ask.

One of the fuckers glances at his friend tied up in the chair.

"I did." The guy in the chair spits at my feet.

I nod at Benoit. "Take the others to the warehouse. They're yours."

He gives me a look of appreciation. It's only fair that he gets to torture and kill them. Gautier was the closest thing he had to a brother.

Half of my men go with Benoit. The other half stay with me.

"You know how this works," I say, standing in front of the man who looks at me like I'm the one doing him the injustice. "Are you going to talk, or must I do my magic first?"

"Fuck you," he says with a grin.

I smile. Good. "I was hoping you'd say that." Taking my gun from my waistband, I aim at his hand.

One of my men shoves a dishcloth in his mouth. He clams his jaw shut on the fabric and clutches the armrest. I shoot off his trigger finger.

The silencer dampens the sound, but he screams like a baby behind the bundle of fabric.

"Who sent you?" I ask.

He's dragging in air through his nose, trying to breathe through the pain. The look he gives me when he can finally focus again says *fuck you*.

I shoot off his thumb. Flesh and splintered bone hang from the knuckle by shreds of skin.

He bleeds like a pig and cries like a pussy. I'd ice the stumps to stop him from bleeding out and shoot off every motherfucking finger and toe until he gives me the answers I want, but I don't have that much time. Zoe is home. Alone. I need to get back to her.

Pushing the gun on his left nut, I ask, "Who sent you?"

He mumbles behind the cloth. My man removes it.

He gulps in air, spit and gob mixing with his words. "*Brise de Mer*."

This idiot isn't part of their family. He's a paid man. If this is about territory, why didn't they come after me themselves? I dig the barrel into his balls. "Why?"

"To take out the girl," he slobbers.

I go still. Every molecule in my body freezes in rage. I know exactly which girl. There's only one girl. There will only ever be one. Still, I grind out the question as atomic violence builds in my veins. "Which woman?"

He looks at me with pain-laced eyes. "*Your* woman. Zoe Hart."

The woman I've paraded for the world to see. The woman I've made a target by showing everyone how much she means to me. My cousin, Jerome, warned me the night I paid a million euros for her in the charity auction, but I was too dead set on showing everyone she belonged to me to care.

I move the barrel down his scrotum and wiggle it under his butt until it rests snugly over his asshole. "Why?"

"Because she's your weakness," he says on a rush, trying to lift his filthy ass away from the gun.

"You thought killing her would weaken me," I say with a cold laugh.

Sweat beads on his face. "Yes."

Fucking wrong. It would've crushed me. "Why are they targeting me?" They should've targeted my father if they wanted the organization to crumble.

"You're the backbone of the family."

I'm the brain. My father is a loose cannon, getting more unstable in his business decisions by the day. The only one who keeps him in line is me. They were hoping on avoiding a war and taking over by weakening the pillar that's keeping the house of cards from toppling.

Gripping his hair in my free hand, I pull back his head. "Who paid you?"

"Stefanu Mariani."

The Corsican underboss. I grin. "That wasn't so difficult now, was it?" I stare into the eyes of the man who was going to snuff out Zoe's life. "Tell me something, how did it feel to pull that trigger?"

He blinks. "What?"

"When you aimed at my woman, how did it feel?"

I relive the moment in stark fucking monstrous detail, the moment I realized they were going to shoot, the moment I felt nothing, not for me or my family or the business, but only for the woman at my side. The moment my heart beat only for her. The moment Gautier threw his body in front of us and took the bullets, three. One in the chest, one in the stomach, and one in the head.

"What's your name?" I ask.

"Dominic."

"What did you feel, Dominic?"

He frowns, incomprehension marring his ugly features. "Nothing."

Wrong fucking answer.

I pull the trigger.

CHAPTER 7

Maxime

On the way home, I call my father. What happened calls for retaliation. The Corsicans need to be shown who runs this city. No one puts a hit on my woman and lives to see daylight.

"You erred," my father says when I've filled him in. "Alexis had reason. We should've wiped out those Corsican bastards the minute they landed on our shore."

I hate to admit for once he's right. I gave them the benefit of the doubt because the Belshaws don't start wars. However, taking a hit at my woman is a fucking cowardice, honorless move, and it just started a genocide.

My fingers curl around the gearstick, my nails cutting into the leather. "I'm taking them all out."

"I'm calling in the Italians."

"I don't need the fucking Italians."

My father's voice rises. "We need them now more than ever. This is exactly why we secured the deal."

"I'll do my own cleanup in my backyard, thank you fucking very much."

"Son." My father sighs. "You can't pretend it's not happening forever."

I clench my jaw. "I'm not pretending."

"Is that why you're avoiding Leonardo?"

I shift gears so violently the gearbox screeches. "I'm not avoiding him. I'm just not in the mood for dragging a tail along."

"I know why you're doing it."

"Do *not* say her name to me. Not now." I'm too explosive.

Wisely, my father keeps his mouth shut.

"I'll let you know when it's done," I say before ending the call.

My father will summon more men and make sure their house is protected. He'll warn Alexis and do what he must. I dial our most effective muscle, one of the men I sent to torture the other motherfucker mercenaries. By now he should have the information I want.

"Where are the Corsicans?" I ask when he answers.

"Meeting as we speak."

Probably weaponing up, knowing their murder attempt failed and we're coming after them.

"They're gathered in a warehouse in the industrial area."

"Blow it up."

"Yes, sir."

By sunrise, no *Brise de Mer* will be left in our territory. Our message will have been delivered. Crystal fucking clear.

My first stop is at Gautier's mother's house. She's a widow, living alone. Fuck. He was her only child, but he knew the risks. He took the bullets knowing she'd want for nothing. We take care of our own, especially of the relatives of those who sacrifice their lives.

I ring the bell.

Her face crumples when she opens the door and sees my face. She knows what this visit means.

"I'm sorry." I grip her shoulder. "He died bravely."

"How?" she asks, her wrinkled eyes dry but sorrow drifting in their depths.

"Drive-by shooting. The men who did this paid. They died slowly."

Her body wilts under my hold, her shoulders folding inward and her spine curling.

I squeeze gently. "Do you have someone to call? Someone who can be with you?"

She nods.

I hand her my card. "You call me. For anything. Any time. Night or day."

She shuts the door.

I leave her to her grieving. There's not much else I can do. Nothing to make it better. Not even time erases this pain.

I get back into the car and make sure I'm not tailed. Driving like a maniac, I head toward Cassis. I only realize how cold I am when I park at the house. I'm eager to go inside, to see Zoe, but I check in with the guards and schedule a shift to make sure everyone remains vigilant before checking the perimeter alarms. Only then do I allow myself to enter and face the fact that I could've lost her tonight. That I most certainly—gladly—would've taken the bullets meant for her if Gautier hadn't.

I shut the door softly. If she's sleeping, I don't want to wake her. I shrug out of my jacket and dump it on the chair in the entrance. I'm halfway across the foyer when she comes down the stairs. Stopping in my tracks, I drink her in as she approaches. She's showered and clean, dressed in a loose T-shirt and a pair of shorts, and I'm pathetically grateful. I don't know how wild my emotions would've run if I'd seen her in her tattered dress and dirt-streaked face.

"You all right?" I ask when she stops in front of me. My vocal cords are tight. They feel unused.

She places her hands on my chest. "You?"

I cup her palms, let her warmth sink into my cold skin. "Yes."

"What happened?" she whispers.

I want to kiss her. I want to fuck her. I want to just hold her. Instead, I let her go. If I touch her in any way, I'll go overboard. I may say things, things I can't mean. Instead, I walk to the library and sink down in the chair behind the desk.

She follows quietly, her bare feet not making a sound on the Turkish carpets. At the liquor tray, she pours a whiskey the way I like and carries the glass to me. Our fingers brush when I take it.

"Thank you," I say, my words laced with surprise at the act of kindness when I deserve nothing of the kind.

She stands in front of the desk, her pretty face so pale I can count every freckle on her nose. "Is he…?" She swallows. "Gautier. Is he—?"

"Dead."

She flinches. Tears blur the blue of her eyes. "I'm so sorry, Maxime."

I take a swallow of the drink. The burn is good. It loosens up my voice, making it easier to speak. "So am I, but not as much as his poor mother."

"Where were you?"

"You shouldn't have waited up. It's late."

"You think I can sleep?"

I hand her the glass.

She turns it and places her lips on the exact spot where the glass touched mine before drinking, then puts it back in my hand. It's become our game. "Were you at the police station, giving a statement?"

I look at her. She says it flatly, her back straight. She doesn't believe it. I bet her question is just one of a long list she's rehearsed to flush out the truth.

"No," I say.

"I heard what you told Benoit about following that car. Did you go after him, the man who killed Gautier?"

"Yes."

Her chest rises with a breath. Her posture is brave, but her hands are shaking. She can't hide the turmoil in her eyes. "Did you kill him?"

I look straight into those pretty baby blues. "Them. I killed *them*."

If at all possible, she goes even whiter. "What are you, Maxime?"

My smile is wry. "A man."

I've never been more of a man since the day I met her. She made me a man who reacts to a woman in the most primal of ways. She made me a man with a weakness, a man with chest full of fear. Most of all, I'm just a man of flesh and blood, a man who wants to live to protect the person he cares about the most in the world.

Zoe plants her palms on the desk, facing me with all forty-six kilos of her feistiness. Her words are measured, each one articulated. "What are you, Maxime? Mafia?" She spits out the word like it's poison.

"You know what I am."

She slams a palm down in front of me. "Say it."

Her anger only makes me smile broader. It's the irony of being caught in a trap I designed for her. It's the knowledge that this little flower has slain me. "Yes, I'm mafia, but you knew that all along."

Fire dances along the tears in her brilliant eyes. "I did *not*."

This changes anything? She thinks I'll let her go? Pretending to be ignorant makes fucking me easier for her?

"Oh, come on, Zoe. Not even you can be that naïve."

She jerks as if I've slapped her. Fine. It was a low blow. Her naivety is part of what I love about her. She's the light to my hell, the hope to my infernal darkness. Men like me are born dark. We're born into the darkness. We inherit it from our fathers and pass it on to our sons. She's the only brightness I'll ever have in my life, and I don't want her as anything other than herself, but she's changing regardless. It happens right in front of my eyes as her features contort with pain. She tries hard to bury her feelings under a mask of indifference, but that's *my* specialty. She's an open book, a flower for the plucking.

"Fuck you, Maxime." Her chin trembles, but she straightens and pulls her shoulders square. "You're right. I'm too naïve. Maybe I was hiding my head in the sand when you took me from my home to teach me your sick lessons, but it was the only way I could cope with what was happening to me, so fuck you again for your petty insults."

"Says the woman who just insulted me twice."

Her dainty nostrils flare. "You could've died tonight, and I don't know why I even care."

I lift a brow. "Is there a point to this conversation?"

She regards me for the longest moment. Her voice is soft but complex, wrapped in layers of weariness, fear, and desperation when she finally speaks. "I want to go home."

"No, you don't."

Her voice rises in anger. "You don't know what I want."

"I know you better than you think."

She balls her small hands into fists at her sides. "I want to go home."

"This is your home, Zoe. You've admitted it yourself, more than once. There's nothing left for you in Johannesburg. This is your dream. This is the life you've always wanted. You want to run because you know who I am now. You want to run because of what you've lived through tonight. It's only natural, but I'm here to protect you. I'll always protect you." Even from my grave.

She's shivering like a daisy in a storm, but she's standing her ground. "If they took a shot at you, you must be important."

If they took a shot at you. Her words still me. She notices. Fuck. It's a heavy truth to lay on her shoulders, but I can't protect her if I keep her head pushed down in the sand.

"How important, Maxime? If you won't let me go, it's only fair that I know."

She's right. I wanted to keep her away from the business, but ignorance gets you killed. Especially now that she'll be attending school in town. Especially now that she'll have triple the guards protecting her day and night. I made an error in showing the world how much she means to me, but I won't let her pay the price.

"Quite important," I say.

"You're not the boss or something like that?" she asks with a nervous laugh.

"Not yet. I still share the power with my father."

Placing a hand over her stomach, she looks at me as if she sees the monster in my soul. "Oh, my God."

"We'll put extra security measures in place. You'll take double the number of guards with you to school."

"Me?" She gives me a wide-eyed look. "It's not me they were after. What if they kill you?"

That coldness spreads through me again. I bury it under the fury and violence still coursing through my veins, but Zoe is perceptive. I may have made it my job to get to know her, but she's gotten to know me in the process, too.

"Unless," she says with a soft gasp, "they weren't after you."

"Zoe." I get to my feet, but she takes a step away.

"They came after me," she says with those big, haunted eyes. I can almost see the gears turning in her head. I see the exact moment she connects the dots. "To get to you."

I stand helplessly, my hands hanging loosely at my sides while the truth turns her face into a mask of horror. I can't tell her it won't happen again. I can't tell her I'll let her go. I can only round the desk and offer her my arms.

"No." She holds up a hand and takes two more steps away from me. "Don't touch me."

Her words hit me like no bullet can. "I'm not going to let anything happen to you."

"You can't promise that," she says on a panicked whisper. "What happens if you're killed?"

I opt for the truth. It's better to give her these weapons than to make her vulnerable by not enlightening her. "It's an option we shouldn't exclude, but I'll make sure you're looked after."

Her breath catches. "That's not what I meant. What happens to me, stuck here in this city without a passport?"

I approach cautiously, like with an injured animal. "You don't have to worry about that. It's my job to take care of the details."

"It's my life. *My* fucking life."

"Zoe." My patience is running thin. It's been a long night. "Don't start."

She folds her arms around her stomach. "A man died because of me."

I slowly continue my advance. "He knew what the job entailed when he signed up."

"Is Damian involved in the mafia? Is that why you're keeping me?"

Stopping, I rub a hand over my face.

"Damn you, Maxime. Tell me! *A man died tonight.*"

The implied meaning hangs in the air. It could've been her. Tilting my head toward the ceiling, I sigh. "Damian is involved with his own mafia in prison. It's got nothing to do with us."

"Then why keep me?"

I wasn't going to tell her, but the game is no longer the same. I'm never letting her go. What difference does it make if she knows? She's right. After tonight, it only seems fair.

Taking a deep breath, I say, "Your brother is planning on taking back a diamond deposit he discovered. The mine currently belongs to Harold Dalton."

"Dalton?" she exclaims. "The man who put Damian in prison?"

"Yes. He stole Damian's discovery and framed him."

"What does that have to do with you?"

"Dalton sells the diamonds directly to us, cutting out the middleman. We want to make sure your brother will sell to us when he takes over."

She gapes at me. "You're that certain Damian will succeed?"

"I've been privy to his plans. My money is on him."

"Just in case, you needed something to blackmail Damian."

My look is level. "Yes."

"That's why you took me." The revelation settles slowly in her eyes. "You were never going to hurt Damian. You need him." Her lips part on a soundless gasp. "You lied to me."

I don't deny it.

Anger washes over her features. "You twisted the truth. You used me. You made me submit to you with a lie. I could've defied you," she says with disbelief. "I could've run. Nothing would've happened to my brother."

I close the distance between us. "One way or another, I had to bring you here. I chose the non-violent way."

Her entire body trembles as the betrayal peels away. Finally, she sees what she's fallen for—the real me, the monster hidden beneath a well-cut suit bearing gifts and kindness. She sees through my plan, and she knows it's too late. She's already caught in my web.

"Why are you telling me now?" she asks, shaking so much her jaw quakes. "You're never going to let me see my brother again, are you? That's why you don't care that I know. I can't tell Damian the truth if I never see him again."

Cupping her cheek, I stroke a thumb over that trembling jaw. "I won't let you go, Zoe. Not in four years. Never. You're mine. Your place is here." I apply the gentlest of pressure, making her pretty lips pout. "What you better understand is it won't end well for you if you run. I will always find you."

She grips my forearms as her knees buckle under the weight of the truth. It's a sugar-coated threat, but she's learned enough lessons to let her imagination run wild with consequences.

I give her time to process it. I give her space when she shoves me away. Her fingers flitter to her lips as she looks around the room like a trapped animal.

"Too much has happened tonight," I say. "Let me take care of you."

"How?" she asks with a mocking laugh. "By locking me up? By lying to me?"

"By taking you to bed. The sun will be up soon. You need to rest."

"If Damian finds out I'm here, what will you tell him?"

"That you're here because you want to be."

She looks at me as if I've slapped her. "How will you explain a lie like that?"

"I went to South Africa to meet with Dalton about business. We had dinner and shared a bottle of wine. I asked about the diamond discovery. He told me about Damian, and how your brother stole a diamond from his house and ended up in prison. I found that hard to believe, seeing that Damian discovered a riverbed full of them. My curiosity was piqued, so I looked you up. One thing led to another."

"Just like that," she says, the strange look on her face not wavering.

"Yes. Now come to bed."

Turning her back on me, she walks to the liquor tray. A drink is probably a good idea. A little alcohol will help her sleep. A glass falls over. She's anything but steady. I cross the floor to help her, and then stop dead as she spins around, pushing the icepick against my chest.

CHAPTER 8

Zoe

The compassion in Maxime's eyes only makes me want to kill him more. This man has betrayed me in so many ways. He lied about killing Damian. He stole me. He stole my virginity. He kept the fact that he's a mafia boss conveniently hidden from me. He teaches me cruel lessons. He controls every aspect of my life. By claiming me, he's put me in danger. He knew how his secrets would impact me, yet he made me dependent on him. He trapped me with his sick games, physically and emotionally, and now I'll always be a pawn for his opponents to get to him. This is as much as I can take.

I push the sharp point of the icepick a little harder, letting it pierce the fabric of his shirt. "Give me the passport you used to smuggle me out of South Africa."

His lips lift in one corner. "When you have it, what are you going to do with it?"

"I'm going to leave," I say through clenched teeth. "You're going to give me money and a car, and you're going to let me go."

He raises an eyebrow. "Go where?"

"Where you'll never find me."

"A place like that doesn't exist, little flower. I'll turn the world upside down if I have to, and you'll only end up right back here."

It makes me feel like a hamster running in place in a wheel. So futile. "Give it to me!" I push harder, feeling the barrier of his strong chest against the weapon.

He looks down at me, his arms resting at his sides. "Go ahead. Stab me, Zoe. You'll want to move the tip up a centimeter and a fraction to the left if you want to hit my heart."

I do it. I follow his guidance and let the point rest against his heart. He's killing me little by little, destroying what's left of me. I can't live like this anymore.

His cold, gray eyes mock me. "What are you waiting for?"

I put my weight behind the pick. I'm shaking so much it's hard to keep the shaft steady. The point meets more resistance, hard muscle and scarred flesh. How many kisses have I planted on that flesh? How many times have I traced his imperfect skin to hear him exhale with a shudder? How many nights have I harbored hope in my chest, hope to escape, hope that he'll return a drop of my feelings? Because if he doesn't, I'm afraid I'll lose my soul. My unrequited affection will slowly poison me. The bitterness of being forever unloved and eternally lonely will chip away at my heart until nothing but hard, polished hate is left. I hate him as much as I love him, but I hate myself more for loving him. It's the worst suffering. Insupportable.

Tears pool in my eyes as I try to harm him. I have to do this. I have to save myself. I start crying when he doesn't stop me as I push harder. A crimson drop flowers over the fabric of his shirt. It's the color of life, of love. It's the color of him. Beneath it all, he's exactly what he said—just a man.

My fingers loosen around the shaft. Every bone in my body shakes. The icepick falls with a clatter on the floor. It's a harsh sound, cruel and devastating. A sob tears from my chest.

Moving like lightning, he grabs my wrist. Even if my hand is empty now, his hold is like an iron shackle. The other hand finds purchase in my hair. He yanks my head back with force and crushes our mouths together. The kiss is as brutal as the threat I couldn't carry out. He forces me onto my knees by my hair, following me down to the floor.

The sting on my scalp makes my eyes water as he unbuckles his belt and unzips his fly. Stretching out over me, he pushes my shorts and underwear over my hips and grabs the root of his cock in his hand. I barely have time to take a breath before he impales me, thrusting so deep it hurts. I cry out, tears of defeat leaking from the corners of my eyes.

Is this what I've reduced myself to? A killer? I don't want to become like him. More so, I can never harm him. It's twisted, but I can control it as little as I can control my love. I care way too much.

Placing a palm over the bloodstain on his shirt, I whisper, "I'm sorry."

He lifts up on one arm and scans my face with his solemn, gray gaze. "I know."

He spears his fingers through my hair, caressing my scalp and wiping away the hurt. Framing my face between his palms, he kisses my eyes and cheeks. He kisses my lips as he starts moving, setting a slow pace. I rock in his arms, letting his gentle strength soothe me. I fall deeper under his spell as his body calls and mine answers. I bow to his magic, gasping into his mouth as my back arches from the pleasure. It's different than how we normally fuck. It's desperate, yet tender. It's a celebration of life. I could've lost him tonight. My threat of killing him was all bluffing, nothing but manipulation to let me go. I don't want him dead. Yet his life is dangerous. I can lose him every day. To live this fear over and over, day after day, I'm not sure I can do it.

I gasp into our kiss. "I'm scared."

He wipes the tears from my cheeks with his thumbs. "You're brave."

"Not enough."

"You underestimate yourself."

I moan when he hits a barrier deep inside. The trauma of tonight makes everything that's churning in my chest spills out. "Will you love me?"

He smiles. For once, the gesture isn't mocking or haughty, but kind. "Am I not loving you now?"

"You know what I mean." I need more than making love. I need the love that bleeds red, the kind that flows from his heart.

A trace of regret softens his features. "I've given you all I'm capable of."

At least this is the one thing he's honest about. Maxime will never be able to love me. The pain is dazzling. It's pure. It's beautiful, because it's born from love. It only hurts as deep as you feel.

Pressing his lips on my ear, he offers me a consolation. He dangles temptation. "Let me give you what I have."

I'm not strong enough. I give in. I follow his lead, rolling my hips to his tempo when he pushes a hand between our bodies to find my clit. I snake my arms around his neck, holding him close to me. I take his pleasure, and give him mine. As I come around him, he comes inside, filling me with his essence for the first time, giving me all that he has.

I'm boneless in the aftermath, depleted by the emotional turmoil and extreme pleasure. Maxime adjusts our clothes, gathers me in his arms, and carries me upstairs. We shower together. When I try to wash away the blood from the nick I've left on his skin, he brushes my hand away. The old Maxime is back, unsettlingly intense and slightly distant.

In bed, he pulls me against his body.

Leaning my head on his shoulder, I trace the bumpy skin of his torso. "Why haven't you come inside me before?"

He stares at the ceiling, gently brushing a palm over my arm, and says in his beautiful accent, "I didn't want to ruin you."

"Ruin me?" I frown. "Ruin me how?"

His voice is like a far-off star in the dark—elusive and intangible, untouchable like every other part of him. "You're pure."

"And now?" I stroke a hand down his stomach to trace the line of hair that starts under his navel. His choice of words makes me smile. "Am I impure?"

His tone is solemn. "Now you're mine."

I trail my palm farther south, cupping his erection. "I thought you said I was that already."

"This is different."

I squeeze gently. "How?"

"Now," he says, still not meeting my eyes, "you're my property."

I still. The declaration slices through me. I didn't think it was possible for him to hurt me more. I pull away from him with a wry smile. I guess that's Maxime, honest to the point of cutting me to the bone.

"Thanks for telling me," I say. "I thought it might've been something a little less coldhearted like enjoying the intimacy of such an act with your fuck toy."

He removes his arm from around me and sits up. Soft light washes over the room when he flicks on the nightstand lamp. Flashing me with a view of his hard, naked body, he walks to the dressing room and closes the door. A short moment later, he exits dressed in sweatpants and a T-shirt, carrying a sports bag.

My gaze is drawn to the bag. "What are you doing?"

He drops the bag on the floor and sits down next to me. "Spread your arms and legs."

My breath catches. "What?"

His look is gentle, encouraging even. "You heard me."

"Why?"

"I'm going to tie you up."

My mouth goes dry. "Why?"

"Spread them, Zoe. I don't want to use force with you after what happened tonight."

Fear snakes up my spine. "Are you going to hurt me?"

"I'll never hurt you." His smile doesn't reach his eyes. "I may frustrate you."

"You're into kink?" I ask, even if it shouldn't surprise me. He's virile, and he has a strong libido. He's also depraved and lacks a moral compass. I bet he's into worse than kink. "You're not into torture, are you?"

His eyes tighten. "I'm not my brother."

Wrong thing to say. His brother seems to be a trigger for his anger. Impatiently, he grips my wrist and lifts it above my head. I keep still because I don't have a choice. I can't fight him off. Doing so will only stimulate his excitement. Maxime loves it when I fight.

My pulse jumps when he takes four coils of rope from the bag. Everything inside me wants to resist, but I'm powerless as he binds me spread-eagled to the bed. It's what he takes out of the bag next that makes me regret my surrender.

"What the hell is that?" I ask, staring at the purple vibrator mounted on a rubber sling and a silicone plug with a flat stopper.

"Sex toys."

"I'm not in the mood, Maxime."

He gives me an apologetic smile. "I know."

He takes a tube of lube from the bag and applies a copious amount to the butt plug and vibrator before inserting both gently. He wiggles the vibrator until the bulbous end fits snugly inside and the smaller one on my clit, then pulls the sling over my folds at the front and through my ass cheeks at the back to attach it to a belt he straps around my waist. Like this, the toys can't slip free.

"Do I need to gag you?" he asks.

"No," I cry out. "I don't like to feel that helpless."

He drags a finger from my temple to my jaw. "Then not a sound, understand?" Taking a small remote from the bag, he pushes on a button. The vibrator starts humming softly. He kicks it up two notches until the vibration penetrates my G-spot and clit. It's pleasant, but not so intense that I want to come.

"Comfortable?" he asks in a husky voice.

I give a nervous nod.

Gripping the sheet, he covers my body. "The toy has eight hours of battery life. After last night, we weren't going anywhere today, anyway."

Wait. What? He can't mean what I'm thinking.

He bends down and kisses my forehead. His deep voice is pure evil. "Sleep well, my little flower."

"You can't leave me like this."

He turns for the door.

"Wait," I call when he grips the handle. "Untie me, Maxime. Please."

He doesn't answer.

"Why are you doing this?" I cry out.

He turns back to face me. "Tonight was the first and last time you threatened my life. I gave you one chance only. You wasted it. It'll never happen again." He drags his gaze one more time over my sheet-covered body before stepping out and closing the door.

I can't believe it. He's serious. He's punishing me by leaving me like this until the vibrator battery runs flat. Indignant anger heats my veins as other parts of my body heat with unwanted arousal. I try to mentally override the sensations by focusing on my vexation, but the physical won't be denied. I feel because I'm human. I become needy despite my desire not to.

The setting is too low to get me off quickly. It takes a long time, and finally I'm so frustrated I wiggle and squirm to set the orgasm off. The relief is instantaneous and intense, but brief. My clit is oversensitive. I can barely tolerate the uninterrupted hum penetrating my flesh and bones. Moving in an attempt to escape the torturous stimulation doesn't help. The toy is strapped on too tightly.

After suffering the relentless vibrations for the longest time ever, pleasure starts to build anew. My need climbs. I'm wet, and it only makes it worse. Somehow, the assault on my lower body parts feels more intense, or maybe it's just because my body is so sensitive after the first orgasm. The need for release rises slowly, driving me to tears. It's like a rubber band that stretches and stretches. When the tension finally breaks, I'm panting. Unfortunately, this time I hardly feel the release, because the need is as constant now as the unbearable sensitivity of my flesh. My clit throbs, and my folds are swollen. My nipples remain hard. My lower body contracts as another cycle of need commences.

I'm clenching my teeth not to make a sound. I won't give Maxime the satisfaction. By the time the sun is bright and high, I'm drenched in sweat, and the sheet around my sex is soaked. It hurts to come, but I can't stop. Every cycle is agonizingly slow, the constant need always outweighing the brief release. It becomes so intense my whole body pulls tight with spasms until my toes curl. My muscles ache. There's a strange burning sensation on the soles of my feet. My hair sticks to my forehead. When another cruel climax takes over my body, my eyes roll back in my head.

At some point during the afternoon, I'm so exhausted I fall asleep, only to be woken with another release that tears me apart. I don't know how many times I come, only that when the battery finally hums too weak to wrench more agony from my body, I sink into the mattress with a sob of relief. It's like falling into a weightless void. It's only when I'm able relax my muscles for the first time that I realize how tense they've been drawn all day. I'm aching all over, but at last I can escape into the blissful reprieve of darkness.

CHAPTER 9

Maxime

The thought of Zoe coming around a vibrator in my bed is a temptation impossible to resist. I go to my study and lock the door behind me before activating the security camera, letting the image reroute to my laptop. I enable sound, too. I told her not to make noise. I can't let her get away with anything, not after she pushed an icepick against my heart and broke my skin. Not after the attempt on her life last night. Her obedience is all the more important. As long as she obeys me, I can keep her safe. It's defiance that opens opportunities for my opponents and puts her at risk.

With her dark hair spread over my pillow and her naked limbs stretched under the sheet, she's too beautiful to be human. I wish I'd left her uncovered to better appreciate the view, but her body temperature will eventually drop from exhaustion, and I didn't want her to be cold.

Watching her wrestle with her arousal, I take the tupper dish Francine had given me yesterday from the windowsill and place it in front of the laptop on my desk. I flick the lid off with a finger. The inhabitant immediately raises its tail. It's a *buthus occitanus,* a black scorpion. Francine found it in the kitchen. They're hardy little buggers to kill, so she threw a plastic container over the invader and slid the lid underneath to catch it inside. It tries to climb out of its prison, but the container is too deep.

A moan pulls my gaze to the screen. Head thrown back, Zoe orgasms so hard I can see her body convulse under the sheet. I smile. She's gorgeous when she comes. I'm looking forward to witnessing every one of her climaxes. I wonder how many times she'll come.

The scorpion turns inside the container. Leaning forward, I study it. Their venom isn't deadly. There are plenty of the small species around here. They favor the rocky landscape. Every year, we find at least a dozen in the garden.

I'm not a huge cigar fan like my father, but I light one now and suck on the end until the tip glows red. I'm a punishment behind, tonight excluded. I never made up for the night I fucked Zoe like a whore in the hotel.

Taking a big drag on the cigar, I roll the smoke around in my mouth before exhaling it into the container. It makes the scorpion furious. They don't like smoke. It swings its claws in the air, snapping its pinches together. I inhale and blow on it again, aggravating the little creature. Smoke is a danger. Its instinctive reaction is to escape that danger and to protect itself by attacking whatever threatens its life. When it's in full-blown survival mode, I stick my finger in the container.

It behaves exactly like it should. It hollows its back and zaps me with the sharp tip of its tail.

Motherfucking Jesus.

It hurts like a bitch. The burn is like nothing I've felt before. It creeps through my finger and up my arm, setting fire to my veins. It's different to the flames that cooked my skin. That burn came from the outside and melted inward with pain. This one starts on the inside, burning outward until it feels like my nails may peel back from my skin.

"Good job, buddy," I say as I sink back into my chair with grunts of agony.

I don't cut off my blood circulation to prevent the poison from spreading. I eat it up eagerly, letting my body's natural functioning carry it farther. My heart pumps faster. My blood flows stronger. The poison burns in my shoulder and down my chest. Sweat breaks out over my body.

Zoe comes.

Perfect. Beautiful.

I take a last drag of the cigar before putting the tip out on my finger, right on the sting.

Fuck, that hurts.

It sizzles and burns, killing one pain with another, but the affected parts of my body continue to hum as the venom works through my system, and Zoe starts crying from frustration.

The only way I can handle her tears is if I hurt myself worse than I'm hurting her. This isn't hurt for Zoe per se—I didn't lie about not physically hurting her—but sexual suffering can sometimes be worse. Her agony is riveting. It stokes my fire, making a different kind of poison burn in my blood. I want her lips around me. I want to fuck her mouth and come down her throat while agony rips through me, while three kinds of fire are wracking my body.

I unzip and take my cock in my hand. I'm so hard I'm aching. Going to my flower now won't serve tonight's lesson. She's got to live this one out alone. I stroke a couple of times, making the burn in my arm brighter. Closing my fist, I squeeze hard and rip my hand up and down. I let the cocktail of pain fuel me, mixing rough pleasure with agonizing suffering and twisted stalking on a laptop screen until my balls draw up and violent release erupts.

I catch my seed in my injured hand. It irritates the cigar burn. Using the en-suite toilet, I clean up. I'm still hurting. It's difficult to breathe. The poison must've spread to my chest. It'll fizzle out there, the crippling effect slowly diminishing. By the time eight hours are over, my pain will be gone.

Taking the container, I unlock the patio door and go out into the garden. A good distance away from the house and the path to the beach, I tip the container over. The scorpion scurries for freedom. It covers a good distance before hiding under a rock. I straighten and let my gaze linger on the house, on the window of the room where my flower is a prisoner spread in a spider's web made of ropes and lust. There's no more freedom for her now. There's no escaping my poison.

CHAPTER 10

Zoe

I wake up to the smell of rose petals. Blinking, I sit up. My hands and feet are untied. The toys are gone. The sheet lies discarded at my feet. Maxime sits on the edge of the bed, still dressed in the sweatpants and T-shirt from earlier.

He hands me a porcelain cup. "I brought you an infusion."

I reach for the offering with mixed feelings. I'm thirsty and the tea smells delicious, but I don't want to take anything from him, not after what he did. My body aches everywhere. Fighting an internal battle, I contemplate if I'm going to accept his peace offering. In the end, my dry throat wins. I take the cup from him and fold my palms around it.

"It's not too hot," he says. "I reckoned you'd be thirsty."

Damn right. I give him a cutting look as I sip the brew. It's become my favorite since he made me try it in Venice. It's not only the herbal tea that makes the room smell of flowers. The scent is stronger than just the rose petal tea. My gaze falls on a small ornate glass container on the nightstand filled with golden liquid.

"Drink up," he says, "and then lie down."

I tense. "Why?"

"I need to take care of you."

My tone is scathing. "Does your care involve ropes?"

He chuckles. "Only rose oil."

I look at the bottle. "It smells good."

"It's pure. I had it brought in from Grasse this morning. It took forty-thousand roses to fill that little bottle, and I'm going to drench your body in it."

I feel like slapping him. The only thing preventing me is the promise I made to myself and him not to ever do it again. "I'm angry with you."

His lips quirk. "I'm sure you are. However, I bet you've learned your lesson."

"Multiple orgasms? Who knew it could be such an effective method of torture?"

"I'll take that as an affirmative."

When he reaches for the cup, I gulp down the last of the tea. "What's with this thing you have for roses, anyway?"

"You," he says, taking the cup from my hand and leaving it on the nightstand.

"Me?"

"You always smell of roses."

"I do?" I blink. "You noticed?"

"There's not anything about you I don't notice. Now lie down."

Cautiously, I shift down the mattress. I'm still not sure I trust him not to inflict some other kind of punishment.

"Your lesson is over," he says as if reading my mind.

I relax a little. I still have much to process after last night. I'm drowning in guilt when I think of Gautier's mother. I'll never trample on the enormous gift of his life by being ungrateful, but a small part of me wishes he hadn't left me with this guilt. Maybe it would've been easier if he'd let me take the bullets meant for me. Shame burns in my stomach for the thought. I'm alive thanks to him. The least I can do is honor him by living it as well as I can. I just have to figure out how to cope with the truth Maxime finally shared with me last night. The deceit is a bitter pill to swallow. I thought I couldn't forgive him for cheating and lying about my admission into a top fashion design school, but this is so much worse. This betrayal goes even deeper. I hate him. I hate him with every fiber of my being. I hate that I care about him, and I hate that I need him even more. I hate what he's doing to me, and I'm powerless to prevent it.

The very subject of my turbulent thoughts rubs his knuckles over my breast.

"Turn over."

I don't want to react, but I can't stop it. The tip contracts. More shame churns in my stomach until acid pushes up in my throat.

"Turn over, Zoe," he says in that sinful accent, his tone non-negotiable.

I turn onto my stomach. At least I can hide my face and his effect on me. A few cold drops dribble on my back. I suck in a breath. When he starts rubbing the oil into my skin with his big, warm hands, I almost forget to think. He finds every knot in my shoulders, every tense spot that aches because of last night's strain, and takes his time to massage the hurt away. He moves down my back to my glutes, legs, and feet, and then my arms before finally massaging my scalp. I can't help but succumb to how good it feels. Like everything Maxime does, he's an expert at this, too. I'm all but melting into the mattress by the time he's done, my body buzzing drunkenly on relaxation. I've only slept for a couple of hours, so I'm about to doze off when he clicks his tongue in disapproval and says, "I'm not done yet."

The mattress dips as he lifts. I tense a little again, some of the agreeable fuzziness evaporating. Turning my head to the side, I watch him. He's pulling the T-shirt over his head, exposing his powerful, scarred chest and broad shoulders. Holding my eyes, he pushes the tracksuit pants over his hips. I trace the deep line of the V that cuts to his groin and the semi-hard cock that hangs heavy between his legs.

After the night I had, I don't want to have sex, but my conditioned body turns wet looking at him. His body is like a statue chiseled from stone. Every muscle is perfectly cut. His cock grows hard under my stare, making my mouth water. The warm, velvety flesh isn't the same as a plastic toy. Not at all. If he can't give me affection, he can give me pain and lust to forget just for a moment how much I hate both of us. I'm already his whore. What's one time more? Nothing in the scheme of bigger things. I can't go back to the virgin I was when he found me. I can't undo the sinful things we've done. Does it really matter if I'm knee-deep or sinking?

Maxime climbs back onto the bed. Dragging his palms up my legs, he spreads them and kneels between my thighs. My body jumps to life. My over-stimulated and over-used parts swell and turn slick. I can stop my reaction as little as I can turn off my love. He's trained me too well. He's a mastermind. The way he played and caught me in his game is brilliant, really.

Stretching out over me, he brushes my hair over one shoulder and kisses the shell of my ear. "I assume your pussy has had enough."

I can never have enough of him. It makes me want to break down with sobs. All I can do is close my eyes and bite my lip in futile denial.

"Get up on your knees for me, *cherie*." He assists me with a hand around my waist. "Lean down on your forearms. It'll better support your weight."

When he's arranged me the way he wants me, my legs are wide open and my ass in the air. I'm stretched open and on show. A flush of heat spreads over my cheeks as I look back and see where his gaze is trained.

His eyes darken. The frosty gray turns into that molten mercury I've come to associate with his lust. Taking his cock in his hand, he grabs the bottle of oil from the nightstand, tips it over his shaft, and stroke a few times to lubricate it. He drags his palm up and down and rolls it over the thick head of his cock. The wet sounds he makes with his hand as he all but masturbates right in front of my eyes turn me on more. I'm still processing this new discovery, storing it away with the rest of my shameful ones when he dribbles the oil in the crease between my globes and uses the slick head of his cock to spread the oil around my dark entrance.

I grip a fistful of sheet in each hand when he leans forward, applying pressure on the tight ring of muscle.

His voice is strained, his accent sounding stronger. "Do you want this, Zoe?"

Zis for *this*. Rounded like a full-bodied wine. The pronunciation drips sensuality. If I get drunk on it, I won't hear the lies.

"Use your voice," he says.

I let go, surrendering my grip to the quicksand of my body's betrayal. "Yes."

Easing forward slightly, he teases me. "Why?"

"Because it feels wrong."

"You're such a good little bad girl," he says, leaning over to caress my breasts and play with my nipples while sliding his cock deeper.

It doesn't hurt like before. I've been stretched all night, ready to take him.

"I need to fuck you hard," he whispers through clenched teeth, "after last night."

Last night.

Neither of us can get it out of our heads. It's a tipping point in time. Our dynamic has shifted. He used to hold back with me, never coming inside my body. I was the fool who silently begged him to let go. I asked for it. I wanted his everything. He reciprocated by giving it. Now that he's marked me, I'm his property, something he can no longer let go. Not after four years. Not ever.

Fuck, I'm such an idiot. I took the noose from his hands and put it around my neck myself. All because he made me love. He made me need more, but he's empty now. He's given everything he was capable of giving. There's no love in his heart, and there will never be. If my heart's to survive, I'll have to find my happiness elsewhere. Even if I got in by cheating, I'll pour my soul into my studies. I'll give it everything I've got, filling the stretching holes in my heart with the passion and purpose Maxime so charitably offered me.

"Fuck, Zoe." His fingers tighten on my nipple, twisting not to hurt but because lost as we are in the midst of this new phase of our forced relationship, he's forgetting his own strength. "If you don't want me to pummel your ass, you have to tell me now. Don't tease me, little flower."

No. I want the dirty. I want the reminder of who I am. I need to remember this wanton woman on her knees is all I'll ever be so that I'll never want things I can't have again. It hurts too damn much.

"Goddamn, Zoe. You're killing me." He kisses my shoulder and starts pulling out.

I reach behind me to grip his wrist. "Give it to me, Maxime."

He hesitates.

"Give it to me, damn you."

"Why?" he asks in a hoarse voice.

"Because I need it too."

Stroking a palm up my spine, he offers tenderness in an advance exchange for the violence we both crave. "I've got you, *cherie*."

In this, he does. On a physical level, he's the king. Gripping my hips, he enters me slowly, taking his time until his groin is pressed against my ass, but that's all the concession he gives me before he lets go. We're rough. He gives me what I need and takes what he wants. Despite *last night* and everything it signifies, despite the endless orgasms, I beg him to make me come.

It's a vicious circle I can't escape. I'll hate him now and be back on my knees tonight, begging him to fill me with the token of his ownership. His name whispers over my lips in a frantic cry as he rubs my clit and makes me explode before spilling his release in my body.

I collapse onto my stomach when my arms give out. Maxime follows me down, keeping his cock buried in my body and his weight on his elbows. He presses kisses and sweet words on my ear, praising me for how well I've taken him.

I'm already lethargic again. It's hard to keep my eyes open. Needing something—someone—to hold onto, I fold my fingers around his hand that rests next to my face. At the hiss of air he sucks through his teeth, I open my eyes. The tip of his index finger sports a nasty, red scab. It looks like a burn.

Lifting my shoulders off the mattress, I turn his finger toward the light for a better look. "Maxime! What happened?"

He pulls away. "Nothing."

I wince at the bite of pain when he frees his cock.

"Did that happen in the fight?" I ask, rolling onto my side to face him. I hadn't noticed it last night, but I've been so wrought out it's possible I missed his injuries.

His laugh is cold. "There was no fight."

Pushing off me, he gets up. "Have a shower with me. I need to go shortly."

My mood darkens. "Business? Now?"

"Yes," he replies in a clipped tone.

Instead of pushing the matter, I let him pull me to my feet.

He washes me in the shower and insists on drying my hair with the hairdryer afterward as if he's scared I'll catch a cold and my death with it. We dress and have an early dinner together. Francine's eyes are red-rimmed from crying. Maxime doesn't comment, and I don't ask, assuming it's because of worry over what could've happened to him.

"Isn't it weird to keep an ex-lover around?" I ask when she's gone.

He shrugs. "It was sex. Now it's over. There's nothing weird about that."

Right.

"You better have an early night," he says. "It'll do you good."

After the main meal, he excuses himself. I follow him to the entrance where he pulls on a jacket and coat, but he's withdrawn again, already preoccupied with the business and the fires I imagine he had to put out after last night. When the door shuts behind him, I can't help but stand in the middle of the foyer with my arms wrapped around myself, feeling lost. I can't help but think that every time he walks out of the door he may never come back.

CHAPTER 11

Zoe

The minute my back hits the mattress, I pass out. I have no idea if Maxime came to bed, because I sleep nine hours straight, and when I wake in the morning, I'm alone. It's still early. Part of me is worried and part of me grateful for the space. My emotions are all over the place. I'm tearful, and my defenses are down. That makes me vulnerable—a susceptible target for more hurt. I need to pull myself together.

I try not to think, but the gears won't stop turning in my head. Where is Maxime? How is Gautier's family coping? Are the police going after Maxime for the killings? Will I ever get away from my captor now? Do I *want* to get away? Can I really turn a blind eye to everything and throw myself into my studies even if I don't deserve a place in the program?

The questions are futile, because the answers, even if I had them, won't change anything. Very little is in my control. By the time I've showered and dressed, I don't feel lighter. The killings and truth Maxime revealed still weigh heavily on my chest.

I go down for breakfast, walking down the dim hallway with the portraits. The faces stare at me, judging quietly. A man died. Several. Some by my kidnapper's hand. How does one live with that? How does *he*? The stairs creak under my feet. The noise is amplified in the big, quiet house. I pass empty rooms and the cold library and stop in front of the locked study door. The phones must be in there together with everything else Maxime doesn't want me to find. It's useless, but I feel the handle. As I expected, the door doesn't swing open under my pressure.

I continue to the dining room. Fruit and croissants are set out on the table. Giving the buttery pastries and fat oranges a long look, I go on, walking to the kitchen. What I need is comfort food. Familiar food.

When I enter, Francine looks up from wiping down the counters. My presence makes her go stiff. I don't bother to say good morning, as I don't expect her to reply. Going past her, I take a mug from the cupboard.

"Can I help you?" she asks, propping her hands on her hips.

"No, thanks."

Her mouth presses into a thin line when I pour myself a cup of coffee. "Don't you drink tea? It's in the cupboard behind you."

"Not today." I blow on the brew. "Oh, was the coffee for you?"

She dumps the cleaning cloth on the counter. "I'll just have to make a fresh pot."

"There's still plenty left."

Grabbing the flask, she pours what's left of the coffee down the drain and rinses it. I take a sip. It's strong. While she polishes the flask harder than necessary with a dishcloth, I look for the sugar. All I find is a box with a corner cut open. Since there isn't a sugar pot, I fill a cup.

"Oh, for God's sake." She pushes a bowl with cubes my way. "This is France. Get used to the way we do things here."

I consider that for a moment. It's a stupid rebellion, childish really.

On any other day, I may not have found her rebuke worthy of a response, but today isn't just another day. Today, I add two heaped spoons of sugar to my coffee, giving her a sweet smile. Her fingers clench on the dishcloth. Making a mental note to never take cubes, I pop a slice of bread into the toaster. What is it with the French and cubes, anyway?

Eyeing the bread, she says, "There *is* breakfast in the dining room." She continues, adding a little jab, "As per Max's orders."

"Does he decide what I'm eating?"

"He pays my salary." Her lips curve into a smile. "That means whatever he decides goes."

I lean my butt against the cupboard. "Exactly. That makes him your boss. So, if I were you, I'd remember my place."

Her eyes flare. "That makes you what? His *girlfriend*?"

The toast pops. I dump it on a plate. "Oh, nothing as romantic as that. I think until yesterday I was a hostage. Today, apparently, the term is property."

She blanches. She doesn't like the statement. That's strange. To me, property sounds like an insult.

"I suppose hoping there's peanut butter is stretching it too far?" I ask as I go through the food cupboards.

"You're nothing but a distraction," she says to my back. "Max is never that careless. You almost got him killed last night."

Inwardly, I still at the words. It's not as if it hasn't been running through my mind. Anyone can die at any moment, but Max's lifestyle puts him—us—at a higher risk. A *much* higher risk.

I settle on the butter and jam in the fridge.

"Don't you have anything to say?" she asks.

"I'll pass your concern to Maxime."

I've lost my appetite, but I spread a thick layer of butter and jam on the toast and take a seat by the window nook to eat.

"Do you mind?" she asks just as I open my mouth to take a bite. "I'm busy, and you're in the way."

She's asking to me leave? I lower my hand. "Actually, I do mind." I don't know where the nastiness comes from. I only know I've reached my limit. "I'd like to eat in peace. You can come back in fifteen minutes."

Color rises in her cheeks as she stares at me with her wide green eyes so perfectly set off against her porcelain white skin.

"If you prefer that the order comes directly from your *boss*," I say when she doesn't move, "you can always call *Max*."

"Your days are numbered." The color of her irises turns brilliant. "We'll see who'll have the last laugh." Head held high, she walks from the kitchen.

If only she knew. Even if Damian's life is no longer the sword Maxime holds over my head, he made it clear he won't let me go. Anyway, running is impossible. I have no money, no passport, and I doubt I'll get far, not if Maxime is the head of the most powerful mafia group in France. I can dial no one except for Maxime from my phone, and I don't have access to a laptop. The only measure of freedom I have is going to school. Phones aren't allowed in class, and Maxime's men are watching my every move outside of class. Even if I did get my hands on a phone or somehow managed to send an email to the South African embassy, Maxime made it clear he'd chase me. After what happened in South Africa, I don't doubt it for a minute. Damian is in jail, unable to help me. I don't have friends or allies here. I can't ask anyone for help.

Even if I wanted to get away, I'm stuck.

Despondency descends on me. I need to get out of this house. After rinsing my mug and plate, I grab my satchel and step outside. Two cars are waiting. Benoit drives me to school while three men follow in the second car. I don't make a fuss. If anything, I'm grateful. I'm scared, but I can't lock myself up and hide from Maxime's enemies forever. Clutching my satchel, I look around for cars with tinted windows as we enter the city. I'm nervous. The tension snakes up my stomach and squeezes my chest.

"You can relax," Benoit says. "We cleaned the streets up."

I glance at him. "I'm really sorry about Gautier."

His jaw bunches.

"I'll understand if you think it's my fault," I say.

"I'm not an idiot."

"That's not what I said."

"Look, it's bad enough that I have to babysit you. Can we please not talk? I'm not exactly in the mood for conversation. If not for you —" He cuts off with a cussword, then swears some more under his breath.

I shrug. "Sure." The nonchalant act costs me. It takes everything I have not to show him how guilty his words make me feel. It's easier to roll the window down and pretend I'm staring outside.

Sighing, he wipes a hand over his beard. "Look, I've got nothing against you—"

"You don't have to explain. I understand."

When he parks in front of the school, I get out before he does. "Thanks for the ride," I say before shutting the door.

I'm early, but when I arrive at the classroom, Madame Page and the other students are already there.

I pull out a chair next to Thérèse, and whisper, "I thought the class started at nine."

"It does." She gives me a bleary-eyed look. "Some of us aren't lucky enough to get a free ride. We're all putting additional time in and working extra hard to pass."

"Mademoiselle Hart?" Madame Page calls from the front. "A word with you outside, please."

All heads turn to me when I follow Madame Page outside. Benoit and one of the guards stand a short distance down the hallway. Madame Page startles at their presence. With their suits and dark glasses, there's no guessing as to who or what they are, and what they're doing here.

Ignoring them with visible effort, she shuts the classroom door and pushes her glasses over her head. "You may think you don't have to attend classes like everyone else, but I won't allow you to make an idiot of me and a joke of my course."

"I'm really sorry I wasn't here yesterday. I know it reflects poorly on me, especially since it was only the second day, but I assure you I'm very serious about this course. My absence was due to circumstances beyond my control."

"Circumstances, mm?" Her look is sour. "That's your excuse?"

"It's not an excuse."

"Then care to tell me why you didn't grace us with your presence?"

"I... Um, personal reasons."

"Personal reasons." She purses her lips. "If this was anyone else, they would've been expelled." She points a finger at me. "No absence without a doctor's certificate. The fact that you're here means someone else lost out on an opportunity, someone talented and willing to work. If you can't appreciate what's been given to you on a silver platter, at least try to respect the rules."

"I'm sorry. I really am." I can't even say it won't happen again, because my life isn't in my own hands. Maxime decides. He controls my days, nights, hours, and minutes.

She drops her glasses back over her eyes. "Apology not accepted. Get inside and try not to disrupt the rest of the class, especially not Thérèse. She's on the bottom of the ladder. If she can't beat five of her fellow students, she's out. Are we clear?"

"Yes," I say, averting my eyes.

Embarrassment heats my cheeks as I follow her back inside, but I ignore the stares and arrange my pencils and sketchpad on the table. For the rest of the morning, I try to catch up on what I've missed. They've completed the first model on business theory. Even if practical isn't until next year, all of them have brought in pieces for Madame Page's feedback. That was what the others were working on until late last night. I'm a good seamstress with three years of experience, but I realize with a sinking heart they're all better than me. If I'm to keep up, I'll have to work at home. I'll have to work harder and longer hours. I don't have a choice but to use the sewing machine Maxime gave me, even if I was adamant about not touching it after finding out how I got into the school.

Madame Page announces a group project where we're supposed to work in teams of two to hand-dye an organic textile for our textile science class. There's a lot of excited whispering about it.

Some of the girls already call out one another's names to pair in teams.

At lunchtime, Benoit and the other guy follow me to the canteen where I grab a sandwich and fruit salad. They get the cooked lunch, pay for their meals and mine, and sit down at a table in the corner. I doubt they'll appreciate my presence, so I approach Christine, the pretty dark-haired girl.

"May I?" I motion at the empty seat next to her.

She blows a sigh from the corner of her mouth. "I don't own the tables or the chairs. You can sit wherever you want."

"Do you want to work together on the team project?" I ask as I sit down.

"Work together?" She laughs. "With you?"

I unwrap my sandwich. "It could be fun."

She snorts. "No, thanks."

The rejection stings a little, but I'm the one who has to put more effort into getting on with my fellow students. I understand why they're mad. I can't give up that easily. "Why not?"

Her fork clanks as she puts it down on her plate. "Why not?"

"Yes," I say, taking a bite from the baguette.

"Here's why. You don't have to work. You don't have to earn this degree. Hell, you don't even have to show up. You'll graduate with flying colors, open an exclusive brand label with a head office on the Riviera that your rich mafia boyfriend pays for, and because you're null and worthless at designing but like to pretend that you're a hotshot fashion guru, you'll pay people like me who worked my ass off to work for you.

"My designs will be branded with your label, and you and your shady boyfriend will carry on drinking champagne with the high society and making more money while I work my fingers to the bone, get paid your peanuts, and watch as you take all the credit. That's fucking why."

It takes me a moment to find words. "Is that what you think of me?"

"That's how it works, sunshine." Picking up her tray, she gets to her feet. "Excuse me if I'm not exactly in the mood for teaming up with you."

"You don't know me. You have no right judging me."

"I have every right. My father works three jobs to pay for my studies. I would've worked six if I didn't have to study day and night. We don't get things handed to us. We earn it." She adds with a sneer, "You won't understand what that means."

"Maybe I understand more than what you give me credit for. Maybe if you give me a chance—"

"Don't you get it? I don't *want* to give you a chance."

Aware of everyone staring, I keep my voice low. "Surely, we all deserve a chance."

"You want me to spell it out for you? Even if your work didn't suck, you'd still be a fake."

The tightness in my stomach grows. "What do you mean my work sucks?"

"Madame Page presented our profiles yesterday while you were playing hooky. Grow up. You're not a princess, and this isn't the eighties. Frills and lace are long since out of fashion. Your designs are cheesy and immature. You're only making a fool of yourself." Giving me a pitiful shake of her head, she walks to the table next to ours. "Can I please sit somewhere I won't get indigestion?"

The girls move up to make space. Someone takes her tray while she comes back for her chair. It makes a screeching sound as she drags it over the floor to her new place. The dining room has gone quiet. Everyone is looking at me.

I bite into my sandwich and chew like I don't care. I swallow like the food isn't a lump of sawdust in my throat that threatens to choke me. From the corner of my eye, I see Benoit wipe his mouth and dump the napkin on the tray. When he pushes back his chair, I give him a small shake of my head. Interfering, and God forbid forcing Christine to sit with me, will only make matters worse. I eat in silence while the people around me go back to their conversations. Their whispers are quieter than before, their gazes often colliding with mine. They don't even bother to look away when I catch them staring.

This is the moment I hit rock bottom, when the day just gets too much. Finishing off the last of the sandwich, I swallow it down with some water and brush the crumbs from my skirt. I grab my bag and walk outside into the heat where I can drag in the salty sea air and bite the inside of my cheek until the urge to cry passes.

Benoit and his buddy come out of the building. I turn my back on them so they won't see the humiliation on my face. God, I could do with a friend right now. In a life that was still my own, I would've called one of the girls from work, and we'd be binge watching a silly series while pigging out on popcorn and wine. Or we would've sewn together, creating *frilly* and *cheesy* creations that are immature and out of fashion. I inhale deeply to steady myself.

Taking my phone from my bag, I stare at it for a long time before I dial Maxime's number.

His deep, rich timbre comes over the line. "This is a pleasant surprise." The way he rolls the R still makes the hairs in the nape of my neck stand on end in both a good and bad way. "A first for us."

I've never called him. He seems pleased that I've finally relented. Now that I'm speaking to him, I hesitate. Maybe this isn't a good idea. "Am I bothering you?"

"Never." I can almost hear him smile. "To what do I owe the unexpected pleasure?"

I study the drops from the wet grass on the tip of my shoe. "Did you come to bed last night?"

His voice turns even deeper. "Why? Did you miss me?"

I bite my lip. Always, but he doesn't need to know that. "I was just wondering."

"Just wondering, huh?"

"Yes," I say, kicking at a stone.

"Were you worried about me, Zoe?" From the satisfaction that sounds in his tone, he already thinks I did. He just wants me to admit it.

Suddenly, I'm too tired for this game. I'm too tired to hide my feelings from him. "How could I not be?" I don't bring up the other night again. We've spoken about it as much as is healthy for both of us.

His manner sobers. "I didn't want to make you worry. I had loose ends to tie up."

"So, you didn't sleep." I glance up to catch Benoit studying me. "You must be tired."

"Don't worry, I can go a couple of nights without sleeping. Is this why you're calling? You want to know if I'm tired?" He adds in a huskier voice, "Or you'd like to see me?"

The hope in his words almost makes me give in, but no, that's not why I'm calling. I'm still too unsettled and angry. I'm upset that I even have to make this call to ask his permission.

"Zoe, what is it?"

I take a deep breath. "I'd like to meet Sylvie for coffee after class."

There's a short hesitation. "You would?"

I drill my shoe into the spongy grass, my stomach hard with the expectation of a negative answer. "You said you didn't mind."

"I didn't think you wanted to see my family again."

"Sylvie's nice," I offer as a weak explanation. I don't want to tell him about what happened today. I don't want to fight about it again. It will remind me of the night—*Stop it!* Harping on it does *not* help.

"Zoe."

"Yes?"

"You don't need my permission to have coffee with Sylvie. As long as you tell me where you're going and take my men with you."

His answer bowls me over. It's not what I expected. "Really?"

"Absolutely. Go out with her and have fun."

My mouth drops open. It's almost too good to be true. "Um, okay?" I frown, fumbling for words. "Can I call Sylvie from Benoit's phone? Does he have her number?"

"You don't have to use Benoit's phone. I added Sylvie's number to your caller list."

"Thank you." I guess?

"Send me a text to let me know where you're going."

"Right, so you know if you shouldn't come fetch me." Hastily, I add, "In case you were going to. I mean, *if* she's available."

He chuckles. "That'll be considerate."

"I'll let you get back to work, then." Or rather his shady criminalities.

"I'll miss you." He waits a beat. When I say nothing, he hangs up.

I check my watch. It's almost time to go back inside, but I can fit a quick call in. When I check my caller list, Sylvie's number is already there. I press dial.

"Hi," I say when she answers. "It's Zoe."

"Oh, hi." She sounds upbeat. "I'm so glad you called."

I'm a little uncomfortable. Maybe I'm putting her out. "Are you back in Paris yet?"

"The university starts in a month."

Gathering my courage, I press on. "That coffee you mentioned, does the offer still stand?"

She gives a small laugh. "Of course."

"Are you available today?" I ask, holding my breath.

"Sure," she says after a beat. "Where would you like to meet?"

"You tell me." My voice is lighter with relief. "I'm still new to Marseille."

"Where are you?"

"At school. I get off at six."

"Okay. I'll text you an address."

We say our goodbyes just as the lunch break is over. Students who've been lazing on the lawn stream back into the building. They're all younger than me, maybe eighteen or nineteen, fresh out of school. I definitely don't belong here.

Benoit comes over, handing me my satchel. "You forgot this."

"Thanks." I don't look at him. "I better get back inside."

"Those girls," he says as I start walking, "they have no business treating you like this."

Stopping, I meet his gaze. "I don't know what you're talking about."

He gives me a narrowed look. "I heard what she said to you. Everyone did."

"Well, maybe I deserved that." Seriously, how are they supposed to feel about having me on board because my mafia *boyfriend* forced it?

"They need to be put back in place."

"Don't say anything to Maxime. It'll only make the situation worse."

He regards me stoically.

"Please, Benoit. Don't make this harder for me than what it already is."

Still no answer.

I can't delay much longer without being late for class. Taking a shortcut over the grass, I head for my building.

CHAPTER 12

Maxime

The last time I visited Dr. Delphine Bisset was before my trip to South Africa. She's a good shrink. I'm not the self-searching or inwardly reflecting kind, but she helped me understand shitloads about myself, which, believe it or not, is imperative in my business. You can't know your enemies if you don't know yourself. Delphine is the only one with the balls to be honest with me. The psychiatrist I tried before her told me whatever I wanted to hear. I guess he was worried I'd shoot him.

Pushing the door to her uptown consultation room open, I walk to the receptionist's desk. I'm alone. My guards don't tag along for this. My visits to the shrink are something I prefer to keep private. My enemies may take it for a weakness.

The girl looks up. Her easy smile vanishes. "Good morning, sir." Her hand is already on the phone. "Dr. Bisset is with a patient, but I'll let her know you're here."

I give her a polite nod and take a seat among the other waiting patients. Five minutes later, the door to the office opens and a young man exits in front of Delphine.

"Max." She offers me a warm smile and beckons me with a wave.

The other patients glare at me when I stand. I don't have an appointment.

Ignoring their nasty looks, Delphine shuts the door and shakes my hand. "It's been a while."

"I've been busy."

"Naturally," she says with wit. "Crime will do that to you." Walking to the informal sitting area, she motions for me to take a seat. "What brings you today?"

I sit down in one of the armchairs and adjust my jacket. "A woman."

"Ah." She takes the seat opposite me and crosses her legs. "You mean one you've seen more than twice?"

"Six months, actually."

She tilts her head. "Very out of character for you. What makes this one different?"

"She's innocent. Pure. I suppose you could say she's naïve."

Folding her hands, she studies me. "You're attracted to these *innocent* traits?"

"Naturally," I say, quoting her earlier remark. "Opposites attract and all that."

Her smile is eloquent. "Why?"

"She's everything I'm not. I'd say that's obvious."

"How is this a problem for you?" she asks in her smooth voice.

Leaning forward, I rest my elbows on my knees and tip my fingers together. I give her a long look as I weigh my words. Their heaviness bears down right in the center of my chest. "Am I capable of love, Doctor?"

"Max." She blows out a short sigh. It's a soft sound laced with compassion. "In order to love, you need to have empathy."

"Whenever I'm the cause of her pain, I hurt myself worse than what she's hurting."

"You're inflicting pain on yourself?"

"Yes."

"As punishment?"

"As a reminder."

"To have empathy?"

"Yes."

"Physical pain doesn't replace compassion, Max. Compassion comes from the heart."

"That's the thing. She makes me feel." I press a palm over my chest where the dead skin crawls from the mere thought of her. "She makes me feel *things*."

"Define things."

"Fear. Fucking loads of it. Weakness. She makes me care."

"Can you put her first, above your own needs?"

I consider that. Putting Zoe first will mean doing what's best for her and what she wants—to let her go. Only, I can't do that, and it has nothing to do with her brother's diamonds. I'll never set her free. She's mine. *Mine*. I fucking claimed her. I took her virginity. I came inside her. No, I'm afraid letting her go has and will never be an option. Tilting my head back, I scrub a hand over my face.

"Do you manipulate her, Max?"

I look back at the doctor. "For her own good."

"Do you lie to her?"

"When I must."

"Do you feel shame or remorse for your lies and manipulations?"

"No."

Her small smile is sad, conveying a wordless message.

"Yeah, yeah." I rake my fingers through my hair. "I'm still the pathologically lying, manipulative, coldhearted prick with the versatile criminal behavior and lack of moral judgment."

"And high intelligence," she adds, "not to mention ruthlessness."

"That's supposed to help me?"

She leans her arms on her knees. "You're the most ruthless person I know, meaning you're willing to take risks. Are you willing to take a risk for her and step out of your comfort zone? You're also a clever man, a man who knows how his behavior impacts others, even if you don't feel guilty about it. You want to do better. That's why you sought me out for starters."

"Even if I do better, I'll still be the fucking psychopath incapable of love."

"You suffer from emotional detachment, but feeling something is a beginning. We can work with that."

Frustration mounts. "I'm pretty much agitated right now. That counts for an emotion."

"Your frustration and anger are manifestations of your selfish impatience. We've already covered this."

"Isn't caring for someone love in its own kind of way?"

"It depends on the root of the caring. Is this about her or you?"

I shift in my seat. "What do you mean?"

"Do you care because of how being with her makes *you* feel, or do you care about how she feels, regardless of yourself?"

"I don't want her to be sad or unhappy."

"How do you feel when she's unhappy?"

"Frightened."

"Why?"

"That it'll slip away."

"That what will slip away?"

"Her. This. What I'm feeling when she's around."

"Right." She raises a brow. "So, this is about you."

"I love my family, don't I?"

"You hate your father, and your brother is your biggest enemy. You have a sense of responsibility toward your mother, and you experience feelings of injustice for your father's behavior, but you lack the empathy that forms unconditional relationships with your family."

"This woman—*my* woman—grew up in a dysfunctional family in a poor neighborhood. She's been exposed to every circumstance you quoted for making a psychopath, yet she's not like me. How come?"

"Max." She sighs again. "It's not a secret you can steal. Every person's internal and external factors are unique. As I've told you before, I suspect in your case it's a combination of your violent circumstances and genetic inheritance."

"So," I say with a wry smile, "you're telling me I'll never be able to love."

"I think you do love in your own way, and I do believe you'll be able to build a trusting and sharing relationship if you can manage to see things from your partner's perspective."

"But?"

"But in this case, your care is selfish. You said it yourself. She gives you what you don't have. You're opposites. You're using her to balance yourself."

Great. This helps a fucking lot, and it changes nothing.

"Thank you, Doctor."

"Always a pleasure, Max." Despite her strict no touching policy, she leans over and squeezes my hand. "I'm here when you need me."

I stand. "I appreciate your time."

"No, you don't." Her intelligent eyes meet mine. "You expect it. In fact, you insist." Not unkindly, she adds, "Next time, try to be considerate to everyone else and make an appointment."

She's right, as always.

I'd give my life to give Zoe the love she deserves, but I am what I am.

I leave Dr. Bisset's office still the same man, a man unable to reciprocate love.

CHAPTER 13

Zoe

As promised, Sylvie sends me a text, suggesting a brasserie in the old town.

Benoit drives me while the men from this morning follow again. With the yellow awning and red window frames, the brasserie looks like a typical French postcard. Before, I would've thought this a dream. Now I can only admire the image abstractly, a deeper part of me hating everything associated with this city.

Loud chatter greets me when I push the door open. The inside smells of coffee and beer. It's busy. People sipping wine or espresso occupy the tables. Not one is free. It seems like a popular place to meet for drinks after work.

Benoit follows behind me and then overtakes to greet some of the customers. I spot Sylvie at the bar. She's wearing a fitted powder-blue dress with a short jacket and ballerina flats. The ensemble is simple but stylish. It's the kind of understated elegance Madame Page and

Maxime's mother favor. Noelle and Hadrienne, too. This is the French bourgeois style.

Benoit raises a hand to catch the bartender's attention. The bartender smiles kindly when he notices me. He says something to Sylvie, who turns.

"There you are," she says when I reach her, kissing my cheeks. She holds me at arm's length to study my leggings and off-shoulder jersey. "You look gorgeous."

I love this jersey. It has pirate sleeves and a drawstring in the hem for a puffy look. "Thank you."

"Come." She takes my hand and leads me to the back. "Let's sit."

The men at the table for which she's headed get up when they see us, take their drinks, and leave.

"That's very gentlemanly," I say.

"Ha. Don't you believe that. It's only because they know who Papa is. Espresso?"

"Tea, please."

She signals the bartender, making a C and a T with her hands. "So, what made you call?"

A man died saving my life. My kidnapper went after the attackers and killed them. Not only did I discover that said kidnapper is a mafia boss, but also that he deceived me when he held my brother's life over my head. I threatened him with an icepick. He tied me up and punished me with multiple orgasms all day. My teacher and classmates think I'm a fake and hate me. I won't even know where to begin. There's no way I can answer her question honestly.

"It's tough," she says, covering my hand with hers, "but you can't let it get to you."

I force myself back to the moment. "What?"

"The shooting. You can't let them win."

"Who?"

"*Brise de Mer.*"

"Is that a gang?"

"The Corsicans. They've been at war with my family for years."

The bartender arrives with our drinks. He serves them with ginger cookies and leaves.

How does Sylvie cope with mafia life? How can she sit there so unafraid, looking so normal? "I don't know how you can live like this."

"Don't worry." She lifts her cup to her lips. "Our men will take care of us."

I consider her words. They strike a chord of irony. "It's funny. I used to have this stupid fantasy of being saved from my miserable life and carried off to a happy ending by a knight in shining armor. Now I don't like that fantasy so much. I didn't like being *saved*." I make quotation marks with my fingers. I can't tell her *saved* is a sarcastic term for kidnapped. "I think I prefer to be in control of my life."

"Oh, honey." She makes a sad face. "The women belonging to the *family* have very little freedom, but we do have control. You just have to be clever about it."

"You mean manipulation?"

She cocks a shoulder. "Papa wouldn't let Noelle and me study, so we got *depressed*." She chuckles. "We started eating so much Maman told Papa no man would ever marry us if we couldn't even fit into a wedding dress."

"That made him agree?"

"Papa's biggest fear is that we won't give him grandchildren."

A life of constant manipulation seems awfully sad, not to mention exhausting, but I'm not going to insult her by telling her so.

"You need to figure out what Max's weak points are," she continues. "You, for one, seem to be a pretty strong weakness. Surely, you must have some bargaining power in bed."

My cheeks heat.

"See?" She wags her eyebrows. "I knew I was right. You need to convince him to let you come visit me in Paris. We'll go out and do some shopping. It'll make you feel a whole lot better."

It's appealing, but a crazy idea. "I doubt that'll ever happen."

"You may be surprised. Max cares about you. He wants you to be happy. I'm sure he'll do anything to make sure you are. He may come along to Paris and bring an army with him, but he'd do that if you go about it the right way."

The right way. He's showed me time and again he'd treat me kindly if I behave, but that's just another form of manipulation, and I'm so tired of the games. I just want to be free. I want to make my own decisions and determine my own actions. I don't want to have hidden agendas. I want to give because I care, not because I need something in return. How can I explain that to Sylvie who's been raised to navigate this world and its myriad of landmines?

"We have to make the best of what we have," Sylvie says, pushing her empty cup aside. "Accept what we can't change. Let's face it, we have it a lot better than many other women." She gets to her feet. "Do you mind if I have a cigarette?"

"Of course not."

She grabs her bag. "You'll have to come with me. I'll have to smoke in the toilet." When I frown, she says, "Papa doesn't know."

"Oh." Of course. The people here all know Benoit. That means they all know the *family*. One of the men will see it as his duty to inform Sylvie's father if she lights up a cigarette in the street.

When I follow her to the bathroom, Benoit takes up a position by the bar from where he can keep an eye on the door. It's a unisex bathroom. The space is cramped with a small basin on one side and a toilet on the other.

She locks the door and takes a cigarette from her purse. "I can't buy a packet, or Papa will know. Every tobacco shop owner in Marseille pays Papa rent."

"Then how do you get them?" I ask, leaning on the counter.

"Some of the guards are friendly." She takes a drag and blows out a thin line of smoke. "I know which ones won't talk. See? You just have to be clever."

I both admire and pity Sylvie. I pity her lack of freedom and admire her survival skills. I admire her outlook on all of this. I wish I could cope so easily. I study her from under my lashes. Can I trust her? She did open up to me about forcing her father's hand to let her study and smoking behind his back, and she was kind enough to make time and meet me.

"Can I ask you something, Sylvie?"

She blows smoke from the corner of her mouth. "Shoot."

"What's the difference between a mistress and property?"

"Where did you hear about that?" She offers me the cigarette.

I shake my head. "Just something the guys talked about."

"A mistress is a lover. It means an open-ended relationship that continues for however long the guy wants."

"What about what the woman wants?"

"In our world, honey, it's always the guy who decides when to call it quits. Property, on the other hand, is a dead end. It means a man has claimed a woman for life. It's like being a mistress, only forever."

The revelation shouldn't shock me. Maxime said as much when he told me he'd never let me go. Still, her explanation settles like an iron ball in my stomach.

She scrutinizes me with shrewd eyes. "Did Max tell you you're property?"

I can't even answer that.

Her smile is sympathetic. "Give him a chance, Zoe. Max isn't that bad. You do feel for him, don't you?"

Placing a hand on my forehead, I say, "I don't even know what I feel anymore."

"It's obvious you care. What are you so worried about?"

"It's complicated."

"Tell him how you feel."

Chewing my lip, I consider that. "I don't know."

"Look, you're stuck, anyway. What can it hurt?"

I inhale deeply. "That's the problem. It can hurt."

"Max really is crazy about you. He's different with you. Just give it a shot. If you don't try, you'll never know." Waving a hand to disperse the smoke, she puts the cigarette out in the sink and drops the butt in the trashcan. "We better get back before they wonder what's taking us so long."

"They? You have men following you, too?"

"Protecting me." She winks. Going through her bag, she takes out an anti-tobacco spray and applies it liberally to her clothes and hair before popping a chewing gum into her mouth. "There. Ready to go?"

I nod.

"You'll be okay. Trust me." She takes my hand. "Promise we'll do this again."

I can't help but smile. "I promise."

"Good." She kisses my cheek. "You can do with a friend."

A man in a suit I don't recognize stands next to Benoit when we exit.

He addresses Sylvie when we reach them. "What took so long?"

She bats her eyelashes. "Period. Changing tampons and all that. Want more details?"

The man coughs. Benoit looks away. She gives me a smile that says, *see?*

She's as trapped as I am. It's an eye opener. I feel sorry for her, but I also feel a little lighter when Benoit drives me home. Sylvie has helped me face a truth, something I've known in my heart for a while but couldn't admit. My love for Maxime isn't conventional. Our relationship isn't healthy or smooth sailing. He's a hardened criminal with a dark heart, and I'm a naïve romantic with an abandoned princess fantasy. Somehow, we work together. Somehow, we've rubbed off on each other. We're diamonds in the rough, cutting our edges together. I no longer want to leave. This is crazy, the craziest thing I've ever done, but I'm going to tell Maxime how I feel. I want to try, because maybe, just maybe, there are ways to survive Maxime, and maybe I don't have to do it alone.

CHAPTER 14

Maxime

When Benoit calls me while Zoe is having coffee with Sylvie and tells me what has happened at school, I'm fucking fuming. I leave my father's office earlier than usual and drive to the campus, bargaining on the fact that Madame Page always works late.

She's alone in her office when I enter just before seven.

"Can I help you?" she asks with her head bent over some sketches and a cigarette dangling from her mouth.

"You most definitely can," I say, striding to her desk.

Her paper-thin skin turns white when she looks up. "Mr. Belshaw."

Yeah. She should be scared.

Her hand shakes as she tips the ash. "I'm busy."

I turn a chair around and straddle it. "Let's get something straight. Zoe deserves to be here the same as everyone else. She has more passion in her style than that shift dress with the fancy label you're wearing. If she's not in class, it's because I need her to be elsewhere. Do you understand?"

Her lip curls. "You're being very clear."

"Good."

"However, this is a serious establishment. I won't let you intimidate me."

I grin. "Let me remind you that the women who earn enough money to afford your label move in the same circles. It'll be a pity if their eyes are opened as to just how undeserving your style is of praise."

Her right eye twitches.

"Is that enough intimidation for you?" I ask. "I can get as persuasive as you'd like me to be."

"Quite enough," she says with a tight jaw.

"Great." I rap my knuckles on her desk. "I'd hate to destroy your career when you're so close to retiring." I get up. "Nice talking to you."

I leave with a smile.

At home, I find Zoe sitting on her favorite bench in the garden, sipping a glass of wine and staring at the sea. I study her profile to make out her mood, but for once her expression doesn't give much away. Her gaze is trained on the distance, her thoughts seeming far-off.

"How was school?" I ask when I stop next to her, observing her closely.

She looks up at me with a start. "Good."

I know why she asked Benoit to keep his mouth shut. After all, it's my fault they all hate her. Perhaps I should've been upfront about how she'd gotten into the school, but she was just so damn excited about it. Her joy made me feel things I've never felt before. It made me *happy*. I just didn't have the heart to disappoint her.

Tracing the curve of her shoulder with a finger, I ask, "How was your coffee date with Sylvie?"

Her face brightens a little. "We had a good time."

"I'm glad."

I mean it. Despite what she thinks, her unhappiness affects me. I don't like it when she's lonely or sad. The attempt on her life still hangs over us. So does everything else that has happened—the icepick incident, coming inside her, tying her up, punishing her…and telling her the truth. The air hasn't been cleared, and all this pollution makes it hard to go back to how we used to be. Then again, do I want to go back? Perhaps this is a step forward.

Tentatively, she lifts a hand. Ever so slowly, she cups my fingers where they rest on her shoulder. I don't breathe. I don't even blink for the fear that she'll move her hand away. Joy surges through my chest. Such a small gesture, yet such a big step in bridging this gap that has fallen between us since the attempt on her life. We stay like this for the longest time as I try to understand this olive branch she's offering. Did Sylvie manage to talk some sense into her?

Fran breaks the spell, calling, "Dinner is ready."

Bloody hell. I turn on her. "You hardly have to announce it."

She pales and wilts. "The food will get cold."

My voice rises with impatience. "Leave it where you always do. In the warm drawer."

"It's all right." Zoe gets to her feet. "We're coming." When my fingers tighten on her shoulder, she adds quickly, "I'm hungry."

I know what Zoe is doing. She's trying to prevent a fight. It's working. My body goes slack, and the earlier tranquility we've somehow found flows back through my veins.

Fran turns away with a wounded expression.

"I think she has feelings for you," Zoe says when Fran is out of earshot.

"Our relationship is strictly professional." Gripping her chin, I note the dark rings under her eyes. "Maybe we should have an early night."

"I can't. I missed a lot in class yesterday. I have to catch up."

I trace her bottom lip with my thumb. "Not at the expense of your health. You need your rest."

"Maxime, stop babying me." She swallows, then glances away. When she looks back at me, she says in a composed tone, "I need this."

"I know you do, *cherie*." Ah, hell. My resolve crumbles. "I'll sit up with you. I won't be able to sleep, anyway." Not if she's not in my bed.

"Honestly, you don't have to."

"No, I don't." In a rare instant, I give her the truth. "I want to."

CHAPTER 15

Maxime

For the next few days, clearing the city of infiltrators dominates my time. I flush out the disloyal men and dole out deaths as examples and punishment where due. It's not only about survival. It's also about keeping the streets safe for the people we protect and the businesses that rely on us.

The attack on Zoe's life left me edgy. Volatile. Even Leonardo stays out of my way. My instincts scream at me to lock her up again, but I understand enough of human nature to know it'll be a mistake. Zoe needs the illusion of freedom. She needs her friendship with Sylvie. She needs to go to classes and chase her dream. I want to own her, not crush her. I want her to flourish, because I need her for who she is. Because of this, when she comes to me one night in the library after I returned home late and another dinner we didn't eat together, I'm attentive to her needs.

"How was your day?" she asks, handing me a whiskey.

She's been nothing but exemplary, a good little girl, and it earns her my kindness. Zoe isn't my enemy. I have no desire to harm or hurt her. I neither take pleasure from teaching her lessons, nor from inflicting pain on myself when I'm hurting her. I much prefer our harmony, to fuck her in earnest and without the tension that comes with complicated games. I know adapting hasn't been easy for her, but I'm trying to make up for it by giving her everything I can. The more effort she makes for me, the more I give back in return. Of all the lessons I've taught her, this is maybe the most important one. It's the answer to both of our peace and happiness, for as long as I can taste her pussy and drink in her existence, I'm as happy as I'll ever be.

"The usual," I say, accepting the drink.

She reaches up to undo my tie. I enjoy the pressure of her slight weight where her body rests against mine. I love the sight of her beautiful face. I fucking revel in knowing she's mine. I get hard knowing I'm going to bend her over the sofa and fuck her before letting her work on her sewing machine in the spare room I've converted into a working space. I don't like the long hours she puts in, but she doesn't sleep more than a few hours anyway, hasn't since the night of the shooting. Working is better than staring at the ceiling with an idle mind. Idle minds are unhealthy. They reflect too much.

I trace the V-neck of her blouse. It's a frilly affair with soft layers. "Did you make this?"

"Yes."

She makes a lot of her clothes now. I like how she dresses. Her garments are feminine and soft, reminding me of sweet smelling roses and gentle daisies.

"It's nice," I say.

"Thank you," she whispers.

Taking a sip of the drink, I bend down and press our mouths together. When she parts her lips, I feed her the alcohol. I let her swallow before using my tongue to taste the whiskey on hers. I lap at her mouth like I'm planning on eating her out later, giving her a preview of what I have in mind for her pussy.

She moans. *Fuck.* It's all it takes. I catch fire. Putting the drink aside, I reach for the buttons of her blouse. The silk is smooth under my fingers, but it's nothing compared to her skin.

"Maxime." She pushes with her palms on my chest and bend backwards to escape my kiss. "I want to ask you something."

I chase after her mouth, catching her around the waist as I lower her onto the couch. "I know."

"Wait." She bites her lip, staring up at me with her big, irresistible eyes. "I don't want you to think I'm fucking you so you'd say yes."

I push my hand under her skirt and trail my fingers up the inside of her leg. So warm. So soft. I barely contain my excitement as I move higher. I'm like an eager teenager on his first date. My hand trembles when I finally cup the juncture of her legs. *Double fuck.*

"How can I deny you anything when you're wet like this?" I groan against her lips, grinding my erection against her sex.

"Maxime." She gives me a little frown. Adorable. "I'm serious."

"So am I." Catching the elastic of her panties, I work them down her thighs. I leave them on her knees and bunch her skirt up to her waist. I use one hand to unzip my fly and take out my cock while keeping my weight on the other that rests next to her face. Her long, silky hair brushes against my fingers.

"I don't want Benoit to drive me," she says. "He hates babysitting me."

I shudder as the head of my cock pushes against her slick pussy lips. "He does what I tell him to do." Pleasure rips from my balls up my spine as I sink deep.

She gasps, threading her fingers through my hair. "I want to drive myself."

Goddamn. Fuck. She feels good. "Why?"

"I haven't driven a car since I got my driver's license in South Africa." She whimpers when I start moving. "I want to be independent."

"Fine." I'm not going to last.

"Really?" She pulls on my hair, bringing our mouths close. "You mean it?"

"After you've practiced driving on the right-hand side."

Her expression softens with pleasure and gratitude.

"Benoit and my men follow wherever you go."

She locks her legs around my waist, lifting her pelvis to take more. "Okay."

"Fuck, Zoe."

That obedience. The easy agreement. Letting me have my way. I break. I fuck her like a madman and come even before I've tasted her or bent her over the armrest like I've fantasized, before I've taken care of her pleasure.

Resting my forehead against hers, I try to get my erratic heartbeat under control. "Now look what you've done."

She smiles. It's not just another smile, but one she smiles for *me*. It's a selfless one that takes my breath away.

"I didn't make you come, you naughty girl."

"I don't mind," she whispers, stretching lazily. "It was good, anyway."

"It wasn't good. It was fucking great, and it's far from over."

She stares at me with sated eyes—trusting eyes—as I push a hand between our bodies and find her clit. She lets me take care of her with her body stuffed full of my cock and cum. It doesn't take long before I recognize the signs. Her pupils dilate and her gaze turns hazy. Rosy pink colors her cheeks. Her inner muscles clench, and her head falls back as she says my name.

The top button of her blouse is undone, a job I abandoned in my haste to get into her panties. I try to finish that intention now, fumbling with the second button. Fuck it. I tear the blouse open in another fit of haste. Her chest heaves with labored breaths as I roll a thumb over her clit, working her fast to bring her up to speed with me. I brush the fabric of her blouse aside and leave her breasts covered in lace. Like this, she looks ravished. Devoured. Undone. Just looking at her makes my cock grow hard again. I swell inside her, stretching her inner muscles.

"Maxime," she moans, every kind of emotion coloring her voice.

"Say it again," I demand with a growl against her ear. I want to hear more of that rainbow, of that complex spectrum of feelings. It fuels me to move harder, to make her shout it.

"I love you," she cries out.

Everything inside me simultaneously combusts and freezes. I fill her up with release even as my body goes as rigid as a rod. I'm ecstatic and devastated. I'm roaring in victory and hurting with something I can't name. For the first time in my life, Delphine's diagnosis is a heavy burden on my shoulders. Pretty little innocent flowers turn their faces to the sun, not to monsters like me. The only reward I can offer is sinking as deep as her body can take me and pounding my ownership into her with a too-harsh rhythm.

Struggling for breath, I push up on my elbows to frame her face between my palms. Tears leak from the corners of her eyes. I kiss them away, offering my lips in exchange for my lack of words.

My thrusts turn even more grueling. I can come ten times more like this. Pleasure already builds again at the base of my spine, but I slow my pace to time our releases. When we finally come, it's a powerful eruption of intertwined relief.

I fucking fly.

She falls.

All I can give is catching her.

CHAPTER 16

Zoe

I wake up to the first glorious day after another freezing winter and realize this ocean has been my view for the past eighteen months. Eighteen months of giving myself to Maxime. The realization jars me. I stare at my face in the mirror, the make-up brush frozen in my hand. I'm trying. I really am. I can't say he's not treating me well. After I dropped the bomb about loving him, nothing has changed for the better, but at least nothing has changed for the worst, either. We're maintaining our status quo.

Maxime steps from the dressing room wearing a white shirt and blue suit tailored to the latest fashion, paired with Italian shoes. He looks smart and impossibly handsome. He's focused on fitting a cufflink, but when he catches my gaze, he walks up behind me and places his hands on my shoulders. Our eyes remained locked for a moment before he swoops down and places a kiss on my neck.

"Good morning, *cherie*." His gray eyes turn a shade warmer. "You look beautiful."

"Thank you." With the restriction in my throat, the words sound thick.

He frowns. "What's wrong?"

"Nothing." I force a smile. "I'm running late, that's all."

The lie comes with effort. He knows me well enough by now not to buy it. Besides, I'm always early.

Kneading my shoulders, he says, "Try again."

He won't give up until I tell him. Biting my lip, I gauge his mood. "I've just realized it's been eighteen months."

Some of the warmth in his gaze dissipates. "We should go out and celebrate."

It's hardly something I want to celebrate, but I know better than to fail this test. "Whenever you want."

He brushes my hair over my shoulder. "I meant to speak to you about tonight."

The way he hesitates makes me tense. "What about tonight?"

"We have to attend a gallery opening." Searching my face, he adds, "With my family."

"Your *whole* family?"

"Everyone, including Alexis. I wouldn't expose you to them if I didn't have to, but this is an important event. We have a lot invested in the gallery."

"I could stay at home?" I offer hopefully.

"No." His tone is curt. "Hiding you at home would send the wrong message."

"Which is?"

"That I don't respect you."

"Oh." His respect never crossed my mind. "Do you?"

"Of course." He twists a strand of hair around his finger. "I admire you."

"If people think you don't respect me, how would that be a problem?"

"People you don't respect are expendable."

Goosebumps break out over my arms. "I see." No one has tried to kill me since the drive-by shooting, but the threat is never out of my thoughts for long.

"All right." My smile is shaky. I don't like Maxime's family. I definitely don't look forward to seeing them at a gala event, which will be stressful enough as it is.

He squeezes my shoulders. "Sylvie will be there."

At least there's something to look forward to.

Gripping my chin, he turns my face to the side and kisses my lips. "I'll see you tonight. Be ready at seven."

I hurry through the rest of my grooming and go down to the kitchen to prepare my latest breakfast craze—a spirulina and berry smoothie.

Francine regards me from where she's rolling out dough for a quiche. She's long since given up on setting out my breakfast, but she still dumps the granulated sugar in the trashcan and replaces it with cubes. In turn, I buy sticky brown sugar and fill up the pot I bought. It's a childish circle of spitefulness, but neither of us is prepared to surrender.

"You better start wearing sunblock," she says, studying me from under her lashes. "You're getting more freckles."

Twisting the lid onto my portable cup, I smile. "Maxime loves my freckles."

She laughs. "Any man who says he likes freckles is a liar."

"I'll let Maxime know," I say on my way to the door.

"That he's a liar? Oh, trust me, he knows, but so do you."

I turn on my heel. "Maybe you should tell him that to his face."

"He knows how I feel. He promised me things when we were together." Leaning her hands on the counter, she returns my fake smile. "What did he promise *you*?"

"What happens between Maxime and me doesn't concern you."

I leave without saying goodbye, holding my head high as I walk through the door, but her words have thorns, and they hook into my heart. I can't get them out of my head during the drive to school or for the duration of my classes.

. . .

My brain feels mushy from a whole day of complicated pattern calculations and mulling over what Francine has said. When I get home by six, I have a headache. The stress of anticipating tonight doesn't help. I take a painkiller and am ready at the hour Maxime has stipulated. At seven sharp, he enters the bedroom with a bouquet of pink roses.

"For the most beautiful woman in the world," he says, offering them to me.

"They're gorgeous." I inhale their scent. "Thank you."

"You're welcome." He runs his gaze over my dress. "One of your designs?"

"Yes." It's a black halter neck with a short train at the back. The skirt is decorated with a few black feathers. They add texture and a focal point to the otherwise simple cut.

"Absolutely stunning." He cups my hips. "Even more so on this body."

I've grown accustomed to his compliments. Maxime isn't someone to offer empty appraisal. He means what he says. I can't help but wonder what compliments he whispered into Francine's ear. For her to be so bitter over their breakup, it had to have been serious.

"Maxime." I put the flowers on the bed, weighing my words. "How committed were things between Francine and you?"

He studies me for a moment. "I told you. It was sex."

"Like us? We're sex, too. Nothing more, right?"

His expression darkens. "There's no comparison between you and Francine."

"What's the difference?"

His fingers tighten on my flesh. "You're a keeper."

"What did you promise her?"

"Nothing." His look is chastising. "I don't make promises I can't keep."

"That's not how she sees it."

He sets me aside and drops his arms by his side. "What did she say to you?"

"That you promised her *things*."

He chuckles. "Believe me, if I promised her *things*, you wouldn't be here."

I'd be with Alexis, and she would've shared Maxime's bed. Yet here I am. "Why?"

"Why what?" He checks his watch. "We don't have time for this, Zoe."

"Why me? Why not Francine or someone else? Is it just because of the diamonds?" I ask, although, I find that hard to believe. He didn't have to keep me forever. He could've let me go when his deal was secured. Maybe he's worried Damian will reverse his decision if he finds out the truth, if this crazy scheme Maxime mentioned ever works out.

A nerve ticks under his eye. "I know what you're asking, Zoe."

"I'm asking why you chose *me* as your property."

"No." He grips my chin. "You're asking if I feel differently about you than other women. The answer is yes. I've never cared more, but you're also asking if I love you. The answer to that, as much as it saddens me, is and will always be no."

His words drive into my heart. They twist and hurt. I lay a palm over the ache, willing it to stop, but I can't turn my feelings off. I can only suffer them knowing there will never be a remedy. Why did I have to scratch the scab off? We were doing so well.

"Maybe..." A suppressed sob turns into a soft gasp. "Maybe you feel more than you realize."

"I *know*."

"How?" I exclaim. "The way you behave—"

"Is designed to make you happy. Love is selfless, like you. Me, I'm the opposite of everything you are. I'm selfish."

Stupidly, I cling to hope. "You're being very hard on yourself."

"No, Zoe." His eyes are solemn. "If I loved you, I would've set you free."

What he says rings true. Yet I don't want it to be. It's too agonizing to bear. I press my free hand over my stomach to where the ache spreads, holding in the raw emotions that threaten to tumble out.

"I wish to God I was capable of love," he says. "I want to give it to you more than I want to do anything in the world, but this is who I am." He strokes a thumb over my chin. "I can't change my nature."

His words are killing me. Between Francine and me, she's the one who's better off. At least she doesn't have to live with him day and night while suffering the knowledge for an unloving eternity. I'm so fucking pathetic. Why do I do this to myself over and over? Why do I keep wanting us to be different?

"If you can't love me," I say, "set me free." It hurts too much to live like this. "Please, Maxime. We can just forget about everything. I won't lay charges. I won't tell a soul. Not even Damian. I promise."

"You know I can't do that."

"Why not?" I cry out.

"Because I can't live without you."

I can only stare at him, trying to get a grip on the old hurt that won't let go. Just when I think I've accepted my situation, I have to go and lift the lid on the pot of my twisted emotions.

"I'm sorry." Folding his arms around me, he pulls me close. "If it makes you feel better, I'm living to make it up to you."

It doesn't, but there's nothing to be done about it. It's not going to change, and I'm not going to cry about it.

My heart must be hardening slowly but surely, because my eyes are dry when I pull away. "Thank you for being honest with me." I'm bleeding inside, but I put on a smile. I've learned from the master.

He kisses my lips. The action is tender, apologetic. It's like a kiss on a child's cut knee. His eyes fold in the corners. Giving me a thoughtful nod like he's just ticked a task off his to-do list, he takes the flowers and walks to the bathroom. I act on autopilot, dumping lipstick and perfume into my clutch bag. Anything to keep my hands busy and hide how I'm feeling.

When he returns, he takes my hand like his words haven't torn me apart. "Shall we go?"

I know the right answer. "Yes."

"Good." He kisses my cheek. "I think you'll like the exhibition."

We drive to town without making conversation. He takes a few calls, but, like always, avoids discussing *business* in front of me. For my own protection, I assume.

The minute we enter the gallery, guests swamp Maxime. To be honest, I'm happy for the reprieve. I need some space from him.

When he hands me a glass of champagne that he takes from a passing waiter, I say, "I'm going to look for Sylvie."

He nods, casts a glance around the room, and flicks his fingers at Benoit.

The place is packed. Making my way through the masses with Benoit following closely, I pass contemporary paintings featuring garbage. Rotting food, one-eyed dolls, and burnt flowers are the subjects. I get the message, but Maxime was wrong. I hate it.

The crowd thins toward the back. A room leads off to the right. I go inside. A mobile light display illuminates nails in the wall. Mumbling, "Excuse me," I push through the spectators who entered behind me and make my way to the room on the opposite side. Just before I reach the archway, Sylvie's bubbly laugh reaches my ears. Oh, thank God. I'm not going to dump my problems on her, but I can do with a friend. I'm about to enter when my name pops up in her conversation. I stop in my tracks.

"I don't know how you can stand her," a female voice says. "Her clothes are so distasteful."

"The princess stuff is the worst," Sylvie says.

"Did you see her dress when they walked in tonight?"

"Hideous."

"Someone should tell her."

"Ha," Sylvie says. "I just can't be bothered."

Sucking in a breath, I lean a hand on the wall. My heart starts thumping with a heavy beat. It's a beat I recognize well, one that pumps with the knowledge of betrayal.

"I hate how naïve she is," Sylvie continues.

They can't be talking about me. Sylvie is my friend.

"I don't see what Maxime sees in her," the other woman says.

"Boobs and ass, obviously," Sylvie replies. "The fact that he won't marry her says a lot."

A wave of heat rises from my stomach to my chest, making me feel sick.

A hand lands on my arm. "Are you all right?"

I look from the hand to its owner. Benoit. "Fine." I down the champagne and hand him the glass. "I need another drink."

Turning around, I go in the opposite direction. I don't stop until I'm somewhere in the middle of the floor, hidden by strangers. Benoit hands me another glass. I thank him and swallow it down.

"Hey," he says, "you better go easy on the booze."

I hand him the empty glass. He's right. I'm not my father, but maybe I am the naïve princess Sylvie described. I fell for her deceit, didn't I? I was stupid enough to believe she was sincere. Taking a glass of juice from a nearby cocktail table, I keep an eye on the archway.

Not long after, Sylvie and Noelle exit. They walk to a small group, smiling as they near. Raphael, Cecile, Emile, Hadrienne, and Alexis are standing together.

"Are those girls being bitches to you?" Benoit asks, following my gaze.

"No."

"I wouldn't worry about their opinion."

I look at him, really look at him for the first time. After he's asked me to keep my distance, I've respected his request. We never drive together any longer, but I've noticed him hastily shoving pastries down his throat in his car before following me to class.

"Do you eat croissants for breakfast every day?" I ask.

His face scrunches up. "What?"

"That can't be healthy or good for your weight."

He drags a hand over his stomach. "The girls aren't complaining."

"From now on, I'll make you a smoothie."

"A fucking what?"

"If you follow me, I may as well watch out for you."

"I'm not following you. I'm protecting you. *I'm* the one watching out for *you*."

I'm hurting inside, my chest throbbing like an open wound, but the banter is like a Band-Aid on a cut. Maybe it's just a really good distraction.

"Well," I smile, "all of that is about to change."

"Here we go." He rolls his eyes. "Now I'm your pet project."

"Nothing like that," I say, swatting him on the arm. "But you're done pushing me away."

"Listen here, lady. I missed five football matches because I'm trailing after you."

"Then maybe we should eat lunch in a brasserie where you can catch up on your matches. Two birds with one stone."

"Getting friendly with the staff?" a voice cuts in.

I turn. Alexis stands in front of me, dressed in a tux. My stomach roils. Vivid images of the woman he tortured run through my mind.

"It's been too long," he drawls.

"Not long enough," I mutter.

He chuckles. "A sense of humor, too. No wonder my brother is so taken with you."

I glance at where I left Maxime. He's talking to his father. Maxime's expression is dark and his gaze narrow as he regards Raphael from under his eyelashes. Raphael moves closer, saying something in Maxime's ear. Maxime's hand balls into a fist at his side.

"Speaking of which, how is my brother treating you?" Alexis asks.

"That's none of your business." I look over his shoulder. Benoit has moved a short distance away, discreetly giving us space, but he's still within earshot.

"I was just going to say you're always welcome at my place if you need saving."

"I don't think Maxime will appreciate you talking like that."

"You were supposed to be mine," he says with a wink. "It's only natural that I watch out for you."

"Like you did for that poor woman we found in your apartment?"

His smile is practiced. Underneath the gesture runs malice. "What woman?"

"I'll never pretend it didn't happen," I say, lowering my voice.

"Calm down, Zoe. You think you know everything, don't you?"

"I know enough."

Laughing, he tips back his glass. "You have no idea."

This evening has gotten too much. "Benoit, I'd like to go home."

"Running?" Alexis asks. "Do I scare you, little Zoe?"

A strong hand closes around my upper arm. I look up into Maxime's thunderous face.

"I told you to stay away from her," Maxime says in a cold tone, slipping an arm around my waist and pulling me against his side.

"I can hardly avoid her at a social gathering." Alexis's gaze moves to his family. "Although, it seems everyone else is."

A muscle ticks at Maxime's temple. "If you want a fight, say so. Don't pick one. I'm happy to take it outside."

Alexis lifts his hands. "I come in peace."

"Is that why you went behind my back again?"

"Father invited me to the club for lunch. The opportunity came up. It would've been foolish to waste it. If you'd been there more often like you're supposed to be, you wouldn't have to accuse me of stealing your fifteen minutes of fame." He trails his gaze over me. "We all know where you prefer to spend your evenings."

Sylvie's voice rings over the noise of the crowd. "Zoe!" She makes her way over and takes my hands. "Where have you been? I've been looking all over for you. Look at you. What a beautiful dress. Did you make it?"

I pull away.

"Has Alexis been keeping you busy?" She pouts at her cousin. "Are you bothering my friend?"

"Just leaving," he says, bowing in my direction.

"You do that," Maxime grits out.

"What's going on?" Sylvie asks when Alexis walks off.

"Nothing new," Maxime says. His eyes remain fixed on his brother's back as Alexis walks to the bar and orders a drink.

"I'm in town until Saturday," Sylvie says. "Shall we grab some pizza? Girls' night. You won't mind, will you, Max?"

"Actually," I say, "I have exams coming up."

"What about the weekend after?"

"I'll be putting all my time into my second level proposal."

She makes a face. "That's too bad. Promise you'll call me?"

I barely manage a smile.

"Ready to go?" Maxime asks.

It's hard to hide my relief. "Please."

He studies my face with a piercing gaze. "Everything all right?"

"I'd just like to go. I'm really tired."

He bends down to kiss the shell of my ear. "Bear with me for another few minutes."

Taking my hand, he leads me to his family. The closer we get, the tighter my insides twist. Cecile looks up. The smile vanishes from her face when she sees me. Hadrienne's expression grows hostile.

"Goodnight, Maman." Maxime kisses her cheeks. "Hadrienne." He barely looks at his father.

I do the forced round of kisses, bidding everyone goodnight like Maxime expects of me. Maxime's family returns the polite greeting, putting up their side of the show while Noelle only stands there with a smirk.

It's only in the car that I breathe again. Sinking back into the cool leather of the seat, I wind down the window and drag a hand over my brow.

"What the fuck is going on, Zoe? And, don't tell me it's nothing."

Taking a deep breath, I blow it out slowly. "Did you ask Sylvie to be my friend?"

Maxime looks at me. "Why do you ask that?"

"Just answer the question."

He taps a thumb on the wheel, seeming to consider the answer. After a moment, he says, "She owed me a favor."

His admission tramples on the heart he's already ripped from my chest. "What exactly did you ask her to do?"

"I asked her to give you her number."

"On that Sunday we met?" I exclaim.

"Yes." He shrugs. "I had to cover for her to go out with a group of friends. She told her father she was visiting me." He repeats, "She owed me."

As if that makes it okay. My spirits sink even lower. "The day I told you I wanted to have coffee with her, did you order her to go with me?"

"I called her and told her to expect a call from you. I suggested taking you to a brasserie where you'd be safe."

My breath catches at the implication. "Did you ask her to talk me into giving you a chance?"

"I told her to try and convince you, yes, but only for your own good."

"How's lying to me and pretending to be my friend for my own good?"

"Accepting your situation is for your own good. I want you to be happy, Zoe. Is that so bad?"

"Don't you realize how wrong what you've done is? Are you even sorry?"

"No." His tone is flat. "I'm not sorry for taking care of your emotional comfort."

"God, Maxime." Gripping my head in my hands, I groan in frustration. "You can't keep on doing this."

He shoots me a sidelong glance. "Doing what?"

"Betraying me. You've pushed me as far as I can go, do you hear me? You've pushed me to my limits, and God help me—" I cut off before I threaten the man who owns my life.

His voice turns hard. "God help you with what, Zoe?"

I sag back. "I'm afraid of what I'll do the day you push me over."

"Nothing," he says with blind conviction. "You'll do nothing, because I'll always be there to catch you."

"Please, Maxime." I sag a little lower. "Please stop manipulating me. Why can't you simply be honest?"

He pulls off on the side of the road and brings the car to a jerky halt. "You want honest?"

"Yes!" I'm tired. Depleted. Empty. I have nothing left to give. "Yes, damn you."

"Get out of the car."

My hand clenches on the door handle. "Maxime."

"Now isn't a time to test me."

I open the door and get out, stumbling in the tall grass with my heels. Before I'm a step away from the car, Maxime is there, his strong arms wrapping around my waist. He pushes me forward, bending my body over the hood. Our shadows fall tall over the road in the headlights, two bodies merged as one. The stark silhouette is a lie. The truth is the invisible picture of our estranged souls.

Flipping my skirt up, he rips off my underwear and pushes a knee between my legs. His zipper makes a tearing sound. His cock is at my entrance before I have time to gasp.

"You want the truth?" he breathes against my ear. "This is the truth."

With one, hard thrust, he buries himself so deep inside me his groin slams against my ass. My body shifts over the warm metal of his car. Grabbing a fistful of my hair, he holds me in place and gives me more truth. My inner muscles tighten around him.

"Show me," he says as he gives me the kind of rough that makes my toes curl.

It's no different than pushing me down and making me kneel. My body's reaction is my bitter truth and his sweet victory. I try to deny it. I fight the pleasure that winds around my insides. I fight the lie of the picture on the ground, but he refuses to let me hide. He folds an arm around my body and pushes the heel of his palm on my clit. The harder I fight, the harder he fucks me. There's no way but down. Falling. There's no way out other than surrendering.

I come with a cry and a shudder, every muscle locking in pleasure, but I take no joy from it. I keep still, letting him use me until he finds his release.

"Fuck. What you do to me..." he says, caressing my hip. "Goddamn, Zoe."

Turning my face to the side, I rest my cheek on the metal and stare with non-seeing eyes at the dark ocean. Just like that, the rebellion is over. He squashed it even before it has started.

He wins. Again.

CHAPTER 17

One year later

Maxime

The wind rips through Zoe's long hair when I steer the boat from the jetty of our family holiday home in Corsica. The place is isolated, a pretty piece of paradise. The stretch of beach is private, meaning I can fuck her wherever and whenever I like without worrying about spectators. This weekend is ours alone. No guards. No business.

She takes an elastic band from her wrist and binds the long tresses in a high ponytail. Then she shimmies out of her bikini bottoms and unties the top. The triangles fall away from her breasts. They jiggle when she climbs down the steps and stretches out on the front of the boat. I battle to tear my gaze from her naked body, only managing when I have to navigate through the dangerous rocks close to the cliffs.

I steer the boat to the small island not far off and anchor in the deeper water so we don't get washed up with low tide. After yanking off my shirt, I adjust my hard-on and grab two glasses of champagne and a bowl of strawberries from the table under the awning. Armed with my weapons, I make my way over to where she's tanning with her gorgeous breasts and pussy exposed to the sun.

She pushes up onto her arms when my shadow falls over her.

I hand her a glass. "Here you go, *cherie*."

Squinting up at me, she smiles. Fuck. That smile. If my life should end now, I'll die a happy man.

I stretch out on my side next to her, propping myself up on an elbow. "Congratulations, little flower." I clink my glass to hers. "I'm proud of you."

A shadow creeps over her smile. I know what's going through her mind.

"You deserved to pass," I say. "You did great."

"Did I?"

Unable to resist, I brush my knuckles over a nipple. "You worked hard."

"Hard work isn't always enough."

Taking a mouthful of champagne, I close my lips around the warm tip of her breast, bathing it in the fizzy liquid.

She gasps. "It's cold."

Letting the champagne dribble over her breast, I set the glass aside to test between her thighs. "Always wet for me." Her reaction pleases me to no end.

"Maxime," she chastises as I roll over her, making the champagne slosh over the rim of her glass onto her stomach.

I lap up the spillage. "Delicious."

"You're impossible," she says with a laugh.

"Happy." I mean it. I can't think of a time I felt happier. I carefully push a finger into her tight heat. "Are you?"

"Yes," she says on a sigh, throwing her head back.

"Show me." I watch her greedily as I move my finger.

Her pupils dilate, and her blue eyes turn hazy. A soft moan falls from her lips. Leaving her glass on the side, she reaches for the elastic of my swimming trunks and pushes them over my hips. My cock jumps free, hard and aching. Always ready.

Freeing the finger I teased her with, I slide it past her lips. She curls her tongue around the tip, making my over-eager cock twitch. When I pull out, she bites down gently. My skin comes alive. Every cell in my body starts to hum. The scar tissue on my chest tingles. I catch her nape and bring her lips closer to mine as I drag a flattened palm down her belly to her sex. I claim her mouth as I rub my thumb over her clit. She goes soft in my hold, surrendering her control. I take it with the same abandonment that I took her life, tangling our tongues while I grab the root of my cock and rub the pre-cum over her clit.

"Maxime."

The way she says my name makes me lose it. I was going to take it slow, but I slide all the way in until I hit a barrier and her back arches.

"Good?" I ask, breaking the kiss.

"Mm."

"Show me."

I fuck her in all earnest. Everything will never be enough. I can't explain it. I can't put a label on or words to it. I only know she makes me want more. She wraps her legs around my ass and slams back when I thrust. Our dance is well choreographed and perfectly timed. We're breathing in tune. She never asked me to love her again, but the words hang in the air. It's in the way she rolls her hips and pants as we pick up our pace. It's in the way she holds my eyes and lets me see the desperate need burning out of control.

"You're mine," I say into our kiss, pounding harder into her.

She takes the roughness and gives it back with good measure, her nails digging into my shoulders as she pushes on them to flip us around. For her, I roll over. The way she rides me with her head thrown back and her breasts pushed out is enough to shatter what's left of my control.

I lock my hands around her waist. "Come with me."

She cries out when I roll my hips and hit that spot that makes her reach her *petite mort* quicker.

"Tell me, *cherie*." I lean forward to steal a kiss. "Tell me how it is."

"You know how it is."

Pleasure coils, ready to erupt. "Tell me, anyway."

"Perfect," she whispers.

I explode, my body contracting as every physical sensation I'm capable of aligns in my dick. An answering shudder runs through her body. Her inner muscles clench on my cock, milking me dry.

Taking her face between my hands, I kiss her. I don't know for how long our bodies are fused like this, our mouths and hips joined, but the shadows are longer when I finally convince myself to pull out.

She lays on top of me in a beautiful disarray of dark hair and damp skin, her breasts pushed flat against my chest.

"Perfect," I agree. "I can stay like this forever."

"Then let's," she says, splaying a palm over the ugly skin that covers my breastbone.

Joy infinitely more powerful than the climax still reverberating in my lower body bursts through my chest. It catches me off-guard, shocking me into silence. It's unlike anything I've felt. Gripping her fingers, I hold her hand over my heart.

"Yes," I say. "Let's."

She snuggles with a content little sigh, burying her nose in my neck.

Like I said, "Perfect."

ON SUNDAY, our forever comes to an end, but the perfect lingers when I hold her hand as we board the ferry. The minute we step into my house near Cassis, my father calls and summons me for dinner. When I kiss her and tell her I won't be home late, the only remainder of the paradise we shared is her tan.

We've fallen into an easy rhythm, Zoe and I. She's adapted. All is good. I *feel* good. My mood sours, though, when I walk through the door of my parents' house and find Alexis in the foyer with a glass of wine in his hand.

"Brother." He gives me a cool smile. "I didn't know you were coming."

He'll never forgive me for the lesson I taught him. Together with his envy of my first-born status, it'll be a rift between us for the rest of our days. Not that I care. It's not as if there were ever any brotherly feelings between us before.

I hand my coat to the housekeeper. "Is that a problem?"

Alexis smiles at the young woman. She's new. They never last long with my mother. "I'm just surprised you were able to tear yourself away from Zoe."

"There you are," Maman says, exiting the kitchen. "Come on, Max. Help me carve the lamb."

Throwing a taunting smile over my shoulder at Alexis, I follow my mother to the kitchen.

She pats my cheek. "It's good to have both my boys at home for dinner. That old table is too big for just your father and me." She smiles. "But soon, it will be filled with grandchildren."

Ah. That explains her happy disposition. Me, I'm apathetic about it. It's a duty, like the business. "Don't start, Maman."

"Oh, no. You're not going to deny me that pleasure."

I take the carving knife from the wooden block on the counter. "Don't expect anything too soon."

She pours gravy into a serving bowl. "You're not getting any younger."

For a moment, I think about children. I think about a boy who'll follow in my footsteps, and a girl who'll inherit Maman's fate. I won't say I'm unhappy with my life, but I'm suddenly not sure if the family future is a gift or curse. Before Zoe, I wouldn't have even posed the question, but she has a way of making me look at things through her eyes, seeing them differently.

"Don't you want children?" Maman asks with big eyes.

"Of course, I do."

She dries her hands on her apron, her posture relaxing visibly.

"Good. The honeymoon is over. It's time to focus on family and making babies, but you shouldn't forget the business. You've been neglecting it, allowing Alexis to fill your shoes. Your place is at the head of the family, Max. Don't let worldly distractions make you forget that." She points a finger at me. "You're the one who's supposed to take over your father's business. Alexis can't run it like you can."

I arrange a slice of meat on the serving platter. "You're not telling me anything I don't already know."

"I have news you don't already know," my father says from the door. He tilts his head toward the hallway. "Join me."

Maman throws her hands in the air. "Seriously, Raphael? We're about to sit down for dinner."

"The lamb is already dead," he says. "It's not going anywhere."

Maman switches on the warming drawer with a scoff. "Make it quick. I've slaved over this meal all day."

My father kisses her cheek when she scurries past him. "You're the one who said Max should pay more attention to the business."

"Were you eavesdropping on our conversation?" Maman asks with a teasing smile.

My father kisses her again, this time on the lips.

She shoos him away.

Alexis leans against a wall when we exit, sipping his wine. He watches me from over the rim of his glass, his gaze following my progress as I follow my father to his study.

"What's up?" I ask when I've closed the door.

Father shoves his hands into his pockets. "Damian Hart is out."

My mind jolts into action, considering the implications. "Since when?"

"This morning. I've just heard from Zane."

Hence the last-minute call to come over for dinner. "Is your informant still on the inside?"

"He got out a week ago."

"That's a coincidence."

"He bribed the parole committee."

"Let me guess. You provided the bribe money."

"Of course." My father walks to the wet bar. "We need to keep tabs on Hart now more than ever. Da Costa is just the man to do it."

"If Hart doesn't play into our hands, I'll have to pay him a visit."

"With his sister." He lifts the carafe. "Scotch?"

"Thanks." I tense when I think about putting Zoe in such a position. What incentive does she have not to tell Damian the truth now that she knows I won't kill her brother? "The fact that she's living in France as my mistress should be enough to convince Hart to keep the business relations good between us."

"She's a means to an end, son. Don't forget that." He pours a stiff shot of Scotch and hands me a glass. "We'll use her as we must, any way we have to."

I don't fucking think so. Zoe is my responsibility. I own her, body and soul. I'll decide what's best for her and how her future will evolve, not my father or anyone else.

My father brings his drink to his lips. "I want Alexis in on the deal."

My fingers clench around the glass. "What deal?"

"The diamonds. I want you to teach him the ropes."

Suspicion goes off like an alarm bell in my mind. "Why?"

"You'll have your hands tied up with the business here when you take over in a few months."

When I honor the deal my father has made, he can finally retire. "The deal with Dalton is the crux of our business. Everything depends on that deal. Alexis can work with the Italians and run the docks."

"No." My father slams his glass down on the desk. "The Italians are your responsibility. Trying to escape it will give them the wrong idea."

"I'm not trying to escape it. I'm just saying Alexis is in a better position to deal with the taxes."

"Leaving you free to deal with Hart or to make sure no one else gets close to his sister?"

"What about you?" I close the step between us. "What's your agenda? Making sure Alexis gets in on the big deals while pawning me off to the Italians?"

He waves a finger at my face. "Watch your tone."

"I don't even know why we're having this discussion. In a few months' time, I'll be calling the shots, deciding how Alexis is involved."

My father's face turns red. "*If* you honor the contract."

I narrow my eyes with a smile. "Are you hoping I won't?"

"Don't put words in my mouth."

"Then don't give me reason to." I leave the glass on his desk and turn for the door. "Maman is waiting. Shall we have dinner?"

When I walk through that door, the power has shifted. I'm holding it all in my fist. Everything. I let the knowledge sink in, soothing my deepest concern—keeping Zoe safe.

CHAPTER 18

Zoe

The shorter and colder the days grow, the harder I work. By December, I'm only sleeping four hours a night. The closer I get to the year-end fashion show, the more my anxiety climbs. Only four of the girls who are left will continue to the final level. Our designs will be judged by an independent panel, and no one, not even Madame Page or Maxime, can determine the outcome.

I want to do well. I want to win Madame Page's approval and show I've earned my place, which is why I put in more effort and hours than anyone in the class. I stitch faster than Thérèse and make fewer mistakes than Miss Page's favorite student, Christine. I always hand in my homework early. I do research at home, and I visit fashion exhibitions and museums with Maxime on the weekends. I pour my heart into my collection. When the day of the fashion show arrives, I'm positive I'll have good results. I'll go as far as to say I'm hopeful of swaying Madame Page.

Maxime takes me early to the performing arts theatre where the event is held so I can add the finishing touches to my garments.

He carries my needlework case to the garderobe where our collections are already stored and leaves it on the worktable to wrap his arms around me.

"You'll do great." His eyes warm with a smile. "I'm proud of you."

"Thank you." I pull away and flip open the lid of my case. The model who'll be modeling my wedding dress has lost weight after a recent bout of gastro, and I have to take in the waist. There's not enough time to remake the bodice, but I can take in a few centimeters on the sides by hand.

"Hey." Maxime catches my wrist.

My cheeks grow hot at the heated look in his eyes.

"Haven't you forgotten something?" he asks in a husky voice.

That voice is enough to make me forget about everything. "I'm sorry." I go on tiptoes to kiss his lips. "I'm a little distracted."

He cups my nape. "I know." Pulling me close, he kisses me in the way that makes every follicle come alive. Lethargic heat flushes my body, making me wet. I throb and ache for him. Just before my knees give out, he breaks the kiss.

My whole being mourns the loss of his touch and warmth. We stare into each other's eyes, wordless understanding passing between us. I'm his. He's mine. Our give and take isn't equal, but there's comfort in knowing we belong to each other and that we've somehow managed to make our warped situation work.

"Good luck," he mouths.

"No." I press my hand over his mouth. "Don't say it. It's bad luck."

Folding his fingers around my wrist, he kisses my palm before moving my hand away. "If I don't let you go now..."

He doesn't have to finish the sentence. We both know we'll end up in a dark corner fucking against a wall if he doesn't leave. How did we get to this point? How did I get so addicted to him? When did he become so handsome and dear to me?

"Break a leg," he says with a wicked smile, turning on his heel and leaving me in a puddle of desire.

I give myself a little shake to break the trance. A tinge of fear slips into my elation. I know exactly why he makes me lose track of everything, even here and now at this critical event. It's because he overshadows everything. He's grown more important than anything else in my life, even more important than my studies and my dream to be a designer. Somewhere in the knotted threads of our unconventional relationship, *he* became my dream.

The realization startles me. It frightens me. Whatever power I've given Maxime over me in the past is nothing compared to this. This is atomic. This can destroy me.

Voices coming from the hallway pull me back to the present. A few classmates file through the door, chatting animatedly. We're all on edge about tonight, over-excited and anxious.

I thread a needle and set to work. My fingertips are already pricked raw. The grand finale, my wedding dress, is my dream design. I've poured everything I am and ever wanted to be into the dress. It's whimsical, romantic, and feminine. It has a sweetheart bodice and a meringue skirt layered with diamante studded net fabric. The color is the softest of pinks, a barely visible hue that bleeds out from the virginal white at the top to the darker hem of the skirt.

After a couple of hours of careful adjustments, my back is aching. Stepping away from the dress form, I study my work. My chest swells. A feeling of peace dawns on me even as my breath quickens. It's a warm feeling, but it's nothing like the arousal Maxime elicits. This is pride. This is my best. I put a hand over my heart. I *love* this dress. I love it for everything it represents, but it's more than pride and love. There's something else underneath the layers, something that causes these reactions of glowing contentedness and combustible love inside me. It's imagining wearing it for Maxime. It's imagining him in a dark suit under the angelic lights of a stained glass window with a ring in his pocket. It's the contrast of his black soul in a holy space, of winning the heart of a man so cruel. It's my girlhood fantasy, the white day and the big dress. It's imagining saying yes.

"Miss Hart?"

I give a start.

A woman with a clipboard breezes past me. "Your models are ready. You're on in ten."

I jump back into action. My dream dissolves in a flurry of activity. The model wearing my day dress cusses when the zipper gets stuck. I work on it while she fixes her lipstick.

"Maxime fucking Belshaw is out there," she says, dabbing powder onto her nose.

"What?" With the noise, I'm not sure I heard correctly.

"God, I hope I catch his eye." She fits her shoes.

"Hart, you're on," the organizer calls from the stage door.

"That's us," the model says, making her way over.

The rest passes in a blur. It's crazy and exhilarating. It's so damn stressful, and I love every minute. I run on pure adrenaline by the time the wedding dresses are paraded. Standing backstage with the rest of my class, I revel in the moment our ultimate creations are revealed on the runway. For an unreal moment, I lose myself in the lights and music as my eyes follow that dress, knowing it's perfect because I made it for *him*.

I search the crowd until I find Maxime. He sits in the front row on the left. The stage lights illuminate his face, making the shadows under his eyes run deep. The groove between his eyebrows begs me to trace the line and drag a finger over the bump at the bridge of his crooked nose. His eyes are bright with pride and his lips pulled into the slightest of smiles. I turn hot knowing what those lips have said and done to me, knowing how deft those strong, slender fingers are. I love watching him like this, when he's unaware and his guard is down, but then there's applause and Madame Page gets on the stage.

I miss most of her speech, my thoughts being scattered in every direction. I'm rerunning the show in my mind. I should've pulled out the seam and re-stitched the body. My head is spinning with everything I've realized tonight. I can't look away from Maxime's face or strong body. I imagine his broad chest and well-cut muscles underneath his shirt. All I want right now is to straddle him and claim him as my very own forever.

Someone takes my hand—Christine—and we form a line to walk

onto the runway. I take my bow like the rest, feeling like somehow this is a dream, and the only real thing is Maxime in his tux, looking as if he may eat me alive.

We stand on stage as the judges call their verdicts. The panel is made up of a mix of fashion editors, designers, and label owners. One by one, our average scores out of ten are called. Seven for Thérèse. Eight for Christine. Loud applause. Six for someone else. Four for another. One for me.

One.

It hits me like a bucket of ice water. The shock travels from my head to my toes, freezing its path down my limbs. I feel the blood drain from my face in shame. Automatically, my gaze finds Maxime's. His jaw bunches, but his gray eyes are sympathetic.

It's over. I blew it. I'm out. I'm not entering the next level. I'm not going to graduate or become a fashion designer. Worse, I suck. The panel agreed. Their decision is irreversible.

We bow. I smile like is expected of me, but inside I'm burning and freezing in interchanging bouts of humiliation and disappointment. I'm devastated. All those hours. All that magic I felt when I held my pencils and needles. All gone.

"Sorry," Christine whispers in my ear. Her eyes glitter when I meet her gaze. "Maybe next time."

The rest of my classmates enjoy their well-deserved glory as family members come up to congratulate them. I escape to the garderobe and start gathering my equipment.

"Hey," Maxime says behind me.

I soak up his warmth as he folds his arms around me from behind and presses his nose in my neck.

"Yours is my favorite," he says. "I'm proud of you, little flower. You've outdone yourself."

Turning in his embrace, I put my arms around his neck. "Don't lie to make me feel better."

He takes my hand and places it over his heart. "I promise. Cross my heart."

And hope to die. "Thank you."

His eyes are filled with understanding. “Shall we get out of here?”

“God, yes.”

“Gather your stuff. I’ll pack your dresses.”

I’m so grateful to him right now. It doesn’t matter that he got me into the course by pulling strings. I’m just happy he’s here for me. I’m happy he’s here when I need him most.

CHAPTER 19

Zoe

It takes me a few days to get over my disappointment. I hang my collection in a closet in one of the spare rooms where I don't have to look at it, but the knowledge that it's there remains. Every time I walk past that room, my failure screams at me.

By the end of the week, I pack everything into a box and donate it to charity, everything except for the wedding dress. I can't get it out of my heart to part with it, not after I've realized what it means. I only hang the dress deeper in the closet, hiding it in a black dry-cleaning bag.

On Saturday, I wander around aimlessly for a while, not having to work on anything for the first time in months. It's a cold, gray day with clouds rolling in from the sea. I try to read in the tower, but the wind howls around the corners.

Hold on. I know why I'm so listless. I've left the debacle about dropping out of fashion school unfinished. There's something I need to do.

I go downstairs to look for Maxime and find him behind his desk in his study. The door stands open. Lines of worry run over his forehead and around his eyes. He's so engrossed in his work he doesn't notice me. I knock because he still keeps the room locked, which means I'm not welcome inside.

He looks up and smiles. "I've just been thinking about you."

"You have?" I wave at the groove between his eyebrows. "It doesn't look like pleasant thoughts."

"Come here."

I pad over the floor to his desk. "I know you're busy, but I just wanted to say thank you."

He gets to his feet and rounds the desk. "For what?"

"For making the fashion school possible. I just realized I never thanked you. I'm sorry for being so rude."

A fresh frown meets his smile. "I didn't take you for being rude, but I appreciate your gratitude." He shoves a hand into his pocket. "You're welcome."

I study him. He seems oddly formal this morning. It's not like him not to touch me when we're standing so close together. Usually, he can't keep his hands off me. He's always looking for excuses to kiss and fondle me. On any other morning, he would've had his hands on my hips and his mouth on mine by now.

"Okay," I say, swiping a strand of hair behind my ear.

"For whatever it's worth, I think you deserve—"

I hold up a hand. "You don't have to make me feel better. I did my best."

"There are other schools."

I shake my head. "It's fine." Madame Page proved her point. I don't have what it takes.

"I know how disappointed you are. You haven't been out of the house since the fashion show."

I glance at the window. "The weather hasn't been good."

"I think you need to get out, Zoe."

"Get out where?"

"Go to a movie. Do some shopping. Have your hair done. Whatever makes women feel good."

"You mean alone?" Except for meeting Sylvie and going to school, he's never let me go anywhere alone. As Sylvie and I haven't spoken since the night I discovered her deceit, I've only been out to school on my own.

"I have a meeting. There's no reason why you should be cooped up in the house." He reaches out, hesitates, and finally cups my cheek. "Go on before I touch you more and change my mind."

The opportunity is too rare not to jump at it. I can take a long walk on the jetty and lick my wounds in solitude. Alone time sounds exactly like what I need.

"Thank you," I say, my heart warming with gratitude.

"Dress warmly and no chatting to my men. They're there to protect you, which they can't do if a pretty woman distracts them."

I roll my eyes. "Yes, Dad."

His gaze heats. "Are you sassing me, Miss Hart?"

"Maybe."

"I'll have to pull you over my lap for that when you get back."

I go on tiptoes to kiss him. "I look forward to that."

He regards me with amusement as I backtrack to the door, the controlling and possessive Maxime silent for once.

"Do I have a curfew?" I ask, pausing in the frame.

"Just let me know where you are. I'll be busy until late afternoon. You don't have to be back before dinner."

There's something intense about him as he watches me leave. It's as if he's fighting with himself to let me go.

I put on my coat and scarf. Making sure my telephone is charged, I drop it with some money into my bag. I always have a stash of cash, courtesy of Maxime. He calls it my emergency fund, as if he doesn't already take care of my each and every need.

Outside, Benoit jumps to attention.

"What are you doing out here?" I ask. "Aren't you freezing?" I wasn't planning on going anywhere. He didn't have to hang around on a Saturday.

"Nah." He rubs his hands together. "I was running errands for Maxime."

"I'm going into town."

"My car or yours?"

"I'm taking some me time." I flash him a smile. "I'm driving alone."

He curses under his breath, hurrying to the Mercedes when I hop into the new Mini Cooper Maxime has bought for me. Two guards follow in his steps.

Throwing the car into gear, I leave the gates before Benoit has had time to start his engine. I grin as I look in the rearview mirror. His wheels are kicking up gravel in his attempt to catch up with me. I can try to shake him off and maybe even succeed, but I do feel better that he's tailing me. No matter how many times I tell him I don't need him, I appreciate the protection.

I take the scenic route. I enjoy driving, and it gives me time to think. However, today I don't find joy in the view or having this time to myself. That strange listlessness from earlier is still there. Something is bothering me. The notion is faint but persistent, like a dull headache or queasy stomach.

Determined to make the best of the time Maxime has granted me, I put my thoughts aside and drive to the main beach in Marseille. The parking is empty. So is the jetty. I'm happy to have the space to myself.

I button my coat up and pull the hoodie over my head against the cold wind. Benoit mutters some cusswords and says something about freezing his ass off as he follows me to the pier. From there, he lets me go alone. I walk all the way to the end. A spray of saltwater blows against my face. A seagull calls out, swooping low and landing in the swell.

I take my phone from my bag and send Maxime a text to let him know where I am. Benoit always lets him know, but texting him my whereabouts is one of Maxime's unbreakable rules. I don't want him to get it into his head to come looking for me just because I disobeyed, or worse, take away my freedom and privileges.

Holding my phone in my hand, I wait for it to vibrate with his reply. Nothing. I check the screen. The tick mark shows my message has been delivered, but the dots don't dance to indicate he's busy typing. That's strange. He always texts me back immediately. I wait a few more seconds, my unease growing, and finally pocket my phone.

It's not like him to ignore my messages. No matter where or when, I always get a reply. Come to think of it, Maxime behaved very out of character this morning. Letting me stand here alone like this is definitely not like him. No matter how much work or how many meetings he has, he never lets business get in the way of spending time with me on the weekends. If he has to attend an event, he takes me along. If I need to get out, he puts everything on hold to accompany me. I've always credited his behavior to making sure I don't escape, but maybe there's more to it. Maybe he's been considerate because he cares.

Then why is today is the exception? It doesn't make sense. He seemed so reluctant for me to go. Did something happen? Is that why he looked so worried? Is that why he's having such a long meeting on a Saturday? He's having it at home?

Wait. That look on his face when I left—the concern and eagerness—wasn't because he didn't want me to go. He couldn't wait to get rid of me.

Every instinct I own goes on high alert. That's what's been eating at me all the way here. Something is wrong, and it's bad.

Turning, I rush back up the pier.

Benoit straightens at my hurried approach, a half-eaten sandwich in his hand. Alarm flashes across his face. "Miss Hart?"

I run past him, pressing the remote to unlock my car.

"Zoe," he calls after me. "Zoe, wait." When I get behind the wheel, he throws down the baguette and runs for the Mercedes. "Fuck!"

I push down on the gas, breaking the speed limit. The Mercedes battles to keep up. My phone rings. Maxime? I yank it from my pocket and check the screen. Benoit. I cut the call and dump it on the seat, calling Maxime on voice command, but the phone goes straight to his voicemail.

Shit. What's happening? Something feels awfully wrong. He sent me away for a reason. For my safety?

My phone rings again. Benoit. I reject the call and drive faster. I think about calling Francine and asking her to check on Maxime, but then I remember it's her weekend off.

My nerves are shot by the time the house comes into view. My hands are shaking when I cut the engine and throw the car door open. The Mercedes races through the gates, Benoit coming to a hard stop behind me. He jumps from the car as I'm racing up the steps, catching up with me just as I grip the handle of the front door.

"Zoe." He grabs my wrist. "Stop."

I look at where he's touching me. "Let go." Maxime will cut his hand off for this.

"Fuck," he groans, releasing me. "Zoe, listen. Don't go in there."

Pushing the door open, I walk inside. I stop in the entrance and listen, expecting gunshots or fighting. What greets me is much worse.

Soft, feminine laughter.

The sound hits me like an arrow in the heart. Nausea rushes through my body. My stomach burns with it.

Maxime's voice reaches my ears. I can't hear what he's saying, but his tone is pleasant. The woman replies, then laughs again.

I follow their voices to the library and stop in the open door. Maxime sits on the couch and a woman with auburn hair and honey-colored eyes sits in the armchair in front of the fire, in *my* armchair, the chair in which Maxime has stripped me naked, draped me over his lap, and made me come more times than I can count. She's impossibly young and beautiful, cultured like his mother, wearing a dress Madame Page will approve of.

It only takes him a second to become aware of my presence. We're attuned to each other. That's what happens when you live together for thirty months. I know he hates lemon juice, and he knows I love sun-dried tomato salad dressing. He has to know this is killing me.

Maxime's expression is stoic. He holds my eyes unfalteringly. The woman is still talking, her voice ringing through the space in a well-groomed Parisian accent, not foreign like mine. There's no funny pronunciation to tease her about or to find endearing. She's perfect. Then she catches on and follows his gaze.

At the sight of me, her back snaps straight. She drags her eyes over me, taking in my Mary Poppins coat and sticky-salty, windblown hair.

Leaning her hands on the armrests, she pushes to her feet. "You *will* get rid of her. I will *not* be humiliated."

Maxime stands.

Picking her bag up from the foot of the chair, she walks past me with a lifted chin. I stare after her, familiar and new pain braiding together, twisting my insides. I know the ache of betrayal. I know the ache of having your life stolen but this…This is new. This is huge. I can't even find a box for it in the wall that makes up my soul. I can't file it with lies or betrayal. Not even jealousy is an accurate description. It cuts much deeper, leaving scars that will never heal.

Silence stretches through the house when she closes the door behind her like a well-bred lady. Me, I would've slammed it. Only her perfume lingers. Expensive. Classy. Everything I'm not. And the memory of that laugh. The torture of imagining what Maxime had said to her to make her so happy.

The silence is infuriating. I want him to explain. I want him to make excuses. I want him to tell me it's a misunderstanding, that she's his cousin or long-lost sister.

I take in his passive stance, how his hands are shoved deep into his pockets and his eyes give nothing away. Always hiding secrets. Never playing open cards with me. Waiting for me to make the first move. It's unfair, but his silence leaves me no choice.

"Who is she?" I ask in a tremulous voice.

"Izabella Zanetti, Leonardo Zanetti's sister." He holds my gaze, not as much as flinching when he says, "My fiancée."

CHAPTER 20

Zoe

The world crashes down around me. I didn't think it was possible to die and still be alive. I didn't think I could be in hell right here on earth. Yet the flames lap at me, mocking me yet again for my stupid naivety.

"The Italian I met at the auction?" I force through the lump in my throat. "That Leonardo?"

"Yes," Maxime says.

I curl my fingers until half-moons from my nails cut into my palms. The pain is the only thing preventing me from breaking down in tears. "How long?"

"My father made a deal."

My voice rises. "How long, Maxime?"

"The engagement party is next Saturday."

I inhale once, twice, trying not to show him how hard it is to breathe, how this minces me up inside. "Is that what you were discussing?"

"Yes." He adds in a flat voice, "Among other things."

I guess other things meaning the wedding. Oh, my God. I'm going to be sick. How long has he been playing me? "For how long have you known?"

"I don't think that matters."

My pulse jumps. Betrayal and humiliation turns to anger. "Don't you dare, Maxime Belshaw. Don't you dare tell me my feelings don't fucking matter. Tell me! You owe me at least this much."

"Two years." He gives me a resigned look. "The contract was signed two years ago."

Fuck. God, that hurts. I stumble back a step. "You made a fool of me."

"No, Zoe. You're not a fool."

"Don't you fucking say my name." I hold up a shaking finger. "Don't you fucking dare."

He takes a step toward me. "I didn't want you to find out like this."

"When were you planning on telling me?"

Another step. "This doesn't change anything."

I take three more steps back. "Like hell it doesn't!"

"We'll still be together, Zoe. Marrying Izabella is a business transaction."

"When?" I manage through trembling lips.

"In spring."

"In April?" I cry out. "You're marrying her in four months?"

"You'll still be my mistress. I'll still spend the majority of my time with you."

I think I'm going to break down, after all. I bite on the inside of my cheek until the urge to turn hysterical passes. "You'll fuck her."

"Only to create a heir."

"To make a baby." My teeth chatters around the words.

"Yes," he says with a frown, as if he's having a hard time understanding why I should be upset about that.

"What about us, Maxime? Have you considered that? What if I wanted a baby?"

"You know I can't do that."

Swallowing my tears, I lift my chin. "Why?"

"Bastard children aren't recognized. I won't be able to protect it with my surname. More so, bastard kids have a hard time adapting. They always come second. That's not fair to any child."

Does he even realize how far his selfishness goes? "And how are you supposed to get rid of me before this marriage?" I ask, repeating his *fiancée's* words.

For the first time, he has the decency to look guilty. "Naturally, as my wife, Izabella will live here."

"So, you're throwing me out." I backtrack to the stairs. "I'll start packing, then. I'll be glad to go home."

He comes after me so fast I don't have time to run. His fist is in my hair before my foot is on the second step of the stairs.

"I'm not throwing you out," he growls against my ear, "and I'm not sending you home."

"I'm not sleeping with an engaged or married man. There's no point in keeping me. You'll have to take what you want with force, but I refuse to be the other woman."

His hold tightens in my hair, making my scalp sting. "Marriage has nothing to do with sex and love. Not in my world. If I want our business to survive, I don't have a choice but to honor that contract and marry Izabella. I'll respect her and care for her as my wife, but it's you I want."

"I can't do this, Maxime. You have no right to ask this of me."

His voice turns cruel. "Oh, but I'm not asking, little flower."

"Fuck you," I cry, pulling so hard his hand comes free from my hair with the long strands stuck to his fingers.

"Maybe it's a good idea to start packing, after all." He reaches for me, but I jump away. "In time, you'll get used to the idea."

"Never," I bite out. "Not as long as I live."

"That's how you felt at first, but you got used to this." He waves a hand around the space. "You're a survivor. You'll adapt."

I can't listen to him anymore. I escape up the stairs, and he lets me. The only mercy he gives me is not coming after me. I keep on moving until I run out of stairs. Rushing into the tower, I shut the heavy door behind me. There's no key to guarantee my solitude. The only door in this house with a key is Maxime's study. That's where he locks away his laptop and the phones, any form of communication with the outside world. My passport has to be in there. I have to find it.

Sitting down on the window seat, I wrap my arms around myself. I'm cold. Shivering. Finally, the tears I'm trying so hard to swallow erupt. They escape with ugly wails of shameless, pitiful crying. I focus my blurry gaze on the distorted vision through the stained glass window. The color twists through my tears like a kaleidoscope. The sounds of footsteps falling on the stairs makes me suck in and hold my breath. The sob trapped between my ribs aches, but I keep it in with all my might. I can't let anyone see me like this, least of all not Maxime.

A knock falls on the door. "Zoe?"

I can't answer. If I do, he'll hear my brokenness. I'm not giving him that much.

"I'm coming in," he says.

I swallow, somehow finding inhumane strength to keep my voice even. "If you care about me at all, even just a little, you won't."

Silence. After a beat, he says, "I'm going to my parents' house. I'll be back for dinner."

"To see her?"

"To smooth things over. She's upset."

No shit. Pulling my legs up, I wrap my arms around my knees.

"Benoit stays here," he says, "in the house."

Another silence. Finally, after a long stretch of waiting, his heels tap an even rhythm on the stairs as he descends.

I let out the breath I was holding. My chest expands with another sob. Suddenly, I'm not sure whose cruelty is worse, Alexis's or Maxime's. Maxime knew all along while he was fucking me and being kind to me, watching me fall for him a little more each day, that he was promised to someone else. This is my limit. This is the straw that breaks the camel's back and sends me over the edge.

Wiping my nose with the back of my hand, I rest my head against the cold stones of the wall and close my eyes. No wonder Maxime's family hates me so much. It all makes sense now. I'm the imposter, the seducer, and the mistress. They're the wives. I think back to a conversation I once had with Sylvie when I still thought we were friends. It was over a glass of wine after class. We talked about made men and how they treated their women. I wanted to know more about what it meant to be property since it had become my label in Maxime's world.

"It usually goes hand in hand with big depth payoffs that can't be honored," Sylvie had said.

The revelation shouldn't have startled me. Still, her words shocked me. "Like selling a person to settle a debt?"

"Or making big, financial sacrifices for a woman. Taking care of her for life."

It sounded too savage to be true. "Why not just marry? Why use such a degrading term?"

"Property isn't degrading. It's a coveted and protected position. It means hands-off to all other men. Whoever dares to touch a man's property is dead. Marriages are made for the business, to further relationships that'll profit the family. Men seldom want or love their wives. As you can imagine, there are a lot of mistresses going around in our circles. Us girls, the ones who are expected to remain virgins and marry a man of our father's choice for the sake of a contract, don't get to be mistresses. We get to remain faithful and suffer their existence pretending we don't notice. Of the lot, I'd say we're the worst off."

She was wrong. They get to be respected. They get to go out with their husbands in public. They're not hidden away somewhere, only taken out of their golden cages on occasion for a quick, dirty weekend in a hotel with mirrors on the ceiling. Maxime won't be able to take me to his events any longer. Izabella will be on his arm. I'll wait alone for the crumbs of his time, tucked away like a cheesy princess dress in a black dry-cleaning bag, a hidden secret in a dark closet. Among women, only the wives are recognized. That's why Maxime never introduced me to the wives when he hoped I'd make friends. That's why I only got to mix with the women who didn't wear diamonds on their ring fingers. No, the wives are much better off. The wives get to have the babies. That is maybe the worst, the part that twists the blade the deepest into my heart.

I sit there until my stomach protests with hunger pangs and my throat is so dry it's hard to swallow. The day turns dark. The tower is freezing cold. Pressing the heels of my palms against my eyes, I rub away the tears. I feel dry and empty. I won't let Maxime find me like this. He's bound to be home soon. I can't even let myself think about what's happening at his parents' house. It hurts too much.

The door squeaks when I open it. I listen. The house is quiet. I walk down the stairs into the deserted darkness, not bothering to flick the lights on or turn the heat up. I walk straight to Maxime's study and test the door. Locked. I have to find a way in. If only I knew how to pick a lock.

I walk to the kitchen and stop in the door. Benoit sits at the window counter with a mug in front of him, reading something on his phone.

He looks up. "Jesus, Zoe."

I hold up a palm. "Don't speak."

He knew. They all knew. Everyone knew and no one bothered to tell me. They're all on Maxime's side. I'm on my own in this, always have been. Just like Damian has always said. Why didn't I listen to him? Why did I prefer to cling to stupid fantasies?

"There's coffee," Benoit says. "You look like you can do with some."

I take a glass from the cupboard and fill it with water from the tap. Taking aspirin from the cupboard where Francine stores the sugar cubes, I drink it for the throbbing pain in my head. Crying always does that to me.

I pop a piece of bread in the toaster, ignoring Benoit's stare as I take butter and jam from the fridge. When I open the drawer to take a butter knife, I pause. The slot for the sharp vegetable knives is empty. I look at the knife block on the counter. All the bread and carving knives are gone. Even the scissors.

Benoit clears his throat. "Maxime thought it was better to lock the knives away."

He thought I'd try to kill him? Harm myself? No, that's not my plan. That's not who I am. An image of Damian and me sitting with our knees drawn up in a dark closet with only a flashlight and a book filters into my mind. I hear the fighting and glasses breaking. I feel the cold fear of violence. I hear my brother's voice, telling me our circumstances don't define us.

Maxime was right about one thing. I'm a survivor. I'm going to follow Damian's advice.

I'm going to save myself.

CHAPTER 21

Zoe

By the time Maxime gets home, I've moved my clothes and toiletries to one of the spare bedrooms, the one the farthest away from the one meant for his wife.

I'm in bed when he knocks on the door. I stay on my side with my face turned to the wall and my eyes closed. Porcelain clatters as his footsteps near. There are no fancy rugs or carpets in this room, only a cold, barren stone floor, just the way I prefer. It reminds me I'm in his prison, not in his home.

A whiff of roses reaches my nostril.

"I brought you a cup of tea," he says.

The cup and saucer click on the nightstand. The mattress indents as he sits down on the edge. When he strokes a broad palm over my hair, I cringe. He withdraws the touch.

"No one can change what you mean to me, Zoe," he says. "You make me feel things I've never felt before. When you touch me, I'm alive. You're the only person in this world who makes me see light.

The only good I have inside me is when you're around." He pauses. "There's not much I can deny you. You know that. I'll make you happy again. I promise."

I turn on my back and open my eyes. His face is beautiful in its imperfection. It's a face I hold dear to my heart, but I won't let him hurt both me and the woman who's been promised to him. I won't be the reason for making another woman suffer the way I'm suffering now.

"If you want to make me happy," I say, "let me go."

"I'll give you anything in my power, but not that."

"There's no point in keeping me. I'm not a cheater. I'm not going to sleep with you."

"We'll go to Venice."

"Venice?" I bite out. "Do you think that place holds any good memories for me?"

He flinches. "Making love for the first time isn't a good memory?"

"You stole my virginity with manipulation." My tears threaten to spill over again. "You stole my love knowing you belonged to another. There's no place in the world you can take me to make me forget that."

"Where's the girl who believed in love and romance?"

"I don't believe in fairytales any longer."

He cups my cheek. "But you want to."

I turn my face away, escaping the touch. "Please. Leave me."

He considers me for a moment, then stands. Staring down at me, he says, "I'll give you time to get used to the change." After another stretch of silence, he walks to the door. In the frame, he turns. "Drink your tea. You'll feel better."

When he's gone, I grab the cup and hurl it at the wall. It breaks with a shattering sound into pieces, the rose petal infusion wasted on the floor.

~

I DON'T SLEEP that night. I lie awake in the dark, thinking. At daybreak, I have a shower and dress in my favorite leggings and jersey. I brush my hair and put on my makeup. I eat breakfast in the knife-less kitchen. I clear out the room Maxime turned into a workspace for me, packing the fabric, buttons, lace, ribbons, and thread into boxes that I seal. Benoit helps me to carry them down to the cellar. I vacuum and air the room, getting rid of my presence and smell. I make sure there's no traces left of me, nothing that can hurt another woman. All that's left when I'm done is my sewing machine. I seal it in its original box and make Benoit carry that to the cellar, too.

By the end of the week, the armchair in the library has been replaced with a new one I've ordered online. The old one I've burned on the beach. Maxime says nothing through it all. He gives me the space he's promised. His guards avoid me. They avert their eyes when I go outside for a walk. Even Francine isn't cruel enough to say she told me so. Like everyone else, she keeps her distance. They're avoiding me as if I'm on death row.

On Wednesday, Maxime comes to find me in my new room. He's holding my coat and scarf in his hand.

"Come on," he says. "We're going for a ride."

"Where to?"

"You'll see."

We haven't spoken since the night he promised to give me time, but I haven't stopped thinking. My thoughts haven't been quiet for a moment. There's something I need to know.

"If Damian doesn't honor the deal you have with Dalton, what are you going to do to him?"

His expression becomes closed-off again. "Whatever it takes."

"That's your plan? That's why you're keeping me? To use me against him?"

"I already told you why I'm keeping you." He holds the coat open. "Come now. You're going to like what I want to show you."

"If you didn't have me, what else would you use?"

He sighs. "There's always someone or something a person cares about."

"You'll hurt him or whoever and whatever he cares about to have your way."

"In short, yes."

I nod. That's what I needed to know.

"Zoe, please. Don't make me put this coat on you. I want this day to be pleasant."

Too late. Pleasant is no longer an option for us. Maybe he should've just given me to Alexis. It would've saved his future wife and me a lot of tears. Turning, I let him help me into the coat and stand obediently while he winds the scarf around my neck.

"That's better," he says with a soft smile.

I follow him to his car, but get in before he can get my door. I don't ask where we're going. For now, I simply go along. He follows the highway to the city and weaves his way through the narrow streets toward the center. Close to the old town, he parks. We make our way on foot through the pedestrian area until he stops in front of a beautiful, old building.

"This is it," he says, looking up at the stone façade. "It dates from 1000 BC."

I have no interest in the history of the building or why we're here. The guards who followed check the street before he punches a code into the panel that opens the street door. We climb all four levels of a winding staircase to the top and exit in a long, narrow corridor with a red carpet and a carved wooden door at the end.

"Here," he says in front of the door, handing me a key with a red ribbon tied through the hole in the top.

I take the cold metal, letting the silk ribbon slide through my fingers.

"Open it," he says.

Inserting the key in the lock, I turn it like he's told me.

"Go on," he says, placing his palm on the small of my back. "Go inside."

I open the door and step inside not because I want to, but to escape his touch. It smells of fresh paint. Pausing just inside the door, I look around. It's a loft apartment, beautifully renovated to leave the antique stone walls bare. A round window with stained glass panels dominates the ocean-facing wall. It stretches all the way from the ceiling to the floor. The floors are polished stone. White mohair rugs are scattered around. All the furniture in the open-space living area is white—the leather sofas, the velvet armchair, the whitewashed table, and the renaissance chairs. Each chair is of a different style, covered with a different white fabric, the textures and weave patterns adding uniqueness while the white gives uniformity. Only the backs are upholstered with fabric portraying images of different flowers in creamy beige.

A wrought iron spiral staircase leads to an open landing with a desk and chair. A study. A bookshelf stretches from the floor of the lounge to the ceiling of the study. The shelves are filled with English and French books, the titles ranging from classics to modern fiction and non-fiction. My gaze falls on The History of Fashion from the Middle Ages. For easy access, a ladder on wheels is hooked to the top shelf. There's a reclining chair and reading lamp under the stairs. Sofas and a low coffee table are arranged around a fireplace with carved flowers on the mantelpiece.

The kitchen takes up the right-hand side of the space. The cupboards are whitewashed and the appliances stainless steel. Through the glass panels on the doors, crockery in pink and gray are visible. Even the wine glasses are a deep pink with roses decorating the crystal stems. A huge bouquet of pink roses stands in an antique white vase on the island counter that serves as a more informal table with two tall chairs.

A door leads off to the right. My feet carry me there, compelling me to take it all in. It's a bedroom. The king-size bed is covered with white linen and pink scatter cushions. The French doors open onto an ornate waist-high rail. The windows face the building opposite the narrow street. White organza curtains provide privacy.

A door leading from the bedroom gives access to a well-organized dressing room with ample cupboard space. Another door opens into a windowless bathroom with Harlequin white-and-black tiles and a skylight allowing natural light. There's a spa bath like at Maxime's house and a shower with double nozzles. The vanity area is spacious with a big mirror and a padded stool. The bedroom, dressing room, and bathroom run along the back of the kitchen. It's huge. One room. For one person. Maybe for a partner who sleeps over on occasion. No rooms for children or visiting family.

Up to now, Maxime has let me take it all in silently, following quietly behind me. I catch his gaze when I turn to exit the bathroom.

His tone is eager. "There's more. Come."

He walks ahead of me to the French doors opening from the living area out to a terrace. We exit from the warm interior into the frosted winter air. My breath is a white puff as I exhale. A splash pool, Jacuzzi, and small summerhouse take up the ocean side. A vine creeps over the metal awning that will provide shade in summer. Potted olive trees frame the summer house and another stands next to a small garden table and two wrought iron chairs. Big pots with winter flowers are arranged around the space to form a terrace garden. A glass greenhouse filled with neatly arranged plants in terracotta pots is constructed on the left. I spot cherry tomatoes, chilies, carnivorous plants, and orchids through the glass.

"What do you think?" Maxime asks behind me.

"It's beautiful," I say honestly. He must've invested a fortune in this place. I turn to face him. "Did you have the renovations done?"

"It took two years," he says proudly.

Two years. All the pain from Saturday comes tumbling out. "Ah. Well, I guessed you didn't just pop out and buy this place yesterday."

"No." His expression sobers as he studies my face. "I bought it two years ago."

He planned it all along. He knew he'd need a place to ship me to.

"The work is only just finished," he says.

Otherwise, he would've made me move in sooner.

"I'll have your clothes sent over," he continues. "A team will unpack everything. You won't have to lift a finger."

The hurt spreads and spreads until I breathe and exhale it, until my heart beats with it and my pulse pumps with it.

"So," I say, "this is the new golden cage."

"It's yours, Zoe. No one can ever take it away from you. The day anything happens to me, this apartment will belong to you together with enough money to allow you to live comfortably for the rest of your life."

I stare at him, my feelings adrift. My emotions won't let me make sense of anything. They won't let me form words.

He approaches tentatively, his arms spread out with his palms facing the heavens. "Will you at least let me hold you?"

The offer tears me to pieces. I need the solace. I so badly need for someone to hold me. Just for a minute. Just for a few seconds. But he belongs to another.

Biting back my tears, I shake my head.

I'm not a cheater, and he's not a rapist. He won't take me by force, not without my consent.

He drops his arms. "I'll let you settle in, then. The fridge is stocked. If you need anything, you only have to call."

The agony is so complete I want to sink to my knees under its force. A silent scream catches in my chest when he turns his back on me and walks through the door. I can only stand there while he rips my life apart with his kindness.

CHAPTER 22

Zoe

It takes me a while to come to my senses. I'm frozen from cold when my limbs finally obey the signals from my brain to move. The first thing I do is go to the front door and yank it open. A man stands on attention in the corridor. My spirits sink. Of course.

"Babysitting?" I ask like a bitch.

"I'm here to protect you, ma'am, and to let Mr. Belshaw know if you need anything."

"What if I need to go out?"

"Your car will be delivered shortly, but you're not to go anywhere without Mr. Belshaw's permission. I'm to accompany you." He adds, "For your safety."

"Where's Benoit?"

"He's driving your car over, but he's no longer your appointed detail."

I suppose Benoit is Maxime's best man. He'd be protecting Maxime's wife.

I shut the door in his face and let my handbag drop from my shoulder to the floor. Crouching down, I turn it upside down, shaking the contents out over the polished stone. I gather all the loose bills, and then the ones in my purse. I have enough money for a plane ticket to Spain. I can disappear from there, but I need my passport.

Sitting down with my back resting on the wall, I bite my nail. I have to get into Maxime's study. I've seen him taking guns from a safe in his room, but there weren't any documents inside. It has to be locked somewhere in his study. Maybe now that I'm no longer living in his house, he'll leave the door unlocked. Which means I only have to get into his house. I have to try, at least.

I scramble to my feet and open the door again. "When Benoit drops off my car keys, can you please ask him to say hi before he goes?"

He gives me an uncertain look.

"I just want to say goodbye. We've been through a lot."

Everyone knows about Gautier. The hard resolve on his face softens. "Fine."

I take my phone to the study and use a paperclip to force it open. After removing the battery, I replace the cover and drop the phone in my inside coat pocket. Then I make tea while I wait.

The doorbell rings an hour later. I open the door to Benoit.

"Your keys." He holds the car keys out to me.

"Thank you," I say, accepting them. "Is Maxime home?"

"He's at the office. Why?"

"I need you to drive me back to Maxime's place. I left my phone there."

He scratches his head. "I'll let Maxime know. He can drop it off."

"No," I say quickly. "He'll be angry with me. You know how he gets when I forget my phone." It's one of Maxime's nonnegotiable rules, especially after the drive-by shooting.

Benoit rubs the back of his neck. "I don't know."

"I'll be in and out. Come on. What am I going to do? Rob him? Please, Benoit. I don't want to get into trouble with Maxime. I'm in enough trouble as it is."

He glances over my shoulder. "Is the place all right?"

"It's lovely. Now will you help me?"

Taking his phone from his pocket, he says, "Maybe it's in your bag. Have you checked carefully?"

I cross my arms. "Of course, I have."

He scrolls down his screen and dials my number. "It's dead."

"Damn. The battery must've run flat."

He sighs. "Fuck. Fine. In and out. Understand?"

"Thanks, Benoit."

Benoit nods at the guard by my door. "No need to report this. We're just going back for her phone."

I swallow a sigh of relief as Benoit leads me to the underground parking and shows me my parking space.

"You'll need the card I left in your visor to lower the concrete pillars that block vehicles from using the pedestrian area," he explains. "Only residents are allowed on these roads."

We get into the Mercedes. My nerves are all over the place. I can't stop myself from fiddling with the tussles of my scarf.

"You all right?" Benoit asks, shooting me a sideways glance.

"Just unsettled." When he frowns at me, I add, "With the change and all."

"Don't be too hard on yourself."

I'm not sure what that's supposed to mean. Don't beat myself up about cheating? Don't be upset about Maxime's upcoming engagement and wedding?

The usual guards are around when we stop at the house, but they don't ask questions. For all they know, Benoit is acting on Maxime's instructions.

Benoit stops in the entrance to take off his coat. I glance around the space in which I already feel like a stranger. It's as if my mind and heart know I'm no longer welcome, whereas my feet carry me along the familiar path to the library wing. Oh, thank God. The door to Maxime's study stands open, just as I hoped.

"Where did you leave it?" Benoit calls after me.

"I'm not sure. I think the last time I used it was in the library."

I listen for sounds of life before I enter. Only the faint clanging of pots and pans come from the kitchen on the other side of the house. There seems to be no one else except for us and Francine.

"Get a move on," Benoit says.

I turn over cushions and feel along the seams of the couch. "Do you mind checking in the kitchen? I don't feel like facing Francine."

"I thought you said you used it here."

"I think so, but I can't remember," I say, straightening. "Maybe I left it in the kitchen where I had breakfast."

"I should just tell Maxime to check the geolocation," he grumbles.

"Only as a last resort. Maxime will be furious with me."

I pretend to look around the desk, watching from under my lashes until he walks through the door. The minute he's gone, I tiptoe to the frame and peer around. When he rounds the corner, I rush to the study, trying to make as little noise with my heels on the floor as possible.

My heart beats wildly in my chest. If Benoit catches me, he'll definitely tell Maxime. There will be hell to pay. I'll lose whatever little freedom I have. Maxime will no doubt think up a cruel lesson to punish me, and I would've wasted the only opportunity I'll ever have of escaping.

Hurrying to his desk, I start at the most obvious place by going through his drawers. I yank open the top one and search through the neat stack of files. The second drawer holds old invoices and receipts, and the third stationary. My hope sinking, I go for the top drawer on the other side. More papers and files. Shit. My hand shakes uncontrollably as I pull open the second drawer. A notepad and diary. My breathing is staccato when I grip the handle of the last drawer. Please, God, let it be here. I pull, but the drawer is stuck. Something has bent upward inside, preventing it from sliding open. I look around on the desk, and settle on a ruler. Wiggling it through the small space at the top of the drawer, I manage to push down the papers blocking it and free the drawer. I almost pull it off its track when it finally gives.

Hurry, Zoe. Hurry.

I stick my hand inside, and then freeze. A stack of envelopes tied with a ribbon is pushed to the back of the drawer. That's what got stuck. The pile is so big it's higher than the drawer.

My breath catches. I can't drag air into my lungs. It's as if I've taken a punch in the stomach. I know what those letters are even before I pull the pile out and turn it to the light. My handwriting. Damian's address in jail.

Maxime never mailed them.

His words ring through my mind. *You can write to Damian as much as you like.*

He never said he'd send the letters. A clever choice of words. Just another sentence constructed to deceive me.

The betrayal stings. Tears burn behind my eyes. I didn't think I had more to shed. Untying the ribbon, I go through the pile. Every week, every letter—they're all here.

A door slams on the other side of the house.

I jump back to life, sniffing as I tie the undelivered words—empty words now, all my warnings worthless—back together and leave it exactly as I found it before closing the drawer.

"Zoe?" Benoit calls from up the hall.

I leave the ruler as it was before, neatly aligned with the desk calendar, and run from the study. I'm not going to make it back to the library. Benoit's footsteps are already falling too close. Slowing to a walk, I smooth down my hair, take my phone from my pocket, and inhale deeply.

Benoit rounds the corner and stops when he sees me, suspicion pulling his brows together.

"Found it," I say breathlessly, forcing a smile to my lips and holding the phone up for him to see. "I left it in the toilet."

He regards me narrowly. I don't know if he believes me, but finally he throws a thumb at the door. "We better get going. Maxime wanted me to bring your sewing machine."

"No, thanks," I say in an upbeat tone as I head for the door. "I don't need it any longer."

He follows me outside and gets into the car when I do.

"You shouldn't give up so easily," he says, starting the engine. "With the sewing, I mean."

"Oh, I'm not giving up." Not by a long shot. I'm only more determined to get away now than ever.

"Good."

Thankfully, he doesn't speak on the way back to the city. It gives me time to process what I've discovered. Damian must think I've abandoned him. He doesn't know his jail mate is his enemy. He doesn't know I've been taken and held against my will. He only knows what Maxime made me write on the fancy hotel stationary in Venice —that I ran away with a foreigner who swept me off my feet.

"You all right?" Benoit asks.

"Mm?" I look away from the ocean. "Yes."

"If you ever want to talk… Nah, what am I saying? I'm probably the last person you'd talk to."

I give him a smile. "I appreciate it, anyway."

"Make sure you charge your phone."

"Yeah."

"Don't let it happen again. Maxime won't like it."

"I know."

He pulls into the underground parking and insists on accompanying me to the door where the other guard is still positioned.

"We'll send a replacement in an hour," Benoit tells the man.

"Thanks, Benoit," I say again before shutting them both out behind the closed door.

Leaning on the cool wood, I drag in a few ragged breaths. I hate him. I hate Maxime with every fiber of my being. I hate him as much as my traitorous heart still loves him. This isn't puppy love. This isn't a fairytale kind of love. It's a love forged with thorns, pain, and suffering. It's a dark love, a habitat conducive to the growth of twisted lust like fungus favors damp places. It's a black stain over the crack in the wall of my heart, a wolf's face in a child's nightmare. It's a real love, a hard-earned love, the kind that lasts forever. I'll carry it inside me like a parasite for the rest of my life. I'll nurture it like a host unwillingly nurtures a cancer by breathing and eating. I'll suffer it like the unwanted burden it is, but I'll suffer it alone.

Pushing away from the door, I go to the foreign bathroom in the foreign space and strip naked. I fiddle with the settings of the shower until I figure out how to operate them and wash my body and hair. I dry off and pull on a robe.

My clothes arrive shortly. A team of three women unpack the rails full of dresses and boxes full of shoes. In under an hour, they're gone.

I go to the fridge and open it. There's rosé champagne and pink caviar, a dinner fit for a celebration. I choose the champagne. Popping the cork, I pour some in one of the beautiful crystal flutes with the glass roses creeping around the stem and walk to the circular window. I stare through the colored glass, but all I see are white envelopes and black ink.

The door opens and shuts.

Silence.

Pain.

When will it stop?

Will time alone ever be enough?

"Zoe."

His voice. I shiver. I hate him, and I want him. God, how I hate myself for needing him, even now. Especially now. He designed this. He made sure I have no one else to turn to. That's how he caught me in his beautiful web. I'm not letting him spin any more lies around me.

"I brought dinner. Chinese. I didn't think you'd feel like cooking."

I turn.

He's unpacking food cartons on the island counter. "What did you do with yourself this afternoon?"

"Why? Do you care?"

He lifts his gaze to mine. "You know I do."

I take a sip of champagne. "Nothing."

"I'm having a home gym delivered. There's space to put it in the dressing room."

I laugh. It's a nasty sound. "You want me to work out? Make sure I don't get fat from staying locked up in here all day?"

He takes two plates from the cupboard. "You don't have to stay locked up. You can go where you want as long as you let me know and my man goes with you."

"To check up on me and report back to you?"

"To keep you safe." He opens a carton and scoops noodles onto a plate. "I still have enemies. They'd still like to get to me through you."

"Don't remind me."

"Only for your safety." He tears a packet open with his teeth and pours sweet and sour sauce over my noodles the way I like. "I told Benoit to bring your sewing machine.

"I don't want it."

"You can putter around in the garden. That's why I had the greenhouse installed. I remembered the plant in your apartment."

"How considerate."

"You'll find plenty of good books. I got all the latest bestsellers. Romance. The flat screen I ordered wasn't ready today, but I'll make sure it's here by Monday. You'll have unlimited access to movies and those soapies you like."

"The news?"

"Not the news or any other channels."

"I suppose that means no laptop, either."

"The pool will make up for it in the summer. You can spend your days outside. There's a fully equipped gas barbecue in the summerhouse. It's easy to operate. I'll show you."

"I would've been happy with a shack, Maxime." No money in the world can buy me. "You shouldn't be here. It's wrong."

His face darkens. Pulling out one of the tall chairs, he says, "Come sit."

I pad over obediently and shift onto the chair.

Taking another flute, he pours himself a glass of champagne. "To your new home."

I don't raise my glass to his.

"I want you to be happy," he says.

Just like that. Like it's a button I can push. On. Off. God, I wish it was that easy.

"You should take up a hobby." He pushes the plate toward me and hands me a pair of chopsticks. "Painting or yoga. Journaling. Knitting. Anything you like."

"I'll keep that in mind."

He leans his elbows on the counter, putting our faces close. "In case you had any illusions about it, I'm staying the night."

It's like slap in the face. "This is what you call respect?"

He walks to the lounge and crouches in front of the fireplace. "This is where I'm supposed to be," he says, throwing a log into the empty fireplace, "and nothing about us is wrong."

I can't listen to it. I hop off the chair.

"Where are you going?" he asks, the darkness that's such an integral part of him surfacing in his voice.

"To the bathroom."

His gaze burns on my back as I walk to the bedroom and close the door behind me. Placing a hand over my stomach, I fight to calm my breathing. My heart thrums in my temples when I rush to the bathroom and go through my medicine box. A long time ago, right at the beginning of our *relationship,* Maxime got me sleeping pills. He thought it would help me to rest better. I've only taken one, and I hated how it made me feel. I was groggy in the morning, feeling worse than when I have a few hours of unmedicated sleep.

Pushing two of the pills out of their foil casing, I place them on the marble vanity, crush them with my hairbrush, and sweep the powder into the palm of my hand. Then I hurry back to the living area before my hands turn clammy from stress and the powder sticks to my skin.

Maxime is building a fire when I enter. He's busy enough with arranging the logs not to notice when I brush the powder into his glass. I give it a stir with my finger for good measure, and rub the rest of the residue that's stuck on my palm off on my robe.

When he returns, I take my seat and pick up my chopsticks. "Aren't you eating?"

He gives me an approving smile. "I wanted to make sure you were taken care of first."

I break the sticks apart and twist the noodles around one.

He grins. "Let me."

Leaning over me from behind, he arranges the chopsticks in my hand and manipulates my fingers to show me how to use them.

His voice is husky, his soft words and accent seductive against my ear. "Like this."

I inhale him, the clean smell of winter. The heat from his body penetrates my skin through my thick robe. I want him badly. I want to use him to take my pain away. I know he'll let me, but it's wrong to desire another woman's man. I stuff my mouth full of noodles. It's all I can do not to give in to temptation and tell myself it would be for old time's sake.

"You're angry with me," he whispers, running his nose along the line of my neck.

Goosebumps break out over my skin. It's a lot more complex than anger. What will he say if I confront him about the letters? He'd tell me he never lied. He'd say he told me I could write them. He never promised to mail them. He'd know I snooped around in his study, and he'd want to know why.

I swivel the chair away from his touch. I'm only a woman, and he makes me weak. The top two buttons of his shirt are undone. His tie sits askew, as if he's pulled on the noose. I trace the outline of his chest with my eyes, remembering every groove and outline that define his muscles. I commit this sin, taking with my eyes, but I can't look lower to where his manhood swells under the expensive fabric of his tailored pants.

"Eat with me," I beg. Anything to not let me give in to temptation. Our love and hate runs too closely together. Fucking, and hating, and loving have all become the same thing.

"Whatever my flower wants," he says, tracing my lips with a finger.

I lean away. "Please, don't," I say with a shaky breath. "Don't call me that, and don't touch me. I'm not ready."

To my relief, he drops his hand. When he takes the chair on the opposite side, the distance is my saving grace. I lift my glass. He does the same. I drink. So does he. I eat and drink, watching him do the same. He tells me we should have a picnic in one of the sheltered coves in summer. One of the coves. We can never swim on his private beach again. I haven't said goodbye to his house. The notion jars me. I never had time. Not enough to find closure. I listen while he talks, happy for him to make conversation for the both of us like only he can.

We finish the champagne in front of the fire sitting side by side on the sofa. Our bodies aren't touching, but I remember with longing how I used to curl up in his lap. The logs are almost burned out when he finally gets to his feet.

Yawning, he says, "I'm tired. Come to bed?"

"I'll be right there."

I wait for him to disappear into the bedroom before going through the pockets of his jacket where he's thrown it over the back of the sofa. No phone. I didn't expect as much. He usually carries it in the pocket of his pants.

I give it a good ten minutes before going to the room. Maxime is passed out in bed, snoring softly. One arm is thrown over his forehead, and the other is resting on his stomach. The nightstand is empty except for the lamp. There's no phone. I go to the dressing room. His clothes are neatly folded on the velvet bench. The sliding doors of the closets are open. Half of the space is filled with his shirts, pants, jackets, and shoes. He must've sent them with my things. I couldn't even pretend to be interested in how his team has organized our clothes. Maxime must've opened the closets to make sure they've done a good job.

Listening to be sure he's still snoring, I feel through the pockets of his pants. Shit. Nothing. I check in the bathroom. No phone. I go back to the room to check the nightstand again. Kneeling, I check under the bed and utter a soundless sigh of relief. He dropped his phone between the nightstand and the bed. He's really knocked out good.

After hastily pulling on a pair of socks, I touch Maxime's hand gently. He doesn't stir. I poke him a little harder. No reaction. Taking his thumb, I push it on the thumbprint button of his phone to unlock the screen, and then slip through the room to the living area. I can't go out into the hallway. The guard will be there. Instead, I pull the

French doors open as quietly as I can and close them behind me. The night is freezing cold.

It's not that late yet. With shaking fingers, I type the number for the correctional services where Damian is held and bite my nail as I wait for the call to connect. My body is shaking from more than the cold. If Maxime catches me, he'll punish me like never before.

"Johannesburg Correctional Services. May I help you?"

"I'd like to speak to Damian Hart, please."

"Sorry, ma'am. Calling hours are from nine to eleven am."

"It's a family emergency. May I leave a message?"

"Do you know his section?"

"A section."

"Hold on, please."

The line goes on hold. A song comes on. *Please, hurry.*

"Ma'am, he's been released on parole."

My mouth parts, but no sound comes out. I cough. "I'm sorry," I squeeze through my tight throat. "Can you tell me when?"

"Almost a year ago."

My lips go numb. "Thank you."

I cut the call. He got out. A year ago. Maxime didn't tell me. He has to know. He said he was keeping tabs on Damian. I clench the phone so hard the edges cut grooves into my skin. Before the screen goes dark, I call up an internet search page and type Dalton Diamond.

The page that comes up takes the wind from my sails. I read through it with growing disbelief. Dalton Diamonds has changed its name to Hart Diamonds after Damian Hart did a hostile takeover by acquiring the majority of the shares. I scroll to the contact section with growing panic, urgency spurring me on as I keep on glancing at the doors, expecting Maxime to storm through them any minute.

I open the icon. There's a contact form. Shit. My hand shakes so much I miss the menu button twice. I select *About the Owner*. There's a separate contact button at the end of that page. Saying a silent prayer, I click on it.

A number appears. A message pops up. *Would you like to connect?* I press yes.

A gruff voice comes on the line. "Damian Hart."

Oh, my God. I press a fist against my mouth to suppress a sob.

"Hello?" It sounds as if he's been sleeping.

"Damian?" I manage with an unsteady voice.

Alarm filters into his. "Who is this?"

"It's me, Zoe."

All traces of sleepiness vanish. He's wide awake now. "Zoe?"

I recognize the alertness and caution that are part of Damian's making. I don't waste time. I tell him, "I need your help."

"Where are you?"

"In France."

His tone is strong, reassuring. "What do you need?"

"I need you to get me out of the country. I'll need a passport. A false identity."

"Where's your nearest airport?"

"Marseille."

"How quickly can you get there?"

"Tell me when." I'll figure out a way.

"Hold on." There's a small pause. "There's a flight on Saturday morning at eleven."

"Perfect." Maxime will be occupied with his engagement party.

"I'll send a man. The name's Russell Roux. Tall, dark, and he'll wear a blue suit and red tie. The code word is apple pie. Meet him at the Air France information counter at eight."

"Okay."

"Can I reach you on this number?"

"No," I say quickly. "You can't call me again."

"Zoe, is there someone I need to take care of?"

I know what he means with *take care of*. "No. Just get me out of here."

"I'm bringing you home, Zee." He doesn't waste time with asking questions. "Whatever this is, we'll handle it."

"Thank you," I whisper.

There's caution in his tone. "Take care."

"See you soon."

I hang up, taking a moment to find my composure before wiping clean my search and call history. The apartment is quiet when I go back inside. Maxime is no longer snoring. My body breaks out in a coat of sweat. I drop his phone into the pocket of my robe and tiptoe back to the room, but he's still passed out in the same position.

Careful not to wake him, I shift the phone back between the nightstand and the bed on the floor. I take another shower to warm up and dress in a tracksuit before getting into bed. I stay well on the edge, far away from Maxime, but sometime during the night when I finally fall asleep, we find each other, because I wake up with his body pressed against my back and a heavy arm draped over my waist.

For a moment, I simply experience us. I take the memory and store it away.

I pretend to be asleep when he gets up. I don't stir while he's having his shower or gets dressed. I sense him staring down at me. I wait for him to call me out on my bluffing, but he only presses a kiss on my temple and quietly leaves.

The room turns colder in his absence. I guess it's something I'll have to get used to.

It's going to take me a while.

Goodbye, Maxime.

A sob catches in my throat. Since Maxime took me, I only wanted to get away. That first night in Venice, I never would've believed how completely I'd end up loving and hating him in equal measures. I never thought leaving him would be this hard or hurt this deeply.

CHAPTER 23

Zoe

I go through the motions. I dress, eat, and do the cleaning. I get through the day by potting around in the greenhouse and watering the plants. Like I expected, Maxime doesn't come to me after work. He's no doubt busy with the arrangements of tomorrow's party. He sends me a text to say he has a family obligation and will see me on Monday, that he will miss me and think about me every minute.

I read the text with mixed feelings through my tears. Sinking to my knees, I imagine him at his party with his strong body filling out his tux, and the look on his face as he slides a ring onto Izabella's finger in front of their families as witnesses. Will his smile be soft? Will his cold eyes warm for her? Will he give her the look of approval he saved for me when I dressed up for him? I let the thoughts punish me. I own the guilt and the pain. I carry the weight of the sin Maxime won't admit. Then I pick myself up from the floor and pack a bag.

I go to bed with the box of chocolates Maxime left in the kitchen cupboard, eating them all. I don't sleep. At five, I make the bed and tidy the apartment. I have a cup of coffee and a slice of toast. After a quick shower, I dress in a wool sweater and my favorite worn jeans. Then I pull a pair of baggy pants on over the jeans and fit my boots. Rolling my red thermal jacket into a small ball, I bundle it with a red beanie and scarf as well as my ballerina flats in my oversized handbag. I tie my hair into a ponytail, but don't apply makeup. I stare at my reflection in the mirror.

My eyes are dull and marred by dark rings. My cheeks are sunken, making my face look hollow. I don't bother with trying to disguise the feelings I wear on my sleeve with makeup. The worse I look, the more convincing I'll be with the guard.

At seven, I pull on my blue puffy jacket, take my car keys, and open the door. A different man from yesterday is on duty.

"Good morning," I say.

"Ma'am." His gaze runs over me. "Everything all right?"

"I need to get out."

He removes a phone from his pocket. "Where to?"

"Anywhere. I don't care."

He gives me a baffled look.

"Maybe the movies," I say. "Preferably a very long one."

Understanding passes over his face. It's the day of Maxime's engagement, after all. Any mistress would want to lose herself in a mindless activity to forget.

Typing something on his phone, he says, "I'm just letting Mr. Belshaw know."

"While we're at it," I say, going back inside and grabbing the bag, "I'll do my dry-cleaning." I dump the bag in his arms and then hand him the key to the apartment. "Do you mind?"

Not waiting to see if he follows, I walk down the hallway toward the elevator. The key sounds in the lock. He overtakes me and pushes the button, my bag slung over his shoulder.

When he holds the key out to me, I shake my head. "Please, keep it for me. I have a tendency to lose things when I'm distracted."

He gives a sympathetic nod. "Which cinema?"

"I don't care. Pick one."

We take my car. I drive while he checks the movie program on his phone. He gives me directions to a theatre near the harbor, someplace in Maxime's territory where we'll be safe.

I park in the underground parking of a shopping mall. I lock the bag in the trunk and ride the escalators up with the guard whose name I don't bother to ask. The earliest screening starts at ten. We're way too early. I buy two tickets at the self-service dispenser and go to a coffee shop to wait. The guard orders coffee. I ask for tea, a rose petal infusion. When the waitress puts the cup in front of me, it doesn't take much for genuine tears to flow.

"Excuse me," I say, wiping at my eyes and jumping to my feet. "I'm going to the bathroom."

The guard pushes to his feet, his eyebrows pulled together. "What can I do?"

"Please." I duck my head. "Just give me a moment."

He doesn't follow me to the bathroom, but moves his chair so that he has a view on the door. I push inside and rush to a stall. Locking the door behind me, I scramble out of my jacket, boots, and pants. I dump everything together with my phone in the trashcan before fitting my ballerina flats and the red thermal jacket.

Stepping out of the stall, I go to the mirror over the basins. I make quick work of untying my hair and shaking it out before fitting the beanie and pulling it low over my forehead. The final touch is adding sunglasses and bright red lipstick. For good measure, I shove my handbag under the sweater and zip up the jacket. I take a step back and study my reflection. I look like a different woman, at least nine months pregnant.

Forcing myself to take long, even breaths, I place a hand over my stomach and exit the bathroom. It takes everything I have to walk slowly like a woman late in her pregnancy instead of running. From behind the dark lenses of my glasses, I keep an eye on the guard. He's still watching the door, ignoring me. I hold my breath until I round the corner, and then I move.

I sprint down the escalator, yanking the bag out from under my sweater in the run. My lungs are burning by the time I reach the underground parking. I don't look left or right. I have the keys ready in my pocket. I push on the button to unlock the car. Only when I'm opening the door do I dare a glance at the doors giving access to the mall. All is quiet.

Shifting behind the wheel, I start the engine and get out of the parking area. Luckily, the first hour is free, so I don't have to waste time by paying. I only have to push the parking ticket into the slot for the barricade to open. I have no idea how much time I have. Maybe not long before the guard realizes I'm gone. Maxime will send men after me. He'll look for my car and license plate. At the nearest bus terminal, I park in an illegal spot and take my bag from the trunk. It won't take long before my car is towed away. Maxime will eventually find it at the impound, but hopefully it wins me more time.

I check the bus routes on the board, and take the number that goes to the airport. All the way there, my stomach twists so tightly I think I may be sick. I grip my handbag in my lap.

Please, God. Please.

After twenty minutes, the bus pulls up at the airport stop. I get out and fall in line with the other passengers, making sure I move in the middle of the group. I've never been to the airport, but it's not big. It doesn't take long to find the Air France information counter.

A tall man wearing a blue suit and red tie stands next to the counter, reading a tourist brochure. He's shorter than Maxime, but bulkier. One look at his strong frame tells me this man is in the security business. His brown eyes have that vigilant light that says he's aware of everything happening around him, even if he seems to be engrossed in what he's reading.

My assumption is proved correct when he looks up while I'm still a short distance away. Our eyes lock. He offers me a warm smile, the appreciative kind a man would only offer to a woman he knows well. He recognizes me. Maybe Damian showed him a photo.

I study his handsome face. He has deep laugh lines around his mouth and eyes. A bit of gray touches the russet color of his sideburns. He looks easygoing, yet alert, competent, exactly like someone Damian would trust and employ.

"Code word?" I ask under my breath as I stop in front of him, looking around to make sure we're not watched.

"Apple pie," he says in a deep voice.

My relief is so great it feels as if my knees may give out. Before I know what's happening, he pulls me into a hug.

I try to push away but he holds tighter and whispers in my ear, "Make this look real. We're a couple traveling together."

Understanding, I return his smile when he lets me go. To anyone looking on, we're just a boyfriend and girlfriend happy to be reunited.

He takes my bag. "Any other luggage?"

"No."

Offering me his arm, he leads me to passport control. "Damian will be so happy to see you."

I know he's only making conversation to help me stay calm. Nodding, I look over my shoulder.

"Act normally," he says, squeezing my hand that rests on his arm. "Just relax."

Easier said than done. I'm expecting Maxime's men to burst through the doors with automatic rifles and kill Russell before dragging me away.

"Who am I, anyway?" I asked in hushed tone.

He glances around before handing me the brochure he was reading. I flip it open to find a South African passport with the familiar green cover inside. Turning the page, I read the name next to my photo, Amanda Clifford.

"I'm Devon Edgar," he says in my ear, pretending to sneak in a kiss. "We spent ten days at the Blue Voile on the French Riviera, our first holiday in France."

The information threatens to scatter with how much I'm stressing. Blue Voile. French Riviera. Ten days. Devon Edgar. I repeat it silently in my head.

"You'll be fine," he says with another easy smile.

We go through the scanners. At the customs counter, I remove my sunglasses. The officer looks from my passport to my face with a bored expression. Taking his time, he pages through the passport. The pages look used—frequently touched and full of stamps.

"Returning home?" he asks me in English.

In a reflex reaction, I almost reply in French, but bite my tongue just in time. "Yes." I smile. "Unfortunately, all good things must come to an end."

The officer turns to Russell. "What was the nature of your visit?"

"Holiday," Russell says.

I nearly sag in relief when the officer pounds the stamp in my passport and shifts it toward me over the counter.

"Thank you," I say in a chirpy voice.

"We're not in the clear yet," Russell says as he steers me to the international lounge. "Not until we're in the air."

I'm very aware of that. A powerful man like Maxime will be able to delay flights and search planes. Since I'm unable to sit still, we wander through the duty-free shops where Russell buys wine and truffle oil.

"Really?" I ask as he bags the goods.

He shrugs. "Just trying to look normal."

"Are you a gourmand?"

He grins. "I like to eat."

I can't help but glance at the biceps stretching the arms of his suit jacket. "You don't say."

He places a hand on my arm to silence me as he listens to an announcement. "That's us."

I close my eyes. "Oh, thank God."

"Come." Taking my hand, he leads me to the boarding gate.

My scalp pricks with uneasiness. By now Maxime must know I'm on the run. It feels as if ants are marching down my spine, but ten minutes later, I'm seated in the plane. Russell puts my bag in the overhead storage compartment before sitting down next to me. Gripping the armrests, I stare through the window. I'm nervous about flying. Technically, this is my third flight, but Maxime drugged me during the first one—I don't recall any of it—and during the second I was too preoccupied with my fate to worry about the plane dropping out of the air.

"It's not my business," Russell says, "but I'm going to ask anyway. Are you okay?"

I look at him. Am I? No. I doubt I'll ever be. There are things I can't un-live, feelings I can't undo.

It takes some courage and strength to produce a smile. "Yes. I'm okay now."

"Good." He pats my hand. "Maybe try to get some sleep. You look like you need it."

"I'm not sure I'll be able to sleep." Ever again.

"I'm here to watch over you. I'm not going to let anything happen to you."

"Thanks," I say, meaning it like never before.

It's not until we take off and the wheels fold under the plane that I relax somewhat. It's only then that I let the emotions catch up with me. Loneliness when you're single is unpleasant but hopeful. Loneliness when you love with all your heart and soul is like walking through fire. It burns yet leaves you cold. The cavity of my chest is hollow. Empty. Only the echoes of painful memories are left.

As the view of Marseille slowly shrinks, I say goodbye to Zoe Hart. When we break through the fluffy clouds, I close the door on the life that lies below.

It's only then I allow myself to cry.

~ THE END ~

DIAMONDS ARE FOREVER

BOOK 3, DIAMONDS ARE FOREVER TRILOGY

A DIAMOND MAGNATE NOVEL

PREFACE

One dark day, a little girl hid in a broom closet and buried her soul in a fairy tale.

"One day, I'll find my prince. He'll buy me beautiful dresses and lots of pretty glasses, and he'll never break them. He'll take me very, very far away from here, and I'll never come back. Just wait and see."

And then she grew up and her wish was fulfilled. Only, she didn't find her prince. The villain found her. He stole her dreams and made them come true. He took her far away, and wouldn't ever let her go back.

CHAPTER 1

Maxime

"She's gone, sir."

I stop dead in my parents' lounge with the phone pressed against my ear. The words bounce off my ribcage and echo in my chest. Damning words. Fearful words. Words I never thought I'd hear.

Everything inside me comes to a standstill—my heart, my breathing, and even my ability to think. The message slams straight into me like you'd collide with someone who suddenly stops in front of you. Those rare emotions only Zoe can raise from the dead of my soul crash into my frozen body when my mind finally catches up. I break out in a sweat. My stomach drops. My pulse throbs in my temples. All the while, I wrestle with the meaning.

"What did you say?" I ask in a voice cold enough to match the frost on the lawn. I heard my guard, loud and clear, but an unfamiliar part of me wants him to deny it. Usually, I don't shy away from the truth. I'm an expert at embracing all its ugly parts. The truth is a weapon in my quarter, a tool I use for designing psychological manipulation—mind games.

Those very games I engineered to trap Zoe turn on me as the guard repeats, "She's gone," sounding uncertain now.

"What the fuck do you mean Zoe is *gone?*"

He swallows audibly. "She was crying. She excused herself to go to the bathroom. When she didn't come out after several minutes, I went to check."

"How many fucking minutes?" I ask, my vision going hazy around the edges.

"Ten. Fifteen. I have a sister, sir." He starts to stammer. "I know how it is when a woman cries."

When a woman cries. I hurt Zoe. I know it. I hated every fucking second of it, but what choice did I have? It'll take time, but, like with all wounds, it'll eventually heal. We'll go back to the way we used to be, back to that peaceful, happy state we achieved in Corsica. Until the day Zoe walked in on that first formal meeting between me and Izabella, my future wife.

Doesn't Zoe know she'll always come first? Didn't I tell her my marriage changed nothing? Well, except for not being seen with Zoe in public and the fact that my fiancée and I are supposed to produce an heir after our marriage. Those things are duties, though, unpleasantries to ensure the survival of our empire. Without the alliance, our business won't develop or thrive. Our families won't be safe. Peace with the Italians will go down the drain. New wars will break out. Men will die. Without this marriage, I can't offer Zoe protection. I won't be able to take care of her or ensure her safety. Why the fuck can't she see that?

"Sir?" my man asks, fear bleeding into his voice.

That fear is nothing compared to the terror ripping through me as the truth finally settles and self-control runs back into my bones with life, allowing me to be the boss who acts fast and efficiently. Zoe is out there. Alone. An easy target. A delicate flower. No resources. No passport and not much money. No fucking weapon to protect herself. She doesn't know my country. She doesn't know my enemies or allies.

I check my watch. It's quarter to nine in the morning. Caterers are scurrying through the house, carrying trays of food to the dining room for a champagne breakfast. My mother invited the Zanettis so the families can get acquainted before tonight's engagement party. Servers are polishing the glasses before setting them on the table. I take it all in with detached attention as a wave of fury rises inside me.

Zoe is *mine*. She made a terrible mistake, one for which she needs to pay, but since I'm the cause of her irrational actions, I'll carry the blame. I understand why she did what she did. I made it my business to get to know her. Marrying Izabella isn't cheating. It's business. Of course Zoe won't see it that way. She's a good person. Her heart is pure. She doesn't want to be a cheater. She told me so herself. Most of all, she's a woman in love. A woman scorned. *That's* why she ran.

"How long exactly since you lost her?" I ask as a chill of violence runs down my spine. The violence is familiar. I know how to control it, but I can't cope with the sickening fear. This fear, it controls me. It won't let me detach myself from my feelings and act rationally. I fucking hate Zoe for it as much as I've ever adored her.

"Twenty minutes, sir. I ran down to the parking. Her car is gone."

I'm already tracking her number with the geolocation app. "Her phone?"

"She left it in a trashcan in the toilets. I monitored her location. That's why I thought she was still in there. I kept on checking her location, sir. I swear—"

"Stop making fucking excuses. Call our connections. Put word out that we're looking for her. Give them her car model and license plate number."

"Yes, sir."

"Nobody fucking touches her. Anyone who lays a finger on her is dead." I cut the call.

Fuck.

Stabbing my fingers into my hair, I stare at the circus unfolding around me while I try to think like Zoe. What would she do? Where would she go?

My mother enters the lounge dressed in her finest. Holding out her hands, she says with a glowing face, "There he is."

The Zanetti clan trickles in behind her—Paolo, Leonardo, Izabella, and her mother, Noemi. I barely spare them a glance.

My hands are shaking with the urge to commit murder. I've lost something precious, and I can't live without it.

I want her back.

Now.

Turning on my heel, I leave the room without offering anyone a greeting. In a far-off corner of my mind, I register Izabella's fallen expression. The manners my mother has drilled into me dictate that I stop and offer an explanation, at the very least, an apology. It would be only that. Manners. I'm too apathetic toward my future fiancée to care how she feels. All I can think about is that Zoe is on the loose in a dangerous city where at least a hundred or more dangerous criminals would love to capture and torture her to get to me. Kill her.

Fuck!

I slam the door open with a palm and rush through the foyer.

"Maxime!" My mother's voice and clacking heels chase after me. She finally catches up with me at the entrance. "Where are you going?" she cries, grabbing my arm. "What's wrong?"

"Not now." I shake her off. "Zoe ran."

Her body jerks. Her face goes white. "What did you say to me?"

"I said, Zoe ran."

"This is your engagement weekend, Maxime."

"I don't give a damn!"

"Oh, God." My mother places a hand over her heart. "This isn't happening."

I follow her gaze. Izabella and Leonardo are standing just inside the door. Izabella's face is drawn. Leonardo looks furious.

How similar they look, my mother and Izabella. So groomed. So composed. So perfect. Like cut flowers cultivated for a vase. Pretty to look at, but their petals have no smell. They've been brought up to accept their fate. Not like Zoe. She's a wildflower, a rose that smells sweet like a rose should. She's authentic.

Leonardo must've told his family what Zoe means to me, yet Izabella hasn't run. She'll never run because of another woman. She'll turn a blind eye and the other cheek, over and over, just like my mother does, no matter how many times my father comes home smelling of whores and infidelity.

Then it strikes me. That's what makes Zoe different from the women facing me. She believes in love. She believes in something beautiful. Not convenience or money or duty or a business deal. She believes in the real thing, the once-in-a-lifetime kind of love you find with a soul mate. That's how she survived, how she managed to stay afloat in family violence and poverty. That's how she survived *me*.

Fuck me.

That's her secret, the knowledge I was chasing so hard, the hope I wanted to steal.

The answer is love.

I'm incapable of love, but I want hers. I want it more than anything. If I don't find her, there's no hope for me. If I don't get her back, my happiest moments will be confined to the stolen years we spent together.

I don't fucking think so.

Trying to hold me back by grabbing a handful of my jacket in her fist, my mother says, "Maxime, if you walk out of here now, I'll never forgive you."

I couldn't give a damn.

Jerking free, I make my way down the porch steps with long strides.

"Your father will disown you," my mother calls behind me. "Is that what you want?" When I don't stop, she goes for the ultimate insult. "You're behaving shamefully, like a lovesick puppy, not the respectable head of your father's business."

Her words still me. I pause with my hand on the door handle of the car.

I guess she's right. In a way, this is my own kind of loving.

Just not the selfless kind.

I'm going after Zoe with everything I've got.

CHAPTER 2

Zoe

Our flight lands just after ten at night. Stepping from the plane onto South African soil is like an out-of-body experience. I feel lost and unanchored. This is home, and it's not. I've become a stranger to my homeland and a stranger to myself. The woman who returns is nothing like the girl who left.

Seeming to understand my hesitation, the man my brother sent to rescue me from France, Russell Roux, takes my elbow and steers me through the throng of people toward the exit. Thankfully, I only have the bag I checked into hand luggage. We can make our way straight to the parking where an SUV waits.

I look at the familiar, yet unfamiliar, dark landscape as he drives. So much has changed in almost three years. There are more buildings and less open land. The roads and signposts are different. It's as if my world has moved on without me while I was stuck in a very bad dream. A bittersweet dream. Despite the bad, there was also the kindness, like when Maxime got me into one of the most reputable fashion designing schools in France or the time he told his cousin, Sylvie, to befriend me. He might've gone about it the wrong way, using his power instead of allowing me to win these things on my own merit, but he did it because he wanted me to be happy. The lies and deceit of his twisted methods hurt, but his intentions weren't always bad. All those tender moments we shared when he made himself vulnerable and opened up to me to teach me how to open up to him had to have meant something. At least that's what I choose to believe. The alternative is much too devastating and bleak for my heart to survive.

I made it this far. I got away from Maxime Belshaw, a French mafia boss who enjoyed toying with me by playing cruel games. Europe and everything that happened there are behind me. From here, I can only grow stronger.

Russell takes the road to the Vaal River and stops in front of a quaint cottage with a private jetty lit by a row of walkway lamps. The dark silhouette of a man is visible in the porch light. He stands by the rail, his hands shoved into his pockets, waiting. I'd recognize that tall, indestructible frame with the permanent tension in the shoulders anywhere.

Damian.

The stance throws me right back into the past to a boy who expected the worst from the people who was supposed to love us, a boy who always had to be ready to defend himself against violence and prejudice. Like a puppy kicked too many times, he grew up into a vicious dog. For the most part, he was a mistrusting and cynical adolescent, but the Damian I remember before he went to jail had hope and ambition. Who is the man today? How does being locked behind bars for a crime one didn't commit change a person?

Russell unlocks the doors. A part of me wants to run to my brother while another part can't get out of the car. Time and everything that filled up that time hold me back. We haven't seen each other in seven years. For six of those, he's been in prison. I've spent three in my own prison, and it changed me. I'm out of place, and I'm scared. Damian and I will be strangers to each other, but Russell is waiting, so I get out and pause.

There's more to my hesitation than just my trepidation. I don't want to put Damian in danger. Maxime will come after me. I'll have to disappear, but before I do, I have to make sure Damian knows about Maxime's schemes. I have to tell him his trusted friend and cellmate, Zane da Costa, sold information to Maxime about Damian's plans to take back the mine Dalton stole from him. He needs to know Maxime kidnapped me to hold a sword over his head, ensuring my brother would continue selling the diamonds from the mine directly to the Belshaw family by cutting out the middlemen.

When I finally manage to put one foot in front of the other, Damian comes down the steps. We meet each other halfway. The moment his face becomes visible in the headlights of the car, all my reservations vanish. He's exactly as I remember, albeit a little older. Yet he's different too. The man who stands in front of me is no longer the strongest boy in the neighborhood. He's grown into something much more powerful. He looks unbreakable, and I feel better for it.

He holds out his arms. "Zee."

The minute he says his childhood name for me, I fall into his embrace, letting his strength fortify me.

"Hey." He brushes a hand over my hair. "You're safe. It's all right. You're here."

I've shed enough tears for a lifetime, but more flow at his words. This is only the first step. There's a long and difficult process of letting go ahead.

"Thanks, Russell," Damian says.

Russell salutes. "You take care of her."

A look passes between the men. It says I'm pretty much screwed up, enough for Russell to have noticed.

Sniffing away my tears, I offer Russell a sincere, "Thank you."

"You're welcome." He hands my bag to Damian. "I'll see you around."

"Come," Damian says, turning toward the house when Russell gets back into the car. "You must be tired."

"I'm sorry for making you wait up so late."

He throws an arm around my shoulders. "You don't owe me any excuses. That's what brothers are for."

He leads me up the steps and opens the door to let me inside. We enter a small entrance with a lounge on the left. It's cozy. The furniture is ethnic with orange, green, and red scatter cushions. Woven rugs cover the wooden floors. He goes ahead of me down a short hallway to a spacious kitchen overlooking the water. It smells of chocolate cookies.

He dumps my bag on the floor and pulls a chair out by the table. "Sit."

I take the seat while he fills a kettle with water and prepares two mugs of Rooibos tea. Putting one down in front of me, he says, "You don't have to tell me anything now. We can talk in the morning if you're tired."

My laugh is strained. "I doubt I'll be able to sleep." Plus, the sooner he knows everything, the better.

His gaze is piercing but his tone gentle. "Is someone after you, Zee?"

"Yes," I admit with a gush of air that tumbles from my chest. Just as I open my mouth to tell him the truth, a boy of about three years with curly hair and blue eyes walks into the kitchen.

"Daddy?" he says in a sleep-thick voice, rubbing his eyes with his small fists.

Damian opens his arms. "Hey, Josh. What's up, buddy?" When Josh walks into his embrace, he picks him up and settles him on his knee. "We have a visitor. This is my sister, Zee."

Dumbfounded, I stare at the child. I'm an aunt? Damian has a child? When? While he was in prison? How's that even possible?

"There you are, Josh," a sweet, musical voice says from the door.

I turn my head toward the sound. A stunning woman with the same startling blue eyes as the boy and golden hair that cascades in waves over her shoulders stands barefoot in the door. She's wearing a short silk robe. My gaze drops to where her hand rests over her big belly. The diamond on her ring finger catches my eye.

Oh, my God.

The change in Damian when he looks at the petite woman is incredible. His features soften. The hardness in his eyes I attribute to our difficult childhood melts to dopey puddles. A gentle smile curves his lips. He looks at her as if nothing else matters, as if she's the focal point of his existence. Wow. My brother is a conquered man. He's a worshipper.

Balancing Josh in one arm, Damian gets to his feet and walks to the woman. He places a hand over hers on her stomach. Concern laces his voice. "Everything all right?"

The woman reaches for Josh. "I heard him getting up and didn't want him to bother you." She glances at me with a shy smile, exposing a dimple. "I'm sure you have plenty to talk about."

"He's too heavy for you," Damian says, lowering Josh to his feet and folding a big hand around the boy's smaller one. "You know what the doctor said about lifting heavy objects."

Josh sticks the finger of his free hand in his mouth while studying me through his lashes.

"I'm Lina," the woman says, making her way over to me.

Coming out of my haze, I push to my feet. Do I shake her hand or kiss her cheeks? How does she feel about housing a fugitive? Because that's what I must seem to be. Before I can decide what to do, she pulls me into a hug.

"I'm so happy to finally meet you," she says, her voice warm.

"Thank you for putting me up."

"Are you kidding?" She holds me at arm's length. "You're family."

I can't help but notice the scars on her arms. What happened to her?

"You're welcome here as long as you like," she continues. "Our home is yours."

"Thank you." I smile for her benefit while anxiety quickens my pulse.

This changes everything. Damian has a wife—a pregnant wife—and a child. There's no way I can tell him the truth now. I can't put his family in danger. I remember Maxime's promise only too vividly. He vowed he'd use anyone and anything against my brother to get his way. As long as Damian honors their deal, Maxime won't have a reason to go after the family my brother so clearly loves. I better make sure Damian honors that deal.

"We'll catch up in the morning," she says, taking Josh's hand from Damian's. "Come on, baby, back to bed with you." With a last smile in my direction, she leaves Damian and I alone.

He stares after them as they walk down the hallway.

"You have a wife? A son?" I ask, still bowled over.

Pride warms his eyes. "Josh is from Lina's first marriage. I adopted him."

"She's pregnant," I say stupidly, still unable to process the information.

"Yes." His chest swells. "Six months."

"Wow, Damian. Congratulations." Emotions clog up my throat. "I'm so happy for you. She's beautiful. She seems really nice."

"Lina is…" Crossing his arms, he leans a shoulder against the wall. "I don't have words to describe her. Amazing doesn't do her justice."

I never thought I'd see the day. My brother really is a lost case. It makes my smile broad and my heart warm. "You deserve happiness. How did you meet?"

He rubs a hand over his face. There's a short hesitation before he speaks. "She's Dalton's daughter."

"The man who put you in jail?" I exclaim. "The man who stole your discovery?"

His regard becomes closed-off. "It's a long story."

"How long have you been married?"

"Little over a year."

I do a quick calculation. "When did you get out?"

Understanding the line of my questioning, he says, "I married Lina a week after I'd gotten out."

"A week?" I exclaim, sensing more behind the story.

"It's complicated. Why don't you tell me why you need a false identity instead?"

I think fast. "I had to get away."

"I've gathered." He scrutinizes me. "Why?"

"I wrote to you, you know," I say, clutching my hands behind my back.

"The last letter I got was three years ago."

"I know." I lower my gaze.

It was the letter Maxime forced me to write in Venice on the luxury hotel stationary. It said I met a foreigner, fell in love, and left the country with him. That I was so happy I was never coming back. The bitter betrayal of finding out Maxime never mailed any letter I wrote to Damian after that is still a pain I'm battling to process.

Since I can't explain why it seems like I abandoned him, I can only say, "I'm sorry."

"I understand." His lips quirk. "Love can be all-consuming."

"It's not that," I say quickly. "Maxime…" Shit, just saying his name is like wringing my heart in my chest. "He's very possessive."

Questions dance in his eyes as he narrows them a fraction. "I see."

"Things didn't work out between us, Damian." It's not difficult to act. The hurt must be written on my face.

"What happened, Zee?"

I give him as much truth as I can. "He's marrying someone else."

Damian's expression darkens. "I'm guessing you're not on the run because he dumped you."

"No." I fiddle with the hem of my jacket. "He didn't want to let me go."

"He expected you to be his mistress?"

"It's an arranged marriage."

Damian drops his arms at his sides. "That son of a bitch."

"You know how it is with powerful families."

"Like hell I do."

This is not how the conversation should be going. I can't turn Maxime into Damian's enemy. I can't endanger my brother's family. Damian deserves this happiness more than anyone I know.

"Oh, come on, Damian. Don't tell me marrying your enemy's daughter the week after you'd gotten out of jail wasn't business."

He stares at me with a broody look.

"Maxime and I," I say, "we couldn't work things out. Let's just say we didn't agree about how I left. It's complicated, to quote your earlier words. I just don't want him to come after me, okay? I don't want to be found, that's all."

He searches my eyes. "You love him."

"I'll get over it."

Walking over, he places a hand on my shoulder. "I'm sorry."

"Thank you." When he pulls away, I say, "There's more you should know."

I sit down again, hiding my expression behind a veil of hair. "You and Maxime aren't exactly strangers to each other."

"What?" He takes the chair opposite me and leans his elbows on the table. "How do I know this asshole?"

"I don't think you've ever met," I say, glancing at him, "but you *are* doing business."

"How's that possible?"

"You sell diamonds to him."

"Wait." He leans back in the chair, a frown pulling his eyebrows together. "The Belshaws? *That* Maxime?"

"Yes."

"Fuck, Zee." He regards me with disbelief. "He's mafia. *The* mafia."

"I know."

"Now I understand why you needed to become someone else." His gaze pierces mine. "How did you meet?"

I think back to the story Maxime told me when he admitted why he kidnapped me, the one he was going to tell Damian if he ever had to manipulate my brother into honoring their diamond deal by confessing our so-called relationship. The lie is a rehearsed one. It comes easily.

"Three years ago, when the mine still belonged to Dalton, Maxime came to see him about business. Maxime wanted to know how the mine came about. Dalton told him about your discovery. He said you approached him for funding but stole a diamond from him and ended up in jail. Maxime said it didn't make sense that someone who'd just discovered a whole riverbed full of diamonds would steal one, so he looked me up to hear my side of the story."

Damian drums his fingers on the table. "Why didn't he look me up in jail if he was so curious?"

"He's mafia. The correctional service isn't exactly a place he likes to hang out. In any event, he invited me for dinner and one thing led to another." At least this part is true.

"So, he asked you to leave with him and took you to Venice."

"Exactly. The rest is history."

"Is it?"

"What are you implying?"

Folding his hands together, he holds my gaze. "Is there something you're not telling me?"

It's hard to maintain eye contact. It's hard to ask him what I'm about to ask, but if Damian rocks the boat, his family will get hurt. "I want you to honor your deal with him."

"You mean continue to sell directly to the Belshaws?" His voice fills with contempt. "I don't fucking think so."

"Please, Damian." Reaching across the table, I take his hand. "Please, don't cut them out."

His jaw clenches. "Why? I was anyway planning on cutting out the direct buyers and go back to selling via the brokers. Why should I favor a man who took you away from your home only to dump you for a pure breed wife?"

"Because I love him," I say, squeezing his fingers. Of everything, this is the biggest truth.

The fire burns cold in his eyes as he considers me, but understanding flashes in their depths. Damian understands love. He knows what it means.

"Rather than cutting him deals, I have a good mind to go over there and kick his fucking ass," Damian says.

"For me," I beg. "Do it for me. Please."

Sighing, he turns his face toward the garden spotlights that shine through the window. After a long silence, he faces me again. "Fine, Zee, but I'm doing this for you. If I had my way, I'd make sure the fucker goes down."

"Thank you." Relief spreads through me. "That means a lot to me."

"He doesn't deserve you."

"No, he doesn't." No one deserves what Maxime has done in the name of power and money.

He pats my hand. "It'll get better."

I doubt that, but I smile for his benefit. My shoulders remain tense. He needs to know Zane is his enemy, but how do I bring up the subject without telling him how I found out? Damian will want to know, and I can't tell him Zane has been spying for Maxime's family.

I clear my throat. "I'm glad you're out." I look around the kitchen. "I'm glad about all of this. You deserve it."

"Thank you."

"How's your cellmate? What's his name again? Zane, right? Do you keep in touch?"

He stiffens. "He's dead."

"Oh." Wow. "I'm sorry."

"I'm not."

From the way he closes off, the subject isn't open for discussion. At least he has one enemy less.

"Come on." He pushes to his feet. "Let me show you the room we've prepared for you."

I stand. "I really appreciate that."

"Anytime, Zee."

"Thank you for the passport and for getting me out."

He smiles. "You can always count on me. What are your plans? I'm not pushing you to make hasty decisions, and I don't want you to think you're not welcome here. I just want to know how I can help."

"I'd like to get a job and find my own place as soon as possible." To hide where Maxime won't find me.

"I have more than enough money to take care—"

"I want to be independent. I need to take back control of my life."

He nods. "I can understand that."

I also need time alone to heal. "If you know of any jobs, the information will be welcome."

"I can arrange a position at the mine for you."

"No." Nowhere where Maxime will think to look for me. When

Damian frowns, I smooth over my error. "I have to build this new life on my own. I don't want to feel like I'm doing it with favors. I want to earn it."

"All right," he says, "but if you change your mind—"

"You'll be the first to know."

"Are we job hunting for Zoe Hart or Amanda Clifford?"

"Amanda. It's safer like that."

He picks up my bag. "Let's get you settled in."

Following him down the hallway, I'm already like two people living in the chest of one. I'm a contrast of feelings.

I'm both hopeful and falling apart.

CHAPTER 3

Maxime

Where is Zoe?

I'm going out of my goddamn mind.

We traced her car to the pound. It was towed away from a bus terminal. There are fifty or more busses leaving daily from that terminal with varying routes, but all of them lead around Marseille. The logical checkpoints are the harbor and airport.

Zoe had enough money on her for a plane ticket to somewhere in Europe—Spain or Italy, or maybe the Netherlands—but she doesn't have a passport. The one I forged to steal her from South Africa is still in the safe in my office. To be sure, I check the passenger lists of all flights that have left since Saturday. With my connections, it's not difficult to get the information. Zoe Hart didn't board a plane.

She could've tried to get away by boat. It's easier to smuggle someone on board a ship sailing to Africa or the States. On this, I can't rely on help from the Italians. That door has closed for me. However, the Balkans owe me a favor. I call it in, sending pirate boats after the ships that have sailed to search each and every one. We track every vessel via satellite. No one escapes, not even the sailboats cruising the Atlantic or crossing the Mediterranean Sea for Corsica and Greece.

At the same time, I run teams through the city and surrounding villages, questioning people and offering a reward for any information about Zoe, which accounts for a lot of false leads from people who are just after the money.

I consider all options—hitchhiking, leaving on bicycle, and hiding right here under my nose. Sparing no expenses, I turn over the south of France, but the search is fruitless. It's impossible for a woman without resources to disappear like this. If my enemies had caught her, they would've dumped her body on my doorstep by now.

At first, that thought gives me nightmares. Then, it makes me an insomniac. I haven't slept more than a couple of consecutive hours in weeks. My life is falling to pieces. Everything around me is going to hell. The pain is insufferable, like nothing I've felt. It's cruel in design, both beautiful and punishing. It's a dualistic pain, a two-headed monster that teaches me the joys of having found something precious and losing it.

It makes me both alive and dead.

Going for a different approach, I start rumors. I plant messages with an evil tiding, saying I'm going after her brother if she doesn't give herself up.

When no clues come up for several days, it leaves me with only one conclusion. Someone helped Zoe escape. She had an accomplice. If not, my threats would've smoked her out like one smokes scorpions out from under rocks. That means she had to communicate with someone. With her only dialing access Sylvie's and my numbers, she would've had to borrow a phone. My guards swear she didn't use theirs, and they never let her out of their sights. There's no chance she used the phone of a random person in the street. I don't get it, and as furious as I am, I can't help but admire this flower of mine for managing what no one else has to date—to slip through my fingers.

The only option left is that she somehow made it back to South Africa. If she did, she didn't do it in her own name, because nothing comes up in my search for Zoe Hart. If she'd made it back to her brother, she would've spilled the beans. By now, he would've pulled the plug on our deal and started a war to avenge her. Yet Damian Hart is oddly quiet, carrying on just as before.

Maybe too quiet.

Hope rises with my suspicion. What if Zoe somehow managed to contact him and asked for help? Hart has his own connections and shady ways of accomplishing things. What if he provided her with a false passport and airfare? If she wants to stay hidden, he won't stir the waters by changing our deal. He'd keep it exactly as is.

I put a detail on Hart, but Zoe doesn't show up on his doorstep or at his office. It looks like just another dead-end strategy. Unless I'm having the wrong person watched. Unless it's not Damian who's going to lead me to his sister.

The more I think about it, the more it makes sense. I've eliminated all other options. Without wasting more time, I book a plane ticket to South Africa.

CHAPTER 4

Zoe

My days are empty and my nights even more so. Not a minute goes by that I don't think of the man who kidnapped me. At night, I lie awake and torture myself with imagining his new life. Was the wedding big and flamboyant? Did he wear one of his tailored pinstriped suits or one of the fitted dark ones? Is the diamond Izabella wears on her finger from my own brother's mine? Are they happy? Are they making things work like we somehow managed toward the end before I found out Maxime had a future wife? Did she move into Maxime's bedroom or the femininely decorated one next to his? Are they fucking? Does he make her come? Is he tender and rough with her like he was with me? Does he drape her over his lap and ask what she's done with herself all day? Does he teach her lessons? Does he reward her vulnerability with kindness?

The questions torment me, but I can't stop. I'm obsessed. I'm obsessed with Maxime Belshaw like only a woman in love can be.

I got a job as a medical receptionist thanks to Lina. The psychiatrist she works for knew someone who needed a quick replacement for a staff member who went on maternity leave. It's not a permanent position, but it's a start. At least I'm earning money while looking for long-term employment. The salary allows me to rent a small first-floor apartment in Fourways. I didn't have a choice but to let Damian pay the deposit to secure the lease. I needed to get out of Lina and Damian's house fast, the very next day after my arrival.

Damian and I are discreet about how and where we meet. He sometimes sends a driver to pick me up after work. We go to restaurants or bars where Damian trusts the owners. I dyed my hair blond and apply a self-tanning lotion on a weekly basis to give my pale skin a darker tone. Contact lenses change my eye color to brown. I'm different on the outside, and even as my new life slowly but surely starts again, what's on the inside doesn't change. The hurt doesn't fade. I've just grown more used to it.

To give myself a jumpstart in the right direction, I set new goals. I want to save enough money to afford a bigger place. I don't want anything fancy, just a place I can call home. A small garden would be nice. I can't get too attached to any place. I always have a bag packed with my fake passport and money so I can flee on a moment's notice.

I still find it hard to make friends. I can't reach out to anyone who knew me as Zoe. The people who meet me as Amanda have questions about where I come from and why I'm not dating. It's hard to answer those questions without lying, and it's easier to simply avoid the curiosity by avoiding people altogether. It's not healthy, but trust doesn't come easily for me. It's difficult to make friends when you're secretive about your past and spending most of your nights alone, bleaching your roots so no one notices it's not your natural color.

Besides for dinners and drinks with my brother, the highlight of my month is the lunch I share with Lina. It's not difficult to see why my brother is so taken with her. She's kind, caring, and nonjudgmental. I have a feeling nothing I tell Lina will ever shock her. It's comforting to be with someone who is undemanding and giving. She's never asked about my reasons for running. I told her what I told

Damian, and she's accepted that without fishing for more information.

Since she's on maternity leave, we meet every Wednesday when I have my monthly afternoon off. Today we're meeting at an outdoor play park in Midrand. I make sure to arrive early, doing a quick walk-through of the Italian restaurant and the outside terrace next to the play area. I note the exits and the quickest getaway routes, and make sure my car can't be blocked in. These precautions are habits, like always keeping a bag packed. A few groups of moms are eating pizza with their kids inside, and two groups are gathered on the terrace. I choose a table close to one of the groups, even if it's noisy. I prefer to blend in with the masses.

Lina arrives with a blush on her cheeks despite the cooler autumn weather, Josh in hand. My heart warms at the sight of them. The weight on my shoulders lifts. That kid is my sunshine and joy. He's the cutest thing since, well, ever. When he spots me, he pulls free from Lina's hold and charges toward the table where I'm waiting.

Taking the chocolate egg from my handbag, I crouch down and catch him in my arms just before he almost knocks me over.

"Easy, Josh," Lina says. "You'll tackle your aunt to the ground."

Laughing, I ruffle his hair and hand him the treat. "This is for after lunch."

He glances at Lina.

"After lunch," she says sternly.

"Thank you, Aunt Zee," he says, throwing his arms around my neck.

I melt. Wrapping my arms around him, I hug his small body. "You're welcome."

"May I please go play, Mommy?"

"Yes, honey, but stay close to our table."

He runs off to the jungle gym.

"Here." I pull out a chair for Lina in the shade. It's the pregnancy hormones that are making her feel so overheated. I would've taken a table where it's air conditioned inside, but I know she likes to survey Josh while he plays. "How are you?"

"Hot," she says with a broad smile, fanning herself with the menu. "I can't wait for this baby to make her arrival."

Damian is nuts about Josh, but I can't even begin to imagine how protective he's going to be with a daughter. If the way he growls when men as much as glance in Lina's direction is anything to go by, the poor girl won't date until she's thirty. If ever. I grin at that.

"I got something for my niece." I push the parcel wrapped in pink paper toward Lina.

"Oh, Zee, that's so kind of you."

It feels too weird for Damian and Lina to call me Amanda, and since Josh started calling me Zee, my sister-in-law adopted the habit. It's less likely for people to connect it to Zoe, and it's less confusing for Josh.

She tears away the wrapping paper and gasps as she holds up the little dress. It's white with silver stars and fairy wings.

"I couldn't resist. I thought it could be nice for her first photo shoot. Maybe." I falter. "If you like. I know it's cheesy."

"This is so sweet." She squeezes my hand. "Thank you so much. You're spoiling them."

"You're welcome. They are my only nephew and niece, after all."

"I'm so happy Damian has you back. We're all happy to have you." Her regard turns pensive. "You've never heard from Ian or Leon?"

"We grew apart while we were still young."

"Will you ever try to find them?"

Leaning my chin in my hand, I say, "Maybe. As soon as I have my own life in order."

"How's that going, by the way?" She pulls the pitcher of water with mint and cucumber slices closer and pours two glasses.

"Great," I say with enthusiasm.

She hands me a glass. "Really?" Her look is intuitive and soft.

"I'm getting there." Taking a sip, I add, "One day at a time."

"I know a great shrink." She winks. "I can even arrange for a discount."

"You mean your boss? Thanks, but no thanks."

It's not that I haven't considered talking to someone about my

Stockholm syndrome. It's just that I'm scared of endangering anyone I speak to. Call me paranoid, but nobody knows how powerful Maxime is better than me. It wouldn't surprise me if he's having all the shrinks in the country's computers hacked for alert words like mafia, Marseille, France, and Stockholm.

Lina says with a glint in her eyes, "Maybe it's time to take the next step."

"What do you mean?" I glance toward Josh, keeping an eye on him as he climbs up the ladder to the top of the slide.

"A date."

I look back at her. "What?"

"You know." She waves with a hand. "Going out for drinks with a guy. Maybe kiss him. Maybe let him stay over?"

"Oh." Dating hasn't crossed my mind. "I'm not ready for that."

"Because you're not moving on."

"You're right. I'm slow at this, aren't I?"

"Do you want to go back to him?"

"No," I exclaim. "Of course not."

"Okay. Just checking, because if you wanted to, I'll be the last person to judge you for it."

"I appreciate that, but I assure you it's not going to happen."

"Damian and I, we had our share of difficulties at the start of our relationship, but working through it was worth every minute."

"He's *married*."

"All right," she says, "but do let me know if I can play matchmaker. I have very strict criteria and valuable insight into the bachelors working for Damian."

I laugh, but my heart isn't in it. Even now, even with this great distance and a wife and a risky escape and all the bad history between us, Maxime holds me hostage. I'm still his prisoner.

"You know what?" I say. "I need to live in the present, not in the past."

"Does that mean I can go bachelor hunting?"

"Nothing serious. Just drinks." Even as I say it, I have the ridiculous notion that I'm betraying Maxime. Guilt settles in the pit of my stomach, making me feel sick. It rises up in my chest and throat, and leaves me strangely unsettled.

The waiter comes to take our order. We both choose a Waldorf salad with honey-drizzled yogurt and berries for dessert. As he leaves, the back of my neck starts to prick. Turning in my seat, I survey the parking. It's fuller than earlier when I came in. More people have arrived. All the tables outside are occupied.

"Is something the matter?" Lina asks.

Shaking off the weird feeling of being watched, I offer her another half-hearted smile. It's going to take me a while to stop looking over my shoulder. "Everything's fine."

"I'm going to take Josh to build his pizza before our food arrives. Would you like to come?"

"I won't miss it for the world."

Getting to my feet, I shoot a last glance at the bushes on the other side of the parking before I follow my sister-in-law to the tables next to the pizza ovens where the kids are rolling out their dough.

God, I really am paranoid. Perhaps I do need help.

Maxime isn't going to find me. I'm being too careful.

Lina is right. It's time to move on, or I'll never be free. At least not truly free.

"You know what?" I say as we dodge a child racing around the mini track in a plastic jeep. "A date sounds like a good idea."

CHAPTER 5

Maxime

Standing in front of my open study window, I take in the view. It's a beautiful late April day, sunny and clear. There's a bite in the spring air. I don't mind it. I like the cold. I like the heat, too. I like all the seasons. I like them because of what this house represents. Home.

It's what I wanted for Zoe, why I gave her the apartment. I only wanted her to have a place of her own where she could feel safe, happy, and relaxed. Since she ran, I had a lot of time to think. I had a lot of time to figure out where I'd gone wrong. I thought reading her needs and meeting every one of them was enough to trap her in my carefully designed web of psychological warfare. Making her fall for me had seemed like the perfect answer at the time. Like my oversight with the one thing she wants more than anything—love—I didn't take her sense of right and wrong into consideration. Zoe isn't the kind of woman who can be swayed with gifts or money. My material weapons are useless. She's immune to them. Not to my charm, but that specific weapon has backfired on me. Falling in love with me seems to have hurt her more than bringing her happiness. She needs love *and* honor. She needs everything I don't stand for.

No matter. She's mine forever. I'm bringing her back, if it's the last thing I do. It's going to hurt her. Badly. For that, I deserve this punishment I'm bringing upon myself. It's going to be hell to bear, but I'll suffer it gladly. It's only fair. It's the only way I can stand hurting her —if I hurt more. Sometimes this all-consuming obsession feels like a vicious circle of never-ending pain. I can never regret finding her. I can never regret the feelings she awoke in my dead heart, not even the blinding pain.

The front door opens and shuts with a bang. Footsteps echo in the foyer and fall louder as they approach the study. I don't need to turn to know to who the lazy gait belongs. Lazy is nothing but an imitation of confidence, a disguise for a lack of self-assurance. Anyway, I expected him.

Alexis stops next to me, close enough for our shoulders to brush. From the corner of my eye, I see his smirk. He's staring at me like an eager child, unable to contain his ugly excitement.

I don't acknowledge him. I continue to take in the view, to remember the moments I loved here most, all of them ironically involving Zoe.

Breaking first, he asks, "How does it feel?"

I turn away from the beauty of the ocean framed by the cliffs. Alexis only taints its perfection with his presence. "Why don't you tell me?"

"Fantastic. Best cunt I've ever had."

I raise a brow. "Does she know how you speak about her? Her honor isn't mine to defend, but I'm sure her menfolk will take up the task."

There are two kinds of hatred. The cold kind that fills you with loathing but leaves you unaffected, and the heated kind that devours your soul and eats you up from the inside. When I look at my brother, it's winter I feel. Cold. The hatred burning in his eyes, on the other hand, is the heated kind. It makes him the loser, always, even when he wins.

"You know they'll kill you if you hurt her, right?" I ask with growing amusement as his face distorts with the realization of how powerless he is against me. A person only has power over you if you give it to them. To give it to them, you have to care, and I don't give a shit.

"I'm going to crush you," he says through clenched teeth, "and I'm going to love every minute of it."

For a second, I almost pity him. Alexis has always resented me for my first-born rights. He's undermined me whenever he could. For as long as he's lived, he's crawled on his knees and kissed my father's ass. He's always hated me, but since I punished him for torturing the prostitutes under his protection, he wanted to destroy me. After making him and his torture buddy fuck each other's asses while whipping them to shreds, it's become his life mission.

Good luck to him. It's not that easy to get rid of a bad weed. Weeds grow tougher than cultured garden plants and flowers.

Sauntering to the wet bar with his fake confidence, he pours my favorite whiskey and carries the glass back to me. Swirling it under my nose, he grins, then takes a sip before flopping down in the chair behind the desk.

"I assume you're all packed." He glances at the door as he speaks. "Bring me a souvenir from South Africa, will you?"

I follow his gaze. Izabella stands in the door, wearing a long-sleeved dress and high heels with stockings, the image of cultured refinement. The perfect wife. Her dark eyes rest accusingly on me. She follows my movement as I cross the floor. When I reach her, I stop and wait. She steps aside without a word. I don't look at her as I push past her. I carry on straight, walking through the front door without sparing either of them another glance.

CHAPTER 6

Zoe

Urgh.

The evening was a disaster. My poor date. He's a nice guy, not bad-looking either, but I decided to be honest with him over a too-sweet fishbowl cocktail we shared at News Café in Sandton. When I told him I was on the rebound, he paid his portion of the bill and left me there alone with a fishbowl full of fluorescent alcohol and two soggy paper straws. Thank goodness I insisted on driving there in my own car instead of letting him pick me up. At least I had a ride home.

It's only nine when I arrive at my complex. At the security gate, I type in my pin to open the gate, and then scan my thumbprint to lift the boom. An armed guard nods from the guardhouse. I give him a friendly wave. The extra security measures almost all the complexes in the area have to combat robberies give me a feeling of safety. Damian had a security slam-gate fitted in front of my door and fortified bars in front of all my windows as well as under the roof. He wasn't taking any chances. My little fortress is safe. With the alarm, there's zero possibility of anyone getting in.

Just in case, I fold my hand around the pepper spray in my bag when I park. A high wall with electrified barbwire on the top surrounds the complex. Spray lights illuminate the parking and the dark corners. Being attacked by someone lurking in the bushes is a very small probability. Still, I scan the grounds and look over my shoulder.

I lived in Brixton before, a suburb a lot more dangerous than Fourways, yet I'd never been this paranoid in Brixton. This constant state of alertness is the price I pay for being kidnapped and smuggled abroad, all in the name of diamonds. Once upon a time when I was young and naïve and had dreams, I wanted a man to put a pretty ring with a shiny stone on my finger. Now I hate those stones for what they represent. Crushed dreams. Greed and ugly truths.

My steps echo on the concrete as I cross the parking lot. There are twelve units with four apartments in each. Mine is on the first level of the second unit. The fact that it's not on the ground level makes the possibility of someone climbing through a window or the roof even more improbable.

It'd been a long day at work. I'd rushed home to get ready, putting on a blouse with wide sleeves I made from tea-stained lace with a pair of high-waist black pants fastening with buttons on the sides. Pairing it with high-heeled booties, I call it my pirate outfit. So much for making an impression. I sigh. Maybe I shouldn't have said I'm on the rebound, but I hate being dishonest. I'll have to tell Lina to limit her matchmaking to guys who aren't looking for anything serious.

Who am I kidding? The idea of a man's hands on my body repulses me. I was hoping tonight was a step in the right direction to get over my phobia of being touched, something I've developed since I escaped. I'm worried sex isn't in the cards for me for the rest of my life. Maybe I'll never be able to tolerate an intimate touch again. Maybe Maxime damaged more than my sense of safety for life.

Climbing the stairs to my unit, I pull free the elastic that ties my blond hair into a ponytail and shake out the long tresses. I use a straightener these days to get rid of my natural curls.

On the landing, I tiptoe so my neighbor doesn't hear me. Mariska is a nice girl, but I'm not in the mood for company. I just want to wash the makeup off my face and crawl into bed. I was worried for nothing, though, because a reggae song pierced with laughter filters through her door. She's got company. Later, I'll have to listen to the banging of her headboard against the wall, lying awake in the dark and pondering all the ways in which I'm screwed up.

Those sleepless nights are the worst. I ache for a touch I can't tolerate from any other man, my body heating with need at the memory of another woman's man. I burn and cry, and eventually make myself come only to hate myself for it in the morning. Maybe I'll take a sleeping pill tonight. I picked up a herbal remedy from a natural medicine pharmacy a while ago, but I haven't tried it yet.

I keep my alarm remote and keys in a zip pocket of my bag that's easily accessible so I don't have to fish for them at the door. It's the small security measures that make the difference. Get inside fast before someone can snatch you on the landing. After deactivating the alarm, I unlock the security gate and door, and blow out a sigh of relief when I'm inside. I lock the gate and door, then double check by testing the handles to make sure I've locked them. Hanging my bag on the coat stand in the entrance, I go through the door on the right to the kitchen and fill a glass with water from the tap. I take a long drink before unzipping and kicking off my booties.

The heat in the overcrowded bar left me sticky. I envision another quick, cool shower as I make my way to my room with the glass in one hand, already unbuttoning my blouse. The lamp I left on in the lounge guides my way. The radio still plays softly. I always leave on signs of life when I go out so that potential robbers would be deceived into thinking I'm home.

I enter the lounge to switch off the light and music, and then stop dead. My heart slams into my ribs. My breath catches, and the glass slips from my fingers. It shatters when it hits the tiles, water splashing over my bare feet and against the legs of my pants.

I don't look at the damage at my feet. I don't look away from the large frame of a man sitting in my armchair. I'm battling to process what's happening as we're staring at each other, my body frozen in shock while he assesses me with an emotionless expression.

"Hello, Zoe," he says in a gruff voice, the foreign accent rich and unmistakable. "Or shall I say, Amanda?"

CHAPTER 7

Zoe

I can't think.

I can't breathe.

Shock pierces my skin like needles. I go hot and cold, then hot again.

Maxime looks exactly as I remember, except for the slightly longer and disheveled hair that matches the dark scruff on his jaw. He's wearing a white dress shirt that's unbuttoned almost to the waist and a pair of dark suit pants. His ankle rests on his knee in a casual stance, but there's nothing casual about the cold light shining in his gray eyes.

He holds one of my water glasses filled with a quarter of amber liquid in one hand while the other lies in a relaxed pose on the armrest of the chair, a gun resting in his slack grip. All the while, he's watching me with the cruel amusement and unsettling interest of a serial killer.

Even from here, the smell of whiskey reaches my nostrils. I don't drink it, but I got the bottle in a crazy bout of devastating sadness one day when missing him hit me so hard it felt like a physical disease. My cheeks heat when I remember how I made myself come on my fingers, fingers I'd dipped into that alcohol and sucked to remind me of the taste of his kisses.

I stare at him in horror as he considers me with that laid back demeanor and strange look that seems indifferent, volatile, cool, and heated at the same time. Despite his quiet immobility, I sense the litheness trapped under the deceptive calm. If he appeared dangerous before, he's danger personified now. The only thing preventing me from bolting for the door is the gun resting in his hand.

His gaze slips down to where my blouse is unbuttoned, heating as it lingers there. My heart is pounding so hard in my chest he must be able to see it.

Terrified, I clutch the ends of my blouse together. "How did you get in?"

"Really, Zoe? That's the first thing you're going to ask me?" His tone is mocking, his accent both familiar and new after all this time. "No greeting or welcoming kiss?" Putting the glass on the side table, he gets up. He executes the action leisurely, but he dominates the small space with his height and mere presence.

Instinctively, I take a step back. Something sharp cuts into my heel. I gasp at the sting.

He holds up a hand, the hand with the gun, but the barrel is turned toward the ceiling. "Don't move."

Lifting the pressure off my heel, I look down. A shard of glass is lodged in my skin, and blood is mixing with the water on the hardwood floor.

Maxime tucks his gun into the back of his waistband and crosses the floor. I shrink back when he reaches for me.

"Don't touch me," I cry, holding up a hand as if that may stop him.

His voice holds a warning that clashes with the melodic quality of his French accent. "I'm not going to hurt you."

He will if he has to. Just like before. Just like always.

"I just want to help you," he says.

Help me? That's not why he's here.

Putting my weight on the toes of my injured foot, I back out of the door as fast as I can. If I can get to the entrance, I can push the silent distress button on my alarm remote that's hanging from the keychain in the door. The security company will be here in a few minutes, and they'll alert Damian.

Maxime has the physical advantage, though. He has longer legs and wider steps. He chases after me with determined strides, in no particular hurry to catch me. Like a fox playing with a rabbit, he backs me up to the door and grabs the keys from the lock before I can reach them.

"Looking for this?" he asks, dangling the keychain in front of my face.

I'm locked in with him. It's a reminder of the first time he broke into my apartment, and it steals my ability to breathe.

Flattening my body against the wood with my palms pressed next to my thighs on the door, I force from dry lips, "What do you want?"

"What do I want?" His laugh is low and wicked as he closes the last step that separates us, putting his body flush against mine. "I think you know the answer to that question."

I can't shrink back any farther. I can only lift my chin with fake bravado. "I want you to leave."

"Oh, I will, my little flower." Dipping his head, he drags his nose over my temple and whispers against my ear, "And you're coming with me."

"You're married," I say with disdain, spitting the next words at him. "Go back to your wife."

He slams a fist against the door next to my face. "You wanted me all to yourself. You've got it, *ma belle*."

I jump. The violence makes me shake. "You have what you wanted. Damian is honoring your deal. He's still selling you your damn diamonds. Now leave me the hell alone."

"Yes." Nostrils flaring, he sneers. "Like hell. Like hell I'll leave you alone."

"What more do you want?" I exclaim, tears burning behind my eyes as fear for Damian and his family rips through my chest.

He regards me with a solemn gaze. "You."

The declaration hangs between us for a moment. I battle to grab it from the air and own it, but then it sinks in, the knowledge like a ball of lead in my stomach.

"I've given you everything," I say on a broken whisper, "and it wasn't enough."

I gave him my love and my heart. He took both and married another woman. He only upgraded me from being his whore to making me his mistress.

He stills. "I gave you everything too. Everything I fucking have." He unclenches his fingers where they rest on the door and curl them back into a fist. "But it wasn't enough for you either."

"Don't you see? We're no good for each other. Please, Maxime. Go back to your wife. Leave me in peace. Please. You can do it. You can let go."

"Is that what you did?" He hits the door again. "You let go?"

"I tried to," I say through my tears. "I *am* trying to."

"By seeing other men? Tell me. Is that how it works for you? Is that why you saw that *putain de connard de merde* tonight?"

My words tumble from my lips with a tremulous breath. "You followed me?"

"Did he touch you?" He leans closer, trapping me with his weight. "Did he kiss you?" His tone is both cold and furious, detached and possessive. "Tell me, Zoe. Did he put his hands on you?" Slipping a hand between our bodies, he cups my sex and rests his thumb on my clit. "Maybe here?" He drags his palm under the hem of my blouse to the exposed skin of my stomach. "Here?"

I suck in a breath as the heat of his hand burns my skin. It's like branding me with a hot iron, but it's not repulsion I feel. It's not a random touch that stirs my phobia. He's not just any other man.

He lowers his head to mine, brushing words over my lips—angry, seductive words—as his palm moves higher and flattens between my breasts. "Or here?"

"No!" I swat his hand away. "He didn't touch me."

"I'll kill him. I swear I will." His lips curve, but the gesture doesn't resemble a smile. "Maybe for this lesson, I'll make you watch."

"Maxime!" My breath catches on a hitch, my pulse spiking not only from the threat but also from his insistent touch. Even if it wasn't familiar and my conditioned body didn't react in reflex, it still would've turned me on. It also scares me with its power and underlying anger. "It wasn't like that."

"No?" He traces my cheek with a finger. "Then tell me. What was it like?"

"It was just a drink, okay? I told him I was on the rebound and he left. That's it."

"How many?" he asks with a tight jaw.

"Just this once."

Spearing his fingers through my hair, he considers my answer for a moment. We're standing too close. His erection is pressing against my stomach and the pull of his fingers is getting tighter in my hair. I'm not sure if he's going to kiss me or snap my neck. There's nothing I can do about it. Whatever Maxime decides will be my fate.

"I have to say," he says, slipping his hand from my hair to curl his fingers around my neck. "I'm impressed. How did you do it?"

Unwilling to implicate Damian, I shake my head.

He squeezes, leaving me little air to breathe. "How did you do it, *ma petite fleur*? I know your brother helped you, but how did you manage to contact him?"

My lungs burn. I suck in what little air I can. On second thought, it's probably better he kills me. That way, I can't betray the only person who's ever cared enough to help me.

"Do it," I croak. "You want to kill me? Go ahead."

He laughs. It's a deep and husky sound. "You think I'll kill you? No, my pretty flower. It's not you who'll pay the price."

The threat makes my throat close up. Stars dance in front of my eyes. I cough when he lets me go, my body spasming as survival instinct takes over and my lungs battle to draw in oxygen.

"I'll ask you one last time," he says. "How did you contact Damian?"

A dull ache starts throbbing in my heel where the piece of glass is still lodged. Rubbing at my neck where he gripped me, I sag against the door. "I slipped a sleeping pill into your champagne and used your thumbprint to unlock your phone."

Admiration lights up his features. "Do go on."

"I called Damian. He sent someone to the airport with a false passport."

"Very innovative." Tracing my bottom lip with a finger, he asks, "How did you know your brother was out of jail?"

"I called the prison first. They told me. I did a search on Dalton's mine and saw it had become Hart Diamonds. There was a contact number on the website." Hurt filters into my voice. "Why didn't you mail the letters? Why did you deceive me?"

A beat passes as he stares into my eyes. "I never said I was going to mail them."

"You know what?" Tears blur my vision. "I knew you were going to say that."

He gives a frustrated sigh. "I thought writing would be good for you. Therapeutic. You thought I didn't know you were warning Damian with your hidden messages?"

"You read them," I say with disgust even if I've always suspected as much.

"You went through my desk. When? The door was always locked."

"I was looking for my passport. When you kicked me out of your house, I told Benoit I'd left my phone there. He took me back for it. The study was open then."

He clenches his jaw. "I didn't kick you out of my house. I gave you one of your own."

Turning my face away as if I can escape the painful memory, I ask, "What does is matter how I did it? It changes nothing."

"It matters because I can't let it happen again. How did you get away from the guard?" When I don't answer, he gives me a little shake. "Tell me!"

I look back at his rugged, angry features. "I changed into a different jacket and beanie I carried in my bag. I stuffed the bag under the jacket to look pregnant."

"Zoe, Zoe, Zoe." His gaze roams over my face. "You're even better than what I gave you credit for." Cupping my chin, he splays his fingers over my cheek. "Hotter when you behave like a little spy."

"Stop it, Maxime." I push his hand away. "Please."

"This is what's going to happen. You're going to tell your brother we've had a fight, but we've worked things out, and you're going home with me."

I give a start. "How do you know I haven't told him the truth?"

"If you had, the deal would've been off. He would've come after me, and we'd be fighting a war right now."

"You have to realize you don't have a hold over him any longer. If you take me, he'll come after you. If you hurt me, he'll kill you. He'll cancel the deal."

"I guess you'll have to be convincing."

"I'm not lying to my brother any more than I already have."

His smile grows broader as he narrows his eyes. "What lie did you tell him not to cut us out of his business and come after me with every weapon at his disposal?"

I swallow. "That wasn't a lie."

"Tell me. Don't make me drag it out of you."

Averting my eyes, I admit the truth. "I told him I loved you."

Gripping my chin, he turns my face back to him. Possession swims in the gray depths of his eyes. "You're coming back with me, Zoe. I don't care about the deal or the diamonds. I'll fight your brother if I have to. I'll wage any war. I won't hesitate to kill any man I must."

No, he won't hesitate. Between Damian and Maxime, I'm not sure who would win. They're both ruthless. Powerful. Determined. I think about Lina, Josh, and the baby. I can't risk Damian's life. Maxime knows. That is his trump card.

My voice is shaky with the tears I refuse to shed. "You're a bastard."

"That, we've already established."

I ball my hands into fists. "I hate you."

"I know, *cherie*, but you also love me."

Scooping one arm behind my knees and the other around my

shoulders, he lifts me like I weigh nothing and carries me back to the lounge where he lowers me onto the sofa before kneeling in front of me. A tremor runs over my body when he grips my ankle. I stare down at his dark head as he inspects my injury as if he cares, as if there isn't a possibility that I can sustain others by his hands. The gray that brushes his sideburns has crept a little farther, like years and not months have passed. He smells of cloves and citrus, a faint mix of a familiar winter that matches the equally familiar frosted landscape of his eyes.

Lifting his gaze to mine, he says, "Stay," before leaving the room.

I hate how much I'm shaking. I hate how powerless he makes me.

The cabinet door slams in the bathroom, and a moment later he returns with my medicine kit. He didn't have to ask where it was. The bastard went through my things. He invaded my privacy and searched my place, just like he did before.

Crouching in front of me again, he reaches for my bleeding foot. His fingers locking around my ankle makes me feel like a trapped animal.

In a knee-jerk reaction, I shove him away. "Don't touch me."

A smile curves his lips. Slowly, he pushes to his feet. His gaze is level on me, those steely eyes hardening enough to contract the skin on my arms. "My mistake. It seems kindness isn't what you need." He moves so close I have to crane my neck to look up at his face. "It seems a different approach will work better with you."

I lean as far back as the couch allows. "Excuse me?"

"Take care of that cut before it gets infected." His smile is unwavering, but it never reaches his eyes. Taking the kit, he shoves it into my hands. "Is that easier for you to understand?"

Yes. I'm well educated in his lessons. He offered to take care of me. Since I rejected the kindness, he's retaliating by being cruel, but I'm done with his games. If it's not real, I don't want it. "If your caring comes with a price, you can keep it."

"If by that you're suggesting I don't care, you're wrong."

"Caring isn't selfish. Caring is giving without expecting something in return."

"Is that so? Then tell me how that doesn't make you selfish. If you love me like you claim you do, shouldn't you give it without expecting my love in return?"

If you love me like you claim you do... "Fuck you!" How dare he demean my feelings by questioning them, feelings he is solely responsible for? It was damn hard for me to admit those feelings. He has no right to use that against me. "The problem with you, Maxime Belshaw, is that you don't understand anything about love. To love means putting someone else's needs before your own. To love someone else, you must first love yourself and loving yourself means not letting a toxic relationship destroy you. I think that is the problem with you. You don't know how to love yourself."

His eyes narrow to slits. "You think you're the expert on me? You think I'm selfish?" His laugh is cold. "You have no idea what I've sacrificed for you."

"I never asked you to."

Gnashing his teeth, he knocks the box from my hands. It falls on the floor with a thump. "Do *not* be ungrateful for what I've done."

The violence jars me, locking me in place.

Dragging both hands over his head, he tilts his face to the ceiling and walks away from me. "Fuck." He stays at the far end of the room for a moment before turning back to me. His hair is even wilder than before when he finally drops his arms to his sides. A war rages in his eyes. For a minute, he's not my kidnapper, but the man who cares about me. He's just a man making himself vulnerable by opening up and dropping his defenses. "I don't want to scare you, Zoe. After your father—"

"Don't."

Sighing, he comes back and picks up the medicine box. "I'm going to tell you a story. A young man goes to a market and sees a beautiful woman admiring a precious object. He can see she wants it, but when she opens her purse, she doesn't have enough money. This man, he was paid to abduct that woman. He has two choices. He can either grab her, tie her up, and drag her away, or he can go up to her and tell her how beautiful she is and buy her that precious object she wants so much. He can do that for her and be kind, inviting her to dinner. They can have a good time, have great sex. He can ask her to go away with him and knows she'll say yes. Tell me, Zoe. Which man is kinder? Which man is the most selfless?"

"The honest one," I whisper.

A shutter drops in front of his eyes. The man who was reaching out to me a second ago retracts back into his shell. I mourn the loss, the almost-intimacy, but I can't lie to him. I can't betray myself. I can't strengthen his warped belief that lies can smooth over his crimes.

"You better take care of that," he says flatly, pointing at my foot and handing me the medicine box.

I act on autopilot, taking out disinfectant and a Band Aid. My hand shakes when I pull out the piece of glass. The sting burns all the way to my heart. I glance up at him. He's watching me quietly, his face an unreadable mask.

"How did you find me?" I ask.

"When I couldn't track you down in Marseille, I knew you'd skipped the country. It wasn't that difficult. I only had to have your family followed."

My heart starts beating in my temples. "Damian?"

"His wife."

I jump to my feet. "Stay the hell away from them, do you hear me?"

"Whether I stay away from them is up to you. However, you will speak to your brother tomorrow and tell him we're back together. You're going to take me to meet him. How things happen from there depends on how convincing you are. We can be like the couple in my story, leaving nicely, or I can kill a few people before we go. As I said, it's all up to you, my little flower."

His voice is even, disinterested almost. It's as if his fire has burned out after our fight, but I know better. I know him too well. He's pulled away, hiding deep inside himself. He's become the cold psychopath again. I can't do this anymore. I can't keep on trying to draw him out of his shell and hoping to reach him. This love I feel, this hopeless, wrong, painful love, I'm not sure it's worth fighting for. It almost destroyed me once. I can't let it happen again.

When he pushes me down with a hand on my shoulder, I'm too weary to resist. I simply sink down into the cushions and let him take my foot in his hand. I watch him disinfect and bandage the cut with the meticulous attention that makes him Maxime. I sit quietly while he cleans up the broken glass and mops the floor. I don't say a word while he boils water and makes tea.

"Have you eaten?" he asks, handing me a cup.

"I'm not hungry." I can't be a complete monster. "If you are, there's food in the fridge."

He doesn't smile at the offer. He waits for me to drink my tea, then helps me to my feet.

"Can you put weight on that?" he asks, looking at my bandaged heel.

I flinch when I put my foot down. "I think it may take a day or two."

Scooping me into his arms, he carries me to the bedroom and lays me down on the bed. He sets the gun on the nightstand and settles next to me before pulling the covers over us. I don't brush my teeth or wash my face. We don't undress. We simply lie next to each other in the layers that protect our bodies and hearts, breathing quietly in the dark, both of us staring at the ceiling.

After a long moment, a big, masculine hand rubs against my smaller one where it lies on the mattress, his pinky locking gently over mine.

CHAPTER 8

Maxime

Waking up early is an inaccurate statement. It's more like I never slept. At the crack of dawn, I take the gun and go to the kitchen, leaving Zoe in bed. She's not sleeping either, but she can do with the rest. We have a long flight ahead of us.

I find bacon and eggs in the fridge and make breakfast. I'm drinking a strong cup of coffee when Zoe walks into the kitchen, showered and changed. My gaze skims over her frilly blouse and fitted jeans. The clothes are her, the woman I got to know. She's as beautiful as ever, even as a blonde. My heart skips a beat. The truth gives me a head rush. She's truly here and not just a vision from one of my empty dreams. I have her back.

I pull out a chair at the breakfast counter. "I kept your breakfast warm in the oven." Using a mitten, I serve her the warm plate of food. "Coffee?"

"Yes." Like an afterthought, she adds, "Please."

I pour a cup and stir in two sugars the way she likes. Gripping a strand of her hair, I twist it between my fingers. "You're going to dye this back to your natural color."

Her words are catty. "I thought men liked blondes."

"I like you for who you are unless you want to be a blonde now."

"Not particularly." She folds her hands around the mug. "Anyway, it's a lot of work to keep up."

Good. It's one step closer to who we used to be, to who we're supposed to be. "Eat your breakfast, then call your brother. I'm going for a shower."

She eyes the door. I smile. The keys are safely in my pocket, the alarm on the door set, and I've already confiscated her phone. If she thinks she can run from me again, she's got another think coming.

While she eats, I shower and pull a clean shirt from my overnight bag. The pants are crumpled from sleeping in them, so I pull on a pair from the suit travel bag I've stored in Zoe's closet. I'm ready in twenty minutes, finding Zoe in a clean kitchen. It would've been fifteen if I didn't have to tend to my painfully hard dick in the shower.

Defeat sits in her shoulders, their proud line slouched. "Damian can meet us at ten."

"If you have any loose ends to tie up, I suggest you do so now."

From the thorough check I did on her, I know she doesn't have any accounts. She pays cash for everything. We only have to give notice to her employer and rental agent.

While she writes a letter of resignation, I make the bed and take the bag she keeps packed from her closet.

I dump it at her feet in the kitchen. "I suppose you'll need this."

She gives me a cutting look.

"Come on." Wrapping my arm around her waist, I support her while she hops down the stairs and to my car on one foot.

"How did you get in here?" she asks as I throw our bags in the trunk.

"I got someone to hack into the rental agency's database. We pulled your code for the gate and your thumbprint for the boom." Smiling, I open her door. "This may or may not surprise you, but there isn't an alarm in this world I can't override or a lock I can't pick."

"Right," she says, letting me help her into her seat.

I fasten her safety belt before going around to my side. Throwing the keys up in the air, I catch them in a fist. My heart beats again. For the first time in months, I feel something other than despair. The autumn day is warm with the fragrance of honeysuckle hanging in the air. It's pretty. It's the only way I can experience these upbeat things. It's the only way I can eat and taste the food, only when I have Zoe by my side.

Zoe gives directions while I drive, even if I know where Damian's office is. The block he owns is a glass skyscraper with a helicopter landing pad on the roof not far from Newtown. Big, silver letters spell Hart Diamonds across the front of the building with the company logo depicted underneath. The place is like Fort Knox. We're searched before we enter the parking. I don't have a choice but to leave my gun in the visitor's safe. Then my car is searched. After a lengthy process of signing in, we go through scanners, are searched again and made to wait in an area with heat sensitive scanners that pick up above normal body temperatures to raise a viral threat alarm. This guy leaves nothing to chance.

A woman in her late fifties meets us when we clear the final checkpoint. "This way, please."

She calls down an elevator that works with voice recognition software and escorts us to the top floor. When we step out, Damian Hart himself is waiting in a large reception area featuring an eclectic collection of art. He's wearing a dark suit like me, and like me, his regard is sharp and observant. If he didn't already know who I was, he would've done an extensive search on me to arm himself with every piece of information he could lay his hands on. Of course I've done the same with him. The little media and company photos I could scavenge don't do him justice. They portray his strong form and handsome features, but not the cunning edge to his manner or the dangerous vibe only someone of the same making can recognize.

Walking toward us with long, confident strides, he pulls his sister into an embrace and kisses her cheek. The resemblance is striking. They have the same good bone structure and dark hair—that is, when Zoe doesn't dye hers. Zoe is a female version of her brother, smaller and paler, but not less stronger. In her own way, she's a warrior, a fighter for justice, a spokeswoman for love, and a formidable little con artist when she wants to be. Or shall I say escape artist?

"How are you?" Damian asks, searching her eyes. The question is loaded.

She gives him a broad smile. Her cheeks are flushed from the stressful situation, but it works in her favor, because she looks like a woman in love. "Good. Damian, I'd like you to meet Maxime."

Damian turns on me with ice in his stare, but he offers a hand. "Belshaw."

His handshake is strong. I like him. "Let's skip the formal address, shall we?"

He tilts his head, examining me like an obstacle he'd love to pull apart. "As you wish, Maxime."

Our voices bounce off the high walls and marble floors. It's a rather unwelcoming reception, but I get the point he's making.

His demeanor only warms when he takes Zoe's arm. "Let's take a seat." When she limps next to him, he stops. "What happened to your foot?"

"Kitchen accident." She waves a hand like it's nothing. "I broke a glass and stepped on a piece."

"You have to be careful," he says. "Is the cut deep?"

"It's just a scrape." She's flustered, but one could easily mistake her reaction as embarrassment for having been clumsy. "Don't fuss."

He leads her to a leather bench facing a wildlife painting. "Tea?"

"No thanks." She looks at me like a considerate girlfriend would.

I shake my head.

Pulling her down next to him, Damian motions for me to take the single visitor's chair. He flinches with annoyance when I drag it closer, the feet scraping over the floor.

"This was speedy," he says, scrutinizing me with his cold smile.

"We've worked things out," Zoe says. "Maxime asked for a second chance."

"You're giving it to him?" Damian asks with a hint of disbelief that makes me want to plant a fist on his clean-shaven jaw.

"She hardly needs your permission," I say, drumming my fingers on the armrest.

Damian looks at me with so much scorn if he was the devil he'd set my chair on fire. "I carry my sister's best interest at heart. Do you?"

Zoe places a hand on Damian's arm. "I want this. I know how I arrived here didn't put Maxime in your good books, but I also carry part of the blame. I've been wrong about many things, including not writing to you, but I'm going to be a better sister this time and be regular about staying in touch so you don't have to worry." She looks at me with a challenge in her eyes.

Clever little sly girl. She knows I'll keep any promise I make to her brother. Promises are not things I like to break, and there's an unwritten code between men like us. I may not be signing a contract for Zoe, but it doesn't mean the regular rules of said contracts don't apply.

"Of course, *cherie*." I lean over to brush a finger over her wrist. "Anything you want."

Damian traces the caress like a rabid bitch about to pounce to protect her litter. "How did you find Zoe?" Smoothing down his tie, he adds in a taunting tone, "If you don't mind my asking."

"She called me."

Zoe's eyes flare, but Damian doesn't notice because his eyes are trained on me like torpedo missiles. I know she hates lying, especially to her brother, but I can hardly tell him I've had his wife followed. Men like him are protective. He'll rip me apart and feed me to the dogs begging downstairs in the street before sending Zoe home with me if that particular piece of information comes to light.

"Is that right?" Damian asks, turning his attention back to his sister.

Zoe blushes. It's the lie, but it looks innocent enough when she says, "I tried to move on, really I did, but I was only lying to myself."

"You should've told me," he says.

She shrinks into herself. "I know you went to great lengths to get me a new identity and start a new life. Please don't think I don't appreciate it. It was a moment of weakness. I'm sorry."

His smile is warm. "Don't be sorry for your happiness. That's all that matters to me."

"Thank you." She takes his hand. "I'll never forget what you did for me."

I don't think her tears are tears of joy. She's playing her role brilliantly. A part of me feels like a bastard for putting her in this situation, but I accept the strange and unfamiliar attack of guilt like I accept the good feelings she gives me. It's a package. I can't have one without the other. What I do know is I'm never giving it up, which is why I draw Damian's focus back to me before Zoe falls apart right in front of his eyes.

"My apologies for the hasty departure, but I have business to take care of. You're welcome to visit. I was hoping soon."

"No," he says a tad too harshly. "Not soon."

Ah. His wife is too far into her pregnancy to be allowed to travel. "Whenever you're ready."

"I'd like to have a word with Maxime in private," he says to Zoe.

She shoots me a panicked look.

"Of course." I get up and straighten my jacket. Kissing the top of her head, I say, "I'll be right back."

Damian leads me into a big office with glass walls and elephant statues. I admire him for building all of this up from scratch. Word is he used the fortune his wife inherited to buy back his stolen mine, but he earned his own riches by doing dirty work in jail and investing that money in the right places. Me, I was born with what I had. A man like him who came from nothing deserves my respect.

He walks to the desk and leans against it, crossing his arms. The fact that he doesn't invite me to sit is another clear message, one I accept not as an insult, but as the ire of a brother watching out for a sister.

"So," he takes me in with a narrowed gaze, "you've worked things out."

"Yes." I go to the window. The view stretches out over skyscrapers to mine dumps that glitter yellow in the distance. "I'm eager to take Zoe home and start our new life."

"What I'd like to know," he says to my back, "is why you came for her when she called."

I turn away from the dizzying height. "I came back for her because I can't live without her."

His eyes have that lively light of someone who's clever and insightful, someone who sums people up well and fast. "What made you realize that?"

"Losing her."

From the way his gaze widens a fraction, I can see he understands this. This particular language, we share. It's a language not consisting of sounds and syllables. Except for that faint recognition of understanding, he gives nothing else of his personal self away. His face is perfectly blank.

He pushes away from the desk. "How did you meet Zoe again?"

I smile, because Zoe and I have rehearsed this on the way over. "You know how we met."

His expression hardens. "Indulge me."

"I had a meeting with Dalton. He mentioned your history, so I looked up your sister to hear her side of the story."

"Why?"

"I didn't believe Dalton."

Picking up a diamond-shaped paperweight, he weighs it in his palm. "Then why not speak out at the time?"

"Would it have changed anything?"

He puts the paperweight back on the desk. "No."

"At the time, you didn't concern me. In any event, your time in jail seemed not to have been wasted. You studied. You made alliances." I let the implied meaning hang. I know about his connections. I know he plays dirty when it suits him. We're two peas in a pod really, or we used to be.

"True." Dipping his head, he studies me. "Conveniently, a relationship with my sister will benefit your business. As your *family*, you're expecting me to honor our deal."

"I don't care about the deal. I'm out of the family business. You can do as you like."

His eyes narrow with more understanding. "You gave it up for her."

"I did." My self-inflicted punishment. I'd do it again. I'll do whatever it takes.

"Then how are you going to provide for her? How do you intend to keep her safe?"

"By running a legitimate business. I'll still be importing and distributing your stones, but I'll acquire them through a middleman if that's the route you choose to go."

"What about your family?"

"How they run their business is up to them."

"Can you guarantee she'll be safe?"

"You and I, with the kind of lives we've lived, no one is ever one hundred percent safe, but you can rest assured I'll die protecting her. She has a property in France. I took out life insurance. If anything happens to me, she'll be well provided for. If she wishes, she can sell the property and come back to South Africa. Whatever she wants."

He nods. "I appreciate your frankness."

"I'll bring her home to visit at least once a year. Of course you're always welcome in France."

The corner of his mouth lifts. "I don't think so."

"Yeah, I didn't think so either." Knowing who we are, he won't risk his family's lives.

"If she didn't love you, Belshaw, I would've been sorely tempted to break your French bourgeois neck."

"Understandably. If I had a sister, I would've felt the same way."

"Glad we're on the same page, because know this." He advances to right in front of me. "If you ever fuck with her feelings again, you'll die a slow and painful death."

"A fate I'll accept as it'll only be fair."

"Good." He gets out of my personal space. "You better make sure she calls me. You don't want me to come after you."

"She'll call." I walk to the door. "Seeing that you're busy, I won't take up more of your time."

"My sister's personal life is hardly my business, but her wellbeing is my concern. You better do right by her."

I grip the handle. "I will."

"There's no place for three people in a relationship, not with Zoe. That's not who she is."

"I know. No triangles. I promise."

His nod is reluctant. He's not happy to let her go, at least not with me, but she's made her choice as far as he's concerned.

I've offered as much reassurance as I could. I close the door on his brooding face. My flower waits by the elevator, her bag clutched to her chest and her pretty face white. All mine.

As far as I'm concerned, there is no choice.

CHAPTER 9

Zoe

There isn't much furniture to get rid of. I picked up a few essential pieces for next to nothing at second-hand stores. Damian offered to buy me what I needed or at least give me money, but I wanted to do this on my own. I wanted this new life to be all mine, earned and not given to me on a silver platter.

Yet here I am again, watching helplessly as Maxime pays the transport company to drive my meager possessions to a charity store. Next, we drop the keys off at the rental agent. Maxime pays the rent for the two months' notice I was supposed to give, and I ask that the deposit is paid into Damian's account once the inspection of the unit has been done. I called in to work this morning to explain the situation. Since I don't have a contract yet, there aren't any legal issues about my hasty resignation.

The little clothes I've brought with me are packed in the bag Maxime carries to his private plane. As I entered the country under my false identity, I'm leaving it under the same name. On paper, Zoe Hart has never left France.

Damian, Lina, and Josh come to the Lanseria airport to say goodbye. It's a difficult farewell, but I do it for the people I love. I do it to keep them safe—Lina, the baby, Josh, Damian, and yes, even Maxime. There's no doubt Damian would start a war if he finds out the truth.

Lina takes my hands and steers me a short distance away from the men. "Is this really what you want, Zoe?" she whispers.

"Yes." I try to say it with a smile and conviction. "Thank you for everything. Thank you for being here for me when I needed a friend."

She pulls me into a hug. "I'm always here for you. Damian and I both are." Holding me at a distance, her eyes turn imploring. "You can always come back if it doesn't work out like you hope. Don't you forget that."

I smile through my tears, knowing it's an impossible notion. There'll be no coming back ever again. This time, Maxime is keeping me for good. He's not going to let me slip through his fingers twice.

Maxime puts a consoling arm around my shoulders, the act tender as he leads me away from the people who mean everything to me. With every step, my heart breaks a little more, and by the time we're stepping on board, the tears flow freely. No matter how hard I try, I can't hold them in.

Handing our bags to a steward, Maxime takes my shoulders and propels me to a double seat. "It'll get better." He sits and pulls me into his lap. "You have to give it time."

Time. Time didn't help the first time round. I doubt there's any remedy. I wiggle off his lap and shift to the far corner of the seat. His jaw clenches, but he lets me.

I decline the champagne and food he offers. Sometime during the night, he lowers the seatback and covers my body with a blanket. It should be impossible to sleep, but after the restless night I spent tossing and turning next to Maxime, I eventually doze off.

. . .

It's early morning when he wakes me for the landing. He calls a valet service, and a driver brings his car from a private parking garage nearby. I'm numb when he drives us home, irrationally expecting the sights to have changed like when Russell took me back to South Africa, but everything looks disturbingly the same.

Instead of driving us to his house in Cassis, he heads for town and parks in the underground parking of the building where he bought me an apartment. The Mini Cooper he gave me is parked in its place. Of course. Life flows back into my body as the blood heats in my veins. His wife is at home. This is me. This is the home of his mistress.

I get out before he can come around the car, and slam the door. He stares darkly after me as I walk to the dingy elevator instead of the stairs, leaving him to get the bags. I test my code. It still works. Getting in, I push the button for the fourth floor. Maxime catches the door just before it closes.

We ride up in silence. I pause when the doors open. There's no one on the landing, no guard in front of the apartment. Maybe Maxime is too certain I won't run again. He knows I won't risk the people I love.

He goes ahead and unlocks the door. The smell of grilled cheese and onions hangs in the air. A quiche is cooling on the island counter.

"I asked Francine to prepare something," he says. "It's leek and onion. You like that, right?"

The mention of her name makes me go rigid. I don't want her here, not in this space too, but I say nothing.

He locks the door and carries our bags to the bedroom. I look around. The sewing machine Maxime bought for me, the one I left in the cellar of his old house, stands on the desk of the upstairs study. Everything else is just like I left it. The champagne glasses I rinsed before running are still standing in the drip tray. He hasn't eaten here since I've left. Why would he? He would've been staying at the big house, enjoying the honeymoon. The thought hurts. Unable to stomach it, I walk to the French doors and peer outside.

The wind has blown the greenhouse door open. I must've not closed it properly. One of the pot plants has blown over. The terra-cotta pot lies in pieces on the ground, the delicate white orchid dying on the heap of dark soil. Unlocking the door, I go out into the cold wind and scoop what I can salvage of the sand in an empty pot before carefully replanting the flower. It's still alive, but I'm not sure it will survive the shock.

The greenhouse smells of damp soil, and the floor is wet. Drops of water shine on the leaves. I look up. An overhead irrigation system has been installed. At least the plants didn't die of thirst in my absence. Whoever did the work must've forgotten to latch the door.

When I get back inside, Maxime waits in the lounge. Taking in his emotionless expression, I swallow.

"Come here," he says with an even voice.

I'm not going to let him touch me like that. His gaze tracks my movements as I slip around him.

"Damn you, Zoe," he says, coming after me with big steps.

I escape to the room, hoping to reach it so I can lock myself in before he follows me inside, but when I get to the door I stop so suddenly he slams into my back.

The air is knocked from my lungs not only by the collision, but also by the sight in front of me. I stare at the dress hanging from the curtain rail in front of the window, illuminated by the soft early morning light.

A white dress with a wide skirt and an embroidered bodice.

A wedding dress.

A bouquet of white roses tied with a pink ribbon lies on the bed. Two velvet boxes are neatly arranged next to the flowers, a square one that holds the diamond choker necklace and a smaller one with the earrings he gave me in Venice. On the floor at the foot end of the bed stands a pair of white Cinderella shoes. The room smells of roses, and I already know I'll find petals and candles in the bathroom.

My throat closes up. It doesn't make sense. Spinning around, I look at Maxime's left hand where his wedding band should be. Why is that finger bare? Why has it escaped my attention until now? Laying a hand on my neck, I take a step back. Many men don't wear rings. It doesn't mean anything. The dress does. The dress and everything else.

"What's going on?" I ask in a hoarse voice.

He backs me up into the room. "I would've explained if you'd given me a chance."

"Explain what?" The back of my knees hit the bed.

"Stay," he says, walking out of the room.

I obey not because I want to but because I'm stunned into a state of immobility, frozen to the spot.

A moment later, he returns with a slice of quiche served on a plate. He sets it with napkin and fork on the nightstand.

"Explain what, Maxime?" I ask with a dry mouth.

"Eat something, dye your hair, have a warm bath, and put on the dress."

"Put on the dress why?" I ask, hysteria creeping up on me.

He only looks at me, looks and looks and looks until I want to scream.

My voice rises in volume. "Tell me."

He just stands there, mechanical like a robot, infuriatingly calm. "You know why."

Banging my fists on his chest, I cry, "Tell me, damn you." My mind begs for an explanation. "Say it."

He catches my wrists in a painful grip. His calm slips, and ice glazes the gray of his eyes. "We're getting married."

I sink down onto the bed, my wrists still captured in his hands. "You *are* married."

"I called it off. This is what you wanted, isn't it?"

No. I didn't want to cheat. I didn't want to be the mistress of a married man, but I don't want to be his wife. Not like this. My breath catches. "I don't understand."

"I gave it all up for you, Zoe."

His words are like lava being dripped over my head. My face grows hot, the heat rolling out over my body to the tips of my toes. "What did you do, Maxime?".

"I paid a price."

He paid a price. He didn't marry Izabella. "The contract..."

"My father made a new deal. Alexis stood in for me."

Alexis married Izabella?

"No cheating," he says through tight lips, lowering his head to mine. "No one else but you. I'm all yours. No more hands-off excuses, Zoe. Tonight, I'm taking what's mine." He lets me go with a shove.

I can only stare at him in dread. He can't be serious. Yet his face says otherwise. His angry steps as he retreats tell me just how serious he is. So does the key that turns in the lock after he's slammed the door shut.

At the sound, I come to my senses. Jumping up, I run to the door and pull on the handle. Locked. I twist around and lean on the wood, sweat breaking out over my brow.

A marriage is forever.

A marriage is for love.

How far will he take his games? How much more betrayal can he manage? Hasn't he broken me enough? Anger rises from the hollowness in my stomach to the empty cavity of my chest. The rage swells through me like a wave. It steals my senses and blurs my sight until all I see is that damning white dress through a veil of red.

He tricked me. Maxime tricked me once again.

I'm done. I'm going to beat him at his own game.

It's as if a devious spirit invades my body. I'm not myself when I walk to the closet and throw it open. It's a different woman who pulls open the drawer with my old needlework tools and takes out the scissors.

With a cry of fury, I attack the dress, ripping into the layers of silk and lace with the scissors. I tear and snip the beautiful dress, a dress with an exclusive label that must've cost a fortune. I destroy what it means, cutting into what it stands for until nothing but a bed of white ribbons is left at my feet.

This is my lesson to teach.

This time, it's Maxime who will learn.

CHAPTER 10

Maxime

I give Zoe enough time to cool down and get ready. She'll have a bath and make herself pretty like she did on the night I took her virginity in Venice. She'll resist me at first, but I seduced her into wanting me once. I'll do it again.

On my way down to the parking, I send a text to Damian Hart to let him know we landed safely. It's what any good boyfriend would do. Hart would expect nothing less. I'm still to give Zoe back her phone, but I leave her number in case he'd like to get hold of her. He replies back promptly with a cryptic note of thanks, saying he'd give us a couple of days to settle in before bothering her with calls.

Today has to be perfect. I go to a lot of effort. A rare flower deserves nothing less. After booking out the quaint restaurant on the hill, I have dozens of pink roses delivered there. The flowers will be everywhere, on every surface and cascading from every wall. I make sure our table has a view and that the others will be moved away to create our own private dance floor. Tonight will be ours alone. I'm too possessive to share this moment with witnesses.

Organizing the singer takes pulling some strings, but Zoe will like her voice and sweet, romantic love songs. I book a room in a hotel like newlyweds do. I order champagne, chocolate-coated strawberries, and sugar-glazed fresh fruit. I have more roses delivered to the room and order the staff to scatter some of the petals over the bed. I tell them to put rose-scented candles in the bedroom too.

On the way back, I stop at the church. The priest is a family friend. He doesn't dare to argue or pose questions. My face is enough to make him gather a choir in a hurry and promise the bells will toll at three o'clock to announce the happy occasion.

I'm elated when I finally pick up the formal suit from my regular tailor. He's worked on it for two days straight since I called him from South Africa. It's a three-piece with a tailcoat jacket, fitted waistcoat, and cravat. My face may not be pretty, but I want to look good for Zoe. I want her to hold fond memories when she looks back at the photos a few years down the line. Fuck, the photos. I almost forgot. I dial a popular photographer in town who immediately clears his schedule.

Zoe will build a new nest, and this time she may even fill it with babies. I know she wants children. I know I hurt her when I said we couldn't bring a child into the world, but it was a different world then. I'm a cruel man, but I'll never be cruel to a child, certainly not cruel enough to spawn bastards and curse them with no recognition, protection, or respect. The more I think about it, the more excited I become about the idea of planting a child in Zoe's belly, of seeing it grow and knowing I've bound her to me by blood.

My mood is so great I stop at the bakery on the way to get Zoe something sweet, something like a box of delicate choux and macaroons. Double fuck. I never ordered a wedding cake. Slamming a roll of bills on the counter, I tell the petrified owner to make sure he gets a *pièce montée* to the restaurant by five. I give him the name and address before taking my box of patisserie and making my way whistling back to the apartment.

All is quiet when I unlock the door. It's a good sign. Smiling to myself, I serve the pastries in a plate. Never mind that it's lunchtime and pastries are dessert. Today is a special day, after all.

Impatient to surprise Zoe, I unlock the bedroom door and push it open. What greets me punches the excitement out of my chest. She sits on the floor, her knees drawn up and her back against the window. Her hair stands in every direction and mascara runs black under her eyes. Next to her lies a pair of scissors, and in front of her the dregs that are left of her wedding dress.

"What have you done?" I exclaim, my vocal cords refusing to rise above a whisper.

"Pay attention, Maxime." Her lip curls up. "This is *my* lesson to *you*. I'm done with your games."

I've never experienced greater rage, neither when I punished Alexis, nor when I revenged Gautier's death. Not even when I killed the man who took a shot at Zoe. The fury mounts in my body until I shake with it. It's not the destruction of the dress. It's what the act stands for.

Uttering a howl loud enough to shake the roof, I throw the plate at the wall. The pastries splatter against the stone, and pink porcelain falls into pieces on the floor. Zoe doesn't react. Not even a flinch. The old Maxime would've been better equipped to handle this. That Maxime would've been able to navigate the situation calmly, to find a way to bend his bride to his will. He would've been able to do that because it's hard to get upset when you feel nothing. However, the new me, the feeling me, has too many emotions clogging up my chest. My ribcage shrinks around my heart until all I feel is suffocating anger and incontrollable madness.

She thinks this is a lesson? I advance on my unwilling bride with big steps. Zoe shrinks away from me, but even that isn't enough to stop me. Grabbing a fistful of her blond hair in one hand and her arm in the other, I pull her to her feet.

She takes the punishment without complaint, hobbling on one foot ahead of me as I march her to the bathroom. Shoving her into the Louis Vuitton chair that stands next to the bath, I keep her there with my hand on her shoulder. I pull the belt of her robe that hangs next to the bath from the loops. I use the belt to tie her hands behind her back, and then drag the chair to the edge of the bath.

"What are you doing?" she cries.

"It's a little late for questions, don't you think?"

Pulling the plug in the bath, I let the rose-scented water Francine prepared drain. I had this all worked out to the finest detail. The timing was perfect. I made sure everything was just right before our arrival. I'd handed Francine a set of keys before I left for South Africa so she could come in and set everything up once I'd found Zoe. All of this, Zoe spoiled by making a destructive choice.

I rip open the box of hair dye I left on the vanity counter and grab her long hair to pull her head back. I'm rough. She yelps. I pull the plastic gloves on before squirting the dye onto her hair and using the comb that came in the box to spread the dark color. After working the black dye through to the ends, I set the timer on my phone.

My next task is fetching the cold quiche on the nightstand.

"Open," I say, stabbing the fork into the quiche and pointing a piece at her mouth like a weapon.

"I don't want it."

"At this stage, *ma belle*, I don't give a damn about what you want. Open the fuck up, or I'll force your mouth open with clamps."

Her lips part even as tears spill over her cheeks, running rivulets through the already smeared mascara. The bite I shove into her mouth is huge. She has to chew a long time to get it all down. I feed her bite after bite, until the fucking plate is empty.

I fill the toothbrush glass with water and hold it against her lips. The water spills over her chin and down her chest when she drinks, wetting her blouse, but I don't care to wipe it away. My alarm pings. I turn on the water and let it run warm before rinsing the color from her hair with the hand nozzle. I don't bother with shampoo. I barely squeeze out all the water. The long strands drip dirty drops over her shoulders when she lifts her head.

Leaving her there, I go through her closet in the dressing room. There are a lot of dresses, the ones I bought for her and the ones she made, but nothing in white that looks suitable. Maybe I should make her wear red. That'll teach her a valuable lesson.

My hand touches a black dry cleaning bag. It's a big bag. Puffy. Unzipping it, I lift out the dress she made for her fashion show, the beautiful princess wedding dress the judges called cheesy and scored one out of ten. I take that dress to the bedroom and throw it on the bed.

When I get back to the bathroom, Zoe's blouse is soaked. I untie her and pull her to her feet by her arm. I all but drag her to the room. Her gaze widens when she takes in the dress.

"Put that on," I say, shoving her toward the bed.

She turns to look at me. "No." Her eyes are bluer with her dark hair. Wider.

"You won't say no to me. Not anymore. Not today."

She shivers. Goosebumps run over her arms.

"Put on the fucking dress, Zoe."

She jumps. Reaching for the buttons of her blouse, she starts to undo them. She undresses until she stands in only her panties. She's even more beautiful than I remember, more delicate and womanly. So pretty. So destructive. For the first time in my life, I'm not in control. She did this to me. She'll suffer the consequences. The old me may have taken pity on her. The me I am now can't fucking think through my furious rage.

Her lip trembles as she reaches for the dress. On second thought, I pick the scissors up from the floor, open the window, and hurl them outside. They drop with a clank in the street.

Cold air rushes into the room. It's barely the end of April. She shivers more. I close the window and watch as she struggles into the dress. She does so quietly, only turning her back on me in silent request when the whole thing is finally fitted. Going to her, I pull the laces through the hoops at the back and tie them together. The dress is beautiful on her. It looks as if it was made just for her.

My instruction is gruff. "Put on the shoes."

She pushes her feet into the heels, flinching when she fits the injured foot. I pick up the flowers and shove them into her hands. I don't have to worry about thorns. I had those removed when I ordered the bouquet. Francine picked it up with the dress and shoes on her way here.

"Come," I say, grabbing her arm and manhandling her to the door.

I arrange the faux fur drape that goes with the dress she's destroyed over her shoulders. Then I push her into the hallway and lock up behind me.

This is how I take her to church—a girl with wet tresses dripping dirty water and mascara running under her eyes.

I don't care about putting on my wedding suit. I guess there won't be any photos to commemorate the day.

CHAPTER 11

Zoe

Maxime drives to the *mairie*. At my horror, Francine and Sylvie wait in the reception room on the ground level of the council building. Maxime must've already supplied all the paperwork necessary for the marriage authorization.

I draw back, straining on the tight hold Maxime keeps on my hand. "What are they doing here?"

"Witnesses," he says through tight lips.

I stumble when he pulls me forward. The cut on my heel hurts in the shoe. "I don't want them here."

"I already told you, what you want is no longer my concern."

"Not them. Please, Maxime."

He doesn't slow down. "Sylvie's your friend."

"Was. She betrayed me. Francine hates me." I can't stand this humiliation.

His gaze lands coldly on me. "You'll patch things up."

Sylvie's eyes grow large when we get closer. Slamming a hand over her mouth, she jumps up from her chair. A smile stretches over Francine's face as she takes me in.

"Maxime," Sylvie exclaims.

He pushes past them without replying, dragging me along.

"Maxime," Sylvie whisper-screams as she runs after us.

"What?" he snaps, pausing in front of a door with a sign that reads marriage office.

"What's going on?"

"Nothing," he says. "Let's get this over with."

He yanks the door open and pushes me inside ahead of him. The man sitting behind the desk gives a start when his eyes land on me. He's a lot younger than the mayor. In order to perform the ceremony, he'll be a representative of the mayor.

"Do it," Maxime says, shoving me to the desk.

The man swallows. He looks from Maxime to me.

"What are you waiting for?" Maxime asks. "I don't have all day."

The man works a finger into the collar of his shirt. Francine and Sylvie follow us inside, but I don't look at them. I can't stand Francine's smug expression and her pristine white, fitted dress or Sylvie's perfectly bourgeois, powder-blue, two-piece ensemble and the pity on her face. Lifting my chin, I jerk my hand from Maxime's.

"Mademoiselle," the man says, "are you sure this is what you want?"

"She wants this," Maxime says.

The man continues, "Are you here out of free will, miss?"

"Do you fucking know who I am?" Maxime bellows.

"I do, sir." The man takes a handkerchief from his pocket and wipes his brow. "I'd still like the lady to answer."

Maxime turns to me with a cruel smile, watching and waiting. He's not worried, because he knows what my answer will be.

Regarding the representative squarely, I say, "Yes."

His brow furrows. "Are you sure?"

"She fucking said yes," Maxime says, his arms drawing tight against his body.

The man clears his throat. Giving me a speculative look, he opens a book. "By the power vested in me…"

The rest of the words float away. They're like burned flakes of paper in a breeze. I tune out of the moment. It's all too surreal, yet so very actual. Before I ran, I wanted Maxime's love. I wanted it because I thought I'd give us a try. He told me he was unable to love, but I still hoped. I hoped that maybe the way he cared about me would evolve into something less selfish, something that made us equals. Now I believe him. The man doing this is incapable of loving.

Maxime lays a hand on my shoulder. His palm is warm on my naked skin where the drape has slipped. I look from where he's touching me to his face. In contrast to the burning sensation of his hand, there's only coldness is his eyes.

"Do you?" the man asks.

A sniffling sound makes me look to my left. Sylvie is crying.

"Please, Maxime," she says. "This isn't right."

"Do you, Zoe?" Maxime asks, those frosted-gray eyes promising nothing but retribution.

"Yes," I say. "I do."

The representative's shoulders sag as if he wanted the answer to be no. With a sigh, he says, "I now declare you man and wife."

Maxime extends a palm. Francine hands him a ring. Her gaze is like acid when it lands on me. He takes my hand in his and slides the ring over my finger. It's a big, square-cut diamond. Simple. Elegant. Pricey. Then he places a ring in my hands.

I look at the platinum band. It's plain. Unassuming. Mechanically, I slip the ring over his finger. Our gazes lock only for a moment, but it feels like the infinity our rings represent. Maxime drops my hand. There's a significant distance between us, at least two steps.

When he turns his back on me and walks out of the room, I don't move. Sylvie chases after him. Francine follows at a leisurely pace. It takes me a while to regain control over my body. I don't want to go after Maxime, but the alternative would mean standing here in front of this man's desk while he studies me with pitiful guilt, as if he's the one who committed the crime.

Finally, I hobble out of the room and stop in the hallway where the others are gathered.

"Thanks for coming," Maxime says.

"I prepared the cocktail party," Sylvie says, fiddling with her clutch bag. "Everything is set up in the reception room."

"Enjoy it." Maxime takes my hand. "We won't be joining you."

"What about the photographer?" she calls after us as Maxime drags me away. "He's all set up."

"Cancel it," Maxime says without looking back.

He bundles me into the car and drives us back to the apartment. My hair is soaking wet, but I haven't realized how cold I am until now. It's freezing outside, and the drape doesn't offer much protection. I study my nails that have turned blue in my lap. I won't admit it, but I'm scared of what's going to happen. I'm scared of being alone with Maxime. When I decided to give him some of his own medicine by teaching him a lesson, I didn't think it all the way through.

We make our way upstairs in silence. He lets me into the apartment and locks the door behind us. While I'm standing in the middle of the floor, he goes to the kitchen and pours a shot of whiskey that he drains in one go.

It starts raining. Drops pelt against the circular stained-glass window and the French doors. Not sparing me a glance, he opens the doors and walks out onto the terrace. The rain washes over his dark hair and the same suit he traveled in until water runs in streams from his face and the clothes are plastered to his body.

He's upset. I've never seen him like this. I've seen him jumping off a cliff into the sea in the middle of winter. I've seen him cold and collected when he took out the men who tried to kill me. I've seen him controlled and distant when he punished and fucked me. Up to now, my choices have only affected me. They've only served as lessons. It feels good to take a stance, to turn those lessons around and show him how it feels. I'm finished with being his puppet. I'm no longer the naïve girl who believes in romance and fairytales. I've done some growing up since he kidnapped me.

Those lessons I hated so much, they did serve one good purpose.

They taught me how much it hurts to love. To hope. To crave scraps of affection. Maybe that's the most important thing Maxime taught me. After what he did today, I'll never open my heart to him again. I'll never make myself that vulnerable for anyone. Love is a joke. It's a laughable weakness. I'm so over it. It's time to woman up. It's time to seal the walls around my heart and grow a thick skin.

After a long time, he comes back inside. A puddle accumulates around his feet on the floor. Grabbing a dishtowel from the kitchen, he dries his hair. He doesn't look at me as he stalks past me toward the room. The water in the shower comes on. I kick off the shoes that are pinching my toes and limp to the bedroom, hovering outside the door. I listen to the sounds Maxime makes as he dries his hair and dresses. I'm still standing on the same spot when he appears in the door several minutes later.

My gaze drops to the overnight bag in his hand. "Where are you going?"

"To a hotel." He presses a phone in my hand. "You know my number."

Without another word, he walks from the apartment, leaving the door wide open.

I stare at the empty space as the quiet slowly fills me up, at the freedom of the open door. It's fake, that freedom, a false promise. The ring on my finger is more effective than handcuffs. The promise I made is more imprisoning than a lock and key. It's a stronger token of ownership than a choker necklace. That's the message Maxime left with the open door.

Footsteps fall on the landing. It's a strong beat. Only a man's stride can tap out that promise of dominance on marble. Why is he coming back? Did he forget something?

Refusing to cower, I limp to the door to meet him head-on.

Then I stop in my tracks.

"Hello, Zoe," Alexis says, pushing inside.

CHAPTER 12

Maxime

Lying in the bed big of the honeymoon suite surrounded by petals and candles, I stare at the ceiling. I haven't even bothered to cancel our dinner. Neither the singer, nor the cake. I've only scavenged enough energy to let the priest know he could send the choir home.

As darkness creeps through the window, a strange sensation grows with the shadows. It's a brand new feeling.

Regret.

I've fucked this up. I'm out of control, which is why I can't be with Zoe. The way I behaved wasn't a well-crafted lesson. I was running on pure, undiluted emotions. I allowed my feelings to control me instead of the other way around.

That has never happened. I'm not sure what to do with these feelings, these *things* living in my chest. It's a godawful sensation, downright depressing. I wish Zoe has never made me feel. It hurts like a bitch, worse than the flames that melted my skin. The intensity with which she makes me experience things is frightening. What if I don't master these emotions? I have to get a grip on myself and fucking learn to control these foreign sentiments.

A knock on the door startles me.

Zoe?

The only way she could've found out where I am is by tracking my number via the geolocation app on her phone. Pushing off the bed, I go to the door with my stupid heart thumping in my chest. I pull it wide open with hope chasing the corners of the shadows away, but my wishful thinking collapses like dominoes.

My voice is dejected. "Francine."

She's wearing the same dress from this afternoon, a white one that shows off her legs. "Can I come in?"

I lean in the frame. "How did you find me?"

"You sent me your itinerary to go over everything and make sure you didn't forget something, remember?"

Fuck. Yeah. I'm not thinking straight. I turn the wedding ring around my finger with my thumb, feeling the weight of it. "What you do want?"

"I reckoned you could do with a friend."

"Wait. How did you know I wasn't at home?"

"I went around to see if you needed anything. The way you and Zoe got married made me worry. Your car wasn't in the parking. Thought I'd take a chance and check here. Bingo."

"I appreciate the concern. Now good night."

I start to close the door, but she slams one hand on the wood and the other on my chest.

The touch is repulsive on my dead skin. I back up a step, giving her the opportunity she needs to wiggle her way into the room.

She shuts the door. "Just one drink. Don't look so scared."

I smirk at that. Walking to the minibar, I take out the vodka and whiskey. "What do you want?"

She saunters over to the table where the champagne stands in the ice bucket. "Nothing too strong for me." Popping the cork, she pours two glasses and hands me one. "Want to talk about it?"

I sit down on the edge of the bed. "Not particularly."

She takes the chair and studies me as she takes a sip. "Mm. This is good stuff. Look, I know you don't want to hear this, but Zoe isn't right for you."

Rubbing a hand over my face, I say, "You're right. I don't want to hear it."

"She doesn't have what it takes to be with a man like you. She needs regular. You know? A nice guy with a nine-to-five job."

"I am a nice guy with a nine-to-five job."

She snorts. "You gave it all up for her, and this is how she treats you."

My muscles tense, tightening my shoulders. "Did you come here to criticize my wife?"

"I knew this was going to happen. I knew she was going to dump you and throw it all back into your face."

"So," I lean back on an arm, "you came here to tell me I told you so?"

She leaves the glass on the table and gets to her feet. Walking over to me, she unzips the dress. "I came here to offer you consolation."

Her perfume makes my nostrils itch. It's young and sophisticated like green apples and cherry blossoms. It's nothing like roses.

Stepping out of her panties, she bunches them in a fist and drags them over my chin before bending down and bundling them in my jacket pocket while whispering in my ear, "You can even keep the trophy."

I shove her away. "Stop it, Fran. Don't embarrass yourself."

She stumbles a step. Hurt twists with tears in her eyes. "I waited for you. I *waited* for you, Maxime. I waited for this day."

"For the day Zoe kicks me out?"

She reaches for me. "For the day you realize how wrong you've been about her."

Catching her wrist, I stand. "I've been wrong about some things, but Zoe isn't one of them."

She yanks free of my hold. "How can you be so blind? You used to be *the* boss. What are you now, Max? Huh? What have you become for her? A weak man, a pussy. With me, that would've never happened."

Her words run off me like water. They don't move me. They don't spark anger. They don't matter. I don't care. I do see now that keeping Fran on my payroll was a mistake.

"I thought you'd moved on," I say. "Clearly, that was my error."

"What?" Nostrils flaring, she locks her fingers into fists. "What are you saying?"

"It'll be better that you hand in your resignation than letting me fire you."

Her face goes white. "I need that job."

"I'll give you a good letter of recommendation. I can even put in a good word for you with a few of my contacts."

She grabs the lapels of my jacket. "No, Maxime. Please!"

Taking her wrists, I move her hands away. "This has gone on for too long. I let it go too far. As I said, it's my mistake. I'll carry the blame."

"I have bills to pay!"

"I'll pay you six months' salary. That should tie you over until you find another job."

"Six months?" she cries out. "That's what I'm worth to you?"

"You're an employee. Nothing more. I'm treating you more than fairly."

Wiping her nose with her hand, she says, "Okay, look, I understand."

"That's a mature approach."

"Just let me finish this month. Give me time to get my ducks in a row. You know how it will look if you make me walk before the month is over."

It will spell out in capital letters that she's been fired. "At the end of this month, you're out."

Pulling her shoulders square, she says, "Your loss."

"You should go now."

She stares up at me. At one time, I thought she was attractive. The only pretty I see now is Zoe. My wife. The irony is too funny not to laugh. The sound is hollow. I married the woman who doesn't want me and am throwing out the one who does.

She pinches her lips together. "You're an asshole."

"I know. If it makes you feel any better, I'm not laughing at you. The joke is on me."

Her green eyes soften. "You really feel for her, don't you?"

"More than I've ever felt. So much, it's fucking frightening." Which is why I'm here. To get my shit together. To find my control. Maybe to punish Zoe a little in a disgustingly immature way.

She sniffs. "It's cold. May I please borrow your jacket? I'll drop it off when I come in to work tomorrow."

Shrugging out of the pinstripe, I hand it to her. "Want me to call you a taxi?"

She slips on the jacket without bothering to zip up the dress. "I'm good." Pulling the sides of the jacket around her, she walks from the room.

I'm left alone once more with these *feelings*, and fuck me if I can make any sense of anything better than before.

CHAPTER 13

Zoe

"What do you want, Alexis?" I ask, backing into the kitchen. The phone Maxime gave me is still in my hand. I clutch it tightly.

Alexis looks around the space. "Nice place."

I stop close to the knife block. "Why are you here?"

"I just thought I'd swing by to congratulate you and Max." He cranes his neck to look over my shoulder toward the bedroom. "Pity I've missed my brother."

I think quickly. "He's having a shower. I'll tell him you stopped by."

Alexis smiles. "Liar. Sylvie told me your wedding didn't go down as planned. Francine said Max is spending the night at a hotel." He drags his gaze over me. "I have to say, you look a lovely mess."

"How nice of them to run to you with their gossip."

"Oh," he tilts his head, "it was nothing like that. I called Max. Since he didn't answer, I called Sylvie. After she'd filled me in, I tried Fran.

Fran and Max have always been close. She was my best bet of finding him. From what Sylvie told me, I was worried about my brother."

Right. If Alexis is trying to hurt me with the Fran and Max being close part, it's working. Maxime shouldn't have forced me into marriage like this. I'm still freaking out about it. That doesn't mean I want him to run into Francine's arms. What Alexis is fabulously successful at is scaring me. I slip the phone onto the counter and close my hand around the shaft of the carving knife. "If you came here just to gloat, you can leave. I want you to go—now."

"Tsk, tsk." He advances. "What are you going to do? Stab me?"

I point the knife at him. "If I must."

"Why would I want to hurt you?" He smiles. "After all, I'm in your debt. If not for you, I wouldn't be the boss."

"What?" My grip falters on the knife. It slips in my sweaty palm. I catch it just before it drops to the floor. "What do you mean you're the boss?"

"Didn't my brother tell you?" He stops by the counter in front of me and leans his arms on the top. "In order to marry you, he had to step down."

Step down? "I don't understand."

"You deserve a golden star for your timing."

"My timing?"

"We were about to sit down for breakfast with Izabella Zanetti's family when Max's guard called to say you'd run. Of course my brother immediately wanted to go after you." He waves a hand in the air and rolls his eyes. "Family dramas. You know how those go. Naturally, Izabella's father was very upset. What a slap in his daughter's face. What a scandal for a man to abandon his engagement party to chase after his mistress. Izabella's father threatened to annul the contract. My father threatened to disown Max if he dishonored the deal by leaving. What did Max do? He threw them both the finger and ran after you."

"Your father disowned him?"

He pouts. "It broke my mother's heart. She'll never forgive you, by the way. You see, Max has always been her favorite. In any event, as the next in line, I took Max's place in the business and family. We made a new deal. I got to marry Izabella and secure the contract with the Italians. The house was a nice bonus. I know Max is going to miss it."

"He gave up his house?" I ask with a growing feeling of sickness.

"The house comes with the business. Max did put a lot of time and heart into the place. Splendid job he did with the renovations." He looks around. "This isn't bad, either."

"Is this why you came here?" The knife suddenly feels too heavy. I drop my arm at my side. "To tell me about Maxime's misfortune?"

"I came here to warn you." All pretense of friendliness vanishes from his face. "Don't get too attached to your husband, because I'm going to squash him like a bug."

My whole body tenses. "Maxime is too powerful."

"He's no one," he says with a sneer. "He has no more power. I'm going to ruin him, and I'm going to kill him when I'm done."

I grip the edge of the counter, fear mixing with that sick feeling. "He's your brother. Why do you hate him so much?"

"Maxime has always taken everything for himself. The business, the money, you."

"He's the oldest. It's not his fault he was born first, and he took me to save me from you."

He snorts. "Save you?"

"I've seen how you treat women, remember?"

"He didn't tell you," he says, his smile stretching.

"Tell me what?"

"Those women, my darling, were prostitutes. You, on the other hand, were destined to be my wife."

The strength leaves my legs. My knees wobble. It's only my grip on the counter that keeps me up. I couldn't have heard right. "What did you say?"

"The plan was that Maxime would extract you from South Africa and deliver you to me. Since he was already promised to Izabella with only the final details of the contract to be ironed out, I would've married you to force an alliance with your brother."

I can't believe it.

"You can understand why I was a little more than pissed off," he continues. "Not only did Max claim the big prize by signing the contract for Izabella, but he needed to take everything. Like the selfish bastard he is, he needed to steal my wife and make her his mistress so he could have both of you."

I think about the windowless room under the water level in Venice where Maxime locked me up to demonstrate my fate with Alexis, to force me to choose between them.

"You would've locked me up," I exclaim with intensifying panic. "Tortured me. Raped me. Let your men have their fun, too."

"Maybe I would've locked you up to keep you from running and have a little fun with my men. Where's the harm in sharing? An orgy can be exciting, especially for a woman. You lucky bitches can have multiple orgasms whereas us poor guys have to wait between hard-ons. I wouldn't have tortured you, though."

"Your idea of excitement sounds close enough to torture."

He shrugs. "Each to his own. In any event, when my brother is dead, you'll need protection." His expression sharpens. "Marseille isn't safe for a mediocre man, let alone a pretty little girl on her own."

I need time to digest all this. "Get out." I point at the door. "Now."

Smiling, he straightens. "You may want to be nice to me, kitten. You may need me sooner than you think. When that time comes, I think I'll claim you as *my* mistress."

Over my dead body. Whereas Maxime specializes in mental and emotional torture, Alexis is an expert in the physical. They're two of a kind. Maybe they deserve each other after all.

He walks to the door with the arrogant stride of a victorious man. Waving his fingers at me, he says, "Chao, *belle*."

The minute he's gone, I run to the door and lock it. To be on the safe side, I pull out the key and push it under one of the books on the bookshelf. Backtracking, I keep my eyes on the piece of wood that stands between Alexis and me. It's nothing to break down a door. Look at Maxime. He got through a security gate and alarm system, not to mention the double security at the complex entrance. How much easier is a thin little door?

With a racing pulse, I retrieve the phone and knife, carry both to the bathroom, and leave them on the chair as I strip out of the dress. I leave the gown where it drops in a heap on the floor. My chattering teeth are not only from the cold.

After a quick, warm shower, I dress in my flannel pajamas and crawl into bed. Too exhausted to stay awake and vigilant, I fall asleep with the knife under the pillow and the phone in my hand.

CHAPTER 14

Zoe

A persistent noise penetrates my dream. I'm not ready to wake up. I'm still tired. The noise doesn't let up, though. As I slowly come to my senses, overwhelming anxiety slams into me when I remember where I am and why. Sitting up, I rub my eyes and squint at the time on the screen of my phone.

Seven o'clock.

It's dark in the room. I haven't closed the curtains, but sunrise isn't for another quarter of an hour. It's still raining.

I'm groggy and starving. My throat aches, and a headache pulses in my temples. Shivers run over my body. Every muscle hurts as if I've completed a triathlon.

The cause of the noise registers in my fuzzy brain. A vacuum cleaner.

Throwing the covers aside, I get out of bed and pull on a pair of socks and a robe. Even the slight pressure of my own hands on my skin hurts. Tying the belt of the robe, the one Maxime restrained me with yesterday, I go to the door. Francine is vacuuming the lounge. I tense. A black suit jacket that hangs over a chair back at the dining room table catches my eye.

Maxime came back?

I look at the terrace, but it's raining hard. I doubt he'd be hiding out there.

The vacuum cleaner stops.

"Morning," Francine says. Her voice turns sweet. "Oh, I hope I didn't wake you?"

"What are you doing here?"

She regards me as if I'm crazy. "I work here."

Going over to the jacket, I lift it off the chair. "Has Maxime been here?"

"Um." She sweeps an imaginary strand of hair behind her ear because not a hair came loose from her perfect bun. "I'm just returning it."

A whiff of perfume reaches my nostrils as I fold the jacket over my arm. "Returning it?"

"He lent it to me last night."

It takes me a beat to catch on. "Last night?"

"You know." She clears her throat. "At the hotel."

She went to his hotel and left dressed in his jacket? What am I supposed to make of that? The answer is obvious.

My headache escalates. The rotten way I feel doesn't help. Turning on my heel, I go to the kitchen to get a glass of orange juice. I need an aspirin and some vitamin C. Something crunches under my feet when I round the island counter. It looks like sugar. I follow the trail. Ants are marching in a line over the kitchen floor. I'm not sure where they're coming from, but their destination seems to be the trashcan. Lifting the lid, I peer inside. Sugar. Granulated sugar.

Dumping Maxime's jacket on the nearest chair, I go to the cupboard and take out the sugar pot. It's filled with cubes. Aware of Francine watching me, I empty the pot in the trashcan. For good measure, I throw the quiche that still stands on the counter in the trash, too. The old me would've never wasted food. The new me has a hardened heart.

My head is aching so much it's an effort just to talk, but I turn on Francine and say, "Leave. Now. You don't have to bother coming back."

She pulls herself straight. "I beg your pardon?"

"You heard me."

"Max is my boss and—"

"That may be, but this is my house."

She drops the vacuum pipe. "I'll work until the end of the month."

"You won't put another foot in here."

Her smile is mean. "Is this about my work or about what happened between Max and me last night?"

Honestly, I can't say if the sugar war is the last straw prompting me to chase her out of my house or if it's the jealous anger eating away at my insides. Maxime and I, we're not an authentic couple, but we *are* married. If he couldn't respect the vows he took yesterday, he shouldn't have made them. Whatever the case, I've reached my limit.

"You're such a spoiled brat," she says. "You don't realize what you have." Taking a few steps toward me, she asks, "Do you know what lengths Max went to yesterday? Do you know what you ruined?"

Placing a hand over my neck, I fight for composure. I fight not to humiliate myself by screaming or saying nasty words I can't take back.

"He booked a whole restaurant out for you and hired a singer," she continues. "Your own private little diva. He spent a fortune on roses and a wedding cake, not to mention the most exclusive photographer in Marseille who cancelled all his appointments just to capture your precious memories. Oh, did I mention the church choir? He did it all for *you*. No guests. Just you. The hotel honeymoon suite sure was pretty with all those roses and candles. At least I didn't waste the champagne."

Maxime always has a reason for doing what he does. He taught me that in Venice. His flowers and candles come with a price. It's not the effort he went to that affects me. It's that he already broke the promise he made when he slipped a ring onto my finger. My chest squeezes until my heart hurts. I can't look at Francine for one minute longer.

"Leave your keys," I say. "You won't need them any longer."

She grabs a coat and bag from the coat stand. "I'll return the keys to the person who gave them to me," she says, slamming the door on her way out.

I lean against the counter. It was hardly a fight, but it took all the energy I had. The smell of Francine's perfume on Maxime's jacket taunts me. It's going straight to the dry cleaners. Furious and hurt, I bundle the jacket up to put it in the washing basket. Something white and lacy peeks from the pocket. I shouldn't. I shouldn't even care, but I can't help myself.

Holding my breath, I slide my hand into the pocket and pull out the item. A woman's thong. White. Like Francine's dress yesterday.

I stand there like a statue, staring at the small piece of fabric in my palm. I have no right to feel like this, but it fucking hurts. It hurts differently to the day I caught Izabella and Maxime having a polite conversation with soft laughter in his library. That hurt was a shock, a mountain of ice dumped on my head I hadn't seen coming. I never expected it. I suppose it prepared me for this second round, because this pain isn't as acute as more drawn out. It's a slow burn, creeping at a snail's pace to bury itself deep under my skin. I'm not sure what's worse, the quick and devastating collision or the slow crawl of agony. In any event, the outcome is the same—pain and more pain.

Maxime fucked Francine on our wedding night.

All the more reason to put a chastity lock and chain around my heart. I throw the jacket and the underwear into the trash can, wash my hands twice, and pour a glass of juice that I take back to bed. After swallowing aspirin, I crawl under the covers and pull the comforter over my head.

If I stay here long enough with my head buried under the covers, the pain eventually has to fade.

IT'S late morning when I wake up again. I'm still alone. I feel like shit. Shaking all over with a cold fever, I pull the covers up to my chin. I need to eat. My body needs energy to heal. When the ice in my bones turns hot and sweat covers my body, I throw the covers aside and drag myself to the kitchen.

There's nothing I can heat up and no baguette to make a sandwich. The quickest meal to fix will be scrambled eggs. I take the carton with the eggs from the fridge, but feel so miserable that I leave them with the pan on the counter and just grab the carton of juice. I take it to bed and swallow another painkiller. My throat is killing me.

I must've fallen into a feverish sleep again, because sounds in the kitchen jerk me from a dream in which I'm walking with Maxime through the freezing rain to a church in the distance that falls farther away the more we advance.

Sitting up, I grab the knife from under my pillow and hold it out in front of me as footsteps approach and a shadow falls over the threshold. A moment later, Maxime's tall body fills the frame. The tension in my shoulders eases marginally.

His angular face darkens as he looks at the weapon in my hands. "What are you doing with the knife?"

Sagging with the breath I release, I leave the knife on the nightstand. "Alexis was here. I thought maybe he came back." I'm so damn angry with Maxime, but too exhausted for a fight.

A thunderous look joins the darkness, making a terrifying tableau of his face. "What?" In two steps, he's in front of me. "What did he want?" He drags his gaze in a frantic sweep over me. "Did he hurt you? Did he fucking touch you?"

Clutching the sheet to my chest, I say, "He told me everything."

"Everything?" Just like that, his emotions turn off. The mask falls back in place. "Everything about what?"

"That you gave up your house and position to go after me. Why would you do that?" Why would Maxime drag me to the *mairie* and marry me if he was going to fuck Francine?

"He said that?" he asks in a flat voice.

He's stalling. He doesn't want to answer me. My energy already depleted, I fall back against the cushions. "You know what? I don't want to know."

He scrutinizes me with a furrowed brow. "Why are you in bed?" Then he says with alarm, "Zoe, you look terrible."

"Thanks." I give him a cold smile. "You can go back to your hotel now."

He presses a hand on my forehead. "You're burning up. You're sick," he adds with a hint of panic. "Why didn't you call me?"

I push his hand away. "It's only a cold. Go away and leave me alone."

"Like hell." Taking his phone from his pocket, he swipes over the screen. "I'm calling the doctor."

"I don't need a doctor." The white dress shirt without the jacket reminds me why I don't want to see him. Even more so, I don't want him to see me like this—weak. "I just need you to go."

He holds my gaze as he makes the call and tells the doctor to come straight over, making it sound as if I'm dying.

"You're wasting the doctor's time," I say when he hangs up. "It's not the first time I'm having a cold. It'll pass in a couple of days."

He paces to the window. "I dragged you out in the cold dressed in a flimsy gown with wet hair."

If only yesterday could turn into a black hole in my memory. "Why do you even care?"

He turns back to me with a somber regard. "Because I can't help it."

I've never understood him. I'm no closer to deciphering my husband. He keeps on saying he cares, but caring lovers don't drag their unsuspecting partners to the altar.

"Why did you do it, Zoe?" he asks with a hint of despair, curling his fingers into fists. "Why push me so far? I wanted to give you a beautiful day."

"You wanted to control me. It was just another one of your sick manipulations."

"The dress and the flowers weren't attempts at manipulating you. Those gestures were genuine. So was the evening I had planned for us. Why is that so hard to believe?"

"I don't know what is genuine and what is psychological warfare with you. In all the time you've kept me, you never let me get close to you. Not even a little. How am I supposed to know when you're real?"

His regal posture slips. "The man from yesterday, the man who lost his temper, that man was real, and I don't like him."

This is the closest to being honest he's ever been with me. "I didn't like him either."

Crouching down, he fists the sheet in his hands. "Then teach me how to be a man you can like."

I barely suppress the urge to trace the crooked line of his nose and rest my palm against his cheek. "Real is good. You just have to learn how to control it."

"This is what you want?" He scrunches the sheet, sounding angry. "This kind of honesty?"

"No more lessons, Maxime. No more manipulations."

A war rages in his eyes. Trust doesn't come easy for us, but we're bound to each other. This is the only way I'm prepared to go forward. I won't expect his love or devotion, but I'm not going back to how we were.

After a moment, he concedes with a quiet, "No more lessons."

At least if he's honest, I'll have a shot at figuring him out. In the meantime, I still have questions.

I consider his actions. "Why did you give up your house?" That house meant everything to him. "Why give up your legacy and birthright?"

Sitting down on the edge of the bed, he takes my hand. "Because you're my obsession."

An obsession. Some people only want what they can't have. I pull my hand from his. "Is it the chase?"

He allows the rejection, but the tight set of his jaw tells me he doesn't like it. "Despite what you may think, I don't enjoy hunting you. I'd much prefer your compliance. I sleep better knowing you're safely in my possession." The wintery color of his eyes turns colder. "How did Alexis get in?" More dangerous. "You didn't open the door for him, did you?"

"You left the door open. He walked in right after you'd gone."

"Fuck." Dragging his palms over his head, he flexes his fingers as if he imagines them around his brother's neck. "He was watching us. Me."

Alexis's warning comes rushing back. "He said he was going to kill you."

Instead of acting shocked, Maxime's laugh is cold. "He can try."

"He said you're powerless."

"I'm out of the mob, but I'm not out of business. The family needs my business. No one can run it like I can. It pumps money into Marseille and opens trade with the rest of Europe. No one is going to be stupid enough to take me out, not even if Alexis gives the order."

"What business?"

"The diamonds. It's legit. Damian decided to continue selling directly to me."

Ah. Hence the reason for our hasty marriage. It's just another business deal. "It's always about the damn diamonds."

"I told you," he says in a hard voice, "I don't care about the diamonds. I didn't care about your brother's decision. I would've made you mine regardless."

"I'm not yours," I force from tight lips.

His smile is wicked. "We'll see." He glances at the glass with the remains of the juice on the nightstand. "Have you eaten?"

"I'll fix something later."

He frowns. "Where's Francine? Why didn't she make you something to eat?"

I tense again. "I asked her to leave."

The line between his eyebrows deepens. "Why?"

I give him a cold stare. "Do you really need to ask me that?"

Comprehension washes over his face. "What did she say to you?"

"Does it matter?" I ask with ice in my tone.

"Of course it fucking matters."

I don't answer. It's the best way of replying when a conversation isn't worth my time.

"Nothing happened, Zoe. She came to the hotel, but I sent her away."

"Wearing your jacket."

"She said she was cold."

I can't help the sarcasm that sounds in my voice. "That must explain why her underwear was in your pocket."

The bastard looks pleased. "My little flower is jealous."

"I have no reason to be jealous, and I'm not your little flower."

"Admit it, Zoe. You're green."

"Go to hell, Maxime."

"Yes, she offered to fuck me." He adds in a gentler tone, "I declined."

I find that hard to believe. "I thought you'd jump at the opportunity."

"Did I jump on it when I first took you?"

I think back to the night when Francine had her arms around Maxime's neck and the fight that resulted, how he punished my mouth and how I slapped him. It was the night I decided I didn't want to revert to violence like my father. "You weren't bothered about fucking me while being married to Izabella."

"That was different. Izabella was business, nothing more. You've made your view on cheating clear. I'll honor your feelings."

"That's it? You won't sleep with other women because you'll honor my feelings?"

"What do you want from me, Zoe? What more do you want me to say?"

That I'll be enough. I suppose, given our situation, that's a bit much to ask. I suppose this is as good as it gets for us.

The intercom buzzes in the kitchen. He studies me for another moment before pushing to his feet to answer it.

When he returns to the room, he says, "The doctor is on his way up. I'll make you something to eat while he examines you."

I don't bother to argue. What's the point? Maxime does what Maxime wants. Nothing has changed.

The doctor who takes my temperature and blood pressure is the same one Maxime took me to for a birth control shot. Dr. Olivier has been administering my quarterly shots since then. Which reminds me, I'm almost due for another.

"You have a bad bout of flu," Dr. Olivier says. "I'm afraid there's not much I can do except recommending a couple of days in bed and painkillers for the fever and ache."

"That's what I told Maxime," I say, embarrassed about wasting the doctor's time. "Since you're here, can we schedule an appointment for the next birth control shot?"

"You won't need it," Maxime says from the door, carrying a tray with scrambled eggs and tea.

I give him a startled look. "I don't want to fall pregnant."

"There's no fear of that if you refuse to sleep with me." He balances the tray on my lap.

Dr. Olivier clears his throat. "Call me when you've discussed it."

Gathering his instruments, he packs everything into his doctor's case. "Keep her indoors," he says to Maxime. "We don't want to risk pneumonia if the infection spreads to her lungs."

Maxime sees him to the door. When he returns, he looks at the tray on my lap. "Shall I feed you?"

"No thanks." I pick up the tea. In all honesty, I am hungry. "You didn't have to do this, but thank you." Just because I'm angry doesn't mean I have to forget my manners. I have to cling to some shreds of decency unless I want to turn into a savage like my husband.

The warm smile clashes with the cold burn in his eyes. "You're always welcome."

CHAPTER 15

Maxime

The doctor is barely gone when Zoe's fever spikes again. Forty degrees. I make her drink another painkiller and take her temperature. The fact that she doesn't argue or slap my hand away tells me how sick she is.

Good going, Belshaw.

Aren't we off to a great start?

Cursing myself, I go to the bathroom to run a bath. Her wedding dress lies in a dirty heap on the floor. The bath is stained with the dye. I clean the bath and let the water run cool. While I'm waiting for the bath to fill up, I gather the dress and carefully fold it into a bag that I store in the dressing room to drop off at the dry cleaners later. Zoe put months and a lot of love into the dress. I don't want it spoiled.

When the bath is ready, I go back to the room for my flower. She's curled into a ball, huddling beneath the blankets.

I pull the covers away. "Come on, *cherie*. A bath will do you good."

She turns on her other side, facing away from me. "Go back to your champagne and your hotel. I don't need anything from you."

Fucking Fran. Letting Zoe believe the worst was a low blow. I'll deal with her later. "Let me help you, Zoe."

"I don't need anyone's help. I'll be fine."

No, she won't be fine. Not for a while. She definitely needs help. Unfortunately, I'm all she's got. She has no one else. Another fault of mine for isolating her when I first brought her to France. Of course I also ensured no one in the fashion design school she attended befriended her when I forced them into enrolling her.

"The water's cool," I say. "It'll help break your fever."

Enough. I'm not arguing with her any longer. She's obstinate because her feelings are hurt, but I know what's best for her. She doesn't have enough strength to fight me when I scoop her up and carry her to the bathroom. An overwhelming sense of protectiveness invades every instinct I possess. She weighs nothing. She's so small and fragile it scares me. Nothing can ever happen to her. I won't survive it. She's weak enough that I have to prop her up in the chair to undress her.

"Don't," she says, gripping her pajama top together when I try to unbutton it.

I move her hand away. "There's nothing I haven't seen before."

The blue color of her eyes looks paler with the dark rings marring them. The adorable freckles on her nose stand out against the unhealthy white of her skin.

"I hate you."

"Maybe one day you won't." A man can only hope.

I must be a sick pervert, because my body reacts when I pull the pajamas off Zoe's body. Fuck, fuck, fuck. She's naked underneath. No underwear. I've missed her full breasts and that womanly triangle of hair between her legs. I've missed the smell of roses in her hair. I miss her laugh so much it's like a gaping hole in my chest. My feelings and lack of control may not make sense, but what does is that I can't live without her. Without her presence, I can't breathe. I can't sleep. Even eating is nothing but a mechanical act.

Before she notices the hard-on straining in my pants, I lower her in the water and make sure I trail her hair over the edge so I don't get it wet. Like that night after I took her virginity—after I all but tricked her into giving it to me—I go down on my knees and serve her. I take care of her like she deserves, washing the sweat from her fever-hot body. Knowing her skin will hurt to the touch, I'm as gentle as I can be. I'm aching to drag my knuckles over the tips of her breasts and test the heat between her thighs, but this isn't the moment to indulge in my dirty fantasies.

After a few minutes, her lips start to chatter as her fever breaks. I make quick work of lifting her out of the water and patting her dry. I dress her in a clean pair of pajamas and make her lie on the sofa, then cover her with a blanket.

I build a fire. When the flames burn high, I strip the bed and put clean linen on. I check the temperature in the room and the living area to make sure it's at a comfortable setting before making her a bowl of noodle soup with chicken stock. By the time it's ready, the color is back in her cheeks.

"How are you feeling?" I ask, handing her the bowl after I let it cool to almost room temperature. I don't want to risk her dropping a scalding hot bowl of soup in her lap.

"I'm good." She avoids my eyes. "Thank you."

Thanking me comes hard for her, seeing that I'm the man who's done her wrong, but her manners dictate she expresses gratitude.

Pushing a strand of hair behind her ear, I say, "There's more soup on the stove and crackers on the counter if you're in the mood to nibble on something later." I hesitate. I don't like leaving her alone like this, but I have a bone to pick with my brother. "Do you want to stay by the fire or would you like me to take you back to bed?"

"Here's good," she says, blowing on the broth.

The television I'd ordered before she ran is mounted on the wall. "Would you like to watch some TV? Maybe you prefer a book. Can I bring you one?"

She gives me an exasperated look. "Really, I'm fine."

Yeah. Right. "I have to go out for a while. I won't be long."

"Maxime." She sighs. "Do what you have to do."

I fetch her phone from the bedroom and check that it's charged. "Here." I leave it next to her. "Call me if you need anything or feel worse, and do not open the door for anyone. Understand?"

She stares at me with those big, irresistible eyes. "Yes."

Kissing the top of her head, I tear myself away from her and put my worry aside for a few minutes to focus on another matter, one no less important—the matter of her safety.

I had the code for access to the street door changed before we got back from South Africa. Too many of the guards who used to work for me knew the old code. He couldn't have gotten in that way. There's only two ways Alexis could've. He would've had to wait in the street until someone left—that someone being me—and slipped inside before the door closed, or he paid one of the residents in the building to give him the code. I'd find out.

Alexis sits in the chair my father used to occupy in the office when I enter. Two men pull their guns. My cousin, Jerome, perks up where he's lounging in the corner.

Alexis holds up a hand, signalling the men to lower their weapons. "Well, well." Tipping his fingers together, he leans back in the chair. "To what do I owe the pleasure?"

"I doubt this is pleasure. If you ever go near Zoe again, you can count on it being torture."

He laughs. "The only reason I'm not shooting you on the spot is because I'm first going to enjoy ruining you."

I advance to his desk. "The reason you're not shooting me is because you can't survive without my business."

I'm paying a hefty fee for the so-called protection service of the very organization I once ran. I'm not doing it because I need that protection. I'm doing it to keep the peace. For Zoe.

Alexis is pissed off that I took the diamond business with me when I left. I have no doubt he'd love to come after me, take me out, and claim said business for himself. He can't, however, shoot the brother-in-law of the man who provides the diamonds without killing the business all together. He knows that, and he hates it. The only way to get rid of me is to make it look like an accident, but I know my brother and how he operates. I'll see him coming long before he strikes.

Gnashing his teeth, he says, "I'll put you six feet under. When I do, your pretty little wife will be mine after all."

I grab the front of his shirt from over the desk. "If you lay a finger on her, I'll cut it off before I kill you."

He smirks. "That'll be hard to do from your grave."

"Don't count on it, *little brother*. I'll bury you long before you get a chance to try." I let go with a shove.

Straightening his shirt, he says, "Are you threatening me? 'Cause the last time I checked, that was reason enough for a man to be taken out."

"This isn't about business. This fight is personal."

"I suggest you leave," he says through thin lips.

"I suggest you stay the hell away from my family. If I catch you sneaking around my building, you're dead."

Hatred burns in his eyes as he watches me leave.

Jerome follows me outside. He grabs my arm when I make to move past him. "Maxime."

I look pointedly at where he's gripping me.

Letting go, he says, "Alexis has it in for you."

"Tell me something I don't know."

"What I'm saying is I wouldn't come around here if I were you."

"You're not me." I start walking.

"Wait." He runs to catch up. "Alexis doesn't have what it takes. He's making bad decisions."

"Complain to my father."

"Your father handed over the power."

"I'm out, Jerome. What do you want me to say?"

He sighs. "I don't know. Fuck. All I know is Alexis is screwing with the wrong people."

"Not my problem," I say, opening my car door and getting inside.

He catches the door before I can close it. "He's double-crossing the Italians, his own brother-in-law. You have to talk sense into him."

"Alexis is a grown man. He's capable of carrying the responsibilities of his actions."

"Dammit, Max." He shakes his head. "It's going to blow up in his face. Don't you care?"

"It seems not." Shutting the door, I start the engine.

He bangs on the window.

My impatience mounting, I wind it down. "I don't have time for this."

"At least talk to him," he says, leaning on the roof with his arms.

"Do you think he's going to listen to me?"

Jerome doesn't answer.

"Neither do I," I say.

When I start driving, Jerome doesn't have a choice but to move away from the car.

Instead of heading home to Zoe, I drive to my parents' house. It's Saturday. My father will be lunching at the club. I'm not welcome here, but the guard who announces my visit to the house lets me through the gates. My mother meets me at the door. With her pale and drawn face, she looks ten years older. It pains me to see her like this.

"You're taking a risk coming here."

"I have news, Maman."

"If it's not offering me an apology, I don't want to hear it."

"I apologized for ruining your party."

"You threw everything away," she says, clutching the string of pearls around her neck. "Alexis isn't cut out for heading the business. He's not a leader. He's making dumb mistakes."

"You're an expert on the business now?" I ask with a teasing smile to lighten the mood.

My mother doesn't bite. "You were born to lead. You were the one."

"It's over. You have to let it go."

"I don't understand," she exclaims.

"I married her."

My mother's face goes even whiter. "What?"

"I found Zoe in South Africa. I brought her home. We got married yesterday."

She staggers. When I reach for her, she holds up a finger, shaking her head. "You married her. Now you come tell me like I'm an afterthought and not your mother."

"Even if I wanted you there, Father wouldn't have let you come." From the way Zoe reacted about Sylvie and Francine's presence, I doubt she would've wanted my mother present. I'm not insensitive to Zoe's reasons. My mother hasn't exactly been welcoming.

Tears shine in my mother's eyes. As always, she fights them. Crying is a weakness, one she's never allowed herself or us. "I always thought you were a clever boy."

"Maman, stop. Don't insult my wife. It's not something I'll forgive."

"You have to go."

"Why don't you give her a chance? She's a good person. Strong. If you can look past your personal ambition for me, you'll see in her what I see."

"All I see, Maxime, is that you threw away your future and broke my heart for a woman who doesn't deserve you."

"I'm sorry you feel that way. I don't regret my decision. If given another chance, I'll do it again."

"Your father will be home soon." She backs up a step. "You better go before he catches you here."

It's a lie. My father won't be home for hours to come, not while the girls are performing.

"Maman," I groan. "Since when have you become so blind?"

The answer I get is the door shutting in my face.

CHAPTER 16

Zoe

Three hours later, Maxime returns with a shopping bag under each arm. He walks straight to the sofa to hover over me. "How are you feeling?"

"I'm okay."

He glances over his shoulder at the fireplace. "You kept the fire going."

"I know how to keep a fire burning."

"You do." The corner of his mouth tugs down.

Is he thinking about how we used to sit together in front of the fire in the library of his old house and all the perverted things we did in my favorite armchair? It's a good thing I burned that chair before I left.

"Sorry I couldn't be here to do it," he says.

"Please, Maxime. Stop apologizing." I don't want him to be kind or polite. It's easier if we both keep our distance and our defenses up.

His chest rises with an invisible sigh. "I got you *velouté de cèpes* and oranges. I would've called to ask if you have any cravings, but I didn't want to wake you if you were sleeping."

Not the consideration I need. It risks denting the armor I'm so carefully constructing around my heart.

"I can go out again later," he says, making his way to the kitchen with the bags.

"I'm sure whatever you got is fine." Uncomfortably, I add, "Thank you."

This new ceasefire between us is strange territory for me. What I know is the constant push-pull of resisting and fighting him, only to kneel to the need he creates inside me. I know how to play nice to avoid a lesson or the discomfort associated with disobedience. Being kind without an agenda is going to take some getting used to.

"It's my job to take care of you." He deposits the bags on the counter. "A job I've sadly neglected already."

"Just stop, okay?"

Splaying his fingers on the counter, he gives me one of those intense looks that used to either set me on fire or made me want to run. "It's not going to happen again, Zoe."

This makes me want to run. Not from fear, but from the commitment he's forcing. He has no right, especially not after yesterday. "I don't think we should make any promises right now."

The stark lines of his face harden. "You don't believe me about Fran, do you?"

I look at the flames leaping up in the chimney to escape his dark stare. "I don't want to talk about it."

"Closing yourself off isn't going to help."

He's deceived me with lies so many times in the past, I'm not sure I'll ever be able to trust him. It's not even a full day since he promised me honesty. He's yet to prove himself. I'm protecting myself against more pain, but I'm not going to admit how much his actions hurt me. That would give him power he doesn't deserve. He may be kind now and promise to be done with his lessons, but I can't forget he still holds my family's lives in his hands. He'll use them against me if he must. That hasn't changed.

When the silence continues to stretch, he says with a resigned tone, "I'll start dinner. We seem to have an invasion of ants in the kitchen. I'll get rid of them."

"No." I turn back to him quickly. "Don't kill them."

"Are you worried about murdering ants, Zoe Belshaw?" he asks with a smile.

Calling me by his last name jars me. It jars him, too. The smile freezes on his face as he goes quiet for a moment. The satisfaction mixed with a familiar look of lust that come over his features are too much for me to handle. My throat goes dry. To me, I'm still Zoe Hart. Belshaw is the enemy's name.

His jaw flexes. He doesn't like what he sees in my face. "I was only going to sweep them out."

Grateful to return to a safer topic, I say, "Sweeping will injure them. They're just doing their job. They'll leave on their own when there's no more food left to carry off. I'll put the trash bag out."

He follows the line of ants to the trashcan. "What are they after?"

"Sugar."

"Sugar?" Stepping on the pedal to lift the lid, he stares inside and stills. After a moment, he pulls out his jacket, and then what I'm assuming to be Francine's underwear, dangling it between two fingers. His face evens out. The earlier broodiness turns to understanding. Finally, he looks up from inspecting the contents of the bin with a frown. "That's a lot of sugar. Did I get the wrong brand or do have you a vendetta against the sugar like you obviously have against my jacket?"

"No vendetta. I actually *like* the sugar."

He drops the jacket and underwear back in the bin. "Then what happened?"

"Francine happened."

The worry line between his eyebrows deepens. "Fine. I get this is about last night, but what sin did the sugar commit?"

"The sugar is collateral damage."

A smile ghosts over his lips. "Do explain. I'm intrigued."

I sigh. "It's a stupid war between Francine and me. I use granulated sugar instead of cubes, so she dumps the sugar in the bin and replaces it with cubes." I make a face. "Apparently, the French way is using cubes."

"I see." He seems to consider it. "Her game doesn't matter now because I fired her last night."

He did? But… "Why?"

"We spent a couple of nights together after I employed her. It was just a fling. I thought she was over it. I was wrong." His smile is grim. "You were right when you said she has feelings for me."

Good, because I really don't want her to come back here. I look at my hands. "I asked her to return her key."

"I'll make sure I get it." Walking to the sofa, he stops next to me. A fire burns in his eyes. "It's hard for me, not touching you."

I swallow.

"I know you're not well," he says, going down on his haunches and sliding a hand through my hair, "but when you're healthy again, I won't be so patient."

The darkness I got used to is still present in his silver stare. It still rules his heart. I've never been immune to his touch, not since the first night he seduced me so tenderly. My body remembers that touch, the contrasting gentleness and wildness, and the roughness I discovered I liked. My heart thuds in my chest as my skin heats with a fever that has nothing to do with my flu.

Straightening, he goes back to his schooled self, the lust replaced with calculated control. "Just wanted to give you ample warning in case the idea needs to grow on you."

It's a command, not a request. He's never forced me, but he has faith in his skills. He knows how to use his hands to turn me into putty.

My breathing is shallow when he finally steps away and gives me space. He unpacks the groceries and fixes an early supper of grilled chicken and pan-roasted vegetables. His manner is strong and confident. His actions say he knows what he's doing. The question is, do I?

CHAPTER 17

Zoe

For two days, Maxime pampers me. He bathes me, dresses me, washes and dries my hair, and massages my body. He does the grocery shopping and replaces the cubes with granulated sugar. He cooks and cleans the apartment before going to work at his new office in town. It's a hectic schedule for him, but he doesn't complain or show fatigue. He's my dedicated and uncomplaining servant.

The rain stops on the third morning. When the sun comes out, the ants disappear. My health returns and everything goes back to normal. Well, as normal as this situation can ever be.

I've been closed inside for as long as I can bear. I've had nothing but time to think. The more I think the more anxious and resentful I become. Resentment comes from Maxime forcing my hand and anxiety from knowing I'm not strong enough to resist him forever.

As promised, he hasn't touched me while I've been ill, but sleeping next to him reminded me of how if feels when his hard body slides over mine, how my skin comes alive when he drags his hands over every inch of me, and worst of all, how it feels when he rocks a gentle rhythm into my body. It reminded me of how he makes me fall apart and come together all at the same time.

When nature gives me this reprieve, I get dressed, pull on a light coat, and step out into the sunshine. The salty air and far-off calls of seagulls are familiar. I stop for a moment on the busy pavement to take it all in. The fact that I can leave the building and go wherever I like doesn't fool me into mistaking this for freedom. I have my phone in my pocket. Maxime can—will—track my movements. I could've easily left the phone behind, but there's something other than Maxime's possession that keeps me prisoner. It's the danger that will always hover over my life. He's no longer the mafia boss in Marseille, but Alexis wants him dead. I have no doubt he'll use me to get to Maxime. With no guards to trail behind and protect me, I'm taking every precaution I can, including taking the busy roads.

The walk and fresh air do me good. I feel invigorated when I get to an open-air textile market I remember from driving past here once. The smell of grilled chestnuts from the vendor stand mixes with the odor of chemical dye from the fabric. Weaving through the aisles, I drag the familiar perfume into my lungs. Despite my situation, my spirits lift. It's like the smell of roasted beans when entering a coffee shop on a cold morning or the welcoming scent of ink and paper in a bookstore on a lazy afternoon. Only, it's the cocktail of threads and colors that makes my heart beat faster. With it comes the rush of memories from the fashion academy and, like an answering echo, a wave of nostalgia. I miss this. I miss the slide of fabric through my fingers and the soothing hum of a sewing machine.

A piece of organza hanging from a wooden rail lifts in the breeze. The floral print catches my eye. It's pink and lilac, soft and lovely. I said I was done with sewing, but maybe it's because I've been stuck on my old designs. Romantic designs. Walking to a stand with a much statelier roll of navy linen, I rub the coarse fabric between my fingers. Maybe I was looking at the wrong dreams.

"Would you like this fabric, ma'am?" the vendor asks.

I look up. The woman has a friendly smile. A red scarf tied around her hair brings out the warm tone of her skin and eyes.

I don't have any money on me. I didn't even know this was my destination when I started walking. "Oh, I'm just browsing."

"Please cut the lady however much she wants," a deep voice says.

I spin on my heel. The sight of him takes my breath away even after all this time. With his hands shoved into his pockets, Maxime's stance is relaxed, but I recognize the power running underneath. As always, he's dressed immaculately. Even his casual street clothes scream of sophistication and a keen sense of fashion. A roll-neck black T-shirt and fitted pants are rounded off with a brown coat, matching scarf, and short boots, but it's not the clothes that define the man. It's his presence. It's how he dominates the space and demands attention. It's what that look on his face promises.

Women stop talking to stare. I stare, too. I take in the familiar sharp chin and deep lines, the crooked nose and bump on the bridge, the gray eyes that cut through defenses and intentions, and the strong mouth that makes knees weak. His hair is ruffled, curlier from the humid air, and the longer sideburns give him an artistic look. He could be an eccentric painter or a brilliant rocket scientist, a mafia boss or a man bathing a woman on his knees. He could be a jet fighter pilot or a diamond tycoon. A woman's imagination could run wild. What every female here knows with instinctive knowledge is that those hands, those hidden hands, can stroke a cheek as gently as they can squeeze around a throat. This is a man who can make a woman's fantasies come true, and his gaze is trained on me with possessiveness. Adoration. Lust.

Our gazes remained locked as he takes his wallet out of his pocket and pulls out a few bills.

The vendor clears her throat. Her voice is husky when she asks, "How many meters would you like, ma'am?"

"Three, please," I say, ripping a number from the sky.

Maxime's lips lift in one corner. The smile makes his unconventionally beautiful-unattractive face seem more predatory than friendly.

Leaning closer, he presses his lips against my ear and says in English, "Let me buy this for you."

The foreign accent hits me between the knees. We've been speaking French since my return. I've forgotten what his deep timbre sounds like when he whispers in my mother tongue. He smells like the king of winter, of cold weather and citrusy days. The perfume of chemical dye retreats as that winter heat rushes over me. The man and everything he stands for overwhelm my senses.

That my mind can focus on his words is a miracle. I think back to his story, to the man who had two choices, the kidnapper who could take his target kindly or with force. I don't want force. I don't want kindness. I want honesty.

"Why?" I ask with a dry throat.

His breath strokes over my ear. His words are self-assured and seductive. "Because I can."

Pulling away, he creates an avalanche of cold when he takes his heat with him. I look down to where he's rubbing the fabric between his fingers in a gesture that seems oddly like a caress. I shiver as if feeling that caress on my skin.

Because he can.

The nuance of the situation isn't lost on me. It's foreplay. It's a preview of what will happen if I follow him home. I don't fight it. I'm already beaten. I lost the minute my gaze landed on him. He hit me full-on when my defenses were lowered, and my armor wasn't in place.

I'm healthy. I'm alive. I'm just a woman. I feel him in the ache between my legs and the heaviness of my breasts. I feel the memory of him in the heat that floods my stomach. I remember him in the anticipation that tightens my lower body.

The woman hands him a parcel. Her hand shakes slightly, and her voice is breathless. "Here you go, sir."

Does everyone feel the sexual tension in the air?

"Thank you," he says, accepting it with a smile without looking away from my eyes.

When he offers me his hand, I take it. I would've taken it if he was leading me to hell. I may have sealed my heart in a dark room, but this is the part of me Maxime fully owns.

CHAPTER 18

Maxime

Zoe is nervous when I let her into the apartment. Her small body is tense. She should be, seeing that I'm about to strip her naked and fuck her until she can't walk. It's been too long. For too many months, I haven't felt the shape of her breasts under my palms or the warm tightness of her body sucking me deeper. I've seen her naked for three torturous days. I've punished myself, abstaining from the release of a hand job in the shower. I won't last much longer.

I know her. If she's to enjoy this, I have to put her at ease. I have to go slowly. I can't jump on her like a tiger and hold her down with my teeth while ramming my cock into her body until she's accepted every inch of me.

I drop the parcel on the table so I can take her coat. "Tea?"

Her shoulders sag with visible relief. "Please."

After hanging both our coats on the stand, I go to the kitchen and boil water.

"How did you find me?" she asks in an uncertain voice, rubbing her hands together as she takes baby steps toward the island counter where I'm putting out mugs and a mix of organic raspberry and rose petal tea leaves.

"Your phone." Picking up the remote, I turn the heat up a notch. "I wanted to make sure you were safe."

She slips onto one of the tall chairs. "You can't follow me around forever. I'm sure you have lots to do at your new job."

I flash her a smile, my eyes meeting hers briefly before I scoop the leaves into the teapot. "I have enough to keep me busy." I dust my hands and make eye contact again. "But you always come first."

Her cheeks flush pink. It makes me want to grab her face between my hands and kiss her, but I miraculously succeed in focusing on the task at hand, which is switching off the kettle before the water reaches boiling point and not kissing her before I've brought us back to a place where she can be naked and comfortable with me.

"Talking about phones…" She wrings her fingers together like she does when she's nervous. "I'd like to call my brother to let him know we've arrived safely."

I pour the water over the leaves. "Then call him."

"But…" She takes her phone from her pocket and looks at the screen.

"I've already spoken to him just after we arrived so he wouldn't worry about his baby sister, but you can call your family any time you like."

"You mean…" She looks at the phone again.

"Yes." The word is curt. Reminding her of her previous limitations isn't where I want to go right now. "You can dial anywhere in the world."

"Thank you," she whispers.

I don't say she's welcome. It's not a novelty she should be thanking me for. Having access to communication is a given in any normal person's life. I don't want her caged. It's no longer necessary. I've effectively clipped her wings with my ring on her finger. Which reminds me of a subject I shouldn't bring up, not ever and certainly not now, but I can't put it out of my head. I can't stop calling up images and allowing my imagination to torment me in every waking minute of my days and every dream-filled hour of my nights.

"Did you move on in South Africa?"

She gives me a startled look. "What?"

My voice is surprisingly even when I pour the tea. "Did you sleep with someone?"

"No," she cries out. "I told you so."

"Just making sure I don't need to have you tested for STDs," I lie.

Her mouth tightens. "How about *you*, Maxime?"

I push a mug and the sugar pot toward her. "No." Meeting her gaze squarely over the too-far distance of the counter, I say, "There's only you. There will never be anyone else."

Questions bounce around in her blue eyes. She wants to know why. She wants to hear the things I can't tell her. She asked for my honesty, but honesty cuts so much deeper than lies when it comes to love. *I love you* could've slipped so easily from my tongue. It's just three little words, but even before I promised her no more games and lessons, I couldn't bring myself to tell her that particular lie. Love has always been the foundation of her dreams. Deceiving her with that ultimate untruth seems simply too cruel.

"All right," she says, adding two spoons of sugar to her tea. "But tell me something." The spoon rings out as she stirs it around the mug. "Can obsession last a lifetime?"

Leaning closer, I give her the conviction that runs in my very veins, the knowledge that comes from a higher place than reason or logic. "You better believe it."

She cups the mug. "People grow old."

"Yes, they do." At least this much I can promise. "I'll be growing old right beside you."

Our gazes remain locked for a precious moment of truth. I can see her weighing the words, testing their meaning, and finally trying to categorize them in her frame of reference. Zoe and I, we can't be categorized. There isn't a file with a label for what we are.

"Married or not, you belong to me," I say. "You always will."

Maybe that was the wrong truth to say. The line of her mouth hardens as she touches the mug to her lips. Pushing the sugar pot aside, I reach across the counter, take her wrist, and pull her hand away from her face. Now isn't the time to hide behind a mug of tea. She wanted honesty without games. We're facing our truths. I won't let her shy away from them.

The black crumbs on the clean counter catch my eye. I'm an OCD personality type. Noticing is a reflex reaction. The crumbs are scattered around the sugar pot. Ants.

Dead ants.

With a sweep of my arm, I smack the mug from Zoe's hands. It smashes against the wall next to the French doors, tea splattering over the curtains and glass panes.

"Maxime!" Her eyes are round in her white face.

A few more ants lie dead on Zoe's side of the counter. They've been hidden from my view until I pushed the sugar pot aside.

"Wash your hands," I instruct tersely, inspecting the floor. The ants never made it that far.

She hops off the chair and stands as stiff as a stick. "What's going on?"

"Zoe, do as I say."

My harsh tone jolts her into action. She grabs the dishwashing liquid from under the sink and washes her hands. I hand her a paper towel to dry them before doing the same.

Her gaze flitters to where mine is lingering on the counter. I can almost see the gears turning in her head as she connects the dots.

"Did you spray poison?" she asks in a hoarse voice.

Mine is strained. "No."

"Do you think…?" She licks her lips, giving me a petrified look.

"The sugar." Taking my phone from my pocket, I dial an old contact from the forensics department. "Don't touch anything," I say as I wait for the call to connect.

Hector's voice comes onto the line. "Didn't think I'd hear from you again." He doesn't sound happy. "I thought you retired."

"I did. I need you to come over to my apartment."

"What now?"

"Now."

"I'm working."

"I'll make it worth your while."

He lowers his voice. "You're not in a position to cut deals any longer. I'm not covering up evidence. You can't protect me."

"This isn't about evidence. I need you to sweep my apartment." Correcting myself, I say, "My wife's apartment."

"If you're hoping to catch her lover, it's easier to hire a PI."

"Cut out the jokes, Hector. Someone tried to poison her. At least I think so." I hope to hell I'm wrong.

"Fuck." He sighs. "You're legit now. There's a police department for that."

"They'll send you anyway." Plus, I don't want the police involved, and Hector knows perfectly well why. I'm going after whoever did this.

He sighs again. "Fuck, Max."

"You owe me, Hector." I have a few favors to call in for all the times I paid off his debts. His wife has expensive taste.

"Goddamn. Okay, fine, but I don't want cash. It's becoming too difficult to hide the extra revenue. I want diamonds."

"Diamonds? That'll be difficult to convert into cash if you don't know the right buyers."

"I don't want to sell it. It's our wedding anniversary soon."

"Ah. What did you have in mind?"

"Earrings."

"I'll make sure you have two of my highest quality stones."

"I'll be there in an hour."

"Thirty minutes." It shouldn't take him longer to drive from his side of town.

"For fuck's sake, Max. I have a boss, you know. What am I supposed to say?"

"You'll think of something."

Cutting the call, I face the woman standing there looking so frail and vulnerable. "A friend is coming over. His name is Hector." I take a pair of rubber gloves from the cleaning cupboard and pull them on.

"Don't open the door for anyone but him and keep your phone with you."

"Where are you going?" she asks as I scoop a little of the sugar into a zip lock bag and seal it.

"I'll be back as soon as I can."

"Maxime!" She runs after me to the door. "You're going to see Francine, aren't you?"

We both had the same thought. Only one person has access to this apartment. Given what Zoe told me about the sugar war, this makes sense.

"Maxime, please." She grabs my arm when I pull on my coat. "What are you going to do?"

"Stay put, Zoe. Don't touch anything and don't eat or drink. Call me if someone other than Hector shows up. Our code word is *bouillabaisse*."

I pull gently from her hold. If I stay a moment longer, I won't be able to leave her at all. Losing her does things to my head, crazy things that boil with a rage in my blood. Still wearing the gloves, I can't even touch her. I only allow myself the luxury of pressing a kiss to her temple.

"Lock the door behind me."

I exit and shut the door. I don't go until I hear the turn of the key.

CHAPTER 19

Maxime

It takes twenty minutes to drive to the small house on the beach. Fran inherited the place from her parents. I fucked her in that house. Although I've never fucked a woman other than Zoe in my bed, I've let Fran into my house. I trusted her.

"Fuck." I slam the wheel.

If I hadn't been tempted to go after Zoe this morning, I could've come home tonight to find her dead. The image is a terrifying visual that tears up my chest.

I shouldn't come to premature conclusions. The ants could've died from something else. Maybe it's coincidence. My gut says otherwise as I park behind Fran's car in the driveway.

The lounge curtains are drawn. It's broad daylight. After three days of rain, she would've left them open to let the sun warm the house.

I get out of the car with the bag of sugar and bang on the door. Fran opens a moment later.

Her face is composed. "Max? What a surprise. Is something wrong?"

Pushing past her, I ask, "Why would something be wrong?"

"Well." She shrugs. "You're here. I thought you didn't want to see me."

I didn't pay enough attention to Fran. If I had, I would've known what a good actress she is.

Glancing at my hands, she asks, "What's with the gloves?"

I close the door and lock it. "I was cleaning."

She smiles, the perfect portrait of serenity. "You? Cleaning? You want me to come back to work? Is that it?"

"We're going to have a drink," I say, going over to the armoire where she keeps her booze.

The bedroom door is open. A suitcase lies on the bed and clothes are scattered over the floor.

"It's not even lunchtime," she says.

I take out the bottle of gin. "That's never stopped you." Pouring a shot in a glass, I place it on the table. "Come here."

She walks to me with confident strides. "What are you celebrating?"

I pour a bit of the sugar from the bag into the glass and give it a stir with my gloved finger. "Drink."

All color vanishes from her face. "What?"

I pick up the glass and hold it out to her. "Drink it."

She steps back. "I told you, it's too early."

"Humor me."

She shakes her head with a laugh. "You're crazy."

"You haven't seen crazy yet." In one step, I'm in front of her, gripping her hair while tilting the glass to her lips. "Drink it, Fran."

"No!" Pushing on my chest, she turns her face away.

"Why?" I shake her by her hair. "Because you may die?"

"Max, please!"

"Did you really think I wouldn't figure it out?" I turn her face roughly toward the bedroom. "Where were you running to, huh?"

Tears leak from the corners of her eyes. "You fired me. I needed a break to think and sort out my life."

"Don't fucking lie to me!"

She cowers in my hold. "It's not a lie."

"Did you go to the apartment this morning when Zoe was out?"

"No." She licks her lips. "I was packing."

"Fine." I relax my tight grip on her hair. "Maybe I'm over-reacting. Maybe it's nothing. So, prove it." Pulling her head back again, I push the glass back to her mouth.

"No!" Slamming her lips together, she turns her head the other way.

"So help me God, I'll make you drink every last drop if you don't talk."

Silence.

"Fine." I dip a gloved finger into the drink. "Let's start with a little teaser."

When I drag that finger just under the outline of her bottom lip, she sinks to her knees.

"Please, stop," she says through her tears.

"What poison did you choose, Fran?"

She stares up at me through her blond lashes. "Botulinum."

"Where did you get it?"

She blinks. Her lips tremble.

I dip my finger back in the poison. "Where the fuck did you get it?"

More silence.

"You will tell me, Fran, or I will make you suck this finger clean."

Gripping her face, I apply pressure to the joints of her jaw.

She says something that sounds like, "Wait," from her wide-open mouth.

I drop my hand. "Speak."

She drags in a breath as if I've strangled her. "Your mother. I got it from your mother."

My mother? She's a lying bitch. I grab her jaw, hovering my wet finger over her lips. "Do not lie to me, Fran. Not about this."

"It was her idea." She folds her fingers around my wrist, not that she'd be able to hold me back if I decide to plunge my finger down her throat. "I swear to God, Max."

I'm shaking with rage. "Why? Why the fuck?"

"Your mother and I," she says in a tremulous voice, "we want the same thing."

They both want Zoe gone.

I take her scrawny shoulders and shake her so hard her teeth clatter. "Where did you put it?"

"Just in the sugar," she shouts. "I swear."

"Like a big fucking metaphor for winning your war?" I spit out in disgust.

She sinks down onto her heels. "It wasn't supposed to be some symbolic victory." She meets my gaze. "I chose the sugar because Zoe is the only one who uses it. You use cubes. I'd never risk you, Max." She grips my leg. "I love you."

"You don't love me." I look at her with contempt. "If you did, you wouldn't destroy the only thing that matters to me."

Her face crumples. "You don't mean that."

Fury burns through my body. "Have you thought it through? What if Zoe decided to bake a cake? What if I took a sip of her tea?"

"I was going to go back and throw out the rest of the sugar as soon as—" Biting her lip, she looks away.

"As soon as she was dead?"

"Please, Max," she says, looking back at me. "What are you going to do?"

"I'm going to give you a choice. You can either drink this," I push the glass into her hand, "or you can let justice run its course and wait until my mother's assassin catches up with you. I'm sure she'll want a painful revenge for your betrayal."

"No." The denial falls in a barely audible sound from her mouth even as her expression shuts down, already accepting the inevitable.

"Your choice." I take a step back. "Make it."

Leaning her back against the wall, she looks at the glass in her hand, the fate she was going to deal my wife. I already know what she's going to choose before she tips back her head and downs the content.

CHAPTER 20

Maxime

Suicide.

That's what it'll look like. I don't wait for the end. I walk out of Fran's house, pull off the gloves, and drive to my parents' place.

My father's Mercedes is parked in front of the house. I don't give a fuck. I get out at the gates and pull my gun as the guards pull theirs. I don't bother to ask them to announce my presence. The security cameras will. A moment later, my father exits the house dressed in his robe and slippers. In the middle of the afternoon. Which means the masseuse is here.

He holds up a hand. The guards lower their weapons.

"You're not welcome here," he says, walking down the driveway.

"Yeah." I meet him at the gate. "I know. I don't exist for you so my presence shouldn't bother you."

"Don't make me shoot you," he says with a scowl.

"This is about Maman, not you."

He spits on the ground. "You're dead to her too, both you and your *wife*."

Ah. He knows we got married. He's keeping tabs on my life like one does with an enemy. Unless Maman told him. "Literally dead, it seems, if Maman had her way."

His face contorts with anger. "I don't like what you're insinuating."

"I suggest we discuss this in private. It's not something you want to talk about in the street."

Nostrils flaring, he flicks a finger. The electronic gates open.

We walk in a strained silence to the house. Inside, he tells the housekeeper to send my mother to his study.

He takes the chair behind his desk while I take a position in front of the window. My mother breezes inside, dressed in Chanel with an apron tied around her waist and smelling of apples.

"Max?" She gives my father an uncertain look. "What is this? What is he doing here?"

"Why don't you tell us, Maman?"

"What on earth, Max?" she says with a surprised smile.

My God. How have I been so blind? How have I never paid attention to the people who truly matter, the most dangerous ones? My mother is a more formidable enemy than my father, because she comes to you with smiles, smelling of apple pie and wrapped in sweet childhood memories.

Bitter loathing coats my tongue. "Where did you get the poison?"

She blanches.

"What have you done, Cecile?" my father asks.

Stubbornly, she tips her chin up.

"Fran confessed everything," I say, "right before she died."

The shock on my mother's face fills me with perverse satisfaction.

My father pushes to his feet. "You better talk, woman."

She turns on him with hatred blazing in her eyes. "The poison was meant for Zoe. She ruined everything. I only wanted my son back."

My father wipes a hand over his face. "Dear God, Cecile. You shouldn't have done that."

"Do you know what it feels like to be powerless?" she asks with clenched hands. "Do you think I'm clueless and naïve?" She points a finger at my father. "Do you think I don't know about your criminal dealings or your women? Who do you think is the backbone of this operation? You think it's you?" She laughs. "You're weak. Pathetic. Who do you think arranged the hit on the men who tried to take you out in front of your beloved club? Who do you think has been giving the orders to get rid of the traitors in your circles?" Turning back to me, she pushes a finger against her chest. "Me. I've carried this family for more than forty years. Zoe was messing with your head, Max, making you weak like your father. It had to be done."

I don't know the woman standing in front of me. I don't know the person who fixed me dinner and slipped extra pocket money into my school bag. All this time, it's been nothing but one, big lie. All this time, it was never about me. It was about what my mother wanted me to be. She would've sacrificed my wife without blinking an eye for her own, selfish goals.

Yet I can't hate her. I can't find it in my soul. She's still the woman who birthed me. I just don't respect her any longer.

"You talk as if she's dead," I say with a cold smile.

"My God." My father looks at me with a slack jaw. "Isn't she?"

It's my mother's gaze I hold. "No." Advancing to her, I peer down at her face. "But you are."

"Max." She reaches for me.

I pull away. "Don't." With a sneer I add, "You're dead to me."

"Did you leave evidence at Francine's that can be traced back to your mother?" my father asks, coming around the desk.

"I wore gloves."

My father's voice is stern. "Where did you get it, Cecile?"

She looks down her nose at him. "I'm not saying."

My father narrows his good eye. "Don't think you'll escape torture because you're my wife. You've crossed a line."

She knows it. Her hands are shaking. She's been dishing out orders behind my father's back to commit murder, no less. That makes her a traitor. My father doesn't have a choice but to carry the consequences of her actions. She's his responsibility after all. He won't stop until he's flushed out every man she's ever commanded, no matter what it takes.

"Your contact at the pharmaceutical lab," she finally says, rambling off a name. The drug factory.

My father sounds tired. "Pack your bags."

My mother's lips part as if to argue, but then she stands taller. "Why?"

"I'm sending you to the house in Corsica. You'll never set foot in France again."

He's condemning her to prison. The holiday house stands on a stretch of isolated beach. No one ever goes there except for my family, and none of them will visit there again. It's nothing short of a cloister. She'll be living the rest of her days out alone and never see her family again. Me, I've already written her off, but the grandchildren she so badly wanted from Alexis and me will never know their grandmother.

Her jaw trembles. "I'm the backbone of this family. Without me, you won't survive a day."

"Get out of my sight. You disgust me." My father turns to me. "You too."

Gladly.

I leave, turning my back for a second time on my family for the woman I love.

Yes, love.

Fuck my shrink and every textbook that's ever been written about psychopaths.

Because what is love other than an obsession?

CHAPTER 21

Zoe

Maxime arrives home just as Hector gets ready to leave. My husband's strong body is coiled with tension. It looks as if he's a soldier on the verge of war, ready to strike.

"We're just wrapping up," Hector says, pulling off his plastic gloves.

Maxime holds my gaze for another beat before he asks, "What did you find?"

"I've collected the dead ants. I'll have to run tests. At least that'll tell us if they died from poison and if so, what kind. To be on the safe side, I took samples of your toothpaste and other toiletries like soap and shampoo. We've cleaned off the counters and vacuumed. I suggest you throw out all the food and perishables and do a thorough spring-cleaning."

"Apparently, it's botulinum," Maxime says.

"Ah." Hector rubs his chin. "In that case, you'll want to use vapor for cleaning and boil the sheets. The toxin is heat sensitive. I'll run tests anyway to be sure."

Maxime nods. "When will you know?"

"I'll push it to the front of the line. I should have something for you in a couple of hours."

"Great." Maxime shakes his hand. "I appreciate it."

"Goodbye, Mrs. Belshaw." Hector nods in my direction. "It was a pleasure to meet you."

"Thanks for your help," I say.

Maxime walks him to the door. "I'll have your payment delivered."

"Try not to call again too soon." With a crooked smile, Hector leaves.

When the door shuts, Maxime and I just stand there for a moment, looking at each other. He moves first. In a few long strides, he eats up the distance between us and folds his arms around me.

"Maxime?" I whisper with my cheek pressed against his chest.

He buries his nose in my hair. "It was Fran and my mother."

My heart trips in its beating. I suspected Francine. After all, who else had a key? Who else knew I'm the only one in the house who uses granulated sugar? However, Maxime's mother? She doesn't like me, but to kill me? That sounds preposterous.

"I'm sorry," he says, pulling away to look at my face. "You needed to know that."

"What...?" I lick my dry lips. "Did you confront them?"

His expression is pained. "Fran confessed about my mother. My mother admitted the truth."

I can't begin to imagine how difficult this must be for him. Maxime and his mother are close. "What's going to happen to them?"

"You don't have to worry about them."

"Maxime." I slip from his embrace. "Keeping it from me doesn't help."

He clenches his jaw. "My father banished my mother to Corsica. She can never come back to France."

Oh, my God. "I'm so sorry."

"Don't be." His eyes are harsh. "She deserved her fate."

"What about Francine?"

He only looks at me.

"Tell me, Maxime. You promised me honesty."

"She's dead," he says in flat voice.

I slam a hand over my mouth. "What? How?"

"She killed herself."

Did she? My stomach flutters with a tremor. "How?"

"She drank her own poison."

It sounds too much like punishment—an eye for an eye.

Cupping my cheek, he says, "Pack a bag. Take clothes for two days."

The shock numbs me. I'm rooted to the spot. "Where are we going?"

"We're staying in a hotel until I've had this place thoroughly cleaned."

"We can do it."

"No." The word is a non-negotiable verdict. "I'm not taking any risks. Go now." He gives me a little push toward the bedroom.

Acting on autopilot, I do as he says and pack hurriedly. We don't take any toiletries, but buy new products on the way to the hotel. Maxime books us into the penthouse suite and puts the *do not disturb sign* on the door. The minute the door is locked, he pounces on me.

Grabbing my face in his hands, he kisses me like the world is about to end. The caress is rough. The pressure of his palms is hard. He bites my bottom lip and sucks it into his mouth before sweeping my tongue with his. Pouring fear and despair into the kiss, he claims my mouth without sparing me his violent emotions.

The kiss is too savage to enjoy, but arousal sparks in my body. God, how I've missed this. How I've missed being held and consumed. My body jumps right back to the past, to the ecstasy it remembers, seeking solace in the relief only he can give. No matter how many times I came on my own fingers, the release was never complete. There was always something missing.

Him.

I consume him right back, tangling my fingers in his thick hair and pressing our hips together. A low growl escapes his throat. Backing me up to the bed, he rips at my clothes. The front of my blouse falls open with the erotic sounds of silk ripping and buttons popping. The buttons bounce and run over the hardwood floor.

Maxime's fumbles with the zipper at the back of my skirt. I pull his shirt from his pants and sigh into his mouth as I run my palms over the hard contours of his abs and the familiar destruction of his chest. Sucking in a sharp breath, he breaks the kiss and goes still. I love how sensitive he is to my touch. It's the one thing he's always been honest about.

I drag my hands over the flat disks of his nipples and back down his stomach to trace the deep line of the V that cuts to his hips. I slide my fingers over the metal and leather of his belt. Pressing my face to his neck, I inhale his spicy winter cologne. He hisses when I cup his erection. When I look back at his face, I catch him watching me with a molten gaze the color of melted steel as I outline the broad head with a finger through the fabric of his pants.

Unable to wait any longer, I unbuckle his belt and unzip his pants. His cock is hard and hot in my palm, the velvet skin pulled tightly around his flesh. I squeeze, then stroke. He studies me with the intense attention of a predator as he lets me fondle him.

"You make me wild," he says, gripping my skirt and bunching it up in his fists. "Be a good girl. Take off your panties for me."

His wish is my command. In this, I don't have a choice. I can only follow my body's lead as it dictates my actions with a selfish need for fulfillment. Letting him go, I grip my thong and pull it down my legs while he looks on with savage hunger. When the underwear pools around my feet, he locks his hands around my waist and lifts me onto the bed.

Our urgency is too pressing for taking time to undress. My fingers fold around his thick, hard length, guiding him to my entrance. With his hands planted on the mattress next to my face, he parts me gently and slides home. The burn is familiar. So is the pleasure erupting in sensitive nerve endings. The rocking of his hips is a welcome rhythm, the only tune my body knows. There's been no one but him. Like the words he vowed earlier, there will never be another. He's all I have. Our union is broken and built on a shaky foundation, but it can't hurt if I don't pour my heart into it. It can only bring me closer to where I need to be, closer to coming.

"Zoe." Framing my face between his hands, he stares into my eyes.

Everything I feel is summarized in the way he utters my name. It's a need for something I can't name. Locking my ankles around his ass, I lift my hips to take him deeper.

"Fuck, Zoe." He groans. "You have to go slowly."

Slowly is not what I want. I want to burn and go down in flames. I want him to catch me, mend me, and pretend we're okay. A growl sounds in his chest when I wiggle out from under him. His fingers spear through my hair. For a moment, he holds me in place, but then he releases one finger at a time, setting me free. The effort it takes shows on his strained face.

"Don't you want this?" he asks with that deep frown running between his eyebrows.

I trace the crease with a finger, dragging the tip over the bump of his nose and along the crooked line. Turning over, I give him my answer. The sharp intake of his breath is always a sweet reward. In a flash, he drags me to the edge of the bed so I'm kneeling on the floor.

I press my cheek on the mattress and look back at him. He pushes to his feet, his face an inferno of lust as he studies me. The way I'm presented with my skirt bunched up over my hips and my ass in the air is dirty. There's something perverse about kneeling half-dressed and knowing what is coming is going to feel as good as it's going to hurt.

Kneeling behind me, he digs his fingers into the flesh of my globes and parts me. My lower body tightens in anticipation as an ache to be touched flowers between my legs. He brings his lips closer to my sex and plants a tender kiss on the apex. The hot glide of his tongue over my folds makes me shiver. A tremor runs all the way up my spine as he trails his tongue along the crease leading to my dark entrance. I bite my tongue not to moan when he traces the tight ring of muscle before softly nipping the fleshy part of my glute.

He can easily drag an orgasm from me with his tongue. I'll come quickly for him, but he only plays with the tip over my clit, making me squirm and clench my thighs in need. Denying me isn't because he's cruel. It's because he's kind. If I come now, I'll be too sensitive to let him take me how I want.

He sucks a thumb into his mouth and presses the tip on my dark entrance. Rubbing the fingers of his free hand in a circular motion over my clit, he gently applies pressure until the muscles give and my body allows his entry. He gives me a moment to adjust before plunging two fingers into my pussy. I'm on the verge of exploding when he starts moving, but he keeps the pace too slow.

Perspiration beads on my forehead when the stretch in my ass increases.

"Just do it," I plead. I don't know for how much longer I can stand the torment.

"Shh, my little flower. I have to prepare your body."

His patience is commendable. I know he wants this as much as I do. It's evident in how hard he is, but Maxime is not to be rushed. The foreplay seems to last forever, until I'm begging him to just go ahead and fuck me. I'm already tired, already raw. The easy pace and probing fingers rocking my body into the mattress are relentless. He lets me feel, and feel, and feel until I'm only aware of the parts of my body he's manipulating with his expert touch.

When every inch of my skin is slick with perspiration, he finally withdraws his fingers.

"Stay," he says, getting to his feet.

My chest sinks into the mattress, the muscles I've kept drawn tight finally relaxing. With my cheek pressed to the sheet, I watch him undress. Fully naked, he walks to the bathroom and returns with lube. He came prepared. He wanted this too.

Going back to his knees, he squirts a generous amount of lube in the crease between my globes and uses the broad head of his cock to spread it around my dark hole.

An uncomfortable sting builds at the base of my spine when he pushes his cock against my dark entrance and applies steady pressure. The ring of muscles finally yields, and cold flames run through my insides as he carefully sinks deeper.

"Harder," I say, my breathing shallow.

He goes slowly, taking his time to fill me.

Still, I beg. "Please, Maxime. Fuck me already."

Pulling back, he sinks deeper, over and over, going a little faster and farther with each stroke. The fire builds. The flame leaps. Pain and ecstasy mix until I don't know who I am or why I'm here. I only know the desperate need for release.

Moving a hand between our bodies, I cup the velvet softness of his balls. He reciprocates by finding my clit. I cry out when he gives the bundle of nerves a wicked pinch. It sets off a slow-building eruption that detonates from my core. My inner muscles tighten. Uttering hot, filthy words, he grabs my hip and holds me in place while punching his hips against my ass. It's beautiful and dirty. Wrong and right. I arch my shoulders and push back, meeting each of his strokes.

The room is filled with our sounds—cries and groans. The air smells like sex and roses in winter. I let go, collapsing in a boneless heap as my aftershocks ebb, simply letting him use me. He slides his hands beneath my body and the mattress to cup my lace-covered breasts. Another few punishing pumps later, his muscles lock. His groan sounds almost painful as he empties himself inside me.

I try to stay with him, but I'm already floating away, exhaustion claiming my senses. He shoves twice more and then folds his body over mine. His broad chest covers my back. Heat seeps from his body and melts into my tired muscles.

Brushing my hair away, he plants a tender kiss in my neck. "I love you, Zoe."

I still at the words. I want to turn so I can face him, but he's still planted deep inside my body, nailing me to the bed with his bigger size and muscular body.

"Shh," he says. "I know that pretty little mind of yours is kicking back into action. Just relax. There's no need to analyze it."

I can't lie to him. Not about this. "This isn't love, Maxime."

"I figured it out on the way home." He twists a strand of my hair around his finger. "Love is nothing but an obsession. Obsession *is* love."

We'll never have the kind of love I dreamed about, but I'm just so damn tired of hurting with the knowledge. "We have a very different view of love."

"Then we agree to disagree," he says, kissing my neck again before sucking on the skin hard enough to leave a hickey.

CHAPTER 22

Zoe

After a shower and a late lunch at the hotel, Maxime calls a company who specializes in toxic waste cleanup and arranges a thorough cleaning of the apartment. While he's on the phone, I step out onto the balcony and dial Damian.

"Hey," he says in a cautious tone. "I thought I'd hear from you sooner."

"Sorry." Gripping the rail, I stare down at the harbor in the distance. "It's been hectic since we got back."

"Yes?" It sounds as if he's shuffling papers. "With what?"

My courage fails me. "You're at work. I caught you at a bad time. I can call back—"

"No. I'm listening."

"We..." I clear my throat and infuse my tone with as much excitement as I can salvage. "We got married."

After a short silence, he says, "What?"

"Just the two of us." I cross my fingers behind my back. "We didn't want to make a big deal out of it."

"You eloped? Is this what you wanted, Zee?"

"Of course." I smile so he can hear it in my voice. "I know it was impulsive, but why wait. Right?"

"Right," he says slowly. "When did this happen?"

"The very day we landed."

"That's a bit rash."

"How long did you wait before you married Lina?"

He sighs. "Is he there?"

"Who? Maxime?"

"Who else?"

"He's busy on a call."

"So you can speak freely."

"Yes, of course."

Damian sighs again. "Zee, you'll let me know if something is wrong, right?"

"Yes. Now stop fussing and congratulate me."

"Congrats. I'm happy for you." He pauses. "You deserve it."

"Thank you. It's good to hear your voice."

I ask about Josh and how Lina is doing. He fills me in on Lina's checkups and the prenatal classes they're attending. His voice is warm with pride when he tells me about the 3D ultrasound and how beautiful their daughter is.

"Have you chosen a name yet?" I ask, my throat thick with emotion.

"No."

"There's nothing you like?"

"No name is perfect enough for her."

"Oh, my God, I sense a very possessive father in the making."

There's a short hesitation. "A good one, I hope."

"A wonderful one." My smile is very real this time. "You're nothing like Dad."

"Sometimes I wonder."

"You don't have to wonder. Dad scared me. You don't."

Turning, I lean against the rail. My gaze collides with Maxime's who's watching me through the sliding door with the intensity of a lion on the prowl as if he hasn't just fucked me senseless.

"I've got to go," I say. "I'll set up an email account and send you and Lina my address."

"Lina will like that. Maybe we can chat on video call."

My smile stretches. "That sounds great."

"We'd love for you to be here for the birth, but we'll understand if it isn't possible. I know you have a whole new life to start over there."

"I'd love nothing more than to be there for both of you." I hold my husband's eyes. "I'll get back to you about that."

"What are your plans for the future?"

"I'm not sure yet. For the moment, we're just, uh, enjoying each other."

Getting to his feet, Maxime walks to the sliding door. He continues to look at me as if he'd like to punch a hole through the glass and snatch me while Damian and I say our goodbyes.

When I step back inside, Maxime grabs the lapels of my coat, dragging me against him. "I missed you."

His words take my reason, but I won't allow them to soften my heart. "It's only been five minutes."

"Five minutes too long," he breathes in my neck.

If I had any doubts about Maxime letting me go to South Africa for the birth of my niece, I'm certain now he won't. Still, I have to try. "My niece will be born in three months." I pull away to look at him. "I'd love to be there."

Regret contorts his features. "I know, flower, but I can't let you go alone. It's much too dangerous."

"You could come with?" I ask hopefully.

Tension invades his expression, making the lines of his face look harsher. "I have to get this business off the ground. There are a lot of changes."

I notice the dark rings under his eyes that, with everything that has happened, have escaped me. He's genuinely concerned about this.

"Are we all right?" I ask.

"Don't worry." He paints a smile over his concerned expression. "I'll take care of you."

I watch him as he sets me aside. "You said you'd be honest with me."

His lips are still curved into a smile, but it's a tight one. "I am. I'd give anything to take you to South Africa for the birth, but this business is our future." Adopting a lighter tone, he says, "In fact, I'd like to show you the office."

"Now?"

"I have to go in to take care of some things."

I suspect taking me with him to work has more to do with keeping me safe than involving me in his professional life.

Trying not to show my disappointment about not being able to be there when the baby is born, I follow him to the car. He drives us to a modern building on the outskirts of the city and leads me through the scanners and security check. There's no name on the outside, but a plaque above the elevator reads Belshaw Diamantes.

His offices are on the top floor, overlooking the hilly side of Marseille instead of the harbor. The interior is modern with gray and white walls and minimalistic furniture. He introduces me to some of the staff members, all of them men, including his assistant. Maxime's office has glass walls affording him a view of the open floor plan where the other employees are installed. Instead of working at desks, the setup is more casual with sofas arranged around workstations and coffee nooks.

While I page through a magazine on the sofa in his office, he makes arrangements for setting up a diamond auction in Paris. From the conversation I overhear, Maxime gets the uncut stones from Damian and sells them to wholesalers in Europe.

Hector calls just before we leave the office, saying he's found traces of botulinum in both the ants and sugar, but not in any of the toiletries he's tested. I still can't believe Francine would've done something like this and even less that Maxime's mother was involved.

Back at the hotel, I switch on the television while Maxime orders room service. We're both too exhausted from the ordeal to have dinner in the restaurant. He didn't allow me access to computers or anything other than movie channels on television before. Watching the news is still a novelty. I flick to the local channel while kicking off my shoes.

A newsflash about a young woman who committed suicide by ingesting botulinum stills me. The reporter stands in front of a house on the beachfront, saying that a neighbor found the body. My knees trembling, I sink down on the bed. For the first time, it hits me, really hits me. Maxime killed her.

"Zoe?"

I look up to see him staring down at me darkly. "She deserved it."

My stomach turns. My husband is a killer. I knew that, didn't I? I knew it right from the start, even if I chose to bury my head in the sand. That luxury is no longer an option. I can't claim to be naïve about the man I married.

"This changes nothing," he says in a hard voice, taking my hand and pulling me roughly to him.

I'm shaking inside. It's hard to keep the fear from showing on my face.

"It's too late for second thoughts, *ma belle*," he says with narrowed eyes, pushing up my sweater and palming my breasts. His hands are angry as he unfastens both our pants and pushes mine with my underwear over my hips. "You already married the devil." Guiding his cock to my entrance, he drives home in a single thrust, consummating the words.

My back arches from the sudden invasion. I grip his shoulders for support when he moves with brutal force, dulling my conscience with his harsh rhythm.

Yes, I did. I married the devil.

What's much worse is that I love him.

CHAPTER 23

Zoe

We move back to the apartment two days later. There's no investigation into Francine's death. Her funeral is to be held the following week. My stomach is constantly wound tight. How does Maxime live like this? Before, he was protected by his position. Now he's on his own. The mafia and their connections aren't going to protect him if the police come after him.

What will happen if he ends up in jail? Will Alexis come after us? Damian managed to build a business from jail. I have no doubt he could've ruled an empire. Maxime is no different. A part of me craves the freedom I could have if Maxime is caught, but another part of me can't bear to see him behind bars. Either way, Maxime will dictate my future, even from jail. He'd never let me go back to my family. Freedom will forever remain my illusion.

We fall into a new rhythm of Maxime leaving for the office after eight and returning for dinner after eight. We eat, fuck, and shower. He spends long hours pouring over reports and statements after I've gone to bed. The more I observe him, the more it's becoming apparent that the business isn't going as well as he'd hoped. The adjustments are taking their toll. When I ask him about it, he only says some clients who are loyal to his family, meaning the mafia, left when he broke away from them and that it will take some time to find new clients and reassure them his service and stones are solid. Keeping the ship from sinking isn't an easy task.

At first, we cut back on entertainment and eating out. Then we start implementing some serious savings, using the heat in the apartment sparingly and relying on the fire to keep the big living space warm. Night after night, I watch Maxime study on his laptop by the dining room table, rubbing his temples while a frown mars his forehead. At least the house is in my name. We'll always have a roof over our heads, but we can't survive like this forever.

After a particularly quiet dinner, I pad to the table where Maxime is working. "Hey."

He looks up. A smile warms his features. "Hey."

"I need a job."

His expression hardens. "No."

I prop a hand on my hip. "Are you going to be *that* man?"

"What man?" he asks, slamming his computer shut.

"The kind of man who tells his wife what she can or can't do."

"Don't I already?"

His answer hurts because it's true. Pushing the ache away, I say, "Yet you let me study once."

"It's my job to take care of you."

"What if I need more?"

His tone is inflexible. "You don't."

Right. It's so typical of Maxime to think he knows what I need. I'm not going to win this argument with words. Leaving him to stew over whatever he was working on, I turn and walk to the bedroom, but his words stop me.

"I've always taken care of you, Zoe. I always will."

He's taken charge of every aspect of my life. It's not the same of taking care of someone, but I've long since given up on making him understand. I've always taken care of myself. I might've been poor, but I did the best I could. The apartment I grew up in was dilapidated and tiny, but when I lived there alone, it was always clean and smelled of the detergent from my laundry drying in the bathroom. I miss the satisfaction that came with my financial independence.

There was a time Maxime wanted to give me passion and purpose. It wasn't a means of letting me earn a living as much as a way of keeping me happy. Thérèse's words that had hurt so much at the time were true, and I'm only realizing it now. I would've graduated to become a mediocre designer using great ones like her to build a brand for myself, and Maxime would've made it possible to keep me content in the pretty cage he'd constructed to confine me.

Without giving him another glance, I go to the bathroom to have a shower, and crawl into bed. Long after he's joined me, I lie awake, thinking.

WHEN MAXIME KISSES me goodbye and leaves for the office in the morning, I fetch the linen he bought at the market and go upstairs to the landing. I run my fingers over the sewing machine standing on the desk. Excitement starts to hum like a distant memory in my veins. My hands itch to transform the cloth into a piece of clothing.

After some deliberation, I pull out my old drawing pad and pencils. I start with a few rough lines, and then fill them in with color. This time, I'm not creating with romantic notions and futile ideas of love. I'm implementing what Madame Page taught me. The design is linear and harsh. There's no place for frills or lace in my new life. Creating a dress that will pass the strict criteria of a reputable French designer is more than survival on a financial level. It's a way of molding myself into someone who can survive my new life. It's an emotional necessity.

By the time Maxime gets home, the dress is stitched together and only missing the finishing touches. I had to set up the dress form in the lounge area since the landing is too small.

He steps inside and stills for a moment as he studies my work. A frown flitters over his forehead, but when he meets my eyes, his lips tilt into a smile. Holding my gaze, he drops his laptop bag by the door and takes off his jacket. The muscles in his back bunch under his shirt as he hangs the jacket on the coat stand. He works his tie loose while he crosses the floor and takes a seat on the sofa in front of the cold fireplace. It was a warmer day, and I try to use the firewood sparingly. In silent instruction, he holds a hand out at me.

Knowing better than to refuse, I walk over and place my palm in his. Gently, he tugs me into his lap. Memories of us sitting like this in his old house when he came home at night fire off in my brain. I settle stiffly against him. I'm wearing a pair of tracksuit pants and a T-shirt because I wanted to be comfortable while working, and it feels oddly out of place next to his business attire. My hair is twisted in a messy bun on my head, and my face is scrubbed clean of make-up. For some reason, being less presentable than him makes me feel like I'm at a disadvantage in a war that's about to play off. Everything between us, even when we fuck, is a war. I would've felt better equipped to defend myself against his manipulation if we were at par, but now I feel like some kind of Cinderella facing a sophisticated, albeit dark prince.

He drags a hand over my thigh, letting it rest on my knee. "What did you do with yourself today?"

I know what he's doing. He's trying to recreate how we used to be, but that dynamic has shifted. I'm still his captive, yet what we were is long gone. It's not our situation that has changed. It's me. Where I craved his affection before, I now fear it for all the ways in which it can destroy me. I made the mistake of thinking he was capable of feelings once. I won't do it twice.

He brushes a strand of hair behind my ear. "Zoe? Don't you have anything to tell me?" I try to shift off his lap, but he tightens his arm around me. "I thought you were done with designing."

"Does it bother you?" I ask in a catty tone. "Maybe you'd prefer I do nothing all day."

My stubbornness to discuss my day with him is born from my resistance to this strategy, one in which he never gave me a choice, but he doesn't get angry or impatient. His voice is gentle as he says, "On the contrary, I'm happy that you're doing something you love."

I'm not going to tell him I'm planning on selling the dress to supplement his income. We need the money badly, although he refuses to admit it.

"The design is very unlike you," he continues.

"Yes, well, it was about time I grew up."

The frown I'd glimpsed when he walked through the door returns as he studies me with a serious expression. "You think you were anything less than grown up before?"

I snort. "I was naïve and stupid."

He searches my face for another moment. "I'd say you have a certain amount of naivety, but that's part of what I find so endearing about you. As for stupid, I have to disagree." When I don't reply, he continues. "Don't you see? I don't want you to change. It's *you* I want, just the way you are."

Too late. I'm already changing. I can't help it. It's the only device I have to protect myself from breaking more, but I keep that to myself. It's a weapon. It's my secret device, and I'm not sharing that with him.

His eyes darken in a way I'm well familiar with just before he pushes his hand under the elastic of my sweatpants. When his fingers find my folds, shame engulfs me for my body's reaction. Need makes me heat from my lower body upwards, sending flames that burn hotter in my cheeks. I hate myself for getting wet when he rubs a calloused finger over my clit. Grabbing his wrist, I try to hold him back, but it's not him I'm fighting. It's myself.

"Let go," he whispers, rubbing his nose over my temple.

With his free hand, he wiggles the pants down over my hips, exposing my humble cotton underwear. I want him inside me so badly it aches, yet I plead, "Please, no."

I feel dirty and weak for wanting this. Instead of obliging, he wraps one arm around me and pushes my underwear down with my pants. Just like before, I'm exposed to him, naked from the waist down. The way he studies me heats my face more, but it also perversely turns me on. I'm lost even before he parts my folds with a finger, testing my arousal. Satisfaction bleeds into his steely gray eyes when he discovers my wetness. Without preamble, he sinks two fingers inside. The stretch makes me sigh even as I hate myself more for responding this way. I feel filthy and depraved as he starts fingering me.

"You want this, don't you?" he asks on a growl, massaging my clit with his thumb. "Open your legs. Show me what a dirty little slut you are."

My body obeys of its own accord. I give him better access and the view he wants as he pushes my upper body down. I should protest when he pushes the T-shirt up to reveal my naked breasts. Already, my orgasm is building, and I'm completely lost before I can salvage enough control to stop this humiliation.

"Fuck," he says through clenched teeth, "you look so good with my fingers in your cunt."

My lower body contracts at the vulgar words. Self-loathing mounts with my desire. I moan when he pulls his fingers free, but the sound quickly transforms into a protest when he roughly flips me over. Some self-preservation returns, bringing me to my senses, but he pushes me face-down with one arm over my back, my body stretched out over his lap on the sofa.

"Show me how you come," he says, teasing my entrance with a feather-light touch.

I don't want to, but I'm lying helpless as he plunges his fingers back inside me.

"Such a dirty little slut," he says, hammering out a rhythm that has my toes curling.

Turning my face away from him, I pinch my eyes shut. I try to imagine that I'm someone else, but all I can think about is how I must look with my ass in his lap and my sex exposed. His brutal movements extract sloppy sounds from my wet sex. It's embarrassing and a dirty turn-on at the same time. When he grinds his palm on my clit, my hips lift to meet the demand.

"What did you do with yourself today, *cherie?*" he asks, battering my body closer to orgasm.

My breathing is too erratic to speak.

"Did you miss me?" he asks in a husky voice.

I did, and I feel like a failure for it. It only makes me close my heart off to him even more, turning off my thoughts and giving over to the physical sensations he extracts with such cruel precision.

"Are you close?" he taunts. "Do you want to come?"

He used to make me ask for it before I ran. I broke every time. Now is no exception. I mewl when he traces a line with his finger down my spine. My body draws tight when he follows the crease between my globes to tease my dark entrance.

"You know what will be even hotter than finger fucking your cunt?" he asks. "Fucking your ass at the same time."

I don't know what had gotten into him tonight, only that this dirty talking is new. He's more intense than ever. I'm so close I don't even fight him when he pushes a digit past the resistance of the tight ring of muscles of my dark entrance. He slips the intrusion in slowly, stretching me with a burn that adds more flames to fire raging through my body. His movements are synchronized, pushing me higher and closer to oblivious ecstasy.

"Every hole in this body is mine," he says with a voice thick with lust. "Say it."

I'm past caring about my modesty or pride. "Yes."

"To do with as I please. Say it."

"Yes," I mumble with my face pressed against the sofa.

"Do you want my cock?"

There's only one answer. "Yes."

"Why?"

This is the only way I can give myself to him. "Because you give me no choice."

"Damn right. There is no choice. You're mine. Forever."

I mourn the answer even as my thoughts start to splinter and my body flies. The orgasm crashes through me in waves, leaving me weak in its aftermath. It's quick and powerful. There's nothing gentle or sweet about it. I'm shaking from the intensity.

Making me go down to my knees, he unzips his pants and frees his cock. His fist is tight in my hair as he grabs my head and lifts it just enough for my mouth to stretch around his cock.

"Suck me like a good girl," he says, spreading his legs.

I barely have time to take a breath before he thrusts past my lips, hitting the back of my throat.

"This is us, Zoe. Me and you. Get it?"

I'm only half cognizant of the question. The meaning of his words doesn't matter. What matters is that I'm degraded and beyond saving, a wife but still a whore. I take what he gives. I breathe when he lets me and allow him to use me to get off. This is what I accepted when I agreed to return to France with him. It's the price I'm paying for keeping Damian and his family safe. I'll do it again and again, whatever it takes.

He comes with a groan, emptying himself down my throat. I don't have a choice but to swallow, but I do so greedily, taking the only thing I'll ever allow myself to take from him again.

"That's it," he says, stroking my hair. "You've been so good."

I'm far from it. I'm his dirty toy, his object to manipulate and defile.

"Now tell me that wasn't perfect," he says.

I don't say a word, because in its own, perverse, ugly way it was perfect.

"I love you, Zoe," he says, stroking my back.

The words cut deep, because he can't possibly mean them.

CHAPTER 24

Maxime

The sun is barely up when I wake. Leaving Zoe to sleep, I have a shower and dress in a pair of black Italian fitted pants and a dark purple tailored shirt with a matching tie. The ankle boots and gray wool coat I choose to round off the ensemble are Italian, too. I like to dress well. It makes up for my lacking physique. My body still fills out the clothes well. The diamond business is less physical than my previous position. I'm no longer using my fists or fighting skills like I used to, but I make sure I stay in shape by working out every evening at an old boxing gym not far from the apartment. It's not about vanity but about survival and being strong enough to keep Zoe safe. I'm no longer in the mob, but Alexis will always pose a danger. I can never let my guard down.

After combing my hair and splashing a dash of cologne on my cheeks, I close the bedroom door so I won't wake Zoe. I switch on the coffee machine and gather my files from the table where I worked last night. I stuff everything into my laptop bag before taking out the leaflets I printed yesterday at the office, alerting the residents of an unauthorized entry into the building. What happened when Alexis got in can never happen again.

While I sip my coffee, I study the dress on the form that stands in front of the circular window. It's just long enough not to be indecent, but the short slits on the sides defy that decency with an almost rebellious intent. The neckline is low, framed by a broad lapel that gives it the look of a male jacket as if challenging femininity. Three-quarter-long sleeves with a fold-back cuff that repeats the sharply pointed lapel add balance to the otherwise too-short hem. It's a dress that demands confidence. Not just anyone will be able to pull off the look.

The worry that ate its way into my mind last night returns. The design isn't like Zoe. She's changing. She's slipping away from me, and I don't know how to stop it. Last night I tried to restore the balance by showing her I'm still in charge. As long as I can manipulate her lust, I can control her body, but it no longer seems to be working. What has changed?

She won't step out of line. She cares too much for her brother. That's still the same. What's different is her attitude. She's closing herself off and molding herself into someone else. If my harsh demonstration on the sofa last night didn't work, then maybe it's the wrong strategy. Maybe forcing dominance isn't the way to go forward. Maybe she needs some power of her own in this relationship. For once, I should let her take the lead. Instead of setting the pace of our sex life, I should let her take the initiative.

With a last glance at the closed bedroom door, I put my empty cup in the dishwasher and leave. On my way down, I push a leaflet under every door. I'm certain now Alexis slipped in behind me that day. I was too blinded with anger to pay attention to what was happening around me, a mistake I won't make again. Only Zoe can push me to such a state of carelessness. Still, I'm not taking chances. Everyone in the building must be aware of what has happened. Vigilance is prevention, and prevention is always better than cure.

There are ten apartments, three on the first three floors and ours taking up the whole of the top story. When I've done my distribution,

I exit into the crisp morning air. Summer is around the corner. It's in the brighter blue of the sky and the way the sunrays already slide over the neighboring building to disperse with wedges that cut through the alleys. At the corner bakery, I take a table outside and order a croissant and an espresso. I'm not taking breakfast outside only to adhere to the French tradition, but also to keep an eye on our building before I head to the office. So far, no conspicuous men that could be connected to Alexis are showing up to watch our street.

While I eat, I read my emails on my phone. There are little confirmations for the auction in Paris. My regular buyers are still skeptical about my split from the mafia. Until I've proven I'm as capable on my own as when I was the mafia underboss and there's no danger of retribution from my family, they're not going to support me. The stones Damian Hart provides are of good quality. They are pure with great color. They don't come free, and whilst I have a vault full of them, it's not going to help me keep the business afloat if I can't sell them.

There aren't that many buyers in the world. The European ones are especially finicky. They know the consequences of being disloyal to my family only too well, ironically thanks to my own doing. For years, I was the one who doled out the lessons. I have no doubt that my brother has something to do with their reluctance in supporting my business even though they need the stones. Ours are conflict free and the quality is much higher than any other on the market. Plus, Hart has recently extended to add black diamonds to his inventory, a craze that has hit the world by storm. For those who can't afford a highly graded diamond, a black diamond is the perfect alternative. It makes diamonds accessible to a broader market. Thanks to Hart, I'm the exclusive importer of black diamonds to Europe. Yet the buyers are not biting. If I don't manage to win them over soon, the business is in serious trouble. I'll be going down, and I'll be damned before I take Zoe with me.

Pushing my concerns aside, I survey the street once more before going down to the parking for my car. The traffic is already heavy despite the early hour. I don't get to the office before nine. When I enter the underground parking, my shoulders draw tight with tension. A black Mercedes is parked next to my regular spot. The windows are tinted, but I don't need to see inside. I know to who it belongs. Drawing my gun out from under my seat, I keep it ready on my lap before I pull in next to the Mercedes and cut the engine. When the driver gets out of the Mercedes and opens the passenger door, I tuck the gun into my waistband before getting out, but I don't slide into the passenger seat as per the silent instruction. I cross my arms and lean against my car.

After a short wait, the backdoor on the other side of the Mercedes opens. My father groans as he folds his body double. He straightens with a flinch. He's put on weight. The trench coat doesn't hide his bigger stomach. His face looks older, his bad eye sagging more in its socket and deeper lines running over his forehead. Through the open door, I glimpse a young woman with red hair and big tits. The dress shows off more skin than a stripper's uniform at the club. My father hasn't waited very long to replace my mother, not that I care. Catching my look, she averts her eyes and pulls the sides of her fur coat together to cover her cleavage.

"Max," my father says in greeting.

I turn my attention back to him. "Why are you here?"

He gives a humorless smile. "No cutting corners, I see."

"Since I'm dead to you, there's no point in wasting time with politeness."

"You're right." He squints at me. "I hear your business isn't doing well."

I laugh. "Spying on me? Are you afraid?"

He shrugs. "I hear things."

"*Things*." I straighten. "Is there a point to this conversation?"

"You need our old clients or you're going under."

I clench my jaw. "They need me too."

"They're buying from De Beers and Anglo. They don't need you."

"De Beers and Anglo don't have the stones I have."

"Yeah." He leans an arm on the door to support his weight. "I heard black diamonds are the latest rage."

So, the old man is keeping up with the business. "Get to the point."

"Cut Alexis in."

This time, my laugh is harsh. "Not a chance."

"If the two of you work together, the old clients will return. They're divided, uncertain where their loyalty should lie."

"Then tell them they have nothing to worry about."

He doesn't respond to my challenge. Alexis is deliberately letting them stew in concern to ensure I don't get buyers, but it seems my father's reluctance to set things straight is also born from another interest. He's not only set on destroying me, but also winning financial gain in the process.

"I thought so," I say, pushing away from the car.

"Wait." My father's voice rings out in the empty garage. "Alexis is making mistakes. Leonardo isn't happy with the way he's dealing with the business. Alexis needs a guiding hand."

From the way he almost chokes on the words, I know how hard this is for him to ask. "Why would I do that?" I ask with scorn.

He raises his palms. "Alexis is your brother."

"*Was* my brother."

His face grows red. "You owe me. I raised you." He stabs a finger in my direction. "Everything you have is because of me."

I advance until we're standing nose to nose. "Everything I *had*, I worked for. I gave it all to Alexis. That makes us even. We cut the ties. You made your decision as I made mine. You're nothing to me. Now get out of my way before I make you."

"You'll regret this," he says, trembling with rage.

"I don't think so."

Turning my back on him, I walk to the elevator. From this conversation, I know two things. One, Alexis is in trouble, or my father wouldn't have come crawling back on his knees begging for help. Two, my father still doesn't give a shit about me. If he did, he'd never suggest I let Alexis worm his way into the business. We both know how that will end up. The diamond business will revert back to the mob, leaving me with nothing and no way to provide for Zoe or myself.

I slam the button to call down the elevator and get inside when it opens. I'm just in time to see the Mercedes pull out of its parking space when the doors close. Taking out my phone, I type a memo to the security overseeing the building. From now on, no one related to me is allowed inside. When you've broken away from the mob, your biggest enemies are your own family.

CHAPTER 25

Zoe

I try not to think about last night or where that leaves me in the unequal standing of my unconventional relationship with Maxime. Instead, I focus on finishing the dress, rounding it off with thick stitching around the lapel and cuffs in the same color as the fabric.

Since I don't have labels, I embroider my initials into the flap under the collar. The rest of the morning I spend setting up a simple website on my new laptop. I keep my CV short, mentioning my passions and vision. Using my phone, I take a photo of the dress on the dress form. An application allows me to change the dress form into a digital model. I choose a woman with a pale complexion to show off the darker fabric of the dress. Her face is avant-garde and as harsh as the simple lines of the dress, a perfect marriage. Then I upload the image onto my site and put a ridiculously high price on the dress.

By the afternoon, I've designed a basic logo with my initials and set up social media accounts. Since it's a beautiful day, I have a quick salad for lunch in the summerhouse before I make a few rough sketches I upload to my new website and accounts. My last task is reaching out to a few industry related accounts, sending them private viewing invitations. Happy with the day's work, I tidy up my material and the apartment before pouring myself a glass of rosé to take a brief break before starting dinner.

The buzz of the intercom in the kitchen is such a foreign sound it makes me jump. I lift the receiver and ask cautiously, "Yes?"

"Zee?"

I go still at the sound of that voice. Impossible. It can't be.

"Zee, it's Damian. Can you let me in?"

"How—" Damian? What is he doing here? "What—"

Oh, my God. My brother is here. Joy mixed with nerves send me into a flat spin. There can only be one reason why he'd be here.

"Of course," I say, pressing the button to open the door in the street for him.

In the time he takes to come up, I leave the wine on the counter and rush to the dressing room to check my reflection in the mirror. I'm dressed in a T-shirt, jeans, and socks. My hair is tied in a high ponytail on my head. I don't have a stitch of make-up on my face, but my cheeks are flushed red from the shock and excitement. Grabbing the make-up brush, I apply a few swipes of powder under each eye to hide the dark rings that make my skin appear bruised. I don't want Damian to see the evidence of my stress and lack of sleep.

I barely make it back to the lounge before the bell rings. Flinging the door open, I jump into my brother's arms.

He stumbles a step and regains his balance with a chuckle. "You'll take us both to the ground."

Holding him at arm's length, I ask, "What are you doing here?"

His smile stretches. "Can I at least come in before answering your questions?"

"Oh, my God. Where are my manners?" Hooking my arm through his, I lead him inside. "When did you get here?"

"I just landed."

I shut the door and lock it. Motioning to the laptop bag slung over his shoulder, I ask, "No luggage?"

"I'm not staying."

I stare at him. "Are you telling me you flew eleven hours and you're not sleeping over?"

"I have a flight back tonight."

"Damian." I search his face. "I'm more happy than I can ever express that you're here, but why would you do that? It's crazy."

His brow pleats. "I didn't want to leave Lina alone for long."

"How is she?" I release him to search his face. "Will she be all right without you?"

"She isn't due for another two months, but…"

Anything can happen. Yes, I understand, and she's too far along to be allowed on a flight. "As happy as I am to see you, you shouldn't have left her. Not now."

"Russell is staying over and Josh's nanny is sleeping in."

"Why are you here, Damian?" I study him carefully. "I'm guessing it's not for business."

"I came to check on you."

"Check on me?" I exclaim. "Why?"

"It's not like you to say you'll call and then not do it. I had to be sure everything was fine."

"Everything *is* fine." I rub my forehead. "I can't believe you came all these miles just to see for yourself."

"Is it?" he asks, still studying me with a serious expression.

"Yes." I plaster a bright smile on my face. "Better than fine." I wave my arms. "See for yourself."

He looks around the space. "Nice place."

"Maxime went to a lot of effort with the renovations. Would you like to see it all?"

"Sure." He drops his laptop bag on the reclining chair under the stairs.

I take him on a tour of the inside, followed by the summerhouse and greenhouse on the terrace.

"Would you like a glass of wine?" I ask when we step back inside. "I was just going to have one."

"Yes, please." He steps up to the dress form and tilts his head as he takes in the dress while I pour another glass of wine. "Thank you," he says when I hand it to him. Nodding in the direction of the dress, he says, "This isn't your usual style."

I smile. "I've evolved."

He regards it thoughtfully as he takes a sip of his wine, and then he winces. I cringe inwardly, but keep a straight face. It's a cheap wine and not the best quality. At least I can get away with not being French and a little uneducated when it comes to the local wine cultivars. I don't want Damian to know about our financial concerns. I don't want to give him any reason to doubt my happiness. His life depends on it. So do Lina's and their children's.

Setting the wine on the table, he rounds the dress. "I didn't know you went back to dressmaking."

"Designing," I say with pride, trying to appear confident.

"It's..."

"Do you hate it?" I ask, wringing my hands together.

"Actually, it's quite stylish. I'm just battling to see you in it."

"Oh, it's not for me. It's for my new brand."

He raises a brow. "You're developing a brand?"

"Yes." I laugh. "I'm trying to."

"Good for you."

I move toward the table where my phone lies. "Let me call Maxime and tell him to come home earlier. We can have dinner together."

"No," he says with a little too much force. "Don't disturb him."

I know what he's doing. He doesn't want to give Maxime a warning that he's here. He wants to study our relationship dynamic with the advantage of surprising Maxime.

"Tell me about this hasty marriage," he says, unbuttoning his jacket.

Our marriage is the last thing I want to talk about. I take his arm and lead him to the sofa. "It just kind of happened."

His look is piercing. "Yes?"

"On the spur of the moment," I add in a happy tone.

He opens his mouth, but the sound of the key turning in the lock saves me from answering whatever my brother was going to ask. The door opens, revealing Maxime on the threshold with a single pink rose in his hands. His gaze immediately finds Damian. For a moment, the two men give each other a measuring look. Not a speck of shock registers on my husband's face. He steps into the room like my brother is visiting every day, dropping his bag before removing his jacket.

I walk to him with my stomach wound tight, praying he'll play along when I go on tiptoes and put my arms around his neck. To my relief, he bends down to kiss me.

Giving me the flower, he says, "I missed you."

"I missed you, too," I whisper.

Maxime rests his palms lightly on my hips, giving a gentle squeeze before setting me aside to face my brother. "Damian. If I'd known you were going to pay us a visit I would've left the office earlier."

Damian gets to his feet. "I didn't want to slow down your business. I know how it is to get a new venture off the ground."

"Very thoughtful," Maxime says with a smile, but the gesture is nothing but empty politeness. He glances at the wine on the table. "Would you like a whiskey?"

"No, thanks," Damian says. "Wine is fine."

I haven't done it since Maxime fetched me back to France, but I walk to the kitchen and pour my husband a whiskey after putting the flower in a thin vase. It's not out of consideration, but to escape the two men's scrutiny for a few precious moments.

When I return with the drink, Damian's attention is back on Maxime.

"Thank you, *cherie*," Maxime says, taking the glass and kissing my lips.

"Congratulations on your wedding," Damian says to Maxime, watching him like a shark circling a seal in bloody waters.

"Thank you." Taking my hand, Maxime pulls me down next to him on the sofa. There's not a stitch of guilt in his voice or comportment.

I cringe in an involuntary reflex, but quickly smooth it over by pretending to be cuddling closer to my husband.

Maxime's arm tightens around me. "We should go out for dinner and celebrate." He adds in a tone that's neither hostile nor friendly, "Now that you're here."

His words are intellectually correct, the suggestion the socially acceptable response that the situation calls for, but they lack emotional substance. He's saying what's expected of him, reciting the phrases like a parrot.

"I don't want to put you out," Damian says.

"I'm sure my brother is tired after the long flight," I add quickly. We don't have enough money for a fancy restaurant and the French cuisine Maxime will no doubt feel obliged to entertain Damian with. Getting to my feet, I make my way to the kitchen. "I'll just throw something together."

I give Damian a bright smile from the counter where I pause to measure his reaction. To my relief, neither of the men pushes the issue, but Damian's next words almost have me gasping out loud.

"Where are the photos?"

Maxime regards Damian with a blunt expression. "What photos?"

Damian's gaze sharpens. "Your wedding photos."

I open my mouth to make up an excuse, to say that in our rush we'd forgotten all about it, but Maxime beats me to it with an even tone.

"They're not ready yet. The photographer hasn't finished developing them."

Damian relaxes a fraction. "You'll send some to us, I hope."

"Of course." Maxime's smile is a little more genuine this time.

Wiping my hair from my suddenly clammy face, I swallow away my nerves.

"How's the business?" Damian asks.

I watch Maxime from under my lashes as I fill the big pot with water and turn on the gas.

"Great," my husband says, not missing a beat. "Thank you for your support. Black diamonds are only taking off in Europe now, but I congratulate you for your vision."

Damian picks up his glass, takes another sip of his wine, and sets the glass aside again. "What's your vision?"

"To follow the trends." Maxime's eyes are fixed on Damian, giving the impression my brother has his undivided attention, but I know he's watching my every move and measuring my expression.

I don't dare to look at him for fear that Damian will catch something passing between us. Instead, I pour a scoop of salt into my palm and add it to the water before dusting my hand on my jeans.

"What about buyers?" Damian asks. "Will *they* follow?"

I'm not stupid. I know the buyers are afraid of showing disloyalty to Alexis by supporting Maxime now that he's broken away from the mob. That's why the business is suffering. If I could've figured it out, so has Damian. I tear open the box of spaghetti with shaking hands, trying not to spill the pasta as I dump it into the bubbling water.

"They'll come around," Maxime says with so much certainty he makes even me want to believe him. "These things take time."

Damian nods, seemingly pacified for the moment.

"Would you like to visit the office?" Maxime asks. "I'd love to introduce you to some of the prominent business players."

Damian's smile is polite. "Maybe another time."

Understanding flashes in Maxime's eyes. "How's your wife doing?"

My brother's features darken. He's taking Maxime's forced interest as a threat.

"We're both excited about the baby," I say.

Damian's gaze finds mine briefly before he says, "She's doing great."

"Good." Maxime sounds sincere. "I'm sorry we can't be there for the birth."

Damian glances at me again. "If Zoe wants to come, I'll make sure she's safe."

"I don't doubt your ability to protect her," Maxime replies, "but I can't let her out of my sight." Rubbing a thumb over his lip as he studies me, he adds, "Yet."

I roll my eyes at the possessive statement, but it's a language my brother obviously understands from the way he relaxes with an agreeable if not satisfied nod.

When I carry plates and cutlery from the kitchen, Maxime gets up to help me set the table. Damian fetches glasses and the jug I've filled with water. While the men instill themselves at the table, I heat a tin of tomato sauce in a pan.

"I'm sorry for the simple meal," I say when I put the pasta and sauce on the table.

Damian's eyes soften as he looks at me. "You know I'm not fussy."

No. When we were growing up, we didn't have that luxury. We were lucky to get anything other than a piece of buttered toast for dinner. I relax a bit. It's easy to forget the wealthy, cultured man in the expensive suit is still my brother. We should never fail to remember where we come from.

During the rest of the dinner I fall quiet as the guys talk business. Damian explains his vision of expanding his finished products, jewelry styled by his designer, to Europe, while Maxime agrees to provide a base for selling them as soon as the foundation of his business is sound again.

When I propose fresh fruit for dessert, Damian checks his watch.

"I'm afraid I have to get going," he says.

Shameful relief mixes with my sadness. "Already?"

"My flight leaves in two hours."

"Coffee before you go?" Maxime asks.

Damian gets to his feet. "I'll get one at the airport."

Maxime follows suit. "I'll drive you."

"It's not necessary," Damian says. "I can get a taxi."

"It's no trouble." Maxime heads to the door to get his jacket. "Besides, I know the safe roads."

My heart is heavy when I walk my brother to the door. Folding my arms around him, I hug him tight. "Give Lina and Josh a hug from me."

He kisses the top of my head. "I will."

"Please let me know the moment there's news," I say, staring up at him.

His smile is tender. "Don't worry. You'll be the first to know."

"A baby." I sigh. "I can't believe I'm going to be an aunt."

"What about you? Getting broody?" Damian asks, but he's looking at Maxime as he poses the question.

"Soon," Maxime says just as I reply, "No."

Damian gives me a curious look, a flicker of caution creeping back into his eyes.

"Something we're still to discuss," Maxime says. "It seems I'm keener than my wife."

I recognize his iron will, but to any onlooker he must appear tender and caring.

Damian relents, releasing me with a smile. "I'm sure you'll work it out."

"Thank you," I say. *Thanks for caring enough to check up on me.*

Damian's expression turns stern. "Call me."

"I'll make sure she does," Maxime says. Taking my face between his hands, he kisses my forehead before retrieving his keys.

The door closes on their backs, and then they're gone. Suddenly, I'm alone in every sense, feeling it all the way to my soul. My hand automatically goes to my stomach, covering the emptiness I feel there that echoes in my chest.

If Maxime is planning on tying me further to him with a baby, he's got another think coming. There was a time I would've given him a child, a time I even craved a baby, but I was stupid then. I believed we were happy in our own way. We're too unstable to be anything other than unhappy. We could never provide a healthy environment for a child.

I clear the table and clean the kitchen, welcoming the tasks to keep my thoughts from drifting into sadness. When there's nothing left to tidy, I have a shower and pull on a pair of comfy pajamas. I'm brushing out my hair in front of the mirror in the dressing room when Maxime gets back.

Our gazes lock where he leans in the frame. He watches me with something that burns fiercely in his eyes, but he doesn't express the sentiment in words.

I put the brush away and get up. "Thank you for driving Damian."

He stares at me like he may eat me alive. "We're family. It's normal."

"I'm going to bed." I squeeze past him. "I'm knackered."

He grips my wrist, holding me back while his gray gaze bores into mine. "That's really what you want to do?"

"Yes," I lie.

Slowly, he releases me.

The minute I'm free, I flee. I walk to the bedroom like I don't want to run, and crawl into bed under the covers while Maxime undresses in the dark. He wants me. I know he does, but for some reason, he doesn't come to bed with his usual seduction skills. He slides into his side and lies quietly on his back, waiting. Waiting for something I don't understand.

CHAPTER 26

Maxime

Zoe isn't taking the initiative. She's not touching me.

She doesn't want me.

Of course she doesn't.

Look at me.

Look at my face. Look at who I am.

What did I expect?

I'm fucking devastated, and it doesn't make sense. I don't understand the feelings beating in my chest.

I'm a fool.

What else is there to say?

On my way to work, I spot the nail sticking out of a plank on the pavement next to a construction site. I lift my foot high and put it down with enough force to drive the nail through the sole of my shoe and into the hollow of my foot.

Fuuuuck. That hurts.

For a moment, I'm nailed to the plank like Jesus to the cross, a rivulet of cold sweat running down my hot back.

"Christ," a workman calls out, making his way over to me. "Are you all right?"

"Does it look like I'm fucking all right?" I ask, gritting my teeth against the pain that burns up my leg.

"Jesus." The man throws his hardhat on the ground and grabs my elbow. "Here, let me help you."

I allow him to pull the plank with the nail from my foot and shoe. The pain reverses, a new kind of fire setting in the minute the nail slips out of my flesh. Warm, sticky wetness coats my sock inside my shoe.

"Man," the guy says, "I'm so sorry. I shouldn't have left the plank lying here. I was just dropping a bag of cement. I was going to move it in a sec, I swear, but you were on me so fast."

I test putting my weight on my foot. Mm. That's going to take a while.

"You need a tetanus shot," the man says. "The nail doesn't look rusted, but—"

"I know." I jerk away, freeing myself from his hand that's back on my elbow.

"Are you going to sue?" he asks, squinting at me as he scratches his head.

"No."

His face relaxes. "Look man, for what's it's worth, I'm really sorry. Better watch where you're going next time."

I shift my laptop bag to my other shoulder to relieve the pressure on my foot and get into the man's space. "You better watch where you leave your material."

When he cringes away from me, I take satisfaction from his fear. He's my size, but he senses the darkness in me. It's a darkness that doesn't fight fairly.

The power shift feeds my soul. Abated, I turn away from him and limp on my way. With every step I take, I recall how Zoe looked when she stepped into a shard of glass and cut her heel.

Her wound has long since healed.
Mine is just beginning.

CHAPTER 27

Zoe

The very next day, I find a female gynecologist in town through an internet search and make an appointment for a birth control shot. That same night, Maxime comes home with an injured foot. He pulls off a blood-soaked sock to reveal a ghastly wound. The nail that went through his shoe penetrated his foot so deeply the point pushed through the skin at the top. He's lucky the bleeding stopped so quickly. When I urge him to see Dr. Olivier, he brushes my concerns away, telling me he's injected himself with a tetanus shot at the office.

"Maxime," I say, kneeling next to him in the bathroom where he's bathing his foot in a tub of Betadine. "You better go see the doctor."

His gaze tightens on me even as his lips tilt with a slight smile. "Worried?"

"Of course I am." I point at his foot. "That looks really bad."

"Why?" he asks, his eyes not leaving mine as he rolls his pants up to the knee.

I sit back on my haunches. "Why what?"

"Why are you concerned?"

I blink. "It's normal."

He rests an arm on one knee, leaning closer to me. "Is it?"

Confusion rages inside my chest. Doesn't he get it? Aghast, I say, "It's called compassion."

"Ah." He sits back, creating distance between us. "In other words, your concern isn't because you care."

About me.

He doesn't say it, but we both know it's what he means.

"What do you expect me to say?" I whisper.

"Nothing." His voice sounds harsher despite the fact that he speaks in a softer tone. "I expect nothing."

I motion to his injury. "Shall I—"

"Leave." He gives me a flat look. "You should leave before I ask you to touch me in a way that has nothing to do with treating my wound."

I gape at him. "You can't seriously be thinking about sex right now."

"If I give you a choice between pulling down your panties under that skirt and straddling my cock or walking through the door, what will you choose?"

Taken aback, I continue to stare at the rough contours of his face. The old me would've never left anyone with such an injury, but living with Maxime has hardened me. The sight of blood still makes me queasy, but I'm also growing desensitized to it.

"That's what I thought," he says. "You put up a good show for your brother."

Anger replaces my concern. Straightening, I ball my fists. "What did you expect? Do you think I want you and my brother to go to war? Who will survive, huh? Tell me who'll win."

He continues to stare at me with his cool gaze. "I'd say it's fifty-fifty."

"Exactly." I look down at him with all the loathing I'm capable of mustering from my soul. "I'm not risking my brother. He did nothing to deserve it."

"Go, then, pretty little flower." His smile turns mocking. "Run."

I don't let him tell me twice. I turn my back on him and leave while I can, slamming the door on my way out. On the other side, I lean against the wood to drag in a few deep breaths and settle my trembling heart.

This new road we're heading down, I have no idea where it's going.

Maxime acts aloof in the day that follows, but I have something else on my mind. Luckily, I only have to wait two days for my doctor's appointment. The gynecologist was willing to squeeze me in between patients. I don't tell Maxime about the scheduled visit. I go during the day when he's at work, knowing no one is following me like before. Maxime will still be able to track my whereabouts via my phone, but he got used to me moving around freely in town to do grocery shopping and window-shopping for supplies. As long as I don't run, he's no longer checking up on me.

I'm not going to seek physical affection from Maxime. On the contrary, I'd rather avoid it. However, I do breathe easier knowing pregnancy won't be a risk.

With my health taken care of, I throw myself back into work. For two weeks, nothing happens. I get a few likes on my social media accounts, but no one calls about the dress. With no money to buy more fabric, I spend the time making sketches and playing housewife. Welcoming the distance Maxime has put between us, I use the space to cram my head full of new design ideas.

During the third week, I finally get a call about the dress, but my spirit sinks when I hear the woman's Texan accent.

"I love the style, and it's exactly what I need for a charity lunch event," she says after a long introduction of telling me about the challenges of finding fashionable clothes for her slim figure and small breasts, "but I'd love a fitting before I make a decision."

"You do realize I'm in the south of France, right?" I could mail the dress to her, but if she needs adjustments mailing it backward and forward can turn out to be expensive and lengthy.

"That's not a problem. I'm due in Cannes for the film festival in a couple of weeks. My flight lands in Marseille. We can meet before I shoot through to Cannes."

I sit up straighter. "You're going to the festival?"

"I'm a nominee," she says in an almost embarrassed tone and then adds shyly, "Vera Day."

I've been out of touch with the news and outside world for so long I have no idea what's going on in the entertainment world. I'm typing her name into the search field of the browser on my laptop even as I ask, "Do you already have a dress for the festival?" Ambition and desperation make me bold. Normally, I'd never have been so forward.

"Of course." She laughs. "It's a Valentino number, and I forked out a fortune for it."

My heart starts beating faster when numerous pages come up under my search. "I bet I can create something a lot more original and fresher for you."

I skim over the information. Vera Day starred in a recent contemporary war drama that's been nominated for a Golden Palm award for the best director, best screenplay, and best actress. I scroll through the photos. Willowy and gracious with an enchanting smile, she's a portrait of humble innocence and self-assured feminism. Idolized by millions, the blond beauty is the perfect spokesperson for a clothing brand.

"Look," she says, "my agent is probably going to steamroller over my choice of an outfit for the charity event anyway, but whatever the outcome, I'd love to own this piece. It's just..." She pauses.

"You?"

"Yes," she says with a sigh. "Perfectly."

"Right, then. Let's schedule a fitting. I can make adjustments and have it ready for you before you head back home. How does that sound?"

"Great." She squeals. "Thank you so much."

"And," I take a deep breath, "I'd really like to present you with a dress for the festival."

"I feel like you get me and what I want, but I can't justify forking out another big amount when I've already—"

"You don't have to buy the dress. I'm only asking that you wear it and if a reporter is interested mention the brand. You can return it after the event. No cost."

"You want advertising?"

"Yes." It's my turn to add shyly, "I'm just starting out."

She sighs. "Now it's going to be hard for me to turn you down. I've started out not so long ago, so I know how hard it is."

My hope surges. "You don't have to promise anything. Just try on the dress and see what you think."

"I suppose there's no harm in that."

We set a date and time, and I take her private email address in case we need to communicate before our appointment. After I congratulate her and wish her luck with the nomination, we say goodbye.

The minute I hang up, I start doing research, downloading every photograph of Vera Day I can get my hands on. In no time, I have a fairly good idea of her figure and style. I go through the list of designers who fashion reporters reckon will pop up at the festival and make sure I'm up to date with their latest trends.

For the first time in months, I feel like I'm living again and not just existing when I put pencils to paper and start sketching a dress. Until the dress I made is sold, that's to say *if* Vera Day decides to buy it, I don't have money for the fabric of a gala dress. However, this opportunity is too big to let it slip through my fingers. I'll just have to push my credit card into the red and explain to Maxime later.

CHAPTER 28

Maxime

"This is unexpected," Dr. Delphine Bisset says when she lets me into her office. Her smile is sly. "You even made an appointment."

"Tell me again a psychopath can't be considerate," I say, taking the sofa facing Delphine's usual chair.

"How are things going with the young lady?" she asks when she's seated.

I stretch my arm along the back of the sofa. "Complicated."

"Mm. What are we discussing today?"

"She's changing."

She tilts her head, regarding me with that smile still in place. "That's a problem?"

"Yes."

"People change. They grow."

I consider that. "I'm not sure you can call this growth."

"Let's take this a few steps back." She smoothes down her skirt.

"Do you see yourself in a long-term relationship with this woman?"

"She's my wife." I let my mind wrap around the word, savoring the permanence of the meaning.

Delphine raises a brow. "Definitely long-term then. When did this happen?"

"Not so long ago."

Her eyes narrow at my vagueness. "Max." Her voice is chiding, but her look turns wary. "Did you manipulate her into marrying you?"

I straighten my tie. "Let's just say I didn't ask."

"Oh, Max." Her shoulders slump. "That's not the way to do it. Haven't we made any progress?"

"You're not supposed to judge me."

"I'm not judgmental, but it's my duty to point out you lack a moral compass."

"It's done. Can we stay on the subject?" I check my watch. "In thirty minutes you're kicking me out."

"What am I going to do with you?" she exclaims.

I give her a pointed look. "We were talking about my wife."

She straightens in her seat. "You said your wife is changing. Change isn't necessarily negative. Change is necessary for growth."

"As I said, I don't think this is growth."

"Tell me about these changes."

"She used to be a romantic. Now she's almost cynical."

"Why do you say that?"

"Her style, for starters. Before, she'd wear frilly things. Feminine things."

She taps a finger on her knee. "What does she wear now?"

"The kind of clothes my mother would wear."

"Stylish?"

She's no longer smiling, but there's still a glint in her eyes. Trust Delphine to see the humor in this, that the woman I chose to be my wife would suddenly turn into someone who resembles my mother.

I shiver with repulsion at the thought. "I suppose you could say so."

"What else is changing?"

Reaching for the jug on the coffee table, I pour a glass of water. "She's becoming harder and less naïve."

"Why is that a problem?"

I take a sip. "She used to believe in love."

"You want her to," she concludes correctly.

"I *need* her to."

"Why? Because you still believe it somehow balances you and makes up for your shortcomings?"

I put the glass aside. "Because love is her survival mechanism. It's how she copes."

"Let's approach this from a different angle." She crosses her legs. "What are you afraid of?"

"That she'll lose the one thing that makes her strong and pretty." Pensively, I add, "Like a wildflower."

"Will she be less pretty to you if she loses her faith in love?"

I frown. "Of course not. This isn't about me. I don't want her to lose the qualities I lack, the ones that make her humane and me a psychopath."

"Because you care," she says.

"I've already told you I do." Goddamn, Zoe is withdrawing from me, and I don't know how to stop it.

Delphine regards me for a moment before asking, "What do you think are the reasons for these changes?"

"I don't know. That's what I'm paying you to figure out."

She drums her fingers on her knee again. "What happened in your lives before these changes started occurring?"

"I fetched her back from South Africa and married her. To do so, I had to break away from the mob and hand my possessions and position over to Alexis. My brother threatened her, and my mother tried to kill her. The person who did my mother's dirty work ended up dead." I tap my fingers on my leg, mirroring Delphine's non-verbal body language. I like to mess with her in that way. "What else? Oh, the diamond business isn't doing that well thanks to my brother who's set on ruining me. I think that covers it." More or less. I'm not elaborating about how the wedding played out or why Zoe was sick for a week afterward.

Delphine's fingers still. She folds her hands back in her lap.

"Do I make you nervous?" I ask with a grin.

"You know you do." Leaning forward, she gives no power to the comment by changing the direction of the conversation. She stays right on track, her worried expression not lifting. "Max, after everything you just mentioned, I'm very concerned about this young woman. What you're describing is a lot to deal with. No wonder she's changing. It's called survival."

"How do I change it back to how it used to be?"

Her look is level. "You take away the cause of the change."

My jaw locks so tightly the joints ache. "My mother is no longer a threat. I'm protecting her against Alexis. I'm working my hands to the bone to get this business off the ground and give her the life she deserves. What the fuck else am I supposed to do?"

She shakes her head. "These are unfortunate side effects. They're not the root of the problem."

I see clearly where Delphine is taking me, but I can't go there. Never. Not a chance.

"Who is the cause of the change, Max?" she asks in her cajoling voice.

I grind my teeth, looking at her with defiance, but Delphine isn't my therapist for nothing. I may make her nervous, but she's never backed down from making me face the truth.

"Who is the cause of the change, Max?"

I bang a fist on the table, making her jump.

She blinks and then charges straight back into the attack. "Who is the cause of the change, Max?"

The admittance tears from my chest. Like a rabid animal, I growl the single word. "Me."

Fuck it.

Me.

She sags in the chair as if our wrestle was physical. "Only one question remains. What are you going to do about it?"

Goddamn. I came here looking for a magic cure for Zoe, for a pill or a session of hypnosis, not for *this*.

Too angry to give expression to my thoughts with more useless words, I push to my feet, bumping the coffee table and making the water spill from the glass.

I turn on my heel and barge from the shrink's office.

That's what I'm fucking doing about it.

CHAPTER 29

Zoe

Lying on my stomach on the bed, I beam at the trio on my laptop screen. Damian, Lina, and Josh are lounging on the couch in their living room. My brother has his arm around his wife's shoulders, and Josh sits on his lap, running a red locomotive over Damian's leg.

"You look stunning," I say to Lina who's complaining about the size of her stomach.

"That's what I keep telling her," Damian says, his eyes taking on that all-consuming light that seems to come from inside of him when he looks at her.

Seriously, she's glowing. I'm overjoyed for them. They found the happiness they deserve. I'm not naïve enough to believe it was an easy road paved with rose petals, but I know what they've built together will last forever. It's just *that* kind of love.

"Tell me more about the dress," Lina says, always diverting attention away from herself. "Vera freaking Day? I can't believe you're designing Vera Day's dress."

"Maybe and a very big maybe at that," I say. "She didn't commit to anything other than trying on the dress."

"That's something, right?" Lina says. "You'll win her over."

I make a face. "She sounded lovely over the phone, but I'm competing against Valentino." Who goes up against Valentino? I must be mad.

"Show it to me," Damian says.

I take the sketchpad from the nightstand and hold it up to the screen.

"That's a nice drawing, Zee," Josh says.

"Coming from you, that means a lot to me," I say with a wink. "Will you make me a drawing?"

"Of a train?" he asks.

My heart melts. "Of whatever you want."

"Okay." He scrambles off Damian's lap. "I'll start now."

"Bye, Josh." I blow a kiss before his small, sturdy body disappears from the screen. "How is he getting cuter each time we speak?"

"He's a great kid." Putting a hand on Damian's leg, Lina gives him a loving look. "Your brother is very good with him."

Lina flushes a little as Damian brings her hand to his lips and gently bites down on a finger. It's tender and possessive, and my body suddenly misses my husband. Not my heart. Never my heart. That part of me, I locked away in a stone chamber deep under the water where a pulse is nothing but a distant sound.

"Maybe I can help you make up Vera's mind," Damian says.

"How?" I ask, resting my chin in my hand.

"I'm sure a black diamond necklace to compliment the outfit will sway her."

"Really?" I sit up. "Do you have something that will work?"

"Nothing that will go with the dress," he says, "but I can get my designer to make something."

"The festival is in two weeks," I exclaim.

"It shouldn't be a problem."

"Are you sure?" I'm breathless with excitement. "That sounds almost impossible."

"Anything is possible when you're the owner of the mine."

"Are you serious? You'll lend something so precious to us just for a night?"

"Anything for you, Zee."

I shift to the edge of the bed, balancing the laptop on my knees. "What about security?"

"She'll have to agree to extra measures and bodyguards, but it's doable. I'm sure Maxime will help you out with that."

Clapping my hands, I say, "Damian, you're a genius." I've seen some of the Hart designs. They're stunning.

"I'll send you a couple of sketches. Let me know what your ideas are, but don't wait too long. Tony will have to hurry if he's to create something before your deadline."

"Won't the courier be a problem?"

"Regardless of what Ms. Day decides, Maxime can keep the necklace to present to his buyers. We were going to extend the business to jewelry anyway. This way, it'll just happen sooner."

"I can't say thank you enough."

"You don't have to." Damian smiles. "It's what brothers do."

We talk for a little while longer, and when we say goodbye, I'm more motivated than ever. Pulling my pencils closer, I sketch in a necklace. The dress boasts a reversed collar with the V running down the back instead of the front. Vera has a beautiful back. In my opinion, it's the most gracious part of her body, which is why I choose to accentuate it. A necklace of black diamonds will form a good contrast and draw attention to her pale skin. I make a sketch of what I have in mind, take a photo with my phone, and send it via a text message to Damian.

Unable to contain my excitement, I pull on a pair of shoes and a fleece jacket and drive to a fabric wholesaler. The shopping is easy. I know what I want. I select a golden fabric with an embossed baroque print and take a few extra meters just in case. My stomach twists into a ball when I present my credit card to pay. The fabric is expensive. I can only hope Maxime won't be furious. If the dress doesn't sell and I can't cover my costs, he'll no doubt be angry. It's debt we can't afford.

On the way home, I make a detour to Maxime's office. It's best I tell him before he gets the bank statement.

CHAPTER 30

Maxime

I'm halfway through the auction stipulations draft when my receptionist announces I have a visitor. I'm not excepting anyone. To say I'm doubly taken back when my sister-in-law walks into my office is an understatement.

"Max," Izabella says when I've seen her inside and closed the door, offering her hand instead of her cheek.

I kiss her fingers, taking care not to touch her skin with my lips. "This is unexpected."

"I believe congratulations is in order." She looks me over. "How's married life?"

Indicating the visitor's chair, I do a quick evaluation of her person. "I should ask you the same." She's wearing a skirt that reaches her knees and a matching jacket. No bruises on her neck or legs. "I take it my brother is treating you well?"

Instead of taking the chair, she drops her handbag on my desk and faces me standing. "Alexis and I don't see that much of each other."

I search her face. "Did he send you?"

She holds my eyes without blinking. "No."

"Does he know you're here?"

She lifts her chin. "No."

"Is that wise?"

"I'm here now anyway." She shifts her weight.

"I guess you are. Tea?"

"No."

Izabella is young, but she's a no-nonsense girl. She's made that clear during the first and only one-on-one audience we'd had when she stated her demands for the marriage that was supposed to take place between us. That's the only reason I'm not throwing her out. It's the history we would've shared if I hadn't stood her up.

"Then I suppose you'll want to get straight to the point," I say.

"Alexis is in trouble."

I move to the door. "You've come to the wrong place."

"Wait." She catches up with me and grabs my arm. "Hear me out."

I look at where she's clutching my jacket. "I've heard enough from Jerome and Raphael."

She removes her hand. "You haven't heard this."

Already gripping the door handle, I say, "I don't want to."

"Someone is blackmailing him."

"Not my problem." I push the handle down.

"Francois Leclerc."

The name stills me. Leclerc is the man who tortured a prostitute with my brother, and I made both pay for by giving them a taste of their own medicine. I drop the handle. "I'm listening."

"Leclerc has information that Alexis doesn't want to come out. Alexis is paying him bribes."

I cross my arms. "You know this how?"

"I heard them talk."

Mm. Izabella is an eavesdropper. "What information?"

"I don't know."

I widen my stance. "Why tell me?"

"Apparently, it's something you'd like to know."

Tilting my head, I consider her. "What are you asking of me?"

"Nothing. I'm just dropping a lead in your lap."

"Why?"

"Someone needs to take care of Leclerc."

I laugh. "You think that someone is me."

Her eyes flash with annoyance. "Alexis can't. Leclerc has measures in place to let whatever he's holding over Alexis's head go public if anything happens to him. You have a reputation of extracting things from people like no one else can. You can make Leclerc give the evidence to you."

"I'm no longer part of the family as you very well know."

"It concerns you. It's a private matter."

She's done her homework and put her ducks in a row. "Why come to me? Why not your brother or father?"

She smiles. "You must know how ambitious my brother is. He's only waiting for the day Alexis goes under so he can take his place. As for my father, he's never been on my side."

In other words, Leonardo and Paolo will rather use the information to destroy Alexis and take the power for themselves, and I'm guessing Izabella doesn't want to fall back under their thumbs.

"All I ask," she says, "is that you share that information with me."

Ah. She wants power, something to hold over her husband's head. Well, well. Ms. Zanetti is a game player.

"I need insurance," she says. "For myself, you see."

I do see. In the family, it's always like a game of chess. The winner isn't necessarily the one with the biggest muscles. It's the one with the brains. Who am I to deny her a survival plan? In any event, my curiosity is piqued. I'd like to know what Leclerc is hiding from me.

"Fine," I say. "I'll look into it."

She holds out a hand. "Thank you."

I don't shake on it, because this isn't a deal. "No more surprise visits." If Alexis founds out she came to me, it won't end well for her.

She opens her mouth, but whatever she was going to say is cut short when the door opens and my wife walks in.

What is this? Surprise me day? Not that I'm not happy to see my wife. Her dark hair is windblown and her cheeks red from the cold. Prettier than a princess. After all the avoidance she's done lately, I can't help but feel a spark of excitement because she looked me up. Isn't that why I gave her space? To let her have some of her own power in our relationship.

Zoe looks between us, her lips parting in a silent oh. "I didn't know you had a visitor."

"I should go," Izabella says, snatching up her bag from my desk.

She walks past Zoe with a straight back, not saying goodbye or closing the door behind her.

Zoe stares at me. She doesn't say a word, but questions run through her eyes. Her expression is tainted with a hint of the pain she carried so openly on the day she caught Izabella and me making engagement arrangements.

"It was about Alexis," I say.

Her mouth tightens. Swiveling on her heel, she says, "I don't want to know."

I cut her off before she can walk out the door. "I didn't know she was coming."

She moves to the right, trying to scoot past me. "I don't care."

I close the door and lean a hand on the wood. "Is that why you're running, because you don't care?"

She taps a foot on the floor. "I'm not running."

"Leaving before you even got here doesn't count as running?"

She motions at the door. "You're blocking my way."

Lowering my head, I study her through my lashes. She's jealous. I'm not going to lie and say I don't appreciate the attention, but she has no reason to feel uncertain of me. "I left her for you, Zoe."

Her nostrils quiver. "I didn't ask you to."

"You didn't give me a choice."

Her blue eyes widen. "You don't want to throw that accusation at me."

I straighten. "It's not an accusation. It's a fact."

"What choice did you give *me*?" She takes a step toward me and stabs a finger against my chest when I don't reply. "Answer me."

I grab her hand. "I'm not saying I regret it."

"Don't you? Can you honestly tell me you don't miss the power and money? Can you honestly say you wouldn't rather be living in your old house as Izabella's husband and still get to fuck me?"

I think about that. I do miss the business. Not having the money certainly complicates matters and gives me sleepless nights. However, I do see it from Zoe's point of view. I understand why such an arrangement would hurt her. Between the business and Zoe, there isn't a choice.

"I'd do it again," I say.

She jerks her hand from my hold. "That's not what I asked. Do you miss it?"

"Of course I do." Looking at her unhappy face, I feel a ping in my heart, an uncomfortable pull where there used to be nothing. "But you're worth it."

She blinks fast. "Do you regret not marrying Izabella?"

Yes, but only because it put us in this godawful position of financial risk. If the business goes under, I'll lose everything. What will I have left to give Zoe? Yet I'd do it again in a wink just to have her. I'd do whatever it takes to keep her.

"Tell me, Maxime."

This isn't the kind of truth Zoe wants to hear. I can only answer it with a question. "Do you regret marrying me?"

The answer flashes across her face, raw and naked in her startling blue eyes before she manages to hide it behind a mask of indifference. We both have regrets. The difference is mine isn't big enough to want to go back in time and change my decisions.

"I don't regret marrying you," I say again for what it's worth. One day, I'll earn enough money so that not marrying Izabella won't be a regret. "She's nothing to me."

"It's not her." She looks away. "I have nothing against Izabella. It's what she reminds me of."

Of the pain I caused. Yes, I get that. "That's over now."

"Is it?" She faces me again. "From where I stand, I still don't have a choice."

Damn right. She's with *me*. I could teach her a lesson about choosing between happiness and misery, but I promised no more lessons. No more manipulation. All she has as a device for happiness is love. Why won't she use it? Why won't she fall back onto it like she did that day on the beach when she begged me to love her? Why won't she be the girl who believes in fairytales? That girl has the power to be happy amidst the grime like me. Me, all I have as a weapon is lust. I can corner her now and shove my hand into her panties. It'll only take a few seconds to make her wet. I know how to drive her to her knees and make her beg, but I promised myself I'd give her power. I told myself I'd wait until she came to me. Well, she's here now, pretty as a flower in the flesh, but if I open that door she'll still be running. I want her so much I have to clench my hands until my knuckles hurt to prevent myself from grabbing her and spreading her legs on my desk.

When she pushes me aside and reaches for the door handle, all I can grab are straws. "You didn't tell me why you came." *Don't go.*

Her tone is flat, her eyes dead. "I maxed out the credit card."

"You did?" She's never been a big spender. "What for?"

"I'm selling that dress, and you're not going to stop me."

I frown. "To who?" I don't want her to have to work to support us, but I never said she couldn't sell the dress.

"Doesn't matter. I came to tell you I made an investment in fabric." She opens the door. "Damian is sending a necklace to go with a dress I'm making. He said you can sell it after I've used it for publicity."

Ah, damn. I lose. My willpower caves. Locking my fingers around her wrist, I hold her back. "Zoe."

"What?"

Touch, me. "I'm happy you're designing again."

She pulls free. I step back, letting her go.

In the threshold, she turns. "I don't regret marrying you, Maxime. I regret how it happened." She takes a shaky breath. "I regret how everything happened."

Hanging her head, she leaves.

I regret how it happened. How everything happened.

It and *everything* are small words for the shitload of dirty water that has passed under our bridge.

CHAPTER 31

Zoe

The day Vera Day steps off the plane in Marseille, the evening gown is ready. I've worked day and night. The necklace Damian promised has arrived. I bought a second-hand mannequin from a thrift store for next to nothing. The mannequin is dressed in the gown and the necklace, standing in the soft light that falls from the circular window.

I step back to study my work. It's striking. The necklace hangs in a single platinum chain down the back, a black diamond caressing each vertebra of the naked spine. Magnificent. Definitely one of a kind but not me. I brush aside the odd twinge of betrayal that nips at my heart. This isn't about staying true to myself. This is about building a brand and making money.

Even if I can't afford it, champagne is chilling in an ice bucket on the counter and macaroons from a reputable baker are set out next to it. The intercom buzzes exactly on the hour. I push the button to open the street door and wait at the front door to welcome Ms. Day.

She flitters from the elevator like a leaf on an autumn day, breezing down the hallway with a bodyguard on her tail. After shaking hands, I invite them both in, but the man takes up a position by the door, politely declining my offer for refreshments.

"Please call me Vera," she says, stepping inside and looking around. "Wow, nice place." The minute her gaze finds the dress, she gasps. "Oh, my God." She waltzes over and slams a hand over her mouth as she circles the creation.

My chest warms. She likes it. There's a good chance she'll wear it to the festival.

"I want it," she says even before I've closed the door.

"What?" I ask, the click of the door sounding loud in my ears.

"I want it. It's perfect." She gives me a panicked look. "With the necklace, right? Please tell me the necklace is for sale."

I lay a hand over my heart. "Actually, yes."

She lifts one of the stones. "Black diamonds? I've never seen one."

"They're from my brother's mine in South Africa." I walk over. "His designer made it."

Her face brightens. "You do have to show me more. Earrings and rings."

"My husband is the importer. He'll be happy to send you a catalogue."

She clasps her hands together. "Excellent."

"Maybe we should try the dress first?"

"Oh, yes." She beams. "I'm so happy I found you."

"I'm glad you like it."

I show her to the bedroom for privacy to undress, but she shakes her head with a laugh.

"Darling, I'm used to undressing on set." Shimmying out of her dress, she says, "It's just a body."

She has a beautiful one for modeling clothes. I help her into the dress and with the zipper before fastening the necklace, and then scurry to bring the swivel mirror from the dressing room into the lounge. She turns left and right, studying her reflection with a critical expression. I give her a hand mirror to see the effect of the necklace hanging down her back. It looks as if the dress was made for her—because it was. It fits like a glove. I hold my breath until she finally tears her gaze away from the mirror to look at me.

"Zoe." She pauses dramatically. "I'm buying this."

My heart almost jumps out of my chest. "But you haven't even asked the price."

"I don't care how much it costs. I have to have it." She turns sideways and admires her reflection again. "I'll need shoes, but I have time to shop, and I know exactly the place in Marseille. I'll have to change the hairdo I had in mind." She takes up her hair, and then frowns. "I'll need a bag."

Having been prepared, I unwrap the tissue paper around the clutch I've covered with the same fabric. It's simple—thin and narrow. "Will this do?"

Her red lips stretch. "You're a genius." She takes the bag and poses with it. "I'm going to own that red carpet."

I have to agree. The dress looks good on her, but most of her presence comes from her attitude. She's enthusiastic and energetic. It's hard not to be swept along.

"Shall we try the day dress for the charity event?"

"Let's," she says with a wink, turning for me to undo the zipper.

The blue dress needs a minor adjustment. I'll have to take the hem down a fraction so that it still passes for decent. We agree on the length, and then I let her dress while I carefully package the dress and the necklace.

"Champagne?" I ask as she writes out a cheque.

"Oh, no, but thank you." She makes a face. "I count every calorie I ingest."

"The effort shows."

"Thank you." She smiles sweetly, giving me the cheque.

We agree on the date the dress will be ready, when she'll be back in Marseille before heading home. I hand her one of the business cards I've designed and ordered online with my logo, website, and contact details. After dumping the box with the clutch and necklace as well as the dress bag in the guard's arms, she leaves with an air kiss in a faint fog of perfume like a dispersing dream.

I stare at the cheque in my hand to be sure it's real, but the numbers are there, four zeros that will put Maxime and me out of our credit card debt and relieve most of our pressing financial concerns.

Elation hits me. I walk to the mannequin on a cloud. For a moment, I can only stare at the plastic model and the naked curves that used to be covered in the dress. I look down at my hands. They're red and my fingertips raw from sewing. My nails are short and torn. These hands aren't pretty, but they earned every cent I hold between my fingers. There's joy in that. There's immense satisfaction in being self-sufficient again, more than I've ever been.

Without Maxime, I doubt this would've been possible. Without him, I'd still be a seamstress in a sweatshop, battling to make a living. I wouldn't have been here in France, sewing designs that look like pictures from Madame Page's instruction manual. I wouldn't have been so unhappily in love that I'd pour my hours and days into a dress for someone else.

Sitting down on the sofa, I consider the whatifs. Damian would've offered me a job, and I wouldn't have taken it. It's too important for me to be independent. I would've moved someplace better, of that I'm sure, and maybe I would've become a seamstress in someone else's factory, in the workshop of a big, local design brand, but I doubt I would've had the courage to do what I've done. I would've been just me—romantic, frilly, and old-fashioned.

I failed at design school, but maybe the failure wasn't all a loss. It's only two dresses. There's a long road still before I can say I've made it, but it's a start, and a good one. For that, I'm grateful to Maxime, no matter how unorthodoxly it came about.

When Maxime comes home an hour later, I'm still floating in my bubble. Usually, I'd have dinner ready, not because I want to be a good housewife, but because I like to be useful. Tonight, I don't feel like cooking. We're not eating pasta. We can order Chinese takeout for a change.

Removing his jacket by the door, he eyes the mannequin. "Finished the dress?"

"Yes." I turn sideways on the sofa. "Thank you."

"For what?" he asks, hanging the jacket on the coat stand.

"For the design school."

He crosses the floor. "You already thanked me."

I did. It was the day he ushered me out of the house to meet with Izabella behind my back. I stiffen at the memory, but then brush it away. It's only fresh in my mind because I saw her at his office last week. It's not her fault. I know that. Knowing about me must've hurt her too. A part of me understands why Maxime regrets not marrying her. I understand he'd want things to be like they used to. I understand what he's given up for me. What I don't understand is why. He doesn't love me and never will. He said so himself. Why go to such lengths to steal me back? I never thought obsession could be so consuming.

In a way, the knowledge that he wouldn't have chosen differently if given the chance of who to marry again is soothing. It placates my bruised ego, however warped that may be, because if given a choice, I'd scurry for freedom. I'd scurry like a mouse, exchanging the cake it had been fed in a cage in the blink of an eye for breadcrumbs in the freedom of gutters.

He stops in front of me. "Aren't you going to show me?"

"I sold it."

"Already? You didn't tell me."

I look up at the man in the stylish clothes. He's wearing a white shirt and dark silk suit. The fitted waistcoat that's back in fashion accentuates his narrow waist and broad chest. Of course, he was always wearing it, long before it became fashionable again. Need stirs in my body. After all, it's been a long time, and I'm only human.

"I wasn't sure she'd take it," I say.

"Who wouldn't?" He unknots his tie, letting it hang loose around his neck. "It's a beautiful creation. Did you put the necklace in the safe?"

I fold one leg under my body. "She took the necklace with the dress." The valuation certificate was in the box. "She'd love to see more pieces. I said you'd mail her a brochure."

His eyes widen a fraction. "Did you sell it at full price? You know how much it's worth, right?"

I point at the cheque lying on the coffee table.

He looks at the amount. "Holy hell, Zoe. Who did you sell it to?"

"Vera Day."

"*The* Vera Day?"

I nod.

He frowns. "Why didn't you tell me?"

"I didn't know if she was going to take it. I didn't want to get my hopes up."

"Jesus." He glances over my shoulder. "Is that what the champagne is for? We're celebrating?"

I swipe my hair behind my ear. For once, I've left it loose in tamed curls down my back and not in a messy bun on my head. I'm wearing a decent dress and heels instead of the sweatpants and T-shirts I favor for working. "I got it for Ms. Day, but she's watching her calorie intake."

"Right." He shoves his hands into his pockets. "I suppose if clients are shopping for clothes with a five digit number price tag, champagne and artisanal macaroons are the least you can offer."

I smile. "That's pretty much how it works."

"It'll be a shame to waste it," he says, making his way over to the counter. He pours two glasses and carries one with a raspberry macaroon, my favorite flavor, back to me.

When he holds the patisserie to my lips, I don't open. I take it from his fingers. The corner of his mouth flicks up even as his eyes dull with disappointment. I've given him nothing since the night he made me come in his lap on this sofa, and he hasn't taken. He wants me, but I can't make myself take that first step. I don't want to give him even as little as that.

Shoving the whole pastry into my mouth, I chew very unladylike. Yet he watches like it's the most erotic sight he's seen. Self-conscious now, I wipe a crumb from my lips with the back of my hand.

"Here," he says, putting the glass in my hand. "You may want to swallow that down before you choke."

There's humor in his words. I ignore it as I take a sip, washing down the cake stuck in my throat. My body is nervous with awareness. If he touches me, I'll falter. When he turns away to study the mannequin, my stomach drops with disappointment. I may hate him, but my body still wants him, and I can only hate both of us more for that.

"She looks strange without the dress," he says, rounding the doll. "With it, she almost looked human."

"They make them very realistically these days."

"Not so much," he says.

"How do you mean?"

Bringing his hand around from behind, he cups her breast. "No nipple. They should make them with nipples so you can see the way it pushes against the fabric of a dress." He brushes a thumb over the tip where the imaginary nipple would be.

My breasts tighten in response. "Why would anyone want to see that?"

"To know how the dress is going to look without underwear." He looks at me as he drags his palm down her side to her hip. "Some dresses don't allow for a bra."

I swallow, imagining his hand on the dip of my waist and the rough feel of his calloused fingers on my skin. The knuckles of his hands are still bruised. He doesn't beat guys up any longer, but he still trains at a boxing club, and he likes to fight bare-fisted.

"You had a dress like that," he says, smoothing his palm over the dummy's stomach. "Several, actually."

I remember each one. I remember on which occasions I wore them. I remember which ones he took off and the ones I took off for him.

He traces the mannequin's stomach, dragging his nails over the plastic. "A navel would be nice too."

My stomach tightens with tingles.

"There's a certain way a dress falls over a woman's hips. There's a dip to her waist and a curve just here." He caresses the doll where her navel should be. "The small valley of a navel is very sensual under the right fabric."

My words dry up when he slides his hand down between the doll's legs. My body answers, my folds swelling in need.

"Here," he says, stroking the center of her legs with his thumb, "should be a line and a triangle of hair. The shape should be visible under bikini bottoms. It's a beautiful part of your female anatomy that's always turned me on."

My pulse jumps. My breath comes quicker.

Holding my eyes, he cups a breast and the juncture of her legs while brushing his lips over her shoulder and along the curve of her neck. "Then again, nothing beats the real thing, does it? I suppose it doesn't matter that they don't look like a woman. Maybe that's not the point."

"It's not," I say in a hoarse voice.

They're only supposed to showcase clothes, not to be an instrument of seduction at the bruised and skillful hands of a dangerous man.

His gray eyes are alight with knowledge. He knows me too well. He knows I'm a shivering mass of need.

When he says, "Come here," I don't argue. I get to my feet and meet him halfway. It's the only way I can do this, if we both take the first step.

He drags his gaze over my halter neck dress, pausing on my breasts. "Turn around."

I turn, facing the kitchen and holding my breath. He pulls the ends of the ribbons that fasten behind my neck. The bodice falls open, revealing my breasts. I gasp when he slips a hand around my body to test one's weight. His thumb mimics the action he practiced earlier on the doll, and my body bows at its reward. My nipple extends when he rolls it between two fingers. My breasts turn heavier when he squeezes.

The warmth of his palm disappears. The zipper on the side of the dress makes a lazy sound as he takes his time to pull it down. The fabric slips over my hips and pools around my feet. His hands are calloused on my hips just like I imagined. His lips are warm and soft as he drags them over my shoulder. I shiver when he kisses my neck. He smells of cloves and citrus, of skill and experience.

Gently, he turns me around. I stare up at the unforgiving lines of his face as he takes off the waistcoat and unbuttons his shirt. He holds my gaze as he unbuckles his belt. When he sits down in the baroque armchair, I follow and stop between his spread legs. He unzips his pants and takes out his cock, all the while watching my face. He only breaks our eye contact when I step out of my underwear. Fixing his gaze on my naked body, he strokes himself twice.

"Get on my lap," he says.

The command is dominant and easy to obey. He's taught me well to follow his orders. I straddle him without bothering to take off my shoes. I rest one palm on the unscarred part of his chest and the other on the damaged part that's hidden underneath the shirt.

He clamps his hands around my middle and lifts me over his erection. It's so easy, this dance. He knows what he's doing. He's taking without making excuses, making it easy for me to follow. There's no guilt or questions, no wondering why we're doing what we're doing. We're simply doing. I sigh as the head of his cock parts my folds. He lowers me slowly, taking care of my comfort. I don't mind it rough, and he knows, but today he wants to give me tender. I close my eyes and lean my head on his shoulder. His lips are warm on my neck. He kisses a path to my jaw, each kiss marking another inch that he slides deeper.

When he's fully sheathed, he grabs my face in one hand and lifts my chin to meet my lips. His hold is rough, but the kiss is soft. I moan when he rolls his hips at the same time as he nips my bottom lip. My hands explore his body under his open shirt, tracing the flat disks of his nipples and the rough edges of his scars. It's a familiar landscape, the only one I know. Maybe the only one I'll ever know. The thought both pleases and scares me. Is a lifetime of only sex enough?

The thought fizzles out when he lifts me a little and moves his hips. It's been so long since he touched me or that I touched myself in the shower, my orgasm builds quickly. I lean back to take him deeper. Always reading my body, he cups my breasts and gives me the pace I need. I'm coming before he's even close to his release. It's instantaneous and gratifying. My skin is sensitive. I gasp when he presses a thumb on my clit and massages in a circle. It makes me want to come again.

He leans back and lets me take over, allowing me to set the rhythm. His jaw bunches when I slide up and down over his length. I'm ruining his pants, getting my arousal all over the dark silk, but he doesn't seem to mind. He abandons my clit when I move faster, digging his fingers into my globes for purchase.

"I'm close," I say, grabbing his shoulders for support.

"Come." He grits his teeth. "Come for me one more time, Zoe."

He's waiting for me to finish before he comes. I can't deny that I'm always turned on when he makes me come draped over his lap, but I prefer it like this, when we're coming together.

So, I do. I come for him. For us. He follows a second later, filling me up with a thrust of his hips. We're both spent in the aftermath, not so much from the physical effort than the emotional toll. Sex with Maxime is always intense on a deeper level. He demands as much as he gives, and if I didn't put a chain and lock on my heart, he'd take that with my release.

"Cold?" he asks, rubbing a hand over my back.

I shiver.

Without pulling out, he removes his shirt and holds it open so I can fit my arms. Then he buttons it up and pulls me against his chest.

We sit like that with him stroking my hair until shadows creep over the floor.

"I'm proud of you," he says after a long while.

I sit back to look at his face. "Do you mean that?"

He tucks a strand of hair behind my ear. "Why wouldn't I be?"

"You said you didn't want me to work."

He smiles. "I don't want you to do something you hate to put the food on our table because my business is suffering. I have nothing against you making money by doing what you love."

I'm not going to ask for his permission to do what I believe is right, but I don't say so. We have little enough peace as it is.

"What are your plans?" he asks.

"Eventually, I'd like to have a small boutique." I add, "If my designs keep on selling."

"I know just the place."

"You do?"

He kisses my nose. "I'll show you tomorrow."

"Do you have time?"

"For you? Always."

I lean my head back on his shoulder. If only we could stay like this. If only we could pretend our love was naked and raw and real, and not a plastic mannequin in an elegant dress.

CHAPTER 32

Maxime

Francois Leclerc is hiding like a cockroach in the drainpipes. It's not as easy to find him as I hoped. I'm certain he's not in Marseille. He won't risk it in the hub of Alexis's organization. Too many men are on the lookout in the city. My bet is on Paris, somewhere where he can lie low until he has enough bribe money to buy a nice, big hacienda in South America.

Even if I'm no longer part of the mob and cut off from my family, many men still respect me. Trust doesn't vanish overnight. It only takes one call to my old bookkeeper to find out Alexis is making transfers to an offshore account. Leclerc isn't a total idiot, after all. I put out word with a few men who owe me favors to keep an eye out for any offshore property purchases or suspicious business activities, and then I contact a banker in the offshore department who laundered money for me before. Now it's only a question of waiting.

I pick Zoe up after lunch and take her to visit the boutique in the old center. It's a small two-story level shop in a prominent trading street with a beautiful façade. The upstairs room can be converted into a working space while downstairs can be made into a showroom. There's a storage room at the back and a kitchen and toilet upstairs. The rent for the prime spot is expensive, but I know the owner, and he's willing to cut me a deal.

I watch Zoe carefully as she pokes her head around doorframes and into empty cupboards. "What do you think?" I ask when I can't keep it in any longer.

She knocks on a wall as if to test its sturdiness. Adorable. "It's stunning."

"The location is right."

"Couldn't be better," she says, folding her hands behind her back.

I lean a shoulder against the wall. "But?"

"It's too soon."

"It's never too soon."

"What if it doesn't work out?"

"We don't have to sign a contract for a year's lease. We can give thirty days notice."

She narrows her pretty eyes. "How did you manage that?"

"The owner owes me."

She doesn't quite smile, but it's close enough. "Of course he does." She rests her chin on her shoulder, looks through the window for a while, and then asks, "Why are you doing this, Maxime?"

Straightening, I walk to her. "I want you to be happy."

She stares at my face. "Why?"

"Don't you want me to be happy?"

I cup her hips to draw her to me, but she twists out of my hold and escapes to the far end of the room, pretending to study the mosaic floor tiles.

"Zoe?" I ask with a nerve twitching under my eye. I don't like it when she defies our connection. No matter what she wants to believe, we have something. A spark.

She shrugs. "I guess."

"You guess?"

"Yes," she says with a sigh. "I want you to be happy."

"Then what's the problem?"

She faces me. "I don't know if I can trust you."

Haven't I proven myself by now? "What more do you want me to do to?"

She doesn't answer.

"Have I manipulated you since our wedding?" I ask.

"Maybe a little yesterday."

When I seduced her with the mannequin. I disagree. That kind of seduction wasn't manipulation. I only reminded her she wanted me. "We both wanted it."

Her cheeks turn pink.

"Have I lied to you since my promise?" I ask.

From the way she averts her eyes and studies her shoes, I'm guessing this is the heart of the problem.

"Have I lied to you, Zoe?"

She looks up. "I don't know." Her voice is pained. "Have you?"

My answer sounds harsher than what I intended. "No."

"That's the issue." She spreads her hands, holding up her palms. "You've lied to me so many times I don't know how to believe you."

The statement stabs me in the chest. I've never been bothered about someone else's opinion, especially not an opinion of me, but this floors me. I don't like it.

"I haven't lied," I say.

"Trust takes time. It doesn't happen overnight."

Fine. I've got time. I have a lifetime of it. I just have to be patient, like with sniffing out Leclerc, but for some reason I want to fix this *now*.

"Zoe, please." I take a step toward her. "Give me the benefit of the doubt."

"I'm sorry." She shakes her head. "You took too much from me. There have been too many betrayals. The lie about hurting Damian, the design school, Sylvie, and Izabella—"

I hold up a hand. "I know what I did."

"Then you must understand how I feel."

The surprising thing is that for once I do. For once in my emotionless life, I get why my actions hurt her. I don't like it, but I can't take it back. For once, I can't have it my way. I don't have a choice but to wait, hoping in time she'll give me the trust I once took for granted and want back at all costs.

"Fine," I say, the word weighing heavily on me. "I can wait."

She crosses the floor and stops short of me. "Don't hold your breath." Squeezing past me, she mumbles, "I'm certainly not."

Fuck me. That hurts, not that I don't deserve it. I've long since made peace with the fear, but the hurt is new, and it's a shock as much as torture. My shrink said I could have a rewarding relationship if I could see matters from my partner's perspective and build trust.

If this is anything to go by, it looks as if we're on our way to a rewarding relationship.

CHAPTER 33

Zoe

The Cannes festival brings in a lot of publicity, not only for me, but also for Damian's diamonds. Since Maxime is the supplier for Europe, he profits from the advertising too.

Within a week, I have five orders for custom-designed gowns. I ask for deposits and use the money to fit out the boutique and hire a seamstress. Maxime's gift to me is a signboard with my logo that goes above the door. He moves my sewing machine, boxes of fabric, and other equipment from the apartment to the new premises.

With the big job of organizing photo shoots, having a glossy jewelry brochure designed, translating it into various European languages, overseeing the printing, and having the website updated, Maxime has his hands as full as I do with the opening the boutique. We're too exhausted for more than a celebration at home in the Jacuzzi with a good bottle of wine.

The weather has turned, and the days are getting warmer, making it possible for us to grill meat on the barbecue outside, which Maxime does more frequently since I work longer hours and arrive home later than him. The business is grueling. My seamstress is good at her job, but she needs a strong hand. If I don't double-check her work, she'll let an uneven hem or a sloppily sewed button go through. Quality is important. It's not in my nature, but I have to be strict.

I call Vera Day to thank her for the publicity, and she places another order. Before I know it, I'm in over my head and need more staff. While Maxime's business is still battling because of the pressure Alexis puts on the buyers, mine is thriving. When the workspace becomes too cramped, I expand to a workshop in the industrial area and transform the upstairs floor of the boutique into a lounge and fitting room for clients who wander in from the street.

An article appears in Le Figaro. The journalist has tracked down Madame Page who takes credit for her influence in my designs. The journalist quotes her saying, "My school delivers the best of the best." When asked about my failure at the fashion show, Madame Page says I was under a lot of stress and my vision clouded, but that she's glad I followed her advice and didn't throw in the towel.

Overnight, I become the success story born from failure, every other potential failure's hope. The media makes me out to be some kind of Cinderella, and I'm lucky to be their new favorite pet. Of course it's nothing other than selling newspapers through sensationalism. Who doesn't like a rags-to-riches story? I tell the truth in an interview, that I simply had a lucky break with Ms. Vera Day, giving credit where it's due. The reporter twists it in such a way that the article makes me appear humble, which adds to my public image of the poor girl gone rich and famous.

There's speculation about my husband, but I try to keep Maxime out of the media frenzy as much as I can. Of course everyone knows about his involvement and break from the mafia. The stories romanticize our marriage. On paper, it's a love story like no other. Maxime becomes the sex idol of many a young, naïve girl, and I turn into the breadwinner as his business continues its downward spiral. The fact that I'm solely responsible for covering our bills and the investments in both of our businesses makes me work extra hard. Despite the taxing hours, I'm enjoying the challenge. It's the purpose and passion I need in my life to make up for what I don't have—the love story the media so ironically idolizes. The harder I work, the less time I have for whatifs. For where I find myself in life, it's much safer like this.

On a hot Friday in summer, my cellphone lights up on my desk. One glance at the number, and I shove all the papers aside.

"Damian?" I say even before I have the phone pressed against my ear.

He sounds tired. "It's a beautiful girl, Zee."

"Oh, my God." I jump up. "How's Lina? How's the baby?"

"Everything went fine. It was a long labor, but Lina didn't want an epidural. She was so brave."

"Are you sending me a baby photo?" I ask, rounding the desk.

"I've just bathed her." His voice fills with awe. "Fuck. She's so small. So perfect, Zee."

"Oh, Damian. Congratulations. I'm so happy for all four of you. When can I speak to Lina?"

"She's sleeping now, but you can call tonight."

"How's Josh with his sister?"

"It's new. I think he feels insecure about sharing us, but he'll come round."

"I'm sure he will. Have you chosen a name yet?"

"Josephine."

"That's beautiful. At what time was she born? How much does she weigh?"

"Just after three. She's a good three and a half kilos. The doctor says Lina can go home if Josie continues to gain weight over the next three days."

Crying sounds in the background.

My heart clenches. "Is that her?"

"Bawls like you can't believe when Lina doesn't feed her fast enough," he says with pride. "I better take her to her mom. I'll speak to you later."

"Take care. Take care of both of them."

"I will."

I stare at the phone when he ends the call. A moment later, a photo drops on my screen of my brother holding a baby in his arms. She's wearing white pajamas with pink bunnies and a pink beanie. Her mouth is open in a wail and her little face bright red with the hungry frustration Damian described. She's so small her head fits in Damian's palm. The expression on his face as he looks at his daughter makes my heart melt into a puddle. A yearning burns deep inside me. A longing stirs. I've always wanted to have children. Two. I imagined giving them a happier home than the one I grew up in. I even know the names I would've given them. What does it feel like to hold that little bundle in your arms?

A knock sounds on the door. I tear my gaze away from my phone. Maxime stands on the threshold with a vase of lilies.

"These are from Damian," he says. "The florist delivered them just as I arrived."

I drop my arm to my side. "What are you doing here?" It's not that I don't want to share the happy news with him. I only need a moment to compose myself. If I tell him now, he'll see the longing in my eyes.

He walks over and leaves the flowers on my desk. "It's Friday."

I inhale their sweet fragrance. It's the third bouquet Damian has sent since the opening of the boutique. Taking the card, I read the message.

Congratulations. I'm proud of you.

It goes both ways.

"And?" I ask, leaving the card on my desk.

"I thought we could go to Paris for the weekend."

"Paris? I'm working tomorrow."

"You're the boss." He perches on the corner of my desk. "You can take off one day."

"Why Paris?" Except for one, blissful weekend in Corsica when I was stupid enough to believe we were happy, we've never travelled. Venice doesn't count. I've scrapped that from my memory. Buried it deep down.

His lips tilt, but it's not a smile. "Because."

I watch him closely, my heart squeezing as I wait for the lie.

"I have to go for business," he says.

I exhale a long, silent breath. I'm always on my guard, walking a tightrope between mistrust and faith, and it's exhausting. It's exhausting not to trust your spouse. It's exhausting to be terrified of the day he'll betray me again.

"Zoe," he says in chastising tone. "I said I wouldn't lie. When will you believe me?"

The day he no longer gives me reason to doubt. Can a bird change feathers?

"I've made mistakes," he says. "Don't let that be our future."

I don't want to talk about our future. "What does this so-called business entail?" He has no diamond auctions planned until the end of summer.

"It's old business."

"Mafia business?" I exclaim softly.

"Just something I need to take care of."

"Two birds with one stone, huh?"

He cups my cheek. "We haven't seen much of each other lately."

It's true, but I refuse to feel guilty about it. Turning my face away from his touch, I harden my heart. "I have a business to run."

He follows me to the door. "The business won't go under in one day."

I charge through the frame into the workshop. "It may."

The girls look up. Their gazes are fixed on my husband with dreamy expressions. They shouldn't believe everything they read in magazines.

"Janice." I flick my fingers in front of my newest employee's face. "Pull out that seam and stitch it again. Make sure it's straight next time."

She snaps to attention. "Yes, ma'am."

"Veronica, that pocket is askew. Do it over."

I evaluate their work with a practiced glance as I walk through the workshop. I never forgot Thérèse's words about being a mediocre designer who pays better ones peanuts to do the work and taking all the credit. That's why I'm extra aware of each of my employee's work quality. My expectations are high, but I don't expect anything of them I can't do myself. My salaries are above the market average. If I spot potential, I move them up in the line of work. For the moment, I still take care of the designs. If anyone shows enough talent, I won't hesitate to promote that person to a position of designer. I don't make them sign exclusivity clauses in their contracts. If they want to go independent, I won't stand in their way. If I believe in their work, I'll even invest in their business.

"You haven't answered me," Maxime says above the whir of the machines.

I stop, making him bump into my back. Iona, who's cutting a pattern, giggles. I turn on him with a huff. Here, between the smell of fabric and the soothing hum of stitching, I feel at peace. I'm safe. Having him here doesn't fit. It's like dropping a stone into a quiet pond.

"Maxime."

I open my mouth to tell him no, but he takes my phone from my hand and swipes a finger across the screen. I'm aware of the faces staring at us as he looks at the photo of Damian and my niece.

"When were you going to tell me?" he asks, not looking up from the screen.

I swallow. "Her name is Josephine."

When he meets my gaze, his eyes aren't filled with the anger I expected. They're filled with compassion. "It'll come. We'll get our turn."

My cheeks turn hot. It's not the subject. It's the lie. I never told him I went for another birth control shot. I justified the omission, telling myself his honesty wasn't going to last. Sooner or later, he'll lie again, but if I asked him for honesty, I owe him the same. Whether he loves me or not, we're in this for life. He's not letting me go. The least we owe each other is the truth.

"Not here," I say, taking back my phone. The meeting room is the closest. I go inside and close the door when he's followed.

"How are Lina and the baby doing?" he asks.

"They're doing well. Damian called just before you arrived."

He searches my face, "Yet you didn't tell me."

I look at my hands. "The moment wasn't right."

"I can see it in your eyes, Zoe."

"What?" I glance at him.

"You want a baby."

"Maxime." I drag a hand over my forehead and walk to the window. "We're not going to have a baby."

The silence is like a knife in my back. I endure it for as long as I can, but when I can no longer take the tension, I turn to face him.

The lines of his face are hard with anger. "What else aren't you telling me?"

The words gush from my mouth. "I had a birth control shot." There. I said it. My chest deflates.

His gray eyes turn glacial. "Without discussing it with me?"

I clench my fingers around my phone. "There's nothing to discuss. We're *not* bringing a child into this twisted marriage. It's not *real*."

His nostrils flare. When he takes a step toward me, I take one back.

"This isn't real," he says through clenched teeth, repeating my angry words in a flat tone. "Tell me something, Zoe. When I come inside you, is it not real?"

"You know what I mean." I back up another step. "Sex alone isn't enough."

I jerk when he folds a hand around my neck, but the touch is excruciatingly gentle.

"This." He strokes a thumb over my pulsing jugular vein. "Is it real?"

His scent wraps around me, familiar and cold like a winter's day. If I reach out, his chest will be warm under his shirt. I'll feel the beat of his heart and hear the intake of his breath when I touch him. If I slide my hand lower, he'll grow hard. Yes, it's real, but only in a carnal way.

"Maybe for you it's not real," he says, letting me go.

I place a palm on my neck over the skin he's left cold. I don't call him back when he walks to the door. The vibration that shakes the frame when he slams it is very real. I feel it all the way to my heart. At least it's not completely frozen yet.

CHAPTER 34

Maxime

Paris has changed. It's dirtier.

Lonelier.

The breeze blows a fast food wrapper down the street. A smell of weed wafts from the sex shop. Following the address one of my connections has given me, I weave my way through the cobblestone streets of the Pigalle district.

I order a croissant with my espresso and take a chair at a street table by the brasserie facing the two-star hotel where Leclerc is renting a room, and then I wait.

It doesn't take long for him to stumble outside, squinting at the early morning sun. His face is unshaven, and he's wearing a creased T-shirt and chinos. He drags both hands through his disheveled hair and crosses the street.

I count the seconds. It takes him exactly five before he spots me. He freezes. His gaze darts right, then left. He chooses left, sprinting downhill. I finish my espresso, leave a bill, and wipe my mouth on the napkin before getting up. At the end of the street, he looks over his shoulder before ducking into an alley.

I'm in good shape. It takes me a short time to run him down. He swings his elbows, putting effort into the escape, but before he's made it to the busy intersection, I'm on him.

Grabbing him by the collar, I slam him against the wall.

He lets out a grunt followed by a frightened sound. "What do you want?"

I look around. We're alone in the alley. "You know what I want."

"Who told you?" he stammers with his cheek pressed flat against the wall.

I turn my nose away from the stench of his oily hair. "What does it matter?"

He lifts his hands. "I've got something you'd want."

"Is that so?" I push his arm up enough to make him grunt again.

"I swear." He swallows. "I swear, Mr. Belshaw. Please."

I apply more pressure. "You're going to give it to me."

He wails. "Yes."

"Tell me what it is."

"Fuck, you're hurting me."

He knows exactly how much I can make him hurt. A bit more force, and I'll dislocate his shoulder. "What is it, Leclerc?"

"Stop!" He pants through an open mouth. "Stop. Please."

"I'm not asking again."

"Evidence," he says when I let up, trying to catch his breath.

"What evidence?"

"Evidence."

The foul smell sweating from his pores tells me he's not taking care of himself. Leclerc is a dirty man. A broken man. They're the most dangerous, because they've got nothing to lose.

I said I wasn't going to ask again. I bend back his thumb, driving him to his knees.

He howls. "Stop! I'll tell you."

I keep him on his knees facing the wall. "Talk."

"I know who—" He gulps, swallowing air. "I know who started the fire."

I go still. Crackling sounds in my ear, the sound of flames melting paint and plaster. I smell it, the smoke. It's thick in my lungs. It burns my eyes. My rage is white-hot. It smolders quietly like coals, a spark waiting to catch and leap.

My voice belongs to someone else. I know, but I still ask, "What fire?"

"*The* fire." He twists his neck to look at me. "The fire in the warehouse."

Ignoring the dirtiness of his hair, I grip the strands and yank his face to the wall. "Don't fucking look at me." I'm too frightened he'll see the anguish I suffered in those moments. That's private.

"I'm sorry!"

Heat devours my skin. "Who?"

"Alexis."

A rush of ice douses the burn. "What did you say?"

"I have it on video. I filmed it."

Blood gushes in my ears, drowning the static crackling. "You were there?"

"I didn't want to. I swear I didn't. I didn't do anything. Alexis told me to empty the can of petrol. He lit the match."

All the evidence, every scrap of DNA, burned away. I walked through that fire. I survived it. I paid the price of living through the ordeal. I searched for the guilty person. I let it fester like the pus that leaked from my charred flesh. Somewhere between fighting for my life and fighting the pain, I lay my hunger for vengeance down. Living took every ounce of energy I had left. I told myself it was enough, that I was lucky to be alive.

Leclerc just struck that match he claims he never touched, and I'm a fire raging out of control.

I think fast. Leclerc's room may be booby-trapped. He may have cameras in place. If I were in his shoes, I certainly would've taken precautions. Plus, I don't know the people in the shithole where he stays. I can't afford witnesses.

"You're going to bring it to me," I say, jerking back his head. "Hôtel du Cadran. Room 118." I know the owner. I can get cleanup in and out unnoticed. "It's not you I want," I lie. "It's Alexis."

"It's going to cost you," he says in a pathetic attempt of bravery.

I let him go, giving him the illusion. "Name your price."

He scurries to his feet. "Twenty thousand."

"You've gotten enough out of Alexis already."

He puts distance between us. "Ten."

I grin. "Deal." I don't even have one thousand in my name, but he doesn't need to know I have no intention of paying him.

"What then?"

Then I kill Alexis. "Then nothing."

He wipes his nose with his hand. "What about your brother?"

I narrow my eyes. "What do you think?"

His beady eyes hop around in their sockets as he considers the outcome of the situation. He's safer with Alexis dead. Plus, another ten grand before he skips the country can't hurt. He knows he's milked this cow dry. He nods.

"One hour," I say. "If you don't show, I'll burn you alive."

Fear widens his eyes. His fat chin quivers.

I hold out a hand. "Give me your phone."

He delves a hand into his pocket and pulls out his phone.

I snatch it from his palm. "If I don't find you, Alexis will, so you better show up."

Pocketing his phone, I turn and walk in the direction of the Moulin Rouge.

"What about the money?" he calls after me. "I want cash."

I don't look back.

He'll show up.

The consequences if he doesn't are much too terrifying for him not to.

CHAPTER 35

Zoe

I work extra late. When I come home, Maxime is gone. He left a plate of grilled calamari and Camargue rice in the oven for me. A note with the name and room number of his hotel in Paris lies on the counter in case I need him.

After kicking off my shoes, I pour a glass of wine. I can't shake my guilt for how Maxime left. I've been a bitch, but doesn't he deserve it?

I owe him nothing.

He's trying, a voice says in my mind.

For how long? How long before he shows his true colors again?

Shaking the thought, I call Lina. She sounds so happy. Damian is staying with her and Josie in the room while their nanny is taking care of Josh at home. I'm glad Damian is an attentive husband and daddy. The bonding with the new baby is important. I've read up about it. We have a quick chat before a nurse interrupts to check on Lina. I ask for more photos of Josie and promise to call back on Sunday. If it was up to me, I'd call every day, but I have to give them some space to adapt to the change in their lives.

I throw the phone on the table and look around the empty space. It's quiet. I've grown used to having Maxime here when I come home. When we're not having sex, he keeps his distance, but his presence has become a quiet given. He'd either be working on his laptop or tidying the kitchen after cooking. If he's not reading, he's always fiddling around, replacing light bulbs or oiling door hinges. The apartment feels lonely without him.

Settling on the sofa, I open my laptop and email a few design drafts and quotes. I get rid of the junk mail in my inbox and upload new social media content. My fingers hover over the search field in my browser. After a short hesitation, I type in the TGV website. A page with travel information comes up. Out of curiosity, I click on the link for Paris. A train leaves at 5 am, arriving in Paris three hours and fifty-three minutes later. I click on the price. The last-minute tickets are selling at a discount. Biting my lip, I hold my finger over the button.

What am I doing? I don't know if it's speaking to Lina and feeling like there's something fundamental missing from my life, the regret of letting Maxime leave in the way I did, or the big glass of wine I finished, but in an impulsive moment, I sweep my finger over the button. My heart starts thrumming with the risk I'm taking when a popup window requests my credit card details.

Without thinking about it more, I get my card and type in the details. Six seconds later, I'm booked on the early morning train to Paris.

I eat, clean the apartment, pack a bag, have a shower, and hardly sleep. I'm up before my alarm, dressing in a red fitted dress with a matching jacket and black heels. I pin my hair up and apply makeup before studying my reflection in the mirror. I look older. I look like someone who's lived ten years in one. Dismissing my image, I grab my bag, lock up, and drive to the station.

On my way to Paris, I send a text message to Veronica telling her I won't be in and instructing her to keep up the fort. I ask Janice, who lives closer to the boutique, to put a sign in the window saying we're exceptionally closed today. I get some work done, and by the time the train pulls up in Paris, I'm nervous. I should warn Maxime of my arrival, but I still don't know what I'm doing or why I'm doing this. I tell myself I want to surprise him, but the truth is I'm keeping my options open in case I want to back out.

I get a taxi and give the driver the address. Less than thirty minutes later, we stop at the hotel. I confirm at the front desk that Maxime is in. Since he booked a double room, there's no need to upgrade. After proving my identity, I convince the concierge to give me a card for the room so I can surprise my husband.

With my heart beating a strange, crazy rhythm, I take the elevator. When I stop in front of Maxime's door, my nerves almost fail me. I consider turning around and going back where I came from, but when I think of taking the train home after I've already come this far, I take a deep breath and swipe the card.

A voice I don't recognize filters from inside when I open the door. I pause. Maxime's louder voice overrides the first, and then they speak simultaneously. Both men stop talking when the door shuts with a click.

A man appears from around the wall separating the bedroom from the entrance.

My throat goes dry.

It's the man I saw at Alexis's apartment on the night they tortured the woman. He smells like sweat and cabbage, clutching a shoebox under his arm.

He bares his teeth in a gesture that resembles a smile. "Your wife's here."

A curse sounds.

Maxime rounds the corner with a glass of whiskey in his hand. His gray eyes are expressionless, his voice flat. "What are you doing here?"

I look between the men. "I thought I'd surprise you."

"Bad surprise," the man says. "At least for you, Mr. Belshaw."

I drop my bag on the floor, my body going rigid in an involuntary flight response. "What's going on, Maxime? What is he doing here?"

"Go downstairs," Maxime says.

The man steps closer to me. "I brought something for your husband, but I think you'll appreciate it more."

I glance at the box, my scalp prickling with premonition. "What is it?"

Unfazed, Maxime takes a sip of his drink. "That wasn't part of the deal."

Maxime is making a deal with a torturer? After what this man did to that woman?

"The deal has just changed." The man turns to me with a feverish light in his eyes. "Your letters."

Coldness travels over my body. "What letters?"

He tips his head in Maxime's direction. "The ones he never mailed."

"She knows," Maxime says with a lazy drawl. "And the letters are at home in my safe."

"I took them out of the envelopes and put blank paper inside," he says. "I stole them from your study when Alexis moved in, before you had time to move everything out."

Maxime regards him with a twisted smile. "You're bluffing."

Fishing a piece of paper from his jacket pocket, he holds it out at me. "See for yourself."

I take the folded paper with a trembling hand, already recognizing the yellow color and ink seeping through the thin sheet before I've unfolded it. It's the first letter I wrote to Damian.

I look at the man. "Why would you steal them?"

"To have something to hold over my head," Maxime says, swirling the drink in his glass.

If he thought I didn't know Maxime never mailed the letters, it would've been something to bribe Maxime with, but what is his motivation for giving it to me? Does he know what it means? Those letters were written in a code language that told Damian I'd been taken and kept against my will. It will give me immense power over Maxime, because if those letters fall into Damian's hands, they'll start a war.

Damian won't let it go, not what Maxime did. If my brother knows the truth, he'll ruin Maxime and then kill him.

My hands shake more as the realization settles. That box could be my ticket to freedom. I could use it to blackmail Maxime into letting me go.

Maxime studies me with a cold gaze, his clever eyes telling me he understands my reasoning.

"I was going to sell them back to him, but they belong to you." The man holds the box out to me. "Take it."

"Why?" I ask.

"I've done some things…" He shoves the box at me. "Just take it."

I stare at the box. I could take it to destroy Maxime and save myself, but a war between Damian and Maxime could go either way. Maxime could still hurt the people Damian loves. It's not a risk I'm willing to take. Those letters aren't safe in anyone else's hands. I have to get them back and destroy them. Damian must never see them.

I reach out.

"Don't take them, Zoe," Maxime says in an even voice.

I lift my gaze to my husband. Is he kidding?

"He's afraid you'll use them against him," the man says. "You can take your letters and walk out of that door right now."

Maxime doesn't reply. He only stares at me with that stoic face that demands blind obedience. I'm standing at the edge of a cliff, and he's telling me to look down. He's telling me to trust him to bid on me, that a million euros won't be too much. Can I give him my trust? Logic tells me no, but my heart says something different. Once again, I'm at the precipice of a test, and I don't want to fail.

I retract my hand.

The man purses his lips. "I didn't take you for stupid." He offers the box to Maxime. "Have it your way. Twenty grand. That's my last offer."

Maxime leaves the glass on the desk. "We're done here."

The man snarls, shaking the box in Maxime's direction. "Take the fucking box."

"You know where the door is," Maxime says.

With a curse, he dumps the box on the bed and charges for the door. Caught off-guard, I step aside as he storms past me and slams the door.

I move to the bed. "What's wrong with—"

"Don't touch it."

I stop in my tracks. Sweat breaks out over my body. "Poison?"

Maxime rounds the bed. "Explosives."

"Oh, my God. Are you sure?"

"No, but there's one way to find out."

When he picks up the box, I utter a shriek. "Maxime, no!"

He walks to the open window, peers down, and throws out the box.

A loud explosion shatters the silence.

I run to the window. Bits of paper drift in a billow of dust in the air. There's a big hole in the lawn next to the pool. Through the dusty cloud, it looks like a sepia picture of paper snowflakes. People storm out onto the terrace. A hotel staff member shouts loud instructions for everyone to stay back.

I grip the windowsill. "If I'd opened the box—"

He rests his hand next to mine, our pinkies overlapping. "I wouldn't have let you."

I'm shaking with cold, even though it's warm. "That man. What about that man?"

He cups my cheek and kisses me. "They'll lock down the hotel. We have to go."

"Maxime," I cry out when he lets me go to grab his bag from a chair.

Picking mine up from the floor, he opens the door and peers around the frame. "Come. Quickly."

I rush out ahead of him. Instead of going toward the elevator, he ushers me to the fire escape. We run down the two flights of stairs and exit into the parking lot. He unlocks his car and dumps our bags in the trunk while I fit my safety belt, and then he tears out of the parking space.

My heart sinks when we approach the boom. It's down. Maxime

has a shady history. He's only cleaned up his act recently. The police are always looking for a reason to arrest him, especially now that he's no longer under the mafia's protection. If they get their hands on him, they'll use any means necessary, including torture, to make him give up information about his criminal family.

When the guard manning the pay booth recognizes Maxime, he salutes and lifts the boom. I sag in my seat, my body running hot and cold with shock and relief. We pull into the traffic, smoothly slipping into the flow.

"Your car," I say. "They have cameras in the parking garage."

"I know the hotel owner." His brow is furrowed in concentration as he focuses on the road. "He'll erase the tapes."

The traffic is heavy. I don't speak again until we're on a quieter road. "What happened back there?"

He glances at me. "The day Izabella came to my office she tipped me off about Leclerc. He was blackmailing Alexis."

"With what?"

His jaw bunches. "It was Alexis who started the fire."

I gape at him. "You mean…?"

"Yes." He takes a sharp turn, making my body press against the door.

"Maxime."

"I only found out this morning."

"Is that what he was doing in your hotel room?"

"I threatened him so he'd give me the evidence. I guess he thought he'd rather blow me up."

I still can't believe it. "How did you know?"

"I didn't. It was a guess. I know how these people operate. I know how they think."

"He would've let me open the box."

"Revenge for how I punished him."

I grip the door handle when he takes another turn. "What did you do to him?"

He clenches the wheel. "Doesn't matter."

The buildings change to more modern ones. "What now?"

"I'm going to deal with them."

My stomach tightens. "Maxime."

"I can't let this go, Zoe."

"The police—"

He takes the exit onto the highway. "You know I can't go to the police." He glances at me again. "Are you all right?"

I shake my head.

He cups my hand. "You shouldn't have been there."

"I should've told you I was coming."

"No." Smiling, he puts my hand on his thigh to change gears. "I appreciate the gesture. Just don't surprise me again. I'm not good with those."

The hard muscles of his thigh bunch under my palm when he steps on the clutch. "What if he comes after you?"

"That's why I have to go after him first."

A sickening thought hits me. "You weren't going to let him leave your room alive, were you?" I remove my hand from his leg. "Is that why he came armed with that box? He knew he needed some kind of weapon? If I hadn't been there—"

"You think too much."

I'm not going to get anything out of him. Why do I even try? I look at the fields on the side of the road. "Where are we going?"

"Home." When I say nothing, he continues, "I'll make up for Paris."

"I don't care about Paris." I care about our safety and our lives.

"What happened this morning isn't going to happen again."

"Please." I close my eyes and lay back my head. "Don't make promises."

"Leclerc caught me off guard. I didn't think he had it in him."

"You don't have to make excuses. You saved my life."

"Because you obeyed me." The pause that follows is strained. "Zoe, if you ever put yourself in danger again, I don't know what I'll do."

I open my eyes. "I couldn't know." My voice is harsh. "Finding two killers in the weekend getaway room your husband organized isn't exactly the norm."

His eyes tighten in the corners. "I would've kept him far away from you if you were coming with me."

"I know."

"Say it."

From the corner of my eye, I see him tensing. "Say what?"

"You don't want to be married to a man like me."

"Who does?" I ask under my breath.

"Leclerc was a loose end. That life is over."

I study his profile. "What about that loose end? Are you going to just let it dangle?"

He purses his lips.

In other words, he's going to kill another man. "What about your brother?" I know the answer, but I want him to say it. I need the confirmation.

Still, he says nothing.

Right. Two murders.

"I'm not letting you go, Zoe."

Crossing my arms, I lean closer to the door. "Did I ask you to?"

"I know you. I know what you're thinking." His nostrils flare. "It's not happening, so you can put it out of your pretty little head."

I turn sideways to face him. "Do you even feel guilty?"

"For taking care of the people who tried to burn me alive?" He utters a laugh. "No, I don't."

I study him in silence. He's dangerous, this husband of mine. He left that life behind for me, to be able to marry me, but it'll always be in his blood. He'll never hesitate to use violence to keep us safe and take lives to protect me. I wasn't a big enough fool to believe that part of his life was behind us. I knew what he was dragging me into when he brought me back from Johannesburg. I didn't want a life like this. He never gave me a choice.

Whatever the case, this is who he is. Under the fashionable clothes and the smooth businessman will always lurk a mafia boss. He's not going to change. I'm stuck with him in this marriage. I know I can live with him. I've done it before. I'm doing it now. It's not that I can't accept who he is. It's that I can't deal with never being loved. I long for it with all my soul. I want to know what it feels like. I know the bitter side of love. I know how it hurts when it's one-sided. I want to know what it's like to be on the receiving end. I want the hurt to end, and the only way to stop making it hurt is to stop wanting what I can't have.

WE DRIVE FOR HOURS. In Clermont-Ferrand, he pulls up at a hotel. It's the big, commercial kind close to the highway that caters for travelers.

"I can't drive anymore," he says, hunching over the wheel.

My chest tightens with compassion. I almost reach out to rub his shoulder, but harden my heart. "We could've stayed in Paris."

"After what happened? Not a chance. I want you safe, not in the middle of fucking danger."

"Will Leclerc tell Alexis what you know?"

"He's blackmailing Alexis. If my brother knows I know, Leclerc has nothing to blackmail him with. Leclerc also knows he'll be a dead man walking if Alexis finds out I know. The only thing preventing Alexis from killing Leclerc is the evidence that will be made public if anything happens to Leclerc." He rubs his neck. "So, no, he won't tell Alexis."

"What's your plan?"

He opens the door. "Let me worry about that." Coming around, he gets mine. "Let's get a room."

We book in and take the elevator to the fifth floor. The room is tiny, barely a shoebox with a bed and shower, but it's clean. I sit down on the bed, staring at the wall while Maxime peels out of his clothes. I sacrificed a whole day of work and closed the boutique for this. I should've known better. It was the last time I made a bad decision. It'll never happen again.

"What are you thinking?" he asks.

I look at him. He's naked. His body is hard and brutal, just like his mind. "Nothing."

"Don't give me that," he says through thin lips. "I want to know."

I lean back on my arms. "Why?"

He walks over. Nudging my knees apart with his body, he steps between them. "I could've lost you."

"Whose fault is that?"

"Mine." His face contorts. "I carry all the blame."

"You do."

With his hands on my knees, he spreads my legs wider. "Don't keep from me. Not now."

My thoughts are not his for the taking. My heart either, not any longer. "It's all right here." I lift my dress to expose my underwear. My pose is slutty. "Take it."

A muscle ticks under his eye. "Why are you doing this?"

"Isn't this what you want?" I support my weight on my elbows. "You can go down on me first. It makes me last longer when I come around your cock."

He clenches his hands at his sides. "This isn't you, Zoe."

"You think you know me?" I laugh. "I think you're wrong."

Kneeling between my legs, he grabs my hips and yanks me to the edge of the bed. I pull on the thong, but I'm not strong enough to rip it like him.

"Tear it off," I say.

He holds my eyes as he grips the elastic. It gives with a snap at the twist of his wrist. Threading my fingers through his hair, I guide his lips to the center of my legs. The kiss he plants reverently on my clit isn't what I want.

"Eat me out like you mean it," I say.

He drags a tongue over my folds before plunging inside.

I lock my ankles around his neck. "Stop playing. Do it."

He does. He nips, sucks, and licks until my toes curl. He does every dirty thing I tell him to do while I lean back and watch. My orgasm comes quickly. I don't savor it. I let it crash through my body and wreck me, devouring it much like downing instead of sipping a good glass of wine.

When I'm done, I put my palm on his forehead and push him away. "I'm done. I don't feel like sex any longer. You can go shower now."

The growl that escapes his chest should frighten me. "You used me? That's how you want to play it?"

I sit up. "It's good to be useful. You'll get over it."

Before I can blink, he grabs me around the waist and flips me around. "Is this what you want?" he asks, throwing my skirt over my hips to expose my naked ass. "Do you want me to fuck you like an animal?"

I look at him from over my shoulder. "I'm sated, but thanks for the offer. Do you need a hand job?"

He digs his fingers into my globes, spreading me open. "Why are you doing this?"

Because it's sex, nothing more. From now on, I'm not mixing it up with emotions. Emotions cloud everything. "Fuck me if you need to get off, but get a move on. I'm hungry, and I need a shower."

Bracing myself, I wait. I don't mind coming again, but I'd rather just have lunch and a nap.

He lets me go with a little shove, making me fall flat on my stomach. "Not like this."

I scoot off the bed. "Suit yourself."

He watches me with narrowed eyes as I make my way to the bathroom. I expect him to come after me, but when I step out fifteen minutes later, showered and my hair washed, he's dressed.

I grab my handbag. "I'm going to see what they have for lunch in the dining room. I'm starving."

He doesn't say a word, but he follows me downstairs, presumably to make sure I stay safe.

"Aren't you going to eat?" I ask when I return to our table with a loaded tray.

"I'm not hungry."

I shrug. Biting into an apple, I say with a full mouth, "Your loss."

CHAPTER 36

Maxime

I'm sitting on the edge of the bed, dressed and my hair damp from my shower. It's early. Zoe is still asleep. I'm careful not to wake her, although I should probably go and get her some coffee to wake her up. We'll have to hit the road soon if we're to make it back before the weekend traffic.

Resting my head in my hands, I drag my fingers through my hair. A weight bears down on me. Everything feels heavy—the atmosphere, my thoughts, and our future. At first, I was angry about yesterday, but now it's just part of the heaviness that won't let me breathe. Zoe isn't my little flower any longer. She's grown into a prickly plant with sharp thorns. Not that I blame her. I brought this on her and myself. It's a survival mechanism, just like Delphine has said.

I still want Zoe. I'll always want her, no matter how she changes. I'll even let her use me like yesterday if it means I get to keep her. I can give her pleasure, and it can be enough. I can live with it, but that pull in my heart when I look at her won't let up. I suppose it's the closest thing to empathy. Regret. She was perfect when I found her, a beautiful wildflower, and I don't want her to wilt in my vase. That's what happens to cut flowers. Eventually, they die. Worse, I'm worried—terrified—she'll grow into something so poisonous she'll turn into someone like me. I'm a bad man. A psychopath. What did I expect? That I could make her happy? Could stealing her have gone any other way?

I chuckle to myself. This is the moment I atone for my sins. I've never paid. It had to catch up with me at some stage. I feel a driving need to hurt myself, but physical pain isn't going to do it this time. I don't need the ache in my body to remind me to have compassion. It's there, all by itself. Maybe it's not full-blown compassion, but it's something. I don't know if it's guilt, or regret, or a mixture of both, but it's a godawful feeling. Thank fuck I never felt those before. How do people live with them?

My phone vibrates on the nightstand. I check the caller ID. It's Jerome. I'm expecting news about Leclerc. I don't know what the hotel owner told the police about the parcel bomb, and I don't care. What I do know is Alexis's men will be on Leclerc's tail after that stunt. A man doesn't throw bombs around Paris. It's only a matter of time before they catch up with him. I already have the evidence Leclerc gave me of my brother starting that fire, so I don't give a damn if he finds Leclerc before I do.

I go into the hallway and close the door behind me before answering. "What?"

"Max." Jerome's voice is shaking. "I think you better sit down."

I walk to the window at the far end and peer down at the highway. "What happened?"

I expect him to tell me Leclerc's body washed up in the Seine or that the police are asking about my whereabouts, but I'm not prepared for his next words.

"Alexis is dead."

My thoughts go still. I drag a finger through the dust on the windowsill. "What happened?"

"Car bomb." He exhales into the phone. "Early this morning, in front of his house."

My house. "Who did it?"

"He made too many mistakes, man. I told you."

"Leonardo?"

"Yes." He hesitates. "I'm sorry, Max. Really, I am."

I dissect my feelings. There's nothing. Then my mind starts working at a mile a minute. Alexis is no longer a threat. Leonardo gets what he's always wanted. Marrying his sister to my brother paid off. Still, there's nothing in my chest, no envy, no anger, and no quest for vengeance. I'm not sorry any longer for having given up my house, my position, and my family. That bomb would've been meant for me if Alexis hadn't taken my place.

"Your father is beside himself," Jerome says.

"I guess that's Leonardo's problem now."

My relief surprises me, not that my brother is dead, but that the consequences are no longer my concern. I've got bigger worries on my mind. Killing has always come easy for me. This *thing* I have to do is more difficult than anything I've done.

"The funeral is tomorrow," he says. "Your father doesn't want to wait."

Manners dictate I thank him. "I appreciate the call."

"If you need anything—"

"I don't."

"Yeah." He sighs. "Of course you don't."

I hang up. Scrubbing a hand over my face, I stare at the passing cars. They're silent thanks to the double windowpanes.

"Maxime?"

I turn. Zoe stands in the door with a towel wrapped around her body and her wet hair combed back.

"Get dressed," I say. "We're leaving."

"What happened?"

I go back to the room and close the door. "Alexis is dead."

Her pretty face pales, making the freckles on her nose stand out more. "How?"

"Car bomb." I take her bag and start packing the clothes she wore yesterday. "Leonardo."

"Oh, my God." She stands like a pillar in the corner. "I'm sorry."

"I'm not." I throw a clean pair of underwear at her. "Get a move on. We'll get breakfast on the way."

"What now?" she asks, dropping the towel and stepping into the panties. Her hands shake slightly as she pulls the lace over her hips.

I look away. I already want her too much. It makes what I must do all the harder.

CHAPTER 37

Zoe

The funeral takes place on Monday. We sit at the back of the church during the memorial service, away from the rest of the family, and stay on the outskirts at the cemetery when the coffin is lowered into the ground. Izabella is dressed in a stylish black dress and hat, her face stoic. Raphael is a different story. His face is red and his gait unsteady. A blonde with fishnet stockings and pink heels clings to his arm.

After the priest has said a few words and the mourners disperse, Raphael makes his way over to where we stand. The woman on his arm has a hard time keeping up with her heels sinking into the damp grass. She keeps on getting stuck, and eventually gives up and lets go of Raphael's arm.

He waves a finger at Maxime when he's still a good distance away. "How dare you show up here? It should've been you." He staggers to a halt in front of Maxime. "It should've been you in that car. I told you. I told you he was in trouble, and what did you do?"

Maxime's doesn't react. He stands quietly, his face expressionless.

Raphael turns on me. "Did you know he played you? Did you know he orchestrated the whole game of making you happy?"

Coldness creeps over my skin.

Maxime jumps forward, gripping a fistful of Raphael's jacket lapel. "That's enough."

"It was just a plan to make you want to stay," Raphael says.

Maxime's eyes go hard like granite. Violence brews under his calm veneer, but I'm too shocked to intervene.

Emile, Raphael's brother, runs up and grabs Raphael's arm. "Time to go." He doesn't look at me.

The blonde has removed her shoes and arrives out of breath with them in her hand.

"Take him," Emile says to her.

She hooks her arm through Raphael's. "Come, sweetie. Let's go home."

Emile takes his other arm. Together, they walk him to his car. What did Raphael mean? I hope to God it's not what I think. I don't have time to analyze it further, because my gaze falls on Leonardo who watches from a distance. When he catches Maxime's eye, he nods, and then he takes his sister's elbow and steers her away.

"What was that about?" I ask, my stomach in knots. I'm petrified Leonardo will come after Maxime too.

"We're even," Maxime says, not taking his eyes off Leonardo's back. "I humiliated his sister. He killed my brother."

At least Alexis is no longer a threat. I cringe in shame for the thought. I've been around Maxime for too long. His blasé attitude toward life and its value is rubbing off on me.

Taking my hand, he leads me to his car.

"Why *did* you come?" I ask as he gets my door.

"Blood is thicker than water."

I get in and fasten my safety belt.

Hadrienne, Noelle, and Sylvie stand a short distance away, waiting for Emile who's telling the blonde to drive Raphael's car while Raphael protests for all the graveyard to hear. Noelle glares and says something to Hadrienne, who turns around to look at me. I can only guess what the hostile stares are about. If not for me, Maxime would never have left his position. He was always a much better mafia boss than Alexis. Maybe then Alexis would still be alive. He would've been alive and at war with his brother. I don't think Alexis would've ever let it go. The conversation we had the day he walked into the apartment when Maxime carelessly left the door open runs through my head. He'd said I was supposed to marry him before Maxime decided to claim me as mistress. He was as bitter about that as he was jealous of Maxime's power.

Maxime gets in and starts the engine. He glances in the direction of the women who turn away as if he's a contagious disease they may catch by sight.

"They were staring," he says, shooting me a glance. "You don't deserve that."

I lean back into the comfort of the soft leather seat. "I don't care. Let them look."

When I meet Sylvie's gaze as we pass, she averts her eyes.

Hugging myself, I ask, "What did your father mean?"

"He's not my father."

I'm not letting him dismiss the question that easily. "What did *Raphael* mean?"

"Nothing." He steers the car into the traffic.

"Nothing." I shake my head. "You're a piece of fucking work, Maxime Belshaw."

He pulls onto the curb and kills the engine. Anger dances in his cold eyes when he looks at me. "Don't insult me. Next time, I won't let it go."

"Then don't insult me with more of your lies." My hands are shaking, but my voice is strong. "Did you make me fall in love with you on purpose?"

He rests his forehead on the steering wheel. "You don't want to go there. Trust me."

The blow I've been waiting for during all the months he's kept his word and didn't tell me a lie hits me full in the face. The fact that I expected it doesn't make it easier. I fall apart. How many times have I excused him for letting me fall in love with him, telling myself I did it all by myself? I want to laugh. Of course it was a well-orchestrated scheme. Does Maxime ever do anything without meticulous planning?

My tone is as flat as his eyes. "How did you do it?"

He lifts his head. "Zoe, please—"

"I want to know, Maxime."

He tips back his head and leans it on the headrest. "I figured out what you wanted."

The hurt slices deeper, twisting into the little that's left of my heart. What kills me, though, is that it was nothing but a psychological game to him.

"Give me an example," I say, needing to hurt myself more with the truth. I need to weed him out of my system for once and for all, and he's just given me the weapon.

He closes his eyes. Suddenly sounding tired, he says, "Don't do this."

I slam a fist on the dashboard. "Tell me!"

He lifts his eyelids and turns his face to look at me with the dead gray of his eyes. "You wanted a fairytale. I gave it to you."

When he took me to Venice, he stole my fantasy. Now I know why. It wasn't only to give me a twisted version of my dream when he fucked me, but ultimately to make sure I stayed by also slowly but surely stealing my love. My eyes are dry, but I'm shriveling up inside. Everything, even *this*, was a lie. I open the door. "All this time, I blamed myself for being so stupid to fall in love with you."

"Close the door," he says through tight lips.

"It was the only thing I still believed was real. My bad." Getting out, I slam the door.

He jumps out when I start walking down the road.

"Zoe, come back."

I lift the strap of my handbag higher on my shoulder and walk faster. He grabs my arm when he catches up with me, but I jerk free.

"Don't touch me."

"Get back in the car." His jaw bunches. "Please."

"Go to hell."

I storm up the road, ashamed of my childish tantrum and unable to stop. He made a fool of me. He made me love him as a part of his sick plan, and I played the role of the needy, naïve girl perfectly. I guess I deserve this pain.

He doesn't come after me again, and I don't hear the engine of his car start up either. I cross the street, turn left, and walk three blocks to a bus stop where I catch one to the boutique. The boutique is closed due to the funeral, but I can't go home.

At the boutique, I leave the closed sign and lock the door behind me, thankful for the quiet solitude. I go upstairs and lie down on the couch. The hours tick by as I try to think, but my thoughts are turning in circles. I recall our history from the day Maxime turned up in Johannesburg to the moment I ran. The design school, Sylvie who I thought was my friend, the fact that Maxime's family planned to marry me to Alexis, everything Maxime has ever lied about turns in my head, all the people who have died, until I have a headache and I can't think anymore. The cushion underneath my head is wet with tears.

I get up and make a cup of tea in the kitchen. I can't stomach food. I drink the tea downstairs, staring at the busy street from a dark shop window. When it gets late, I take my bag, lock up, and set the alarm. I take the tram to a nearby hotel and get a room for the night before buying some essentials from the pharmacy across the street. I send a text to Maxime to let him know I won't be home so he doesn't go looking for me, but receive no reply. My phone lies on the nightstand of the strange room, the screen remaining black.

By morning, there's still no answer. I take off the underwear I slept in and have a shower. Donning the same outfit, I use the new toothbrush and hairbrush to make myself presentable. Still not having an appetite, I grab a coffee on my way to the boutique. I arrive early enough to change into one of my own creations before anyone else gets there. My shop assistant, Camille, arrives just before nine to put up a new window display before we open at ten.

For the rest of the day, I throw myself into work. It helps me forget I'm unhappy. It's helps me forget what happened yesterday. I've walked out on my husband, and he didn't come after me. In relationship terms, it means our marriage is in trouble. In our terms, it means nothing. I'm a prisoner in Maxime's golden cage. My feelings aren't going to change that.

We get a lot of traffic from the street. With the peak summer wedding season around the corner, many women come in asking for a wedding outfit. I've expanded to a selected range of wedding and bridesmaid dresses. Camille arranges the new collection in the showroom while I brew a fresh pot of coffee and catch up with my emails at the front desk. I'll drop by the workshop tomorrow to check how the girls are progressing with the orders. I simply don't have enough energy today.

A girl with dark hair and slanted eyes walks into the shop. I notice her because she reminds me so much of Christine from the design school.

"Can I help you?" Camille asks.

"I'm looking for a wedding dress," she says, "but I'm very fussy."

"I'm sure we'll find you something you love." Camille walks to the mannequins modeling some of the dresses. "If not, we can always design one for you."

I cut their conversation out, focusing on an order of fabric as they go through the showroom. Camille is a great saleslady. She's much better at selling than me.

The young lady browses through the dresses hanging on the rail when Camille goes upstairs for a tape measure.

"Oh, my," she exclaims, taking down a dress. "This is exactly what I want."

I get up and go over to assist her, and then I stop dead. The dress she's holding up to the light has a sweetheart bodice with a wide skirt of diamante studded net tulle. It bleeds from white to the softest of pinks that ends with a darker hue at the hem. I have no idea how the dress got here or why it isn't stained with hair dye and splashes of mud from the gutters. Maxime must've had it cleaned. He must've accidently moved it with my sewing material from the apartment, and Camille must've unpacked it with the other wedding dresses.

My mouth is suddenly too dry to speak.

"Can I have it?" The woman presses it to her body. "Please, please, please tell me it's not for someone else."

Finally finding my voice, I say, "Actually, that one isn't for sale."

She pouts. "This is exactly what I've been looking for."

My smile is impersonal. It gives nothing away of my turmoil. "That was my wedding dress. It must've ended up here by fluke."

"Oh, shucks." She lowers the dress. "You can't sell it then, can you?"

I think back to the moment I realized for who I'd made that dress at the fashion show. I remember why I loved it so much. It wasn't the design. It was imagining wearing it for Maxime. I had hope for us then. I wanted to say yes so badly. I told Maxime yesterday everything was a lie, but my love has never been a lie. My love might've been a victim of our twisted circumstances, but it was never anything other than solid and real. However it came about doesn't take away from its truth or depth. I fell in love with Maxime, and I love him still.

"Can you make me one along similar lines?" she asks. "Not the same, but the same style, if you know what I mean?"

I force myself back from the past to focus on her face. "Of course. Are you sure though? It's not according to the latest fashion."

"I don't care much for fashion." She beams. "I just want my dream dress."

"Whatever you want. Camille will take your measurements and contact details. I'll draw something and email a draft and quote, and then we can take it from there."

She jumps on the balls of her feet. "Wonderful."

Going to the desk, I take my handbag. It's almost seven o'clock. "Will you please lock up?" I ask Camille when she comes downstairs with the measuring tape. We usually close at seven.

"Sure." She smiles. "See you tomorrow."

My heart beats with an unsteady rhythm when I take a bus and get off close to the apartment. I rush the last two blocks home in my heels. Maxime normally leaves the office at six. Urgency makes me forego the lengthy elevator and take the stairs. I'm out of breath when I reach our landing, and then I stop.

Maxime stands in the door, a suitcase in his hand.

Panic rushes through me in a hot flush. "What are you doing?"

"Leclerc is dead. A jogger found his body in a park this morning. Alexis's men got him eventually."

The information boggles my mind, but my head is stuck on that suitcase. "What are you doing?"

"Telling you so you don't have to be scared."

"That's not what I'm talking about."

He looks at the keys that he holds in his hand. "I was going to drop this off at your workshop, but it's better like this."

I advance a few careful steps, frightened he'll flee if I corner him. "Where are you going?"

"It's time to face the facts, Zoe." He looks back at me. "This isn't working."

The panic turns into anger, hot and all-consuming. I walk until I stand in front of him. "You don't get to make this decision on your own."

He pushes me aside. "Don't make this difficult."

I move back, blocking his path, standing my ground and demanding my answers. My throat is so dry it hurts to speak. "Why?"

"You're changing."

I'm changing? The anger creeps up my neck and heats my cheeks. "You made me." I push a finger on his chest. "You'll live with me."

His smile is tender, apologetic. "I'm afraid you'll wake up one day and not know who you are any longer. I don't want to be the reason you hate the person you've become."

"Is it because of the hotel, of what I did?"

He puts down the suitcase. "It's because of what *I* did."

We both know what he's referring to. He's talking about stealing my life and cheating his way into my heart. He used every possible means of making sure I can't escape, even forcing me into this marriage and holding my family's lives over my head. After everything he's done to keep me, he's prepared to let me go?

I stare at him as the enormity of what he's doing hits me. Because I'm changing, he's willing to set me free. He cares enough. It's nothing short of a declaration of love.

"Maxime," I whisper.

He picks up the suitcase again. "You'll be fine with money. The apartment is paid for, and you're the one making the big bucks now." His smile is wry. "You've taken care of me for long enough."

He's proud. I get that. "The business will recover now that..." *Alexis is dead*. I can't bring myself to say it. It sounds too selfish.

"I know."

"I'm sorry."

"Not as much as I am." He moves around me.

"I'm sorry for the hotel," I say. "I was upset. I was trying to..."

He looks back. "Survive me."

"Yes," I say, biting my lip. "Yet..."

"Yet what?"

I inhale deeply, and admit the truth. "I want you to stay."

His smile only turns sadder. "You jumped off a cliff and ran away to escape me. I think it's also time to admit to myself you don't want me."

I lock my fingers around the wrist of his hand that's holding the suitcase. "I do. I do want you. That's what I realized tonight when I looked at my wedding dress. I made it for you. I wanted to have something you couldn't give me so badly that I didn't see what was right in front of me."

"What?" he asks, intertwining our fingers.

I smile through the tears burning in my eyes. "You."

Pain contorts his features. "I'm not a nice man, Zoe."

"I know who you are."

"I have nothing to offer you, no money and no love."

"Today you've given me everything."

His lips tilt. "Have I?"

"You've put my needs before yours." I search his eyes and recognize the conflict. "That's love, Maxime."

Dropping the suitcase, he folds his arms around me and crushes me to his body. The pain I saw in his face reflects in his voice. "You can teach me to be the man you want me to be."

"No." I burrow into the safety of his arms. "Don't change. I've always loved you just as you are."

He rests his chin on my head. "I don't deserve this. I don't deserve *you*."

I pull away and take his hand. "Come back inside?"

He scoops me up in his arms, making me squeal. "I think I'm supposed to carry you over the threshold."

"I'm not sure how it's supposed to work, but we'll figure it out together."

"Starting with this," he says, lowering his head to catch my lips.

The suitcase remains forgotten in the hallway like the baggage I've carried for too long when he carries me inside. The door closes on our past as we make our first decision together, to love with all we're capable of.

Love.

He doesn't say it, but it seems fitting. This is who he is. His actions speak louder.

It's the first moment of a new beginning.

Eat, sleep, love, and repeat.

With him, I can do this forever.

EPILOGUE (ZOE)

Zoe

The bells toll in the tower. Their music rings out over the harbor city of Marseille, their message one of joy. As if the angels are playing along, it's a warm autumn day with a clear blue sky. I'm standing in the nursery, facing my reflection in the mirror. The girl looking back at me is hardly the girl from a few months ago. This one's eyes are sparkling, and her cheeks have a blush. This one believes in love.

Love.

My heart beats with a wild rhythm when I think what I'm about to do. Nerves tighten my stomach, but they're the good kind.

Lina fiddles with the dress, separating the layers of tulle.

"It's fine," I say.

My sister-in-law doesn't look at me. She's hiding behind the mass of golden hair that tumbles over her shoulders. "It has to be perfect."

Josie fusses in her stroller.

"Hey." I take Lina's hand to still her. "It's okay. The dress is fine.

We're okay." Meaning both of us. This is emotional for her, more than what it should be. There's more to her state than feeling sentimental about the ceremony.

Turning her face to the ceiling, she blinks away the moisture in her eyes.

I squeeze her hand, those same emotions clogging up my throat. "Don't cry."

She gives an awkward laugh. "Now look. I'm making you sad."

Josie complains, making a ruckus with her rattle. I go over and lift my niece from the stroller.

"Oh, wait." Lina runs to us and takes Josie from my arms, but not before I've inhaled the sweet baby scent of her hair. "I've just fed her. You don't want her to burp on your gown."

I give a soft laugh. "I'm so happy, Lina." I brush a hand over Josie's blond curls. "Really, happy." Lina has asked me twice this morning if I am. I don't want her to doubt it for a minute.

"I know." She sighs. "Weddings bring back memories for me, that's all."

"*You're* happy, right?"

She beams. "More than I can ever be." Shifting Josie to her hip, she drags a finger under her eye to catch the tear that has spilled over. "It's just that you look so beautiful, Zee. I can't believe you made this dress."

I look at the dress in the mirror. It's a princess dress, down to the diamante detail on the meringue skirt. It's not fashionable, but it's me. It's who I am. It's hard to say if it's genetic or my past that's shaped me. Maybe it's a little of both. Whatever the case, I'm comfortable in my skin. I'm designing the clothes I love, and I found a market for them. I've put frills and lace back in fashion. Romantic has become my trademark, and it caters for an existing need. My label is for women who like to feel feminine and who don't shy away from going just a little overboard.

After everything that's happened, our lives are finally back on track. I'm lucky. Thanks to celebrities like Vera Day, Zoe Hart became a leading international label in a short time. Maxime's business is solid again. He won back his old clients and made new ones. Not having to look over his shoulder makes him more relaxed, although he still fights at the boxing club. That part of him will never be over. It's him. It's the man I love.

With our businesses booming, we can afford a bigger house, but we love the apartment. Leonardo has moved into Maxime's old house near Cassis. Even if the house were available, we wouldn't have wanted to go back there. We deserve a new start. When we need a nursery, we'll upgrade to a house with a garden, but I'm keeping the apartment. It's mine, and Maxime gave it to me with love. A lot of my memories were made there, and I'm embracing all of them, even the bad ones. Even Venice. Especially Venice. They hold a deep sentimentality, because everything that happened led us to this moment.

A knock sounds on the door. It creaks open, and Damian's face appears in the crack. "Hey, Zee." He looks at my face and the dress, and then he swallows. "Can I come in?"

"It's bad luck to see the bride," Lina says with a chastising smile.

Damian grins. "Only for the groom." He comes inside and shuts the door.

We look at each other. I know what he's thinking, because I see in his eyes what I feel in my heart. We're back under a blanket in the dark, holding hands for comfort. All we have is each other, but in our make-believe tent we're safe. We came a long way. I rescued myself with my fairytales, and Damian saved himself with his truth. We made it. We created the realities we wanted. We're okay. We'll always be, because no matter what, no one can take this strength away from us.

"Zee." His eyes glitter with pride. "You're lovely."

"Isn't she?" Lina says, blinking away fresh tears.

A look passes between them, something I can't decipher, but it's profound.

"I have something for you," he says, taking a small box from his pocket and handing it to me.

"What is it?"

"Open it."

I flip back the lid. A pink heart shaped diamond on a thin platinum chain glitters on the velvet cushion. My breath catches. I know how rare pink diamonds are, how precious.

"Damian," I exclaim. "You shouldn't have."

He takes the necklace from the box and motions for me to turn around. When he fastens the chain around my neck, I trace the heart with a finger. I can't help but admire the beautiful color and perfect cut.

"It's you," he says, meeting my gaze in the mirror. "A real princess."

The bells toll again.

"It's time," Lina says with a tremor in her voice, bouncing Josie on her hip.

Damian kisses my cheek. "Thank you for giving us this. Photos could never compare."

My cheeks heat when I think about the lies, but then I push it away. Today is a day for the truth. "It was Maxime's idea."

Lina hands me the bouquet of roses tied with a pink ribbon.

Damian offers his arm. "Ready?"

I smile.

When the tenor starts singing Bon Iver's *I Can't Make You Love Me,* Damian leads me down the aisle. There aren't many guests, mostly our work colleagues and associates, but the people who mean the most to me in the world are here, and that's all that matters.

I lift my eyes and look toward the end. Maxime stands in a pool of angelic light that fans through the window. In tailored pants and a fitted waistcoat underneath a swallowtail jacket, he looks cultured, beautiful, untamed, and wild.

The crazy beat of my heart evens out. When his gray gaze homes in on me, isolating me in his vision like nothing else exists, everything falls into place.

His eyes shine with a possessive light as he tracks my movement. When we stop in front of him, he only breathes one word, but it's charged with the history of a lifetime. "Zoe."

Damian shakes his hand. "You know what'll happen if you don't take care of her."

"You don't have to worry," Maxime says. "No one and nothing can ever mean more to me."

When Damian, Lina, and Josie join Josh, who sits in the front row with his nanny, Maxime folds his broad hand around mine. His skin is warm and calloused. Those skilled fingers can play many different sensations over my body, but right now his touch is gentle, a promise to protect and hold.

Lowering his lips to my ear, he whispers in his seductive accent, "You're beautiful. So damn much. Just like a flower." His voice turns hoarse. "I'm never letting you go. You know that, right?" He leans closer, letting our shoulders brush. "You know what you're promising, don't you?"

I stare up at his face. He's a fallen angel in a holy place with a ring in his pocket and a question in his eyes.

When he asks me for my answer, I'm going to say yes.

Every time.

That little saying about being careful of what you wish? It's science, really. We attract what we think. That's the law of energy. Our deepest desires shape our paths. I dreamed about a prince. It's the villain who found me. It just took me a while to figure out it's the villain I wanted all along. My light attracts his darkness. His darkness is a canvas for my light.

I've waited for him for a long time. He conquered my heart in a dark broom closet. He broke it in real life. He took me far away and gave me beautiful dresses and lots of pretty glasses. He mended my heart with the biggest sacrifice a man can make. He gave me a fairy-tale, and he never broke those glasses.

Our love isn't conventional. It's so much more. It's bigger than us, even bigger than life. It's a bond that follows soul mates beyond death into eternity. Our love shines like a diamond. It's the kind that lasts, because diamonds are forever.

~ THE END ~

BONUS EPILOGUE (LINA)

Lina

Damian's deep timbre comes from down the hallway. "The spaceship landed on Earth, and the Goollie monster lifted the hatch." His voice deepens. "I'm hungry. Bring me some toys to eat."

I make my way to the bedroom and peer around the frame. The sight melts my heart. Damian lies in the middle of our bed with Josh under one arm and Josie curled up against him on the other side. Josh's eyelashes brush his cheeks. His chest rises and falls with even breaths. Josie's eyes are closed too. The bottle has slipped from her perfect little rosebud mouth, but she clutches it like a life buoy in her tiny fist.

Damian catches my gaze over the book. It's a giant book of sci-fi tales, a gift from their beloved Auntie Zee. His lips tilt into a sexy smile. With those new reading glasses, he looks extra hot, like a rocket scientist with a male stripper's body.

I lean a shoulder on the frame. "I think they're sleeping."

He gives me a sheepish grin. "Have been for about fifteen minutes."

My smile is soft. It comes easy. He has that effect on me. "You're still reading."

"The story was almost finished. I read kids absorb words even in their sleep. I think we should play audiobooks in their rooms at night. Maybe they'll learn to speak French like that."

"Zee said she'll teach them during the holidays."

"A head start can't hurt. Besides, Josh is a natural with languages, and Josie is a genius. She already said daddy."

"Is that so?" My smile stretches. "She's ten months old."

"As I said, genius." He drags a heated gaze in a slow evaluation over me. "Since they're sleeping…"

The desire burning in those bitter chocolate eyes instantly sets me on fire. My voice is husky. "Since they're sleeping what?"

He closes the book. "I can spend time with my wife."

Biting my lip, I say, "Maybe."

A calculated look comes over his handsome features as he narrows his eyes. "Are you teasing me?"

I keep my face innocent. "Never."

He puts the book and glasses aside, and gently removes his arm from around Josh. I stand quietly. This is my favorite part of the evening. It warms my chest and fills my heart, night after night. I'll never run out of love or grow tired of witnessing this.

Careful not to wake Josh, Damian lifts him in his arms. I step aside for Damian to squeeze past me and pad behind them to watch from Josh's door as Damian lies him down on his bed and pulls the comforter with the space rocket motive up to his chin. My big, strong husband bends down to plant a kiss on Josh's forehead before brushing away a curl. He leaves the blue lamp on so that Josh doesn't get scared of the dark if he wakes in the night.

Flashing me a smile, he leaves the door ajar and goes back for Josie. Damian works hard, but he comes home before dinner every evening without fail so he can read the kids their bedtime story and tuck them in. That's his special time with them, his time to unwind from the stress of the diamond business.

We're lucky. Josie's been sleeping full nights since she was five months old, and we never had to rock her to sleep. Put her down, and she's lights out after a few minutes. Damian steps from our room with our daughter in his arms, staring down at her with such a tender expression I know this is one of those moments I'll remember forever. It's one of those images a person revisits on a deathbed, a moment of profoundness that gives meaning to life.

Like a puppy, I follow behind them. I can't help it. I'm still telling myself every day this is real, that I won't wake from a beautiful dream to discover I'm back in a nightmare.

Damian pauses next to Josie's crib. Even if she's fast asleep in his arms, he rocks her for a while.

"Love you, baby girl," he says, planting a soft kiss on her head. "Sweet dreams, little angel." He lies her down and puts her favorite cuddle toy within reach.

I slip around the frame and lean against the wall, listening to him move around the room as he flicks on a night lamp and switches on the baby monitor. When he finally exits and looms over me, my heart starts thumping like it always does when he stands so close. His masculine scent washes over me. He's barefoot, wearing a pair of dark jeans and a faded T-shirt. I long to run my hands over the hard ridges of his chest, but I resist for as long as I can. When I finally break and touch him, it always feels like the first time.

"What would you like to do, Lina?"

The way he says my name, hot and husky, makes me clench my thighs. I can't help but toy with him a little. "I need to study."

Leaning a hand on the wall next to my face, he cages me in. "Do you now?"

I'm doing a correspondence degree in Psychology. I love being a psychiatrist's assistant, but I love helping people more. People like me.

"How about this?" He presses closer, letting me feel his hardness. "I read your textbook to you in bed."

I stare up at his beautiful face. "Will I get any studying done in bed?"

"Plenty." He drags his fingertips from my shoulder down my arm to my wrist. Then he reverses the path, brushing a light caress over my scars. "I'll test you to make sure you've paid attention."

My breath catches when he lowers his head and drags his lips over the arch of my neck. "Will there be punishment involved?"

He kisses my jaw. "Absolutely."

"Mm." My knees grow weak as he trails a finger up my leg, lifting the hem of my dress in the process. "I'll have to think about that."

"Do you need some persuasion?" he asks as he reaches my underwear.

I'm helpless against the seductive tone of his voice. I have no defenses against the skillfulness of his hands.

"I love you, Lina."

But those are the words that slay me, time and again.

"So fucking much," he says with a sudden dark, desperate urgency. "Let me show you, princess."

When he takes my hand and leads me to our bedroom, there's only once choice.

I follow.

Anywhere he wants.

Wherever he takes me.

Always.

ALSO BY CHARMAINE PAULS

Standalone Novels

(Enemies-to-Lovers Dark Romance)

Darker Than Love

(Second Chance Romance)

Catch Me Twice

Diamond Magnate Novels

(Dark Romance)

Standalone Novel

(Dark Forced Marriage Romance)

Beauty in the Broken

Diamonds are Forever Trilogy

(Dark Mafia Romance)

Diamonds in the Dust

Diamonds in the Rough

Diamonds are Forever

The Loan Shark Duet

(Dark Mafia Romance)

Dubious

Consent

Box Set

The Age Between Us Duet

(Older Woman Younger Man Romance)

Old Enough

Young Enough

Box Set

Krinar World Novels

(Futuristic Romance)

The Krinar Experiment

The Krinar's Informant

Seven Forbidden Arts Series

(Dark Paranormal Romance)

Pyromancist (Fire)

Audiobooks

Standalone Novels

(Enemies-to-Lovers Dark Romance)

Darker Than Love

Diamonds are Forever Trilogy

(Dark Mafia Romance)

Diamonds in the Dust

Diamonds in the Rough

Diamonds are Forever

The Loan Shark Duet

(Dark Mafia Romance)

Dubious

Consent

Krinar World Novels

(Futuristic Romance)

The Krinar's Informant

ABOUT THE AUTHOR

Charmaine Pauls was born in Bloemfontein, South Africa. She obtained a degree in Communication at the University of Potchefstroom and followed a diverse career path in journalism, public relations, advertising, communication, and brand marketing. Her writing has always been an integral part of her professions.

When she moved to Chile with her French husband, she started writing full-time. She has been publishing novels and short stories since 2011. Charmaine currently lives in Montpellier, France with her family. Their household is a lively mix of Afrikaans, English, French, and Spanish.

Join Charmaine's mailing list
https://charmainepauls.com/subscribe/

Join Charmaine's readers' group on Facebook
http://bit.ly/CPaulsFBGroup

Read more about Charmaine's novels and short stories on
https://charmainepauls.com

Connect with Charmaine

Facebook
http://bit.ly/Charmaine-Pauls-Facebook

Amazon
http://bit.ly/Charmaine-Pauls-Amazon

Goodreads
http://bit.ly/Charmaine-Pauls-Goodreads

Twitter
https://twitter.com/CharmainePauls

Instagram
https://instagram.com/charmainepaulsbooks

BookBub
http://bit.ly/CPaulsBB

Printed in Great Britain
by Amazon

64898290R00366